By E.T. MALINOWSKI

BL ENTERTAINMENT
Night Kiss

Published by DSP PUBLICATIONS
www.dsppublications.com

NIGHT KISS

E.T. MALINOWSKI

DSP PUBLICATIONS

Published by
DSP PUBLICATIONS

5032 Capital Circle SW, Suite 2, PMB# 279, Tallahassee, FL 32305-7886 USA
www.dsppublications.com

Night Kiss
© 2019 E.T. Malinowski.

Cover Art
© 2019 Kanaxa.
Cover content is for illustrative purposes only and any person depicted on the cover is a model.

Trade Paperback ISBN: 978-1-64080-881-2
Digital ISBN: 978-1-64080-880-5
Library of Congress Control Number: 2018947737
Trade Paperback published January 2019
v. 1.0

Printed in the United States of America

This paper meets the requirements of
ANSI/NISO Z39.48-1992 (Permanence of Paper).

This book is dedicated in memory of Sandrine Gasq-Dion. I began Night Kiss in October 2017, and during the time of its writing, Sandrine passed away very suddenly. She was an inspiration to me not only as an author of my favorite gay romance series, but also as a human being. She treated her fans as friends, and shared her adventures and her wacky sense of humor with us. She was our Alpha and is our Spirit Alpha now. We miss you, Sandrine. This Night Kiss is for you.

Author's Note

HONORIFICS ARE an important part of Korean culture and relate to whether the person being addressed is older or younger than the speaker. Koreans place a great deal of emphasis on respect for elders—parents, grandparents, etc. To drop honorifics without permission of the addressee is very disrespectful. Honorifics will change as the relationship between the speaker and the addressee changes, becoming more familiar to indicate a closer relationship as the two parties deem appropriate. Honorifics are also defined by the gender of the addressee. Familial relation names, such as aunt or uncle, will differ depending on whether the person is from the mother's or the father's side of the family in addition to age.

The honorifics are hyung, nuna, oppa, unnie, and dongsaeng.

"Oppa," is used when a younger woman addresses an older man or an older brother. "Dongsaeng" is used to address anyone younger than the speaker. It is also used to address a younger brother while "hyung" is used for both an older brother and an older man by a younger man.

While the use of given names is more frequent, these honorifics will be used when speaking. In a mixed group, it is possible to use the given name plus the appropriate honorific to identify which person the speaker is addressing.

-a/-ya are often used to indicate a close relationship between speaker and addressee, and are not used until both feel comfortable doing so. These are not necessarily considered honorifics.

http://www.worknplay.co.kr/index.php/article/titles-of-coworkers-people-and-family-in-korean/mod/article/act/showArticle/art_no/163

GLOSSARY OF TERMS

KOREAN WORDS, PHRASES, AND DEFINITIONS

Abeoji — Father, when talking to parent.

Abeonim — Father, with honorific when talking to parent.

Adeul — Son, when talking to child.

Aish — Oy vey.

Antifan — Someone who hates an idol so much that they will attempt to physically harm them.

Bam Kiseu — Night Kiss.

Bias — A favored member in a group.

Boojangnim — Division Head, with honorific.

Eomeoni — Mother.

Eumak Nabi — Music Butterfly.

Godaeui — Ancient one.

Gomabseumnida — Thank you very much (more formal).

Gomaweoyo — Thanks.

Halmeoni — Grandmother.

Huijang-nim — President, with honorific.

Hwaiting — A form of encouragement used to cheer someone on, like "Let's go!" or "You've got this!"

Jal meokkesseumnida — I will eat well (said at the beginning of the meal).

Janggyo-nim — Officer (formal).

Joesonghaeyo — I am very sorry (more formal).

Ihaehaesseo — I understand.

Ments — Sections of concerts where the idols talk with fans at length.

Mudangnim — Honorific form of address female Shinto Priestess.

Nae Adeul — My son, when talking to child.

Namdongsaeng — Younger brother.

Oesamchon — Mother's older brother.

Pogseu Paieo — Fox-fire.

Sajangnim — Boss.

Sasaeng — Obsessive fan to the point of stalking behavior.

Seonbae/Hubae — Coworker higher/lower, also used in terms of mentoring.

Seonsaengnim — Teacher, with honorific.

-ssi — A suffix used with the surname to address someone you do not personally know.

Stan — A fan who actively follows a K-pop band or idol, often overzealous.

VCRs — Short clips to full music videos used specifically for a concert as transitions.

Yah — OMG.

Chinese Words and Phrases

Bù kèqì — You're welcome.

Chāoguò yībǎi gè lièkǒu -- Over a hundred lacerations or so.

Dàn wǒ bù zhīdào rúguǒ wǒ chénggōngle — But I don't know if I succeeded.

Duōchóushàngǎn — Teddy bear, softie.

Fēng Líng — Wind Spirit.

Fùqīn — Father, when talking to parents.

Géxiá — Literally "Beneath your pavilion." Equivalent to "Excellency." Used to address important people or to show respect.

Gǔpén gǔzhé — Fractured pelvis.

Húli jīng — Fox-Spirit.

Jiānbǎng suì liè — Shoulder blades are shattered.

Jǐ gè chuígǔ bèi pòjiě — Couple of vertebrae are cracked.

Lǎodà niáng — Grandmother.

Méiyǒu yīyuàn — No hospitals.

Nǎi nai — Grandmother, father's side.

Nǐ bú xūyǎo baochí — You do not have to remain (roughly).

Qíngfù — Mistress.

Qù nǎlǐ nǐ huì juédé ānquán hé shūshì — You may go where you feel comfortable (roughly); You will be safe and comfortable there (literally).

Shi — Yes.

Táozi — Peaches.

Wǒ bù likāi wǒ de jiārén — I will not leave my family (literally).

Wǒ de àirén — My love.

Wǒ de érzi — My son.

Wǒ de sūnzi — My grandson.

Wǒ de xīn — My beloved.

Wǒ hěn bàoqiàn — I am very sorry.

Wǒ míngbái — I understand.

Wǒ shìguòle — I tried.

Xiǎo húdié — Little butterfly.

Xièxiè — Thank you.

Xīn'ái — Beloved.

Xuè huǒbàn — Blood partner.

Yuǎnli tā — Stay away from him.

Zhēn — Truly.

JAPANESE WORDS AND PHRASES

Baka — Idiot.

Gomen nasai — Excuse me (after the fact), I'm sorry.

Kitsune — Fox-Spirit.

Okaa-sama — Mother, with honorific (very formal).

Okasan — Mother, with honorific.

Ritorukitto — Little kit.

Saiai — Beloved.

Segare — My son.

Shitte iru — I know.

Watashi no Kokoro — My love.

Watashi wa, anata o aishiteimasu — I love you.

Yandere — A term for an anime character, usually female, who is romantically obsessed with someone, often to the point of violence, particularly against someone they perceive as a threat to their relationship with their crush. https://www.urbandictionary.com/define.php?term=yandere

NIGHT KISS

E.T. MALINOWSKI

JIN-WOO

CHEONG JIN-WOO stared, shock freezing him in place. By the label on her shirt, the clipboard dangling from her hand, and the headset she wore, the woman had to be one of the stadium's technicians. The soft little moans she emitted tightened his belly. Then Ki-tae opened his eyes, opened his silver eyes, and stared right back at him. He held the technician to his chest with one arm around her waist and his other hand cupping her chin, lifting it and holding her head at an angle. The perfect position for feeding. Those sinfully full pouty lips pulled back, fangs sliding slowly from her flesh, and Ki-tae smirked. Jin-woo ran.

His long legs carried him quickly down the back halls of the stadium, but he got turned around and had no idea where he was going. The deeper he got into the bowels of the building, the more disoriented he became. Cement walls surrounded him. Cords and cables, crates, and trunks lined the hallways, blending one into the other. Finally Jin-woo had to stop. Bending over and putting his hands on his knees, he tried to catch his breath. It couldn't be. It just couldn't be. They didn't exist. It wasn't possible.

"I'm the 'stan' of a Vampire."

"You interrupted my snack."

Ki-tae's voice, like smooth milk chocolate, caressed his ear. Jin-woo whipped around, throwing himself off-balance. He stumbled backward, colliding with the wall in what appeared to be the delivery area of the stadium. There were large overhead doors to the right and bays where trucks could be backed in to unload. The ceiling rose high above his head, the beams bare and the lighting dim in the corners. Ki-tae continued to move closer.

"I... I didn't mean to," he murmured, his breath catching as Ki-tae stalked toward him. Jin-woo didn't know whether to be terrified or turned-on. His mind voted for terrified, but his body wholeheartedly voted for turned-on.

"Yet you did," Ki-tae said as he came to a stop in front of Jin-woo.

Mere centimeters separated their bodies. Jin-woo could feel his heat. He pressed up against the wall, his body trembling, as Ki-tae leaned forward. If Ki-tae moved any closer, he was going to find out exactly how much Jin-woo liked his proximity. He whimpered softly, squeezing his eyes closed as he felt the soft brush of Ki-tae's nose against his sensitive skin. Without realizing it, Jin-woo tilted his head, exposing more of his neck. He heard Ki-tae's soft chuckle and then the gentle stroke of lips against his skin. The touch sent a shockwave of pleasure through his body, forcing a loud moan from between his lips. He'd never reacted that strongly to anyone before. Granted, it had been a while, but still, he shouldn't react so powerfully to someone he'd just met, even if it was Ki-tae, even if he was the one idol Jin-woo adored above all others: the one he "stanned."

"You… smell… delicious," Ki-tae murmured, bringing his hands to rest on either side of Jin-woo's head. "And since you interrupted my meal, it is only right that you provide a replacement."

"I—" Jin-woo began.

"It's not going to hurt," Ki-tae purred. "Trust me."

"Famous last words," Jin-woo whimpered.

Ki-tae

Ki-tae CHUCKLED at his words, his breath puffing back in his face, bringing Jin-woo's scent with it. Never had a human smelled so intoxicating before. He opened his mouth, allowing his fangs to descend, and sank them slowly into Jin-woo's neck. The sweet rush of blood filled his mouth, and Jin-woo's moans filled his ears. Energy flooded through him, along with the most intense pleasure Ki-tae had ever experienced. He pressed his body flush against Jin-woo's, feeling the hard evidence of desire against his stomach, an answer to his own erection.

Jin-woo gripped his shoulders with surprisingly strong hands, clutching at him. Ki-tae growled softly, pulling more of the sweet liquid into his mouth. He shifted his hips, rubbing their cocks together, the cloth of their pants an annoying barrier. Slipping one knee between Jin-woo's thighs, Ki-tae parted them slowly. He brought his hands down and filled them with the rounded curves of Jin-woo's ass, the muscles quivering in his hands. Ki-tae lifted him, settling more firmly between his thighs, and hooked Jin-woo's legs over his hips.

With each pull on Jin-woo's neck, Ki-tae gave a slow thrust of his hips. He'd never experienced this much pleasure from feeding. He'd never encountered someone who smelled so damned good. The feel of Jin-woo trembling in his arms thrilled him, and he gripped tighter, causing Jin-woo to whimper. When he had his fill, Ki-tae withdrew his fangs. He licked the wound, sealing it with his saliva. He slowly worked his way up Jin-woo's neck and along his jaw until he captured those lips in a searing kiss. Ki-tae thrust his tongue deep into Jin-woo's mouth, tasting him once more. Though he no longer needed to feed, Ki-tae continued the movement of his hips, savoring the way Jin-woo eagerly moved with him.

"That's it," he whispered against Jin-woo's mouth. "Let go. Show me how good it feels. Let me hear you."

"Oh God," Jin-woo cried out, clawing at Ki-tae's back.

"Such sounds you make." Ki-tae purred again. "Such sweet, needy sounds."

"Ki-tae," Jin-woo whimpered. His trembling increased, the movement of his hips erratic.

"Cum for me," Ki-tae whispered directly into his ear.

Jin-woo screamed.

Ki-tae was stunned. Jin-woo was so beautiful as he came, so stunning. Ki-tae's gut clenched, and he followed, spilling in his pants as they pressed and rubbed together, panting. He leaned his head against Jin-woo's shoulder, trying to catch his breath. Ki-tae held him tightly. When he was finally able to breathe normally, Ki-tae lifted his head. Jin-woo's eyes were closed, his breathing still irregular. He brushed Jin-woo's hair back from his face, delighting in how silky and soft the black strands felt, how they curled around his fingers.

"Such a delight to the senses," Ki-tae murmured as he studied Jin-woo's face. "Such a sweet taste, and so responsive to my touch. It's a shame I have to leave you."

Ki-tae cupped Jin-woo's cheek, brushing his thumb along his full bottom lip, his top lip a perfect bow shape but thinner than the bottom, such a kissable mouth. He lowered Jin-woo to the ground, gently unwrapping his legs from Ki-tae's waist. He looked down and chuckled as he saw the dark stain on Jin-woo's pants. "I've made a mess of you."

The sounds of 2NE1's "Scream" filled the loading bay, and Ki-tae sighed. He pulled his phone out of his pocket, slid the Answer button over, and held it to his ear.

"Where in the world are you?" the stage manager, Seung-gi, demanded angrily.

"I… needed a little snack," Ki-tae said with a chuckle.

Seung-gi murmured, "I told you we'd get you something on the way home. You risk too much eating at the venue."

"Don't worry. I'm finished," Ki-tae said, caressing Jin-woo's face once more.

"Please tell me there's nothing for me to clean up," Seung-gi said with a sigh.

"No, but there is someone who needs to get home safely," Ki-tae said. "I'm in the loading bay."

Seung-gi arrived shortly after they hung up. It was as if he had a homing beacon for Ki-tae. On the one hand, such an ability could be very annoying. On the other, it had saved his life on several occasions. Ki-tae was sitting next to Jin-woo, the human's head on his thigh as Seung-gi approached.

"Please tell me he's still—"

"You know I don't do that anymore," Ki-tae admonished.

"I know," Seung-gi acknowledged. "Where does he need to go?"

"25-9 Jongsan-dong Ilsandong-gu, Go-yang-si, Gyeonggi-do. Do you think you can get him home safely?" Ki-tae said after fishing Jin-woo's wallet out of his pocket and opening it.

"I'll have Min-ho hyung take him," Seung-gi said as he pulled out his phone. "You'd best get back. The others are looking for you."

"They're always looking for me," Ki-tae murmured as he gently shifted Jin-woo's head from his thigh and rose to his feet. He took one last look at Cheong Jin-woo. Dark lashes fanned across his high cheekbones, softly curved and perfect for his face. He looked so sweet and innocent, an immediate draw for Ki-tae. His black hair was short on the sides and longer at the top, styled in slender spikes over his forehead. After a moment's hesitation, Ki-tae brushed his bangs aside, kissed his forehead, and then walked away. It wouldn't do to get infatuated with a human.

Those relationships never seemed to work out. No relationship ever worked out for him. Absently Ki-tae licked his bottom lip and Jin-woo's taste burst to life on his tongue. He stumbled and then caught himself. He would never forget that taste, never in a million years.

JIN-WOO

JIN-WOO AWOKE to the feel of warm sunlight on his face. He smiled at the pleasant pull as he stretched each of his muscles. After throwing back the covers, Jin-woo got out of bed, only to freeze in his tracks. He looked down. Why was he still dressed? Thinking back, Jin-woo realized he didn't remember coming home last night. He remembered the concert and the intermission, wandering around backstage as part of the University Media Club. He had learned a few new tricks from the cameramen that would help if and when they began filming their web series. After that, nothing. Jin-woo shifted and felt a pulling sensation at his groin. After lifting his shirt, he stared at the dark stain on his pants. He scrunched up his nose at the mess.

Jin-woo dropped back onto his bed, his eyes wide with shock. "It wasn't a dream. My Ki-tae is a Vampire. He... drank from me and... oh my God."

Heat flamed in Jin-woo's face. The things he'd allowed Ki-tae to do. He was shameless. He should have.... Well, Jin-woo didn't know what he should have done in the face of a Vampire, but it probably wasn't a good idea to let Ki-tae rub against him like that. Letting Ki-tae drink his blood, yeah, that probably hadn't been a smart thing either. How was he ever going to watch his favorite idol? How was he ever going to look at those pouting lips and those soulful brown eyes and not remember how Ki-tae had made him cum so hard he passed out... from frotting?

"If that's what frotting did to me, what would sex do?" Jin-woo whispered, covering his face with his hands. "No, no, I am *not*, absolutely not going to think about that. It would probably kill me.... Heck of a way to go, though."

Jin-woo giggled, actually giggled, and that sobered him up quickly. He was a man; he shouldn't be giggling like some high school girl with a crush. Glancing at the clock, Jin-woo swore softly. He was going to be late for class if he didn't get his ass in gear. He jumped off his bed, stripping his clothes off as he did so. Forty-five minutes later, Jin-woo was out the door and on his way to Jeonjin University. He made it to Pungson Station by 7:20 a.m. Granted, he'd had to jog most of the way, but he didn't miss his train, and that's all that mattered. Another thirty minutes later, the train stopped at Jeonjin University station in Mapo-gu, Seoul. Jin-woo had another ten-minute walk until he reached the campus, but he didn't mind. Well, in the spring, summer, and fall, he didn't mind. Jin-woo glanced at his phone and groaned. Fourteen degrees Celsius? Seriously? He loved his country and adored Seoul, but January weather sucked and it wouldn't start to warm up for another two months. Jin-woo pulled the hood of his parka tighter around his head and kept walking. The sooner he got to campus, the sooner he could warm up.

"Jin-woo-ya!" a familiar voice called, and he paused on the sidewalk outside the station, his boots making a squishing sound in the slush. He waved as his best friend, Yi Min-su, came running up to him, her ponytail bouncing in time with her backpack. "Are you all right?"

"I'm fine, why?" he asked as she hooked her arm with his and they walked to class.

"You disappeared last night. I waited for over an hour, called your phone a billion times, and sent you message after message. You didn't respond, so I got worried."

"No, I, uh…. I'm sorry, Min-su-ya," Jin-woo said, blushing. "I—I got really sick and, uh, and headed home."

Min-su punched him in the arm and then hugged him. "I forgive you, but don't do that ever again."

"I missed the rest of the concert," Jin-woo said, rubbing his arm. She always hit so hard. "How, um, how was it?"

"Oh my God, it was amazing!" Min-su bounced. "I so want to have Cheongul oppa's baby!"

"You're such a fangirl," Jin-woo teased.

"Ki-tae oppa was pretty amazing too." Min-su looked at him sideways. "He did this slow dance. The things that man can do with his body. He's like walking sex!"

"He certainly is," Jin-woo murmured.

"Well, fortunately for you, I filmed it." Min-su smiled brightly. "I sent it to your email this morning. You can watch it at lunch and drool to your heart's content."

"Would you mind keeping it down, please?" Jin-woo said, looking around as they entered the university. "I'd rather not advertise that particular bit of information."

"I don't know what you're afraid of," she said softly.

"Yes, well, people are stupid, and while I don't deny it, I don't advertise it either," Jin-woo answered. Min-su hugged his arm once more. She'd done the same thing when she first found out he was attracted to men. That was an interesting conversation. He should have been more careful when watching the older boys in PE, especially Jae-wook hyung. Man, Jin-woo crushed on him so bad.

"I know," Min-su said. "So you can watch it when you get home or find a private spot. We have a club meeting today, and Seonsaengnim said we would be having a special visitor to our class, so don't be late."

"I won't," Jin-woo said with a smile as he tugged on her pigtail. "And if I am, it's usually your fault!"

"Oh, not true!"

"Very true," Jin-woo said. "Now, pull up your hood. You're making me cold. How can you run around in this weather with no hat or gloves and your coat unzipped? Are you trying to get sick?"

Min-su shrugged and looked away. "I don't feel it."

"I'd kill to have that ability," Jin-woo grumbled.

"No, you wouldn't." Min-su's voice was odd and Jin-woo looked at her sideways. What was up with that?

"Well, well, what have we here?" Jin-woo sighed as Ki-bom's voice cut through the air behind them.

"Doesn't she have anything better to do?" he asked Min-su. When she would have stopped, Jin-woo pulled her along. They didn't have time for Ki-bom's attitude this morning. If they stopped, they'd be late, and Jin-woo didn't relish the idea of standing in the hall or extra cleaning duties.

"I'm talking to you," Ki-bom called out.

Min-su tried to turn around once more, but Jin-woo kept a tight grip on her arm, pulling her along the graffiti-covered walkways toward the campus. This section of the city was a little… gritty, but the small areas of evergreens and barren trees were kind of pretty in their own way. He liked it better when the trees were in full bloom and gave some color to the otherwise boring gray concrete and cement. He wished the city would put more of them in. Seoul needed some nature to counter all the industry and urbanization in his opinion. "She is so not worth being late for class, Min-su-ya. Just ignore her."

"I cannot stand that bitch!" Min-su hissed. "Who the hell does she think she is?"

"I'm not a psych major, so I don't care about her mental deficiencies. I care about getting to class on time because I hate cleaning classrooms!" he said.

Finally Min-su gave up trying to go back to face Ki-bom. From what Min-su had told him, she and Ki-bom had been friends in elementary school. Then Ki-bom moved away for a short time. Min-su said they hadn't gotten along since Ki-bom came back. She didn't go into detail about it, and Jin-woo didn't press. It seemed to be a sore subject for her. Of course, she also said she didn't care because now she had Jin-woo, and that was just fine with her. Jin-woo smiled. Min-su was his best friend, and there were so many things he could tell her. Honestly, she was the only person who knew the real Jin-woo, about his dreams, about what he wanted to do with his life, and about his past.

KI-TAE

KI-TAE GAVE a little purr as he languidly stretched beneath the silk sheets of his bed. The floor-to-ceiling windows allowed sunlight to filter through the dark blue sheers. He hadn't felt this relaxed, this sated, in a very long time. He let loose a happy chuckle. He felt really good, and he could, more than likely, lay that at Jin-woo's feet. Something about his blood had given Ki-tae this energy, this pleased feeling. He had been so responsive, so vocal in his pleasure. There was nothing Ki-tae enjoyed more than knowing he was pleasing his partner, and Jin-woo had certainly let him know how good he was feeling.

"Too bad he's human," Ki-tae murmured. "Otherwise I would consider playing with him for a few centuries."

After a couple more moments of fantasizing about Jin-woo in his bed, Ki-tae rose and padded, naked, to the shower. He had dance practice, a voice lesson, and several interviews ahead of him, and he needed to get moving. Otherwise Soon-joon, his manager, might have kittens. Well, he was more than just a manager, but he took all his roles very seriously.

Once he was clean, Ki-tae threw on a pair of worn jeans with holes in the knees, followed by a long-sleeved T-shirt and his black Chucks. He grabbed his bag, shoved several bottles of water inside, along with some snacks, and headed out to the studio. The sun was just peeking over the horizon, and he had to be at the dance studio in thirty minutes. His apartment in the capital wasn't that far from headquarters and he would be taking company transportation to his interviews, but at the end of the day, he didn't want to walk back to his place. It would be too damn cold. Their choreographer, Rah Goo-ji, was a slave driver, but Ki-tae had to admit the results she pulled from them were phenomenal.

Several hours later, he was not so fond of their choreographer. His entire body ached, and sweat slicked his skin, and it took a lot to make him sweat, reminding Ki-tae why they had nicknamed her Gojira. He wanted to chug the bottle of water in his hand but forced himself to drink it slowly. Stomach cramps would not be fun. He might be a Vampire, but his body didn't function all that differently from a human's. He had greater endurance and could take way more damage than a human before being incapacitated, but everything else was pretty much the same. Well, except for the additional need to consume blood. Cheongul dropped to the floor next to him. He handed one of his best friends—brother, really—a bottle without a word.

"You smelled like sex and blood when you came back last night," Cheongul said after taking a long pull off the water bottle. "And you had an early costume change."

"My two favorite scents," Ki-tae said with a smirk.

"*Dongsaeng*—"

"Nosy," Ki-tae said, elbowing Cheongul. "I had an… encounter with someone backstage. He caught me having a little snack, and I chased him through the stadium to the loading dock."

"Shit, he knows?" Cheongul said and sucked air through his front teeth as he pressed his tongue against them. Ki-tae realized he made that noise a lot when they talked.

"Yes, he knows," Ki-tae said. "I don't think he's going to say anything, though."

"Why not?"

"First, who's going to believe him? Second, if anyone did believe him, there's no proof, and third, frotting with me definitely ruins his credibility, don't you think?" Ki-tae said, raising his eyebrow.

Cheongul stared at him, his mouth hanging open. "You're shitting me."

"Not in the slightest. Plus he tasted absolutely fucking delicious," Ki-tae said before taking another swig of water.

"You're telling me you chased this guy through the Seoul Olympic Stadium after he caught you feeding, cornered him in the loading docks, and he let you drink from him *and* get off?"

"Well, the last was definitely mutual."

"Even so, dongsaeng, *Abeoji*'s not going to be happy someone knows we exist," Cheongul said with all seriousness. "And you know Seung-gi hyung has to tell him."

"I'll tell him. I don't want to put Seung-gi hyung through that," Ki-tae said, looking down as he fiddled with the bottle cap. Their sire could be… intimidating, but he wasn't an unreasonable man. "Abeoji will at least listen."

"He's still not going to be happy. You know how he feels about keeping us safe," Cheongul said.

Before Ki-tae could respond, Gojira came in and put them back to work. They would practice another two hours, followed by his voice lesson, and then it was off to interviews, after a shower and clothing change, before rehearsal in the evening. Afterward they were supposed to meet their sire for dinner, as they did every month. Ki-tae loved what he did, but it was hard work. Perhaps that was why he loved it. Work gave him purpose, something to look forward to, something to make it worth getting out of bed. Immediately an image of Jin-woo came to mind and Ki-tae smiled. Well, maybe there were more reasons to get out of bed in the morning.

JIN-WOO

JIN-WOO CURLED up on the window ledge, sketching. His morning classes were done for now, and he had a few moments before his last class started. Then it would be off to the studios to work on his various projects. Min-su had yet to arrive, so he figured working on his storyboards was a good way to pass the time. Honestly, he loved his faculty, loved the combination of art, music, and technology. That's what had drawn him to Jeonjin University and why Jin-woo chose the School of Design and Media. He could indulge in both his passions.

Jin-woo jumped as Min-su slammed her books down on the desk next to him. For a moment he couldn't breathe. Then his heart slowed and he could focus on her. She looked mad as hell.

"What's happened?" he asked, setting his drawing pad aside.

"Ki-bom *seonbae* happened," Min-su snarled. "I don't get her. Why can't she leave me alone?"

"You have to ignore her."

"It's hard when I get cornered by her and her cronies in the girls' bathroom," Min-su said, crossing her arms over her chest. "It took forever to get out of there without punching someone."

Jin-woo smiled. "Well, I am proud of your show of restraint. It proves you're the better person."

"Thank you." Min-su looked slightly mollified. "Did I miss anything?"

"Not really. I've just been working on my storyboards while waiting for everyone to arrive."

"Really? Can I see?" Min-su asked, a smile blossoming on her face. She practically bounced with excitement.

"They're not very good, just preliminaries. I won't be able to do more until we hammer out the story itself," Jin-woo said as he handed her the pad.

"Your work amazes me every time I see it," Min-su said softly, flipping through the pages. "Even your rough sketches are awesome. You have such a natural talent."

"I'm not all that," Jin-woo muttered, ducking his head to hide the blush he knew was on his face.

"I swear every creative thing you touch, you excel at, Jin-woo-ya," Bak Jong-in said as he plopped down in the desk next to Min-su. Jong-in was the only other person he felt close to. A quiet man, Jong-in was a god on the soundboard. "You play several instruments, the artwork is amazing, even the writing—although you don't get involved in that part too much, you're good at all of it."

"That's not unusual, and I only play two. You play drums, guitar, bass, and piano. And if you saw the marks I got on my last 3-D art project, you'd realize I'm not good at everything. And have you seen me trying to balance my checkbook? Math is not my forte. Really, I'm not—"

"Stop," Min-su said with a smile as she grabbed his arm. Jin-woo smiled at her. It made him feel good when they liked his work. It meant he was doing things right.

"Most of us are really good at one aspect of digital media production, maybe two," Jong-in said. "You're really good, and it's nothing to be ashamed of. You have natural talent."

"Until you put me in front of an audience and I pass out or puke. I just... you all do great work," Jin-woo said. "It's not just me."

"We do better work with you," Mei said, joining their little group. She moved close to Jin-woo, almost touching. He shifted away slightly, her proximity making him uncomfortable. He wished she would stop standing so close to him all the time. "So does anyone know what this special announcement is?"

Jin-woo gave her what he hoped was a polite smile but didn't respond to her compliment. He always felt slightly unsettled around Mei. He wasn't sure what, if anything, to do about the blush that colored her cheeks. He really hoped it didn't mean she *liked* him liked him. She was guaranteed disappointment on that front. Before he could think further on it, the teacher entered the classroom and called for everyone's attention. They took their seats.

"Good afternoon, everyone," he began. "As I mentioned last week, we have a special visitor today. He is an alumnus of Jeonjin University and a dear friend of mine from my own school days. Currently he is one of the most successful managers at BL Entertainment. Please welcome Park Soon-joon-nim."

As the distinguished gentleman entered the room, Jin-woo nearly fell over. Park Soon-joon was known as the God of K-pop. Every group he put together never failed to soar to the top of the charts. He was known for managing bands that were a strong cohesive unit in talent and personality. Park Soon-joon just had the gift. He knew who to mix with whom, how many members, what would work and what wouldn't. There was no one with his success rate in the industry to date.

Jin-woo stared wide-eyed at the man responsible for bringing Ki-tae and Bam Kiseu into his life.

KI-TAE

KI-TAE ARRIVED at his sire's home in one of the more affluent districts of Seoul. Beyond the walls, it was as if he'd stepped from the city to the country. In the spring, summer, and fall there was greenery everywhere. Zelkovas, alders and birch trees, though they were bare of leaves at present, abelia shrubs and camellias in various shades creating a transitional rainbow affect when they were in bloom. Snow blanketed the entire area at the moment, but the soft burble of water could be heard in the quiet of the night. He truly did enjoy coming to his sire's house. It made him feel... safe, secure, and that was a feeling he cherished. There was a time when he wasn't either of those things, and Ki-tae never wanted to go there again. A chill danced up his spine, and he immediately shook it off.

He turned off the main walkway and followed the stone path curving around the right side of the house. It took him through a small garden and over a little wooden bridge spanning a decent-sized koi pond. A sheet of ice covered the surface, but the pond had been installed with a heated edge used only during the winter which kept the pond from completely freezing and allowed for ventilation with the use of the aerator. The path continued between two peach trees standing to either side, as if they were sentries guarding the emperor's castle. Ki-tae chuckled. He paused long enough to remove his shoes and place them on the tidy wooden shelves nearby, noting three other pairs already settled. Then he walked through the open doors and into a spacious sunroom. He continued through, weaving around the low table and cushions into the dining room. The room was a long rectangle, its walls showing serene landscapes of Korea, China, and Japan, all places they had lived at one point or another.

Beyond that was the kitchen, an ode to their love of food with sleek appliances and maximized counter space. They would make breakfast together in the morning, able to move around the kitchen easily and freely. This weekend visit was always their time to be a family, something all of them had lacked for a long time. Ki-tae pushed his fingers through his hair as he walked into the small nook to the right of the kitchen. It was a cozy room filled with warm, welcoming color. He found Cheongul, HanYin, and their sire all seated at the medium-sized square teak table, waiting for him.

"*Adeul*, so good of you to join us!" his sire called, lifting a hand and beckoning him closer. "We have waited for you."

"You didn't need to do that, Abeoji. I'm sorry for being so late," Ki-tae said as he walked to Soon-joon's side and placed a kiss on his head after he bowed. "You should have started without me."

"I will not eat until all my sons are at my table."

"Stubborn old goat," Ki-tae teased affectionately.

"I am at that." He gestured toward the food spread across the table. "Eat. Then we will talk."

Ki-tae took his seat to Soon-joon's right. In the privacy of their home, certain protocols were not observed unless company was present, though there was very rarely any company present. Sometimes, it still struck Ki-tae as odd to eat regular food. He remembered asking once, as many of the stories he'd heard said they only existed on blood. His question resulted in a lengthy—very lengthy—explanation of how blood maintained their qi and thus their enhanced senses, reflexes, and healing ability while regular food maintained their physical body. Why Soon-joon couldn't have just told him the food was for the body and the blood for the qi and leave it at that, Ki-tae didn't know. His father seemed to like lengthy explanations.

Once Soon-joon picked up his spoon, they dug in, chattering about nothing in particular as they served themselves and each other. Soon-joon invariably placed more food in their bowls, exclaiming they didn't eat nearly enough when they tried to protest.

"*Aish*, do you want me to get fat?" Ki-tae cried as another heap of shrimp was placed in his bowl. "I won't be able to dance onstage! I'll have to waddle!"

"As if fat stays on us with our choreographer. She must have been a slaver in her last life," Cheongul complained, scrunching up his face. "My legs *still* hurt from practice today."

"Quit complaining. You're all too skinny as it is," Soon-joon said, turning back to his own food.

"Not me. This is all healthy!" HanYin said with a smile, yanking up his shirt to show off his muscles.

Ki-tae smacked his firm stomach. "*Yah*, look at you, so proud."

As soon as they were all settled with their food and had taken several moments to eat, Ki-tae felt Soon-joon's eyes on him. He looked up into his sire's gaze. It was intense but beyond that, unreadable.

"What is it, Abeoji?"

"I went to Jeonjin University today to see an old friend." Soon-joon began shifting the food around in his bowl with his chopsticks. "He is a professor there. We had lunch together to discuss an idea I had for your next project."

"The minimovies?" Cheongul asked, glancing at Ki-tae. "I like Ki-tae's idea. I think concept will make our music videos stand out more if there's a story being told visually as well."

"People love good stories and good music," HanYin agreed.

Ki-tae glanced away for a moment. He had been hesitant to present the idea, thinking they wouldn't like it, would think it too gimmicky, but he was tired of all the videos just being them singing and dancing. He had nothing against those types of music videos, but he wanted their fans to have more.

"It was just a thought," Ki-tae mumbled, staring down at his food.

"It is a good idea, Ki-tae," Soon-joon said with a small smile. "That's why I went to my friend with it. I had been looking for a way to help the digital media students from Jeonjin. It is so hard to get into this business. I want to give them a foot in the door, so to speak."

"I thought that was what your scholarship program was for?" HanYin said as he examined a piece of pork before putting it in his mouth. At his father's place, he used his manners... for the most part.

"It is, but that's just money, and it's from one of the subsidiary companies. I want to do a little more. Pretty much every aspiring artist, musician, filmmaker, director, or sound engineer must have examples of their work these days. Our companies want to see what they can do, measure if the risk to hire them is worth it," Soon-joon explained. "Therefore, Seonsaengnim and I worked out a program whereby the students in the design and media school will have a chance to begin building their portfolio and earning an internship with BL Entertainment."

"How does that relate to my suggestion?" Ki-tae asked.

"Beginning this year, the students will divide into groups. During the first part of the program, they will each be assigned one of Bam Kiseu's songs, one we haven't done a video for. They will take that song and come up with a video concept that tells a story. They will need to create storyboards, mock-ups, go through the whole process. Once that is completed, they will present their ideas to a panel made up of Seonsaengnim, myself... and you three. Once all ideas have been presented, we will determine which group had the best idea. That group will then be involved in the making of the video."

"You said that was the first part. What's the second?" Cheongul said, pushing his bangs out of his face.

"In part two, each student will write an original song. They will compose it, record it, and produce it," Soon-joon said.

"What's the catch?" Ki-tae looked at his sire.

"The song will need to take into account the vocal style of not only Bam Kiseu as a group, but each of your individual vocal styles." Soon-joon smiled almost beatifically.

"And this is going to be a yearly thing?" Cheongul asked.

"Well, the requirements will be the same, but it would be better if the idols we manage are rotated year to year. I want to give them variety. Creating music videos and writing songs for a group is different than doing it for a solo artist."

"The average student is going to have difficulty with this," HanYin said. "And the ones who don't listen to us will have a harder time of it."

"True, but they will have to put together examples of what they *can* do, and any manager worth their salt will be able to see the potential in them," Soon-joon said. "Also, I've arranged for each student to receive small grants to assist them with establishing their full portfolios."

"You're just an old softie," Ki-tae teased as Cheongul nodded.

"*Duōchóushàngǎn,*" HanYin agreed. "A teddy bear."

"What made you do this?" Ki-tae asked, suddenly seeing a bit of regret in Soon-joon's eyes. When those eyes met his, he could see pain as well.

"I met a young man today," Soon-joon said, his focus solely on Ki-tae. "He was shy, but not to the point of inaction. Once the announcement had been made, the students all clamored to have this young man as part of their group. Apparently he was considered the most talented one in their class. He was very polite when speaking and responded easily to the teasing he received, but he had one other thing that made him stand out."

"What was that?" Cheongul asked hesitantly, glancing at Ki-tae.

"His scent was overlaid by that of one of my children," Soon-joon said. "Can you tell me which one?"

"You already know it's me," Ki-tae said with a sigh. "Why pretend?"

"Can you tell me why you fed so deeply from him that he smells of you, even after bathing?" Soon-joon said. There was no heat in his voice.

"How?"

"There is only one way to embed our scent on a human so deeply," Soon-joon said. "You fed from his neck, from his carotid, didn't you?"

"I… yes," Ki-tae said softly, hanging his head. At the time he hadn't been ashamed at all. Now he felt very guilty.

"There are reasons why I teach you to feed the way I do," Soon-joon said just as quietly. "Blood from the carotid artery comes straight from the heart. Freely given, it is the most amazing feeling in the world, but it also has consequences. It can bind you to that individual."

"What do you mean, bind me to him?" Ki-tae asked, snapping his head up to stare at Soon-joon. He… he couldn't go through that again, couldn't belong to someone, controlled by them, not ever again.

He started shaking in his seat, his grip on the table causing it to vibrate. The roaring in his ears made their voices fade away. He dug his claws into the wood, leaving deep furrows. His fangs descended, puncturing his lips as they hadn't done since he was first turned. Hands grabbed him, and Ki-tae struck out with a roar. Vague sounds of crashing and shouting followed. He tried to get away, tried to break free, and then he heard that voice in his ear, the sound of love and safety and peace.

Ki-tae curled against Soon-joon as they fell to the floor, his face pressed into his father's chest. Tears streamed down his face; he curled his fingers tightly in the fabric of Soon-joon's shirt. He couldn't think, couldn't breathe. It all hurt so much. What was he going to do? He could never go through that again. It would kill him this time, Vampire or not. Gentle fingers stroked his hair, soothing him into sleep.

Soon-Joon

SOON-JOON ROSE gracefully, heedless of the weight of Ki-tae in his arms. He carried his youngest son down the hallway that opened slightly off-center from where Ki-tae had entered. To the right was a line of windows, a small Zen rock garden beyond. The hall connected with an open living room with a more Japanese influence, harking back to Soon-joon's very early days. He had lived in many different places, but he always came back to Asia, whether it was Japan, China, or Korea. Here, Soon-joon felt most at home, and he wanted that same feeling for his sons.

On the opposite side of the living room were their private quarters. Made up of four rooms, each with a hallway separating them and no doors facing each other, it gave them privacy but also a sense of closeness. He carried Ki-tae down the right hallway and into his room, bumping against the black cabinetry to the left of the door as he entered. Gently he placed Ki-tae on the bed after Cheongul drew back the covers. Soon-joon tucked them up under Ki-tae's chin. Slowly he reached up and pushed Ki-tae's bangs to the side with a sigh.

"Abeoji," Cheongul said quietly. "What are we going to do?"

"He hasn't had an episode in so long," HanYin said, then nibbled his lower lip. He leaned against the corner, part of his body hidden behind the wall.

"We will have to wait to see if binding took place first," Soon-joon said as he rose from the bed. "Only then will we know what course to take. In the meantime, you two should stay with him. He knows I am here, but he needs the comfort of his brothers."

They nodded and immediately climbed into bed with Ki-tae, sandwiching him between them. Soon-joon watched them as they cared for their brother. HanYin would have a nice bruise along the left side of his jaw later, and Cheongul's right eye was already swelling slightly. Fortunately both injuries would be gone by morning. He had tried to do his best with them. Each of his sons had his own story. Each had something in his past that affected him to this day, and each one showed a strength of will, of spirit, that was all too often squelched by those who should know better, by those who thought to control and dominate everything around them. It continued to amaze him how arrogant humans could be, to think they had such power and the right to wield it so.

Soon-joon withdrew quietly. Questions rattled through his mind. Ki-tae was not a careless man, impulsive, but not careless. There had to be a reason why he'd been feeding at the stadium during a concert. He would have to look into it later, talk with Ki-tae after he was more settled. If the ancestors were smiling on them, no bond had been established between Ki-tae and this young man. He could only hope. Ki-tae and bonds were not a good combination, as attested to by the shattered table, dishes, and food scattered all over his floor. Soon-joon sighed. Then he went into the kitchen, grabbed the garbage can, and pulled it into the breakfast nook. It was a good thing he always made extras. His boys would be hungry when they woke.

JIN-WOO

JIN-WOO SAT in the student cafeteria with Min-su and Jong-in. He stared at his food, not seeing it. Seonsaengnim's announcement spun around and around in his head. A chance to film a video with Bam Kiseu. A chance to write a song that would be performed by Bam Kiseu, by Ki-tae. Jin-woo started to breathe faster and faster. The crack of a hand across his face brought him back quickly.

"Ow! What the hell, Min-su-ya?" he demanded.

"You were hyperventilating... again," she said. "I know it's incredibly amazing and wonderful and the dream of a lifetime, but if you pass out and end up in the hospital, then what?"

"I'm sorry. You just—"

"Do not tell me I don't understand. Who is the president of the Cheongul oppa fan club? Who has his image plastered all over one wall of her room?" Min-su said, pointing at him.

"All right, you do," he said.

"Yeah, well, you two can keep Cheongul hyung and Ki-tae hyung and leave HanYin hyung to me," Jong-in muttered.

"HanYin oppa? Since when have you been more than a casual fan of Bam Kiseu?" Min-su demanded.

"I've always been his stan," Jong-in said defensively, sticking his chin out.

"You never said a thing! You were all over G-1 and their short-shorts," Jin-woo said.

"I... I just didn't want you guys to think less of me because I like him so much."

"Geu-rae-yo?" Jin-woo said. "You have listened to me going on about Ki-tae hyung... not nearly as much as Min-su-ya goes on about Cheongul hyung, but still, what would have given you the idea we'd think less of you?"

"I don't know." Jong-in hung his head, chuckling as Min-su smacked Jin-woo.

"You're an evil midget," Jin-woo hissed at her as he rubbed the back of his head. She raised her hand again and Jin-woo held up his sketchpad in defense.

"That is an insult to little people and you shouldn't talk that way," Min-su said, giving him a dirty look.

"Fine, you're an evil bitch."

"Thank you."

"All right, stop it, you two. We have work to do," Jong-in said with a laugh. "We need to come up with a killer concept *and* a kick-ass video for Bam Kiseu. You have the notes, Min-su-ya. Which song did we get?"

The two settled down, and Min-su pulled pencils and her notebook from her backpack while Jin-woo opened his drawing pad. He took the pencil from behind his ear.

"We were given 'Crossing Time,'" she said after checking her notes. "That's off their third minialbum, *Eternity*."

"Damn. That's the one I just had to throw out because it got all scratched to hell with no hope of saving it," Jong-in grumbled, flopping back in his chair.

"I can't believe you still use CDs," Min-su said.

"What? I get sick of the streaming sites asking me if I'm still listening," Jong-in said. "No commercials either, which is always a plus and… no buffering."

"He's got you on that one. Buffering sucks," Jin-woo said, absently moving his hand over the paper. "Do you have it on your phone, Min-su-ya?"

"No, the file got corrupted somehow and won't play." She pouted as she looked at her phone. "We don't have time to listen to it now. Lunch is almost over."

"All right, why don't you guys come over to my house after school. We can listen to the song and brainstorm," Jin-woo said.

"Looks like you're already doing that," Jong-in said as he stood up to see what Jin-woo was drawing. "Ki-tae hyung, big surprise… as a Vampire?"

Jin-woo jerked his head up, and he stared, wide-eyed, at Jong-in. "What?"

"Your drawing. I think that's an awesome idea. Think about it. The album is called *Eternity*, and the song is called 'Crossing Time.' It'd be perfect. How often do music videos go with a supernatural theme? At most you get the super sad ones where one of the lovers dies, leaving the other to grieve alone."

Min-su tapped her pencil against her bottom lip. "We could work with two or three eras. Costuming wouldn't be that hard. We don't have to get real elaborate with them, and I'm sure we can find a props house to work with."

"But… why a Vampire?" Jin-woo said, swallowing hard as he recalled his very intimate encounter with the real thing. He stared at his sketch: the way Ki-tae had looked up from the woman's arm as he continued to drink. Without thinking, Jin-woo had sketched his first encounter with Ki-tae. Well, before he ran. But Ki-tae had caught him, hadn't he? He certainly had. Jin-woo shook his head. "What if we just imply he's immortal without actually identifying exactly *what* he is?"

"What other creature lives forever?" Min-su said.

"Tons. There are hordes of beings that are immortal," Jin-woo said, hoping they would drop the whole Vampire thing.

"Okay, you come up with a list of other beings we could use and how we can show what they are without coming right out and saying it. If you can't, then we go with the Vampire because then all we have to do is flash some fangs," Min-su said, pointing her pencil at him.

"I'll start working on setting ideas," Jong-in said.

After bidding Jin-woo goodbye, Jong-in and Min-su left for their afternoon classes. Jin-woo didn't have one immediately following lunch, for which he was very grateful. Food made him sleepy, but right now, he was wide-awake and twitchy. They couldn't make a video of Ki-tae being a Vampire! They just couldn't. It wouldn't be right to expose him like that, and Ki-tae would think Jin-woo told them what he was, and Jin-woo was pretty sure that would not make Ki-tae happy. In fact, it might just make him angry, and while Jin-woo might like Ki-tae to be aggressive like he was in the loading dock, he was pretty sure Ki-tae would not be looking for sex. More like he would be looking to permanently shut Jin-woo's mouth.

The rest of Jin-woo's day passed in a blur. He was sure he went to classes, but he wasn't quite sure he didn't do anything stupid or out of the ordinary. All he knew was he needed to come up with a way to avoid portraying Bam Kiseu as Vampires. Why did everyone always think of Vampires when they thought of immortals anyway? Weren't the gods immortal? There were hundreds of those. Why did they go for the fanged ones first? Okay, fangs were hot; he could attest to that. They had felt amazing in his neck. Of course, having Ki-tae pressed against him the way he was probably went a long way to convincing Jin-woo fangs were a good thing.

He had to stop thinking of that... encounter? Hookup? Jin-woo didn't even know what to call it. Every time he remembered, his body responded, and he didn't want to have his friends show up while he was sporting an erection. Besides, it wasn't ever going to happen again. He would just have to cherish the memories... in private... when he wasn't expecting anyone. Then he could take care of the resulting problem at his leisure. Remember every touch, every kiss, the way Ki-tae had pressed between his thighs, hot and hard, and.... Jin-woo shook his head. He *really* needed to stop.

The knock came at his door just as Jin-woo pulled food from the oven. He figured they would get hungry while brainstorming, and all three of them could eat. Well, Min-su could out eat him, but he wasn't about to tell her that. He liked living, and she'd make his death a lingering one if he ever said anything of the sort. Jong-in could pack it away, too, but he wasn't as bad. Jin-woo couldn't help it. He loved food, which was why he also exercised rigorously. If he didn't, he would look like a waddling marshmallow. Okay, so he wasn't exactly a gym sort of guy, but he liked to dance. He wasn't very good at it, but that's how he exercised.

"Jin-woo, what's taking so long?" Min-su said after she opened the door. "I almost expected the door to be locked."

"I was just pulling our snacks out," Jin-woo answered as he set the bowls and plates on the small table in the center of his living area. "But if you aren't hungry, I can always put it away."

He laughed when he heard the *thunk* as she immediately kicked off her shoes, ran around the corner and across what little space separated them to snatch a bowl out of his hand. Immediately she popped a chicken wing into her mouth, pulled off all the meat in one go, and smiled at him with puffed-out cheeks.

"You're a crazy lady, you know that, right?" Jin-woo said, shaking his head as he turned to get their drinks.

His apartment was long but narrow and made the most of the space by having the bedroom above the kitchenette and living area. In all, his home was maybe nine meters wide but about fifteen meters long. From the little entryway, there was a very short hall forming a U-shape from the door, around a corner, and then into the main room. His couch, armchairs, coffee table, and ottoman formed a living room of sorts along the right side of the main room. His stove, counters, refrigerator, and sink ran along the left side. The stairs leading up to his bedroom jutted out slightly about a meter from the end of his kitchen counter. A little area beyond them gave access to a set of sliding glass doors that led to a little balcony overlooking his neighborhood. He loved his apartment. It was tiny but cozy, and Jin-woo didn't need more space.

Once everything was all settled, Jin-woo sat down on the floor and rested back against his couch. He leaned his head back, closed his eyes, and sighed. It had been a long day and an even longer night. Well, at least the ending. He still couldn't remember how he got home. It was not a little disconcerting. He lived by himself, mostly because his aunt wanted nothing to do with him if she could help it, and that worked for him because Jin-woo really didn't want to deal with her either. While she would have preferred otherwise, he was family, and she felt a certain sense of duty where he was concerned. After all, his mother was her baby sister. When he started university, they both agreed it would be more beneficial for him to get his own place close to campus, and so Jin-woo did so with very little input from his aunt. If she had her way, he would be living destitute on the streets. Fortunately his grandparents hadn't been unaware of her feelings toward him.

Wiping his hands down his face before pushing them back up and into his hair, Jin-woo mentally shoved the thoughts aside. He didn't even know why he was thinking about that. He had his family right here, and that was all he would ever need. They were both staring at him, chewing on chicken wings.

"What?"

"What is up with you?" Jong-in said. "You've been a bit off all day today."

"I'm just tired. We did go to the Bam Kiseu concert last night," Jin-woo mumbled. "And I had to leave early because I wasn't feeling good."

"You should have told me. I would have driven you home," Min-su said, pointing a chicken bone at him.

"I didn't want you to miss the concert because of me." How easily the little lie rolled off his tongue.

"Are you feeling better now?"

"Yes." Jin-woo smiled to reassure them. "I'm just still a little tired from it all, I guess. Now what ideas have you guys come up with?"

"I still like the Vampire idea," Min-su said. "I think it's the easiest to portray on film."

"Yes, but because it's easy, it tends to be overdone," Jin-woo pointed out. "We have to stand out, and we can't do that if we go with easy."

"All right, Mr. Smarty Pants, what ideas did you come up with?" she said with a pout.

"Well, I had some, but I think we need to listen to the song. Jong-in-a, would you pull up a good copy of the lyrics? We'll compare them to the song," Jin-woo said. "I think I got most of them, but there are spots where I can't hear them clearly."

"And that's why you have me," Jong-in said.

Min-su snorted. "As if you're the only sound engineer."

"I know I'm not. I'm just the best at it." Jong-in beamed.

"I'm surrounded," she said with a huff. "You're Mr. Ego, and he's Mr. Humble!"

"Hey!"

"Well, you are. I swear half the people who speak with you are flirting with you, and you have no clue. Li Mei hubae is trying hard-core. She wants you, my friend. 'We're better with you,'" Min-su said in a fair imitation of Mei. "I mean, seriously? I have nothing against her, but that made my teeth hurt, it was so sweet."

Jin-woo blushed. "Back to the music."

"Okay, give," Jong-in said, wiping his hands clean on a napkin before pulling the laptop from in front of Jin-woo and turning it to face him. He reached into his backpack, grabbed his headset, and then plugged them in. Jong-in took in about five slow, deep breaths and then nodded. Jin-woo hit the Play button, and Min-su got her pen ready. Jong-in was insanely good with sound. Now all they had to do was wait for the music to start.

KI-TAE

HE BLINKED slowly, coming back to consciousness in bits and pieces. The smells reached him first, as usual, and he knew he wasn't alone, but neither was he in danger. The comforting scents of his brothers soothed him. HanYin's face was right in front of him, and he could feel Cheongul at his back. The arms wrapped around his waist were tight. Ki-tae smiled softly, reaching up to brush a finger down HanYin's cheek. Immediately silver eyes greeted him.

"Shhh," Ki-tae whispered. "It's all right. No need to be on alert."

"How do you feel?" HanYin asked.

"I'm good," Ki-tae said. "You still wake up expecting to be attacked."

"We all have our issues," HanYin said.

"True, such as Cheongul's death grip on me." Ki-tae chuckled as Cheongul tightened said grip.

"Well, you kind of lost it last night," HanYin said with a small smile. "You even took a swing at Abeoji."

"Shit," Ki-tae said. "I didn't hurt you guys, did I?"

"Not really. You threw Cheongul and me around a little, but not too bad. Nothing we haven't done to each other roughhousing."

"Still, I… I thought I'd gotten over it," Ki-tae whispered.

"Ki-tae, you don't 'get over' something like that. He controlled *everything* for years. You just need to remind yourself you're free, that Abeoji turned him into a smear on the ground, and the only person who controls you is you."

"*Joesonghaeyo.*"

"Don't apologize," Cheongul said, the words muffled against Ki-tae's shoulder. "You never have to apologize to us… for anything."

"Not even when I borrow your favorite black shirt without asking?" Ki-tae teased.

"You need to keep your hands off my clothes, Ki-tae." Cheongul bit his shoulder. "Of course, I've taken to buying two of everything. That way I don't have to worry about not having what I want to wear!"

"You shouldn't have to… holy shit," Ki-tae said, panting sharply as every nerve ending in his body fired all at once.

"Well, that answers my question," Soon-joon said as he came around the corner.

"He's bound, isn't he?" Cheongul asked.

"Yes."

"Fuck!" Ki-tae screamed, a terrifying combination of rage, fear, and uncontrollable lust colliding inside him.

"Just let it happen, Ki-tae," Soon-joon said as he moved HanYin out of the way and sat on the bed. "It will be easier to deal with that way. If you fight it, you'll only hurt yourself."

"I am not going to do what I want to do in front of my family," Ki-tae hissed.

"And we appreciate that, believe me," HanYin said with a blush. "I can practically taste your pheromones."

"Yeah, and you stink," Cheongul said, though the look in his eyes belied his apparent lack of concern. "I'm going to go get something to eat."

HanYin followed Cheongul out the door, giving Ki-tae a little wave as he did so. Soon-joon looked down at him, and Ki-tae could see the sadness in his eyes.

"This isn't your fault, you know," Ki-tae said, suppressing a groan. "I did this to myself by being stupid."

"You're not careless, Ki-tae," Soon-joon said, brushing Ki-tae's bangs off his forehead. "This boy, he must be something special."

"I couldn't tell you what it was about him. When I chased after him, it was because he'd seen me feeding, and I had to take care of that. But when I caught him… he smelled so good. It sent my whole body humming… like now."

Ki-tae knew he was blushing furiously.

"I'm going to give you some privacy," Soon-joon said with a smile. "When you're… finished, we'll be in the tearoom."

"Is there any way to break the bond, Abeoji?"

"Yes, but we'll discuss it later."

"Okay."

Ki-tae whimpered as another wave of desire hit him hard. What in the hell was Jin-woo *doing*? He'd better not be doing it with anyone else, that was for damn sure. Ki-tae would shred them! He felt his fangs slide down from their sheaths to prick at his lips. Jin-woo's smell filled his nose. Not just his normal one, no; that would have been easier on Ki-tae, sort of. The scent filling his nose right now was Jin-woo aroused, Jin-woo on the very edge of orgasm, just about to fall over. What. The. Fuck?

Ki-tae kicked off the blankets and pulled his shirt out of his pants. He tried to unbutton it, but his fingers were shaking too much. With a snarl, he ripped the soft cotton fabric and shoved it off as he sat up. Another wave of pleasure, and Ki-tae fell back against the bed. The next things to go were his pants and underwear. He couldn't have anything against his skin. It was too much. He was too sensitive. When this was over, Ki-tae was going to find Jin-woo and beat his ass for making Ki-tae go through this by himself.

"Jin-woo, you little pervert," Ki-tae said with a breathless chuckle as he stroked his hands down his body, lifting his hips slowly. He closed his eyes, allowing his mind to follow the pull on him, on his being, and there was Jin-woo lying in his bed, naked. It was a dream, of course, but Ki-tae had walked them before, just not while so fucking aroused. He'd certainly never walked someone's wet dream… about him! Ki-tae laughed. He was going to do every single thing Jin-woo was dreaming about in person when he got his hands on the little bastard. Such a sweet, innocent face and a wickedly dirty mind. When he had full control of his faculties, he was going to explore that mind and make Jin-woo beg to cum.

He couldn't stop himself anymore. He couldn't just lie there and not do *something*. Ki-tae tried to take a steady breath and failed. He let go and allowed himself to just experience the pleasure. Once he stopped fighting, he could wallow in it, savor the sensations racing over his skin, through his muscles, making everything so much more aware of each touch, phantom though they were. Biting his knuckle, Ki-tae tried not to scream, but it was almost impossible. He had never been a quiet lover. Finally he slid his other hand down along his abs, lingering on them for a few moments as Jin-woo's dream touch did. Then he continued until he felt the soft hair of his groin, his fingers sliding through the precum dripping from his aching cock. Ki-tae cried out at the first touch, like an electric current shooting through him. Strong, sure strokes from root to tip, and Ki-tae moaned at each pull. He dug the fingers of his other hand into his hair, pulling just enough.

He could hear Jin-woo's sweet moans, the way he whimpered and clawed at Ki-tae's back. He remembered how Jin-woo had turned his head to the right, offering his throat without conscious thought, how his blood had tasted on Ki-tae's tongue, and Ki-tae wanted more. He wanted Jin-woo above him, straddling his hips as Ki-tae pumped into him from below. Ki-tae wanted to dig his fingers into those lean hips and hold Jin-woo steady as he fucked him. He wanted to hear Jin-woo scream as he came all over Ki-tae's chest.

The base of his spine tingled and then jerked tight. Ki-tae reached up and grabbed the headboard, digging his claws into the fabric as he planted his feet and pumped his hips upward. He cried out as his orgasm shook him, spilling his seed over his hand, his lower stomach, and thighs. He strained, arching until the last few drops, the last electric sensations passed over him, before collapsing to the bed once more. Eyes closed, panting for breath, hand still loosely wrapped around his softening cock, Ki-tae couldn't give a damn. Everything prior to that moment, that blissful glimpse at heaven, was wrapped in a fuzzy haze of satiation. The only thing that would make it better was to have Jin-woo, blacked out from the pleasure, sprawled across his chest.

"Damn, Jin-woo," Ki-tae chuckled breathlessly.

When his body decided to stop telling him to fuck off with the moving thing, Ki-tae rose and went around the wall to the right of his bed and into his bathroom. This was one of his most favorite rooms of the house. The glass wall around the concrete tub offered privacy but still maintained a sense of openness. To the left was the shower with waterfall showerhead, his personal favorite. The rest of the bathroom was accented with smooth black marble walls and silver fixtures. The outer wall was all glass that opened onto a stunning view of Soon-joon's garden.

As he walked into the bathroom, Ki-tae flipped a switch, and the soft whir of curtains being drawn filled the room. A double layer of white sheers slid along a track in the ceiling in front of the outer windows, granting privacy for the room's occupants while maintaining the open feel. Grabbing a towel from the shelves built into the wall shared with his bedroom, Ki-tae tossed it over the edge of the tub before he entered the shower. He would have preferred to stay in bed, savoring the languid, sated sensation sex always left him with, but he had things he needed to discuss with his father.

While he would certainly be all for sex with Jin-woo *frequently*, the binding part had to go.

JIN-WOO

JIN-WOO JOLTED up in bed with a cry, wet heat rushing over his groin. He jerked his head down, staring at his lap, embarrassment making his cheeks flush. He hadn't had a wet dream for years. That he had one now, he blamed on Ki-tae. It was all his fault. He really had no right to be that damned sexy, and he certainly didn't have the right to turn Jin-woo into a shivering mass of want just by the mere thought of him. No, sir, he did not! Jin-woo climbed out of bed. Then he pulled the sheets and covers off and threw them in the empty laundry basket before heading into his bathroom to clean up. He was not going to spend the rest of the night a sticky mess and then become a crusty mess by morning. That was not on his list of things to do.

Once he was cleaned up, Jin-woo found he was wide-awake. With a sigh of resignation, he pulled out his books. He opened his laptop and clicked on his study playlist. Immediately the sultry sound of Ki-tae's voice filled the room, the lyrics of "Heat" giving Jin-woo goose bumps. He hit the fast-forward button, only to be confronted with "Master." Jin-woo let his head drop to the table with a *thunk*. Was this some sort of sign? He hoped not, because it was never going to happen. He had thought of Ki-tae too much before the concert. Now if he didn't force himself to focus on school or projects, he was thinking of Ki-tae all the freaking time, and it had been less than two days! It was utterly ridiculous.

In an act of desperation, Jin-woo hit the fast-forward button again. This time, VIXX came on with "Hyde." This he could deal with. Finally Jin-woo could focus on his studies.

Morning found Jin-woo with his head on his coffee table, out cold. He could just hear his alarm clock in his bedroom. Slowly he raised his head, rubbing his eyes, and looked around the room, disoriented for a few moments. Then he remembered his dream and taking the shower, only to find himself unable to sleep afterward. He glanced at the clock on his wall. It was too damn early to think about anything other than getting his coffee. Since he'd woken up on time, Jin-woo didn't have to rush getting ready. That always made the day start out well. It was his experience that waking up late made him feel rushed for the rest of the day.

Jong-in, Min-su, and he had brainstormed late into the night. They had come up with a few other ideas for the video, and Jin-woo had sighed with relief. Jong-in managed to figure out the lyrics Jin-woo missed, and he trusted Jong-in's ear. Had he been able to find the damned CD, it wouldn't have been an issue, but he'd rearranged his room and now couldn't find anything he needed. Of course, he'd probably find the stupid thing in the next few days when he didn't need it anymore. He had, fortunately, come up with another immortal being to use rather than the Vampire. The *dokkaebi* were a type of goblin. The Chonggak Dokkaebi was known as the bachelor, and it wasn't inconceivable that he could make himself attractive to humans. It was that whole magic thing. Jin-woo would have to do a little more research before he began his storyboards, but that wasn't a true hardship. He had an interest in the supernatural… and that was before he knew Vampires existed.

Vampires. Were. Real.

If Vampires were real, then what else was real? Werewolves? Goblins? Ghosts? Well, he'd always believed in ghosts, but the other stuff? No, he didn't want to think about inanimate objects becoming sentient entities capable of hurting people, and he certainly didn't want to think about demons and devils and evil creatures being real. Nope, not for him, no thank you. Except… were all Vampires as sexy as Ki-tae?

Jin-woo dropped his head. There he was, his thoughts circling back to Ki-tae yet again. He was getting as bad as any fangirl. At least he wasn't at the stalker stage. He drew the line there. Still, he was going to have to learn to keep a straight face when the judging began. He was going to have to not giggle like a freaking idiot when he saw Ki-tae again. Of course, that wasn't the only thing he was going to have to *not* do. He certainly couldn't tackle Ki-tae and ride him to the ground, no matter how tempting the idea was. Pulling his thoughts from contriving ways to keep Ki-tae occupied on said floor, Jin-woo headed into his bedroom to get ready for class. He could do this if he forced his mind not to wander back to Ki-tae. It was a case of easier said than done because he'd always been a wee bit obsessed with Ki-tae.

After several hours of school, extra study, and working on projects, Jin-woo was ready to scream. His brain could no longer fire on all cylinders, and he needed to stop thinking about work. He needed to relax. He needed to cut loose. What it all really boiled down to was Jin-woo needed to go to the club and party. He might even need a little bit of intimacy therapy just to get Ki-tae out of his head. He had to be realistic. Beyond this scholarship program, he would never see Ki-tae anywhere but onstage again.

Two and a half hours later, Jin-woo was dancing at Club Bound in Gangnam-su. It wasn't one of his usual choices, but he wanted something different and he'd chosen this place on a random impulse. Bodies pressed close all around him, and the energy was high. He laughed as he moved to the beat. They'd been playing EDM most of the night and it kept everyone moving. Hands clamped onto his hips and pulled him backward. Jin-woo looked over his shoulder to see a man smiling at him and then let his gaze sink toward the floor in a full examination. Tall, ruggedly handsome, muscled, nothing like Ki-tae. Yeah, this is what he needed to get Ki-tae out of his head. Jin-woo smiled and pressed back even as his brain screamed at him for being stupid.

Twenty minutes later Jin-woo wrapped his arms around the guy's neck as he was pressed up against a wall in the back hallway. He hadn't even bothered to get a name. What was the point? Hands groped him in turns too rough and not rough enough, but his cock was not even half-hard. Then the guy was kissing him and Jin-woo's stomach churned. No. He couldn't do this. He put his hands on the guy's shoulders and pushed hard.

"What?" The guy looked confused, his eyes glazed with more than just lust. Shit, he was on something, and that was so not Jin-woo's scene.

"I can't."

"What do you mean you can't? You were just into it."

"No, not really," Jin-woo said. "Look, I have to go. The dance floor is full of other people. You have a crapload of choices."

"I want you." The guy growled, and it wasn't even remotely as sexy as Ki-tae's was.

"And I'm saying no," Jin-woo said moving from between the guy and the wall.

"You don't get to say no."

"Yeah, actually, I do," Jin-woo said and then he turned and walked away. This had been a bad idea.

"You're a cocktease," the guy snarled after he grabbed Jin-woo's shoulder and spun him around, invading his personal space. This really wasn't a good idea.

"Maybe I am," Jin-woo said refusing to back down. "But I'm not doing anything with yours tonight."

"You're going to—"

"Problem?" His former hookup backed off, eyes wide with fear, and Jin-woo turned to see one of the bouncers standing behind him.

"No, Jae-woo hyung, none at all," the guy said. "I'm… going to go dance some more."

"No," Jae-woo said. "You're going to leave. I told you never to come back here while you're tripping. You want to fuck yourself up that's your business, but you don't bring it here."

"Yes, Jae-woo hyung." The guy practically ran to the door.

"Thank you."

"Look, I couldn't give a shit who you want to fuck, but most of this crowd is not like-minded," Jae-woo said as he put his hands on his hips. "Don't make my job harder."

"I didn't ask him to hit on me," Jin-woo said.

"No, but you didn't stop him either," Jae-woo said. "I'm just saying there are safer places for you if you want a hookup. Here may not be one of them."

Jin-woo walked out without a word. He didn't need that kind of shit. Yes, this had definitely been a bad idea. He rarely had problems with people taking offense at his sexuality, mainly because he didn't flaunt it, but sometimes, like tonight, it was brought home that people could be assholes about something that didn't even concern them.

KI-TAE

KI-TAE WAS annoyed. He'd been trying to get Soon-joon to tell him how to break the bond between Jin-woo and himself for the last week. Every time he thought he had his father nailed down, Soon-joon managed to either vanish or talk his way around what Ki-tae had on his mind. It was almost as if Soon-joon was doing it on purpose. It was as if he didn't want to break the bond, but Ki-tae couldn't have it remain. He just couldn't.

He looked at the clock on the practice room wall and growled in frustration. He still had another hour and a half left of dance practice. His frustration was making him mess up, and that pissed him off even more. Gojira, unaware of the situation or the danger Ki-tae presented when he was in a pissy mood, kept getting on his case about missing steps. He was about ready to tear her fucking throat and watch her bleed out. He walked to the side where he'd thrown his bag and grabbed a water bottle. He felt HanYin come up beside him.

"What's the matter, dongsaeng?" HanYin said softly. "Your eyes keep flashing silver, and you're growling. It's low, but it keeps getting louder."

Ki-tae grumbled, "I don't want to be here now. I'm this close to ripping her fucking throat out. She gives me that snide look one more time, and I won't be responsible for my actions."

"I can see that," HanYin said with a smile. "And while my legs would wholeheartedly agree with you at the moment, Soon-joon-nim would be most displeased. Why don't you head home? I'll clear it with seonbae here."

Ki-tae snickered despite himself. "You're bad."

"You love me anyway." HanYin grinned.

"Yeah, I do, you brat." Ki-tae grabbed HanYin in a headlock and rained kisses on his head. "You're my brat, though."

"Get out of here, cranky bastard." HanYin slipped free and shoved Ki-tae toward the door. "I'll take your stuff with me."

"You sure?"

"Yes, get out before you make a mess," HanYin said with a wink.

Ki-tae didn't ask again. He headed straight for the door, pulling out his phone and then dialing Soon-joon's number, ignoring Gojira. He needed to get this straightened out as soon as possible. When his call went to voicemail *again* he almost threw his phone. Was Soon-joon avoiding him? Really? It hurt. He was tempted to head to the corporate offices, but this wasn't something they could discuss there. Too many nosy people in the entertainment industry. Yes, BL Entertainment was a family, but that didn't mean they had no curiosity. Instead he headed to the house. He would wait until Soon-joon came home and corner him there.

Five hours. Ki-tae waited five hours for Soon-joon to return, and his patience, not something he was necessarily known for, paid off. When he heard his father coming inside, he stood up and headed out into the living room. Soon-joon looked very surprised to see him. Of course, he was still supposed to be working, but Ki-tae didn't give a damn about that right now.

"I've been trying to get ahold of you for the last few days," Ki-tae said softly. "You sent my calls to voicemail… why, Abeoji?"

Soon-joon sighed. "I am sorry, Ki-tae. I am not sure how to approach this subject."

"How about 'We can break the bind by doing this…' and then explaining," Ki-tae said. "It doesn't seem that hard to me."

"That's because you don't know the answer to your question. It is simple, and yet, it is not."

"Please, no riddles. I can't handle riddles today. I came really close to killing our choreographer, I was so mad." Ki-tae rubbed his forehead. "I just want to know how I can be free."

"Even freedom has a price, Ki-tae," Soon-joon said as he approached and took Ki-tae by the upper arms. He waited until Ki-tae looked him in the eyes. "To break this bond, you will either have to turn Jin-woo dongsaeng… or kill him."

"What?"

"I'm sorry, Ki-tae. Do you see now why I have been avoiding the conversation? Neither solution is really a solution. One changes a life forever, and the other ends it," Soon-joon said softly.

"He didn't ask for this," Ki-tae said, his brain still trying to process. "It was my stupid mistake. Why does he have to be punished for it?"

"This is why I tell you from the right or from the wrist, anywhere else but the left side of the neck," Soon-joon said.

"I can't believe you just gave me a roundabout 'I told you so,'" Ki-tae muttered as he pulled free to pace back and forth. "This isn't right. Are you sure there's no other way?"

"Not that I am aware of. I could reach out to some who are older than myself, but it will take time," Soon-joon said as he shrugged out of his suit coat. "They are… reclusive, is the kindest way I can put it."

"Take all the time you need. I will deal with this damn bond until we can find a way to break it without hurting Jin-woo in the process."

"You care what happens to a light snack?" Soon-joon asked, watching Ki-tae carefully.

"He's more than food," Ki-tae snarled. "He's a human being. He's feisty and beautiful and sweet."

"All this from one encounter?"

"It doesn't matter. We're not doing either to him!" Ki-tae practically shouted. He felt the pounding in his ears, a clear sign he was losing his shit.

"You had best check your tone," Soon-joon warned, his eyes flashing gold. "I am not too old to take down a youngling such as yourself, and you're dangerously close to crossing the line."

Ki-tae forced himself to take a deep breath and let it out slowly. Then he did it repeatedly until he felt more in control of himself. He wasn't going to let his anger make him do something incredibly stupid.

"*Joesonghaeyo, Abeonim,*" Ki-tae said softly, hanging his head. He was startled when Soon-joon grabbed the back of his neck and pulled him into a hug.

"It is all right, *nae adeul,*" Soon-joon said, pressing a kiss to his temple. "We will get you through this. We will not abandon you."

"That's Cheongul's issue," Ki-tae mumbled.

"Yes, he does not like people to leave him," Soon-joon said. "And we will not leave him."

"I… I don't want to hurt Jin-woo dongsaeng," Ki-tae whispered.

"I know. You are a good man, Ki-tae. You only fight back. You never attack. I will contact my friends and see what we can find. I do not want you to hurt Jin-woo dongsaeng either."

"Please don't tell Cheongul and HanYin," Ki-tae said. "They would try to spare me, and I don't want them going after him either."

"It wouldn't do them any good. It has to be you to break the bond," Soon-joon said.

"Of course it does." Ki-tae sighed. "There are times when I wish we could just be normal human beings."

"There are times when I still wish that as well, but we are not human beings anymore. We are… other."

"And in this case, it sucks," Ki-tae grumbled.

"Have you eaten?"

The sudden change of subject threw Ki-tae off. He stared at his father for a few moments. "I could eat."

Soon-joon headed for the kitchen, not waiting to see if he followed or not. Ki-tae shook his head. Soon-joon could be very focused when he wanted to be. Apparently his mind had turned to food, and now he would focus on nothing else.

It wasn't an uncommon occurrence for the four of them to make a meal together. They would chitchat, talk about their day, go over new songs, new videos, and public relation ideas. That was the nice thing about Soon-joon. As a manager he valued the input of the bands he managed, and it wasn't contained to the music. He encouraged them to be creative, to give him input on the things they wanted to do and where they wanted the band to go. He was good at getting bands through quarrels and maintaining cohesion.

Yet he was most special when he was just being their father. Ki-tae hadn't known his parents. Honestly, it had been so long, and he had been so young that he could no longer remember their faces. When someone asked about his parents, he thought of Soon-joon. He thought of Cheongul and HanYin as his brothers. Did they fight and argue? Of course they did, but so did any healthy family. If there were no arguments, there would be resentments hidden beneath the surface that festered and caused soul rot.

Ki-tae and Soon-joon had just finished setting the table when HanYin and Cheongul walked in. They both looked utterly exhausted. Soon-joon simply gave them a gentle smile and gestured to their seats. They trudged over and sort of fell into the chairs, rather than sitting.

"That bad?" he asked.

"Gojira seonbae is a monster," HanYin grumbled. "Or a control freak… or both. I'm going to go with both."

"She seemed to take personal offense at you leaving practice early," Cheongul said. "And decided to take it out on us. I don't know what her problem is. If she weren't so good, I would say get rid of her."

"Gojira?" Soon-joon asked as he served the rice.

HanYin blushed and ducked his head. "Rah Goo-ji seonbae, our choreographer, she's…."

"Driven, I believe, is the polite word you're looking for." Soon-joon chuckled. "She wants you to be successful, and pushes you because she knows you're capable of everything she throws at you. She pushes you to be the best dancers you can be."

"We know, Abeoji. It doesn't stop us from grumbling when our bodies don't want to move anymore and complaining vehemently the next morning! She works us so hard we don't even need to use the gym!" Cheongul said. "All we have to do is attend dance practice, and any bit of fat is seared away!"

"Oh, come, she cannot be that bad," Soon-joon said.

"Come to practice tomorrow and see for yourself," Ki-tae said. "Just don't tell anyone, or she'll be on her best behavior, and that's just plain creepy."

"I think she's sweet on you, *Fùqīn*," HanYin teased. "She blushes every single time she sees you."

"Do not be ridiculous," Soon-joon said.

"I'm not," HanYin said. "A lot of the women at the studio giggle and blush when you walk down the hall. You're a very attractive man, Fùqīn. We can tell when you're visiting by the way they're behaving. Some of them giggle around us, but I swear half of them nearly faint from knowing you're nearby."

"You do know they call you the God of K-pop, and it's not just because you handle the most successful groups in the business." Ki-tae chuckled. "There isn't another manager who could take that title from you."

"If people admire me, it is because I treat them well and do not abuse my power," Soon-joon said. "As I have taught you boys to respect people and to understand the responsibility of being what we are. We must live in this world with humans and other beings. If we want respect, we must give it, not because it is the only way, but because it is the right way."

"I understand, Abeoji," Ki-tae and Cheongul said.

"*Wǒ míngbái*, Fùqīn," HanYin said, and then all three bowed to their father.

JIN-WOO

"OH. MY. God," Min-su said as she stared at his storyboards. "There's no doubt about the story. This is something we can really work with."

"Good, because I was up all night finishing these," Jin-woo said with a yawn as he reached for his drink. They were sitting in Hoho Myoli Café about twenty minutes from campus. It was quiet and cozy and one of their favorite places to eat and relax after classes. "I also have the set designs done. There's four in total: two historic and two modern contemporary. I tried to keep away from too extravagant. We want to keep the cost low and the quality high while being able to shoot quickly."

"What?"

"What do you mean, what?"

"What you just said." Min-su slapped his arm. "What did you mean, 'the cost low while keeping the quality high and being able to do it fast'?"

"I was doing research a while back and just caught an interview with this young guy. I can't remember the name now, but he said there's a triangle to production. The points are quality, speed, and cost. He said people tend to want things good, fast, and cheap, but that isn't realistic. A product can be cheap and it might even be fast, but it isn't going to be good. It can be high quality and done fast, but it more than likely isn't going to be cheap. However, if a client is looking for high quality, then it isn't going to be fast and certainly not cheap. A good engineer, or in our case, a good production team, should aim for the middle, leaning toward quality. We should aim for a good-quality product while producing it in a realistic amount of time and at a reasonable cost. While he was talking sound engineering, I think that applies to any aspect of business where a product is being made."

Min-su nodded. "That makes sense. The bigger the idea, the costlier the creation of it, and the more chances for problems and delays. The more complex, the more difficult it is to produce, which will make the project take longer."

"You two don't stop, do you?" Jong-in chuckled as he came up to them. "The minute you have a project, you're like hounds on the scent. You focus solely on that. What are we talking about?"

"The triangle of production, quality versus speed versus cost," Min-su said and then turned back to Jin-woo. "I wish you could remember that guy's name. I want to watch the interview."

"I'll see if I can find it. I know he was a YouTuber as well as a sound engineer. He's probably in my history. I'll look it up when I get home today."

"No, when you get home today, you're going to go to sleep. You'll need all your rest for our presentation tomorrow. We have to sell this thing," Min-su said, pointing a french fry dripping with ketchup at him, before popping it into her mouth.

"Don't remind me," Jin-woo said. "This is the worst part of the whole project."

"Why?" Jong-in said. "Your work is brilliant."

"My work may be brilliant, and I still disagree with that idea, but my public speaking is not," Jin-woo cried. "I get tongue-tied, and feel as if I'm going to pass out, and I want to throw up."

"You did fine with our last project," Jong-in pointed out.

"Yeah, and that was much better than the first time you presented to the class," Min-su reminded him. "So you're getting better with it."

"But that's in front of people I pretty much know. This is Park Soon-joon hyung, a giant in the South Korean entertainment industry, the God of K-pop. I have to impress this man not only with my work, but with my ability to present it in a confident and professional manner. I'm going to die. Die, I tell you!"

"Ah, okay, I get what this is," Jong-in said as he turned to Min-su. "He never remembers, does he?"

"Nope, not once," she agreed. "I keep hoping, though."

"What are you two talking about?" Jin-woo demanded. "I'm talking about my impending doom, and you're talking nonsense? Where's the love?"

"The love is in the fact you never remember what happens when you start talking about music or art or digital production," Jong-in said.

"You never remember these are topics you love, and you get so absorbed in talking about them you forget everything else. It doesn't matter who you're talking to," Min-su said with a gentle smile. "You once explained the entire Western neoclassical art movement to the Dean of Student Affairs and didn't stutter or throw up once."

"Granted, he got a glazed look on his face because he was completely lost, but still, he was a very important authority figure whom you talked to without a problem," Jong-in said with a smile. "You can do this, Jin-woo-ya. You just need to do you."

"Listen, we've all been working really hard these last few weeks, and this project is super important, so we've been more stressed about it," Min-su said, putting a hand on each of their shoulders. "Tonight we're going to go out and relax, but not too much, and then we'll hit that presentation and make it bow down before us! We will win this. *Hwaiting*!"

"Hwaiting!" Jin-woo and Jong-in laughed.

"Okay, Club Cocoon or M2?" Min-su said with a clap.

"I thought you said we couldn't relax too much?" Jong-in said.

"Well, we could go to I Love K-pop," Min-su said.

"That sounds like a plan," Jin-woo said. "I really just want to relax."

"Then I Love K-pop it is," Min-su said. "I'll see you guys later. I have to run some errands for my mom before I head home. Jin-woo-ya, go home and get some sleep. I'll call you to make sure you wake up."

"I still have some work to do on my sound mix project, so I'm going to head back to the university," Jong-in said. "I'll see you guys later."

Jin-woo watched his friends leave and then laid his head on the table. He could fall asleep right here but knew it wouldn't be a good idea. He had a half-hour-plus trip home. Someday he'd be able to afford a car and wouldn't have to switch buses and trains so much. He could just go whatever route he wanted if he chose to drive. He could meander if he wanted, seeing aspects of the city and his neighborhood he might not otherwise see. He could even go beyond Seoul without having to coordinate train schedules.

Yet Jin-woo knew that was a long time off. He would have to focus on paying off his university fees, rent, and so many other things. He still had his parents' hospital bills. His aunt refused to pay those, so he had to use the monthly stipend from the trust fund his grandparents had established for him. She hadn't approved of Jin-woo's father at all.

Jin-woo shook his head. He wasn't going to think of that spiteful woman. He was going to go home and get some rest, hopefully without dreaming about Ki-tae. Three weeks straight of wet dreams; it was no wonder he was exhausted. There had to be something wrong with him.

CHEONGUL

"Ki-tae?" Cheongul knocked on the door but got no response. With a sigh, he checked the handle and found it unlocked. He walked inside, pausing at the corner. Ki-tae was sprawled across his bed, facedown. He looked exhausted, and if the scent filling the air was any indication, he hadn't gotten any rest. Dream walking could be a pain in the ass. Cheongul hated to wake him, but they had to go to the presentation today, Soon-joon's orders.

Much like HanYin, Ki-tae had issues waking up, especially if he was on his stomach. Cheongul moved to the end of the bed, well out of arm's reach. The trick was to wake him up slowly. With HanYin, it didn't matter. Slow or fast, he was going to come up fighting if anything other than his alarm clock woke him up.

"Ki-tae," Cheongul called. "Time to wake up, *namdongsaeng*. We have the presentation today."

Ki-tae grunted and turned his head to face the other way. Cheongul sighed. He was going to have to do it the hard way. He knew he should have made sure Ki-tae set his alarm clock last night. Cheongul took Ki-tae's left foot and shook it gently. "Ki-tae!"

As expected, Ki-tae jerked into a ball and exploded out of the bed at Cheongul. Thankfully he was prepared and moved out of the way. Ki-tae stared at him with silver eyes, not quite awake yet. It would take a minute or two for Cheongul's scent to register and for Ki-tae's brain to process the information. If Cheongul stayed still while that happened, Ki-tae wouldn't attack again. Ah, the trials of living in a household of Vampires with tragic pasts, including his own.

Finally Ki-tae blinked and straightened. "What time is it?" he asked.

"Seven in the morning," Cheongul said. "We have to be at Jeonjin University by nine. Abeoji says we can dress comfortably but presentable. Think you can manage that?"

"I dress better than you," Ki-tae muttered, rubbing a hand through his hair.

"Hardly." Cheongul snorted. "When did you start sleeping naked?"

"About three weeks ago," Ki-tae grumbled. "Now go away so I can get dressed in peace."

"HanYin's making breakfast," Cheongul said as he walked out of the room. "Coffee is already waiting."

KI-TAE

"AWESOME." KI-TAE smiled as he headed to the bathroom. Of the three of them, HanYin was the best cook. Ki-tae swore HanYin would have been a chef if he didn't love music so much. Either way, if he ever decided to retire from the business, he had another skill to fall back on. Ki-tae wished he could say the same. He really wasn't good at anything but singing, dancing, and making music. Well, there was one other thing he was good at, but he would never sell his body, never again. Shaking the dark thoughts from his mind, he turned on the waterfall showerhead.

When Soon-joon decided to build this house, he had asked their opinions on how they wanted their rooms to look. He said they would always have a place in his home, even if they moved far away. Ki-tae had few good memories of his past, but one of them was finding a secluded waterfall deep in the wilderness. The grotto was so serene, untouched by anything. He had been hiding, running, and was completely filthy. He looked more animal than man, and finding that waterfall was a blessing. He remembered standing naked in it and letting the water wash away everything. Not just the dirt and filth, but the negative energy he had been trying to escape. He was fourteen, maybe fifteen, at the time. He couldn't remember his birthday. After that he felt cleaner than he ever had before. It hadn't lasted long, but it was one of his better memories. That was why he had the showerhead changed when waterfall ones became available. He wanted that sensation every time he showered. He wanted to feel the water cascading over his body, making him lighter, cleaner again.

Twenty minutes later Ki-tae stood before his closet, trying to decide what to wear. Comfortable but presentable. With a smile, he pulled out a high-neck shirt with long sleeves, his black skinny jeans, and followed those up with his black leather jacket and combat-style boots. Yes, he would be all in black, but he would look damn good.

He quickly styled his hair, blowing it dry partway before using gel to get a wet, messy look. Then he grabbed the makeup kit. Since they more than likely wouldn't be asked to perform, Ki-tae kept it light, just lining his eyes and using a tinted lip gloss, and he was done. He grabbed his jacket off the bed, met the others in the entryway, and burst out laughing. It couldn't have worked out better if they had planned it. The only differences in their ensembles were shirt colors and shoes. Cheongul preferred his white high-tops and had paired them with a white top and three beaded necklaces. HanYin had chosen his glittering purple top, sleeveless, of course, and his side-zipped high-tops, but they all wore black jeans and a leather jacket.

"I see we have a common theme today." Soon-joon chuckled. He himself had chosen to wear a white T-shirt under a pastel-patterned vest and a dark gray wide-collared, thigh-length coat paired with charcoal gray slacks. He looked casual and yet sophisticated.

"What do you mean, Abeoji?" Ki-tae asked with a cheeky grin. "This is us every day."

Soon-joon laughed. "Get in the car. HanYin packed breakfast. We can eat on the way. I want to get there a little early so we can sit down with Seonsaengnim. The room should be secured by the time we get to the university, and we can meet in there."

"How publicized was this?" Cheongul asked as they settled in the car. "I don't recall seeing it on any of the social media."

"I wanted the students to be able to work undisturbed by reporters, so the story will break today. We all know how annoying they can be on occasion. If they weren't necessary, I wouldn't deal with them at all," Soon-joon said. "There will be a press conference after the presentations. Production will begin in a week's time."

"You think these students are ready for it?" HanYin asked.

"I think so, and we'll have our normal team on hand. I've arranged for on-site mentors for the group that wins, who will work with the students and help teach them with hands-on experience," Soon-joon said.

"You've thought of everything as usual," Ki-tae said absently as he stared out the window. He wasn't really paying attention to the conversation. His mind was focused on one student in particular. This would be the first time he would see Jin-woo since the concert, and Ki-tae wasn't sure how he was going to react. He needed to remain professional, but it was going to be damned difficult. Jin-woo just did it for him in a way he'd never experienced before. Not to mention he had no idea how the bond was going to affect their interaction.

Chatter filled the car for the remainder of the trip, but Ki-tae really didn't contribute. What good mood he'd had upon waking had slowly faded until he was left with a sense of numbness. It was as if he were suddenly wrapped in cotton, unable to feel anything. A part of him wanted to maintain this detachment until they left the university, but Ki-tae knew he wasn't that lucky. It would probably last until they arrived, and then everything would slam into him once he stepped foot on campus.

Suddenly HanYin bumped his shoulder. When Ki-tae turned to face him, HanYin gave him a reassuring smile. "You're not alone," he said quietly. "We're here with you, and we will help you get through this."

"Thank you," Ki-tae whispered. HanYin nodded but didn't say anything further. He didn't need to.

All too soon, they arrived at Jeonjin University. There were some curious stares as the two black cars pulled through the main gate to the left of the athletic field, but no one rushed the cars. Students stopped to watch. Soon-joon exited first, sunglasses firmly in place. It wasn't until Cheongul and HanYin exited either side of the car, their bodyguards holding the doors, that a more… vocal response was heard. Cries of "Bam Kiseu" filled the air as the more diehard fans recognized them, even from a distance. They would have to walk the rest of the way to Lecture Building I, where the presentations were to be held.

Kim Kyu-won met them at the door, a young woman standing to his left and slightly behind him. He and Soon-joon greeted each other as old friends.

"I would like to introduce you to the group," Soon-joon said, turning to face Ki-tae, Cheongul, and HanYin. "Please allow me to introduce Ki-tae dongsaeng, Cheongul dongsaeng, and HanYin dongsaeng. Boys, this is Kim Kyu-won seonsaeng-ssi."

"It is an honor to meet you, Seonsaengnim," they said as they bowed.

"The honor is mine. Welcome to Jeonjin University. This is my assistant, Park Sung-yi hubae," Teacher Kim said politely as he gestured to the young woman. "Please. Follow me, and I will show you to the room we will be using."

"Wonderful. I have some things I wish to go over with you before we begin," Soon-joon said.

"The presentations are scheduled to begin at ten. I wanted to give them plenty of time to prepare," Seonsaengnim said as he ushered them into the building.

"Excellent."

Ki-tae didn't pay much attention to their surroundings. He could hear the clicking of phone cameras going off, hear the excited chatter of the students. There were a plethora of scents filling the air, but one scent rose above them. Ki-tae stopped in his tracks just before entering the building and lifted his head. He inhaled deeply, pulling the smell into his lungs. He knew that smell, knew it intimately, even mixed with the faint scent of Shifter and something else, something… wild. He turned around and scanned the area. Far down the walkway, he spotted Jin-woo walking with two other students, a male and a female. They stood close together, indicating a close relationship. Suddenly Cheongul grabbed his arm.

"You're growling," he whispered in Ki-tae's ear. "And if you pull off your sunglasses, you're going to give everyone here a perfect shot of your silver eyes. Let's go. You'll see him in a little bit."

"They're touching him."

"They're probably his friends. We touch each other all the time," Cheongul said. "It's normal. Come on, Ki-tae-ya. People are beginning to stare harder than they should."

Ki-tae allowed Cheongul to push him into the building. He tried to ignore the urge to rip Jin-woo away from the other two, but it was incredibly difficult. How the hell was he going to react when they were in the same room? Was he going to turn into some slavering beast bent on claiming what was his and destroying anything that got in his way? The idea terrified him.

He caught Soon-joon watching him when he lifted his head. Ki-tae gave him a smile and a nod. He would be fine. He had to be. As they continued walking, Cheongul and HanYin flanked him, and Ki-tae chuckled. His brothers could be overprotective at times, and this was, apparently, one of those times. They smiled and waved as if everything was normal, because that's how it had to be, and they had been playing this game for quite some time. Granted, they hadn't been at it as long as Soon-joon, but they weren't brand-new either.

They were led into a medium-sized room with a small raised dais and a large projection screen hanging behind it. There was a podium to the left of the screen. The seats were about ten feet from the dais itself and stretched several rows back, with a center aisle splitting them into two sections. Each row was six seats deep and slightly higher than the one before it. HanYin gave a low whistle and then turned to Ki-tae, smiling.

"This room has great acoustics."

"No kidding." Ki-tae chuckled.

"You wouldn't have to raise your voice much to be heard in the back without a mic," Cheongul agreed.

"The university has made sure every room where formal presentations may be made has the proper sound quality as part of the design," Teacher Kim said. "The original idea was to use the seminar rooms, but they hold, at most, fifteen people, and as these presentations may be multimedia, we felt the rooms might be too small, so we rescheduled for this room."

"This is perfect, Seonsaengnim," Cheongul said with a smile. "As HanYin-a said, the acoustics are excellent. Don't you agree, Ki-tae-ya?"

"Yes," Ki-tae said.

When Teacher Kim looked a little confused, Soon-joon explained. "Ki-tae dongsaeng has the occasional habit of taking over the soundboard. He has also been known to rerun an entire mic setup when he's not happy with it. The crew has learned to accept it because he's usually right."

"I didn't realize you were trained in other aspects of the business. I am sorry," Teacher Kim said.

"It's okay, Seonsaengnim," Ki-tae said. "Most people don't. We have spent time working with the various crew teams so we may better understand and appreciate what they do for us."

"BL Entertainment is truly unique," Teacher Kim murmured.

"Indeed it is." Soon-joon smiled. "Shall we take a seat and go over the presentation schedule?"

"Of course," Teacher Kim answered. He bowed to Ki-tae, Cheongul, and HanYin before moving to the dais and pulling out a small book. Soon he and Soon-joon were engrossed in their discussion.

"I bet if we left, when we came back, they'd still be like that," HanYin said.

"Probably," Cheongul agreed as he took a seat in the front row closest to the aisle and shrugged out of his jacket. "Has anybody looked at the schedule yet today?"

"No," Ki-tae said. "We probably should. I know we don't have dance practice today, thankfully."

"Oh yeah, Gojira seonbae has it in for you now." HanYin chuckled.

"She's making me work twice as hard as you two," Ki-tae grumbled. "I miss one practice, and she holds a grudge."

"She's evil that way," HanYin said as he took the seat next to Ki-tae. "What do you think these presentations are going to be like?"

"I don't know. Hopefully they'll be at least halfway decent. We should probably find out how many presentations there's going to be and how long each one is."

"Excuse me," Sung-yi said as she bowed to them, a pile of papers and three clipboards in her hands. "Seongsaengnim asked that I give these information packets to you. Each one contains the list of presenters and which song they are presenting for. Each presentation will be twenty minutes. There is a total of eighteen students per class, and Seonsaengnim has two classes. Each class has been divided into groups of three. Class One will be presenting first, followed by Class Two. There will be a thirty-minute break between each class. The last pages of the packet are for notes on each of the groups and a scoring box. Once the presentations have been completed, the students will be escorted out of the hall, and you, along with Seonsaengnim and Park Soon-joon hyung, will have an hour to compare notes and scoring on each of the presentations. Once the voting has been completed, the students will be brought back into the room to hear your determination. If you would like to take a few moments to review the packets, please do so. We will be starting the presentations shortly. *Gomabseumnida*."

"She made it through that whole speech and didn't take her eyes off Cheongul-a's chest once." Ki-tae watched Park Sung-yi scurry across the room and out the door. "Too bad she's not your type, poor thing."

"I happen to prefer cute blondes," Cheongul said absently.

"No, you prefer cute blondes with attitudes," HanYin said. "You like them feisty."

"I do at that." Cheongul smirked. "The feistier the better. You're too picky, HanYin-a, and Ki-tae-ya not picky enough."

"That isn't true!" Ki-tae smacked him in the arm. "I'm... selective."

"You so are not." HanYin chuckled. "Now I—I am selective."

"No, you're a monk," Cheongul deadpanned. With an outraged gasp, HanYin pounced on him. The two wrestled back and forth, catching Ki-tae in the middle. When Soon-joon came over to see what was going on, they were all laughing in a pile.

"Could you three stop beating on each other? We're going to be occupied for the next couple of hours."

"I didn't realize we had this many songs without videos," Ki-tae said as he flipped through the packet. "Sometimes I feel as if all we do is eat, sleep, sing, and make videos... oh, and dance torture, uh, practice."

"I only chose six songs," Soon-joon said. "There will be two presentations on each song: one group from each class."

"Please tell me we're going to at least time the break for lunch?" HanYin said.

"Of course. The caterers will arrive shortly before the break." Soon-joon almost looked offended. "Did you think I would let you starve? I know how often you need to fill those hollow bellies of yours."

"Did he just call us fat?" HanYin asked.

"No, he said we eat too much," Ki-tae said.

"That's it. He's going in the pond when we get home," Cheongul grumbled.

"I believe the term youngsters use is 'as if.'" Soon-joon chuckled as he walked away. They burst out laughing.

An hour and a half later, Ki-tae was ready to scream. Of the five presentations so far, four of them had done a decent job, but decent wasn't good enough in his book. He could tell the current group hadn't listened to the song. There was a big difference between listening and hearing. In this case, they had heard it but they hadn't focused on the lyrics. He wanted to bang his head against the desk, except he wasn't sitting at a desk.

"Please make them stop," Ki-tae muttered as he laid his head on HanYin's shoulder. "'Heat' is not about the weather!"

"Did they even listen to the words? Maybe they only had the Chinese version and don't speak the language, because damned if they have a clue!" HanYin said. "I can only hope this was meant to be funny or some kind of headtrip, a video about weather with a song about sex. A parody? Were they trying for a parody?"

"I... I have no words," Cheongul said, and that was saying something. He always had something to say. "Only seven more to go, guys. Hwaiting!"

Ki-tae glared at him. "Shut up."

"The next one is 'Master,'" HanYin said. "Talk to us after that."

Twenty minutes later, Cheongul looked as if someone had slapped him. He stared at the students on the dais. They were stammering and forgetting what they had just said. Their visuals were subpar, and he had yet to figure out how they associated the circus with the words he'd penned.

"Now you know our pain," HanYin said. "The circus? Really?"

"Not another word... or I just might cry," Cheongul said softly.

The lights went up, and the students broke down their presentation. Once they were clear, the caterers began wheeling in food and setting up a nice buffet. The smell of meat filled Ki-tae's nose, and his stomach rumbled loudly.

"Hungry, Ki-tae-ya?" HanYin laughed.

"I should have had another breakfast sandwich on the way in," Ki-tae said sheepishly. "I'm starving."

"Let's get some food and go over the first class," Cheongul said.

"Do we have to?" HanYin almost whined. "Wasn't once painful enough?"

"As much as I would love to say no, especially the last two, we have to be professional about this and really look at what they did," Cheongul explained.

"I know," HanYin sighed.

Soon-joon

Soon-joon watched as they got food and then sat down on the floor near the wall in a circle, packets and clipboards in hand. He was proud of them. They weren't dismissing the first group out of hand, and they were multitasking to boot. How long had it taken him to convince them they could focus on more than one thing at a time? Soon-joon chuckled.

"They are very professional," Teacher Kim said.

"They can be, when called upon to do so." Soon-joon smiled. "They can act like rambunctious toddlers too."

"They're still young," Teacher Kim said with a nod.

"They are good boys," Soon-joon said. "This is a good experience for them as well. They're seeing how others interpret their songs. It is hard because they know what the songs mean, but not what they mean to other people."

"I will admit I had not heard their music," Teacher Kim said. "It is not my style. However, I listened to it a lot over the last three weeks to get a feel for it."

"Of the many bands I manage, I enjoy Bam Kiseu's music the most," Soon-joon admitted. "There is such feeling in their words. They each have their own style, and yet they are adaptable to each other. They work well together, and they always present a united front. They are family."

"I can see that in the easy way they interact with each other. They are close."

"As close as brothers," Soon-joon said softly.

JIN-WOO

JIN-WOO WAS late and Min-su was going to kill him, but if he hadn't gone back to the studio, they wouldn't have their visuals, and then she would have killed him slowly. He'd had to scramble to find someone with the keys, too, forcing him to miss all the other presentations. He never realized how hard it was to find maintenance personnel on a campus this size. When he finally reached Min-su, she looked scared as hell.

"What?" he asked. "What is it? What's wrong?"

"Um, I... I can't breathe. I really... can't." Min-su puffed out her cheeks and fanned her face. "I didn't.... If I had known, I would have chosen a different outfit. I would have done my hair, and my makeup is just.... Dammit. Why didn't anyone tell me they were going to be here?"

"What the heck is she talking about, Jong-in-a?" Jin-woo demanded.

"We're not just presenting to Park Soon-joon hyung," Jong-in said quietly.

"Of course we aren't. Seonsaengnim is there as well," Jin-woo said. "This isn't new."

"It's.... We're.... Jin-woo-ya, Bam Kiseu is in that room!" Min-su said, grabbing him by his vest and shaking him back and forth. "HanYin oppa is in that room! Ki-tae oppa is in that room! *Cheongul oppa* is in that room!"

Jin-woo did the only thing he could think of. He slapped her.

Min-su stumbled back a few steps and just stared at him. Then she narrowed her eyes and came at him.

Jin-woo threw up his hands in defense of the punch coming his way.

"I'm sorry!" But it never landed. He peeked with one eye. Min-su looked completely calm.

"Thank you," she said with a sigh. "I was losing my shit, and that's not acceptable."

"You're good?" Jin-woo said.

"I'm good."

"Good," Jin-woo said as he began to shake. "I'm going to pass out now."

And he did just that.

Jin-woo didn't remember hitting the floor, but he figured that must have happened, as he was staring up at the ceiling with Min-su slapping his face and Jong-in looking terribly concerned. He caught Min-su's wrist and held her hand to his face for a few moments, closing his eyes once more.

"No, you cannot pass out on us again. We're up next, Jin-woo-ya!" Min-su said, an edge of desperation in her voice.

"I'm not going to pass out again. I just wanted you to stop slapping me and calm down," he said. Then he slowly sat up, rubbing the back of his head. He looked at Jong-in and teased, "You couldn't have caught me?"

"Nope, Min-su-ya was in the way."

"Hey, this is not my fault," she said, putting her hands on her hips.

"Well, you were shaking Jin-woo-ya pretty hard," Jong-in pointed out. "There's no need to panic. They're people, just like us."

No, not just like us, Jin-woo thought but wisely kept the words to himself.

All too soon they were up, and Jin-woo was so nervous his hands were shaking. He hadn't seen Ki-tae in person since *that* night. His dreams had been consistent and incredibly realistic, and he could describe the scent of Ki-tae's skin if asked. He could describe the taste of it, if pressed. That was how vivid they were. How in the hell was he supposed to form coherent sentences while in the same room with him?

Min-su entered the room first, and then Jong-in followed. Jin-woo was last, and he paused at the door. He took a deep breath, and finally, after a last desperate thought of *How badly will Min-su kill me if I run away screaming*, entered the room.

Immediately he sought out Ki-tae and found those intense eyes locked on him. Jin-woo swallowed hard and couldn't seem to tear his gaze away. He noted how Ki-tae sat up and leaned forward, saw how his nostrils flared as if scenting Jin-woo, which was kind of hot, in a predatory sort of way. Jin-woo's breath caught in his throat as he realized Ki-tae was hunting him. Even though they were in the same room and neither one of them had moved, Ki-tae was hunting him.

The stirring in his groin had Jin-woo turning away and rushing to the dais. He turned his back to the crowd and set up the storyboards on the easel placed in the center. Glancing to his right, Jin-woo noted Jong-in expertly managing the media station, and Min-su was already handing out the lyrics and informational packets. She paused and bowed before Bam Kiseu. Jin-woo was amazed at how she maintained her professionalism, refraining from staring at the man she stanned, Cheongul. Then she was back on the dais with them, and they started their presentation.

"Good afternoon, honored guests and classmates. My name is Yi Min-su, and these are my colleagues, Cheong Jin-woo-ya and Bak Jong-in-a," Min-su began with a pleasant smile, and they bowed to their audience. "Our presentation is for the song 'Crossing Time.' We have provided you a packet containing the lyrics, as well as the major points we will be addressing. Bak Jong-in-a will begin our presentation with a breakdown and analysis of 'Crossing Time.'"

Once Min-su finished speaking, Jin-woo followed her to the two seats they had set up on the side. The focus, at this point, would be solely on Jong-in. Jin-woo envied him. Jong-in had such an easy way about him. He could charm anyone just by flashing those adorable dimples. Combined with his round wire-framed glasses, they were killer. Jong-in's smooth voice was low and melodic. No matter how many times he heard it and knew it was coming, Jin-woo was still amazed by Jong-in's singing voice. His low tones suited the beginning verse of "Crossing Time" perfectly.

I never went looking for love
I never wanted that weakness inside me
Over the years, I've been successful
Keeping my heart always free.
But then I chanced upon you
Your gentle smile was a knife inside of me.

As Jin-woo looked at the crowd, purposefully not seeking out Ki-tae, he noticed HanYin sitting up a little straighter, his eyes locked on Jong-in. Interesting. It seemed he wasn't the only one impressed by Jong-in's voice.

"The introduction to 'Crossing Time' is a slow drawing in of the audience. It is a symphonic melody in minor. The beat is a subtle pulse beneath the synthesized strings, a soft echo of a heartbeat, slow and steady," Jong-in began. "On the screen behind me, you'll see I've pulled the song into its individual tracks. When overlaid with each other, they create a beautiful, melodic, yet melancholy sound. The first verse tells us a story. It tells of a being who was afraid to love, afraid of being weak because of it, afraid to be vulnerable. Yet love finds him and with a single glance, captures his heart."

Jong-in pointed the remote and clicked Play, allowing the slow introduction and opening melody to fill the room. Cheongul's voice, his tone conveyed exactly what Jong-in described. Jin-woo could hear the slow beat of the percussion, the melancholy in the strings. He could feel what the narrator felt, and it made him shiver. The song paused, and Jong-in spoke once more.

"Our narrator is still resistant. He keeps himself away from the one he loves, tries to maintain his solitude, but he can't. The intensity of emotion is building within him, conveyed in the increased pace, the beat picking up speed, just as our hearts speed up when we see someone we desire. The chords change to major, showing more energy, more passion, more desire. The words come a little faster, a little sharper, showing his primal desire for the one he loves."

I thought I could let you go,
Never tell you what I feel.
I thought I could ignore the pain,
Of being only me.
I think of you all the time.
I can't get you out of my mind.
You're in every thought and every dream,
Haunting me.

The song began again. Ki-tae's voice grabbed the audience, carrying the increased energy, the passion, the intensity. Jin-woo cursed under his breath. This song got to him when he was alone. Knowing Ki-tae was about ten feet away, he had a hard time not getting out of his chair and climbing into Ki-tae's lap.

"And then the music grabs you by the throat," Jong-in said. "It hits you with a strong, fast beat drop, the harmony of all three voices slamming together to show how everything is breaking free within our narrator. He can't control it anymore. He can't stay away. He must have the one he loves. He'll do anything to have this one person… even cross time itself. Four simple lines to convey the determination and dedication of a being in love."

Through the walls and through the chains,
Through the ice and through the rain,
You found your way into my heart,
And now, I'm crossing time to find you.

"However, he is still surprised, still amazed at what he feels, at this thing he saw as weakness. He finds strength in love. He feels it pick him up, grant him the strength to carry on, to search for the one he loves. The beat softens just the tiniest bit, fluttering like butterfly wings. The melody is no longer melancholy. It is light and sweet and pure. Yet it is as strong as it appears delicate."

What is this weakness that turns to strength?
This ice that turns to fire?
Deep inside of me, something flutters,
A love to last the ages.
This is what you've done to me,
By simply being you,
And now, nothing less than your eternity will do.

HanYin's clear vocals echoed through the hall. Jin-woo could hear the wonder in it, the surprise. He could feel the power and the strength being in love granted. Jin-woo wanted a love like that. He wanted it to make his knees weak and his heart strong. Smiling, Jin-woo glanced up to see Ki-tae watching him again. Well, Ki-tae might have paid some attention to Jong-in, but every time Jin-woo glanced in his direction, Ki-tae was staring at him. It was as if he sensed when Jin-woo was going to look at him. He was so intense, more so than when he was onstage. Jin-woo wasn't sure how he felt about that. With a shake of his head, Jin-woo brought his focus back to Jong-in's part of the presentation.

"Once more we feel the intensity of our narrator's emotions, the strength of his heart. The three voices harmonize, weaving a wall of sound that captures us, holds us there, showing us how determined our narrator is. The pace picks up once more, the frustration, the guilt of what he's done in the past, of the things he needed to do to survive, making him wonder if his love will be returned."

I've done things I'm not proud of,
Things I needed to survive,
I walk in darkness, blinded by the light.
I can't go on without you.

The years, they stretch on too far.
I'm crossing time to find you,
Wherever you are.

"He's not ready to give up, not yet." Jong-in's voice softened almost to a whisper. "He can't go back to what he once was. He can't let go of this love he's found. He'll travel as far as he needs to claim it. The tempo slows, the beat softens, the melody remains hopeful but cautious. It almost starts to fade away. That crescendo comes rushing at you, bursting into existence in another beat drop that carries into the last chorus. He will not give up. He will not return to solitude. He will have his love, even if he has to cross time forever."

Through the walls and through the chains,
Through the ice and through the rain,
You found your way into my heart,
And now, I'm crossing time to find you.

"Each section of this melody, of the underlying beats, the drops and the pacing, all convey the intensity of emotion, the whirlwind that is falling in love for the first time, of learning how painful and how sweet it can be. The baseline keeps the song strong, even as it rises and drops in tempo. The symphonic overtones and the strings keep this firmly in the ballad arena while making it a good song to dance to… unless your name happens to be Bak Jong-in of the two left feet!" The crowd laughed, and Jong-in took a bow amid loud applause. "Thank you. Cheong Jin-woo-ya will now present to you our conceptual designs for a music video of 'Crossing Time.'"

Jin-woo wanted to throw up, but he fought the urge and rose, perhaps a little shyly, from his seat. He moved to the center stage, standing to the right of the easel. He took a moment to close his eyes and calm his breathing. He could do this. He really could.

"'Crossing Time' speaks of traveling far to be with a loved one. It speaks of years spent alone in protective exile, only to find no protection was needed. It speaks of doing the impossible in the pursuit of love. Or is it truly possible to cross time?" Jin-woo asked, tilting his head to give visual emphasis to his question. "That was the question we asked ourselves as we listened to the song. The idea took root as we acknowledged there is more to this world than what we can see with our own eyes."

Jin-woo pulled the first board off the easel, revealing a series of nine storyboard panels. They were projected on the screen behind him for those farther back. He could hear the "oohs" and the "ahs" and a few gasps and knew the heat in his face meant he was blushing. The panels depicted, in detail, three men in historic clothing, their hair flowing down their backs from the topknots. They studied and they played *Yut Nori*, a board game with dice, and performed moving meditations to improve their energy. Yet the horns upon their heads marked them as nonhumans. The last set of three blocks showed them sneering at human couples, dismissing them.

"In our cultural mythology, there are many beings that are immortal, but surprisingly, few stories tell of them interacting with human beings in a positive way, let alone falling in love," Jin-woo said. "One of the few that attract humans are the Chonggak Dokkaebi, the bachelor goblin. He is a being who lives many centuries, who watches mortals in their fumbling, and has decided we are most stupid when we love. He eschews love, seeing it as weakness."

Jin-woo removed the panel, so engrossed in his topic that he barely noticed the suddenly very attentive looks of four of his audience members. The second panel began with three blocks showing three women resting by a pond. One was reading while another played a gayageum, a string instrument, and the third did needlework.

"Here we see three human women sitting by a pond. They are relaxing at their leisure. They love music and literature and crafts. They are quiet and serene, happy," Jin-woo said. "They are simply going about their business, but it is their quiet beauty that captures the attentions of our dokkaebi, ensnaring them with little effort. They are fascinated by these women but have yet to figure out why."

Another panel, and Jin-woo continued, "But time cannot be stopped. It is ever moving forward, and soon it claims the three women. Our bachelors are heartbroken, having never spoken words of love to their maidens. They cannot understand the loss and resolve to find their loves again, even if they must travel across time."

Finally the last three panels were moved in slow succession. "The bachelors search for them across the ages, feeling the fluttering in their chests grow stronger and stronger each time they reconnect with their lost loves, until finally, in our time, they find them once more. Here they resolve to never be without their loves again."

Jin-woo set the panels aside and turned to face the audience, not really seeing them. He paused for a moment before speaking once more. "What are our memories but little leaps across time? We go back to moments where we were happy or sad, where we felt loss and pain, joy, and hope. Our concept for 'Crossing Time' is a journey both forward and back, traveling the memories of our bachelors as we go."

With a nod to Jong-in, Jin-woo stepped to the side as the screen switched from projecting the panels to a video. The first series was of historical sites in the local area. He sat down as Min-su took the dais.

"Our bachelors are old. They have seen many things, but their pursuit of love begins in the past. This song tells a story, and its music video will be an extension of that. From ancient times to modern, we will watch them find love, wonder at it, pursue it, and finally win the ones they love," Min-su said, a small smile gracing her almost cherubic features. "'Crossing Time' is its own hook, from the slow rise to the beat drops and final fade. Its video can do no less."

Jin-woo tried to listen to Min-su. Yet he kept getting distracted by the humming in his body. He couldn't keep his leg from bouncing with the energy. He nibbled on his lower lip, trying to keep his eyes from straying to Ki-tae and failing. He found him in deep conversation with HanYin. Cheongul, on the other hand, was watching Min-su like a hawk. If Min-su noticed, she gave no sign. On second thought, this was Min-su. If she had noticed how intently Cheongul was focused on her, she would be freaking out.

Jin-woo glanced at the clock. They were almost done. Once Min-su finished reviewing their projected production schedule, including filming, editing, and postproduction, they would hit the audience with their final visual, a concept trailer that had taken them the full three weeks to complete. Jin-woo could only pray it looked and sounded as good as they hoped. The applause brought him out of his reverie, and Jin-woo almost shot from his seat to join Min-su and Jong-in at center stage.

"We hope you have enjoyed our presentation. It will come as no surprise that we are huge fans of Bam Kiseu and their music. We hope our efforts today have done your work justice. The final portion of our presentation is a concept trailer we created to give a more concrete idea of what we feel this video should be. Thank you."

They bowed and left the stage as Jong-in started the video. They walked up the center aisle, right past Ki-tae and the others, and took their seats several rows back. He saw Min-su blow out a slow breath and Jong-in rub the bridge of his nose, pushing up his glasses. Once they were finally able to get out the door, Jin-woo figured he was okay to pass out... again.

KI-TAE

KI-TAE WAS floored, absolutely floored by what he heard, and now by what he saw on the screen. He'd seen professional videos not half as good as the concept trailer playing in front of him. They done this in three weeks? It was, simply put, amazing.

"Holy shit," HanYin muttered. "They got it. They really got it."

"That they did," Cheongul murmured.

"Should we even bother discussing the others?" Ki-tae said with a chuckle. "Save for the video, you could hear a pin drop in this room."

"You know we have to do this professionally. We have to review all of them and discuss them with Soon-joon-nim and Seonsaengnim," Cheongul said. "He will expect nothing less."

"That boy can sing," HanYin murmured. "And he's got the most delectable dimples."

Ki-tae looked at HanYin for several moments before his brother seemed to realize what he'd just said. The blush coloring HanYin's cheeks was freaking adorable. "So that's what it takes to get your attention: a great singing voice and dimples?"

"Shut up," HanYin muttered, looking away.

Ki-tae decided to take it easy on his monkish sibling. He threw an arm around HanYin's shoulders and pulled him into a side hug. Then he kissed his temple. HanYin poked him in the side, and they were good once more. They turned their attention back to the front of the room as Teacher Kim took to the dais. He waited for the noise to quiet down before he began speaking.

"I would like to thank everyone for their efforts today. I know you all worked very hard on your presentations. I am proud of your efforts," he began. "I would like to thank our honored guests, Bam Kiseu and Soon-joon-nim, for taking the time out of their busy schedules to provide us with this wonderful opportunity. The presentations are complete. The students will now have a short break while we deliberate on the many wonderful ideas we've seen today."

The students rose, but they certainly weren't as energetic as they were earlier in the day. He bit back a groan as Jin-woo's scent pretty much kicked him in the groin. Even those other two scents couldn't distract him from Jin-woo. A small growl escaped, and his eyes locked on that sweet ass walking away from him. Cheongul's hand on his arm was the only thing preventing him from tackling Jin-woo. It took several deep breaths *after* the door closed behind Jin-woo for Ki-tae to get control of himself. This was going to be hell. He followed HanYin and

Cheongul when they rose and went to the dais. Jin-woo's visuals were still on the easel. They stood before them.

"He's got talent," Cheongul said.

HanYin chuckled. "They actually look like us."

"Dokkaebi are usually pictured with long fangs," Ki-tae said with a smirk. "Notice how he didn't put those in there, just the horns."

"I'd say it says a lot about Jin-woo dongsaeng," Cheongul said. "Maybe he can be trusted."

"Maybe," Ki-tae agreed. "That doesn't mean I want to be bound to him. He doesn't even seem to feel it the way I do."

"I don't know," HanYin said. "Between the two of you, there are enough pheromones to knock out a Dragon."

"He has been dreaming of you every night for the last three weeks," Cheongul pointed out. When Ki-tae gave him a look, he just shrugged. "What? Your room is next to mine, and you're not quiet by any stretch of the imagination."

"Do you know the meaning of the word tact?" Ki-tae said.

"Yes. I just choose not to bother with it." Cheongul smirked at him.

Ki-tae went to punch him in the arm, but Soon-joon clearing his throat stopped him. He glanced at his father and saw the raised eyebrow. With a sigh, Ki-tae lowered his hand, but the look he shot Cheongul promised retribution. Ki-tae moved out of Soon-joon's way and leaned against the desk immediately next to the podium.

"Soon-joon-nim?" Teacher Kim said with a smile. "I thought we might adjourn to one of the seminar rooms, stretch our legs a little, and have a change of scenery while we discuss the presentations."

"Of course. That is an excellent idea."

"I agree," Cheongul said with a smile. "We've been here quite some time. It almost feels like dance practice… without the work!"

They laughed. Ki-tae shoved Cheongul's shoulder as they followed Teacher Kim and Soon-joon out the door. Cheongul shot him a wink. Ki-tae gave a soft "oomph" as HanYin pounced on his shoulders and wrapped his legs around Ki-tae's waist like an overgrown spider monkey. He bounced HanYin-a a couple of times to adjust his weight on his back and then carried his brother down the hall. This wasn't unusual for them. The three of them were very close, although some people took it the wrong way.

Teacher Kim was right when he said the seminar rooms were too small for their needs. If they had tried to cram so many people in that one spot, things would have gotten super tense. There were certain scenarios where he and HanYin did not function well.

Sung-yi brought them refreshments as they took their seats. Ki-tae opened one of the waters and downed half of it in one long gulp. He needed something to cool him off. Although he wasn't sure water would ever do the trick, not when he knew Jin-woo was near.

"Shall we begin?" Soon-joon asked, looking at each of them in turn.

"Of course," Teacher Kim said.

The discussion went back and forth on each group until they reached group four of Class One. There was no way for Ki-tae to be nice about this one.

"I don't mean to be rude, but they were awful," Ki-tae said bluntly. Soon-joon winced a little. He'd apologize later.

"How so?" Teacher Kim asked.

"Ki-tae-ya and I wrote that song," HanYin said. "It was as if they hadn't even bothered to listen to it before putting their presentation together. They were so off the mark it was almost insulting."

"In addition, how could a video about the weather be remotely interesting unless one is a meteorologist?" Cheongul added. "Their visuals were subpar, and their presentation was poorly organized and sloppy."

"I don't know if you've ever listened to the song, but it has absolutely nothing to do with the weather. From the very first verse, there is no way a person could mistake it for anything other than a song about... being intimate with someone," Ki-tae said, changing the words he was going to use at the last minute.

"I did feel as if they had no real interest in what they were doing," Soon-joon said. "It was my impression that our style of music was not to their taste, and so their efforts were... lacking. This does not bode well for them in the entertainment industry. You don't always get to choose what projects you work on. Sometimes you must complete assignments that aren't to your taste, but you can't let that affect your work. You must give 100 percent to every project you do. Otherwise you will soon find yourself without work. I would not want to work with them until they come to understand and accept that fact."

Teacher Kim smiled gently. "I had hoped this project would inspire them to put more effort into their work, but it seems I was wrong."

"It isn't your fault," Soon-joon said. "It is hard to find motivation for others. Honestly it is something they must find within themselves. The only thing you can do is give their creativity nurturing. They're the ones that have to run with it."

"Those are wise words," Teacher Kim said. "I will keep them in mind as I continue to teach."

"Group six of Class One," Soon-joon said. When Cheongul groaned, he had a hard time suppressing his smile. "You have something to say, Cheongul dongsaeng?"

"The circus. That is what I have to say," Cheongul said calmly. "If 'Master' made them think of the circus, I don't ever want to go to the ones they visit."

"Again we have a situation where they didn't listen to the music. I mean really listen to it," Ki-tae said. "That song speaks of the beast inside all of us: the beast of wrath, of anger and rage. It is about how it can control us, smashing our hopes when let loose from its cage. I didn't see that in their concept at all."

"It appeared as if they didn't prepare for the actual presentation. Their material was falling apart. They lost their thread and repeated things they had already said. I understand some people have a difficult time with public speaking, but rehearsing can help to alleviate that," HanYin explained.

"Dedication shows in the willingness to prepare," Soon-joon said. "The boys complain about dance practice, but they're there for six hours every Tuesday and Thursday. On Mondays and Wednesdays, they have two hours of voice coaching and two hours of rehearsal. Then they have another two hours of dance practice in the evening. This is in addition to the many other engagements they have throughout the day. The only time these schedules change is when they record in the afternoon. Since the recording is the actual product, they rest in the mornings, so as not to strain their vocal cords and cause injury. Sometimes we must force them to leave the studio because they are working long after everyone else has hit the end of their stride. That is dedication."

"By the end of the day, we're beat too," Ki-tae said. "But we love what we do, so every ache and pain is worth it."

Teacher Kim nodded. Ki-tae liked the way he listened not only to Soon-joon, but to them as well. He jotted down notes on what they said and didn't dismiss them out of turn as some people tended to do. They appeared young, but they weren't, and it shocked people when they didn't act as expected. Teacher Kim made Ki-tae, at least, feel as if he took them seriously and that their apparent age didn't matter. They made it through the rest of the groups, reaching Jin-woo's team last.

"The Class Two groups were very good and I want to keep an eye on them as they continue their education, especially Group Three. That was Tae-ri dongsaeng, Hyung-ri dongsaeng, and Kwon-soo dongsaeng. They have a lot of potential, but this team," Soon-joon said, tapping the packet with his finger. "They know what it means to work and to prepare. Everything was on point. They were organized and had their pacing down. Each section easily flowed from one to the next, and they clearly took their time."

"They got the song right off the bat," HanYin said. "They nailed it."

"Their visuals were incredibly detailed and professional. Nothing was falling apart or got misplaced," Cheongul said.

"Jong-in dongsaeng took the time to rehearse that part. He sang it perfectly," Ki-tae said. "They were the only group that included actual production information in their presentation. Not a single other group mentioned filming, editing, or postproduction estimates, time frames, or any of the behind-the-scenes work."

"Jong-in dongsaeng, Min-su dongsaeng, and Jin-woo dongsaeng often work together and function as a very cohesive team," Teacher Kim said with a smile. "They are in the top ten of their faculty. I would not be surprised if they opened their own production company one day."

"Gentlemen, I feel we have come to a determination." Soon-joon smiled. Then he rose from his seat. "I will speak with our staff. The press should be here shortly, if they have not already begun to arrive. Seonsaengnim, I have something for each of the students, which we can present to them once the press has left."

Teacher Kim nodded and followed him out of the room, presumably to get the students ready for the announcement. Ki-tae leaned back in his chair and rubbed his hands over his face. He was mentally exhausted. Every time Jin-woo nibbled on his bottom lip, and it was often, Ki-tae had to resist the urge to scoop him up and carry him off. His muscles ached with how tense the last hour and a half had been.

"Are you okay, Ki-tae?" Cheongul asked quietly. "You look wiped out."

"I am," Ki-tae said with a sigh. "I didn't realize how much energy I was using fighting myself, of all people."

"He really does it for you," HanYin said.

"Yeah, I guess he does," Ki-tae said. "But is that really me, or is it the bond? Is what I feel real? Okay, the arousal… that's real, dammit, and persistent, but this… need to be with him…. Is that really coming from me?"

"Ki-tae, at this point, you and Jin-woo dongsaeng don't even know each other," Cheongul said, putting his hand on Ki-tae's thigh and giving a squeeze. "You've had one actual encounter, and the rest has been dream walking. Right now what you feel is more than likely the bond, because you know nothing about him. However, he is already your type. He's sweet and innocent-looking, and that gets you every time. If he's got a dirty mind, and your nocturnal activities, dream or not, seem to indicate he does, you're a goner. You cannot resist someone who looks so sweet on the outside and is so naughty on the inside. Hence 'Heat.'"

"Was that whole spiel supposed to be helpful?" Ki-tae asked with exasperation. "Because it sucked."

"It was meant to be practical. You two know nothing about each other," Cheongul said, popping Ki-tae upside the head. "What I'm saying is you have an excellent opportunity to get to know him over the next several weeks. Use it… and not just to get in his pants!"

Ki-tae pouted. "Is that option completely off the table?"

Cheongul did a facepalm while HanYin laughed so hard he fell off his chair. "You're too much!"

"Come on, we'd best go find Abeoji." Cheongul sighed. "We have fans to greet and reporters to smile at."

"Shall we play three-way Pocky again?" HanYin asked. "They seem to love that!"

"Only the fangirls do." Ki-tae chuckled. "They love to see us kiss."

"There's actually a YouTube video out there counting how many times we stick our hands in each other's pockets or in the waistband of each other's pants," HanYin said with a grin. "Ki-tae does it the most."

"My hands get cold," he complained, bumping his shoulder against HanYin.

"I know, because you're usually shoving your freezing cold hands down *my* waistband," HanYin pointed out. "Cheongul is pocket boy, and I prefer hugs!"

"It's not my fault you run the warmest of the three of us," Ki-tae grumbled.

"That is a really weird thing to count," Cheongul said. "It's funny how wound up people get with the way we touch each other. Remember when that one fan hid in my hotel room, only I never went back there that night because I crashed in HanYin's bed with him? She was still there the next day after we'd left. Then there was all that back-and-forth on the social media sites, fans making such a fuss out of us in the same bed."

"I remember Abeoji was *not* happy she'd gotten into the room in the first place," HanYin said.

"I'm glad I wasn't the hotel manager," Ki-tae said. "Abeoji can be downright frightening when he chooses to be."

"This is why we never want to piss that man off," Cheongul said, and then he paused as they approached the lecture hall. "Smiles on, gentlemen. Get ready to charm them."

"Aren't we always ready?" HanYin asked innocently, then grinned wickedly. "I have Pocky with me, you know."

"After the press conference, we'll play," Ki-tae said.

"Promise?"

"I promise."

"You two are going to get me in trouble again," Cheongul muttered as he opened the door.

"Yeah, but you still love us." Ki-tae grinned as he rucked up HanYin's coat and shirt, shoving his cold hand down the back of his pants. HanYin yelped a little but didn't pull away.

"Yeah, I do," Cheongul agreed.

JIN-WOO

JIN-WOO SLOUCHED in his chair. He was beat. They had stayed later at I Love K-pop than he wanted. When he had gotten home, he couldn't fall asleep. Then there was the whole issue with the visuals. He just wanted to go home and sleep. He jerked awake when Min-su poked him in the arm.

"Why must you abuse me?" he demanded grumpily, rubbing his arm.

"If I try to be nice, you don't hear me," she said. "You sleep like the dead. Are you okay?"

"I'm just beat." Jin-woo sighed. "We've been working our asses off for three weeks straight. There were nights when my hands completely cramped up. I had to soak them in hot water to get them to relax. Honestly, I'm glad this part is over."

"Me too," she said with a soft smile. "I had it easy compared to you and Jong-in-a. All I had to do was figure out how long it would take to do the filming, editing, and postproduction, and estimate how much it would cost. Jong-in-a spent so much time practicing that one verse he almost lost his voice. I told him he wasn't allowed to talk at all for the last two days."

"Easy?" Jong-in snorted. "You're the one who did all the rendering and production work on the concept trailer in addition to doing all the planning and estimates. Don't sell yourself short, Min-su-ya."

She blushed and looked down, not a normal reaction for her, but Jin-woo figured being so close to Cheongul was making her weird. Well, weirder than usual.

"But your part was important, Min-su-ya," Jin-woo said with a smile. "No one else covered deadlines and financials. That's going to give us an advantage, I think. We made a full project presentation, not just a creative one."

"True, but I'm still really nervous," she said. "I mean, I know what their music means to me, but to try and put their words on screen? That's hard."

"I think we did a great job," Jong-in said quietly, then sipped a ginger tea. "I think we worked really hard, and we're feeling it. I could sleep for a week."

Before Jin-woo could comment, the sound in the room dropped to almost silence. He looked up to see Park Soon-joon enter with Teacher Kim. They walked up to the dais and stood at the very front. Bam Kiseu followed, standing behind and off to the left. They looked so serious. Jin-woo decided he liked it much better when they were all smiling, especially Ki-tae. He didn't like the almost sad look on Ki-tae's face. He wanted to go to him, rub away the little worry lines between his eyes. Jin-woo shook his head. What in the world was he thinking? Before Jin-woo could berate himself further, Teacher Kim began speaking.

"First I would like to thank you all once again for your presentations today. We will discuss them over the next few weeks as we continue our lessons," Teacher Kim said to soft groans. He smiled. "As you are aware, this was just the first part in the program Soon-joon-nim and BL Entertainment have presented for Jeonjin University's Art and Digital Media Production Faculty. The second part involves less public speaking, but not less work. In part two you each will be required to write an original song. No collaborations allowed. Soon-joon-nim and I have decided to grant a very generous four-week deadline to complete the song, as we want you to be able to keep up in your other classes. This will be a completed song, which means composing, recording, and postproduction. With that time, I suggest each of you become familiar with the work of the artists standing with us today. They are your clients. Therefore your song will need to take each of their vocal styles into account as well as combining those styles cohesively. Do not doubt this will be challenging, but it is not impossible. These young men and their team do it on every album. Remember we are a creative faculty, but we still must rely on things such as research to accomplish our goals. With that being said, we will continue with part one of the BL Entertainment program. Soon-joon-nim, will you do the honors?"

"Of course, Seonsaengnim." Soon-joon stepped forward, his hands behind his back. Jin-woo thought he looked very intense, very mature, and handsome. The God of K-pop lived up to his name visually as well as in his business dealings. His presence took command of the room, but it was subtle. There was no sense of demand. Jin-woo sat up straighter. It felt as if slouching while Soon-joon spoke would be disrespectful. He clasped his hands and rested them on the long desk in front of him, giving his full attention to Park Soon-joon.

"In my line of work, I deal with artists, businessmen, craftsmen, many different types of people all day, every day. I interact with dancers and choreographers, voice coaches and singers, sound engineers, and production managers. I deal with accountants and sales representatives. Each interaction must convey my intent clearly, concisely, and quickly. When a young singer brings me his demo CD, I must evaluate and analyze not just the music but the musician. I must not only listen to the product but evaluate the risks involved based on what I see. That musician has precisely three minutes to impress me, to show me his or her potential, to show me he or she is worth the risk of taking them on. Poor presentation and poor product means poor risk. There were presentations I saw today which would not have made it past the first thirty seconds, let alone the full three minutes. I saw lack of motivation. I heard lack of product knowledge. I saw lack of effort. On the other end of the scale, I saw many presenters that I would have advised to rework their ideas and come to me again in six months."

Jin-woo wrinkled his nose. What manager gave someone who flubbed an interview a second chance? He'd read that BL Entertainment was unlike other companies, such as GT Entertainment and MS Tune, and Park Soon-joon proved it. Without realizing it, Jin-woo leaned forward, intent on whatever else Soon-joon had to say.

"Then I saw a group that hit every point I look for in a potential protégé. This presentation went beyond the creative to include the practical. This group knew the song they were presenting and knew it well. They incorporated it into their presentation in multiple ways. I saw the culmination of hours of hard work. I was impressed within the first thirty seconds. Class Two, Group Six, Yi Min-su dongsaeng, Bak Jong-in dongsaeng, and Cheong Jin-woo dongsaeng, please join us."

Jin-woo stared, shock freezing him in place. He felt numb and shivery at the same time. Min-su had to pinch him hard before he jerked out of it. After rising shakily to his feet, Jin-woo led the way out of the row and down the main aisle. He kept his eyes on where his feet were going, lest he fall flat on his face and embarrass the hell out of himself. He moved to the right, sort of slipping behind Jong-in's slightly larger frame. He was going to be sick... or pass out again, one of the two. Thankfully Min-su had always been the de facto leader of their group. She had the most control over herself.... Well, for the most part. She did have her moments. They bowed to Park Soon-joon and shook his hand. It was a strong, firm grip, but not overpowering, as if he knew his own strength and contained it.

"I was very impressed with your work," Soon-joon said after the applause had died down. "Tell me, what made you use 'Crossing Time' that way?"

"The presentation was for a music video of that song. It didn't make sense not to use it," Min-su said. "We began our first brainstorming session by listening to the song, to the words, and breaking them down by verse and chorus. Then we focused on each section and what we felt the words might mean. In the end we concluded it was about a love that defied even time."

"What made you choose a supernatural theme?"

"What other being could cross time for the one they loved?" Min-su asked with a cute little grin. "Originally we were going to go with the Vampire myth, but Jin-woo-ya was adamant we try something new, something different. So I challenged him to find another immortal being that would fit the song, and damned if he didn't do it."

Jin-woo wished they would stop talking, wished they could just leave already. His senses were overloaded, he was exhausted, and he just wanted some peace and quiet. And sleep, sleep would be good too. He wanted to nudge Min-su, let her know enough was enough already and to move things along. Yet he couldn't. That would be unprofessional. He didn't want to ruin the image they had created, but if he stood there much longer, he was going to collapse.

When Soon-joon turned to the desk and picked up a pile of papers, Jin-woo couldn't help but think, *Finally*. But then it was another eon before they finally got to sign the agreements. It was official. He, Min-su, and Jong-in would be making a music video with Bam Kiseu. Jin-woo could feel the puffy sensation in his temple and knew he was going to pay for all this stress within the next twenty-four to forty-eight hours. It would be worth it, though, for this experience alone.

Teacher Kim approached the group and turned to face the rest of the room. "I have obtained permission for all of you to take the rest of the day off. You may spend it as you wish, although I do recommend getting a start on your next project. Have a good day."

When he turned to face them once more, Jin-woo couldn't help but return his warm smile. "I am very proud of you three. I always see good work from you, but your presentation was nothing short of amazing," he said.

"Gomabseumnida, Seonsaengnim," they said, bowing.

Min-su added, "We have learned much from you."

"And much of it is natural talent," Teacher Kim said.

"It is a pleasure to formally meet you," Soon-joon said with a smile. They greeted him politely, Jin-woo practically whispering the words. He could feel eyes on him, knew Ki-tae was watching him again. In a few moments, they would be formally introduced to each other. How did you politely greet someone who'd made you cum so hard you passed out? This was not within his realm of experience, and Jin-woo was hard-pressed to figure out how to behave.

"I would make introductions, but I have the feeling you three know exactly who these young gentlemen are," Soon-joon said with a smile as he motioned Cheongul, Ki-tae, and HanYin closer. "Still, polite is polite. Let me introduce Cheongul dongsaeng, Ki-tae dongsaeng, and HanYin dongsaeng, Bam Kiseu. Boys, this is Yi Min-su dongsaeng, Bak Jong-in dongsaeng, and Cheong Jin-woo dongsaeng, the winners of the Music Video BL Entertainment program for Jeonjin University."

Everyone murmured the appropriate greetings and bowed. Jin-woo found his gaze jumping around. Each time he would look at Ki-tae, see him watching intently, and then look somewhere else. He couldn't seem to keep his eyes on one spot. Ki-tae looked incredibly hot in his black leather jacket and jeans. His hair had that messy look Jin-woo adored on him, and his eyes popped with the subtle makeup around them. His already tempting lips looked more so with the hint of color. No man had the right to look that hot and *not* come with a freaking warning label. Jin-woo nibbled on his lip absently, twisting his fingers together behind his back, and he bounced on his toes.

Cheongul, as the oldest, always seemed to be the unofficial spokesman for the group, and today was no exception. "We look forward to working with you. I must say we were very impressed with your presentation. You really understand the song, and, Jong-in dongsaeng, your singing was spot on."

"It was beautiful," HanYin said quietly. Jin-woo wondered if Jong-in noticed how HanYin was staring at him.

Jong-in smiled shyly. "I almost lost my voice practicing."

"After a long concert run, HanYin-a always loses his voice for about a day and a half," Ki-tae said, smiling. "We count our blessings, because then he can't talk nonstop!"

HanYin smacked Ki-tae in the shoulder. "No steamed dumplings for a month."

"Steamed dumplings?" Jong-in's voice perked up.

"You caught his attention," Min-su teased. "If there's one thing Jong-in-a loves beyond music, it's food."

Jong-in blushed harder and ducked his head, pushing his glasses back up his nose as he did so. "What? I like to eat."

"Good to know, because HanYin-a likes to cook," Ki-tae said as he threw his arm around HanYin's shoulders. "We're going to be spending a good deal of time together over the next several weeks, so now HanYin-a will have someone else to experiment... I mean cook for."

Jin-woo chuckled as Ki-tae's comments earned him a jab in the ribs.

"Well, boys," Soon-joon said once Ki-tae and HanYin had settled down. "It's time to show our new partners what it's like to be pop stars."

"I'm not sure I like the sound of that," Jin-woo muttered.

"Don't worry, we'll protect you from the rabid mongooses," Ki-tae said with a wink.

"Wouldn't it be mongeese?" Min-su asked suddenly. "Or is it like the English word *moose*?"

"No, no, no, not another one!" Ki-tae did a facepalm and shook his head.

"I believe the most common plural form is 'mongooses,' but it can be, on the rare occasion, 'mongeese.' Of course, either one sounds ridiculous," Cheongul said.

"Very true," Min-su said. "Of course, if you say a word often enough, it starts to sound odd."

"Word geeks." Jin-woo leaned over and poked Jong-in, who was staring at HanYin. "I thought she was a rarity."

"Looks like there's more of them out there."

"Regardless, we're about to encounter the human version, and it can be overwhelming," Ki-tae said. "It's been my experience that it's best to let Soon-joon-nim take the lead unless asked a direct question. At which point try to keep your answer brief and to the point. They'll jump on anything."

"They can't possibly be that bad," Jin-woo protested.

"You have *no* idea, and I hope you never have to deal with the more vicious ones," Ki-tae said quietly.

"Let's go," Soon-joon said, putting a hand on Ki-tae's shoulder. He smiled, and Ki-tae returned it, although Jin-woo still thought it looked a little sad.

While Ki-tae might prefer to let Soon-joon take the lead and simply stand at his side, Jin-woo had his own preferred method when dealing with people and attention. He stood slightly behind anyone who was taller than he was. That way he sort of got lost in the shuffle, and people didn't notice him as much. He didn't have to say much of anything during the press conference. Mostly he just nodded and bowed and thanked people, and honestly, that worked for him. This wasn't his thing. He didn't want to be onstage. He wanted to make it all happen. Well, not all of it. He didn't want to be a manager. He wanted to be involved in the actual process of creating the finished product.

When it was finally over, Jin-woo sagged against Jong-in in relief. "Can I go home now? Please?"

"You're whining," Jong-in said with a smile as he ruffled his hair. Jin-woo slapped his hand.

"I can't help it," Jin-woo said with a pout. "I'm beat. I got *maybe* two hours' sleep last night. I hit the ground running this morning and feel as if I haven't stopped."

"We still have to set up a meeting with Soon-joon hyung," Min-su said as she stared at her phone, tapping away. "We'll need to fill out some paperwork, get photos taken for temporary badges, contact information, meeting schedules. If I remember correctly—"

"And of course you do." Jin-woo sighed.

"Bam Kiseu has a couple of appearances in and around the area," she continued as if Jin-woo hadn't said anything, which, he supposed, was better than her usual response of smacking him upside the head. "We'll have to hammer out what sort of budget we're looking at. My estimates were conservative. Then we'll need to meet the crews, the director, art director, sound engineers. I wonder how many meetings I can squeeze in between classes?"

"Pocky?"

"What?" Min-su's head shot up, and she stared at HanYin.

"Would you like some Pocky?" he said with a smile.

"Thank you," she said, taking the proffered treat.

HanYin gave her a nod, and after offering some to everyone, bounced over to Ki-tae. Jin-woo wondered what HanYin was up to. The mischievous look on his face said it was something naughty. Glancing around, Jin-woo saw more people than normal milling around the building entrance. Many of them were female students, but there were a good number of male ones. They were smiling and, in some cases, giggling behind their hands. Some of them held autograph books. Yet they seemed hesitant to approach. One or two reporters were still present, mostly the teen-magazine types.

Nibbling on his own Pocky, Jin-woo nearly choked when Ki-tae grabbed the back of HanYin's neck and started nipping his way down the stick held between HanYin's lips. Giggling and screaming echoed through the air, getting louder the closer they got to each other's mouths. HanYin's hand rested on Ki-tae's shoulder, and from his angle, Jin-woo could see he was smiling. Then they got too close to see, and Jin-woo felt his breath catch. He turned away, trying not to whimper. He knew what Ki-tae's kisses felt like, knew what Ki-tae tasted like, and damned if he'd ever been more jealous of another human being than he was of HanYin right now. He shifted in his seat on the rock wall, bringing his coat into his lap. Ki-tae was hugging HanYin, and they were both laughing. Jin-woo could sense what was coming next. No sooner had the thought crossed his mind than they grabbed Cheongul, who looked incredibly put upon but humored them. Normally people would use Pepero, but for whatever reason, when Bam Kiseu played the game, they always used Pocky.

The three of them faced one another in a sort of triangle. HanYin held the Pocky in his mouth. He turned to Ki-tae, who then took the stick with his teeth, biting off a bit before turning to face Cheongul. They went around and around, each one nipping off a little more until the very last round. Cheongul looked at Ki-tae, shook his head, and proceeded to kiss the Pocky right out of his mouth. Then he tapped Ki-tae on the nose with a smile on his face, chewing the final piece while he pulled Ki-tae to his side and stuck his hand in Ki-tae's pocket. If it wasn't already doing naughty things to his thought processes, Jin-woo would have laughed too.

Jin-woo took a deep breath. How in the heck was he going to get through this? Here he was, sporting an erection from watching Ki-tae play a game, hiding said predicament under a coat like a teen in the locker room. The sad thing was Ki-tae probably didn't even remember who he was. He probably didn't even recognize Jin-woo, and that hurt more than Jin-woo thought it would... or should. Did Ki-tae do that so often that one more face was hardly going to stand out?

"Give me your phone."

Jin-woo jumped at the sudden sound of Ki-tae's voice. He swallowed hard. "What?"

"Give me your phone," Ki-tae said again, holding out his hand.

Jin-woo handed it over without thinking. He watched as Ki-tae tapped at his phone. "Why?"

"I'm giving you my phone number," Ki-tae said. "You'll get a company phone for the duration of the project, which will have everyone's phone number in it. It makes it easier to communicate because business messages and phone calls don't get lost among the personal ones, but I wanted you to have mine in your own phone. Call me later tonight."

"Why?" Jin-woo seemed to be stuck in one-word response mode. He tensed when Ki-tae leaned close to him, his breath brushing Jin-woo's ear and sending shivers racing over his skin.

"Because I remember."

Jin-woo couldn't breathe. He watched Ki-tae walk over to Soon-joon, who was speaking with Teacher Kim. Did he just say what Jin-woo thought he said? Did he say he remembered? Did he? Jin-woo couldn't believe it. He quickly unlocked his phone and pulled up his contacts. He scrolled through the list and tapped Ki-tae's name. Jin-woo groaned and dropped his head. Ki-tae had made his contact icon a shot of him with the killer little smile Jin-woo loved. It was just one corner of his mouth kicked up, and it always made Jin-woo's belly quiver. Ki-tae was going to be the death of him; he just knew it.

Soon-Joon

"LADIES AND gentlemen, I am afraid it is time for Bam Kiseu to depart," Soon-joon said to the reporters still asking questions and snapping photos. He should have known when he saw the box peeking out of HanYin's pocket what they were going to do. "They have a pretty tight schedule tomorrow. If you have any further questions, please contact the main office of BL Entertainment and ask about the program. I wish you all a good day."

He ushered Ki-tae, Cheongul, and HanYin into their car. While the boys would get to rest, he had to return to the office after speaking with Teacher Kim and handing out the individual grants to the other students. There was always work waiting for him. He liked it that way. It didn't give him time to brood over things. He had sent missives to each of his mentors and his sire but knew it would take them a while to get back to him. They could be irritating like that, but it was their privilege and their due. They had lived many centuries and knew much. He just wished it was easier to get in contact with them. Although perhaps once Ki-tae and Jin-woo got to know each other in a less intimate sense, it wouldn't be necessary to break the bond.

Once they were settled in the car, Soon-joon leaned his head back and closed his eyes. Jin-woo knew what Ki-tae was. This was an undeniable fact. Had he purposefully avoided the Vampire theme because of that knowledge? If so, that spoke well of him. There were very few people who knew they existed and for good reason. Today people would not be able to handle the idea of the spiritual world being a real thing. It would get violent and ugly. Soon-joon missed the days when people accepted these things as fact and didn't try to destroy everything they didn't understand. He wished for simpler times every now and then. He had walked many paths in his long life, and his desire for some of those simpler times in no way negated his love for his current one. He just had the benefit of seeing how simple things could be and how people complicated things unnecessarily.

Absently Soon-joon reached out and stroked Ki-tae's hair. He was the youngest of Soon-joon's children, and Soon-joon would dare say he was the most damaged. Had it truly only been 275 years since he'd found Ki-tae in that monster's brothel? That was horrible in and of itself, but when he learned the master was a Vampire and forced a bond upon Ki-tae, Soon-joon became enraged. It was a bloodbath despite Soon-joon sparing those who did not fight or those who knew no other way.

It had taken years to wean Ki-tae from the Vampiric blood that bound him. The withdrawal was a hundred times worse than with any drug. Even now he,

Cheongul, and HanYin had to be careful when injured and Ki-tae was near. He was and always would be a recovering addict, and they did everything they could to help him. Yet Ki-tae was strong. There was no doubt about that. He had survived in that nightmare for close to eight years before Soon-joon found him, not an easy feat for a child.

"You're thinking very hard, Abeoji," Ki-tae said softly. "I'm okay."

"I worry."

"I know you do. You all do, but I will be fine," Ki-tae said, trying to reassure them.

"I saw you talking to Jin-woo dongsaeng," Cheongul said. "How did that go?"

"It was… brief." Ki-tae chuckled. "He only gave me one-word answers, but I put my number in his phone and told him to call me later tonight. Whether he will, I don't know."

"Did he mention that night?" HanYin asked.

"No," Ki-tae said. "I did."

"*You* did?" HanYin was clearly surprised. "That couldn't have been an easy conversation."

"It really wasn't a conversation. When he asked me why he should call me tonight, all I said was because I remember."

"Why would you say that?" Cheongul looked confused.

"I didn't want him to think he was just one of many. I wanted him to know he stood out, that I remembered him specifically. I don't know if he caught that with those few words, but that was what I was trying to convey."

"We shall have to wait and see," Soon-joon said.

KI-TAE

LATER THAT night, Ki-tae sat at the grand piano in the great room. He placed his fingers lightly on the keys and, closing his eyes, began to play. He had nothing in mind, but the haunting strands of Beethoven's *Moonlight* Sonata floated into the air. He loved the way the piece started out so slowly, just a gentle brushing of the keys and the deep notes holding the listener as if they had an anchor tied to them. This was the most recognizable part of the sonata to most people, but Ki-tae knew there was more. The piece was fifteen minutes long stretching over three movements, and it didn't have any blatant hooks, but it still resonated within him. Just when you thought it would end, and indeed it could with the movements being separate yet also part of the whole piece, the scherzo picked up with a happier tune, still in the lower keys but with higher-toned accents and a slightly faster pace. It was a bit brighter, lighter, freer. He never played just the first movement. Ki-tae always felt compelled to play all three movements unless he was interrupted.

For the longest time, Ki-tae had thought he would never be free, but Abeoji had changed all that. He thought he wouldn't be allowed to stay long, to pollute everything with his filth, but here he was, two hundred-some odd years later, and they still loved him. Then the sonata moved faster and faster, more powerful, more strength, the will to endure, to carry on. It became more complex, more challenging, much like his life. There were calmer moments but still that underlying frenetic pace, the rush forward to, or away from, something. What was he running to? He did not want to recall what he was running from.

Finally the sonata came to a close. Ki-tae felt a little bit better. Music always did that for him. It was his outlet. Cheongul often commented how he could determine Ki-tae's mood by two things: the music he was listening to and the colors he wore. Ki-tae had to admit he had a point. His feelings were reflected in the way he dressed and what music he played. Right now he was feeling a bit sad, a little melancholy. Jin-woo hadn't called, and Ki-tae wasn't sure he would call this late at night. Was it late? He didn't think so, but he didn't have what anyone would consider a normal schedule. He should have gotten Jin-woo's number instead of just asking him to call.

"Ki-tae, you left your phone on vibrate in the kitchen again. No wonder you miss so many text messages. You know that's how people communicate these days, right?" HanYin said as he set the phone down on the piano. "There's homemade noodles in the refrigerator when you're done. And you missed a call, but it wasn't blocked, so you can just call them back."

Ki-tae immediately grabbed his phone and ran into his room. Well, maybe not ran, but walked very quickly, much to HanYin's amusement; Ki-tae heard the chuckle. He pulled up his missed calls list and hit the last number. He held his breath as it rang and rang. He tensed when he suddenly heard Jin-woo's voice.

"What? You tell someone to call you, and then you don't respond to my text or pick up? How rude is that?" Jin-woo said with a huff. Ki-tae laughed softly, relieved.

"I left my phone on vibrate and, apparently, in the kitchen, so I didn't hear it," he explained.

"Well, I suppose I can forgive you. I do that all the time," Jin-woo said. "It's a good thing you called back immediately. I was going to say forget it and go to bed."

"I'm glad HanYin hyung brought me my phone," Ki-tae said.

"He did? I guess I have to thank him the next time I see him. This is easier on the phone. You don't quite turn my brain to mush when we're talking like this." Ki-tae chuckled, and he heard Jin-woo sigh. "I said that aloud, didn't I?"

"Yes, but it was adorable. I like knowing I turn your brain to mush," Ki-tae said.

"Well, I'm not sure I like knowing that you know you turn my brain to mush. It seems as if it would be an unfair advantage, don't you think?"

"If it makes you feel any better, I haven't been able to think of much else but you since the concert," Ki-tae said.

"This is…. I don't know what this is," Jin-woo said.

"I guess it's two people who had an amazing encounter getting to know each other on a different level," Ki-tae said. "I want to know more about you."

"Why? I'm not that interesting," Jin-woo said softly.

"You're interesting to me," Ki-tae said. "It was difficult today. I didn't know how to behave."

"I felt the same way. I didn't know if you remembered, and then you said you did, and I was like, 'Oh my God,' and then everything kind of just went poof."

"Poof?" Ki-tae asked as he fiddled with one frayed edge of the hole in his jeans.

"I don't really remember doing anything else. It's just all kind of a blur." Jin-woo paused a moment, and Ki-tae held his breath. It was so strange how easily they were talking. "Is it just me, or are we talking as if we've known each other for a while?"

"It's not just you," Ki-tae said. "I was just thinking the same thing, how easy it is."

"I'm sorry."

"Why?"

"I really didn't mean to bother you that night. I was just curious about what it was like backstage. I mean, you see all the behind-the-scenes stuff, but you know the video is edited to make things look good, and you can't feel the energy through the videos, so I went exploring, and I really shouldn't have."

"Do you regret meeting me?" Ki-tae asked, a knot of pain settling in his chest.

"I…," Jin-woo began, but then he stopped, and Ki-tae felt the knot expand.

"You?" Ki-tae prompted.

"I have to admit, stumbling on you the way I did, sucking the blood out of some random woman's neck, wasn't the best way to meet. Having my whole worldview turned upside down, where the monsters are real, is not something I'd planned that day and it was terrifying. I didn't wake up and say 'I want to meet a fanged beast in the middle of feeding today,'" Jin-woo said.

"Monsters, huh?" Ki-tae tried to keep the hurt from his voice. It wasn't the first time that word had been thrown at him, but he could have done without the revulsion in Jin-woo's voice.

"Well, I figure if you're real, then the others are real too. You know, werewolves, ghosts, and other things that don't bear thinking about." Jin-woo's voice trembled slightly as he spoke, and Ki-tae wondered if he only called because he was too afraid of Ki-tae not to. "When I think about the idea that all the fairy tales and creatures that go bump in the night are real—I mean, really real—it scares the crap out of me."

"It's okay. I understand. Good night, dongsaeng," Ki-tae said softly.

"Ki-tae hyung, no, wait—"

Ki-tae ended the call. Turning it to silent, he placed it on his nightstand and then rolled to face the other way. It really didn't surprise him Jin-woo regretted their meeting. He'd not only revealed the demon inside him, but he pretty much assaulted Jin-woo in the process. It seemed his past still stained him with blood no matter how many years passed. No matter how far he ran, he was still the monster. It would be best if he tried to forget how Jin-woo made him feel, forget how much Ki-tae wanted him, because relationships with humans never worked out. It would be safer for Ki-tae if he just forgot everything, safer for Jin-woo too.

How the hell was he going to get through the next several weeks?

JIN-WOO

JIN-WOO STARED at his phone. Ki-tae had hung up on him. Jin-woo dialed his number again, but it just rang and rang before going to voicemail. Why wasn't Ki-tae taking his call? When he got no answer the third time he called, he went to text messages. After the first twenty received no response, a little stone of dread wedged in his belly. Had he said something wrong? Could Ki-tae have misunderstood his silence? His voice had changed at the end of their conversation, as if he were saying more than just goodbye for the night, and Jin-woo didn't like that idea, not one bit. And why in the hell wouldn't Ki-tae just talk to him? It wasn't as if they hadn't been having a decent conversation up until that point. The more he thought about it, the more annoyed Jin-woo got, but underneath was a small kernel of worry. Ignoring things never made them go away, and for a Vampire that was pretty childish too.

Finally Jin-woo had to stop. He had to get some modicum of sleep if he wanted to function in school the next day. Yet he couldn't stop bouncing between annoyance and worry. Did Ki-tae really think he regretted their meeting? While he could have done without the vision of Ki-tae feeding on the tech, he couldn't regret what happened after. Well, maybe he could have done without the fear that prompted his run into the bowels of the building. He certainly did *not* regret his experience with Ki-tae.

Jin-woo wasn't a virgin, but his experiences were infrequent. What art student, who actually enjoyed his classes, had time to get laid? He didn't have time to date either, so any knowledge came from hookups and were so brief as to be unmemorable. Ki-tae, no, the encounter with Ki-tae was *un*forgettable. The frotting had been amazing, messy but amazing. Sex would probably kill him… in the best way possible. No, he didn't regret meeting Ki-tae. Now he just had to find a way to convince Ki-tae of that, because Jin-woo was pretty sure Ki-tae was as upset by the idea as he was.

Morning came way too early, and Jin-woo just wasn't ready for it. He hit Snooze and ended up making himself late. He tried to sneak into a lecture, but Teacher Park wasn't having it.

"Nice of you to join us, Jin-woo," Teacher Park said drily.

"It is a pleasure to be here, Seonsaengnim," Jin-woo said with a bow, earning some chuckles from the other students.

"Perhaps next time you could arrive on time, if it's such a pleasure," Teacher Park said. "Hurry up and sit down. We're waiting on you."

"I'm sorry, Seonsaengnim," Jin-woo said and hurried to his seat next to Jong-in. Jong-in looked at him strangely, raising an eyebrow, and Jin-woo mouthed, "Later." He didn't want to get on Teacher Park's bad side. It was not a nice place to be.

Jong-in pulled Jin-woo to one side as they left the room after class. He waited until the hall was clear before he spoke.

"Okay, what is going on?"

"It's complicated." Jin-woo sighed. "And I can't really talk about it in detail."

"You'd better tell me something, Jin-woo-ya," Jong-in said. "I've known you a really long time, and you don't run this late."

"Yes, I know," Jin-woo said. "Let's find somewhere a little more private."

It took them several moments to find an empty classroom. Jin-woo closed and locked the door so they wouldn't be disturbed. Then he set his bookbag on a chair and sat on the desk, his feet on the chair. "You remember the concert?"

"I couldn't go. Pissed me off," Jong-in said.

"Well, I managed to get backstage with the DM club. The area we were in was boring, so I kind of slipped away and wandered around backstage. It was amazing. The videos really can't capture all the energy. Anyway, I bumped into Ki-tae hyung."

"Why are you blushing?"

"Shut up."

"What happened, Jin-woo-ya?" Jong-in said, trying to catch his eye, but Jin-woo couldn't look at him.

"Well, we… sort of…."

"Did you have sex with Ki-tae hyung?" Jong-in's voice was a shocked whisper.

"No!" Jin-woo said hotly. "Well, not full sex, frotting, but still, amazing!"

"Let me get this straight," Jong-in said, putting his fingers to his temples and rubbing small circles. "You dry-humped Ki-tae hyung backstage at a Bam Kiseu concert, and you're just telling me now?"

"Hey! You know I'm not the kiss-and-tell type!" Jin-woo protested. "Stuff like that is private."

"Okay, okay, you're right. So why and how could that possibly make you late today?"

"Well, yesterday was really awkward for me. At first I thought Ki-tae hyung would behave differently, and when he didn't, I thought he didn't remember, that it wasn't uncommon for him to do that."

"But?"

"He came over and gave me his personal cell phone number," Jin-woo whispered. "He said he remembered and wanted me to call him last night."

"Holy shit!"

"You're telling me?" Jin-woo said. "I mean, it's a drama come true! Anyway, I texted first and when I didn't get a response, I called him, but he didn't pick up, and I thought, well…. I didn't have good thoughts, but then he called back because HanYin hyung had found his phone in the kitchen and it was on vibrate, so he didn't hear it ring."

"Jin-woo-ya, you're babbling," Jong-in said calmly. "Breathe, or you'll pass out."

Jin-woo took a deep breath and let it out slowly. "We got talking, and Ki-tae hyung asked me if I regretted meeting him because of what happened. I didn't know how to answer, and I think he took my silence to mean I do regret our meeting, but I really, really don't! He hung up on me, saying goodbye, and it sounded like the permanent goodbye, not the goodbye for just the night. I tried calling and texting for a while afterward, with no luck, which was really fucking annoying and childish of him to ignore me, and so I didn't go to sleep until really early this morning. I missed my alarm and then my train, and that's why I'm late. He sounded so sad, Jong-in-a! Like me regretting our meeting really hurt. But I don't regret it. I don't!"

"I get it, Jin-woo-ya," Jong-in said, resting a hand on his shoulder. "This is just a misunderstanding. Here's what I recommend. Text him after classes are done for the day. Even if he doesn't respond, he'll still see it. He more than likely took your silence as a rejection, and idol he may be, but he's still a person."

"Yeah, you're right." Jin-woo took another deep breath. "You can't tell Min-su-ya. She'll kill me for not telling her."

"You think she's not going to figure it out eventually? That girl is like a bloodhound when it comes to romance, and if sex is involved, she's worse."

"Well, if I have to tell her, I don't want to do it anywhere public. She will be so loud!" Jin-woo grumbled.

"Oh hell yeah, she's going to scream like a rabid fangirl." Jong-in chuckled. "We'd better get going. I didn't grab breakfast, and you probably didn't either. If we hurry, we can get something at the commissary before our next class."

Jin-woo nodded and, grabbing his backpack, hopped off the desk. It was going to be a long day, and he was going to worry about Ki-tae constantly, but what choice did he have? As much as he wanted to call Ki-tae right then and work things out, he knew he couldn't. Chances were Ki-tae either couldn't or wouldn't pick up the phone.

By far, Teacher Kim's class was Jin-woo's favorite. With their different focuses, he didn't get to have class with both Jong-in and Min-su often. He wanted to clarify something with Teacher Kim before class, so Jin-woo headed to the room early. He was fortunate enough to catch Teacher Kim alone.

"Good morning, Seonsaengnim," Jin-woo said. "May I speak with you for a moment?"

"Of course, dongsaeng. How can I help you?" Teacher Kim said with a smile. Jin-woo smiled back and hurried over, taking the seat next to his desk.

"I wanted to clarify something about part two of the BLE program," Jin-woo said.

"You and the others did a wonderful job yesterday. I was very proud to be your teacher."

"Gomabseumnida, I am very excited," Jin-woo said.

"What did you want to know about part two?"

"I wanted to know if we are able to seek advice and brainstorm with other students," Jin-woo said. "Bounce ideas off each other and such."

"Ah, collaboration verses assistance," Teacher Kim said with a nod. "You must write the song yourself. You must record and edit it as well. It must be *your* work. However, that doesn't mean you can't borrow Jong-in dongsaeng's ear or ask for Min-su dongsaeng's input. Your friends are valuable resources and provide an outside point of view for you to work from. You provide the same for them as well. They just cannot help you actually write and produce the song."

"Gomabseumnida, Seonsaengnim," Jin-woo said. "I wanted to make sure I was understanding clearly."

"It is better to ask the question than guess the answer," Teacher Kim said. "Midweek you and the others will be heading to BLE headquarters to go over the essential paperwork, get your badges and work phones, as well as go over everyone's schedules. Make sure you bring a list of current projects for other classes. This is a wonderful opportunity, but Soon-joon-nim does not want it to be detrimental to your studies."

"It is still hard to believe," Jin-woo said. "I will make sure the others know to bring the list as well. Gomabseumnida, Seonsaengnim." Jin-woo rose and bowed before heading to his seat and getting his things out for class.

JUST ONE more edit, one more effect to make the image clear, and it would be done. It hadn't taken much to get the product just right. The two cameras in the loading bay had caught everything and were of decent quality. Often security cameras tended to be rather grainy, meant only to capture the basic area. But the Seoul Olympic Stadium wasn't one of those low-grade facilities. It hadn't taken much to get the footage either, just the big, wide eyes and the slightly pouty lip. People were so easy to manipulate when they cared.

When the time was right, this video would go viral, and his world would come crashing down. When he was at his lowest, that was the time to let him know the error of his ways. That was the time to show him his folly. Then and only then would forgiveness be granted... if he did what he was told and never, ever showed the least bit of disinterest and rejection again. And if enough money to live comfortably for a very, very long time could be had, so be it.

HANYIN

WHEN HANYIN was worried or upset, he cooked. The kitchen was his space to regain his balance and find his center. Currently the counters and table were covered with dishes, the island was strewn with ingredients, and he was still worried. Ki-tae was not okay. No matter how many times his little brother told him otherwise, HanYin could see it.

The biggest problem for HanYin was he could do nothing to help Ki-tae. He knew it had something to do with Jin-woo. Well, he suspected it had something to do with Jin-woo; Ki-tae was unusually reluctant to talk about it... or anything else for that matter. Every day he woke up, dressed in the darkest, most somber colors, choosing baggy clothing and donning dark sunglasses and baseball hats before leaving the house. When he came home, Ki-tae would kick off his shoes and head straight to either his room or the recording studio they had in the house, not even bothering to put on house slippers. HanYin had tried to see what he was working on in the studio, but Ki-tae had password-locked the file—again, uncharacteristic of him.

So, no, Ki-tae wasn't "fine," and if he wasn't fine, HanYin wasn't fine. HanYin needed his family to be happy. They were supposed to begin shooting tomorrow. Anyone who knew Ki-tae would know something was wrong. And how was Ki-tae going to react when he saw Jin-woo again? These questions swirled around HanYin's head as he made dish after dish. Some of them hadn't been seen for over three hundred years.

"You worry." Cheongul's quiet voice startled HanYin.

"And you don't?" he said. "You've seen him. He won't say anything, won't talk about what's bothering him, and that mask he wears when he's out of the house? I hate it."

"I do too," Cheongul said as he moved behind HanYin and hugged him. "We have to be patient with him. In time he'll tell us what's wrong."

"Will that be before or after we have to save his life again?"

Ki-tae

Ki-tae was exhausted. He was trying to do the right thing, trying to keep Jin-woo at a distance, but between the voicemails and the texts, which tore at him every time he read them, and the damned dream walking, Ki-tae wasn't getting any rest. He'd never wanted to scare Jin-woo, to make him afraid, and he cursed himself for feeding at the venue that night. He'd managed never to be alone with Jin-woo these past several days, always having either HanYin, Cheongul, or one of the staff nearby, thus avoiding the conversation Jin-woo clearly wanted to have. When Jin-woo had arrived on set a few minutes ago, Ki-tae had made some excuse to leave and now, he was hiding in a bathroom stall. He'd even gone so far as to maneuver Min-su and Jong-in to be buffers between him and Jin-woo. He couldn't take the knowledge of Vampires from Jin-woo's mind, but he could keep the daily reminders to a minimum. After all, Jin-woo knew nothing about Cheongul and HanYin, so they wouldn't scare him the way Ki-tae did.

Ki-tae's stomach growled. While he'd eaten regular meals, as regular as could be expected with their schedule, he hadn't been able to feed beyond sips here and there. No one tasted as good as Jin-woo. No one satisfied him as Jin-woo had. In truth, when he tried to feed from someone else, he wanted to puke afterward. Finally, he just stopped trying. He never thought he would miss Jin-woo while still being in the same room with him. He leaned his head against the stall wall, attempting to find some sense of quiet in his own head, his stomach cramping with the need for blood. He had to be in wardrobe in about fifteen minutes, and he was going to use all that time, if necessary.

The banging of the outer door and angry muttering pulled him from his thoughts. Then Jin-woo's scent hit him, and Ki-tae cursed silently. His luck had just run out. Then he caught the sound of his name amid the mutterings and paid closer attention.

"Twice-cursed Vampire, what does he think he's doing? He can't avoid me forever. Oh, he makes me so angry," Jin-woo growled, and Ki-tae clenched his teeth at the sensations it sent through him. "Won't answer my texts, won't take my calls, won't stay in the same room if he can help it, stupid man. And if he thinks I don't know what he's doing by always being around people when he can't fucking run away from me, he's got another thing coming! Stupid ass won't let me explain, so stubborn. I want to just punch him!"

Before he could stop himself, Ki-tae stepped out of the stall. "That would be incredibly unprofessional, don't you think?"

He wasn't prepared for Jin-woo to launch himself at him. Jin-woo moved his hands over him, shoulders, chest, back, thighs, all the while he kept talking rapidly.

"Oh my God, Ki-tae hyung. You're okay! Thank God. I was so worried. You wouldn't respond, and I... I didn't know what to think and... oh, you jerk!" Jin-woo started pounding on his chest, cursing at him. "You wouldn't respond! How could you do that to me? So damned stubborn and childish, and immature for a however the fuck old Vampire you are! Oh, you are such an ass!"

Stunned, Ki-tae couldn't get a word out. Then he was wrapped in the tightest hug he'd been in since HanYin cornered him two days ago.

"I don't regret meeting you, not one minute of it. I never will regret it. I won't ever regret you!"

"You're scared of me," Ki-tae whispered. Jin-woo immediately stepped back and stared at him as if he'd lost his mind.

"Scared of you? Whatever gave you such a fucked-up idea?" Jin-woo demanded as he crossed his arms.

"You said you were terrified of the monsters being real, that meeting me scared the crap out of you."

"I said having my worldview turned upside down terrified me," Jin-woo said as he poked Ki-tae in the chest. "There are some scary-ass fairy tales out there and the idea that they might be true does frighten me, but never once did I say *you* scared me."

"But I *am* one of those monsters."

"You're not a monster, Ki-tae hyung," Jin-woo said softly. "Monsters don't care if they scare people."

Something broke inside Ki-tae, and he clutched Jin-woo to him. Jin-woo rained kisses on his face, his neck, and finally his mouth, thrusting his tongue hard past Ki-tae's lips. The aggression was an incredible turn-on. Ki-tae scooped Jin-woo up, and Jin-woo wrapped those lean legs tightly around his waist, aligning their groins. The feel of Jin-woo's erection against his spurred Ki-tae on.

With a growl he turned and slammed Jin-woo up against the wall. Jin-woo felt so good pressed against him, so right. Ki-tae never wanted to let him go. He kneaded the firm muscles of Jin-woo's ass, earning little whimpers and moans of pleasure. Finally they broke apart, and Ki-tae rested his forehead against Jin-woo's with a breathless chuckle. Jin-woo cupped his face and lifted it, his eyes traveling over Ki-tae's face.

"What?"

"You're so pale," Jin-woo whispered. "Just like you were that night. Is... how... dammit, this is awkward."

"What is?" Ki-tae said, trying to focus on Jin-woo's words when all he wanted was to kiss him senseless for a start.

"Do you need to feed?"

That caught his attention.

Ki-tae tried to look away, but Jin-woo wouldn't let him. With a gentle smile, Jin-woo tilted his head to the right and guided Ki-tae's head forward. "I don't regret anything about you, Ki-tae hyung."

Ki-tae whimpered, moving his hips back and forth as his nipped Jin-woo's throat. He wanted to, by God, how he wanted to sink his fangs into Jin-woo, to taste the sweetness of blood straight from his heart, but he couldn't. He didn't know what that would do… to either of them.

He pulled back and shifted to hold Jin-woo in one arm. He slid his hand lightly from Jin-woo's shoulder all the way down to cup his wrist and brought it to his mouth. Bare flesh greeted him, and Ki-tae smiled. He lipped the tender, sensitive skin as he spoke. "The next time I feed from your throat, I will be buried balls deep in your sweet ass at the same time. For now I will feed here."

Ki-tae brushed his lips across Jin-woo's wrist once, twice, three times before letting his fangs slowly sink into his flesh. Sweet ambrosia filled his mouth as Jin-woo's muffled cry caressed his ears. Somehow he knew Jin-woo was biting his bottom lip to keep from screaming. He drew on his wrist softly, steadily, matching each pull with a pump of his hips. He wanted Jin-woo to experience only pleasure in his arms, wanted only his cries of sweet sensual torture. Ki-tae withdrew, swathing his tongue over the wound—the enzymes in his saliva would close it, leaving no trace—and turned to look at Jin-woo. The smile that greeted him almost made him cum, but he couldn't let that happen.… He had nothing to change into.

Jin-woo wiggled, releasing his waist, and Ki-tae looked at him in query, raising an eyebrow. "My turn."

Before Ki-tae could respond, Jin-woo was on his knees, opening Ki-tae's pants and taking him down in one long slide. Ki-tae bit his fist, containing the roar that so desperately wanted to escape. He slammed his other hand against the wall, bracing himself as Jin-woo did beautifully wicked things to his cock with his mouth.

He couldn't have stopped the thrusting of his hips even if he wanted to. Jin-woo teased his tongue along the ridge, flicked it into the slit, tormented him with every stroke. Where in the fuck had Jin-woo learned to suck cock like a god? Never mind, Ki-tae didn't want to know; it would only make him jealous. He rested against his forearm, pushing his other hand into Jin-woo's hair, gripping but not guiding. Jin-woo didn't need any guidance. He knew exactly what he was doing.

All too soon, Ki-tae growled low and loud and spilled down Jin-woo's throat, hissing at the caress of muscles as Jin-woo swallowed. Ki-tae struggled to breathe as little kitten licks sent shivers through his body. He caressed Jin-woo's hair, soothing them both. Finally he pushed away from the wall and looked down at a smirking Jin-woo. Ki-tae laughed before hauling Jin-woo to his feet and kissing him soundly, licking deep and tasting himself.

"You are wickedness incarnate wrapped in a sweet, innocent package.... I love it."

"I was... inspired," Jin-woo said.

"But you...."

"I did," Jin-woo said as he rose to his feet, gesturing to the front of his uniform pants.

"I've made a mess of you again." Ki-tae chuckled.

"It's okay," Jin-woo said, then pulled Ki-tae in for another kiss. "I came in here to change anyway... and gripe about you."

"I'm sorry I worried you," Ki-tae said quietly.

"Just don't do it again. Talking is better than running away and it's less likely to piss me off. I won't be ignored or brushed off. If I say something that bothers you, talk to me about it. Don't make assumptions," Jin-woo said, caressing Ki-tae's cheek.

"You sound as if you want more than just a fling, as if you want... a relationship?"

"Yeah, I do. Do you?"

"Yes" was Ki-tae's simple answer. What more could he say? What he felt, it was bigger than anything he'd felt before, and he really didn't know how to express it. Not to mention it was probably way too soon to say those kinds of words. And he still didn't know what was real and what was the bond. Just the thought of the bond and what his options were made Ki-tae tense.

"What's wrong?"

"I... I just.... I'm not...."

"Ki-tae hyung, this isn't going to be easy for either of us. We don't know much about each other and we're probably not going to have a lot of chances to learn while doing this project, and this... attraction between us is.... I don't know what it is," Jin-woo said. "Still, I've always been drawn to you, even before we met, and I want to see where this can go. However you'll have me, I want to be with you."

"Why would you want someone like me?" The question was out before Ki-tae could stop it, and dread filled him.

"I can't explain it, but you just make me all soft and squishy."

"Well... not all of you." Ki-tae grinned wickedly, hoping to change the tone of the conversation. He stroked Jin-woo's cock through his pants.

"No, not all of me," Jin-woo gasped, gripping Ki-tae's shoulders as his cock made a valiant effort to harden. "And as much as I would love to continue this, people are waiting for us. We don't want them to come looking."

"Damn, you're being practical and responsible," Ki-tae teased.

"And you're being naughty and distracting." Jin-woo laughed. "But we have a job to do."

Ki-tae sighed and stepped back, putting himself away and zipping up his pants. "Yes, we do, although it's going to be hard to concentrate when I now know how those lips feel wrapped around my cock."

"No more from you!" Jin-woo said forcefully, turning Ki-tae around and then pushing him toward the door.

"Spoilsport." Ki-tae pouted, but he left Jin-woo to change in peace.

JIN-WOO

BY THE end of the first week, there wasn't a crew member around who didn't absolutely adore Jin-woo and company. They loved the way the three students asked relevant questions, listened actively, and applied what they learned. The easy way Min-su moved from team to team with her perky smile and cherubic face made her a popular girl. Her sharp, practical mind earned their respect. The sound engineers wanted to adopt Jong-in, charmed by those dimples, his quiet demeanor, and his amazing ear.

In turn, Jong-in, Min-su, and Jin-woo hadn't met a single person they didn't like. The set and the studio were warm, friendly places with people who honestly wanted to help them learn the trade. They made them feel so welcome, as if they were members of the BLE family. Yet no one took to the three students as strongly as Bam Kiseu, and the crew joked about it constantly. It didn't take long for Jin-woo and the others to feel comfortable enough to relax and bug each other the way they normally did when not at work or school.

Jong-in sighed dramatically, making Jin-woo laugh as Min-su smacked his arm. "I've showed you the steps a hundred times now!"

They were in the middle of a lunch break, and Min-su was still trying to master the dance steps to "Heat." She was always obsessed with the choreography of Bam Kiseu's videos. He couldn't blame her. Dancing was fun, and though he claimed to have two left feet, Jong-in was, in fact, a talented dancer. He just didn't like to brag about things. He didn't really brag about anything. Okay, every once in a while, he did boast about his engineering, but those moments were few and far between, and not undeserved.

"Show me again," she insisted. She pulled him to his feet once more, dragging him away from his lunch, and made him stand next to her.

"I'll do it slowly, and you just watch my feet. Then copy my steps," Jong-in said. Min-su nodded, already focused.

After about ten minutes, the frustration was clear on Min-su's face.

"I don't get it. I've been able to learn all the other dance steps but this one," she said. "I don't know why I can't seem to get that first move right."

"You're moving your entire body at once, and that's throwing everything off," Cheongul said, suddenly right next to her. "You start with sliding your front foot back like this, shifting your weight as you go so you can slide the other foot back next. Your shoulder leads the motion, and then the rest of you flows right into the body roll."

Min-su gave a yelp and smacked Cheongul on the arm, her standard response to being startled.

"Don't do that! You're not supposed to be helping. You're supposed to be over there looking all hot and sexy and completely edible, not over here teaching me dance moves and being all nice and shit." When Jin-woo snorted, nearly sending milk through his nose, her eyes got wide, and she looked back and forth between him and Cheongul. "That wasn't in my head, was it?"

"No, no, it wasn't," Jin-woo said solemnly, trying very hard not to laugh as she blushed furiously.

She turned to Cheongul and bowed formally. "If you will please excuse me, I must go find a very deep, dark hole in which to bury myself for the rest of eternity."

Then she turned on her bright red Chucks and walked away as regally as any empress. Jin-woo and Jong-in lost it, falling over with their laughter. Cheongul looked flummoxed as he stared after her. He turned back to Jin-woo. "What just happened?"

"Min-su-ya prides herself on being able to remain professional, no matter what she may be feeling on the inside. She doesn't get overly emotional or demonstrative around people she's not comfortable with," Jin-woo explained.

"She hit me," Cheongul said.

"She hits Jin-woo-ya all the time," Jong-in pointed out, taking a sip of his ginger tea.

"But not you?" Cheongul asked.

"I dodge, but he never sees her coming until she's already smacked him," Jong-in said, earning a cheese puff thrown at his head. "What? It's true!"

"You make me sound like an unobservant wimp," Jin-woo grumbled.

"Unobservant? Depends on the situation, but wimp? Hardly." Jong-in snorted. "Either way, Min-su-ya doesn't do shy and demure. She can be poised and confident or feisty and hilarious. It just depends on where she is and who she's with. You startled her, and she reacted the same way she would with me or Jin-woo-ya. That's a good sign. It means she's comfortable with you."

"Provided, of course, you like that in a woman," Jin-woo said, contemplating a cheese puff before popping it in his mouth. His casual tone didn't quite match the look he shot at Cheongul.

"You're acting like her older brothers," Cheongul said with a smile. "Not as overprotective as I am of my mine, but subtler."

"Are you *seriously* doing the 'if you hurt my brothers' shit? Already?" HanYin demanded from behind Cheongul.

"I didn't realize you three were related," Jin-woo said.

"Not by birth, but we might as well be. We're just very protective of each other, and some of us take it a little too far." He glared at Cheongul as he set several bags on the table. "He really doesn't mean anything by it."

"No, that's a good thing," Jong-in said. "It's good to know someone has your back. Wait... do I smell... steamed dumplings?"

HanYin smiled as he pulled containers out of the bags. "You have a good nose."

"We were not lying about Jong-in-a and food," Jin-woo said. "And steamed dumplings are one of his favorites."

"He may have to fight Ki-tae-ya for them." Cheongul chuckled.

"There's enough for everyone, and I made Ki-tae's Shiu Mai dumplings, so no worries," HanYin said. "Help yourselves while I take this batch to Tae-hwa nuna."

"He made her a special batch?" Jong-in asked as he carefully took one of the dumplings, his voice soft and almost sad.

"Yeah, Tae-hwa nuna is a vegetarian, so he always makes sure to have a dish she can eat," Cheongul said

"Are they a couple?" Jong-in asked, nibbling on the dumpling.

"HanYin-a and Tae-hwa nuna?" At Jong-in's nod, Cheongul laughed. "No, her husband would kill him... or try, at any rate. He is very much in love with his wife, and she with him. See?"

Cheongul pointed over to the director's seat, where HanYin was handing a very large man the container of dumplings. "That's Cho Shin-bai hyung. He's head of off-site security. Well, all of security, but he tends to handle off-site for us personally. He's so far gone on Tae-hwa nuna it's not even funny. Ancestors help anyone who makes her even sniffle. He'll kill them, and he's going to be worse when the baby is born. HanYin-a isn't seeing anyone at present."

Shin-bai then ruffled HanYin's hair and began hand-feeding his clearly pregnant wife as she bounced like a little kid, clapping. She and Shin-bai were a distinct contrast. Where she was petite, topping *maybe* five feet, Shin-bai towered over her at six and a half feet minimum. He had a dark head of hair cut close, deeply tanned skin, narrow eyes, and thin lips, while Tae-hwa had a white-blonde pixie cut, large doe eyes, full lips, and lightly tanned skin. She was slender and willowy while he was built like a tank. Yet the gentle way he scooped her up and set her on the nearest table to feed her conveyed more than words ever could, just as her smile and the look in her eyes told the same story; they loved each other.

"Oh." Jong-in's voice seemed a little lighter than before, and Jin-woo looked at him, saw him smiling, those dimples peeking out. It looked as if Jong-in's interest in HanYin was deepening. He just hoped Jong-in wouldn't get hurt. They didn't even know if HanYin was interested in men, and that was a very delicate question in and of itself. It could get so many different responses, not all of them good.

JONG-IN

JONG-IN FELT giddy, as if he'd drank too much. HanYin was single. He was simply amazing, beautiful, talented, and adorable as hell. He was exactly the type of person Jong-in often pictured himself with. And HanYin could cook. The dumplings were amazing.

"If you keep smiling like that, your dimples are going to crack," Jin-woo murmured softly, elbowing Jong-in in the side. "You're grinning like an idiot."

"I can't help it," Jong-in said.

"Well, then, do something about it," Jin-woo said as he nudged Jong-in in HanYin's direction. "Go talk to him."

"What could we possibly have to say to each other?"

"How about 'these dumplings are amazing'? That would be a good start," Jin-woo said, taking one and biting into it.

"What's the point?" Jong-in lost his smile as he watched HanYin move through the people, everyone vying for his attention, male and female. "No, better I just keep these thoughts to myself."

"You truly don't see it, do you?" Jin-woo said. He sounded surprised.

Jong-in turned to look at him, confused. "Don't see what?"

"I had wondered why you wore your glasses to the presentation when you normally wear your contacts."

"I have no idea what you're talking about," Jong-in said, feeling the rock settle in his stomach. He glanced at Jin-woo and knew he didn't want to continue this conversation. It was too complicated, too personal, and he wasn't ready to discuss it with anyone. "I have to get back to work."

He rushed away, not giving Jin-woo a chance to stop him. He couldn't talk about this right now, not here, where anyone and everyone could overhear them. Jong-in found a secluded corner and hopped up to sit on one of the large equipment cases. He could hear the words bouncing around in his head, feel the fear settling in his gut, and couldn't take it.

He pulled out his phone, put his earphones in, and hit Play as he pulled his legs up to his chest and wrapped his arms around them, dropping his forehead to rest on his knees, hiding. He wanted to lose himself in the music. That way he wouldn't have to think about anything. He wouldn't have to think about how attracted he was to HanYin, the only man, the only *person*, who had ever caught his eye. He wouldn't have to think about how he was going to continue to pay for university. He wouldn't have to think about what would happen if his father found out Jong-in liked a man. He would never be allowed to see his mother or sister again. He was barely allowed to see them now. He was only permitted home once or twice a year, if he was lucky. His father hated him. Well, no, he wasn't his father. He was Jong-in's stepfather, and they had never really gotten along.

He hadn't been able to go to the concert with Min-su and Jin-woo because he had to work. When he wasn't studying, he was working all the time. That's all he ever did: study, work, and on the rare occasion, sleep. Jong-in smiled sadly. His mother was the best cook in the world and had made all his favorite meals when his father was alive. She would make special little cakes for them. She would make their noodles from scratch, their dumplings, everything was done by her hands. Every bite was filled with her love for them.

Then Jong-in's father died in a train accident on the way home from work, and the food was flavored with her sadness. When she married again, Jong-in's stepfather put an end to all that. He never tasted his mother's cooking anymore. Jong-in turned the sound up louder.

HanYin's food tasted like his mother's food once did. It broke something in him. Something he needed to prevent him from thinking about everything that was lost to him: his father, his mother, his family. It was just one more thing about HanYin that wrapped around Jong-in's heart. He hadn't expected it. When he first saw a picture of HanYin, Jong-in felt as if he'd been kicked in the chest. Then he listened to the full album online and knew immediately which one was which. He could be blindfolded and in a darkened room, and Jong-in would be able to recognize the voices from a single note.

HanYin's voice sent a shiver through his body that made nerve endings fire in ways he hadn't ever experienced with a woman, no matter how he tried. Jong-in knew he wasn't meant to be with a woman, but what could HanYin possibly see in Jong-in? He was a poor boy struggling to stay in university. He worked two jobs when he wasn't studying. He never had time to have fun with his friends. He wasn't boisterous or talkative around most people. Jin-woo had mentioned his glasses. He was right. Jong-in normally didn't wear them because contacts were easier at his factory job. And they were a shield. He hid behind his glasses because when he wore them, people didn't notice him as much. And if they didn't notice him, they couldn't find out he was a poor boy who had fallen in love at first sound with another man. If they didn't notice him, Jong-in could go about his business without being bothered or harangued or beaten. That was an experience he could do without repeating.

It was weird being here with the BLE team. They were so welcoming, but would they remain that way if they knew how he felt about HanYin? Or would he be ostracized or made to leave? He didn't know the answers to those questions, and so he wouldn't take the risk. Just like he didn't know what HanYin's response to his overtures would be, should he be foolish enough to make them. It was best to not take the risk of being mocked, beaten, or worse.

JIN-WOO

"WHERE DID Jong-in dongsaeng go?" HanYin asked as he served himself some dumplings. "He was here just a few minutes ago."

"He, um, he needed a few moments to himself," Jin-woo said, feeling guilty for upsetting his friend.

"Is he all right?" HanYin asked, pausing and looking around for Jong-in.

"He'll be okay." Jin-woo tried to give a reassuring smile, but he was worried too. "He's probably sitting in a quiet corner somewhere with the music turned up. Don't worry. He won't be late. He's really good with time management."

"Oh," HanYin said. "I was hoping to see what other types of food he likes. I tend to make food for everyone when we're shooting. I don't want to make something he doesn't like or is allergic to."

"That's very sweet. He really likes the steamed dumplings. On the rare occasions we go out, he always wants crispy, crunchy fried chicken and kimchi fried rice. He loves it," Jin-woo said. "They asked you about that in an interview one time, didn't they?"

"Yes. Apparently it was just such an odd concept that an idol would do something nice for the crew," HanYin said. "BLE is family, and I like to see my family happy."

"Everyone does seem to get along really well," Jin-woo said.

"So what do you think of the experience so far?"

"It's amazing." Jin-woo laughed. "There's so much energy here, so much positive support from everyone. And everyone is being so nice. I know I ask a lot of questions, and I know it can get really annoying sometimes, but it's just because I want to know about all of it."

"You can't expect to learn if you don't ask any questions," HanYin said with a nod. "Soon-joon-nim tells us that all the time. No one here will be bothered by your questions. And honestly, everyone already adores you three!"

"I don't know if I'd go that far," Cheongul said as he approached.

"You like him, admit it." HanYin poked Cheongul in the arm, furrowing his brow when Cheongul winced. "What happened? Why did you wince?"

"It's nothing," Cheongul said, rubbing his upper arm.

HanYin said, "Roll up your sleeve and let me see."

"No, it's nothing."

"You don't wince for nothing," HanYin said. "Don't make me force the issue, Cheongul-a. You know I will. It's just easier to do as I ask now, rather than when I have you pinned."

"That happened once," Cheongul pointed out. "It's truly nothing. I just have a bruise, and you managed to hit right on it."

"How did you get a bruise?"

"Min-su-ya packs a wallop." Jin-woo smiled. At HanYin's confused look, he explained, "Cheongul hyung startled her earlier today, and she smacked him. Only her smacks to anywhere, except the head, tend to involve a closed fist."

"Oh, Ki-tae-ya is going to love this."

"Where is Ki-tae hyung, anyway? He disappeared when they called break," Jin-woo asked. He tried to be nonchalant about it but wasn't sure he succeeded.

"Ki-tae-ya hasn't been sleeping well lately," Cheongul said quietly, shooting a glance at HanYin. "He probably went to lie down in the dressing room."

"Is he all right?" Jin-woo asked, looking up in surprise. "He seemed very energetic when we started this morning."

"All part of being in this industry. We have a job to do, and that sometimes means working when we're exhausted, sick, or just plain need downtime. That doesn't happen often. Soon-joon-nim doesn't allow it. I think it mostly happens on tour. We've never been so bad off that we couldn't perform, but he would have no problem canceling and compensating people if we were," HanYin said. "Still, we have a responsibility to our fans to give them 100 percent, at the very least. We just try to take care of ourselves so that we don't get sick or worn down too often."

"Still, you should rest when you need to," Jin-woo said. "You can't give that 100 percent if you're hospitalized."

He wondered if Ki-tae did get tired or if he just pretended to hide his secret. He didn't seem tired when he was onstage, but Jin-woo had seen a number of backstage videos and some candid shots, not to mention fancams following Ki-tae everywhere, where Ki-tae just looked exhausted. Did Vampires get exhausted? Did they get sick? The sunlight thing was complete crap because Ki-tae had done outdoor concerts on more than one occasion, looking hot as hell literally and figuratively standing in the bright light. He was going to have to pin Ki-tae down and ask all the questions swirling around in his head: Did Ki-tae have any special powers? Could he control people's minds? How often did he have to have blood? He'd seen Ki-tae eat. Did it do anything for him? Did it make him sick? Dammit, there were just so many questions.

"Very true, so we work with Soon-joon-nim and make adjustments when necessary," Cheongul said with a smile. "Ki-tae-ya is just a little more stubborn than the rest of us when it comes to working and his health. He pushes himself very hard. Ofttimes we have to make him take breaks because he gets so focused on what he's doing he'll forget to eat or sleep. Granted, the results are amazing, but then he crashes for at least two days."

"I knew idols worked hard, but I didn't realize how hard," Jin-woo said quietly as he looked down at his cheese puffs. "I've heard of idols fainting onstage and such. I always thought it was because they were sick and those lights are stupid hot. It never occurred to me it might be because they're pushing themselves for their fans."

"We're here because of our fans. We can do no less than give our all," HanYin said. "Some fans understand, and some don't. I'm glad you're one of the ones who does."

"Me too." Jin-woo smiled at them.

He was just about to say more when they announced lunch was over and everyone needed to return to the set. Jin-woo put the cover back on his cheese puffs and set them with his things. He grabbed his notebook and a pencil and shoved the pencil behind his ear. He'd been taking notes and comments since they began filming. It was fascinating to watch the crew plot out the filming schedule. Seeing his storyboards next to theirs made him feel giddy.

Much like a film production, the video wasn't shot in order either. Since Bam Kiseu had other commitments to prepare for, they had to work on the shots with the band in them first. Some of it was done on a green screen, as arranging to use historical or near-historical sites was time-consuming. They could recreate those sites on the computer in postproduction, which was a bit more cost-effective than on-site shoots… and involved less paperwork.

Each morning Jin-woo and Min-su would sit down with the director and go over the boards for the day. Jin-woo often found himself so caught up in the conversation that he would ramble and Min-su would be forced to rein him in, but the director didn't seem to mind. Once that meeting concluded, he would go to the set and help get everything ready. That's when he'd see Jong-in working with the sound crew.

What made it even more special was if he wanted to make a change to what they were shooting, maybe change how the band entered the shot or how the camera panned, they would listen to him. His ideas were not always implemented, but often the director would have them shoot it the way he suggested. When they did the final editing, they would choose the best shots, so the director was happy to have a lot of material for the editors to work with.

The hard part came when Ki-tae stepped on set. The first time Jin-woo saw him in costume, he barely caught his whimper in time. Ki-tae in modern clothing was hot and distracting. Ki-tae dressed in a period costume was incredibly sexy and alluring, especially after he'd already been to makeup and had the wig in place. Apparently long sapphire hair and curving black horns were a turn-on for Jin-woo. Who knew?

Shooting a music video was more hectic than Jin-woo had thought, and as the days passed, Jin-woo and Ki-tae were only able to find brief moments of privacy. Ki-tae would catch him backstage and steal heated kisses. They'd find an empty dressing room on break and engage in some heavy petting. While Jin-woo loved to give blowjobs, he had yet to experience one from Ki-tae, which seemed to bother Ki-tae a lot. The last few times they had been able to catch a moment, Ki-tae had refused to let him go down on him.

"Am I doing something wrong?" Jin-woo finally asked. "Don't you like when I do that?"

"I love when you do that," Ki-tae said, caressing his cheek. "What I don't like is not being able to return it. I enjoy the dry humping, too, but I want to give you as much pleasure as you give me. I want to take you to bed and make you scream all night long. I want to make you cum so hard you pass out again."

"You talk like that, and I can't think straight for imagining it," Jin-woo whispered, laying his forehead against Ki-tae's chest. "I... I want that too, but there's just... no time."

"We're almost done with filming. Postproduction will take...." Ki-tae paused for a moment.

"Postproduction should only take about a week, week and a half at most, only because we have classes. Soon-joon-nim said that was a priority, and our on-site mentors had other projects they could work on but would save this for when we're there. Normally shooting wouldn't take this long either, but these aren't normal circumstances," Jin-woo said, trying to focus while Ki-tae teased his hands along his spine. It was very difficult to think with Ki-tae's touch on his skin.

"We have public appearances the beginning of next week. HanYin-a has some commercials to shoot. Cheongul-a will be working on the charity events, and I have three magazine spreads to do. I believe we have a group interview two weeks from now, and then there's the meet and greets all over the country. Dammit, I don't get to spend enough time with you," Ki-tae complained with a growl.

"Somewhere in there you have to eat, right?" Jin-woo asked. "Look at your schedule tomorrow, and we'll see about having dinner together."

"I'll take you anywhere you want to go," Ki-tae said with a smile as he kissed Jin-woo's nose, laughing when Jin-woo scrunched it up in response.

"Nope," Jin-woo said.

"What do you mean, 'nope'? You just said you wanted to have dinner together," Ki-tae said, looking confused.

"I want dinner with just you, not you and any fans or businesspeople that conveniently happen to show up," Jin-woo teased with a smile. "So we'll set up a date, and then you'll come to my place, and I will make dinner for you. A nice, quiet, *private* dinner."

Jin-woo punctuated the last four words with a fleeting kiss. Then he found himself scooped up into Ki-tae's arms and kissed breathless. When Ki-tae finally released his mouth, Jin-woo couldn't help but tease him. "You're determined I walk out of this room with a hard-on tenting my pants, aren't you?"

"If I must suffer, so do you," Ki-tae growled as he nibbled on Jin-woo's neck. "Your scent alone is like a kick to the gut. It gets me hard so fast. Your voice is a caress, sweet and sensual. I love the needy sounds you make when I touch you just so."

Ki-tae skimmed his hands down to cup Jin-woo's ass. He slid his nails over the sensitive inner area where thigh met buttock, making Jin-woo whimper and bite his lip. "I love the way you catch your bottom lip between your teeth when you look at me. It reminds me of all the wicked things you've done with that sweet-looking mouth. The way you suck my cock all the way down is nothing short of mind-melting."

"See? You're doing it again." Jin-woo was panting. His entire body tingled, and he dug his fingers into Ki-tae's shoulders. Letting his head fall back, he tried to regain some semblance of control, but it was useless. With Ki-tae so close, he could feel the heat of their cocks pressed together. "You're going to make a mess of me."

"Not today, unfortunately," Ki-tae said, his voice strained as he stepped back. "We have five minutes before break is over, and then it's work for the rest of the day."

"You're an evil bastard. You know that, right?" Jin-woo chuckled. "I want to cum so badly right now."

"I want to watch you cum. Hell, I want to make you cum, but we're out of time, sweetling," Ki-tae said as he pulled Jin-woo close once more and stroked his hair as if gentling him.

It took them the full five minutes they had left, but they managed to regain control of themselves. Jin-woo reminded Ki-tae to check his schedule so they could set up their date and then headed to the set. He paused to adjust himself, muttering at the unfairness of time when horny. It was going to be a bitch to work for the next several moments, but hopefully no one would notice.

KI-TAE

KI-TAE WALKED into the dressing room and found Cheongul and HanYin smirking at him. "What?"

"You were with Jin-woo dongsaeng again," Cheongul said. "The perfume fills the air."

"What the hell are you talking about?"

"You reek of pheromones and Jin-woo dongsaeng," HanYin said with a laugh. "Fortunately for both of you, only Cheongul and I have to suffer with it. Although I think several members of the crew have suspicions."

"Has anyone said anything?"

"No, no one," Cheongul said. "It's a matter of time, though. You two keep sneaking off together. You hide being a Vampire better than your attraction to Jin-woo dongsaeng."

"So much for being discreet," Ki-tae muttered, running a hand through his hair.

"You guys are discreet, but people here notice things," HanYin said before biting off the end of a Pocky stick. "Jin-woo dongsaeng can hide his emotions pretty well, I must say. It's only in the unguarded moments, when he thinks no one is watching, that his feelings for you show on his face."

"Feelings for me?" Ki-tae whispered.

"He's falling for you, Ki-tae," Cheongul said softly. "You know you have to make a decision about him soon. The temptation to feed from his neck will grow too strong."

"Do you know what my choices are?" Ki-tae asked quietly, coldly.

"No, neither you nor Abeoji will tell us, which really pisses me off because I want to help you," HanYin said.

"That's exactly why I asked him not to tell you. This is something only I can do," Ki-tae said tightly. The very idea of hurting Jin-woo made him sick, but to turn him? Would that be the right thing to do?

"What are they, Ki-tae?" HanYin asked softly. "What are the choices you have to break the binding between you and Jin-woo dongsaeng?"

"I can either turn him into one of us… or kill him. Both can only be done by me, otherwise the bind remains, and that could kill me too."

"What the fuck?" HanYin shot to his feet. "There's got to be another way."

"I said the same thing to Abeoji," Ki-tae said as he sat in his chair. "He said he would reach out to some of his connections, but so far, he hasn't heard anything from them. I should leave Jin-woo-ya alone, but I can't seem to do that.

It's like I have this invisible thread always pulling me to him, and the thing is, I really don't want to fight it. I want to be with him, but is it something I truly feel, or is it the bond?"

"We will be able to find out soon, Adeul," Soon-joon said as he closed the door behind him. "I have received word from my old teacher. It was not what I expected, however."

"What do you mean?"

"She is traveling here to meet with you. She did not give specifics, only that she would need to see you first before she could say anything," Soon-joon said. "She will arrive in about two weeks' time, as she prefers not use any modern form of transportation."

"At least I'll finally know," Ki-tae said quietly.

"You've gotten rather close to Jin-woo dongsaeng these last few weeks," Soon-joon said as he walked over and laid a hand on Ki-tae's shoulder.

"It was Cheongul's idea," Ki-tae said, smiling. "At first I thought I would be able to stay away from him, but it was as if Fate laughed. He won the competition, which meant I would be around him constantly. Jin-woo-ya is a good man. He's sweet and kind and funny, and he's talented. I can't deny I find him incredibly attractive either."

"Even if you did deny it, we'd know it's a lie." HanYin smiled before pinching his nose. Ki-tae threw a makeup sponge at him, which he easily batted away.

"This bond… perhaps it is not a bad thing," Soon-joon said carefully, watching Ki-tae's face. "It is not like the one you experienced."

"I…. It terrifies me," Ki-tae whispered. "I don't want to go back to that. I don't want to lose… me again."

"I know, Adeul," Soon-joon said. "This bond is different though. We will wait until Godaeui-nim arrives."

There was a knock on the door before anyone could say anything else. The stage manager's voice came through. "We're ready for you."

"We'll be right out," Cheongul called as he rose from his chair and straightened his robes. "Are my horns on straight?"

"Weirdest question ever. Yes, they're straight." HanYin chuckled. Then he walked over and touched his forehead to Ki-tae's, cupping the back of his neck. "We'll see you out there, Ki-tae."

The last day of Bam Kiseu being on set was coming sooner than Ki-tae wanted. It meant he wouldn't see Jin-woo daily anymore, and that bothered him. No more stolen kisses or making out in an empty room. No more watching him laugh at something one of the crew members said or sitting quietly, sketching everything and everyone around him, or working on his other projects, writing incessantly. No more watching him lick the cheese powder off his fingers and wishing those fingers were something else. Ki-tae stopped walking as he realized he would miss Jin-woo *a lot*.

"It's not goodbye, you know," Cheongul said suddenly from in front of him. Ki-tae contained his response just in time. He didn't like to be startled. "You have his phone number. You know where he lives and goes to school."

"How did you know what I was thinking?"

"Because I know you," Cheongul said as he put his arm around Ki-tae's shoulders. "I also know a little of what you're feeling. I'm going to miss that spunky little wench."

"Min-su dongsaeng?"

"Yeah. She is… one of a kind." Cheongul said. "I have the bruises to prove it. That girl has a solid punch."

"She…."

"She what?" Cheongul asked.

Ki-tae focused on his words. "There's something about her scent. It's as if it's, I don't know, muted or something. Jong-in dongsaeng, I don't think he's human, but it's not my place to say anything. He doesn't smell like most humans and I can't place what he *does* smell like."

"I noticed that too," Cheongul said. "It's almost as if there's something masking her scent, making it impossible to identify. As for Jong-in dongsaeng, honestly, he reminds me of Hyun-jo seonbae. Really, that's not something you can bring up in casual conversation, you know? What would you say? 'By the way, you smell funny. Why is that?'"

"I see she stopped avoiding you," Ki-tae said as they sat down to wait for the director. "How are the dance lessons coming?"

"Are you kidding?" Cheongul laughed hard. "I have never seen anyone take on Gojira seonbae the way Min-su-ya does! She really gave Gojira seonbae an earful the first time they met and saw how hard Gojira seonbae pushes us. It was spectacular to watch!"

"I thought they were going to come to blows." Ki-tae chuckled.

"Apparently they went for drinks afterward and are now friends," Cheongul said. "I still have a hard time picturing Gojira seonbae as anyone's friend."

"You only say that because I don't let you three slack off in practice." The voice was firm and lyrical. Cheongul and Ki-tae turned to see Gojira standing behind them, arms crossed. "It is why you dance well enough to bring tears to the audience's eyes. Now hurry up. We have one more quick practice before they begin, and Ki-tae dongsaeng, you're still sloppy on that last series of moves. Up, up, up!"

"She is…," Ki-tae began.

"A slave driver!" Cheongul finished with a sigh as he pushed himself up from the chair. "Where's Min-su-ya when we need her?"

"Already waiting to begin practice!" Gojira said. "She works harder than you two!"

Ki-tae's legs were protesting and it had only been fifteen minutes while the lighting team replaced two blown lights. Granted it wasn't anything he wasn't used to. Gojira took it easier on them when on-site. It was her idea to have Min-su, Jong-in, and Jin-woo practice the steps with them. He had no idea why, but he wasn't going to complain. Jin-woo moved incredibly well. That boy should not be allowed to do body rolls anywhere near Ki-tae when others were present. Now, in private, that was another story. Jin-woo could roll that sweet little body of his all he wanted.

"Ki-tae dongsaeng, Jin-woo dongsaeng, you two in the middle. Cheongul dongsaeng and Min-su dongsaeng, you to the right, Jong-in dongsaeng and HanYin dongsaeng to the left," Gojira said raising an eyebrow when they were too slow in her opinion. "This is practice, not a stroll in the park."

"Tyrant," Ki-tae muttered, making Jin-woo chuckle.

"And begin…."

The music started playing. Gojira counted off the steps as she moved around them, correcting as she went.

When the music stopped, she was standing in her original position, studying them one by one. "Better, but not perfect. Again!"

By the time they were done, everyone was bent over, panting. Everyone except Jin-woo, that is. He seemed full of energy and was bouncing off the walls. "How? How in the world can you have any energy after dealing with her?"

"Are you kidding me?" Jin-woo laughed. "My regular exercise routine is dancing. This was fun!"

"It's official," Cheongul said drily. "You are insane!"

"Admit it," Jin-woo teased as he poked Cheongul in the stomach, something Ki-tae was sure he would have never even considered doing a few weeks ago. "You have fun dancing together."

"I will admit nothing of the sort," Cheongul said.

"I saw you smiling," Min-su pointed out. "If you weren't having fun, why were you smiling?"

"The company," he said with a shrug. Ki-tae glanced over and saw the blush on Min-su's cheeks.

"Why did we get dragged into it?" Jong-in said from his spot on the ground, flat on his back. "I mean, I understand you three, but us? We're not going to be on camera."

"I gave up trying to figure out why she does anything." Ki-tae sighed before chugging half a bottle of water. "Personally I think she's a sadist."

JIN-WOO

ONCE THEY had recovered, they hit the showers. They were using one of the smaller sets, and so Jong-in and Jin-woo went to use a separate shower while Ki-tae and the others used the one in their dressing room. Jin-woo wished they could shower together, although he would not have an easy time of it. It was Ki-tae, a naked, wet Ki-tae, and Jin-woo so wanted the privacy to explore all that dark, honey-toned flesh. He closed his eyes and counted to ten, breathing slowly. Then he did it again, going to twenty. No, the breathing exercise just wasn't working. There would be too much Ki-tae on display.

"It's all going to be over soon," Jong-in said quietly, leaning his head against the tile wall, his shirt in his hand and his shorts hanging low. "All of this will be just another memory. How long before they forget us? How long?"

"Jong-in-a?" Jin-woo moved closer. He wrapped his arms around Jong-in and held on tightly. He could feel the shaking of his body. "You'll miss him."

"It was pointless, but it still hurts," Jong-in said. "Why does it hurt so much when there was nothing there to begin with?"

"Tell him, Jong-in-a," Jin-woo said softly. "Tell HanYin hyung how you feel."

"And run the risk of being laughed at? Beaten? I don't think so."

"What in HanYin hyung's personality ever gave you the idea he would purposely hurt you?" Jin-woo said. "He is one of the sweetest people we know. He wouldn't do something like that. I doubt that man can hurt a fly."

"Do you know that for sure? Can you promise it?" Jong-in demanded, turning to face Jin-woo and making him step back. "No, some dreams are better left untainted by reality."

Jin-woo didn't know what to say as Jong-in went into the showers. As he replayed the words in his head, Jin-woo realized Jong-in would never act on his feelings for HanYin. He would never put himself out there to get hurt. He had always thought Jong-in preferred girls, but he never seemed to have any. At least not voluntarily. Some of the girls at university harassed him, trying to get him to accept their chocolates or other presents. He was polite to everyone, but he never accepted the gifts. After his admission a couple of weeks ago, certain things made more sense, and Jin-woo was surprised he hadn't clued in earlier, but in the end, it didn't really matter to him. What mattered was Jong-in and his happiness. He always seemed to be rushing off, too, as if he didn't have time to breathe. It really bothered Jin-woo, as he had the suspicion there was something going on, something that was causing the dark circles under Jong-in's eyes.

Yet Jin-woo had watched him with HanYin. Jong-in had smiled more in the last few weeks than ever before, all because of HanYin. He'd even stopped wearing his glasses and went back to his contacts. Why would Jong-in give that up? It was scary. Jin-woo could understand that. Acknowledging that you weren't like everyone else, that you were attracted to other men, was hard. He understood how people's reactions were different, even hostile, but living a lie, not being yourself, that killed your soul. He didn't tell anyone unless they straight-up asked, but he didn't hide from it either. He learned to defend himself, and he refused to let other people's problems dictate how he lived his life. How could he inspire Jong-in to do the same?

When the last day Bam Kiseu was on set arrived, Jin-woo was very quiet. He was going to miss seeing Ki-tae every day. He loved watching Ki-tae, sketching Ki-tae, kissing Ki-tae, and he certainly enjoyed blowing Ki-tae. There would be no more of that until filming was done. Then it would be postproduction time. He, Min-su, and Jong-in would be inside the studio from the moment they arrived in the building, making sure everything came out perfect. It was still so damned exciting. Now if he could just figure out his song and dinner for Ki-tae, life would be beyond good.

"You look very sad today," HanYin said as he approached.

"I am sad. I'm going to miss you three and your antics," Jin-woo said, pausing in his sketching. "And not having to cook, that was definitely a plus."

HanYin laughed. "I see how you are. You only want me around for my food."

"Well, yeah," Jin-woo teased.

"I'm going to miss you guys too," HanYin said, and Jin-woo watched his gaze go straight to Jong-in.

"Give me your phone," Jin-woo said, holding out his hand.

"What?"

"Give me your phone."

"Why?"

"Are we going with 'when' and 'who' next?" Jin-woo laughed. "Just give me your phone."

Finally HanYin gave up his phone after unlocking it. Jin-woo smiled at a beautiful shot of a lotus flower as the phone's wallpaper. He quickly opened the contacts app and put in Jong-in's information. Then he smirked at HanYin and handed the phone back after saving the information.

"Call him," he said.

"Call who?" HanYin mumbled, even as he stared at the screen.

"He's not going to make the first move," Jin-woo said. "You'll have to show him you're interested in him."

"What makes you…? Never mind, that's a stupid question," HanYin said. "You know I'm gay."

"I had my suspicions, but I try not to assume anything," Jin-woo said. "I'd think the same thing of Cheongul hyung, especially with the way he keeps stuffing his hands in yours and Ki-tae-ya's pockets, if he didn't watch Min-su-ya's ass and catch his bottom lip between his teeth every time she walks by."

"She is definitely his type," HanYin said. "Cute, adorable, and feisty."

"Feisty doesn't even come close." Jin-woo chuckled. "She's a force of nature."

"I can't argue that," HanYin said. "You guys head into the studio soon, don't you?"

"Yeah, the director figures we can wrap up the rest of the video in about a day or two, and then into the studio. I have a feeling we're going to be working harder there than we did here," Jin-woo said. "Plus, we still have our classwork and the song for part two of the BLE program."

"I like being in the studio. Cheongul-a gets twitchy, though. After about a day or two, he starts bouncing off the walls, usually after Ki-tae-ya has made him sing the same section over a hundred times in a row because he's not happy with it."

"I noticed you guys seem to take turns being the lead writer on different albums. How did that happen?" Jin-woo asked.

"We all write lyrics. Sometimes we'll come into the studio with about fifteen or twenty songs apiece," HanYin said. "Then we'll go through what everyone's written and see which ones share a similar theme. Once they've been sorted that way, we'll pick a theme to start with, and the person who wrote it will sit down at the piano and sing it, playing the melody that went through our head at the time we were writing. We'll do that a couple of times, and then we'll pick apart the melody, tweak things, and we'll see what works and what doesn't. After that it's a matter of putting down the tracks. I'll warn you now. When Ki-tae-ya doesn't have any other commitments, he'll be in that studio, driving everyone insane."

"He's that bad, huh?" Jin-woo said.

"He is, but he's that good, too, so they put up with it." HanYin smiled. "Every song he writes, he records. They don't always get released, but he has everything that ever popped out of his head. There are some tracks we've recorded that will never see the light of day. They're just… too personal."

"I completely understand that," Jin-woo said quietly. "There are some drawings of mine that will never appear anywhere outside my room. Drawing is my therapy on occasion, and those things are private, personal… intimate."

"Exactly." Suddenly HanYin grinned wickedly. "Want to see how much trouble we can get Cheongul-a into?"

"What do you mean?" Jin-woo asked warily.

"We cannot leave this set without getting either Cheongul-a to kiss Min-su dongsaeng or her to kiss him," HanYin said.

Jin-woo smiled. She'd kill him, but it would be so worth it. He nodded.

"Does she like Pocky?" HanYin asked.

"She does, but she adores Haitai Choco ThinThins," Jin-woo said. "I watched her chase down a thief on a bike because the bag he'd stolen had not her wallet, but her ThinThins in it. One does not mess with Min-su-ya's ThinThins."

"Oh, this is going to be good," HanYin said. "Those are Cheongul-a's favorite too."

Arrangements needed to be made, and HanYin hurried off to make them. He was almost cackling with glee when he left Jin-woo. Clearly he was going to enjoy this... whatever it was... immensely.

Jin-woo looked around the set at the milling people, some working on equipment, others going over paperwork. The director was looking at the dailies from the previous day. Jin-woo would miss the busyness of it, but he figured the studio would have its own kind of busy.

He turned back around just in time to see Ki-tae walk through the door. Jin-woo smiled, and Ki-tae made a beeline for him. He closed his sketchbook, putting his finger between the pages, and tucked the pencil behind his ear. It was hard to sit there and wait for Ki-tae to reach him. Jin-woo wanted to run to him and envelope Ki-tae in a tight hug.

"I thought you weren't going to make it," Jin-woo said as Ki-tae stopped in front of him. "What kept you?"

"Last-minute radio interview." Ki-tae sighed. "Soon-joon-nim is not happy. He told them not to schedule anything for days when I'm shooting, yet someone manages to do it every single time. Heads are going to roll. He went back to headquarters after he dropped me off."

"That is not something I want to see," Jin-woo said. "Soon-joon hyung seems very easygoing, but sometimes there's a fierceness in his eyes that kind of scares me."

"His bad side is not pretty, I can tell you that." Ki-tae chuckled.

"Well, let's get you into wardrobe," Jin-woo said. He set his sketchbook aside and rose to his feet. Ki-tae smiled at him. "What?"

Ki-tae took the pencil from behind his ear and then placed it on the table next to his sketchbook. "You're forever forgetting to leave your pencil with your sketchbook, and then getting upset when you lose it."

Jin-woo could feel the heat in his cheeks. He smacked Ki-tae's chest and then started walking to wardrobe. He gasped as Ki-tae came up behind him and pressed close, wrapping one arm around Jin-woo's waist, then pushed him through the door and locked it behind them.

"Ki-tae-ya, what?"

His words were cut off by Ki-tae's mouth hot and insistent on his. Jin-woo whimpered softly, wrapping his arms around Ki-tae's neck as they maneuvered through the racks of clothing. Ki-tae's hands seemed to be everywhere: on his back, his shoulders, his hips, and especially his ass. Jin-woo wasn't complaining, though. He loved the way Ki-tae touched him, as if he couldn't resist.

When Ki-tae nuzzled his neck, Jin-woo tilted his head without thinking, giving Ki-tae easier access. He expected to feel the delicious sensation of Ki-tae's fangs sinking into his throat, but all he got was a sharp nip before Ki-tae continued down to the collar of his shirt. Jin-woo's brain was too far gone to figure out how Ki-tae was undoing his buttons when his hands were still filled with Jin-woo's ass, but he was enjoying the licks and nips to his bare chest.

Jin-woo cried out when Ki-tae nuzzled his shirt out of the way and sucked hard on his nipple, digging his nails into Ki-tae's shoulders as he tried to steady himself. His breath came in short pants punctuated by whimpers. He rocked his hips uncontrollably. Vaguely he felt his shirt being tugged from his pants. The sound of a belt buckle clanged gently, and there was a tugging sensation at his hips. Cool air caressed his heated skin, and Jin-woo shivered.

He looked down to see Ki-tae staring up at him from beneath long lashes, making his breath catch at the heat in his eyes. Jin-woo couldn't have looked away even if he wanted to. He watched as Ki-tae leaned forward, still holding his gaze, and slowly ran his tongue up the length of Jin-woo's cock. He cried out, his hips jerking forward. After a moment the sensation faded, and Jin-woo looked down once more, only to see a flash of fang in Ki-tae's smile and watch his cock disappear down Ki-tae's throat in one slow slide. He dug his fingers into Ki-tae's hair, his body on fire with the sensations racing through him. By God, the wait had been worth it as Jin-woo felt Ki-tae's throat ripple against him.

"Oh fuck!" Jin-woo moaned, drawing out the word as Ki-tae tortured his body with his tongue. He thought he was good at giving head. He was an amateur compared to Ki-tae. He could hardly catch his breath. Every time Ki-tae pulled back, the cool air on his wet shaft tormented him in an exquisite way, and then the molten heat of Ki-tae's mouth surrounded him once more. Short bobs, long strokes, Jin-woo couldn't have remembered his own name if he were asked. He repeatedly clenched one hand in Ki-tae's hair, gripping the shelf he was shoved up against with the other. Ki-tae kneaded his ass with strong hands, stroked his balls, and teased between his cheeks as he used his mouth to work him into a frenzy.

He tried to focus, tried to warn Ki-tae he wasn't going to last much longer. All he could do was moan and bite his bottom lip to keep from screaming. The pulling at the base of his spine and through his scrotum was all the warning Jin-woo had. Then his body was one big explosion of pleasure as he spilled down Ki-tae's throat on a loud cry, slamming his head back into the shelving. Black spots danced in front of his eyes, and Jin-woo fought not to pass out again... and failed.

KI-TAE

KI-TAE CAUGHT Jin-woo as he slumped, holding him in his arms and settling him astride his lap. He laid Jin-woo's head on his shoulder with a smile, chuckling softly. "Such reactions you have."

As much as Ki-tae wanted to let Jin-woo come to on his own, they didn't have the time to wait. Last time it took several hours. Seung-gi, being Seung-gi, stayed to watch over Jin-woo, observing his apartment from outside. When he reported back in, it was the next morning. They didn't have several hours. They only had several minutes before wardrobe would fill with people. Gently Ki-tae tapped Jin-woo's cheek until he got some sort of response. The fluttering of Jin-woo's dark eyelashes signaled his return to consciousness.

"You're good for my ego, you know that?" Ki-tae teased when Jin-woo finally opened his eyes.

"Huh?" So eloquent.

"You passed out the first time too," Ki-tae said.

"I'm almost hesitant to have sex," Jin-woo said sleepily. "It might just kill me."

"You don't want to have sex with me?"

"I said 'almost.' Pay attention," Jin-woo grumbled as he snuggled closer to Ki-tae, tucking his head against Ki-tae's neck, making Ki-tae chuckle again. "Sleepy."

"You can't go to sleep. We have work to do," Ki-tae pointed out.

"Meh."

"Aren't you the one always trying to get me to be responsible?"

"Feh."

"If you don't get up now, I'll never blow you again," Ki-tae said, knowing it was complete and utter—

"Bullshit," Jin-woo said.

"Okay, you got me on that one, but we still need to clean up and get going. Do you want the others to burst in here and see us like this?" Ki-tae said. "What would Min-su dongsaeng say?"

"Her exact words would be 'Lucky bastard... I want deets,' and then she would attempt to harangue me until she got them," Jin-woo said. "She's a Boy Love fangirl. Won't admit it though. She hates being called a fangirl."

After a few more minutes of cajoling, Ki-tae managed to get Jin-woo back on his feet and straightened up. Then they chitchatted as Ki-tae pulled out the costume he was supposed to wear for the first scene they were shooting that day.

Fortunately they were done with the historic scenes and could work with clothing that was easier to dance in.

"Whose suggestion was it to have the top part historically influenced and the bottom leather?" Ki-tae asked as he pulled up the pants, tucked himself inside, and zipped up.

"That was Jong-in-a's idea. He figured after the way the period costumes restricted movement, these would be much easier and still carry the historic feel to them, especially since the dance steps for this section are more complex," Jin-woo said almost absently as he sat on a worktable. Ki-tae turned to see him staring at his leather-clad ass and smiled. "You're not letting me return the favor. Don't think I didn't notice."

"We don't have time," Ki-tae said quietly.

"I understand why," Jin-woo said, looking at him with serious eyes. "I just don't like it."

Ki-tae walked over and cupped Jin-woo's face, making him tilt his head up. "I would love nothing better than to spend hours loving on you," he said earnestly before placing a sweet kiss on Jin-woo's lips. "And I intend to do just that, but not here. I don't want any interruptions when I finally take you."

"I'm supposed to function normally with that thought in my head? Not likely," Jin-woo grumbled, but he stretched up to give a kiss of his own.

"If I can do it, you can," he said, returning to the rack to pull out his shirt.

"Hello? Vampire," Jin-woo said, pointing at Ki-tae and then at himself. "Human. Big difference in the control department, right?"

"Not really. I've met Vampires who have less control than most humans," Ki-tae said. "And there are some, much like with humans, who are obsessed with control. We're different in some ways but alike in many others."

"What's it like being a Vampire?" Jin-woo asked. Ki-tae could hear both curiosity and concern in his voice and it made him smile. Jin-woo seemed to be able to do that a lot, make him smile in a way only his brothers usually could.

"That is a complex question and I'm surprised you haven't asked it long before this," Ki-tae said. "However, it is best saved for another time and more secure location."

"Oh man, I forgot," Jin-woo said, his cheeks flushing an adorable pink. "It was stupid of me to ask a question like that."

"No, Jin-woo-ya, it's not stupid. It's actually a very good question. Most people would not bother to ask it. They would rather destroy what they don't understand," Ki-tae said. "It takes intelligence to learn about something that is, ultimately, frightening."

"I think it was more a matter of shock rather than fright. No, no, at first, it was very much fright right there with the shock, but part of me was really turned-on, watching you with the tech," Jin-woo admitted, his blush getting brighter. "It wasn't as good as when you fed from me because, oh my God, amazing, but it was still… arousing."

"You liked me feeding from you?" Ki-tae purred as he stalked closer to Jin-woo, still bare-chested, his shirt tossed onto the back of a chair.

"One of the most amazing experiences of my life," Jin-woo said as Ki-tae came to a stop in front of him. His eyes were locked on Ki-tae's abs.

"You liked the feel of my fangs in your throat?" Ki-tae stroked his neck where he'd bitten Jin-woo and watched the minute shivers race over his skin.

"Yes."

Ki-tae took hold of Jin-woo's wrist as he dropped to his knees in front of him. He brushed his lips over the sensitive skin. "You like the feel of my fangs in your wrist, the feel of my mouth sucking on you, bringing the exquisite taste of your blood into my mouth?"

"Oh God, you know I do." Jin-woo moaned.

"Your cum tastes just as delicious," Ki-tae murmured before sinking his fangs into Jin-woo's wrist to the sounds of his moans.

"Oh fuck."

MIN-SU

MIN-SU REREAD what she wrote and snarled in frustration. She tore the paper from her notebook, crumpled it, and threw it in the waste bin. The bin was filled with similar attempts at writing. Tilting her head back, Min-su tried to give herself a pep talk.

"Your journal is filled with lyrics and poems. You can do this," she said out loud. "You can come up with a really good song. This is Bam Kiseu, your favorite band! You know their vocal styles. You know how Ki-tae hyung likes the low sultry sounds that bash you in the head with the beat drop. You know HanYin hyung's voice is perfect for melodic ballads that blend into an R&B 808 rhythm. And you sure as hell know Cheongul-a's voice is perfect for the harder, almost rock heavy metal sound with a pop beat that vocally rips you apart with his growl. You can do this. You *can* write for them."

"You're having trouble too, huh?" Jong-in said quietly from behind her. Min-su jumped only a little. She turned to watch him approach and take the seat next to her.

"I'm having a bitch of a time." She sighed. "I can't seem to find the right words. I can hear the melody in my head and I can hear the beat, but the words just aren't coming to me. All I can hear is a rehash of stuff they've already done, and that is as far from 'original' as you can get."

"I know the feeling," Jong-in said as he leaned his head back.

Min-su watched him closely. He seemed so much more worn-out lately. It worried her. Getting Jong-in to talk was always one of the hardest things for her and Jin-woo to do. She knew he told Jin-woo things he didn't tell her, and it did bother her a little bit, but it was more important that he was at least talking to someone. Honestly she had her suspicions, but she was going to wait until he was comfortable telling her. It wasn't something a person should push.

Of course it probably didn't help that he was physically working himself ragged. Min-su wasn't the type of person to let things go, for the most part. When Jong-in first started hanging out with them at the beginning of high school, he was quiet but still had a certain amount of energy inside him. Over the last few years, that energy had seemed to drain away, so Min-su followed him one day. She was amazed at the sheer drive and determination Jong-in displayed. There were times when he worked three jobs on top of going to school. That was impressive, not conducive to good health, but still impressive. She hadn't said anything then either, figuring he would tell her, but it seemed he was going to continue with his "strong, silent type" act.

Eventually it was just going to piss her off and she would call him on it, but now was not the time. She wasn't sure when that time would be, but she would figure it out. Now if she could just figure out what was going on inside her own head that was preventing her from writing lyrics, she'd be at least a little bit happier. It wasn't until Jong-in reached for the bottle of water next to her, and she saw the raw state of his hands, that Min-su decided to throw her timetable out the window.

"Do you think I'm stupid?" she asked angrily as she grabbed a hold of his hands.

"What? No. Why would you ask me that?" he said.

"Do you think I'm completely unobservant? That I don't notice things about the people who are dear to me?" she said, trying not to let the emotions boil over as she saw cracks in his skin, his poor hands. Without looking, she reached into her backpack and pulled out her first aid kit. It was homemade and so had a lot more in it than a regular kit.

"Min-su-ya, what are you talking about?" Jong-in demanded, trying to pull his hands out of her grip, but she wouldn't let him, and he stopped when she glared at him.

"I know you're working multiple jobs after school," she said quietly as she applied a homemade herbal salve to his hands. "I know you go straight from here to work, sometimes three jobs in a row, and then go home to crash, or go right back to campus to work on projects. I've watched you. I figured you'd confide in me at some point, but you never did. And now your hands are raw and bleeding in places, you're exhausted, you're so sad, and I can't stand it anymore. I can't take seeing you in pain like this, both physically and emotionally, Jong-in-a. You're one of my best friends, and no matter what, I love you."

"I'm fine."

"No, you're not 'fine,' dammit!" she said angrily, the tears tightening her throat as she wrapped some bandages lightly around his hands so he could use them. "You're not! And it's killing me not to be able to help you! Why won't you talk to me, Jong-in-a?"

"I—" He looked away. "I don't want—"

"If you tell me you don't want to be a burden, I will smack you so hard," she hissed. "You and Jin-woo-ya are the only friends I have. You could *never* be a burden to me."

She hauled him into her arms and held him tightly, refusing to let him go even when he tried to pull away. Finally she felt his body relax, and he wrapped his arms around her. Though he made no sound, Min-su could feel the tears soaking her shirt, matching the ones sliding down her face. He wasn't talking, but he was holding on, and that was something. She turned her head and placed a kiss on his cheek, and he did the same before burying his face against her neck.

CHEONGUL

"WELL, I guess that answers my question," Cheongul said quietly as he watched Min-su and Jong-in from several feet away. The kiss was tender and sweet, and it kicked him in the gut. "Figures, you always go for the ones who don't want you, Cheongul. When are you going to learn? It's been well over four centuries, and you still fuck it up."

He turned away from the touching scene, leaving the couple alone. He had to admit they were incredibly discreet. Cheongul didn't think anyone on set suspected Min-su and Jong-in were together. He certainly hadn't. In fact, he could have sworn Jong-in was interested in HanYin. He paused in his walk to wardrobe. He supposed Jong-in could be bisexual, but he didn't think Min-su was the type to share, and he *knew* HanYin wasn't.

Why did his chest hurt?

Cheongul rubbed his chest absently. He should have known someone like Min-su was taken. How could she not be? She was intelligent, beautiful, and sassy. She worked hard and was determined to make sure she got something, no matter how many times she had to do it over again. What man in his right mind would resist her? Seriously, if he, a Vampire, a being who lived centuries, couldn't get Yi Min-su out of his mind, what chance did a human being have? If Jong-in was human. Cheongul had his doubts just as much as Ki-tae did.

Despite the time they had spent together over the last few weeks, no matter how he had taken the time to teach her the dance moves to their songs, repeating it without complaint and flirting with her, it was clear Cheongul was firmly ensconced in the Friend category, regardless of her "hot and sexy and edible" comment from before. Cheongul paused again. Thinking back over his many years, he realized he'd probably done that to several people too, put them in a group of purely platonic people he would never sleep with. There had been no term for it back then when he was still inclined to try for more than just a simple hookup. It didn't really make any difference, did it? If there was one thing Cheongul wouldn't do, it was poach another man's girl, especially when he considered that man a friend. He was just going to have to put his feelings for her aside. Thankfully this was their last day. It would give him time to adjust, a little break to get his head in the right space. Now after seeing the two of them together, Cheongul was glad he hadn't said anything about his feelings to Min-su. He didn't think she would laugh in his face, but what person liked being rejected? They could be friends, he supposed, but would that be a wise idea? Would he be able to keep his feelings buried or would the temptation prove irresistible over time? He wasn't sure what to do. It had been literally hundreds of years since he'd last wanted more with someone.

Thinking about Min-su and Jong-in brought on memories better left forgotten. He had to stop and take a deep breath. Memories were not his friends. They brought with them all the emotions that had triggered him that day. He'd been young, but that was no excuse for what he'd done. Sometimes, being a Vampire sucked. Everything was so much more intense: the emotions, the senses. When a human got angry, there was a good chance they could pull out of it and remain rational enough to function and not hurt anyone. For a Vampire, the feelings were almost overwhelming, especially for the younger ones. For Cheongul, he never really lost that weakened control over his emotions. Even now, he struggled a lot with the intensity of his feelings. Mostly, he worked them out in the weight room or dance practice. Sometimes, he took a trip into the underbelly of whatever city they were in at the time and found fight clubs for Spiritual Beings. They were mostly filled with Shifters of varying species, but other species competed as well. The money was good and it could be a heck of a lot of fun. There, in the ring, he could work out his anger with little fear of killing someone. Shifters were some of the heartiest and more aggressive Spiritual Beings out there. It took a lot of damage to kill one. Yet they were one of the most community-oriented groups he'd ever met. Once you befriended one, you would have to do something horrendous to make them leave you. He'd made a couple of friends in the ring and had kept one or two through the centuries.

When he reached wardrobe, Cheongul wanted to smack his head against something. It just wasn't his day. He could smell the pheromones from where he stood. It was a good thing human noses weren't as sensitive. Jin-woo and Ki-tae would send everyone into a tizzy. The energy coming off his brother meant Ki-tae was feeding too. After he made sure no one was around, Cheongul pounded on the door.

"Put it away, Ki-tae-ya. We have work to do," he growled. He really wasn't in the mood for another loving couple, even if they didn't realize they loved each other yet. If he could, he would just avoid people altogether, but Cheongul prided himself on being a professional… antics with HanYin and Ki-tae notwithstanding. He would finish his work here and get gone as soon as possible. The hurt was building inside him, and he knew himself well enough that he could tell he was going to spiral downward quickly. He wouldn't be safe to be around when he hit rock bottom, and he didn't want to lose someone else he loved to his rage.

The door opened a few seconds later. As he leaned against the wall, Cheongul watched Ki-tae look up and down the hall. He hadn't realized he'd hidden himself from sight, a habit he developed when he was first turned. For the most part, he cloaked himself at will, but sometimes, he did it without thinking and it usually happened when he really wanted to be left alone. It was one of his admittedly few extra abilities. With conscious effort, Cheongul tried to relax. "I'm right here."

Ki-tae was immediately by his side, staring at him intently. "What's wrong?"

"Nothing."

"Bullshit."

"Fine, but I don't want to talk about it, so just fucking let it go, okay?" Cheongul growled, feeling as if he was going to split at the seams. He headed into wardrobe, having to make a concerted effort not to shove Jin-woo aside when he came to the door. "Excuse me."

Jin-woo didn't say a word but quickly moved out of his way, and for that, Cheongul was grateful. He had to get this day over with. He was deteriorating fast. He yanked the clothing down, thankful at the last second it didn't tear. Was he going to be able to sit still for the makeup artists? It wasn't as if he had an option. He was going to have to. Cheongul sighed. He hated when this happened to him. It was as if the control he'd built up over the years just eroded, leaving him raw and broken and angry at everything, especially himself. The worst part about it was knowing it was happening but not being able to stop it. He could fight, could push it off, but in the end, his rage always won out. It was the beast inside of him, the master he fought so hard against. He could hear Ki-tae's whispered words sending Jin-woo away and knew the moment Ki-tae entered the room.

"What? You're my guardian now? Or my warden?"

"Both," Ki-tae said. "You don't want to talk about it, fine, but I know if you lose it and hurt someone, you'll never forgive yourself. I won't let you do that to yourself, not now, not ever."

"And you're going to stop me." Cheongul laughed. "We've been down this road before, Ki-tae, and it wasn't pretty."

"Yes, I am," Ki-tae said softly, "if need be."

"*We* are," HanYin added as he walked into the room and closed the door behind him.

"You called HanYin-a? I didn't hear that part," Cheongul said.

"I didn't say it," Ki-tae said as he moved farther into the room.

Cheongul glanced between the two of them. They'd flanked him in just that one move. Good, because he was close to losing it. He was shaking. The thing of it was, there was really no logical reason for him to be like this. It wasn't like the first time because Min-su and he didn't have any sort of romantic involvement. Hell, it wasn't like the fifth or sixth time, but at least those hadn't ended in death, and love hadn't been involved then either. Why were they doing this anyway? What the fuck did it matter? Didn't HanYin and Ki-tae get tired of going a round with him whenever he got too upset?

Cheongul's mind spun in circles, trying to figure out what else could have caused the beast to stir within him. It wasn't Min-su; he knew that. Yes, he found her incredibly attractive, but she always kept her distance from him, even if they were standing right next to each other. Of course, now he knew why. It wasn't as if he was in love with her, so this was nothing like before. He liked her a lot, but love would never be in the cards for him. He tried that once with disastrous results. He'd tried it what felt like a hundred times, but it always ended in pain. He was too dangerous to love. Even his family, his brothers, were cautious right now.

Rationally Cheongul knew Ki-tae and HanYin loved him. He knew Soon-joon loved him. They were a family. They had been for the last seven centuries as their household had grown to first include HanYin and then Ki-tae. He knew he could trust them with anything and everything. He knew he wasn't a bad person, but the rage didn't care. It wanted the violence, the blood. It wanted the pain and anguish that happened when he lost control. It wanted the death that would result from the snapping of the reins. It made him feel like a passenger in his own body, able to think, but not control the things he did. The haze settled over his eyes like a hot blanket, dulling his mind but sharpening his senses.

The door slammed open, startling him and drawing everyone's attention.

"What's wrong with Cheongul-a? Why does he need help? Someone damn well better tell me what's going on!"

A switch flipped inside him and Cheongul stopped thinking. He flew at Min-su, taking her to the ground. He grunted as she planted her foot in his stomach and grabbed his shoulders, rolling with their momentum until he was on his back. The only thing that prevented them from rolling a second time was Min-su. She stopped the motion and then slammed him back into the ground, his head hitting so hard black dots danced across his vision, her eyes a blazing red.

"Bitch, please. I will rip you apart if you ever try that shit with me again," she snarled.

Cheongul's eyes widened as he saw fangs in her mouth, not two like his, but four: two on top and two on the bottom, long, glistening white fangs. What. The. Fuck?

He looked into her red eyes, saw the horror filling them. She slapped her hand over her mouth. "Oh... oh no!"

Without another word, she bolted. Cheongul had never seen her move so fast. He sat up, staring in the direction she went. Ki-tae and HanYin were immediately at his side. Soon-joon stepped through the door, taking in the scene in a single glance. He merely raised an eyebrow.

"She's a Shifter," Cheongul whispered. "Min-su-ya is a Shifter."

JIN-WOO

"SHE'S A what now?" Jin-woo said from the doorway. "Where's Min-su-ya?"

Everyone was staring at Jin-woo, and as he looked from one man to the next, he noticed something very important: save for Soon-joon, they all had Ki-tae's silver eyes. Soon-joon's were gold, a beautiful shade of bright gold.

"Jin-woo-ya," Ki-tae whispered.

"Well, that makes a hell of a lot of sense," Jin-woo said. "You're all the same, and Soon-joon-nim is the… what? Sire? Leader? Master? Work with me, people. I just learned my bestie is not completely human and I'm trying not to pass out because that floor looks like it will hurt… a lot."

HanYin burst out laughing as he turned to Ki-tae. "Does anything faze him?"

"I haven't found it," Ki-tae said with a smile as he helped Cheongul off the ground.

"I wondered how Ki-tae-ya kept his secret around all of you. Now I get it. He didn't have to," Jin-woo said. "And while all of this is really fascinating and I have hoards of questions I want to ask, should have asked Mr. Bites First over there, but didn't want to be rude, I have to find Min-su-ya."

"Where would she go if she's upset?" Cheongul asked as he wrapped his arms around his torso. He was still shaking. "Because it's a safe bet she is really upset."

Soon-joon moved over to Cheongul and took him by the chin. He raised Cheongul's head, their gazes meeting. Jin-woo could have sworn they were speaking to each other without words, and it was kind of cool and just a wee bit creepy.

"It depends on *how* upset she is," Jin-woo said. "She'll either go to my place, head to Jong-in-a's, or disappear for a day or two. I'm really hoping it's not the latter."

Cheongul looked down at the ground as Soon-joon moved to his side and rubbed his back, making Jin-woo tilt his head in curiosity. This didn't strike him as the Cheongul he had come to know. "I… I hope I didn't hurt her."

He'd never heard Cheongul speak in that tone of voice, low, hesitant, almost timid, and scared, definitely scared. Jin-woo walked over and hugged him, causing Cheongul to stiffen up. Was he shaking? He kept at it until Cheongul relaxed. "She ran out of here. Safe bet she's fine, and you were the one laid out on the floor."

"True." Cheongul sighed. "I just…."

"Hey, stop it," Jin-woo demanded. "Don't beat yourself up. Sometimes things happen that are beyond our control, and sometimes people get hurt because of it. All we can do is try to be better next time. You may be supernatural, but you're just as flawed as the rest of us, so knock it off, or I'll find a way to kick your ass. Got it?"

"You *really* need to keep him," HanYin said as he threw his arm around Ki-tae's shoulders.

"I will talk to the director," Soon-joon said. "We will see how long we can delay filming for today."

"Thank you, Soon-joon-nim. I greatly appreciate it," Jin-woo said with a bow. Soon-joon nodded and then walked out the door.

About thirty minutes later, Jin-woo walked into his and Min-su's favorite coffee shop. He went to the very back corner and found her curled up on the bench, her hands wrapped around a steaming mug of some frothy beverage high in whipped cream and sweet as hell. He slid into the booth next to her but didn't say a word. She would tell him when she was ready.

"I'm surprised you bothered to come looking for me," she said quietly.

"You're my friend. Of course I came looking for you," he said.

"I'm a monster," she whispered.

"You're Min-su-ya, the best friend a guy could ask for. You're always there for me, and I will always be there for you. So, you have some… extras. Doesn't bother me a bit because, when all is said and done, you're still Min-su-ya, my best friend since forever."

"Is Cheongul-a okay?" she asked.

"Yes and no," Jin-woo said, really thinking about the answer. "Physically he's fine, as far as I can tell, but emotionally, mentally, I think he's all sorts of hurting. He was really upset at the idea he might have hurt you."

"You guys are usually pretty breakable, and I slammed him pretty hard," she muttered.

"Let's just say you and Cheongul hyung have a lot to talk about and leave it at that," Jin-woo said, bumping her shoulder. "So, what happened?"

"No fucking clue," she said after taking a sip of her drink. "I overhead Shin-bai hyung on the phone, saying something about Cheongul-a needing help and I just, I didn't stop to think about it. I just ran into the room. Next thing I know, he's launching himself at me from halfway across the room and I just… acted on instinct."

"Well, I guess we can safely say that Cheongul hyung has a fight response when startled."

"Are you mad at me for not telling you sooner?" Min-su asked, looking at him.

"Are you mad at me for not telling you I prefer men?"

"No."

"There's your answer," Jin-woo said. "Some things are still really big, even if we trust the other person. It's hard to say them, and it's not because we don't trust, but because we're afraid. It's like Jong-in-a. I really wish he would talk to me about all the shit he's going through, but I only get bits and pieces, and I have to kind of put together a puzzle of what's going on inside his head. I know he trusts me, but he's the type to think he'll burden his friends if he tells us his problems."

"I hate that," Min-su said. "He's not a burden. You two are a blessing to me, and I hate when I'm not able to help you."

"We feel strongly," Jin-woo said. "That's why we get so upset when we can't help."

"I made a complete ass out of myself, didn't I?" Min-su said. "Running off like that. I didn't know what else to do. I didn't ask for this, and it's a big secret to keep. It makes a lot of things hard. Cheongul-a probably thinks I'm a freak."

"Trust me when I say he'll be more understanding than you think," Jin-woo said with a smirk. "But if you don't go back to the set, you'll never know."

"Do you have any idea what it's like for me there?" Min-su sighed. "I feel so wound up it's not even funny. If I let myself go for even a second, I'm going to jump him and ride him to the ground... in front of everyone!"

"He might not mind," Jin-woo teased. "Are you kidding me? Every time you walk by, he stares at your ass and does that lip thing you love so much!"

"You lie!" she said, smacking his arm.

"Would I lie about something like that?" Jin-woo tried his best to hold a straight face, but the look on hers was priceless. He burst out laughing. "I love that dazed expression you get when you fantasize about him. But truly, he does watch you."

She snarled at him and then took another sip of her drink. "I guess I could go back. I mean, I really should apologize, right?"

"Definitely." Jin-woo managed to keep a straight face this time. He really could picture her riding Cheongul to the ground, and the expression on Cheongul's face would be worth the scarring of his retinas. He wouldn't be able to unsee that shit. He thought she would get up, but instead she just stared at him for several moments. "What?"

"How come you're not freaking out?" she demanded.

"I'm going with shock."

"Shock?"

"Yup."

"That's your theory?"

"Yup," he said. "I figure at some point I'm going to have just one too many surprises or this is all going to hit me at once and I'll pass out, hopefully on something soft."

"And you don't have any questions?" she said raising an eyebrow.

"Oh, I have so many questions for all of you, I don't know where to begin," Jin-woo said. "But I think I've filled my quota of boo-shit today."

"Boo-shit? Really? That was a horrible pun," she said with a laugh.

"It was awesome. Now, hurry up. We have to get back to work before something else weird happens, like gremlins come out of the kitchen dancing the waltz."

"Okay. I'll get this put in a to-go cup." She pushed him out of the booth and hurried to the counter.

Jin-woo shook his head. Sometimes Min-su was so serious it almost hurt, and others, like now, she was so damned adorable. He was pretty sure Cheongul didn't stand a chance of resisting. That she was smiling was his primary goal, and he'd accomplished that. Now they just had to get back to the set and finish work. It would be interesting, to say the least.

"Okay, it's driving me crazy," she said, stopping in the middle of the sidewalk. They were about ten minutes from the studio and she just stopped.

Jin-woo turned around. "What is?"

"You, your reaction, or lack thereof. This is a major thing you've learned and you haven't asked me a single question. It's not natural, Jin-woo-ya."

"I'm not asking because I don't know if I want to know the answers," he said throwing his hands up. "I wonder how it happened. Were you born this way? Were you changed? Are there others? Does it hurt you to… change? Would you still be you if you did? I have so many questions, but I've been pretending nothing's changed because I don't want it to. I liked how things were before I found out myths walk among us looking just like everyone else. And why in the hell would someone with that type of secret go into such a fucking public career? Does that even remotely make sense?"

Why did she have to poke at his little shell of alternate Jin-woo-friendly reality? So many things spun around his head, never leaving him alone until he pushed them into a mental closet and locked the door.

"Jin-woo?"

"I thought I knew you so well and you have this huge thing," he said quietly. "Ki-tae hyung has this huge thing. Hell, they all have this huge thing, and I… I feel small and… weak, and insignificant. I'm not…. I don't have a secret. Yeah, it's a little overwhelming. I was perfectly content walking around in purposeful ignorance, and here you go, popping my bubble of happy."

"*Joesonghaeyo*, Jin-woo," she said, and he could see the tears shimmering in her eyes.

"Dammit, I didn't mean to make you cry," he said as he pulled her into his arms and hugged her tight. "I guess I still need to process and am just not ready to ask all the questions in my head."

"I'll answer what I can when you are," she said. "I don't know how informative it's going to be. I'm sort of stumbling along figuring things out on the fly. I don't know if there's anyone around here who can answer the questions I have, let alone the ones you have."

"Does your mom…?" He didn't even have to finish his question before she nodded.

"To answer one of your questions no, I wasn't born this way," she said quietly. "Let's get back to work."

CHEONGUL

CHEONGUL SIGHED, wishing Soon-joon had been able to delay the filming a little bit longer, at least until they knew if Min-su was okay. As it was, he was having a hard time concentrating on what he was supposed to be doing, and it showed. He could feel himself getting worked up, but then the strangest thing happened. Cheongul inhaled deeply, filling his nose with the most delicious scent he'd ever smelled, and it all seemed to melt out of him.

He looked up to see Min-su and Jin-woo approaching. He held his breath, waiting for her to look at him. When those beautiful chocolate-brown eyes lifted and caught his, Cheongul felt the tightness in his chest ease. She was okay. Well, as okay as anyone with such a secret could be after unwittingly outing themselves. Min-su gave him a tentative smile, and he nodded. They would talk later. Now was not the time, and if there was one thing he learned about Min-su in the time they'd been working on this project, it was that she was a professional. Everyone had their off moments when they just wanted to run away, and earlier had been one of hers. It was going to be hard enough to talk about it in the first place without adding a poorly chosen, public location.

Once everyone had greeted Min-su and made sure she was okay, they got back to work. Cheongul found he could focus once more, and by the pleased look on the director's face, it showed. They danced in perfect sync, each movement precise and sharp as they went through their choreography. The music played over the speakers, and they managed to hit each cue right on time. It was, for lack of a better word, perfect. Cheongul felt it deep inside. They had nailed it.

"Cut!"

The applause began immediately after. Cheongul smiled, feeling the heat in his cheeks. He enjoyed what he did, and he wasn't as prone to blushing when hearing such things from their fans, but when the crew did it, it made him feel a little self-conscious. These were people who knew him on a more personal level, people he saw frequently, and it just seemed weird when they applauded. He felt as if he didn't deserve their applause as much as the crew did. After all, they made it all possible. Still, he should accept the compliment, and so Cheongul bowed to them. Then after their applause died down, he turned to his brothers and nodded. They clapped for the crew. "You all are awesome!"

Finally they could leave the set, and Cheongul headed straight for the drink table, grabbed a water bottle, and downed it in one long go. He sighed as he put the cap back on. It had been a long day, and the whole morning had been terrible. Right now he just wanted to go home to bed. He couldn't, but he still wanted to. Honestly

Cheongul just didn't want to be around people. He knew Jin-woo had been trying to be helpful, but he still felt guilty, ashamed, and that was never conducive to positive social interaction.

"Cheongul-a." Min-su's voice pulled him out of his thoughts. He turned to face her, swallowing hard. She looked like he felt: broken. "I... I wanted to apologize for... for this morning."

"I'm the one who owes you an apology," he said. "I shouldn't have done that."

"I... can we go somewhere more private to talk?" she asked. "This isn't something I want to do out in the open."

"Sure, I get it," Cheongul said.

They found a quiet room not far from the set. Cheongul ushered her in and closed the door, locking it. He took one of the chairs next to the makeup table, and Min-su took another. For several moments neither of them said a word, and then, finally, Min-su chuckled softly.

"I don't know where to begin," she said.

"Then allow me." Cheongul had been staring at the floor until that point. When he looked up at her, he allowed his fangs to drop and his eyes to go silver.

Her eyes widened. Cheongul remained still, waiting to see what she would do. She rose from her chair and approached him, stopping when their knees bumped. Slowly Min-su reached her hand forward and stroked her finger across his bottom lip, pushing it down a little farther to see his fangs. He tried to contain his shiver, but it wasn't easy. When she stroked a fang, he couldn't stop his groan.

"You're not like me," she whispered.

"No," he said, feeling a little breathless. "I'm a Vampire."

"A Vampire. I thought you smelled deliciously weird, but that never crossed my mind. Wow," she said. "I've never met another.... I don't even know what to call us, call me."

"Those who change shape from one form to another are Shifters and there are many different types: wolves, bears, snakes, birds, cats.... I met a panda Shifter once. He was just as cuddly looking in his human form as he was in bear form and could be just as mean in both, but when referring to all of us in general, we are just called Spiritual Beings. Some people call us spirits, but that's not accurate as all spirits are Spiritual Beings, but not all Spiritual Beings are spirits," Cheongul said. "We don't meet many like us either, just enough to know we're not the only ones."

"Us?"

"Myself, HanYin, Ki-tae, and Soon-joon-nim," he explained. "We're all the same."

"How did you become one, a Vampire?" Min-su said.

"That's... a long story, and not one I like to talk about a lot. Let's just say a lot of unpleasant things led to my change, and while there have been some dark times since then, everything has been much better than before."

"I don't like to talk about my... change either," she said, tracing the curve of his cheek with her fingers.

"I really want to kiss you," Cheongul said quietly, trying to keep his urges in check.

"I really want you to kiss me," she whispered.

Slowly Min-su leaned over, pulling her hair to one side. Cheongul tilted his head up. He knew he shouldn't, but he couldn't resist. The soft touch of her lips on his sent bolts of pleasure through his body. He gripped the arms of the chair to keep from grabbing Min-su and pulling her into his lap. The choice was taken out of his hands when she straddled him all on her own. Cheongul was not that strong. He gripped her hips and pulled her tight against him. She gave a little gasp and he took advantage of the opportunity, sliding his tongue deep into her mouth. He growled when she clenched her fingers in his hair and tugged just enough to sting. Cheongul couldn't get enough of Min-su's taste. He wanted more. Slowly he worked his way along her jaw. The soft mewing, growling sounds were sweet music. The urge to bite was strong, especially when she tilted her head as if in offering.

"Has anyone seen Min-su-ya?" Jong-in's voice echoed through his head.

Cheongul pulled back, panting. He held Min-su away from him slightly. "We can't do this."

"What?"

"We.... I can't do this," he said as he rose, setting her on her feet. "I'm sorry, Min-su-ya."

Cheongul hurried out of the room, rushing past Jong-in and Jin-woo as he left. He had no clear destination in mind. He just knew he had to get away. Putting on a burst of speed, he left the studio behind. Jong-in was his friend. Min-su was his, not Cheongul's. He wasn't going down that road again. He would *never* go down that road again. He would do the right thing this time. He would not give in to what his heart wanted, and he would not fight for someone who was already with another. Someday he would stop hoping to find someone who would love him for him despite what he was, despite his flaws. Someday.

KI-TAE

KI-TAE FOUND Jin-woo sitting with Jong-in and Min-su. None of them looked happy. When Jin-woo looked up, Ki-tae was surprised to see how angry he was. He tilted his head in curiosity. Had something happened?

"What's wrong?" Ki-tae asked, squatting down before Min-su, as it appeared she was the one in need of comfort.

"I...."

"Cheongul-a is what's wrong," Jin-woo said angrily. "I didn't realize he was a bigot."

"What? He's nothing of the sort," Ki-tae said.

"Of course you'd say that. He's your brother."

"I don't say that because he's my brother. I say that because I know him," Ki-tae said. "I don't know what's going on, but I think you'd better start from the beginning."

"I—" Min-su took a deep breath and then started again. "We went to one of the unused rooms to talk about... what happened earlier."

"You mean when you sort of kicked his ass a little?" Ki-tae smiled, trying to lighten things a little.

"Something like that," she said, giving him a little smile in return. "Anyway, wow, Vampire? So, we, um... that is I, we, dammit, this is embarrassing."

"He kissed her and then fucking ran away!" Jin-woo snapped.

"*I* kissed *him*, Jin-woo-ya," she corrected. "It was definitely mutual until he just, he said he couldn't do this and then took off. It's because I'm a... Shifter, isn't it?"

"What else could it be? You're awesome and he's an ass!" Jin-woo said.

Ki-tae listened, but it wasn't much. Yet he knew Cheongul, and so there had to be some other explanation for his behavior. From what Min-su said, his words didn't indicate why he left, so as far as he could tell, the leap to "bigot" was a bit of a stretch. Looking into Min-su's sad eyes, Ki-tae wanted to make her smile again, but this wasn't something he could really crack a joke at, even if he'd gotten her to smile a few minutes ago. Besides, that tended to be HanYin's thing. He took her hand in his.

"Don't lose hope," Ki-tae said. "I'll talk to Cheongul-a. It may take a few days because if what you described is any indication, he's going to be extremely antisocial unless forced to do otherwise. But I will find the answer, and I can guarantee it's not what you think."

"How can you be so sure?" Jin-woo demanded.

"Because of the four of us, Cheongul-a has had the most exposure to Shifters," Ki-tae said. "He goes out of his way to help them, especially the lone ones."

"Why?" Jong-in asked.

"That's his story to tell, if he chooses to do so," Ki-tae said quietly.

While Ki-tae wanted to rush out in search of Cheongul, he couldn't. Commitments had been made that he had to fulfill. When he reached their father's house that night, Cheongul's car was not there. Where could he be? Usually Cheongul would head to Soon-joon's house, especially if he was upset and spiraling. It was a haven for all of them, and Ki-tae was pretty sure his brother needed that sense of safety. Was it possible he'd gone back to his apartment in Seoul? Ki-tae didn't think so, but it was worth a shot. He'd been trying to call Cheongul off and on since he left the set, but his calls went straight to voicemail each time. All his text messages went unanswered. He pulled out his cell phone and dialed.

"Hey, HanYin," Ki-tae said as soon as HanYin picked up. "Have you talked to Cheongul?"

"Not since lunch, why?" HanYin said.

"Something happened between him and Min-su-ya, and now I can't get ahold of him. He's not answering his phone or texts," Ki-tae said. "He's not at Abeoji's house either."

"I'm still in Seoul," HanYin said. "I'll stop by his apartment and see if he's there."

"Thanks, HanYin."

"Are you going to call Abeoji?"

"Not yet," Ki-tae said. "I don't want to if we don't have to. He had to leave town today. If we tell him, he'll do nothing but worry."

"Okay. Talk to you later."

"Talk to you later."

Ki-tae ended the call and put his phone back in his pocket. He hoped they found Cheongul soon. It wasn't good for him to be alone when he was in a dark state of mind. Something had made Cheongul walk away from Min-su. What that something was, Ki-tae didn't know, and the only place he was going to get answers was from Cheongul.

CHEONGUL

KI-TAE AND HanYin looked up as they heard footsteps in the garden. Thirty seconds later there was a small dogpile outside the dining room with Cheongul on the bottom. Finally they let him up and knelt next to him. Then HanYin punched him in the arm, and Ki-tae smacked him upside the head.

"Ow!"

"Don't you *ever* scare us like that again," Ki-tae growled. "If you need time to yourself, at least answer the fucking phone and say so!"

"No dim sum for a month!" HanYin said with an adorable pout as he crossed his arms over his chest. His eyes flickered back and forth between their normal warm brown and silver in his agitation.

"Aw, come on, HanYin!" Cheongul complained. "A month? It wasn't that bad."

"It was two fucking days, Cheongul," Ki-tae said. "I was this close to telling Abeoji we couldn't find you."

"Did you?" Cheongul looked down at the ground.

"No, but it was close. He's due back either tonight or early tomorrow morning, but you know how he is. He'll take one look at you and know something's up," Ki-tae said softly. Then he pulled Cheongul into a hug. "We need to talk about it, though. Min-su dongsaeng thinks you took off because she's a Shifter. Jin-woo-ya was pissed when he found out."

"It wasn't that," Cheongul said.

"Then what was it?"

"She's...." He glanced at HanYin. "Involved with someone else and... I saw her and... Jong-in kissing...."

"You don't poach," HanYin finished. God, he couldn't stand that look on HanYin's face, as if his whole world was crumbling. "Jong-in? Then why did you kiss her?"

At Cheongul's surprised look, Ki-tae explained, "I told him when we couldn't find you."

"I didn't kiss her, per se," Cheongul said. "She kissed me and I... I didn't resist, and the, well, it really was a mutual thing. I'd been wanting to kiss her for so long. It was.... I couldn't turn away."

"Then what stopped you?"

"How do you know she's with Jong-in?" HanYin asked.

"I saw them together. They looked very happy. She was hugging him so tightly, and he was returning it with equal strength and then they started kissing, and that's when I left."

"That was a dumb thing to do and you really need to not assume things. Are you sure they're together? Because she was really upset when I talked to her and it was Jin-woo doing the comforting while Jong-in-a was sort of a silent support. That doesn't strike me as couple behavior."

"We understand, Cheongul," HanYin said after shooting a "shut up" look at Ki-tae. Sometimes, HanYin's face was so easy to read. "Honestly the three of us are seriously screwed up in the head. We try very hard to put it behind us, to let it go, but Fate seems to have a vicious sense of humor and keeps throwing these situations in our path."

"Life is a series of natural and spontaneous changes. Do not resist them. That only creates sorrow. Let reality be reality. Let things flow naturally forward in whatever way they like. Laozi, a wise man. You could learn much from his teachings, young ones."

The voice was whisper soft and echoed the sound of the ages. They were on their feet in a heartbeat, Cheongul in front with Ki-tae and HanYin immediately behind him. All three bared their fangs and growled. The woman standing before them merely raised one delicately arched eyebrow. She wore a thin blue tunic with sleeves ending in large bells over what appeared to be a T-shirt and jeans. A narrow red belt with golden Chinese dragons twisting along the length wrapped around her waist. On her feet she wore a pair of red Converse high-top sneakers. Her ebony hair was swept up in the front and on the sides into a small topknot. The rest fell to her knees. She had a small three-petaled flower on her forehead above the bridge of her nose. Her lips were a bloodred and echoed in the faint red eyeshadow around her eyes. Her long, sooty eyelashes were emphasized by the extended sweep of eyeliner. She folded her hands into her sleeves and smiled gently.

"Do I pass inspection?" she asked, her voice still quiet, almost musical.

"Who are you?" Cheongul said, his voice low.

"She is Godaeui-nim, my teacher and friend," Soon-joon said as he came up behind them. He laid a gentle hand on HanYin's shoulder.

"And more. It is good to see you, again, Táozi-chan," she said with a smile. "You have been distant far too long."

"Táozi?" Ki-tae snickered and winced when Soon-joon's hand connected with the back of his head. "What? It's cute."

"I do not do 'cute,'" Soon-joon said. "And she is the only being on this planet allowed to call me that."

"It is what your mother named you, Táozi-chan. She was a good woman. Do not dishonor it," Godaeui said. "Shall we adjourn inside, or should we have our discussion out here? I can see the situation is most… complicated."

Soon-joon stepped to one side and ushered Godaeui inside. Ki-tae followed Cheongul's lead and bowed. He noticed how HanYin stepped away from her as she walked past him, but also bowed. Ki-tae walked over to him and looped his arm around HanYin's shoulders.

"Are you going to be okay?" he asked quietly.

"I don't know," HanYin said quietly, his usual good humor not present. "I....
She is... old, very old, and that... that scares me, Ki-tae."

"I know," Ki-tae said, giving him a hug. "But Abeoji would never invite
someone into our home who was a threat to us. He must be very trusting of this
woman."

"I am... not good with people of such... power and age," HanYin said.

Ki-tae couldn't say anything further to that. He knew his brother's story,
knew this was going to be hard for HanYin, knew his brother didn't like to feel
weak and helpless. There was nothing he could do except be there for him. It
wasn't as if he could tell Godaeui to leave. That would be dangerous, not to
mention incredibly rude, and that would make Soon-joon mad. The only thing
he could do would be to keep in constant contact with HanYin, and that's exactly
what he did.

When they entered the tearoom, Godaeui and Soon-joon were already
seated, Soon-joon at the end and Godaeui sat facing him. When Ki-tae took his
seat, he made sure HanYin was between him and Soon-joon. Cheongul took the
seat to Soon-joon's left, folding himself onto the mat with practiced ease. For a few
moments, no one said a word. Godaeui looked at each of them in turn, pausing on
HanYin.

"I have no wish to harm you, young one," she said quietly. "Be at ease. You
are as a beloved grandchild, for not only am I Táozi's mentor, I am his sire as well."

"*Wǒ hěn bàoqiàn, Géxiá*," HanYin practically whispered, bowing low.
Ki-tae rubbed the small of his back, hoping to soothe his nerves. The Mandarin
was a clear sign HanYin was highly agitated. His normal pattern of speech often
combined Korean and Mandarin, even English on occasion, but full-on Mandarin
was reserved for times when he felt threatened, unsafe, and in danger.

"It seems I have delayed this visit for far too long, that your sons feel
threatened by me," she said quietly. "It was not my intention."

"We understand, Godaeui-nim," Cheongul said.

"*Wǒ de sūnzi, Nǐ bú xūyǎo baochí,*" Godaeui said, speaking solely in
Mandarin and addressing HanYin directly. "*Qù nǎlǐ nǐ huì juédé ānquán hé shūshì.*"

"*Wǒ bù líkāi wǒ de jiārén, Géxiá,*" HanYin responded quickly. Godaeui
smiled at him and nodded. Her expression showed she was proud of HanYin, who
chose to remain with his family when offered the option to leave, even though he
was afraid.

"Ki-tae dongsaeng, tell me of this young man, Cheong Jin-woo dongsaeng.
How did you meet him?" she said as Ki-tae poured tea for all of them. As the
youngest, it was his duty, and he was cool with it. It was relaxing at times to have
a set definition of his role. Soon-joon had taught them all the traditional tea rituals
and ceremonies for China and Japan, as well as Korea, and so he knew exactly
what to do.

"I met him backstage at our last concert tour performance in the Seoul Olympic Dome," Ki-tae said. "I was feeding."

"And why were you feeding in such a location?" There was no censure in her words, just curiosity.

"I...." Ki-tae sighed. He hadn't wanted to share this information with anyone. They would only worry. "I was... hit in the parking lot on my way in. It was bad, but not enough to keep me from performing. By the end of the first half, however, I was hurting, and wouldn't have been able to do the second half without some quick healing."

"What?" Soon-joon's voice was deadly quiet, not a good sign.

"Shit," Cheongul hissed. "Why didn't you say anything?"

"Because you all would just worry and try to stop me from going onstage. We all agree our fans deserve the best performance we can give them, no matter what," Ki-tae said.

"Not at the expense of your health," Soon-joon said.

"So you fed from the tech to heal," Godaeui said, redirecting the conversation. "Is this Jin-woo dongsaeng the tech?"

"No," Ki-tae said. "I had just started when Jin-woo-ya came around the corner and caught me."

"He interrupted you feeding?"

"Yes, after standing there for several moments, he fled deeper into the stadium. I followed him. I don't know why, other than needing to deal with my slip-up, but I did. I cornered him in the loading docks and... well, I fed from his neck, from his artery," Ki-tae said quietly.

"He is human?" she asked.

"Yes."

"There is nothing unique about him?"

"Well, other than being absolutely beautiful inside and out, no, I wouldn't say there was anything else unique about him," Ki-tae said. "Why do you ask?"

"While bonding is not uncommon, it usually only happens this quickly with someone who has some spiritual blood in them, either fully or small amounts," Godaeui explained. "That it took place with a full human is not unheard of, just incredibly rare and indicative of a deeper bond. I will need to meet Jin-woo dongsaeng to ascertain if he truly is fully human or not. Then I will know what other options will be available to us."

"I'm not sure how we are going to arrange that," Soon-joon said. "They started postproduction work yesterday."

"It is simple, Táozi-chan," Godaeui said with a chuckle. "I own half of BL Entertainment, remember? It is not unusual for the owner to observe their workers on occasion."

"You…. I thought Abeoji owned the company?" Cheongul said as he took a sip of his tea. Ki-tae watched his hand shake as he set the cup down and felt guilty. That was the other reason he didn't want to tell them what happened. Cheongul would have taken it harder than anyone else. Losing people terrified his oldest brother, especially if the demise was… violent.

"He owns the other half," Godaeui said. "We began this company a long time ago. It has had many names but always supported the arts we love so much and the unique and beautiful people who grant us the gift of their creativity. It has gone through many changes, and there are several subsidiary companies all over the world, but the stock is split solely between myself and Táozi."

"She is right. It is not uncommon for owners to make surprise visits to their companies," Soon-joon said with a smile. "As much as you dislike the modern world, you are still involved with it."

"I may dislike it, but that does not mean I am so foolish as to not pay attention to it," she answered. "I have seen more of this world than many of our kind. I have seen dynasties. I have even helped some of them… in both the rise and the fall. It is a fool who ignores the world around them just because they find it distasteful."

"Very well," Soon-joon said, still smiling. "You can accompany us to the studio tomorrow, and I will introduce you to Jin-woo dongsaeng and the others. Ki-tae, your schedule is free, I believe. You will come with us. Now let us finish our tea, and then we can go over the schedule for the next few days."

It was several hours before they retired for the evening, and Ki-tae went to shower before bed. He stood under the water, eyes closed, head resting against the tiles. He hadn't thought about the accident since that day, but the more he did, the more he realized there was a good possibility it wasn't an accident.

He had heard the rev of an engine right before the headlights blinded him and he was hit. It wasn't his first car accident, but it was certainly the first time someone had hit him on purpose. Who was the driver? Why did they want to hurt him? Was his family also in danger? The questions bounced around inside his skull, making it impossible for him to relax.

He turned off the water and dried off. After throwing on a pair of lounge pants and a white tank top, Ki-tae headed out of his room and to the living room. He sat down at the piano, resting his fingers lightly on the keys. Ki-tae closed his eyes and let his fingers move. The song began slowly, soft and sweet. He let his mind wander, the memories carrying the music. Ki-tae had only the music to soothe him inside. His brothers tried, as did his father, but it was the music that reached deep inside him and eased the pain.

He didn't know what to do. So far there was no other option for Jin-woo. He cared for Jin-woo, but this bond was…. It was not something he wanted. He wanted a choice, and he wanted Jin-woo to have that choice as well. He didn't want to take it from him. The music reflected his thoughts, growing darker and more somber. Ki-tae felt the wetness on his face, the tears falling on the backs of his hands.

"You are troubled," Godaeui said quietly as she entered the living room. Ki-tae stopped playing. "Please do not stop. Your playing is beautiful."

She gracefully lowered herself to the couch, tucking bare feet beneath the skirt of her nightgown. Ki-tae placed his fingers on the keys once more. For the next several moments, the only sound in the room was the music as it poured from inside him. Somehow it seemed right that she was there, listening to him play. Finally he stopped, his hands coming to rest where they had begun.

"Feel better?" Godaeui asked quietly.

"Yes, thank you," he said as he rose and joined her on the couch. "Did I wake you?"

"No." Godaeui smiled. "I do not sleep much. I do not need it anymore. It has been quite some time since Táozi-chan and I were last together. I miss him."

"He said you chose to withdraw from the world."

"I did, for a time. Our world follows a circular path. There are high points and low points. Sometimes those low points show us the darkest side of humanity and others like us, and last for so long we lose hope of the return to light. People, all peoples, are also capable of great good. For a time I lost sight of that and no longer wanted to deal with people. And so I withdrew into my mountain home, only keeping abreast of the barest things, usually through my children, when they permitted. Much has changed since I last walked among humans, but I am nothing if not a quick study," she said with a wicked grin.

Ki-tae chuckled, but then his thoughts turned back to Jin-woo. "I don't want to hurt him."

"Once I see him and then the two of you together, I will know what our options are," Godaeui said. "Given what you have told me, there is a good chance you may not have to."

"I don't want to take his choice away either," Ki-tae said. "He shouldn't be punished for my mistake."

"Do you truly see us as a punishment?" Godaeui cocked her head to one side, much like a cat.

"I don't know how to answer that," Ki-tae said softly.

"You have been bound before," she said suddenly, narrowing her eyes.

"I… yes." Ki-tae felt the panic welling up inside of him. He did *not* like talking about his past.

"What was done to you was an abomination," she said quietly. "A twisting of something sacred and special to our kind, done only when there is the deepest love between the Vampire and his or her lover."

"I had… nothing of myself." Ki-tae stared at his hands, watching them shake. He barely registered the shifting of the couch, and then Godaeui wrapped her strong arms around him. He leaned his head on Godaeui's shoulder, listening to soft humming, a gentle tune he found oddly relaxing.

"Shhh, young one, be at ease. You are free of him, and he is no more," she whispered softly. She kept humming and the sound of her voice lulled him to sleep.

JIN-WOO

JIN-WOO STARED in amazement. When they had come to have their photos taken for the temporary badges, they were given a brief tour. He hadn't gotten a good look at the studios they would be working in until now. He stood in the center, turning slowly in a circle. Monitors, speakers, everything down to the custom-made walls for the best sound was top-of-the-line. Clearly BLE spared no expense when it came to any part of their process. The giggling from behind him drew his attention. Jin-woo turned to see Min-su and Jong-in grinning like idiots. He stuck his tongue out at them.

"You're like a kid in a candy shop."

Ki-tae's voice was filled with amusement. Jin-woo whipped around to face him, his cheeks straining with the size of his smile. He contained the urge to run at Ki-tae and pounce-hug him... barely. The way Ki-tae's hands twitched, Jin-woo was pretty sure Ki-tae was resisting a similar urge.

"Oh geez, you two are making my nose twitch!" Min-su complained. "Again!"

"Try living with it," HanYin said quietly, but his eyes were all for Jong-in. "Say 'Jin-woo-ya' in his presence and you're choking on it."

"Same with him!" Min-su poked Jin-woo in the side. "That's for keeping it from me."

"Ow, stop it, you evil little thing!" Jin-woo said.

"What are you two talking about? I don't smell anything except Min-su-ya's perfume," Jong-in said, shifting his eyes back and forth nervously.

"You and I need to have a talk later," Min-su said quietly.

"Okay." Poor Jong-in looked really confused.

Jin-woo glared at Min-su but said nothing. What could he say? He couldn't help it if she had an oversensitive nose, and it wasn't like he could really control his body's reaction to Ki-tae. He turned to Ki-tae. "What are you doing here? I thought your schedule was pretty full up for the next two weeks."

"It was cleared for today," Ki-tae said. "Soon-joon-nim asked HanYin-a and I to escort a VIP around. She was very interested in you three, so I figured I would see if you were in the middle of something before I brought her over. I didn't want to interrupt. I hate when people do it to me."

"He gets super cranky," HanYin said with a small smile. Jin-woo could tell he wasn't comfortable. Was it because of this VIP? It seemed like it. Normally HanYin was all smiles.

"Kind of like you when someone interrupts a writing spree?" Ki-tae said with a raised eyebrow. HanYin just shrugged. Sadness filled Ki-tae's eyes, and

Jin-woo wanted to make it go away. He just wasn't sure how, other than to find out what was bothering HanYin. He decided redirection was a better tactic at present.

"We had an early-morning meeting with Seonsaengnim, otherwise Min-su-ya would have had us here at the crack of dawn," Jin-woo said.

"This is a bad thing how?" she said. "The earlier we get here, the more time we have to work before we have to leave for classes. I see nothing wrong with this thought process."

"Of course not. It's your thought process," Jin-woo said. "I, however, like to sleep in on the mornings when I don't have a class."

"You sleep too much," she grumbled.

"I do not."

"Do too."

"You two act like siblings." HanYin chuckled. Jin-woo smiled; mission accomplished for the moment.

"We might as well be," Min-su said.

"Siblings are good," Jong-in said quietly. He was looking down at his feet, the walls, anywhere but at HanYin. Jin-woo sighed inwardly. Those two were going to mess it up if they didn't take a chance on each other.

"Why don't you three get settled, and I'll go get Soon-joon-nim and our VIP?" Ki-tae said.

"That works," Jin-woo said. "See you in a few?"

"Definitely," Ki-tae purred.

"Oh, stop it!" Min-su snapped. "You're enough to give me cavities."

Jin-woo and Ki-tae laughed as they went their separate ways. When they had come in for their badges, they had been given small desks where they would be able to put their things and do some individual work that didn't have to be done in the studio. Jin-woo liked the setup because his desk was right by the window, and he could glance outside to get a bit of a break when he needed to.

For the first day, they were organizing the media files. They needed to go through what they had filmed and pull the shots they wanted to use and those they would leave out while Jong-in went over the sound recordings. Right now it was a matter of making sure they had received all the media and were able to access it. It surprised Jin-woo when the director told him they would keep everything they shot, but not everything would be used in the video. Some of it would be used as promotional pieces, and the rest would be used as a behind-the-scenes video. The whole process was so fascinating to him.

It seemed odd, sometimes, to be here. It would strike him at random moments. He was standing in the headquarters of one of the most successful entertainment companies in South Korea. He was interacting with his favorite idols.... Well, okay, "interacting" had an entirely different meaning when Ki-tae managed to catch him alone, but still, it was something Jin-woo had never dreamed would be possible. He fully expected to be on the bottom rung of the entertainment industry ladder for several years before slowly moving his way upward. This experience only made him more determined to reach this point after he graduated.

"Oh my God, she is gorgeous," Min-su whispered from beside him.

He looked at her and then turned to see who she was staring at. He caught his breath. He didn't know a single individual who wouldn't stare at the woman who walked between Ki-tae and Soon-joon. He didn't know what anyone else noticed first, but for Jin-woo, it was her eyes. They were so dark as to appear black and seemed as if they had seen many ages and learned much. Her ebony hair, that was the only way to describe it, was swept back from her face and pinned, the rest falling loosely around her. Yet it didn't make her seem less elegant or less mature. Her makeup and jewelry were understated, used to enhance rather than overpower. The top she wore was a crimson with deep gold trim, and the collar fit snugly around the neck yet was open at the base of the throat, and the edge followed into a diamond shape. The fabric looked embroidered with small golden designs, and it flared out slightly at the hips. She had chosen black slacks, and the heels she wore, in the same shade of crimson, brought her closer to Ki-tae's height. Who was this woman? She looked elegant, beautiful, and powerful.

And just a little bit intimidating. Jin-woo was hard-pressed not to think such thoughts. There was no doubt in his mind this was the VIP. Even if Ki-tae and HanYin hadn't been standing with her, Jin-woo would have known this was not a person to mess with. Then she was standing in front of him, and Jin-woo didn't know what to say. He mumbled something, he couldn't exactly say what, and bowed. She lifted his chin with gentle fingers, and he was staring into her eyes.

She smiled. "You will join me for lunch today."

"I would be honored," Jin-woo said.

"Perhaps introductions should be made first?" Soon-joon said with a small smile. "Allow me to present Cheong Jin-woo dongsaeng. He and his fellow students, Yi Min-su dongsaeng and Bak Jong-in dongsaeng, are the winners of the first part of our BLE Scholarship and Internship program. Jin-woo dongsaeng, Min-su dongsaeng, Jong-in dongsaeng, this is Lyang ChenBao-nim, owner and president of BL Entertainment."

Jin-woo nearly passed out. The owner... the *owner* of the company.

"Soon-joon-nim, you've overwhelmed the poor boy," ChenBao said with a soft chuckle. "Shame on you."

Jin-woo was jarred back into himself by a gentle caress to his face. He looked to see Ki-tae smiling at him.

"Breathe," Ki-tae whispered with a smirk. Jin-woo glared at him but was able to pull himself together.

"I am disrupting your day," ChenBao said. "I will let you get back to work but will see you at lunchtime. I look forward to it."

"I do as well, Huijang-nim," Jin-woo said with another bow. Her laugh was musical and a delight to his ears. Jin-woo couldn't help but smile. It was that kind of laugh. He watched them walk away, sticking his tongue out at Ki-tae when he looked back and winked at Jin-woo. Then Ki-tae rounded the corner and was out of sight. Jin-woo turned to find Min-su and Jong-in staring at him.

"What?"

"You just make an impression wherever you go," Min-su said. "I'm trying to figure out your secret. I have yet to meet anyone who doesn't like you."

"You haven't met my aunt," Jin-woo said quietly as he took his seat.

"We'd best get settled," Jong-in said, laying a hand on Jin-woo's shoulder, and then he went to his own desk.

Once their on-site advisers came to get them, the day was a blur of activity. He and Min-su had done a good portion of the sorting, each picking which shots they thought were the best. When they were filming, some days seemed so long and others short, but when they looked at the actual footage, it was impressive what they had. At about eleven in the morning, their advisers, Kim Hyung-jun and Li Cheong-bo, both premier production engineers and editors in the field, sat down with them and looked at what they had selected.

"Hyung-jun-seonbae, are you thinking what I'm thinking?" Cheong-bo asked as he flipped through Min-su's selections.

"Definitely," Hyung-jun said. He turned to Jin-woo and Min-su. "We're going to split you two up."

"What? Why?" Min-su asked, surprise filling her voice before she regained control of herself.

"It's not a bad thing," Cheong-bo said with a laugh. "Sometimes we find enough to really make doing more than one video worthwhile. Given what you two have selected, this is one of those times. Min-su dongsaeng, you focused a lot on the dancing, with just enough of the story shots to convey the concept of the video, so you're going to work with me on a performance version of 'Crossing Time' while Jin-woo dongsaeng and Hyung-jun-seonbae work on the regular version."

"Seriously?" Jin-woo asked. He couldn't stop the smile on his face.

"Seriously," Hyung-jun mimicked with a laugh. "You two have a really good eye, a definite feel for it."

"Are you sure that's feasible with the budget?" Min-su asked. Jin-woo could already see the calculations running through her head. She had narrowed her eyes slightly, and one eyebrow kept going up and down as she worked·the numbers.

"The biggest portion of the budget is the filming. This part is less of a strain for us because we're a company, not an independent. We have more leeway with postproduction," Cheong-bo said. "It's not as if we're shooting more footage. We have everything we need right here for both videos."

"Stop overthinking it." Jin-woo laughed.

"It *would* be cool to be able to do two of them," Min-sun said.

"Then let's do it," Jin-woo said, giving them his best encouraging smile.

"Knock it off," Min-su grumbled, but she did smile... a little.

KI-TAE

KI-TAE AND HanYin followed Soon-joon and Godaeui into the CEO offices of BL Entertainment. He studied her as Godaeui took the seat behind the desk. It seemed so natural for her to be there. Yet it was also very odd. They'd never really been in the offices. Then something struck Ki-tae, and he turned to Soon-joon.

"So when you say you're going to talk to the president of BLE, are you talking to yourself in here?" Ki-tae asked. Soon-joon chuckled.

"No, I actually contact Godaeui, and we discuss whatever problem or concern I'm dealing with at the moment."

"I thought you were just the CEO and a manager," HanYin said.

"Well, my official title is CEO, but most people just see me as a manager. They bring things to me because they know they can and it will get addressed," Soon-joon explained. "I cannot sit behind a desk all day and push papers. The results would not be pretty, so I keep myself more directly involved with the business, as you know."

"Who else knows you're the CEO?" Ki-tae asked.

"All of upper management," Soon-joon said.

"And they know you're the owner?" Ki-tae turned to Godaeui. She nodded.

"They believe I travel a lot but know Soon-joon-nim keeps me abreast of everything. The only thing they do not know is Soon-joon-nim owns half the company. We have many business interests here and abroad. It is how we survive, by being smart and frugal. There are few things we splurge on, usually our living space, as that is our haven. The house is gorgeous, by the way, Táozi-chan. I love how you've combined the modern and traditional cultural styles of Korea, China, and Japan."

"I cannot claim total credit," Soon-joon said. "The boys had a hand in the house and how it looks. They helped make it our home."

"I wish the rest of the world was so," she said.

"Is ChenBao your real name, or is it just an alias?" HanYin asked suddenly.

"It is the name I was born with. Táozi-chan likes to call me 'Godaeui' to remind me I am so much older than he is," she said, shooting a teasing glance Soon-joon's way. "I call him by his given name to remind him he is Chinese as well as Japanese, and the two need not be mutually exclusive within him. He is stubborn, however."

"Is that why you keep switching honorifics? You call him Táozi-chan, but also Soon-joon-nim," Ki-tae pointed out.

"I try my best to adjust to the environment. In private he will always be Táozi-chan. While in public I will address him by his current cultural name and honorific."

"It also reminds me of happier times when I was a boy, so I don't mind when she addresses me that way," Soon-joon said. "I think we need to get back on track, though."

ChenBao sighed. "Yes. Please, take a seat."

"Why does that sound so ominous?" Ki-tae said as he sat in one of the wingback chairs placed in front of her black teak desk.

"It isn't," she said. "You are just worried about what you might hear."

"I think I have good cause to be," Ki-tae said.

"Such an adorable pout," ChenBao said, lightening the mood a little. "It is not as bad as you think."

"The options he has are not pleasant ones," HanYin said as he took a seat on the matching love seat along the wall to the left of the desk, nearest Ki-tae.

"True," ChenBao agreed. "Like calls to like, and it is the same for Vampires. Often if a Vampire falls in love, it is with another Spiritual Being: a Shifter, a water spirit, a Sorcerer, etcetera. That loved one will either be full-blooded or half or less, but there will be spiritual blood in their line within two or three generations at most. Vampires are the only Spiritual Beings, other than Shifters, that can be both made and born. You three are made. I am born. The whys and hows of that are unknown to me. We have no documented record of the origin of our species. Apparently we're a very secretive bunch, even from each other."

"That is very interesting," Ki-tae said. "But what does it have to do with Jin-woo-ya?"

"Patience," ChenBao said. "Once Jin-woo dongsaeng, you, and I have finished lunch, I will be able to more fully understand the bond between you. There have been occasions when a Vampire has fallen in love and bonded with a full human, but they are very rare."

"People would do this to themselves on purpose?" Ki-tae murmured. The idea was completely foreign to him. He couldn't even contemplate bonding with someone voluntarily.

"There are those who corrupt the bond, use it, and those they bind for their own purposes. They are rogues, abominations, and when discovered, they are hunted down and destroyed," ChenBao said softly. "We live a very long time. We watch the people around us grow old and die. We bury fathers and mothers, sisters and brothers, daughters and sons and lovers. To commit ourselves to someone is to show how much they mean to us. It is sacred."

"It doesn't feel that way," Ki-tae said, lowering his gaze to the floor.

"Ki-tae dongsaeng, the bond placed on you when you were younger, it was a perversion, an addiction forced on you," ChenBao said. "This bond between you and Jin-woo dongsaeng… it is very different."

"How?"

"Because there is mutual desire there," she said with a smile. "Or did you think I'd lost my sense of smell?"

Ki-tae could feel himself blush. He glared at HanYin when he heard his chuckle. "Shut it."

"I didn't say a word," HanYin said.

"You were thinking it."

"True, but I didn't *say* it, so you can't be mad at me," HanYin said with a grin.

"Yes, I can."

HanYin just smirked at him.

ChenBao raised an eyebrow and looked at each of them in turn until they settled down. Ki-tae shot his brother one last glare before turning his attention back to her.

"I believe Jin-woo dongsaeng is one of these rare humans, but there may be something more to it. As I said, I will need to spend more time with the both of you to ascertain if it is just a matter of his spiritual blood being more than three generations back, or if he's simply blessed to be *Xuè huǒbàn*, a blood partner."

"I've heard that term before," Soon-joon said, speaking for the first time in several minutes. "I have never seen one, though."

"As I said, they are extremely rare and sacred," ChenBao said. "There hasn't been any Xuè huǒbàn for at least a thousand years."

"How will you know if Jin-woo dongsaeng is one of these humans?" Ki-tae asked.

"You young ones do not pay attention to all your senses." ChenBao eyed Soon-joon. "Have you taught them nothing of their abilities? They should have mastered spirit sight by now."

"Do you know how long it took me just to get them to pick their clothes up off the floor?" Soon-joon said.

"Only half as long as it took us to teach you the same thing!" ChenBao shot back.

Soon-joon said softly, "I began with survival. I am… out of practice with the spirit senses. I have done my best."

"And you have done well, Táozi-chan." ChenBao smiled at him. "I know it is not easy to be a mentor and a parent. Your sons are strong, good men, and that is because of you and your love for them."

He hadn't just loved them; he'd saved them. Ki-tae was sure he would have been dead had Soon-joon not found him. He would have been one more unidentified body, someone no one would miss, food for the scavengers, had he continued to be bound. Soon-joon had saved him, clothed him, and fed him. He had taught Ki-tae how to read and write, to do math and to play the piano, among other instruments. He had taught Ki-tae so many things, had given him purpose, a way to express the music inside his head. There was no way Ki-tae could ever repay that, no way to truly show Soon-joon how very grateful he was. He lifted his head and looked at ChenBao.

"How will you know?"

"Your qi will reach out to each other, try to merge, to form a stronger connection than you have now. Right now you can only receive Jin-woo dongsaeng's dreams. You dream walk. It is… ephemeral."

"It doesn't feel ephemeral to me," Ki-tae muttered before clearing his throat and glancing around the room.

"Because it is you who consumed his blood, and not vice versa," ChenBao said. "He offered you his neck, did he not?"

"I…." Ki-tae paused, thinking back to that night, shifting in his seat. "I was feeding from the tech's wrist, but when I got close to him, he tilted his head, so yeah, I guess he did."

"Despite his lingering fear after discovering Vampires were real, he was still drawn to you, still offered you his blood," ChenBao said. "That is an interesting bit of information. Because he offered willingly and you drank willingly, you are connected when you dream. Intent is important in any type of magic or ritual. The will of those involved plays a large part as well. Have you drunk from him since?"

Ki-tae grimaced. He'd hoped she wouldn't ask that question.

"I can see you have." She laughed.

"Always from the wrist," Ki-tae reassured her.

"You may feed from others, but it will not be as satisfying, as fulfilling as when you drink from Jin-woo dongsaeng, and it may even make you ill," ChenBao explained. "Until we know more about Jin-woo dongsaeng, we can make no further plans."

Ki-tae wasn't sure he liked that idea. He didn't like not knowing what options he had. A part of him wanted to tell Jin-woo what was going on, but a part of him was afraid to. What if it was too much for Jin-woo to handle? What if he just decided to avoid Ki-tae altogether, to stay away from him and have nothing to do with him anymore? Ki-tae didn't know if he could handle that. In the time they had been working together, Ki-tae had gotten to know quite a bit about Jin-woo. He certainly knew how to please him. That would never be an issue.

"While I am here, I might as well go over the reports," ChenBao said. "You and HanYin dongsaeng are free to go, Ki-tae dongsaeng. I will see you in a few hours."

Ki-tae nodded and then turned to HanYin. All it took was a look for HanYin to understand. His arm landed heavily on Ki-tae's shoulders. When the door closed behind them, Ki-tae gave a sigh.

"Everything will turn out all right," HanYin said, always trying to make him feel better. "In the meantime, let's go into the studio. I have some tracks I want you to listen to. They sound off, and I can't put my finger on what exactly is making it not work."

Ki-tae nodded. The work would keep his mind off Jin-woo. At least he hoped it would. He needed a respite from the images that kept popping into his head when he thought about him. ChenBao and Soon-joon kept telling him this bond was not a bad thing, but he had only one incident to compare it to. Granted, matters were very different this time around, and granted, he was the one who caused the situation, but it was still terrifying to him, being bound to another.

Yet Jin-woo never made him feel threatened, never made him feel less than what he was, and never put him down. Threatened him? Sure, but in that playful way, and his growls were freaking hot. He was the perfect mix of sweet and innocent and sexy. He was smart and creative, talented, incredibly talented, and humble. Jin-woo didn't brag about his work. He was confident without being arrogant. Thinking about it, Ki-tae couldn't find a single flaw in Jin-woo. He knew he had them, everyone did, but Ki-tae hadn't seen them. Everyone seemed to love Jin-woo, and as long as they did it from a distance, and without laying hands on Jin-woo, Ki-tae was okay with it.

"You're thinking about Jin-woo dongsaeng again," HanYin said with a smile. "When are you going to admit you have feelings for him... and not just the carnal ones!"

"Aren't those the best kind?" Ki-tae asked, knowing he wasn't pulling off the innocent look by HanYin's eyebrow. "All right, all right, there may be some truth to what you're saying."

"Seriously? That's the best you can do?"

"What do you want from me, HanYin-a?" Ki-tae snapped, suddenly frustrated with everything. "I've never felt like this before. I don't know what the fuck to call it!"

"Love. It's called love, Ki-tae-ya, and it's a gift. You should cherish it."

JIN-WOO

JIN-WOO FOLLOWED behind Rhim Hyun-jo, Soon-joon's assistant, quietly. Nervous butterflies filled his stomach. He didn't understand why he'd been singled out to have lunch with the president. He wasn't anything special. He was just Cheong Jin-woo.

Hyun-jo stopped before a set of double doors. He bowed low, opened the door, and ushered Jin-woo inside. It was too weird. Hyun-jo didn't say much, apparently, being a man of few words, but he had a certain grace and elegance about him, a quiet confidence Jin-woo liked. It fit for him to be Soon-joon's assistant. When he walked into the office, he found Ki-tae seated in one of the chairs in front of a beautiful teak desk, and ChenBao in the large leather chair behind the desk. Ki-tae winked at him again, right before he licked his lips and smiled. Jin-woo gave him a pointed look. It was not nice to push Jin-woo's buttons while they were in the presence of BL Entertainment's president.

"Stop being an instigator, Ki-tae dongsaeng. You can pursue that later," ChenBao admonished with a grin. "Boys these days."

Jin-woo gasped in shock and dropped his gaze to the floor. He was so freaking embarrassed, and it was all Ki-tae's fault. Oh, he was so going to kill Ki-tae later! He bowed, muttering an apology.

"Do not apologize for being a normal, healthy young man. I'm not so old-fashioned as to not understand the way of things between people," ChenBao said with a chuckle. "Now lunch has already been prepared and laid out in my small conference room. Shall we eat, then?"

"Yes, please," Jin-woo said.

"After you, Huijang-nim," Ki-tae said as he rose to his feet.

"Such wonderful manners… when he wants to use them," ChenBao said as she led the way into a small room off her office. "You are quite the charmer, aren't you, Ki-tae dongsaeng?"

Jin-woo had never seen so much food outside a restaurant in his life. Did people really eat this much for lunch? He glanced at Ki-tae, who was watching him again, smirking.

"I didn't know what you liked, so I ordered a bit of everything," ChenBao said as she took a seat at the table. Then she patted the seat next to her, smiling at Jin-woo. He sat down, feeling incredibly nervous, although having Ki-tae there seemed to help calm his butterflies. When Ki-tae took the seat next to him, rather than sitting on ChenBao's right, Jin-woo smiled at him.

He turned to ChenBao. "*Jal meokkesseumnida.*"

Jin-woo waited for ChenBao to pick up her chopsticks and then took up the pitcher of water to pour for her and Ki-tae. Then he looked at the dishes spread before them. There was such a plethora of choices, and he wanted to try them all. Apparently Ki-tae thought he should too because he kept putting food in Jin-woo's bowl.

"Are you trying to make me fat?" Jin-woo whispered.

"I was just...."

Suddenly Ki-tae looked very self-conscious. He tried to draw his hand back, but Jin-woo caught his wrist. When Ki-tae looked him in the eye, he smiled. "It's all right. I was just teasing. It is very sweet of you. Thank you."

"I know I'm not very good at it, but I do try," Ki-tae said. He ducked his head and turned back to his own food, but Jin-woo could see the small smile on his face.

CHENBAO

CHENBAO WATCHED them silently, not saying a word as they whispered to each other. She huffed inwardly, as if she couldn't hear everything they said. It was very sweet, though, and so she chose to ignore any breaches of etiquette as Ki-tae kept selecting the choicest meats for Jin-woo. Each time another piece of meat was placed in his bowl, Jin-woo blushed. She was sure if she weren't in the room, Ki-tae would have fed Jin-woo, and Jin-woo would have let him. Ah, to be in love once more. It was a sweet feeling. Yet as much as she just wanted to watch them, ChenBao knew she needed to focus on her task. Soon-joon had explained Ki-tae's background to her. His phobia regarding bonds was justified, but it could also cost him the very person who could heal him.

Continuing to eat, ChenBao began chitchatting with Ki-tae and Jin-woo. She wanted to laugh at the surprise in their eyes when she easily conversed with them regarding the technical aspects of music production. While Jin-woo had no way of knowing exactly how much experience ChenBao had, Ki-tae should have known better.

"Are you enjoying yourself, Jin-woo dongsaeng?" ChenBao asked. "It seems a lot for you with school as well."

"I am, very much so, Huijang-nim," Jin-woo said, his smile honest and bright. "I'm learning so much, and it all makes a little more sense than just reviewing lecture notes."

"Good. I'm glad to hear it," ChenBao said. "Soon-joon-nim tells me you have remarkable talent. He said your presentation was amazing."

"Oh, it isn't just me, Huijang-nim," Jin-woo said, turning to face her fully. "Min-su-ya and Jong-in-a both are incredibly talented, just in different areas. Jong-in-a did a complete song analysis, and Min-su-ya is amazing, not only with the postproduction, but the financials as well. She also has a wonderful grasp of the creative aspect too. It was very much a group effort."

She smiled. "It pleases me greatly to see you sharing the credit with your friends. Too many people in this industry would not be so honest and humble. I will be having lunch with Min-su dongsaeng and Jong-in dongsaeng as well. I like to get to know people individually before conversing as a group. People act differently when with others, and it can be difficult to gauge what kind of person they truly are. I trust Soon-joon-nim's judgment; however, I do not rely solely on it. He said you were a good man, and I can see he was right."

ChenBao caught Ki-tae's proud smile and had to hide her own. She could see their qi swirling around them, reaching out to wrap around each other. Jin-woo was, indeed, one of those rare humans who could be a Vampire's xuè huǒbàn. Ki-tae was truly blessed by both the Gods and the Ancestors. It only needed the ritual and the binding of Jin-woo to Ki-tae to be a complete partnership. The question then became whether Ki-tae would willingly complete the ritual, and if he would reveal things to Jin-woo before he did so.

Once she assisted Ki-tae in resolving his romantic dilemma, she could then turn her focus to not only her other two grandchildren, but her child as well. She would not stand by and see Táozi spend the rest of his years alone. ChenBao smiled. Romance and love was a wonderful thing, yet the men she knew continued to mess it up. To be honest, the women of her acquaintance didn't do that great of a job with relationships either.

HANYIN

HANYIN SHUFFLED through his papers, the words playing through his head as he tried to work out the melody. The beat was clear, but the melody was giving him issues. He hummed a couple of different tunes, but none of them seemed to fit. He'd tried just writing, but that wasn't working either. He needed to hear it outside his head, and the best place to do that was in the instrument room. He nibbled on the tip of his finger as he kept walking. HanYin grunted as he encountered something warm and solid. Strong hands caught his upper arms, preventing him from falling on his ass.

"Whoa there. Are you okay?"

HanYin shivered at the sound of Jong-in's voice. "Please keep talking."

"What?"

"Uh." Heat filled his face, and HanYin took a step back, looking everywhere but at Jong-in. "Are you okay?"

"Yeah. I'm okay," Jong-in said quietly, pushing his glasses back up on his nose. "Where were you going?"

"The instrument room. I'm having some trouble with a song," HanYin said absently, staring at the page in his hand. Then it struck him. "You wouldn't like to help me out with it, would you?"

"Me?"

"Yes. I mean, your voice is… amazing… and your ear…. I could use someone else's ear," HanYin said, feeling hope blossom in his chest when Jong-in didn't immediately try to leave. "I was able to lay the beat track, but the melody is not quite right and it's driving me nuts."

"I suppose I could give it a listen," Jong-in said.

HanYin smiled at him. Impulsively he grabbed Jong-in's hand and ran to the instrument room. This was the first time since filming Jong-in had voluntarily stayed in his presence, and he wasn't going to waste it. He didn't even mind the chuckles that followed them. It wasn't as if he hadn't run through the building before.

When they reached the instrument room, HanYin let go of Jong-in's hand and closed the door behind them, then flipped the switch for the In-Use light and locked the door. It wasn't an overly large room, but it was built with soundproofing and didn't have any distracting features, such as a window where people could watch others working inside. HanYin didn't like being watched while he worked. It made him uneasy, especially when he was working on something personal. He ran to the piano. After setting the pages of lyrics on the music stand, he turned back to see Jong-in still by the door.

"Is something wrong?"

"No, I just haven't been in this room before." Jong-in made his way over to the piano. HanYin sat down and patted the seat next to him. Jong-in looked hesitant; HanYin thought he might decide to leave. He was surprised when Jong-in sat down. He pulled out his phone and ear buds, handing one to Jong-in. Inwardly he smiled because it meant they had to sit closer together.

"I put the beat on my phone so I could hear it while I worked on the melody," he said as he queued the track. He hit Play and then put his hands on the keys. As he played the first melody, HanYin glanced over at Jong-in. His eyes were closed, and HanYin could see he was actively listening to the music. Jong-in was so beautiful, and he smelled delicious, an earthy aroma. His fingers stumbled as his gut clenched with Jong-in's scent. He glanced over and saw Jong-in's eyes still closed. Perhaps he hadn't noticed the little stumble.

"This is a ballad?" Jong-in's voice caught him by surprise.

"Yes, a bit of a sad one." HanYin looked down at his hands sliding over the keys. "About loving someone and not knowing how to tell them how you feel, or even if you should."

Suddenly Jong-in put his hands next to his, on his, guiding them to different notes. He gasped, feeling the simple contact throughout his body. HanYin couldn't breathe. He'd never responded to someone so quickly before, never let anyone close enough to touch before he was ready. Yet with Jong-in, it was… right that he should touch HanYin whenever the desire struck him. HanYin wanted that, wanted to give him that permission. He looked away, feeling the blush in his cheeks.

"This is awkward. Hold still," Jong-in muttered as he rose. He moved the piano bench out with little problem, even though HanYin was still sitting on it. When he moved behind the bench and stopped right behind him, HanYin tensed. "Scooch forward a little."

Not knowing what he was up to, HanYin did what he asked. He nearly lost it when Jong-in sat back down, straddling HanYin from behind. He couldn't move, didn't dare to. He was pressed against Jong-in from ass to shoulders, and it was short-circuiting his brain. His hands trembled on the keys until Jong-in covered them once more.

"The words are sad but hopeful," Jong-in said, right next to HanYin's ear, torturing him with sound and touch as his breaths caressed the delicate whorls. His personal space was completely compromised, but HanYin couldn't and wouldn't have changed it for anything. He'd probably kill anyone who tried. "It has to have some lighter notes to show that hope. The beat track starts out slow but picks up a little at about midverse. There's where the melody can go to major, not too powerful, though. You don't want to change the energy."

"Hm," HanYin said, listening with only part of his brain. The rest of it was focused on the delicious sensation of Jong-in pressed against him from behind, a particularly favorite position of his.

"HanYin-a?"

"Hm?" HanYin turned to look at him, tilting his head up slightly. He got caught in Jong-in's eyes, the heat there, the intensity of his gaze. That look, so hot, sent his body into high speed. He whispered, "Please kiss me."

JONG-IN

THERE WAS no way Jong-in could resist the plea in HanYin's voice. He wasn't strong enough, not pressed up against him as he was, not feeling HanYin in his arms finally. He took his fingers off the keys and, cupping HanYin's face with one hand, wrapped the other around his chest. He took his lips slowly, brushing back and forth until HanYin opened with a whimper. Then he swept his tongue deep into HanYin's mouth, turning the whimper into a full-fledged moan. The sound vibrating against his lips only heightened the delicious pleasure that was kissing HanYin. HanYin gripped his wrists in his strong hands, but he didn't push Jong-in away. He only held him closer.

He wanted skin. He had to feel HanYin's skin beneath his hands. Still kissing, Jong-in slowly bunched up the fabric of HanYin's shirt until there was bare flesh beneath his fingers. Pressed so close, he felt HanYin's entire body tremble at the first contact and growled as his cock jerked in his pants. He rolled his hips, pressing against HanYin's ass tucked firmly between his thighs, only to feel HanYin press back. Jong-in wanted… so much. He pulled his hand from beneath HanYin's shirt and reached for the buttons, undoing them as quickly as the trembling would allow. They had to part to breathe, and he savored the way HanYin was panting. HanYin added his hands on the buttons, and soon the shirt went flying… somewhere. Jong-in pulled his shirt up and over his head, and it went the way of HanYin's. Flesh against flesh, Jong-in leaned his head down and licked HanYin's shoulder, tasting the salt of his skin. He nipped and kissed his way up the side of his neck, growling when HanYin tilted to give him more access.

"Yes, more, please more."

He ran his hands over all the exposed skin, catching HanYin's nipples and pinching them. HanYin cried out, tossing his head back and digging his fingers into Jong-in's thighs. So beautiful, he was so beautiful in his passion. Jong-in wanted to know what he looked like when he came. He didn't care if it was right or wrong. He wanted to give HanYin more pleasure than he'd ever experienced before. He wanted to ruin him for anyone else but Jong-in.

"You want more?"

"Yes," HanYin panted. "I want more… with you."

"HanYin."

"Please, Jong-in," HanYin whimpered. "Don't stop. Feels so good when you touch me."

Suddenly Jong-in stood up, taking HanYin with him. He kept his mouth on his shoulder as he gripped his hips and pushed him around the piano. He grabbed the longish hair on the back of HanYin's head, pulling his head back so he could kiss him again. He kept a hold of him as he worked the button and zipper on HanYin's pants. Jong-in could feel his cock pressing against the fabric, hard and insistent. He savored the whimpers each brush against that hot flesh brought from HanYin. He growled when the zipper caught, and then it gave way, and he wrapped his fingers around HanYin's cock. The hiss of pleasure was so worth it. He was going to do this. He was going to make love to HanYin, and damned be the consequences.

HANYIN

OVERLOAD. HANYIN was in sensory overload, and he still had clothes on. He pushed his pants down and off, hands trembling with each stroke of Jong-in's hand on his cock. God, it felt so good to have someone touch him again after so long, but he wanted more than Jong-in's hand. HanYin reached back and pressed his fingers against Jong-in's still confined cock. It felt huge. He managed the zipper and snap—wonderful invention, snaps. Silky heated steel filled his palm. HanYin caught himself against the piano as Jong-in shoved him forward. He dug his fingers into HanYin's hips, teased between his cheeks, and then stroked his opening and pressed deliciously against it.

"Yes," HanYin whimpered as he shivered and parted his legs as wide as he could before leaning farther over the piano.

"I...." Jong-in's hot breath puffed against the back of his neck. "I have no...."

"Don't stop," HanYin almost cried. He'd never been so aroused in all his long life. He felt as if he would burst into flame any second. He needed Jong-in inside him, one with him. "Please don't stop."

"I'm not going to," Jong-in whispered, his breath a lot lower than it was before.

HanYin's eyes went wide, and he bit back a scream as Jong-in speared his warm, wet tongue into him, moving it in and round his anus, working the muscles, preparing him. HanYin shook violently, biting his lip and tasting blood. Only one man had ever rimmed him before this, and it had definitely not been as good. He couldn't have said which way was up as Jong-in pushed and licked and teased him. Then he added his fingers, and HanYin couldn't stop his scream. He clawed at the piano even as he pressed back against Jong-in's mouth.

Then it was gone, and HanYin whimpered in protest, dropping his head to thunk against the piano. Jong-in buried his fingers in his hair and pulled his head up, stinging just enough. Jong-in took his mouth, claimed it, as he pressed his cock against HanYin's ass, parting the guardian muscle slowly, making HanYin feel the stretch just the way he liked it. He curled his fingers into Jong-in's hair as he accepted his tongue into his mouth, stroking it with his own.

Jong-in covered him completely, pressing him down as his cockhead finally pushed through. The stretch, the burn was perfect, and HanYin pushed back against it. Jong-in kept thrusting forward, barely giving him time to adjust until he was fully seated inside HanYin, hips flush with his ass. He paused, panting heavily in his ear. He wove his strong fingers through HanYin's, and HanYin almost cried at the sight of their hands entwined. Was there hope after all?

"HanYin," Jong-in whispered, his voice husky and low, filled with concern.
"You feel... so good inside me," HanYin said. "So tight and deep, perfect."
"HanYin."

Jong-in gently kissed the back of his neck, up the side, and along his jaw. HanYin turned to meet his lips, cupping Jong-in's face.

"Please... love me."

There was so much more to his plea than sex, but HanYin didn't want to think about that, at least not yet. He wasn't ready. He just knew he wanted Jong-in, wanted him to move, to feel him sliding in and out of his body, bringing them both incredible pleasure. He whimpered at the withdrawal, feeling empty for the briefest moments before Jong-in slid back into him. Jong-in nibbled his flesh, bringing stinging pleasure. He canted his hips slightly, feeling as well as hearing Jong-in's groan.

JONG-IN

SWEAT SLICKED their skin as Jong-in stood up, gripping HanYin's hips, and set a steady pace. Every other stroke pressed hard against HanYin's prostate, forcing a grunt of pleasure, a moan, a whimper. Jong-in could see the tremors shake his body, awed that he brought such a response from this beautiful man, awed he was even in this position. He wanted to make this so good for HanYin, but he wanted to see his face. He pulled out, drawing a cry of protest from HanYin, but he simply spun him around until they were face-to-face.

Jong-in saw the passion, the emotion in his eyes. He pounced, claiming HanYin's mouth once more, lifting him at the same time. HanYin wrapped his lean legs around his waist tightly and twined his arms around Jong-in's neck, participating fully in their kiss. Jong-in held him with one arm, guiding his cock back to HanYin's entrance. He pulled him down onto his shaft, swallowing HanYin's moan. Tight, he was still so tight and hot.

Jong-in pulled back, staring into HanYin's eyes. He slowed the pace, watching every emotion dancing across that beautiful face. They stared at each other, panting, quivering with the pleasure flowing through them just from being connected, joined. HanYin cupped his face, still staring into his eyes, and slowly rolled his hips, He caught his bottom lip between his teeth, letting it slide out slowly as he continued to move on Jong-in. Wrapping both arms around HanYin's waist to hold him securely, Jong-in moved to meet each downward movement of HanYin's hips. The only music filling the room was the sound of their moans. Jong-in took a few steps forward, bracing HanYin against the piano. He dropped his forehead to HanYin's shoulder, the feel of breath against his skin adding shivers to the pleasure wracking his body.

"So perfect," he murmured, barely able to get the words out.

"You feel so good," HanYin whimpered softly. "Jong-in… faster."

Jong-in turned once more and dropped to his knees, then laid HanYin on the floor. He bent one leg, keeping HanYin's thigh hooked high over his hip as HanYin unlocked his ankles from around Jong-in's waist. He leaned down and took one taut nipple into his mouth, sucking hard as he thrust faster, deeper. HanYin cried out, arching his neck and holding Jong-in's head to his chest. Heat surrounding his cock, the press of HanYin's firm body beneath his, the scent of their sex in the air, Jong-in took it all in, savored it, changing the angle to hear more of HanYin's sweet voice raised in pleasure. He left nipping bite marks in his wake as he sought HanYin's mouth once more. He reached his goal, growling softly when HanYin bit, a sharp pain stinging his lip. Jong-in chuckled at his aggression, enjoying the thrill it sent through him.

Too long had he denied himself this pleasure, this connection with another person. No, not with another person: with HanYin. With anyone else, resisting had been easy, but HanYin was different. HanYin made him feel things he'd never felt before, made him want things he knew better than to want. But this moment, right here, making love with HanYin, he would never regret it. He would never regret the joy he felt at HanYin's pleasure, at knowing how much he pleased his lover. If this was all he was ever going to have, he was going to make it impossible for HanYin to love another without thinking of this moment.

HANYIN

HE HAD been alive for well over five hundred years. In all that time, HanYin had never had anyone who made him feel this way. He gripped Jong-in's back, lifting his hips to meet each thrust into his body. He didn't even register the taste of Jong-in's blood in his mouth as more than an added pleasure buzzing along his nerve endings. He never wanted this to end. He wanted to spend forever tasting the line of Jong-in's jaw with the tip of his tongue, feeling the weight of Jong-in pressing him into the floor. He loved that sensation, of the strength. It took everything he had not to bite when HanYin ran his lips down along the line of his neck.

"Your eyes," Jong-in whispered. "So beautiful, glittering silver."

"So deep in me," HanYin murmured, wrapping his arms around Jong-in's neck once more as Jong-in slid his fingers up his back and curled over his shoulders from behind. Each thrust was harder than the one before, driving him forward, making the pleasure knot and pull inside him. HanYin would never complain. He wanted it, wanted Jong-in, wanted to hit that precipice and fly in Jong-in's arms. He wanted Jong-in with him when he did.

"Faster, please, faster, Jong-in."

Flesh slapped against flesh, whimpers turned to moans, and HanYin was on fire. He tossed his head back and forth, lost in the sensations wracking his body, tightening the pleasure at the base of his spine. He knew he wouldn't last much longer. Pressed between their bodies, his cock emitted waves of precum, slicking their bellies in a delicious slide.

"HanYin, I... I'm...."

Jong-in dropped his head, biting down on the curve of his neck. HanYin screamed as his entire body exploded with pleasure, arching sharply as he dug his claws into Jong-in's shoulders. The rush of seed between them was matched by the rush of heat as Jong-in came deep within him. He clamped down tight with his body, wanting to hold Jong-in there inside him. Jong-in's thrusts stuttered, faltered, and slowed, and still HanYin held him close. His muscles shook with the effort. Jong-in's hot breath puffed fast against his neck, his weight fully pressing him down, pinning him. He closed his eyes, reveling in the feel of Jong-in around and inside him. He could feel the little aftershocks, the occasional twitch of Jong-in's cock, the rug leaving imprints on his back, Jong-in's hair brushing his cheek. It was perfect.

When he felt Jong-in start to withdraw, HanYin tightened his grip. "Please don't leave just yet."

"I'm heavy," Jong-in-murmured against his neck, brushing his lips over HanYin's skin and leaving little lightning bolts in his wake.

"Not for me," HanYin said, placing a small kiss on Jong-in's shoulder. "You feel perfect, and I like the feeling of you pressed against me, like the weight of it."

"I don't want to crush you."

So happy, HanYin let the laughter bubble from within him before he bucked his hips and rolled them over until he was sprawled across Jong-in's chest. He placed a quick kiss on his nose and then stole a second from his lips, lingering over that theft. "Is this better?"

"I could get used to it," Jong-in teased as he kneaded HanYin's buttocks, then slipped his fingers between to stroke where they were still connected. HanYin's eyes widened, and he shifted his hips experimentally.

"Oh," he whispered as he stared down at Jong-in. "You don't soften right away."

"I…." Color flooded Jong-in's cheeks. "I…. It usually takes at least another before I start to… soften."

"Oh, such promise," HanYin said as he sat up and pushed himself fully down on Jong-in's still hard cock. "Delicious, you are so very…. Um, you feel so good."

Jong-in gripped his hips, and HanYin grabbed his wrists. He pulled them off and turned them until he could twine their fingers together.

"Let me," he whispered. Jong-in nodded but didn't let go of his hands.

Slowly HanYin rose, flexing his thigh muscles until he was almost clear of Jong-in's cock. Holding that intense gaze, he lowered his body gradually, watching Jong-in's eyes go wide and then close as his head fell back and thunked against the floor. HanYin smiled, happiness rushing through him at the obvious pleasure on Jong-in's face. He was going to give him as many orgasms as he could handle. There was no way he was going to let this go until it was unavoidable. If this was all he had, he was going to ruin Jong-in for anyone else.

KI-TAE

KI-TAE AND Jin-woo stood next to each other, waiting for the elevator. As much as he wanted to, Ki-tae didn't reach for Jin-woo's hand. On the set they had places he could drag Jin-woo off to, but there weren't many empty rooms at headquarters, and he wasn't one for janitorial closets.

"Oh, I am so stuffed," Jin-woo said.

"I wish," Ki-tae mumbled.

"What did you say?" Jin-woo demanded, his hands on his hips.

Just as he was going to say he'd said nothing, the elevator binged and the doors slid open. Ki-tae let out an internal shout of triumph. They stepped on the elevator. As soon as the doors shut, he pressed Jin-woo up against the wall and claimed his mouth in a hot, biting kiss. When he pulled back, they were both breathing heavily, and Jin-woo followed the kiss for a few seconds.

"I've been wanting to do that since this morning," Ki-tae murmured.

"Good, because I've wanted you to kiss me since this morning," Jin-woo said. "I still want to smack you for teasing me while we were with Huijang-nim, giving me that smirk, licking your lips. You're evil."

"No," Ki-tae said with a chuckle. "I just know what turns you on when I can't touch you as I want to. And I am not above using it to torment you with sweet anticipation."

"I cannot walk around the building with a hard-on, you ass!" Jin-woo said with a laugh, smacking Ki-tae's chest.

"Should I take care of that for you?" Ki-tae purred as he reached down and stroked Jin-woo through his pants. With his other hand, he hit the Stop button. "You're in quite a state. We can't have you distracted while you're working."

"Ki-tae-ya, don't you... holy shit!" Jin-woo shouted, banging his head against the elevator wall. "Ca... camera!"

"Maintenance had to disconnect this one this morning and the replacement won't be in until tomorrow." Ki-tae grinned, pointing to the wires dangling from an open panel in the ceiling.

"You planned this."

"Pure luck as to which car would open first."

Ki-tae would have chuckled, but his mouth was full, and he wasn't about to stop his current activity, not even on pain of death. As much as he wanted to take his time, work was not the place to do it. Ki-tae kept the pace steady, pulling Jin-woo's pants down far enough to reach the other interesting places between his legs. He loved the way Jin-woo tugged at his hair and how his hips bucked involuntarily.

Looking up from beneath his lashes, Ki-tae watched everything Jin-woo felt move over his face. When Jin-woo caught his bottom lip between his teeth, Ki-tae moaned. Jin-woo wasn't the only one who found that gesture hot as fuck. He cupped Jin-woo's balls, rolling them gently while taking a long, slow pull up the length of his cock. He loved that sweet taste and the musky smell of Jin-woo's arousal. It filled the tiny compartment, surrounding Ki-tae in its decadence. He wanted that scent all over his body. But more than that, he wanted Jin-woo's seed in his mouth.

Moving faster, Ki-tae stretched his fingers out and pressed against the sensitive skin behind Jin-woo's scrotum. He continued until he could tease that wonderful little opening between his cheeks. On a cry, Ki-tae got what he wanted and swallowed every drop. He caught him as Jin-woo's legs gave out. Ki-tae held him up and gently licked him clean. Then he tucked him back in his pants and rose, gathering Jin-woo in his arms.

"I cannot wait to get you into my bed, where we can take all the time in the world," he murmured against Jin-woo's hair.

"I want that too," Jin-woo said. "Shouldn't you start the elevator again?"

"I should, yes," Ki-tae said but made no move to do so. That would require letting go of Jin-woo, and he didn't want to do that. Jin-woo chuckled and then pushed on his chest. Ki-tae sighed but followed the unspoken suggestion. He hit the Start button reluctantly.

"Soon," Jin-woo said as the elevator moved again.

"Not soon enough," Ki-tae grumbled before kissing Jin-woo one last time as the bell dinged but before the doors opened. He smiled at Min-su as he walked out of the elevator, smirking when she covered her nose with the back of her hand and then glared at Jin-woo, who just shrugged and smiled.

CHEONGUL

CHEONGUL HELD the back of his hand against his nose. He glanced to his right; the instrument room, he wasn't going to go in there anytime soon. If his nose was right, and it generally was, HanYin had someone in there…. HanYin had Jong-in in there. Cheongul growled. How could Jong-in do that to Min-su? It was… it was just plain wrong. He made a move toward the door but then heard his brother's laughter. HanYin had been quiet since ChenBao's arrival. Could he really rob him of what joy he was finding now? No, he couldn't do that to HanYin, but he was going to have a talk with Jong-in the next time he got him alone.

"Oh my God, no place is safe!" Min-su grumbled. "I'm getting assaulted everywhere I go."

"What do you mean?" Cheongul was on full alert. "Who's assaulted you?"

"Not me, per se. Between Jin-woo-ya and Ki-tae hyung in the elevator and HanYin hyung and Jong-in-a in there, my nose is taking a beating!" Min-su said. "How do you stand it?"

"This is usually a safe spot to be when Ki-tae-ya's found someone he's interested in," Cheongul said with a small smile, but then he realized what else she'd said. "Wait. You know Jong-in dongsaeng is in there with HanYin-a?"

"Yes."

"And you're not mad?"

"Oh, I'm mad, all right. My nose can only take so much pheromones, you know," she growled. Cheongul tried his best to contain his shiver… and the urge to carry her off, consequences be damned.

"I mean you're not mad at Jong-in dongsaeng?" he clarified.

"Why would I be mad at Jong-in-a?"

"Aren't you… two… aren't you together?" Cheongul asked hesitantly, looking everywhere but at her. Then his gaze shot to her as she laughed a full belly laugh, nearly doubling over with it. "What's so funny?"

"The idea of me being romantically involved with Jong-in-a," she said after she could breathe again. "He's like a brother, and eww."

"But I thought… you were hugging on set." Cheongul couldn't get a complete sentence out. His mind had gone numb. "And… kissing."

"Hugging him on…. Oh, I remember. No, he is having a lot of issues right now. He pushes himself really hard, and it was starting to wear on him. I could see it, but he wouldn't talk to me, so I finally had enough and made him tell me. Then I hugged him, kissed his cheek, and we cried, and everything is a little better now."

"I'm sorry. I shouldn't have assumed anything," Cheongul said with a low bow.

"Wait... is that why you.... Is that why you left that day?" Min-su asked. "Because you thought I was with Jong-in-a?"

"Well, I... yes. I don't poach, ever. Period," Cheongul said, looking her dead in the eye. "And I don't share."

"Hm, that's good to know," Min-su said with the sexiest little smile Cheongul had ever seen. "Because I don't share either."

With those words, she walked away, leaving a stunned Cheongul behind her. What had just happened? He wasn't sure, but he thought she just told him she was single... and still interested. Cheongul tilted his head. Did that... mean what he thought it meant? No, couldn't be. He wasn't that lucky, and relationships never worked out for him. He turned and continued to the locker rooms. He had missed dance practice because of an interview, and if he didn't make it up, Gojira would put him through hell for who knew how long. She was not a forgiving woman.

KI-TAE

KI-TAE WALKED into the house, only to find everyone seated in the living room, staring at him. He looked from one to the other. HanYin gave him a small smile, Cheongul smirked, which was never a good sign, and Soon-joon wore his calm mask normally reserved for annoying business meetings or the three of them acting like toddlers on a sugar high. Yet of all the people looking at him, Ki-tae figured ChenBao's bright smile was the scariest thing of all. He slowly continued into the room.

"Why are you all staring at me like that?" he asked.

"Sit down, Sūnzi," ChenBao said as she patted the seat next to her. "I have news for you."

"Am I going to like this news?" Ki-tae said warily as he joined her on the couch.

"I'd like to think so, but it is all dependent on you and what you want," she said.

"Okay, I'm listening."

"Our luncheon was very enlightening," she began as she shifted to face him, crossing her legs tailor-fashion. "It told me a great deal about the relationship between you and Jin-woo dongsaeng. By the way, not very nice to tease him in public."

"He said the same thing." Ki-tae chuckled.

"I know." ChenBao gave him a smirk when he stared at her. "I heard him. I have very good ears… and my nose works exceptionally well."

HanYin chuckled, and Ki-tae threw a pillow at him.

"I wouldn't be so quick to laugh," Cheongul said. "Min-su-ya and I got a noseful outside the music room too!"

HanYin blushed furiously and hid his face in the pillow, curling around it.

"Delinquents, the three of you," Soon-joon said with a straight face, though his eyes twinkled with mirth.

"Much like their sire," ChenBao said pointedly. "Now back to Jin-woo dongsaeng and Ki-tae dongsaeng. You are very fortunate. Jin-woo dongsaeng is one of those rare humans who can be your xuè huǒbàn."

"What exactly does that mean for him and for me?" Ki-tae asked.

"It means he doesn't have to die, and he doesn't have to be turned," ChenBao said. "It means he can choose to complete the bond with you and be with you for as long as you live."

"What?"

"Xuè huǒbàn is a sacred bond between a Vampire and a human. We do not know what makes them special or so rare. All we do know is once the human chooses to accept the bond, they eventually stop aging. They and the Vampire become bound so deeply they share each other's lifespan. He will become like us, yet not. He will be harder to injure. He will be faster, stronger, his senses sharper, but he will not need the blood. In fact, it is his blood that will be most satisfying, most fulfilling and energizing to you. His blood will heal you faster. His blood will make it so you do not need to feed as frequently. He will sustain you, and you, him," ChenBao explained.

"How will I sustain him?" Ki-tae said, his curiosity getting the better of his fear.

"From observing the few xuè huǒbàn I've met, I've learned there is a constant exchange of qi happening whenever the two are near each other. Jin-woo dongsaeng's energy kept reaching out to yours, but since the bond isn't fully in place, the connection couldn't be made."

"What does completing the bond entail?" Ki-tae asked.

"Ki-tae?" The surprise in Soon-joon's voice was clear. "Are you sure?"

"I don't know," Ki-tae admitted honestly as HanYin scooched over to lean his head against his knee. Ki-tae absently ran his fingers through HanYin's hair. "I... I care about Jin-woo-ya—a lot. The more time I spend with him, the more I want to spend with him, if that makes sense. I even like the way he smacks me when he's mad at me. I don't get why he's so different."

"Many of my compatriots feel the xuè huǒbàn bond is predestined," ChenBao said with a gentle smile. "I don't know if that's true or not. I would like to think so."

"This bond, it does not frighten you anymore?" Soon-joon asked, his gaze intense.

"It's still a frightening thought," Ki-tae said, running his fingers along HanYin's neck and jaw, making him purr like a kitten. It was a soothing sound. "I hear the word 'bond,' and I get flashbacks. I... I still dream about him, and they're so *real*. It's as if I'm back in that brothel, chained to the bed, able to think of nothing but Sashin."

"Every night for over the last month," Cheongul said quietly.

"When you're away from him, you start thinking about the bond. It becomes the focus of your thoughts, rather than how you feel when you're with Jin-woo dongsaeng," Soon-joon said quietly. "It isn't so much the bond with Jin-woo dongsaeng as it is the *idea* of a bond."

"Yet the idea fades away when you're with him. You're no longer scared of it," Cheongul said. "I watch you smile at him as you haven't done for quite some time. He makes you happy."

"He does," Ki-tae said softly, hearing the wonder in his own voice. "Jin-woo-ya makes me happy."

That was a lot for Ki-tae to take in. He rose from the couch with one last ruffle to HanYin's hair and made his way to his room, lost in thought. When had that happened? When had he started to feel happy with Jin-woo? He couldn't pick any one moment. He just knew he liked being with Jin-woo, liked talking with him. He liked how they bantered and picked on each other. He loved Jin-woo's sweet kisses and his wicked tongue. He loved his laugh and his twinkling eyes. When had Jin-woo gotten past his defenses and under his skin?

Ki-tae crawled beneath his sheets and curled up on his side, staring out his window over the garden. There was so much going on inside his head. He'd spent years avoiding any kind of true commitment to anyone. Well, anyone save his family. He owed them everything, and he loved them more than his own life. But other people, he kept them at arm's length, so to speak. His relationships didn't last long. If he remembered correctly, his longest relationship was a month, maybe two. Eventually his lovers started talking living together, getting married, doing something to cement the relationship. That's when he walked away. No one was worth giving up his freedom, his sense of self... until now. And there was still one big question everyone had failed to ask.

What if Jin-woo said no?

SOON-JOON

"PARDON ME, *Sajangnim*," Hyun-jo said from the doorway. He approached the desk at Soon-joon's nod. "This arrived for you by courier, but there is no return address."

"Thank you, Hyun-jo hubae," Soon-joon said as he took the envelope, trying not to stare at him. Yet as soon as Hyun-jo turned his back, Soon-joon couldn't pull his eyes away.

Once the door closed, Soon-joon sighed. The envelope was nondescript, a normal courier's package from a company they used all the time. He opened it and let the contents slide out on his desk. Photographs spilled across the surface.

He picked up the top one, his hand shaking with fury. The intent was clear, and someone had just made a very big mistake. He studied the photo. Jin-woo's face was clear as day, as was Ki-tae's. The position they were in was, in a word, compromising. He shifted the other photos around until he located the note.

It wasn't uncommon for people to attempt to take advantage of a situation they stumbled upon. Some paparazzi used their photos to make a little extra money or as leverage for exclusive shots, and some companies went along with them. BL Entertainment wasn't one of those companies. Their entertainers were their family. In this case his children, and Soon-joon did not respond well to threats against his children. He glanced out the floor-to-ceiling windows to the right of his desk, where the evening sun colored the sky with pinks, blues, purples, and violets. It reminded him of all the things he should be thankful for. His sons were the most precious gift he could ever have, and he'd be damned if he was going to let someone hurt them.

Soon-joon turned back to his desk and reached for the phone, dialing as he read the note.

Ki-tae's reputation may not survive the backlash. You know how vicious the fans can be. And what would happen to his little friend? Take a good look. I'll contact you with the appropriate arrangements. After all, we wouldn't want Ki-tae to get hurt, now, would we?

"Yes, sir?" Hyun-jo answered.

"Contact Sara hubae and her team. Have them clear their schedule for this evening and secure the small conference room on the fifth floor. Have the social media teams closely monitor any references to Ki-tae dongsaeng until I say otherwise. Later in the week, set up a meeting with the head of security at the Seoul Olympic Stadium. Not his assistant. The head of security," Soon-joon said, surprised his voice sounded so calm. He felt anything but calm. "Contact ChenBao-nim's assistant and see if she can arrange for a meeting as soon as possible with myself and Sara hubae's team."

"Is everything all right, Sajangnim?" Hyun-jo had been with him for a very long time and had earned the level of trust Soon-joon afforded him.

"No," Soon-joon said. "But it soon will be."

JIN-WOO

THURSDAY MORNING, Jin-woo stepped off the train and headed toward campus, rubbing his hand through his hair. He had a meeting with his mentor, and then he had to head straight over to BLE headquarters. It seemed as if he hadn't been on campus for more than an hour in so long. He waved as people called his name. It was weird being noticed by others, and he wasn't sure he liked the idea.

"Oppa!" an almost perky voice called. Jin-woo turned to see who it was and spotted Mei sort of trying to run toward him but trying not look like she was running. Sometimes women really confused him. If he wanted to run, he ran.

As much as he was on a timetable, Jin-woo didn't want to be rude, so he waited for Mei to reach him. She was out of breath and doubled over, panting, when she finally stopped. Jin-woo chuckled softly. Mei was such a skinny thing. Shorter than Min-su, she was practically tiny, almost childlike. Wearing her hair in pigtails so often didn't help either. He wondered if that was why she did it, to look younger.

"I didn't think you would be on campus today," she said once she finally caught her breath. "I've looked every day."

"You looked for me? Why?" Jin-woo asked.

She looked down at her feet and said, "You haven't been around since you, Min-su unnie, and Jong-in oppa won the first part of that scholarship. It's been very hard getting along without you here."

"I'm sure everyone is doing just fine while we're away. Besides, this is a great opportunity for us," Jin-woo said with a smile.

"But you want to stay here, right? On campus?"

"I don't mind being on campus, but BL Entertainment headquarters is amazing," he said as he began walking once more. "And working there, they're like family."

"Don't you have to put up with those idols?" Mei's voice sounded colder. Jin-woo looked at her sideways. "I wasn't impressed with them. Do they bug you often for stupid things?"

"What are you talking about, Li Mei dongsaeng?" Jin-woo laughed. "The guys from Bam Kiseu are just as cool as the rest of BLE's staff. They really know what they're doing."

"I think you're just biased," she huffed. Her attitude was starting to irritate him. "I'm sure you could do much better than they could."

"Not hardly," Jin-woo said. "Look, I have to go meet with my mentor. You have a good day."

"Why don't we go out to dinner on Saturday?" she said, smiling at him and grabbing hold of his arm suddenly. She'd never done that before. She often crowded him and had little respect for personal boundaries, but she'd never touched him uninvited before. Only Min-su could do that. Well, Min-su and Ki-tae. Jin-woo glanced down at her fingers wrapped around his wrist. Was there a polite way to say "get your hands off me"?

"I can't. I have plans," Jin-woo said.

"Plans?" she demanded. "Who do you have plans with?"

"I don't think that's really any of your concern, Mei dongsaeng," Jin-woo said, getting tired of her behavior. They weren't close friends. She had no right to ask him such questions and touch him so familiarly.

"Cancel them." She smiled brightly, tightening her grip on his arm. "It will be much more fun with me."

"Look, I already made plans, and I'm not going to break them. I have to go, Mei dongsaeng. Have a good day," Jin-woo said.

He tried pulling his wrist free, but she wouldn't let go. Jin-woo ended up having to pry her hands off him. He turned and walked away when he was finally free. He could feel her gaze boring into his back. When he checked, she was staring at him, and her face was anything but perky and happy. A shiver raced up Jin-woo's spine. He'd never seen her like this before.

His phone alarm sounded, reminding him of his appointment with Teacher Kim, and Jin-woo picked up his pace. He had about ten minutes to get across campus to his mentor's office. If he didn't hurry, he was going to be late, and Teacher Kim didn't like tardiness. Fortunately Jin-woo managed to make it on time.

"Dongsaeng, it is good to see you," he said as he rose. Jin-woo bowed and then moved to take his seat by the desk, setting his backpack on the floor.

"It is good to see you as well, Seonsaengnim," he said with a smile.

"How are things going at BLE?" Teacher Kim asked, resuming his seat.

"They are going well," Jin-woo said. "We finished filming last week and started postproduction. After they had Min-su-ya and me go through the footage, Hyung-jun seonbae and Cheong-bo seonbae have decided to do two music videos: a regular version and a performance version. I'm to work on the regular, and Min-su-ya is working on the performance. It's amazing. I didn't think we'd shot enough to do that."

"It sounds as if you two are making quite the impression. What about Jong-in dongsaeng?" Teacher Kim asked. "I haven't been able to arrange a conference with him. He always seems so busy."

"He's doing well." Jin-woo smiled. "He's working with the sound engineers, and the other day, he helped HanYin hyung with a melody he was having trouble with. Everyone loves him. They even asked him to help with the initial recording of a band debuting soon."

"It seems to have worked out quite well for all of you," Teacher Kim said with a bright smile. "I am so glad. Now we need to discuss your academics. Some of your credits can come from your work at BLE, but there are other courses where you'll need to work on additional projects."

"I have several projects ready to submit for my fine arts classes. I sent in two engineering projects just this morning before I left home," Jin-woo said. "I talked to my other professors about the papers that are due next week, and they've agreed to allow me to email the papers and do a video conference presentation instead of coming to campus, to limit the disruption to my time at BLE. It seems they all recognize how important and beneficial this program is. I'm very lucky."

"You are not just lucky, dongsaeng. You are talented and have willingness to work. You are very personable and pleasant to be around. These are good traits to have in the entertainment industry. You also have the strength of will to hold fast in a sea of sharks." Teacher Kim chuckled. "Also a good trait to have when working in the entertainment industry."

"I hope to work with many great artists, engineers, and managers," Jin-woo said. "I've wanted to be involved in the music industry since I was old enough to understand what it was to make music."

"You are well on your way to making that dream come true," Teacher Kim said. "I am very proud of you. You have worked very hard to get where you are, and you deserve it. You, Min-su dongsaeng, and Jong-in dongsaeng are establishing a very strong network now, and that will work to your advantage after you graduate."

"Everyone there is so nice." Jin-woo laughed. "I met the president the other day. She asked me to have lunch with her. She wasn't at all what I was expecting."

"Oh? And what were you expecting?"

"I don't know, a matronly lady. You know, someone reserved and calm, traditional, maybe a little cold and distant," Jin-woo said, really thinking about his answer. "She was very approachable and laughed a lot. She teased Ki-tae-ya and Soon-joon hyung as if they were old friends. Yet she was graceful, elegant, and incredibly intelligent. I didn't expect her to know a lot about the ins and outs of the music production process, but she did. Talking with her was amazing, and I think I learned just as much from that conversation as I have anywhere else."

"Huijang-nim is an amazing woman," Teacher Kim said with a nod. "She can be very no-nonsense when the situation calls for it. She can also be very playful and friendly, teasing people as close friends."

"You've met her?"

"Yes. Soon-joon-nim and I have kept in touch over the years. One day we ran into each other by coincidence in a restaurant near BLE headquarters. I can't remember the name of it now, but he was there with Huijang-nim. I found her incredibly lovely both inside and out," Teacher Kim said.

"This is such an amazing experience. I'm glad other students will be able to go through it as well. I'm very happy that I am one of the first." Jin-woo grinned.

Teacher Kim and Jin-woo talked a little more, going over his grades and his reviews, adjusting his schedule to work around his time at BLE. When they finally got things arranged to where they worked for all involved, Jin-woo bid his mentor farewell and left.

As he left campus and walked toward Hongik Station, Jin-woo felt a strange sensation come over him. There was a niggling feeling right between his shoulder blades, as if he were being watched, and the person doing so was focused on that one spot. He stopped and looked around but didn't see anyone. It made him nervous, and Jin-woo quickened his pace. He felt a little better when he reached the station and boarded the train. Jin-woo found an empty seat, sat down, and pulled out his phone. He plugged in his headphones and put the buds in his ears, letting the sound of Bam Kiseu soothe his nerves.

When he got home that night, he was going to have to work on his song. He still hadn't figured out exactly what it was going to be about, but he had several ideas floating around on scraps of paper in his apartment. Jin-woo had to admit, to himself, at least, he hadn't been thinking about much of anything beyond sleep when he went home at night. The dreams of Ki-tae had not been as frequent, probably because of the many times Ki-tae cornered him somewhere to steal kisses or dragged him off to an empty room for something more. Not that he was complaining. Jin-woo would never complain about being with Ki-tae.

The day had been a long one. He'd been going since he woke up that morning, and Jin-woo hadn't stopped since. It took him three tries to get his key in the lock, he was that tired. After opening the door, he entered his tiny foyer-type space and kicked off his shoes. That felt so good. Jin-woo didn't really like shoes and preferred to be barefoot. He rounded the corner and stopped dead in his tracks.

His apartment was... trashed.

His TV was shattered, facedown on the floor. His chairs and sofa were slashed, the stuffing yanked out and thrown all over the room. His coffee table had been smashed, and shreds of paper were mixed with the stuffing. Jin-woo took several steps into the room. He knelt and picked up pieces of paper. One held the beginnings of a song, his project for part two of the scholarship. The others.... Jin-woo hiccupped, and tears slid down his cheeks. The others were pieces of a drawing he'd been doing of Ki-tae. Jin-woo snapped his head up, and he bolted up the small set of stairs to his bedroom, and another shock.

It was... pristine.

It was clean and tidy, too much so. Jin-woo wasn't a slob, but he wasn't a neat freak either. Someone had cleaned his room. Had more than one person invaded his home today? Could the same person have done both? It didn't make sense. He rushed over to his desk, searching frantically. His laptop had been with him, but his sketchbooks, save one, weren't. Jin-woo pulled open the cabinets. He stumbled backward when it hit him.

Every last sketchbook was gone.

Someone had gotten into his apartment, trashed his place, but cleaned his room, and then stolen all his sketchbooks. It didn't make any sense. Without realizing it, Jin-woo pulled out his phone and dialed the police. He didn't even remember the conversation. When he called Min-su, he was a little more coherent. Her calm voice helped him not to lose it. After he hung up, Jin-woo sat down where he was. Right in the middle of the chaos. He couldn't stay in his room, but being in the living room wasn't much better. Who could have done this?

KI-TAE

KI-TAE DROVE faster than the law allowed, and he didn't give a fuck. He wove through traffic and barely made it through a stoplight. He didn't care. Shifting almost faster than the car was capable of, Ki-tae stepped harder on the gas. Finally reaching his destination, he screeched to a halt and bolted out of the car, barely remembering to lock it, not that he cared if the damn thing was stolen right off the street. The flashing lights bothered his eyes, blowing his night vision to hell and back for a few moments. Then he was past them and inside the building. He didn't need to know what apartment Jin-woo was in. Ki-tae could sense his distress, and that was enough to drop Ki-tae's fangs. The elevator would be too slow. Ki-tae slipped into the emergency stairwell and looked up. Then he leaped, jumping from railing to railing and propelling himself up to the tenth floor. He pulled back just in time to *not* rip the metal fire door off its hinges.

"He's already told you he doesn't know who could have done this." Min-su's voice was angry. "How many times are you going to ask him?"

Ki-tae paused outside the door. If he went into that room in full rage, he wasn't going to do Jin-woo any good. In fact, he would probably make matters worse, because someone would be dumb enough to shoot him, and that would just piss him off even more. When he felt his fangs slide back up, he opened the door. Knocking was for when Jin-woo wasn't in distress. The minute he rounded the corner, Jin-woo cried out and was in his arms. His feisty man was really upset. He laid his hand on Jin-woo's hair, stroking it gently.

"It's all right," he whispered. "I'm here now."

"They… they stole all of my sketchbooks," Jin-woo cried against his chest. "They trashed my home and tore up all my work down here. They… they…."

"Shhh," Ki-tae said. "It will be all right, I promise."

He looked over at Min-su and mouthed "thank you." If she hadn't called him on her way here, he didn't think Jin-woo would have. It was clear Jin-woo was too upset to think of calling anyone but his best friend. While it hurt a little bit, Ki-tae could understand it. He would have called Soon-joon first.

"Who are you?" the officer asked, his hand poised over a notebook. He appeared to be the older of the two and seemed more laid-back, patient even. Ki-tae glanced at his tag, taking note of his name: Officer Lee.

"Jung Ki-tae. Janggyo-nim," he said, not letting go until Jin-woo pulled back slightly. He reached up and wiped the tears from Jin-woo's face. "Better?"

"A little," Jin-woo said. "I'm sorry I didn't call you."

"It's all right," Ki-tae said, giving him a little smile. "Min-su-ya did. I got here as fast as I could."

"What's your relationship with Cheong Jin-woo dongsaeng?" the other, Officer Kim, asked, clearly not pleased with having such a short answer to his partner's question.

"Very close friend," Ki-tae said, looking hard at the man. He didn't like the tone of that question. "We also work together."

"I thought you said you were a college student?" Officer Kim said, glaring at Jin-woo.

"I am a college student. I'm also doing work at BL Entertainment as part of an internship program," Jin-woo said. "After I left the campus, I headed over to BLE headquarters, and that's where I was all day."

"Jin-woo-ya and I are both part of that program, along with our friend Jong-in-a," Min-su said. Ki-tae could hear the slight growl in her voice, and he couldn't blame her. The tone of some of their questions was irritating him too. He just wanted to take Jin-woo out of there, at least for a little bit. He needed to not be surrounded by the remains of his home. It was a terrible thing to have your haven from the world invaded. It had happened to Ki-tae on a few occasions, and it always left him feeling unbalanced and vulnerable.

"You said you felt as if someone was watching you earlier today," Officer Lee said, flipping back in his notebook. "Was that the first time?"

"I mean, when the program was first publicized, I got recognized when I was out shopping a couple of times, but nothing like this," Jin-woo said. "It was almost a physical sensation, if that makes any sense."

"Believe me, it does," Ki-tae said with a wry chuckle.

"And you would know this because?" Officer Kim almost sneered. Ki-tae was getting sick of his attitude.

"On any given day, I can be followed by as many as thirty people who want to know my every move, every breath, what I ate, where I shop, what I do when I'm home alone, and whether I dress right or left," Ki-tae said.

"Why would anyone do that?"

"Because he's an idol," Min-su said. "While a fangirl or boy will obsess over an idol or group, a sasaeng will fixate on an idol and take it the point of invading the personal and private lives of their idols. They've been known to cause car accidents while following or chasing their idols, break into the idols' homes, tap their phones, all sorts of crazy and sometimes illegal activities. They're stalkers and can be dangerous."

"Have you ever reported these people?"

"Only the ones who do something illegal," Ki-tae said. "It's irritating to have them follow me everywhere, but as long as they don't cross that line, there's not much I can do about it. It's why we have a security detail."

"And where's yours right now?"

"Right here." Shin-bai entered the room, looking huge and intimidating. Ki-tae gave him a smile, and he nodded. "I am Cho Shin-bai."

It took another twenty-five minutes before the officers left. Ki-tae didn't think they were going to do much, but he knew Shin-bai would.

When the lights pulled away and no longer flashed on the ceiling, Shin-bai bowed to Ki-tae. "I'll be downstairs. Please don't take off like that again. It takes years off my life that I can't spare, watching you drive like a maniac!"

Ki-tae chuckled. "I'll try. That's all I can promise."

"It will have to do." Shin-bai sighed before turning to Jin-woo and handing him a business card. "If you need me, call. You are part of the family now. I do not take kindly to threats to my family."

"Thank you, Shin-bai hyung," Jin-woo said as he took it with both hands. "That means a lot."

Shin-bai nodded and then left the room. Ki-tae turned Jin-woo to face him, gently cupped his face, and kissed him. Then he pressed their foreheads together, feeling a sense of calm surround him and settle Jin-woo.

"Better?" he whispered softly.

"Yes, thank you," Jin-woo said. "I... I can't stay here tonight."

Min-su came up behind Jin-woo, watching Ki-tae carefully. "You don't have to. You can stay with me if you want. Or you could probably stay with Ki-tae hyung, right?"

"Of course." Ki-tae smiled at Jin-woo, hoping to get a response. While he got one, it wasn't Jin-woo's usual smile, and that bothered Ki-tae—a lot.

"I don't want to be a bother," Jin-woo said. Min-su immediately smacked him upside the head. Ki-tae couldn't help the growl. She just raised an eyebrow at him.

"I reserve the right to smack him when he says something that freaking stupid," she said with a huff. "I don't care how fangy you get at me. Mine are sharper, and I have four."

That got a bigger smile from Jin-woo, and Min-su stuck her tongue out at Ki-tae. In response, he reached out and flicked her nose lightning quick. She actually yelped and jumped backward. "Ow, you evil little bloodsucker!"

"That's not all I suck," Ki-tae said, leering down at Jin-woo.

"Oh, gross!" Min-su snapped. "Not an image I want in my head, damn you! At least not with you and Jin-woo-ya!"

"She's very visual." Jin-woo chuckled.

Ki-tae smirked at Min-su before turning back to Jin-woo. "Why don't you put a bag together for a couple of days. I'll take you to my apartment. It's near headquarters, so you won't have far to travel to get there."

"Do you have a lot scheduled this week?" Jin-woo's voice seemed small, and Ki-tae pulled him close once more. "I.... It's stupid, but I don't really want to be alone."

"It's not stupid, Jin-woo-ya," Min-su said as she rubbed his back. "Someone broke into your home and did some nasty and decidedly weird shit. It's understandable to be scared."

"I've never had this happen before. They trashed my living room and cleaned my bedroom. They stole all my sketchbooks but left the drawing of Ki-tae-ya torn to shreds in the living room. Why would they do that?"

"For right now, you're going to stop thinking about it as best you can," Ki-tae said. "You're going to grab some clothes and necessities and come to my place. We'll worry about cleanup later."

"Okay," Jin-woo said. "I'll just throw some things into a bag. I'll be back in a minute."

Ki-tae watched Jin-woo slowly climb the stairs to his room. When he was out of sight, Ki-tae turned to Min-su. They walked farther away from the stairs. Then he glanced around, inhaling. Something niggled at his senses, but he couldn't place it. There was an overlying chemical scent that was masking a lot of scents in the room.

"I can't get a clear mark on anything," Ki-tae said. "I mean, I can smell Jin-woo-ya, but his scent would be the strongest and the hardest to disguise. I haven't been here before, so I don't know what scents are supposed to be here and what aren't."

"Whoever did this cleaned more than just his bedroom," Min-su said. "They wiped down the place to get rid of fingerprints, and they used some sort of chemical to distort what couldn't be wiped away. That's one smart bastard... or someone who watches way too many crime dramas. I can't get a clear scent either, which pisses me off even more. Everyone needs a place where they feel safe, and this bastard just took away Jin-woo-ya's."

Ki-tae pulled out his phone and tapped out a message. "That's my address and home phone. You have my cell. I'll put you and Jong-in dongsaeng on the list at the security desk. On Sunday we all have dinner at Soon-joon-nim's house. When he's feeling a little more settled, I'll see if he wants to come with me. I don't have anything scheduled for tomorrow, so I can stay with him if he isn't up to going in."

"Thanks. I feel better knowing he's not going to be alone," Min-su said. "Hopefully this was a one-time thing. I want to say it was random, but there's no way."

"What are you two plotting?" Jin-woo asked as he came down the stairs, a small suitcase in one hand and his backpack on his shoulder. He looked exhausted.

"Nothing," Ki-tae said with a smile. "I just gave Min-su dongsaeng my address and phone number. I'll also put her and Jong-in dongsaeng on the security clearance list so they can come visit you when you want them to."

"I really feel like...."

"If you say the word 'burden,' I will hit you twice," Min-su growled. "You're my friend, Jin-woo-ya. This is what friends do."

"Is it?" Jin-woo looked at Ki-tae. "Is this what friends do?"

"Well, I'll be honest. The idea of having you in my home makes me very happy. I just wish it wasn't under these circumstances," Ki-tae said, rubbing his hand through his hair with a chuckle. "I've been dreaming about you in my house for a while now."

"And there go the pheromones," Min-su grumbled with a sneeze. "Can't you two contain it until I leave at least?"

"Then go already," Jin-woo said with a halfhearted smirk. Min-su hugged him and then bonked his forehead with hers.

"Call me when you get there, okay?" she said. "Don't make me come searching, because I will not respect a closed door in this case."

"Nothing is going to happen," Jin-woo protested.

"Then I will lose all respect for you," she teased. "I'll talk to you later."

She gave him another hug and then walked out the door, leaving Ki-tae and Jin-woo alone among the chaos. Ki-tae held out his hand. He didn't like how Jin-woo's hand shook as he took it. "Come on. Let's get you out of here."

Once Jin-woo had closed and locked the door, Ki-tae pulled him to his side and wrapped his arm around him. He didn't say anything. There was only so much to say in this situation. No matter what, Jin-woo's haven had been taken from him. They took the elevator down. Ki-tae leaned against the corner, Jin-woo held firmly against him. Outside Shin-bai was waiting by Ki-tae's car. He took Jin-woo's suitcase and stored it in the trunk.

"You will drive more responsibly on your way home, correct?" Shin-bai said. "Do not shave any more years off my life."

"I will," Ki-tae said, giving Jin-woo a side hug.

Shin-bai nodded and then opened the passenger door for Jin-woo as Ki-tae slid into the driver's seat. He closed it and then tapped on the roof before getting into his own vehicle. Ki-tae waited until Shin-bai was ready and then slowly pulled out onto the street, his speed much more sedate than when he arrived earlier.

"I always wondered," Jin-woo said absently.

"Wondered what?"

"What you listened to in the car," Jin-woo said. "I mean, do you listen to your own songs? You sing them for weeks on end. Do you ever get tired of hearing them?"

"Not really," Ki-tae said as he checked his mirror and then changed lanes. "I mean, I listen to other groups. I like 2NE1 and Big Bang, Rain, and BTS. B.A.P. is pretty good too, and Block B, they're funny as hell, but when they get serious, it's still damned good music. I also listen to Mozart and Bach, and I like Wagner."

"What is the one band you listen to that no one would ever picture you listening to?" Jin-woo asked.

Ki-tae glanced at him and smiled. "You really want to know?"

"Yeah, I wouldn't have asked if I didn't."

"I listen to Motionless In White and Asking Alexandria," Ki-tae said and then hit Play on his stereo. "This is one of my mixed playlists. The first song is called 'Reincarnate' by Motionless In White. I usually do about three songs in the same genre and then change to a different one, so the next two should be either Asking Alexandria, probably 'Death of Me' or Five Finger Death Punch 'Jekyll & Hyde.' It's pretty eclectic."

"I'd say so," Jin-woo murmured as the music began to play. He leaned his head back and closed his eyes, taking in the heavy guitar and drums and the deep screams of the vocalist. When Ki-tae glanced over again, he was bobbing his head to the beat. For several minutes the car was filled with nothing but music, and that seemed to soothe them both.

"So what do you listen to that no one would suspect?" Ki-tae said as he made the turn onto his street.

"You really want to know?" Jin-woo shot his words back at him.

"Of course. I wouldn't have asked if I didn't." Two could play that game.

"I listen to Right Said Fred, Shakira, and Paul Young," Jin-woo said. Ki-tae chuckled. "What? What's so funny?"

"I love the song 'You're My Mate,'" Ki-tae admitted, turning into the parking garage. "Paul Young I haven't heard, but Shakira dances like a dream. No one should be able to control their body that well. She has a unique voice too. I always thought she looked like she was having so much fun doing her thing."

"I think the really good ones do enjoy it. I mean, what's the point if you don't love music?" Jin-woo asked.

"I couldn't even begin to answer that question," Ki-tae said as he parked the car. "We're here. You ready?"

"Yeah. I'm so tired, Ki-tae-ya," Jin-woo said. His voice sounded distinctly watery.

"Come on. Let's get you upstairs." Ki-tae leaned over and gave him a gentle kiss.

By the time the elevator reached Ki-tae's floor, Jin-woo was practically asleep standing up. Ki-tae chuckled softly. He carefully shifted Jin-woo until he could squat slightly and get him on his back. Ki-tae hoisted him up and then grabbed his suitcase before wrapping his arms securely around Jin-woo's thighs. If he didn't have to grab the suitcase, too, he would have just hooked his hands under Jin-woo's ass. When he reached his door, Ki-tae dropped the suitcase to fish for his keys without dropping Jin-woo. That would not be an auspicious start to Jin-woo's stay.

As tempted as Ki-tae was to put Jin-woo in his bed, he was a good boy and put him in the guest bedroom across the hall. After removing only his shoes, he tucked Jin-woo in and left the small lamp on the nightstand on so there would be some light if Jin-woo woke up. He tiptoed out of the room and put Jin-woo's shoes by the door. Then he padded, barefoot, to his own room.

This was his home away from home. He grabbed the cordless phone on his way and, after taking the two steps down into his living room seating area, he curled up on the couch and dialed the security office. It didn't take long to get that squared away. Then he pulled out his cell and sent a text message to Min-su, letting her know they'd made it and that Jin-woo was out cold. He'd call Soon-joon in the morning and let him know what was going on. Right now he was beat and wanted his bed, preferably with Jin-woo in it, but he would have to deal with that disappointment for right now.

Ki-tae was not necessarily a neat person. His clothes ended up strewn over the soft leather chair set at an angle about three or four feet from the foot of his bed. Everything in the room was a shade of that dove gray, with darker gray and black accents. His bed was a platform style in a light pinewood. The headboard was padded and covered in almost the same shade as the wood. His linens were a darker shade of gray, not quite the same color as a stormcloud, but rather the medium gray of a storm building. He had matching nightstands, with a single shelf and two box storage slots underneath, on either side of his bed. Pillar lamps sat on each nightstand. Perhaps Ki-tae's favorite piece in his room was the cherry blossom tree branches stretching across the ceiling and down the wall behind his bed, giving an impression of lying beneath the trees. He really liked that sensation.

Ki-tae sighed as he slipped, naked, between the soft sheets of his bed. He was exhausted. He might be a Vampire, but it wasn't like in the movies. He got tired, had to eat food as well as consume blood, and could get hurt, just not as easily as a human could. He'd been on the go all day, starting with dance practice at eight in the morning. Then interviews, guest appearances, radio shows, and a photo shoot for a new clothing line. Plus the minute he sensed Jin-woo's distress, he went into heightened defense mode, making it hard to function without doing damage to people who were in his way. He was beat. Five minutes after his head hit the pillow, he was out.

A few hours later, there was a gentle knock on his door. Ki-tae mumbled and then rolled over. The knock came again, a little louder, and then he heard Jin-woo call his name. Ki-tae was immediately awake. He called for Jin-woo to come in as he sat up and rubbed his eyes. He normally didn't wake up well, but he'd wake up for Jin-woo. His door opened, and Jin-woo came around the corner.

"Are you okay?" Ki-tae asked softly.

"I, yeah…. No, no, I'm not," Jin-woo said. "Can I…."

Before Jin-woo finished speaking, Ki-tae held up the edge of the blanket. Jin-woo rushed to the side of the bed, shucked his jeans and T-shirt, and climbed in. He snuggled close as if uncaring Ki-tae was completely naked beneath the sheets. Ki-tae bit back a hiss as Jin-woo's legs tangled with his, and he laid his head on Ki-tae's chest. It was going to be a long night, but Ki-tae didn't care. Jin-woo needed this, not sex, right now. He closed his eyes and went back to sleep, his arms firmly around Jin-woo.

Sunlight filtered through the pale gray sheers covering the floor-to-ceiling windows. Ki-tae's eyes snapped open, and he sucked in breath as hot, wet heat encased his shaft. Immediately he buried his fingers in Jin-woo's hair as he dug his other hand into the sheets, his claws sliding from his fingertips, tearing them. He panted for breath as Jin-woo flicked his tongue against his frenulum, sending sparks shooting… everywhere. Ki-tae gasped, his fangs dropping, his neck arching, his eyes rolling back in his head. Jin-woo knew exactly what did it for him. The pinches to his nipple made Ki-tae growl, while the rolling of his balls between Jin-woo's fingers stole his breath away. Ki-tae parted his legs wider, giving Jin-woo more room.

And then the wonderful sensations went away. Ki-tae opened his eyes, searching for Jin-woo, only to find him straddling Ki-tae, completely naked. He grabbed Jin-woo's hips and lifted, stopping him from dropping any farther.

"Please tell me this isn't gratitude for letting you stay," he said huskily, trying to maintain control when all he wanted was Jin-woo wrapped around him.

"No, it's not," Jin-woo said with a smile. "Gratitude is the breakfast I'm going to make you once we're awake again. This is because I've wanted to make love with you since our first kiss. This is because I want you buried deep inside me, making me feel so hot and sexy and desirable. This is because I know you want me too."

"Good," Ki-tae growled before he surged upward and twisted, holding Jin-woo so he didn't go flying off the bed and taking his mouth in a hungry kiss. Then he changed it, sipping at Jin-woo's mouth, lightly licking his bottom lip until Jin-woo gasped, and then slowly thrusting his tongue deep. He gentled his hands, stroking lightly over Jin-woo's arms, his sides, over his hip and thigh. Ki-tae hooked Jin-woo's thigh and lifted it over his hip as he settled between Jin-woo's legs. Then he stopped and looked into those gorgeous brown eyes.

"Ki-tae-ya?" Jin-woo questioned.

"Are you sure, Jin-woo-ya?" Ki-tae asked softly, nervousness filling him.

"Yes, I'm sure," Jin-woo said, cupping his face. Ki-tae turned and kissed his palm.

He followed the line of Jin-woo's arm down over his shoulder, pausing long enough at the bend of his elbow to give it a little lick, making Jin-woo giggle. He continued upward, nibbling along the line of his shoulder, then nipping at his neck, making Jin-woo arch and give him more access. Ki-tae chuckled against his skin, feeling the full-body tremor he caused. Jin-woo really liked that.

"You want me to drink from you, don't you?"

"Not until you're inside me," Jin-woo panted, gripping Ki-tae's shoulders and digging in his nails. He moved his legs restlessly.

Ki-tae smiled. He definitely liked that answer. He reached over to his bedside table and grabbed the lube from inside the drawer. He paused at the condoms. He couldn't transmit or carry, but he didn't know how comfortable Jin-woo would be with bareback. "I can't give you anything, but do you want me to use a condom anyway?"

"Really?" Jin-woo's eyes widened in surprise.

"Really." Ki-tae smiled. "Our bodies kill any diseases."

"We'll never have to use a condom?" Jin-woo asked again.

"Not unless you want me to," Ki-tae said, placing a kiss on his nose.

"Are you kidding?" Jin-woo smiled. "If we don't have to use one, then we don't. I want to feel you without anything between us."

"As you wish," Ki-tae purred, then took his mouth in a deeper kiss as he dropped the lube on the bed next to Jin-woo's hip.

He pulled away, sucking gently on Jin-woo's bottom lip before kissing his chin, then licking his neck, then sucking on the hollow at the base of his throat. Ki-tae took the time to nip the length of each collarbone before circling down to take one dusky nipple into his mouth. Jin-woo's sweet cries filled his ears. His lover was not quiet, and Ki-tae adored that. He began gently and then increased the pressure before biting slowly. Jin-woo bucked beneath him, and Ki-tae chuckled, his breath teasing the wet nub. Then he moved across Jin-woo's chest and lavished the same attention on his other nipple. One day he was going to make Jin-woo cum just from playing with his nipples, but not today.

He loved the slick wetness Jin-woo's cock left on his belly as he slid down, pausing to run the tip of his tongue along the ridges of his abdomen. Jin-woo still gripped his shoulders. He could feel the trembling in his hands as Jin-woo tried to hold on. Ki-tae took that as a personal challenge, to break that control. Instead of continuing to the lovely hard shaft oozing precum against their skin, Ki-tae followed the line of Jin-woo's Adonis belt, up to his hipbone. He nibbled and licked and kissed, listening to the sounds of Jin-woo's whimpers and pleas. Then he made the return journey, only to bypass Jin-woo's cock in favor of following the same path on the other side of his body. That earned him little snarls of frustration. Ki-tae grinned.

"You are deliberately trying to drive me insane," Jin-woo panted breathlessly.

"Something like that," Ki-tae murmured against his flesh. He pushed Jin-woo's left leg out and followed the bend with his tongue, his cheek brushing Jin-woo's scrotum, eliciting a cry. He rubbed his nose along that sensitive sac on his way to the bend of Jin-woo's other leg, licking delicately at the crease as he went. Each little cry sent jolts of pleasure through Ki-tae. This close, he could see the fine trembling of Jin-woo's body. He wanted more. He wanted Jin-woo to come apart.

"Ki-tae," Jin-woo moaned. "I'm going to seriously hurt you if you don't get on with it."

"I thought I was," Ki-tae purred.

"I want you inside me," Jin-woo whined.

"So you want me here?" Ki-tae lathed the tip of his cock slowly, making sure to catch all the precum, savoring the taste. Jin-woo screamed and bucked once more.

Ki-tae rode out the movement of his hips before pinning them to the bed and taking his cock on one fast slide, allowing it to pass into his throat with ease. He bobbed his head, twisting slightly and sucking hard. Jin-woo clenched his fingers in his hair, giving just enough pain to heighten Ki-tae's pleasure. Then he slowed. Shifting his weight, Ki-tae grabbed the lube. He flicked the cap open with the tip of his thumb and poured some onto his fingers. He slid his shoulder underneath Jin-woo's left leg and pushed the right outward, giving him greater access. He looked up at Jin-woo from beneath his lashes, catching his gaze.

"Your eyes are silver," Jin-woo whispered with a small smile, reaching out to run the tips of his fingers from Ki-tae's temple down his cheek and along his jaw. "So beautiful."

It pleased Ki-tae that Jin-woo liked his eyes, that he cared enough to comment on it. He'd never been able to be this relaxed with a lover, this... free. He didn't have to hide his eyes or his fangs from Jin-woo. He accepted them as part of Ki-tae. With care, Ki-tae slid one finger inside Jin-woo's passage, circling gently to the soft whimpers and moans. He watched Jin-woo's face for any signs of pain, continuing the leisurely suction on his cock. It became all about pleasing Jin-woo. Soon one finger became two and then three as Jin-woo's body adjusted to the intrusion. When he began rocking his hips down on Ki-tae's fingers, he knew Jin-woo was ready.

Ki-tae pulled his fingers free, smiling at Jin-woo's almost mournful cry. "Easy, my beloved, I am not leaving you."

Jin-woo didn't respond, and Ki-tae quickly looked up. Jin-woo's eyes were closed, his head turned to the right, the line of his neck exposed. His lower lip was caught between his teeth, and he played with his own nipple. Ki-tae groaned at the sight. His Jin-woo looked so sweet and innocent but was deliciously wicked. He shifted, moving up Jin-woo's body until they were face-to-face. Jin-woo turned to him, his pupils blown with his desire. Ki-tae's gut clenched. Such an erotic sight, his Jin-woo. There was no way Ki-tae couldn't have kissed him at that moment. He pounced, feasting on already swollen lips as he positioned his aching cock against Jin-woo's entrance. When he pulled back, Ki-tae gave him the smirk he knew Jin-woo adored and pushed forward slowly. Jin-woo's eyes practically rolled into the back of his head, and his hands flew to Ki-tae's shoulders. He lifted those lean legs and clamped them around his hips just as the muscle gave way and Ki-tae slid inside him with an almost audible sound. Then he stopped and watched Jin-woo's eyes snap open.

"Watch me," he whispered. "Feel me within you."

He didn't thrust fast into Jin-woo. Ki-tae wanted him to feel every inch of his cock sliding deep, just as Jin-woo wanted. He took his time watching the emotions, the pleasure, chase across Jin-woo's face.

"You feel…," Jin-woo gasped. "So good. Deeper, Ki-tae, please."

"Not going to stop until I'm all the way in," Ki-tae promised.

Hot, so hot and tight and perfect, that's how Jin-woo felt as Ki-tae slid deeper and deeper. He kissed his cheeks, his mouth, his neck, his chest, anywhere he could reach. Then their groins were pressed together, and Ki-tae was all the way in. He took a deep breath, trying to stop himself from cumming immediately. Jin-woo felt so… perfect, so right. It was almost surreal.

After several attempts, Ki-tae finally managed to get words out. "Are you all right?"

"I'm… perfect," Jin-woo said on a soft moan as he twitched his hips, his arms wrapped around Ki-tae. He whimpered softly. Ki-tae could read it on his face. Jin-woo wanted more, wanted Ki-tae to move, to push them along until they both came hard.

He pulled back, feeling Jin-woo grip at him, trying to hold him in. When just the head of his cock remained, Ki-tae thrust fast and deep. Jin-woo's scream echoed through the room. Again and again Ki-tae withdrew slowly, only to sink back in fast, pressing his cock against the gland, the source of Jin-woo's pleasure. Soon they were both slicked with sweat, Jin-woo not being a passive partner. He met each of Ki-tae's thrusts, kissed him just as hungrily, tortured him with pinches to his nipples, and dragged his nails down the length of Ki-tae's spine. Ki-tae gasped as Jin-woo found the hot spot at the base of his spine, the two little dimples above his buttocks. Ki-tae laughed softly when he could breathe again.

"Found one." Jin-woo grinned.

"Oh yeah?" Ki-tae gave a twist of his hips, and Jin-woo groaned long and loud.

"Still found one," Jin-woo panted. He pulled Ki-tae down for another kiss and thrust his tongue forward. Ki-tae loved it when Jin-woo got aggressive. The next thing he knew, Ki-tae was fighting his body not to cum as Jin-woo stroked his fangs with his tongue. He tore his mouth away on a loud feral roar. "Another one."

Ki-tae didn't say a word. He simply moved, rolling his hips and thrusting deep. He reached down and pulled first one leg and then the other over his shoulders, nearly bending Jin-woo in half as he increased the speed of his movements. Jin-woo could do nothing but scream and moan and cry out his pleasure as he was driven to the edge, the sounds punctuated by the smack of flesh against flesh. The smell of sex filled the air, encompassing them in the warm, hot scent of their loving. The urge was so strong. All he had to do was lean down and sink his fangs into the column of Jin-woo's neck and drink. He could almost taste the sweetness. He wanted that, but he wanted it to be Jin-woo's choice. He didn't want to take that from him. He struggled to keep his thirst in check, struggled to prevent himself from losing control.

"Ki-tae…," Jin-woo said as he turned his head.

Ki-tae could no more resist that silent offer than he could resist breathing. He grabbed hold of Jin-woo's hair, clenching his fingers tight, and sank his fangs deep into Jin-woo's neck, taking blood straight from his heart for the second time. He drank, listening to the harmony of Jin-woo's voice raised on a cry as hot wetness spread between them. Jin-woo's body clenched around his cock, pulling him along, and Ki-tae continued to drink even as he came. He continued through the fine tremors shaking their bodies and only stopped when Jin-woo passed out from the pleasure. Then his strength gave out, and he collapsed on top of Jin-woo, breathing heavily against his neck, his nose pressed against him. Ki-tae snaked his tongue out and licked delicately at the wounds, getting the last little drops and sealing them. Then he closed his eyes and slept.

IT WAS unacceptable, simply unacceptable. Things would have to be taken to the next step. The plans would have to be accelerated. Unacceptable but unavoidable. Clearly the lesson had not been learned. Cleary further instruction was needed. He would learn the folly of his ways. He would learn to do as he should. He would learn or he would pay in blood.

The leather buckles on his boots jangled as he walked over to the board. Pictures, notes, pushpins, the map of Seoul was covered with them. To the left was a map of Asia marked with more pushpins. Each location carefully noted with date and time. Each one a music venue. Each one a potential target location. One of them would prove to be the right place, but he had yet to determine when to strike. The time wasn't right yet. It was too soon to begin the lesson in earnest, but soon. Soon he would learn to obey, or he would bleed.

CHENBAO

CHENBAO STUDIED the photograph of Ki-tae and Jin-woo, tilting her head this way and that. She set it down and picked up another. Each one had been enhanced to show their faces clearly. That photo was discarded and another lifted from the pile. Someone had gone through a great deal of effort to clean up what was obviously security footage. It was a half-decent job, but if one knew what to look for, it was easy to spot the changes.

"Do you feel it wise not to inform them of this?" ChenBao asked, glancing up to see Soon-joon pacing in her office. Agitation and an inability to remain still replaced his normal calm. She could certainly understand that. Ki-tae was his son, his youngest. Any parent would be disturbed, infuriated, by a threat to their child.

"Honestly, Okasan, I am not sure how to tell him," Soon-joon said. "How do you explain such greed?"

Now she knew he was more than just nervous. He only called her Mother when he was scared.

"This is not something new to us, Táozi-chan," ChenBao said quietly.

"This is the first time it has happened to one of my sons," he pointed out. "They have never been targeted before. This isn't about getting an exclusive story or photo opportunity. This is about money, and the threat is clear. This person will hurt Ki-tae and Jin-woo dongsaeng if they do not get what they want."

"We will deal with this as we have always done," ChenBao said firmly, rising. "And we will do so with the full knowledge of Ki-tae dongsaeng *and* Jin-woo dongsaeng. They deserve to know of this threat, not be kept in the dark. Given last night's events, I would think these might be connected. Ki-tae dongsaeng and Jin-woo dongsaeng tried to be discreet on set, but people notice these things."

Soon-joon sighed, rubbing his face with his hands. He kept alternating between furious and terrified for his son's safety as seen by the rapid change in his eyes from brown to gold and back again. "I know. Yet who in our clan would do such a thing?"

"I do not believe it is one of our own. Shin-bai dongsaeng's report of the break-in said Ki-tae dongsaeng and Jin-woo dongsaeng have been arriving here together. It is something to keep in mind."

"You're right, Okasan. These incidents occurred too closely together to not consider the possibility." Soon-joon said. "I just...."

"You are his father as much as his sire," she said softly as she approached him and wrapped her arms around him. ChenBao kissed his temple. "No true parent will tolerate a threat to their children. I know this from personal experience, so you must listen."

Soon-joon smiled. "I remember. I could have taken care of that one myself."

"Yes, but as your mother, it was not acceptable to me to do nothing," she said. "And so I took action."

"You first took everything he owned and then drained him dry."

"I was less inclined to be merciful back then," she said with a shrug. "Samurai, shogun, or daimyo, no one hurts my son."

"They still tell stories of you in the province." Soon-joon chuckled.

ChenBao smiled. "I am spoken of in many provinces, with mixed feelings of awe and fear. It is as it should be. Now back to Ki-tae dongsaeng."

"I will have them meet us here as soon as they arrive." Soon-joon glanced at his watch. "HanYin took his motorcycle today. Cheongul had an early-morning interview. Only Ki-tae had nothing scheduled for today."

"When is Jin-woo dongsaeng due in?" ChenBao asked as she resumed her seat.

"I believe he and Min-su dongsaeng generally arrive at eight. Jong-in dongsaeng tends to arrive earlier, around seven," Soon-joon said, using the tablet he'd set down upon entering ChenBao's office to pull up the schedule. She knew he kept track of everything, though he did leave certain tasks to members of his team. He could trust Hyun-jo with much more. Hyun-jo would not return without the information Soon-joon wanted, and though he was a small man, he would not allow them to stop him. Hyun-jo was a force to be reckoned with when he chose to be stubborn. Soon-joon smiled.

"And what brings that smile to your face, Táozi-chan?" ChenBao said with a smirk of her own.

"I sent Hyun-jo hubae to the stadium today," Soon-joon said. "They had been very reluctant to arrange the meeting, but Hyun-jo hubae was very persistent. It occurred to me he would be the best person to get me the information I seek."

"And what are you looking for?" she said absently as she studied the pictures and noted with more than just her regular eyesight.

"A list of people who had access to the security footage. Once he has the list, he will begin researching each person on it, evaluating them for motive, opportunity, and financial situation. Money, as we know, makes people do things they normally wouldn't do."

"So you think it is someone inside the facility? Or someone connected to them?" ChenBao said.

"It is entirely possible," Soon-joon said. "I would think only employees have access to that footage."

"Very true," she said. Then she turned her full gaze on him. "It is after eight. Why don't you go get HanYin dongsaeng and then see if Jin-woo dongsaeng has arrived yet?"

"As you wish," Soon-joon said. Then he did something out of character. He walked over to her and kissed her temple. She looked up at him, surprised, and then smiled. He didn't do that very often, but it always made her smile when he did. He was a grown man, a Vampire sage in his own right, but he was still her son, the little boy she had helped raise and watched grow from a precocious toddler to a strong, honorable man. ChenBao watched him walk out the door.

"We did a good job, Mai-Qi-chan," she whispered, bringing her most favored handmaiden and dearest friend to mind. "He is a good man, our son."

KI-TAE

KI-TAE AWOKE to the glorious smell of coffee. He reached for Jin-woo, only to find the other side of the bed empty. He frowned for a moment, but then it came to him. Jin-woo had promised to make him breakfast as a thank-you. Ki-tae smiled and threw back the covers. He headed straight to the kitchen and found Jin-woo stirring a decent-sized pot on the stove. The smells coming from it were mouthwatering. Ki-tae slipped up behind him and wrapped his arms around Jin-woo's waist, laying a kiss on his neck.

"Good morning," Jin-woo said with a chuckle as he pushed his hips back against Ki-tae's erection snug against his ass. "Someone's all happy this morning."

"There's food, coffee, and you," Ki-tae purred, nibbling. "I can't decide which one to eat first."

"The food," Jin-woo insisted with a laugh. "It will get cold if you don't, and I don't know about you, but I've never been a fan of cold kimchi. Now go sit down."

"You made kimchi?" Ki-tae was surprised.

"On second thought," Jin-woo said as he turned around and ran his eyes up and down Ki-tae's naked body. Ki-tae smirked at him. "Go put on at least a pair of pants. I want to eat my breakfast in relative comfort!"

"Spoilsport," Ki-tae said with a pout. "What's wrong with the way I'm dressed?"

"You're *not* dressed, Ki-tae-ya." Jin-woo laughed. "That's the problem. Go on!"

"Drop the honorifics, and I will," Ki-tae said.

"Really?" Jin-woo said. "You're negotiating with me about putting on pants?"

Ki-tae continued to pout, but it didn't last long. He laughed and pulled Jin-woo into his arms for a resounding kiss before releasing him and then going back to the bedroom. He grabbed a pair of blue plaid sleep pants and a white tank top from the drawer. He made a minor effort to find his house slippers but gave up in the end. He didn't often wear them in his apartment, so he wasn't all that put out by not being able to find them.

When he went back to the kitchen, Jin-woo was setting out breakfast. He had several banchan waiting and a large tureen of what appeared to be bokimchi. He hoped it was the kind with seafood. Ki-tae could deal with fruit bokimchi, but he really liked it with seafood instead. There was also a large mug of coffee at each of their seats, and Jin-woo was just setting down the bowls of rice. When he looked up and smiled, Ki-tae felt as if he'd been punched in the solar plexus. He walked over and cupped Jin-woo's face before kissing him sweetly, brushing his lips back and forth until that tiny little whimper signaled Jin-woo's surrender, and he opened that delectable mouth to grant Ki-tae entrance. When Ki-tae finally released him, they were both panting for breath. It was hard to focus on anything other than Jin-woo's mouth and all the things he wanted Jin-woo to do with it for several moments. He stared into Jin-woo's eyes, still holding his face.

"The... the food is... going to get cold," Jin-woo whispered.

"I'd rather feast on you," Ki-tae purred.

"Ki-tae," Jin-woo moaned as he leaned into him, sliding his arms around him.

"I want to make love with you again," he whispered.

"You're being evil again," Jin-woo whimpered. "We have to go to work. Well, I have to go to work, and then I have school, and then... then I have to go back to my apartment...."

"You're determined to be responsible right now, huh?" Ki-tae said with a chuckle.

"I have to be. Otherwise we'd spend all day in bed," Jin-woo pointed out as he stepped back.

"Why is that a problem?" Ki-tae said with wicked smile. "I'm sure I can make you forget all about being responsible."

"I know you can, which is why we're going to stop," Jin-woo said. "Now sit down and eat your breakfast."

"Later, then?"

"Later," Jin-woo promised. With the words spoken, Ki-tae took his seat. He dug right in.

There were certain foods Ki-tae adored, and usually only HanYin made them. Mainly because HanYin knew more about cooking and more recipes than many professional chefs, and he knew them as they were originally created. He adored HanYin's steamed dumplings and Oi-sobagi. While he did enjoy red meat and chicken, Ki-tae preferred seafood, crab and shrimp being his favorites. HanYin made some of the best seafood dishes Ki-tae had ever tasted.

"It smells delicious," Ki-tae said, giving Jin-woo a smile.

"Your kitchen is very well-stocked," Jin-woo said as he served. "I didn't know what you would like, but when I saw how much of the leftovers were seafood, I figured it was a safe bet to go with bokimchi. I did see one thing in there that surprised me."

"And what was that?" Ki-tae asked absently as he took his first bite of the kimchi. He moaned loudly. It was perfect.

"Dammit, don't moan like that," Jin-woo grumbled, his face bright red and his pupils blown. He was staring at Ki-tae, and Ki-tae grinned at him, biting his lip.

"You keep staring at me like that, and I'm dragging you back to the bedroom, breakfast be damned."

"You... you're not making this any easier, you know," Jin-woo said, shifting restlessly in his chair.

Ki-tae made a decision at that moment, and it wasn't the responsible one. He grabbed Jin-woo's wrist and pulled him out of his chair, turning his own in the process. Then he yanked Jin-woo down onto his lap and took possession of his mouth.

Breakfast got cold, and Jin-woo was late… again.

JIN-WOO

JIN-WOO LAUGHED as he walked out the front door of Ki-tae's apartment building. Ki-tae was right behind him, looking hot as fuck in tight light blue jeans and a long-sleeved blue Henley with blue Converse high-tops. He turned around, walking backward as he dodged Ki-tae's hands.

"No, no more tickling!" Jin-woo cried as he jumped to the side. "I'm late as it is!"

"You could call in, and we could go back upstairs," Ki-tae purred before licking his lips. Oh, the evil bastard.

"You're a horrible influence. You know that, right?" Jin-woo said, dodging another grab. He knew Ki-tae could catch him anytime he wanted, and it was an incredible turn-on.

"Yes, and you like it." Ki-tae chuckled. "I want to take you back upstairs."

"Well, I have to go to work," Jin-woo said, coming to a stop next to the car. Ki-tae was standing a few feet away, a bright smile on his face that crinkled his eyes. He loved that smile. Jin-woo froze. No, he didn't just love that smile… he loved Ki-tae. Oh crap, when had that happened? It was a shock, but a good one. Jin-woo looked at Ki-tae and smiled. He loved this amazing man.

The screech of tires was incredibly loud, mixed with the roar and rev of an engine. The car drifted hard around the corner, fishtailing as it reached the intersection. It jumped the curb, heading straight for them. Jin-woo watched Ki-tae turn his head in slow motion. He saw those beautiful eyes widen and flash silver. Jin-woo stretched out his hand, not realizing the screams were coming from him as Ki-tae moved. As fast as he was, the distance was just too short, and the car clipped him. He spun with the impact, and Jin-woo lunged forward, catching him as he hit the sidewalk. The car continued, screeching around the next corner and speeding away.

"Ki-tae!" Jin-woo sobbed. "Dammit, are you okay? Oh my God, Ki-tae!"

"Shhh." Ki-tae's voice was calm amid the pounding in Jin-woo's ears. "I'm okay. A little broken, but I'll heal quickly."

"Not funny," Jin-woo said as he held him.

"Into the van," Shin-bai said, his voice brooking no argument. "You are not driving today."

"Goes without saying. They clipped my driving leg." Ki-tae chuckled. "Bastards. My hip's busted, and there's a fracture in my upper thigh at the very least."

Shin-bai pulled Ki-tae's arm around his shoulders and easily lifted him. Ki-tae hobble-walked to the van, his grip on Jin-woo's hand tight but not painful.

Jin-woo winced when Ki-tae slid into the seat, his face scrunched in pain. Durable but not invulnerable. Jin-woo wished that weren't the case. He wished Ki-tae were invulnerable because then his heart wouldn't be beating like a dubstep mix on fast-forward. He wouldn't feel like throwing up and passing out at the same time. He wouldn't feel this horrible nausea-inducing sense of déjà vu.

"Get in before you pass out," Ki-tae murmured, his voice sounding sleepy.

"Go, Jin-woo dongsaeng. You can help him," Shin-bai whispered.

"You… know."

"Of course. I have been with them… many years." Shin-bai smiled with a hint of fang. "Get in and let him feed. It will heal him."

"I'm surrounded," Jin-woo muttered as he climbed into the car and settled carefully next to Ki-tae.

"You have no idea."

"That is not reassuring," Jin-woo grumbled.

"Help him," Shin-bai said. "Just do not make a mess of my van."

"Oh em gee, you people," Jin-woo snapped. "As if he's in any condition…."

Shin-bai chuckled as he closed the door and then went around to the driver's side. The glass was up, so Jin-woo at least had that semblance of privacy. However, he had a feeling it really didn't make a difference with Vampires.

Ki-tae's eyes were closed when Jin-woo looked at him. When he gently brushed Ki-tae's bangs, they popped open, a beautiful glittering silver. Jin-woo could see the tips of his fangs and shivered in anticipation.

"Come here," Ki-tae purred, patting his lap.

"Oh hell no," Jin-woo said. "We are not having sex with Shin-bai hyung in the front seat, and definitely not when you're hurt."

"So if he wasn't here…."

"Jung Ki-tae, no," Jin-woo said firmly.

"But I want your neck," Ki-tae whined softly.

"You'll get my wrist for now. Then we're heading for the police station," Jin-woo said.

"We don't involve the police for things like this," Ki-tae said. "It's too difficult to explain why I'm not in traction."

"Oh," Jin-woo said, realizing how stupid going to the police would be for a Vampire. "I should have thought of that."

"It's okay, Jin-woo. You haven't been around us long enough to have such thinking be the norm, and we haven't really sat down and talked about what I am," Ki-tae said with a smile as he stretched out his hand. "Now give me your wrist. Heal me, *Wǒ de xīn*."

Jin-woo gave him a soft smile as he placed his hand in Ki-tae's. "What language is that?"

"Mandarin. It's HanYin-a's native language. We all learned it," Ki-tae murmured as he brushed his lips over Jin-woo's wrist. It was such a light sensation that it tickled and tingled at the same time. His cock hardened as he watched Ki-tae drag out the anticipation of his bite. He started panting, and the car was getting way too hot. His eyes snapped open when Ki-tae chuckled. He hadn't even realized he'd closed them.

"What's so funny?" he said, his voice low and husky. That's what Ki-tae did to him.

"I wonder if I could make you cum just from feeding," Ki-tae murmured, flicking his tongue against Jin-woo's skin, tormenting him with little bolts of pleasure that shot straight to his groin.

"Ki-tae," Jin-woo moaned. "I have nothing to change into."

"You're going to cum for me, Jin-woo," Ki-tae said as he slowly sank his fangs into Jin-woo's wrist.

There was nothing quite like the sensation of Ki-tae's bite. When he did it slowly, it was a building of sensations; tingles began where his fangs met Jin-woo's wrist. Then he pushed, and an overwhelming rush of pleasure shot out from that point of contact and slammed into Jin-woo's body like an ocean wave. It swamped his senses, and his entire body shook with it. He couldn't stop his moans any more than he could stop his body from spilling his seed in his pants. He lost track of where he was, floating on the river of pleasure Ki-tae threw him into. Jin-woo chuckled softly. He didn't mind at all.

Clarity returned with Ki-tae's sweet kisses to his temple, his cheek, his forehead. He registered the feel of Ki-tae running his hand along his side, down over his hip, and then back up. The car was filled with their mingled scents. He snuggled against Ki-tae's chest, a sense of peace settling over him, knowing Ki-tae was healed, but he asked anyway.

"You're okay now?"

"Yes," Ki-tae murmured against his hair. "I'll be a little sore for about another hour or so, but other than that, I'm fine... thanks to you."

"Anyone could have—"

"No, Jin-woo." Ki-tae's voice was suddenly very serious, and Jin-woo immediately lifted his head to look at him, giving Ki-tae his full attention.

"What do you mean, no?"

"There's something we need to discuss," Ki-tae said with a sigh. "I'm not sure how to begin."

"At the beginning usually works." Jin-woo sat up fully, feeling the sticky mess Ki-tae had made of him. He shot a glare in Ki-tae's direction and was met with a completely unrepentant wicked smile. "You made a mess of me... again, and I have no clothes."

"Check your backpack." Ki-tae smirked.

When Jin-woo opened it, he found a change of underwear and pants. He turned and raised his eyebrow at Ki-tae, causing him to laugh. The sound filled Jin-woo with joy, and that scared him a little bit. After only a moment's hesitation, Jin-woo pulled his essentials pack out of his backpack, grabbed the wipes, and stripped out of his pants and underwear. He cleaned himself as best he could, batting away Ki-tae's "helpful" hands.

"Ugh," he said as he pulled up his pants. "Min-su-ya's going to take one sniff and know."

"My scent is all over you, and yours is all over me, just the way I like it."

"You mean to say I smell like you?" Jin-woo asked, tilting his head as he really thought about the idea. He found he didn't mind. In fact, he liked it a lot.

Ki-tae, his brows furrowed, said, "Well, you smell like us."

"Us?"

"Yeah," Ki-tae said as he sat up, looking at Jin-woo intently. He was serious again, and Jin-woo didn't know if he liked it.

"You said we had something we needed to talk about," he said as he pulled a shopping bag out of his pack and stuffed his dirty clothes in it. Before Ki-tae could respond, the privacy glass slid down, and Shin-bai glanced back at them.

"Soon-joon-nim just called. You and Jin-woo dongsaeng are to go to the president's office upon arriving."

"Seriously? I have today off," Ki-tae whined.

"He says it is very important, Ki-tae dongsaeng," Shin-bai said quietly. "And I think, after recent events, you have something to discuss with him as well."

"You think it was deliberate?" Jin-woo said, hearing the tremble in his own voice. He heard Ki-tae's sigh. "Wait, Ki-tae? Why don't you seem surprised by this?"

"Would you mind waiting until we get to the office?" Ki-tae said, sounding exhausted. He shifted to lean against the side of car, away from Jin-woo. It hurt, and Jin-woo looked down at his hands.

He didn't know what to say. There was so much going on inside his head. Now that Ki-tae was going to be okay, he could feel the fear setting in. He'd never been so scared in all his life, watching that car careen toward Ki-tae. He didn't know how much it would take to kill Ki-tae, and he never wanted to find out.

Jin-woo moved to the other side of the car, bringing his feet up and wrapping his arms around his knees. He rested his chin on them. Obviously there was more going on than he knew, and that didn't sit well with him. Jin-woo preferred knowing things up front. If he knew about them, he could prepare and plan. He didn't like being kept in the dark. He remained silent for most of the ride, but when they finally reached the offices, he couldn't stay silent anymore.

"I…." Jin-woo paused when he felt Ki-tae's eyes on him. "I know I'm new to all this. I'm just a regular guy, a regular human being. But I don't like it when people treat me as if I can't handle things."

"Jin-woo."

"No, just listen," Jin-woo snapped. "I know I'm extremely young compared to you and the others, that I haven't had as much experience and doubtfully ever will, but you don't know my story any more than I know yours, the things that made me who I am. I won't be coddled. I won't be sheltered from shit. I'm an adult, and I refuse to be treated as if I'm still a child. When you can accept that and not hide things from me because you think they might upset me, then you let me know. Until then, I think it's best if you just leave me be."

Jin-woo didn't let Ki-tae say anything further. He opened the door and got out, walking quickly inside the building. It hurt that Ki-tae was keeping things from him. It might not seem like such a big deal, but it was the idea that Ki-tae thought less of him, thought he couldn't handle unpleasant things. Jin-woo knew about unpleasant. He knew about pain and loss and betrayal. He just refused to let these things make him a bitter, jaded person who saw the world as a dark, nasty place where everyone was out to step on anyone else to get what they wanted. Yes, there were people like that, but Jin-woo refused to think everyone was. He chose to believe most people were good. Everyone had a dark side, and some people chose to indulge that side often. Jin-woo was not one of those people, and he would not paint everyone with the same brush.

Did it hurt to walk away from Ki-tae like that, especially after what happened and how he felt? Of course it did. It hurt like hell, but Jin-woo wasn't going to let it slide. A relationship couldn't be built on one person hiding things from the other. If they couldn't be open with each other, then they simply couldn't be. Either Ki-tae would accept it or he wouldn't. It was better to know now than to find out much later in the relationship. At least, that's what he kept telling himself all the way to his desk.

KI-TAE

KI-TAE STARED at the open door, his mind too confused with the need to sleep and heal to think clearly. What had just happened? It sounded an awful lot like he'd just been dumped, but that didn't make sense. He wasn't sure what to make of Jin-woo's words. Granted, he had been keeping something rather important from Jin-woo. It wasn't exactly easy to tell someone you either had to kill them or turn them into a Vampire to break the bond you'd inadvertently made with them. Not exactly a common topic of conversation. Ki-tae slowly slid out of the van. While feeding from Jin-woo had repaired the major damage to his busted hip, there were still fractures all down his thigh and into his calf, and it still hurt. He would be able to walk, but there would be a limp for a couple of hours, days if he didn't allow his body to slip into its healing state to repair the damage. Being highly in tune with his personal energy flow because of his Vampiric nature made finding all the little breaks and bruises easier.

"Where is Jin-woo dongsaeng?" Shin-bai asked, glancing from Ki-tae to the car interior.

"He's already inside," Ki-tae said softly.

"Why didn't he wait for us?" Shin-bai asked as he helped Ki-tae out of the car.

"I… I think I made him mad, although I'm not exactly sure how," Ki-tae said. "Damn, this hurts more than the last one."

"Last one? What last one? You need to stop getting hit by cars," Shin-bai said as they maneuvered through the front doors. The receptionists began to fuss the minute they saw him, but a quick word from Shin-bai had them back at their stations.

"No, people need to stop trying to run me over," Ki-tae grumbled once they weren't surrounded. "We might as well head up to the president's office."

"What of Jin-woo dongsaeng?"

"I… I don't know," Ki-tae said. "He probably went to put his stuff in his desk before he headed upstairs."

"I will get you settled and then make sure he is okay," Shin-bai said as they entered the elevator.

It was going to be a long day. Ki-tae sighed. It had started out with such promise too. If he had told Jin-woo from the beginning, would they ever have made love? Of course not. Jin-woo would have run from him as fast as he could. It wouldn't have done him any good because the bond would have still been in place, but Jin-woo would have run. Who wouldn't? Ki-tae absently rubbed his chest. It hurt to not have Jin-woo beside him. No, it was knowing he was why Jin-woo left him. That wasn't a new scenario for Ki-tae, but it was the first time having someone leave him hurt so damn much he felt as if there were a gaping hole in his chest.

"What the hell happened to you?" Cheongul demanded, rushing over to Ki-tae's side and taking his other arm as the three of them entered the elevator.

"I'm fine," Ki-tae said. "Stop making such a freaking fuss or you'll draw attention. I'm just a little bruised."

"Bullshit," Cheongul said succinctly. "Bruises don't make you limp this badly and need assistance walking."

"Well, it may be because I had a busted hip until about, oh, twenty minutes ago, give or take," Ki-tae said casually.

"What happened?" Cheongul said, his hands shaking as he held Ki-tae.

"I'm too damn tired, so I'm only going to tell this story once. You'll have to wait until we reach Huijang-nim's office," Ki-tae said. "I figure if I'm being called in, then you and HanYin-a would be as well. So any idea what the heck is so important I have to give up part of a day off?"

"You're just mad you can't spend the morning seducing Jin-woo dongsaeng," Cheongul chuckled. "You reek again."

"Well, that may not be an issue anymore," Ki-tae said softly.

"What do you mean?" Cheongul said, trying to catch his eye. Ki-tae refused to look at him. "Ki-tae-ya?"

"Just... not right now, Cheongul-a. I need time to process everything," Ki-tae said. "I...."

He had to stop talking for the tightness in his throat. He felt the tickle of a tear sliding down his face and cursed silently. Ki-tae detested crying, or, more precisely, he hated it when *he* cried. Tears were a waste of time. They didn't resolve anything. As a child he never cried. That had been beaten out of him within a month. He'd always been stubborn. He barely registered when Shin-bai departed and Cheongul took his full weight.

Jin-woo had left him.

What had he done wrong? He'd been so tired in the car, he just wanted to sleep. When he was hit before the concert, it was more of a sideswipe, and there wasn't as much damage, just torn muscles that hurt like a bitch. Broken bones and shattered hips took a little more to heal. Jin-woo's blood had accelerated it a lot, but the need for rest, for inactivity to allow his body to finish knitting his bones back together, had been almost overwhelming. He'd wanted to answer Jin-woo's questions, but he started having difficulty focusing as his body fought to put him to sleep. It was still fighting him, and it was winning.

"Cheongul-a... I'm... so tired. I just.... Sleep.... Jin-woo."

Ki-tae passed out.

JIN-WOO

JIN-WOO PUT his head down on his desk and took several deep breaths. Had he done the right thing? Was there any other way he could have handled the situation? He'd been second-guessing himself since he got off the elevator. Now sitting and staring at the top of his desk, he was even more unsure. Was he too unyielding when it came to secrets? He hadn't really given Ki-tae a chance to say anything. The man had just been hit by a car, for Pete's sake. He could have waited until they reached the office and asked the questions again. Now he'd made the impulsive decision to tell Ki-tae to leave him alone. He didn't want Ki-tae to leave him alone. He wanted Ki-tae to harass and seduce him every chance he got.

"I'm such an idiot sometimes." Jin-woo sighed.

"You won't get any argument from me," Min-su said as she set her backpack on her desk. "What's got you all upset?"

"I… I broke…."

"You did not," Min-su said, putting her hands on her hips. "Don't even complete that sentence, or I'll feel the need to smack you more than I already do."

"You don't even know what I'm going to say," Jin-woo snapped back.

"Well, if it has anything to do with the way you smell and the scent of pain and despair that filled the elevator I just rode up in, I figure you just did something stupid, like pushed Ki-tae oppa away," Min-su hissed after glancing around the room, noting they were alone.

"I might have had good reason," Jin-woo said defensively. It sounded weak even to his ears.

"Jin-woo-ya," Min-su said, pulling a chair around to sit facing him. "A relationship takes work, right?"

He nodded.

"That work can't happen if you guys don't talk before making stupid, rash decisions, can it?" She smiled, and it was the "I'm containing my urge to hit you" smile. "Did you give him a chance to explain or did you make some sort of stupid statement like 'unless you accept blah, blah, blah, stay away from me'?"

Jin-woo felt his cheeks heat up and he saw her eyes narrow.

"You're going to fix it today," she said, grabbing the front of his shirt. "You have never been happier than you have been with Ki-tae oppa these last few weeks. Don't fuck it up because of things that happened in the past."

Impulsively Jin-woo hugged her. "Thank you."

"You're welcome," she said softly. "Just remember, the past is the past. It makes us who we are, but it doesn't control how we live our lives going forward."

"I, I can't have him keeping things from me, Min-su-ya," Jin-woo said softly.

"I understand, but you can't just shove him away without at least trying to talk it out either," she said. "It's not fair to him, Jin-woo-ya. If you expect full disclosure from Ki-tae oppa, then you need to give him your story too. Your go-to response can't be to push him out of your life constantly. Otherwise, one day, you're going to push him away and he's not going to come back."

Jin-woo nodded. He turned at the sound of someone clearing their throat to find Shin-bai standing a few feet away. He looked... very official, and it was kind of creepy. Jin-woo smiled hesitantly, but it didn't seem to get him anywhere with the big man.

"Jin-woo dongsaeng, Soon-joon-nim has requested you meet him in Huijang-nim's office," Shin-bai said.

"What's going on, Shin-bai oppa?" Min-su asked as she rose with Jin-woo.

"I am not sure at present," Shin-bai said. "We will know more after the meeting. We must hurry. He does not like to be kept waiting, especially when it is an important matter."

"Okay," Jin-woo said, rising. "Let's go. I'll talk to you later, Min-su-ya. Will you let Hyung-jun seonbae know where I am?"

"Of course," she said with a smile.

Jin-woo followed Shin-bai to the elevators in silence. He didn't know what it was, but something had changed since he got into the car that morning. When the doors closed, he turned to Shin-bai.

"Have I done something to upset you?" he asked directly.

"Yes," Shin-bai answered. Jin-woo waited a few more moments for him to continue, but he remained silent.

"What have I done, Shin-bai hyung?" he finally asked.

"Did you know if a Vampire is injured badly enough, he or she will go into a comatose state after a healing feed to allow their bodies time to complete the repairs it needs to?" Shin-bai said, turning to look down at him. "Bones take a long time to knit together."

"I didn't know that," Jin-woo said, having an inkling of why Shin-bai was upset with him. "I hardly know anything about them."

"It becomes very hard to focus," Shin-bai continued. "Thinking coherently is a struggle because our bodies are trying to put us in an inactive state."

"Why are you telling me this?" Jin-woo asked, confused.

"It is something you should know," Shin-bai said. "I am mad at you for getting out of the car without waiting for my men and me to make sure it was safe for you to do so. It was an incredibly stupid move considering someone just tried to run Ki-tae dongsaeng over not forty minutes ago."

"I... I didn't think. Joesonghaeyo, Shin-bai hyung," Jin-woo said with a bow. "Am I forgiven?"

"No. That is not the only reason I am mad at you," Shin-bai said.

"What else did I do?" Jin-woo said.

"You made Ki-tae dongsaeng cry. I don't know if I can forgive that."

"What?" Jin-woo barely heard his own whisper.

"I will not repeat it," Shin-bai said.

"No, that's… that's not what I meant. I'm just surprised," Jin-woo said.

"I have been with the Jungs for over one hundred and fifty years," Shin-bai said quietly. "First as a human retainer and then as a protector, not that they really need one. They are good men. *Ki-tae dongsaeng* is a good man, but he is still a man. He makes mistakes. He does not deserve to be abandoned because of them."

"I didn't—"

"You did," Shin-bai said. "You left him in that car, door wide open, and walked away, leaving not only yourself but Ki-tae dongsaeng exposed, vulnerable. You abandoned him physically and emotionally. You walked away because he didn't live up to a standard he probably had no idea you had."

"Shin-bai hyung."

"I tell you this because you are a part of this family now, and our family speaks plainly at times," Shin-bai said. "If you care for him as much as I think you do, you will make this right, and you will *never* make him cry again."

Jin-woo nodded as the elevator doors slid open. Shin-bai gestured for him to go first, and he walked out. Hyun-jo was waiting by the door. He bowed to Jin-woo, which still seemed so very odd, and then opened the door. The room was filled with tension as he walked in, and Jin-woo glanced from one person to another until he spotted Ki-tae on the divan, eyes closed, unmoving, Cheongul standing like a bodyguard at his head. With a soft cry, Jin-woo headed in his direction, only for HanYin to stop him. He blocked Jin-woo's way, shifting when he would go around him.

"I like you," Jin-woo said softly. "But you're in my way."

"*Yuǎnli tā*," HanYin growled, actually *growled* at him. His eyes were bright silver, and his fangs flashed from between his lips.

"That would be great if I knew what the heck you were saying!" Jin-woo snapped. "Get out of my way, HanYin hyung. I want to see Ki-tae."

"You will not get by him," Soon-joon said quietly. "HanYin dongsaeng will not allow you near Ki-tae dongsaeng until he is satisfied you pose no danger to his little brother. He is at his most dangerous right now, and it would be best for everyone involved if you withdrew and came to sit by me."

"But Ki-tae…."

"He is in a healing sleep, nothing more," Soon-joon said with a gentle smile. "However, since he was brought into the room unconscious, we do not know why, and that set HanYin dongsaeng off. Please. If he hurts you, he will never forgive himself."

"I thought he was healed," Jin-woo said softly as he took the seat Soon-joon offered. He watched HanYin move backward until he crouched beside Ki-tae. His eyes still burned silver, and his fangs, slightly longer than Ki-tae's, pricked his lips. "He said he was fine."

"Never believe Ki-tae dongsaeng when he uses the word 'fine.' Invariably he's lying through his teeth." Cheongul snorted.

"What happened, Jin-woo dongsaeng?" ChenBao said, speaking for the first time from behind her desk. "Shin-bai dongsaeng said there was an incident outside Ki-tae dongsaeng's apartment building?"

"We had just come outside and were about to get into Ki-tae's car when another car came careening around the corner. The engine revved, and it jumped the sidewalk, heading straight for Ki-tae. There was no time for him to get completely out of the way, and it... it, oh my God, it hit him," Jin-woo said, letting the tears finally fall. He covered his face with his hands and curled into a ball on the chair. The tears streamed down his face, but he barely made a sound. His body shook as memories long buried tried to push to the surface. "It hit him, and I couldn't do anything to stop it."

Gentle arms wrapped around him, and Jin-woo was pulled into a solid chest. He buried his fingers in the soft white shirt as he cried out his fear and helplessness. Words he didn't understand, but were soothing nonetheless, brushed against his ear. He didn't know how much time passed while he bawled, but Jin-woo was mortified to realize the person he'd used as a tissue was Soon-joon-nim. He jerked backward.

"Joesonghaeyo, Soon-joon seonbae," Jin-woo exclaimed, searching for something to clean Soon-joon's shirt with.

"Do not worry about it, Jin-woo dongsaeng," Soon-joon chuckled. "It is nothing."

"Except incredibly embarrassing," Jin-woo murmured, forgetting for a moment that four out of the six people in the room could hear him anyway. Soon-joon handed him a handkerchief with another smile.

"What happened after Ki-tae dongsaeng was hit?" ChenBao pressed gently.

"Well, um, we got him into the car." Jin-woo looked around the room desperately.

"Oh, Jin-woo dongsaeng." ChenBao laughed, drawing his attention back to her. He nearly jumped out of his seat when he saw her eyes were completely white and her fangs were... much more impressive than any he'd seen so far. A loud snarl came from HanYin. "While your efforts are admirable and appreciated, there is no need to keep their secret from me. You see, I am Soon-joon dongsaeng's sire."

"I really am surrounded," Jin-woo whispered, overwhelmed by everything. "I'm sorry, but I'm afraid I'm going to pass out now. It's a thing."

SHIN-BAI

"ENTER," CHENBAO said, smiling when Shin-bai slipped quietly through the door. He glanced around the room, taking stock of the situation within seconds. He bowed to ChenBao and then to Soon-joon. Then he positioned himself before the desk, but with a clear view of HanYin, should his skills be needed. He hoped they would not, but when HanYin was in such a state, he was a bit unpredictable.

"Is Jin-woo dongsaeng okay?" Shin-bai asked.

"He was a little overwhelmed by me." ChenBao smiled. "He thought I was human and was trying very hard to keep Ki-tae dongsaeng's secret. That is a good sign. How badly was Ki-tae dongsaeng injured, Shin-bai dongsaeng?"

"He said his hip was broken, and he had a fracture in his thigh. I believe he downplayed the extent of his injuries in Jin-woo dongsaeng's presence," Shin-bai said as he straightened. "After he fed from Jin-woo dongsaeng, I believe most of the damage was healed during the twenty-minute drive from his apartment to headquarters, but he was still in extreme pain and had difficulty moving. Given his current state it is more than likely only the hip was healed enough for him to walk with aid."

"Was anyone able to get photos of the car?" Soon-joon asked.

"Yes, they are a little blurry, but I already have my digital monitoring team working on the license plates. Although it is more than likely stolen," Shin-bai said as he shifted into an at-ease position. "Hyun-jo seonbae was also able to provide me with copies of the CCTV from the parking lot outside the stadium. He has a list of everyone with access to the indoor security footage archives."

"Why is that needed?" Cheongul demanded. "What's going on?"

"I had Soon-joon dongsaeng request both you and HanYin dongsaeng to meet with us because this will, more than likely, affect you as well," ChenBao said. "Jin-woo dongsaeng is here because he is a part of it, but I would prefer to wait until Ki-tae dongsaeng regains consciousness before we discuss it."

"And for HanYin to calm down," Soon-joon said as he settled Jin-woo more comfortably in the chair. "Jin-woo dongsaeng should wake up shortly."

"This is all really freaking frustrating," Cheongul said angrily.

"I know, but they are the focus," Soon-joon said. "However, I will not doubt that you and HanYin could be pulled in. We must prepare for all contingencies."

JIN-WOO

"JIN-WOO."

Ki-tae's voice seemed far away and very sad. Jin-woo frowned. He didn't like Ki-tae to be sad. Shifting, he struggled to open his eyes. Finally he blinked and winced as light filtered in before he was ready. He brought his hand up to shade his eyes and tried again. When he felt he was ready, Jin-woo moved his hands to find Ki-tae sitting next to him, filling his vision, a uncertain smile on his face. Jin-woo reached up and cupped his cheek. Then he curled his hand around the back of Ki-tae's neck and yanked him down for a deep, aggressive kiss.

"I think he's feeling better." Cheongul chuckled.

That caught Jin-woo's attention, and he reluctantly withdrew. "I'm sorry."

"It's okay, Jin-woo," Ki-tae said.

"No, it's not," Jin-woo said. "I was unfair to you. I didn't give you a chance to say anything and laid into you right after you'd been hit by a fucking car. It is most definitely not okay."

Ki-tae pulled him into a hug, and Jin-woo wrapped his arms tightly around him, no longer caring who saw them. He didn't ever want to let go, and he wouldn't unless Ki-tae told him to go, and then he'd be stubborn about not going. He hoped that would never happen, Ki-tae sending him away. After several moments, Ki-tae pulled back slightly, looking down at him. Jin-woo could feel his eyes and looked up at him. Ki-tae smiled and kissed his nose. He scrunched it, the kiss tickling and making his nose twitch.

"Much better," Shin-bai said quietly. Jin-woo smiled at him hesitantly. He didn't know if he was on Shin-bai's good side again, but the amusement in his eyes had to be a good sign, right?

"Ki-tae dongsaeng, Jin-woo dongsaeng," ChenBao called. When they looked at her, she signaled for them to approach her desk. What he saw there nearly made him pass out again. With trembling hands, Jin-woo picked up one of the pictures. Heat flooded his face and the back of his neck. He looked like such a wanton little slut.

"Hm, I might have to have this one blown up and placed in my bedroom," Ki-tae chuckled, looking at another picture. Jin-woo gasped and smacked him in the arm on pure instinct. "What? You look amazing!"

"I look like a whore," Jin-woo grumbled.

"Nope, there's no way to fake that expression," Ki-tae teased, and while his voice was light, the twinkle wasn't quite in his eyes.

"You're just trying to make me feel better about being caught on film," Jin-woo grumbled but had a hard time not smiling.

"Maybe a little," Ki-tae admitted, and then he sighed and looked at ChenBao. "What else came with the photos?"

ChenBao handed him a plain white piece of paper. When he was finished, Jin-woo took it and read it himself. He didn't know which part of the note bothered him more: the threat to him or the threat to Ki-tae. No, no, that wasn't true.

"Jin-woo?" Ki-tae's voice drew him from his thoughts, and when he looked down, the paper was vibrating, his hands were shaking so hard.

"I can tolerate a lot of things," he said quietly. "But threats to people I care about? No, that is *not* allowed."

"You definitely need to keep him." Cheongul chuckled.

"Interesting," ChenBao murmured.

"What's being done about this?" Jin-woo asked. "I assume some sort of action has been taken already."

"These were taken, obviously, from the CCTV cameras in the stadium," Soon-joon said. "Shin-bai hubae and Hyun-jo hubae have already been working on that. Were we able to get anything on the car from the stadium parking lot?"

"Wait, what car from the stadium?" Jin-woo asked, turning to look at Ki-tae.

"The day we met," Ki-tae said with a sigh. "Before the performance, someone tried to run me over. That one I had a little more time to move, but it still did some damage. That's why I was feeding. I had to heal a couple torn leg muscles."

"You didn't do that until intermission," Jin-woo said in shock. That meant Ki-tae had been dancing on an injured leg. He slapped his chest. "Don't do that again! You could have made things worse, dancing on an injury like that."

"So feisty," Ki-tae chuckled as he pulled Jin-woo into a hug. "The damage wasn't that bad, but it was getting worse toward the middle of the show. But when I drank from you, it was healed completely. Thank you."

"You need to stop getting hit by cars," Jin-woo mumbled.

"That is what I told him," Shin-bai said as he stood near Soon-joon, arms crossed over his chest.

"It's not like I woke up and said, 'Hm, I think I'll get run over today, sounds like fun,'" Ki-tae said. "But that one happened before these photos showed up, so it's possible they're not connected."

"It is possible but unlikely, and the threat to you is clear," Soon-joon said with a sigh.

"Does this happen often to you guys?" Jin-woo said quietly, twisting his hands together and not looking directly at anyone.

"No, not really," Cheongul said.

"This kind of leverage? Usually it's some tabloid journalist looking for a quick buck or an exclusive opportunity," Soon-joon explained. "As we have never condoned such behavior, after a while, they stopped trying. We always have responses ready in the event they follow through with their threat to release the photos or whatever they have. After being countered so many times, they eventually gave up. This? This is different. This is out-and-out blackmail. This person isn't looking to get the jump on other photographers. I will not be surprised if there is another note delivered with a dollar amount attached to it."

"I've seen other companies ditch the idol shortly after having something like this come out," Jin-woo said, gesturing to the pictures spread over ChenBao's desk. "They send them away or put them on some sort of hiatus. What would happen if this person does release these pictures?"

"The papers would have a field day. The fans, at least a portion of them, I would think, would be furious. They don't mind when we kiss each other playing the Pocky game or hang on each other, that's just how we are, but if they saw these and thought I was gay, they could get vicious, especially the netizens," Ki-tae said.

"If they 'thought' you were gay?" Jin-woo asked, raising an eyebrow. He was pretty sure having sex with another man counted as gay. Was Ki-tae saying....

"Silly," Ki-tae murmured. "They prefer to believe I'm straight. They've never seen me with a woman, and they don't acknowledge the few times I've had a relationship for longer than a week or two with a guy. I like men and always have, and I like you in particular."

"Aw, I'm so proud of you, Ki-tae dongsaeng." Cheongul clapped dramatically. "You've admitted to liking Jin-woo dongsaeng… instead of just lusting after him. Good for you."

"I hate you," Ki-tae said.

"No, you don't," Cheongul said with a grin and then added with a sigh, "So sweet."

"Shut up."

"Are you two finished?" Soon-joon said. "I swear, toddlers."

ChenBao chuckled. "They are brothers. It is their duty to pick on each other."

Soon-joon shook his head at their antics. Jin-woo had to smile. Cheongul and Ki-tae bickered back and forth, but he figured anyone who tried to harm the other one wouldn't be breathing for long. He wondered what it was like to have a sibling. Jin-woo was an only child, and he had no cousins, his aunt never marrying. It was… nice to watch them together. This was a serious situation, he supposed. It was clear Ki-tae was in danger. Not only could he be seriously hurt in one of these attacks, he could also be exposed as a Vampire. Neither situation would end well.

"Honestly the person who would be most harmed by these pictures is you, Jin-woo dongsaeng," Soon-joon said, settling on the corner of ChenBao's desk.

"What do you mean?" he asked. He hadn't thought about it because he wasn't anyone famous.

"Well, this could affect your college career," Soon-joon explained. "Too often students who are outed experience more threats from their classmates than from the person who outed them to begin with. They are ostracized and tormented to such a degree they often leave school or, worse, harm themselves."

"I've never hidden my orientation from anyone," Jin-woo said with a shrug. "I know how people can be. I don't advertise it, and I haven't had anyone at school come right out and ask me if I was gay."

"You seem… unfazed by the idea," Soon-joon said.

"There isn't much, save ChenBao nuna, that phases Jin-woo dongsaeng." Cheongul smirked. He appeared a little more relaxed now that the discussion was underway. Jin-woo figured Cheongul was the action type. He didn't like sitting around waiting to learn things. He wanted to get the information, make a plan, and then implement it. Jin-woo had often watched him pace during filming when technical difficulties of one type or another would hold things up.

"Well, I can sit here and worry it to death, or I can plan," Jin-woo said with a shrug. "I would like to think my classmates wouldn't turn on me, but I know it's a possibility. I wouldn't let them drive me out of school, though, and I certainly have no intention of harming myself because someone else has issues with who I sleep with, even though it has nothing to do with them, which is really stupid, if you think about it."

"I take this to mean you are fine with our company policy regarding such things?" ChenBao said. "We will not negotiate, and we will not comply. We will address and counter."

"That has always been how we handled things," Ki-tae said.

"The public relations team is monitoring social media sites. I have had Hyun-jo hubae adjust what commitments he could to this location. Not all of them could be changed, so security has been increased for off-site locations," Soon-joon said.

"That man should really be a manager," ChenBao said. "If he can manage you, he can manage anyone."

"I am not that bad."

"You have a terrible time letting go of control, Táozi-chan." ChenBao sighed. When she next looked up, Jin-woo could have sworn her eyes sparked. "You need someone to take your mind off work."

Ki-tae and Cheongul snorted in amusement. They hid their smiles behind their hands and turned away from the rest of the room. He couldn't figure out why they did that, but then Jin-woo realized they were laughing at how their sire was sort of getting scolded by their grandsire. Vampires were weird… or maybe they were too human. It seemed as if Ki-tae and the others acted just like anyone else, and being Vampires was just another thing about them, like being tall or having brown eyes.

"This has got to be the weirdest meeting I've ever been to," Jin-woo said, turning to look at Shin-bai standing next to him. "It's like one minute, everything and everyone is all serious, and the next, they're all picking on each other or laughing about something. And who is Táozi-chan?"

"Welcome to the family," Shin-bai said with a smile. "That would be Soon-joon-nim."

"Okay, I'm not going to touch that because my brain already hurts. Are they always like this?" Jin-woo asked. "When they were on set, they goofed around, but not all that much."

"That is work, and they pride themselves on being professional, but not off-putting. The threat of exposure is a mild annoyance to them," Shin-bai explained. "It is the threat to you and Ki-tae dongsaeng that they are serious about."

"This is all kind of surreal," Jin-woo murmured. "It makes the break-in seem petty and insignificant."

"Neither you nor Ki-tae dongsaeng have mentioned it. Why not?"

"I guess because it's not related," Jin-woo said.

"Are you sure?"

"Well, of course. I mean, what could someone who is trying to blackmail BLE possibly gain from breaking into my apartment, trashing my living room, cleaning my bedroom—and that seriously creeps me out, by the way—and then stealing all my sketchbooks?"

"You could be right," Shin-bai said. "However, it is still something Soon-joon-nim should be aware of."

"We've already been contacted about the incident," ChenBao said suddenly. "The police wanted to confirm you were working here. I sent a team over to your building to speak with the landlord about it. They checked the door, and it was not forced. Whoever invaded your home had a key."

"A key? How could they have gotten a key?" Jin-woo said, confused. The only way to get a key was to be given a copy. Other than himself, Jong-in, and Min-su, the only people who had copies of his keys were the landlord and the maintenance guy. "This means they can come back anytime they want."

"We'll take care of it," ChenBao said, waving her hand. She then gave Ki-tae a hard look. "There are other things that need to be taken care of. We have discussed everything we can, and now we must play the waiting game to see if this person is going to back up their threats, or if they're going to slink off with their tail between their legs."

"You know, watching her flash fang like that is… terrifying," Jin-woo said as he caught sight of ChenBao's still impressive canines.

"Flash fang?" Cheongul burst out laughing. "I like it!"

"I do too." ChenBao giggled, and it just was so incongruous with her appearance Jin-woo couldn't comprehend it for a second. "Now I do have more work to do today, so you all must leave my office."

Jin-woo turned to see Cheongul and Ki-tae talking, and that's when something hit him. "Where's HanYin hyung?"

HANYIN

HANYIN SAT in the middle of the darkened rehearsal room, his arms wrapped around his knees. There was very little light, but he could see some of it bouncing off him in the mirror he stared at, illuminating one side of his face and neck, touching his shoulders and along the length of his arms. He'd been there for the last hour or so, ever since Ki-tae woke up and everyone had got distracted. He'd been able to slip out of ChenBao's office without anyone noticing. They didn't need him in there. He'd overreacted to seeing Ki-tae unconscious. He knew at the time it was an overreaction, but he couldn't stop himself from switching into that protective mode. HanYin brushed the tear off his face. He knew he would have hurt Jin-woo if Soon-joon hadn't said anything. He would have done anything to protect his little brother, and Ki-tae would have hated him for it.

He hated when he lost control like that, hated how much of an animal he became, reacting to any perceived threats with violence, the way he snarled and snapped and hissed. He hated how exhausted he was afterward, how he had no energy left inside him, it seemed. HanYin didn't like how he had to have an alarm clock wake him up so as not to run the risk of hurting Cheongul or Ki-tae, because he couldn't seem to *not* wake up on the defensive.

Cheongul teased him about being a monk. That wasn't it at all. He didn't take lovers because they would invariably want to spend the night, and HanYin was too scared he'd hurt them if they did. Crowds still bothered him to a certain extent. It was a confusing situation. He had issues being surrounded by people, but he loved being an idol. He loved the singing and the dancing and the whole process. He loved what he did, and he put himself through hell every time he went out to an interview or a guest appearance. He'd taken to chewing some valerian root after major concerts, just so he could not freak out when they were invariably swamped on the way to the tour bus. The door opened with the barest of sounds in the silent room.

"What are you doing here?" he said.

"I came to see if you're all right," Jong-in said quietly.

They hadn't gotten a chance to speak since their... encounter in the instrument room. He figured Jong-in regretted what they did. It wouldn't be a first for HanYin, but it still hurt. He refused to look at him. He could see the silver glow in the darkened mirror across from him.

"I'm fine."

"Bullshit," Jong-in said. "You've been in here for over an hour, lights off, no music playing. You're not fine."

"How would you know when I'm fine or not?" HanYin demanded.

"When you're fine, your smile lights up whatever room you happen to be in," Jong-in said softly.

He didn't know how to respond to that. HanYin hadn't turned to look at him, didn't dare, but he could hear his footsteps getting closer. He turned away when Jong-in came up on his right. He hadn't fully recovered from earlier. The next thing he knew, Jong-in was pressed up against his back, his legs on either side of HanYin's. He brought his arms around him, and Jong-in placed his chin on HanYin's shoulder.

"If you're trying to hide your fangs and eyes, it's kind of too late for that," Jong-in murmured. "I already saw them when we made love."

"Made love? Is that what we did?" HanYin said stiffly.

"Yes, HanYin," Jong-in said. "We haven't really gotten a chance to talk since then, have we? We've been busy with so many other things."

"I figured you regretted it. Before you avoided me as much as you possibly could. If we had to be in the same room, you looked everywhere but at me. If I came into the room, you made an exit as soon as possible," HanYin said, his voice cold. "Was I just scratching an itch for you? Would any willing body have done at that moment?"

"Are you trying to pick a fight with me?" Jong-in asked, his surprise clear in tone. "No, I was not just scratching an itch."

HanYin shot to his feet. He couldn't stay pressed against Jong-in while they talked like this. He couldn't stop the tremors that wracked his body when he was close, and HanYin didn't want him to know how badly their contact affected him. He couldn't seem to get control, couldn't seem to pull back the beast inside him.

"Perhaps that's all it should be, dongsaeng," he said, turning to face Jong-in. "You don't want to be involved with someone… like me."

"Good thing you don't make decisions for me, then," Jong-in said. "I think I'll stick around, thanks. I didn't say to hell with hiding how I feel and make love to you, only to go back to the way things were before. And we're past honorifics. Either call me Jong-in-a or just Jong-in. Your choice."

HanYin didn't think. He just reacted. He pinned Jong-in against the wall, his entire body pressed against Jong-in's, holding his wrists above his head. His fangs scraped his lips. "Don't you get it? I'm dangerous."

"You're not the only one," Jong-in said as his eyes flashed.

"I could hurt you," HanYin whispered softly, laying his forehead against Jong-in's shoulder as he let his hands slide away from his wrists. HanYin gripped the material of Jong-in's shirt at his waist.

"HanYin," Jong-in murmured, turning to kiss his temple, gently stroking HanYin's hair.

"I can't even have you sleep in my bed for fear of hurting you," HanYin said softly. "I want to wake up with you in my arms... and I can't because I always wake up violently."

"It's all right."

"No." HanYin lifted his head, staring into Jong-in's eyes. He desperately needed Jong-in to understand what he was saying. "No, it's not okay. I nearly attacked Jin-woo dongsaeng because Ki-tae was unconscious and he was trying to get close. I was a complete animal.... I... I don't want to hurt you, Jong-in. It would kill me to hurt you."

HanYin fell to his knees at Jong-in's feet. He couldn't take it anymore. He tried to be happy and to live as normally as possible, but he wasn't normal. He was a Vampire. A Vampire with some serious aggression issues. He didn't have to fight all the time anymore, but he couldn't seem to make his mind believe that. He couldn't stop himself from waking up in midfight response. He couldn't stop himself from going animalistic when faced with a threat to his brothers or when they were injured. He couldn't control the part of him that wanted to rend and tear anything that threatened what was his.

"I just... want to be as normal as I can be, to be me, but not so... violent."

He hung his head, his hands curled into fists on his thighs, the claws digging into his palms and drawing blood. The coppery scent filled the air, and he didn't care. He watched the tears splash on the backs of his hands, raining dark spots on his jeans. He didn't deserve Jong-in. What good was he? He was either attacking or slinking away from someone or something more powerful than he was. ChenBao terrified him, absolutely terrified him. When she revealed even the tiniest bit of her power in the office, HanYin had barely contained the urge to launch himself at her. He would have gotten his ass handed to him, but he thought if he attacked first, got the upper hand, he could survive.

"I'm trying to be normal... and it's killing me," Jong-in said.

HanYin looked at him. The little bit of light in the room illuminated the right side of his face. He blinked, and his eye went from the beautiful brown HanYin knew to a light purple. A flicker of movement caught HanYin's eye, and he followed it, spotting an almost delicately shaped ear on the side of Jong-in's head. Jong-in shifted against the wall, pushing his hips out slightly, and something, a soft sound slithered into the room. The shadows hid the movement, but there was something there.

"Jong-in?" HanYin questioned.

"I don't know what I am. It started when I was... fourteen, fifteen, maybe," he said softly. "My dad had just died, and it was really hard on my mom. When she cooked before, I could taste the love in her food. I could taste her desire to see us happy and healthy and protected. Afterward her food tasted like ash, but there was still a hint of the love she had for us, my sister and me, in there... until he came."

HanYin reached up, took hold of Jong-in's hand, his clawed hand, and pulled him down until they were curled around each other.

"Sometimes when I get too stressed, I change. I don't remember anything that happens while I'm... different. If I get too agitated, I sprout these. I keep a hat in my bag just in case." Jong-in gestured to his head. "I've shredded more sheets than I care to think about, usually from having a nightmare. I was kicked out of my home about six years ago. I was just about to turn seventeen. My stepfather.... He and I never got along. He hates me, I think. I look like my dad a lot. I'm a reminder. I get to see my mom and my sister once, maybe twice a year if he's feeling generous. I work two or three part-time jobs while going to school, just to pay for it. I barely sleep for trying to be a normal person, to afford the things a normal person needs, and to make myself so exhausted that when I do sleep, I'm too tired to dream."

"Jong-in."

"Then you came along," Jong-in continued as if he hadn't heard, and HanYin just let him go. He knew Jong-in didn't talk a lot. To have him say so much, even if it wasn't happy things, was a gift. "I heard your voice first. I was walking down the hall toward Jin-woo-ya's apartment. The door was cracked because Min-su-ya doesn't always remember to close it all the way. We were supposed to study, but we ended up watching music videos all night. I heard your voice, so clear, so perfect, singing. God, I can't even remember the title of the song. Your voice was high, and then it dropped to this growl. I swore it was a different person, but the sound was still, it was still the same voice echoing through my head. That's when you hooked me, with that song, and I can't even remember the title."

"Call the Dragon," HanYin murmured against the side of his neck. "I wrote it during the Year of the Dragon. I wanted to do something different, blend more genres together in one song and write about some of my cultural history."

"When Jin-woo-ya showed me the video.... You should not be allowed to wear leather pants with no shirt and do body rolls," Jong-in mumbled, laying his head on HanYin's shoulder. "I about came in my pants watching that video. That was it. I became your stan at that moment. Every time I close my eyes, you're there. Nebulous at first, sort of hazy, but since this program started... I can't get you out of my mind. I try pushing myself harder, drowning myself in music, in work. Nothing helps."

"If it makes you feel any better, I've felt the same way from the first moment you stepped on that dais and sang," HanYin said.

"How can you still want me? Not knowing what I am?" Jong-in lifted his head, and they looked at each other.

"The same way you still want me, knowing I'm not human either," HanYin said. "We have our issues, the two of us, but when I'm with you... I'm happy. I like cooking for you, watching you enjoy the food I made. I love listening to you when you're singing because you think no one's around. And the dimples just kill it for me."

"That's the most I've talked in a long time," Jong-in said. "I don't even talk that much to Min-su-ya and Jin-woo-ya."

"I'm honored," HanYin said. "And thank you."

"For?"

"You pulled me out of my funk," HanYin said. "You matter to me—a lot. I need the people I care about to be happy. It's weird, I suppose, but when they're not happy, I'm not happy."

"HanYin?"

"Yes?"

"Kiss me."

"As you wish," HanYin purred, and then he leaned forward and brushed his lips slowly against Jong-in's. He savored the soft whimper. He cupped Jong-in's face and tilted his head to get a better angle. As much as he desired Jong-in, HanYin felt no urge to take things further. Just kissing him was the sweetest pleasure he could imagine. He pushed his fingers through Jong-in's hair, brushing along a silky ear. HanYin smiled against his mouth as he felt Jong-in shiver.

"What?" Jong-in said between tiny kisses.

"I think you are a Shifter," HanYin said and absently licked along his jawline.

"What being has multiple tails?" He tilted his head, and HanYin hummed happily at the greater access. He loved the taste of Jong-in's skin.

"*Húli jīng.*" HanYin worked along his neck, nipping, feeling the urge to drink slowly building within him. "Fox-Spirit."

"I can't think when you do that," Jong-in said breathlessly, gasping when HanYin bit a little harder at his neck.

"Thinking is overrated."

"This floor is hard."

HanYin pulled him into his lap and continued exploring the length of his neck.

"I should...." Jong-in moaned. "I should be... getting back. Shit."

"I don't want to let you go."

"They've got me working on different mixes for 'Crossing Time.'" Jong-in shifted restlessly in his lap, and HanYin growled at the stimulation to his hard shaft. He wanted them both naked, but he knew he had to stop. He didn't want Jong-in to get in trouble. BLE was a pretty accommodating place, but there were limits. Reluctantly he pulled away from Jong-in's neck.

"Meet me for dinner tonight?" he asked in a rush.

"What?"

"I'd like to take you to dinner," he said again. "Will you let me?"

"I... I'd love to, but I have to go to work right after I'm done here. I won't have time to eat before I have to catch the train," Jong-in said.

"What if I drove? Would you have time to eat, then?" HanYin said as they stood up.

"I think so. It's probably a little quicker by car."

"Good. I'll meet you at your desk after work, then," HanYin said, stealing another kiss.

"Do me a favor, HanYin?" Jong-in said, pausing just inside the door. "The next time you feel like this, come talk to me, okay? Don't try to face it alone."

"Only if you do the same," he said. "If you can't reach me, talk to Min-su dongsaeng or Jin-woo dongsaeng. They love you."

"Okay."

Just outside, HanYin pulled Jong-in to him for one last kiss, lingering over the taste of his mouth, savoring it. Then he let him go about his business. Their conversation hadn't started out that good, but it ended on a positive note. He was pretty sure Jong-in was a Fox-Spirit. It would explain a lot of things, like his ability to sort of disappear in plain sight. HanYin had watched him do it on a couple of occasions. He was sure if he weren't so aware of Jong-in's every move, he would have lost sight of him too. It was amazing to watch him just stand still and then see how people didn't know he was there, at least not on a conscious level. They did move around him without looking at him, as if something told them they needed to shift their path. Cheongul did it sometimes, too, but HanYin didn't think he was aware of it.

As long as he'd been alive, HanYin still didn't know what the range of his abilities were. They'd trained with their physical abilities, learning to control them to blend in better with humans. Every once in a while, he caught sight of things that shouldn't be there. Perhaps that was the spirit sight ChenBao was referring to. ChenBao. HanYin bit at the tip of his thumb absently. He couldn't seem to be completely at ease around her. Cheongul and Ki-tae had managed it, but he still found her qi overwhelming. Ki-tae was right: Soon-joon wouldn't invite someone into their home who was a threat, and he hadn't exactly made an effort to get to know her better either. HanYin figured he should try to become more comfortable with her, but he wasn't sure how to start.

"I wonder what she likes to eat," he murmured as he headed for one of the smaller recording studios.

JIN-WOO

JIN-WOO STARED at the computer screens, watching the time counts and jotting them down on a notepad. He rewound the footage a couple of times, making sure he could get the precise count for the cut. Going through the costumed footage, he found several shots he wanted to mix together, close-ups with midshots, and he wanted to include group shots as well. Bam Kiseu was a trio, and he didn't want to favor one over the others. Yet it still had to convey the story.

He smiled as he remembered how much of a fuss Cheongul had kicked up about the wigs. Jin-woo couldn't blame him, though. Those things were hot to begin with, but the temperatures were on the high side when they were filming. They looked so comfortable in the clothing, though. The topknot and long hair looked completely natural on HanYin, Cheongul and Ki-tae only less so. He wondered when they were all born. How old were they? How old were Soon-joon and ChenBao? How did they become Vampires? There were several comments that made Jin-woo suspect asking Ki-tae about it would be a bad idea. He knew there were still some things they needed to discuss, but he figured it could wait until after work.

Jin-woo shook his head. He needed to focus on what he was doing, not on Ki-tae. Well, not on Ki-tae in a personal capacity. He glanced down at his notes. Jong-in had said they were working on new mixes, something to make the song stand out from the original. Having the lyrics helped Jin-woo get an idea of what he wanted to do, but without the actual new audio tracks, it would be difficult to get the timing. He grabbed his phone and tapped out a text to Jong-in.

When do you guys think you'll be finished with the new mixes? I think I should wait before I really work on the timing.

Jong-in: *I should be finished later today. Working on a debut track now. Guy thinks he's already on top, won't listen to what I'm telling him.*

They're letting you run the board? That's awesome!

Jong-in: *It's cool. If this* IDIOT *would listen, we'd get something great, but he doesn't want to push. Thinks I'll back down.*

Doesn't know you. Keep pushing! Hwaiting!

Jong-in: *You realize you're a bit of a goof, right? Hwaiting? Seriously?*

Trying to be supportive... jerk. Get back to work!

Jin-woo laughed as he set his phone back down. Jong-in didn't usually call people names unless he was tired and they were irritating him. It sounded like this guy was doing more than just refusing to follow direction. It was important to listen to the sound engineers. It was their job to make a singer sound fantastic. In this case Jong-in was going to have to stand his ground and make this guy put out the sound Jong-in wanted. While Jong-in was laid-back and had an uncanny knack for maneuvering people when necessary, he could be incredibly stubborn when the situation called for it, and as far as Jong-in was concerned, the music always called for it.

About an hour and a half later, Jin-woo's phone pinged, pulling him out of his work zone. He grabbed it from on top of the desk and swiped it open. It was a message from Jong-in.

Jong-in: *You busy?*

Sort of, what do you need?

Jong-in: *Need you to come to the studio. Have something I want you to hear.*
On my way.

Jin-woo locked up his computer and grabbed his notepad and pencil. Chances were he would need them. He leaned his head into Hyung-jun's office and knocked on the doorjamb. Hyung-jun looked away from his monitors and smiled when he spotted Jin-woo.

"Seonbae, Jong-in-a has something he wants me to listen to. May I go?"

"Sure. Cho-ree-ssi wanted him to work on the mix for the performance video after they finished that trainee's debut single. Have them send me a copy if it's finished," Hyung-jun said.

"Okay." Jin-woo bowed and then headed to the recording studios.

As he walked, Jin-woo started humming, a melody coming together inside his head. Something sweet and sad, wistful, and then it struck him. This could work with the lyrics that had been spinning around his head for the last few days. With everything that had happened, Jin-woo hadn't gotten a chance to sit down and work on his song. Four weeks was very generous, but it passed quickly. With all the work they'd been doing on the videos, between filming and now postproduction, plus all the other drama, time was in short supply.

When he reached the studio assigned to Bam Kiseu, Jin-woo found Jong-in slouched down in his chair, his hood pulled low over his eyes and a set of over-the-ear headphones on, the band curling under his chin. Jin-woo smiled. If not for the telltale bob of his head, Jin-woo would have thought Jong-in was sleeping. Of course he knew him better than that. He had always thought it was a Jong-in thing, to sit like that when he was mixing, until he looked over and saw Cho-ree doing the same thing, only with a baseball cap sitting backward on his head. He gently tapped Jong-in on the shoulder.

"Hey, Jin-woo-ya." Jong-in smiled, something Jin-woo hadn't seen in while. "I didn't think you would get away so quick."

"Hyung-jun seonbae was actually kind of eager, I think. He said he wants you to send him a copy via email when it's done," Jin-woo said. He waved at Cho-ree when the engineer finally opened his eyes after tapping the space bar on the keyboard in front of him.

"Jin-woo dongsaeng." Cho-ree smiled. He was always smiling. "How are you?"

"I am good, Seonbae," Jin-woo said. "Jong-in-a said he had something he wanted me to listen to. I don't know why. He's the sound guy."

"We're a team. Sound and visuals go together," Cho-ree said, nodding at the same time. "We create the sound, you create the visual. To be a good-quality product, the sound needs to encourage and create that visual inside the audience's head. If we don't talk, we won't get that cohesion."

"I never thought of it that way," Jin-woo admitted. "I guess I do have something to contribute."

"You do. You're the most visual of all of us, at least storyboard-wise. Min-su-ya was in a meeting, Otherwise, I would have asked her to be here too. I'll have to catch her later," Jong-in said. "Pull up a chair. We'll get this started, and if you and Hyung-jun seonbae are happy with it, you can really start work on the video."

"That's if Ki-tae hubae doesn't come in before we're done and redo everything," Cho-ree chuckled.

"Is he really that bad?" Jin-woo asked.

"Not really, but we all pick on him about it," Cho-ree explained. "Ki-tae hubae has a really good ear. It's as if he can pick up the smallest sounds on the recording, and he'll use that to tweak the heck out of individual tracks. The best part of working with Ki-tae hubae, Cheongul hubae, and HanYin hubae is they listen to what you're telling them, and they'll give you what you're asking for. Sometimes they give you more than what you ask for. I'm thinking we should have them relay the vocals, really give 'Crossing Time' a makeover."

"Do they have time for that?" Jong-in asked. Jin-woo could see him turning the idea over in his head.

"Three hours tops, one for each of them." Cho-ree held up the last three fingers of his right hand. "And that's if they're happy with what comes out of the session. If not, they'll do it until the rest of us pass out from exhaustion, and then they'll keep going until it meets their standards. They're not one of the most popular bands in South Korea by sheer luck. They work hard, give it their all, and produce some fantastic music."

"Sometimes I wonder if there are times when they don't get along with each other," Jin-woo said. "They seem so close, but I can't imagine they don't have disagreements."

"They do." Cho-ree nodded. "Usually it's Cheongul hubae and Ki-tae hubae going head-to-head, with HanYin hubae trying to mediate. Well, he tries until he gets sick of it and smacks them both. This usually prompts a break, and then when everyone has their head back on straight, they'll come back into the studio, replay the tracks in question, and then go over the contending points until they get an answer they can all live with. They do everything as a team. They are Bam Kiseu."

"Then we need to do our best to give them a video they can be proud of," Jong-in said as he turned to Jin-woo. He then handed him a set of headphones, and they got to work.

JONG-IN

JONG-IN SIGHED as he leaned his head back against the chair. Putting his arms high above his head, he stretched the entire length of his body. He was tired, and although he had already been working for ten hours, his day wasn't done yet. He still had his first part-time job to go to, and there would be several more hours before he would be able to go to sleep. The door to the studio opened, and Cho-ree stuck his head inside. Jong-in worked up a smile for him, but it was an effort.

"Good work today, dongsaeng," he said before fully entering the room. "You have a great ear and an easy way with people. I was impressed with how you handled the trainee today. He was being a bit of a diva, and he doesn't have the chops to back it up yet. He's got raw potential, and you pushed until we got him to give what we knew he was capable of. On top of that, you finished the two remixes. I've sent them over to Hyung-jun-ssi and Cheong-bo hubae as well as Soon-joon-nim and the boys."

Jong-in felt his cheeks heating. He dropped his gaze to the floor. "I…. It wasn't anything special. I had really good material to work with."

"It's more than that," Cho-ree said. "You have natural talent, much like Jin-woo dongsaeng, just for sound rather than visuals. I think a lot of people are going to be impressed with what you've created."

"Gomabseumnida, seonbae," Jong-in said. He didn't have any further words. It was always awkward when people complimented him. He didn't quite know how to take it. He just… he just heard what the music could be and helped it get there.

"Get some rest. You've had a long day."

"Yes, seonbae."

"Have a good night, dongsaeng," Cho-ree said, and then he left with a wave of his hand.

Jong-in shook his head. He very much wished he could take that advice. With a sigh, he shut down the computers, turned off the lights, and left the room. He paused at his desk. It was still so weird to be here, to be in the headquarters of BL Entertainment. It was even more bizarre to be producing music, to be working with these amazing people. He'd laid everything out when he got kicked out of his home, but his plan hadn't included this for another several years. He was so sure it would take a long time to get to this point, and honestly, a part of him doubted he would make it. He had stopped allowing himself to hope for things because, most of the time, it didn't work out for him. This whole trying-to-be-normal thing kind of sucked.

And then there was HanYin. He hadn't seen that coming, hadn't even considered it would happen for him, let alone with someone like HanYin. Jong-in hadn't been a monk, but he'd never been able to fully enjoy the moments because he had to make sure he kept his secret. He never even considered there might be others. Well, okay, given the fact he existed, others had to exist, but he didn't think to ever meet one. Off and on throughout the day, Jong-in had found himself wondering just how many different types of nonhumans there were. HanYin had called him a Shifter, had in fact seemed very familiar and comfortable with the term. He'd also called him a Húli jīng, a Fox-Spirit. That would be *Gumiho* in Korean. Min-su had made him sit down with her and explained some things about herself. And while he felt honored she was trusting him with the truth, he wasn't able to tell her about himself. She knew what she was. He didn't... or hadn't at the time. Thinking about what his ears and tails looked like, Jong-in could see the reference to foxes. Maybe that explained why walking past cemeteries always bothered him. Every time he got near one, Jong-in heard whispers, voices so soft he couldn't make out what they were saying. He knew deep inside those voices were spirits. The older the cemetery, though, the louder the whispers became, yet, they were still unintelligible to him. Could he hear them because he was a Gumiho?

Jong-in didn't realize he'd reached his desk until he was standing in front of it, staring down at HanYin dozing. He smiled. HanYin looked so sweet and innocent, his dark lashes fanning across his high cheekbones, his lips slightly parted. His deep purple hair, a recent change that looked sexy as hell, was all tousled, and Jong-in was loath to wake him. He reached out to shake HanYin's shoulder but paused, recalling their conversation earlier in the day. He took a half step back and called his name instead.

"HanYin," he said quietly, not wanting to startle him awake. "HanYin, it's time to get up."

From adorable innocence to snarling, silver-eyed, and fanged, HanYin jerked awake. Jong-in held perfectly still, functioning on pure instinct for those several seconds. Slowly the silver bled from HanYin's eyes, and his fangs slid back... wherever they were kept when he wasn't using them. Jong-in shivered, remembering the way HanYin had scraped them against his skin, sending electric currents of pleasure all over his body. The scent of his arousal perfumed the air, and HanYin zeroed in on him, quirking up the corner of his mouth in a sexy smirk.

"Are you awake now?" Jong-in asked quietly, feeling as if he were in the presence of a superior predator, which, he realized, he was, and damned if that didn't jack up his arousal another notch.

"Yes, thank you," HanYin said as he rose and moved closer, almost too close for Jong-in to think clearly. Before he could say anything, HanYin leaned in and kissed him gently. He gasped and received a little kitten lick before HanYin drew back. Jong-in looked at him, confused as to why he'd pulled away. "If I continue to kiss you, I'm going to want to do other things, and you have to go to work."

"I'm glad one of us has a functioning brain," Jong-in muttered, and HanYin laughed.

"Are you ready?"

"Yes, I just have to grab my backpack," Jong-in said. He moved around HanYin to the desk and pulled his backpack out of the bottom drawer. Then he patted his pockets, making sure he had his keys, wallet, and phone. Once he was sure he had everything, Jong-in turned to HanYin and smiled. "Okay, I'm all set."

"Let's go, then," HanYin said as he grabbed a bag Jong-in hadn't seen. As they turned to leave, he handed it to Jong-in.

"What's this?"

"Your dinner," HanYin said, his cheeks turning rosy.

"You made me dinner?" Jong-in whispered. While he'd enjoyed HanYin's cooking while they were filming, this was different. This was just for him. It made him feel… all sorts of funny and hot. He hadn't had anyone cook just for him since he left home. His throat tightened, and he had to look away to compose himself. When he finally turned back to HanYin, he could see the confusion and the concern in his eyes.

"Are you okay?" HanYin asked. "I didn't mean to upset you. You don't have to eat it if you don't want to."

"No… yeah, I'm okay. I just…. It's been a very long time since anyone has cooked for me like this, Hyung," Jong-in said. "Thank you."

HanYin smiled. "Who said we were past honorifics? It's HanYin only. I hope you like it. There's steamed dumplings, which I know are your favorite. There's some pork spring rolls because they're a finger food, no chopsticks or utensils required. And there's a manju roll for dessert."

"When did you do all of this? I thought you were working on songs for the next album?" Jong-in said. "Cho-ree seonbae said you and the others were in and out of the studios, driving the rest of the department insane."

"He likes to tease us." HanYin huffed. "I made them this afternoon. I had some time between my interview and meeting you, so I headed to my apartment and put this together. I didn't want you to go without food, especially if you had to work several more hours."

"This is very thoughtful… and amazing," Jong-in said as they exited the elevator into the parking garage. "Thank you for taking care of me."

"No thanks needed," HanYin said, ducking his head, but Jong-in saw the corners of his mouth turn up just before he did so. "I just…."

"You just… what?"

"No, I… I can't." HanYin looked everywhere but at him, a clear sign he was getting twitchy.

"Hey." Jong-in put his hand on HanYin's arm, stopping his restless movement. "It's okay. Tell me when you're ready. In the meantime, where's your car?"

"That's the other thing. I took my bike in this morning, so I had to go get my car in order for you to eat on your way to work," HanYin said, clearly thankful for the change in topics.

They walked a little farther. As they did, Jong-in got this niggling feeling, as if someone were staring at him. He paused, looking around. Then he took a surreptitious sniff. There was a scent, something vaguely familiar but off somehow, something he'd smelled before. He turned this way and that, trying to pinpoint the scent trail. Suddenly the sensation vanished, and that was even stranger than having experienced it to begin with.

"What's wrong?" HanYin asked quietly.

"I just felt... as if someone was watching," Jong-in answered just as quietly. "There's a scent, something... I don't know, something I've smelled before, but I can't place it. It smelled... wrong, sort of twisted, if that makes any sense."

"Let's get to the car. We can talk about it on the way," HanYin said, bringing his hand to rest on Jong-in's lower back. It was soothing.

"You believe me?"

"Of course I do. I learned never to doubt my instincts a very long time ago," HanYin said. "It's kept me alive on more than one occasion."

"Exactly how old are you?"

"That's a discussion for another time," HanYin said with a self-deprecating smile. "Needless to say, I'm old enough."

"Uh-uh, I'm not going to accept that answer," Jong-in said with a chuckle as they stopped at a brilliant blue sporty-looking car. The lights flashed and the horn beeped, and HanYin gestured for him to get in.

Driving significantly reduced the time it took for Jong-in to get to work, and he had time to eat the delicious food HanYin had prepared for him. Their conversation had been easy and relaxed, although Jong-in wanted to ask more about HanYin's age, where he came from, and how he became... whatever he was. Jong-in realized HanYin had never really said exactly what he was.

Outside of the store where Jong-in worked, there was a small picnic table where they took their breaks. He and HanYin sat there now in a companionable silence that was immensely relaxing and incredibly bizarre. HanYin occasionally stole bites of food, but Jong-in didn't really mind. Well, he didn't mind when HanYin, Min-su, or Jin-woo did it, but anyone else would have gotten smacked.

They talked about a wide range of things: music, books, movies, the video and how it was coming. In truth, HanYin did most of the talking, but Jong-in knew he was like that, and it was fine because Jong-in wasn't much of a talker. His little diatribe earlier in the day was a prime example of "things Jong-in rarely did." Even so, he talked more with HanYin than he did with just about anyone else.

"Isn't your shift starting soon?" HanYin asked, bringing Jong-in out of his thoughts.

"Yeah. I really have to get going," Jong-in said.

"Then I'll see you tomorrow?" HanYin said as he climbed off the picnic bench.

"Definitely," Jong-in said, smiling. "Have a good night, HanYin."

"You as well," HanYin said. He glanced around and then leaned in and kissed Jong-in again. "Something for you to remember."

"As if I could forget." Jong-in snorted. "You're just as bad as Ki-tae hyung is with Jin-woo-ya, only you hide it better."

"I'm older," HanYin said with a chuckle, and then he walked away. Jong-in had the ridiculous urge to call him back, to keep him from leaving, but he fought against it. He had to work, and HanYin was not conducive to him working.

Min-su

Min-su stared at the words on the page, a sandwich in her other hand. She scanned them repeatedly, rolling them around in her head. For the first time since this whole adventure started, she had been able to put pen to paper and come up with something halfway decent. It still needed tweaking, and the beat wasn't clear in her head yet, but it was a start. She had the words, and they meant something. She just hoped when it was time to present the song, no one else got how personal it was.

This was how she felt about Cheongul. Yes, she had been a fangirl, not that she would ever admit it, not even under pain of torture, but since this project began, her feelings had only gotten stronger. She wasn't going to stalk him or anything creepy like that, but it was getting harder and harder to keep things casual. He was… amazing, and she didn't have to hide being a Shifter. That very thought made her feel lighter somehow. There was no doubt they were attracted to each other, and if they jumped into bed, it would be incredible, she was sure, but that wasn't all she wanted. The problem was she wasn't sure how Cheongul felt about her, and she was having an incredibly hard time working up the nerve to just ask.

She was the unconventional girl, but she wasn't *that* unconventional. Okay, perhaps she was, but when it came to Cheongul, she didn't always act as she normally would. Min-su leaned her head back against the chair, closing her eyes. She took a deep breath and then let it out slowly. It was getting harder and harder for her to be calm and professional. Every time she caught a whiff of him, it was as if she shifted into heat like some bitch. All she could think about was how he'd felt pressed against her, his cock tight against her core. Min-su whined softly, squeezing her legs together. This was definitely *not* the place for such thoughts. Her next deep breath only made her conscious mind realize what her body already knew.

"Why the hell do you always have to sneak up on me?" she snapped as she opened her eyes and looked at him upside down. "It's a really annoying habit of yours."

"It's not my fault you weren't paying attention," he said absently, his eyes roving over her as they flickered from black to silver and back again. "You're distracted."

"That *is* your fault," she muttered.

Suddenly Cheongul let out a low growl. He wrapped his fingers around her wrist and pulled her to her feet. The next things she knew, Min-su was staring down at the floor, and Cheongul's very fine ass, through the curtain of her blonde hair. She braced one hand against his back and pushed her hair to one side as she lifted her head. Just as she opened her mouth, she felt him clench his hand around her thigh… high up on her thigh, under the hem of her skirt. The pleasure wracked her entire body, robbing her of the ability to formulate coherent sentences.

"What?" was the best she could do.

Cheongul didn't respond, but he tightened his fingers again. Min-su glanced around in fear. Had anyone seen them? Was someone watching them now? She would never be able to show her face again if someone saw her being carried like a sack of potatoes through the offices. "Put me down."

"Not until I find us some privacy," he rumbled, and that was doing absolutely nothing to help her calm her body.

She knew he could smell her, how aroused she was. She covered her face with her hands. A part of her mind screamed at her to fight against this, to claw at his back and try to get away, but the other part, the larger part, didn't want to. She wanted to be alone with him. She wanted to feel him against her again, to kiss him again, feel his tongue in her mouth. She really was a bitch in heat.

Then she heard a slam, the clicking of a lock, and the flick of a switch. Cheongul set her on her feet and she immediately started pushing her hair out of her face again. Before she could do more than open her mouth to speak, Cheongul's lips were on hers. He was pressed against her from thigh to hip, and if her mouth wasn't full of his tongue, Min-su would have howled. She smelled his musky scent of sex and Min-su knew he was as affected as she was by the hard erection pressing against her stomach. This time they weren't going to stop. This time he wasn't going to run and leave her confused and horny. This time she was going to make sure of it.

Min-su pushed him back, following him, her mouth still feasting on his. She yanked the hem of his shirt out of his pants and only broke their kiss long enough to pull it over his head and toss it over her shoulder. With so much new skin to explore, Min-su didn't waste any time. She worked her way over his chest, feeling him curl his fingers in her hair and clench tight as she sucked hard on his nipple. He snarled, and she practically purred, knowing she was pleasing him.

Licking, nipping, teasing with flicks of her tongue, Min-su worried that nub until it was swollen from her attentions. Then she moved to its mate as she worked the button and zipper of his jeans open. Pushing the placket aside, she let out a little cry of delight when Cheongul slid, hot and hard and silky, into her hand. Slowly she stroked him, looking up into his face. His eyes were silver, and his fangs pricked at his lips.

"That is so fucking hot," she murmured, giving him another long stroke.

"You like my fangs, do you?" he growled softly pressing forward, pushing his cock into her grip. "Like the feel of my cock in your hand? You have the perfect touch, just hard enough to really make me feel it."

She murmured against his chest, throwing his words back at him. "You brought me in here for a reason, Cheongul. Why are we talking?"

"I like the sound of your voice," he said as he leaned down and nipped her shoulder. Little bolts of electric pleasure shot through her, and she shuddered.

Panting, she continued to stroke him, running her nail gently through the slit, giving a twist as she reached the head every other stroke or so. Each pass was made easier by his heavily leaking cock, slick and hot. Min-su let out a cry when he gripped her thighs and lifted, pulling his cock from her hand as she grabbed his shoulders to stay upright.

"I'm going to make a mess of you."

"Promise?" she growled as she bit his shoulder.

"Definitely."

Cheongul found a chair; she had no idea how he managed it, as focused as he was on driving her insane with his fingers teasing between her thighs. Her muscles trembled with each stroke, and if she hadn't had her mouth firmly planted against his shoulder, she was pretty sure she would have screamed her head off from that stimulation alone. Cheongul had seriously talented fingers. He sank down into the chair, her thighs now on either side of his, parted wide as he moved his legs outward. She felt her panties being pulled to one side and the hot, slick head of his cock pressing against her. Dammit, too slow.

"Ready?" he purred against her throat.

"I want you inside me," she moaned, rocking her hips, trying to press down on him.

He nudged once, twice, and then she couldn't take it anymore. She pressed down just as he gave one hard thrust upward, sinking fully inside. Min-su threw back her head and howled long and loud as pleasure slammed into her. Energy coursed through her, heightening… everything. This was not going to be gentle. She couldn't do gentle right now. She buried her claws in his shoulders, and she cut her own lip as her fangs burst forth.

"That's it, Min-su, honey, let me hear you," Cheongul said, nipping her ear before swirling his tongue along the delicate edge. "Let me feel you. Let me see you come apart for me."

Min-su matched him thrust for thrust, the sound of flesh meeting flesh echoing through the room. She could feel him in her soul, feel his heart beating in time with hers. He was so hard and thick inside her, filling her perfectly. She slowed, circling her hips, feeling him rub her deep inside. The scrape of his teeth against her skin was a sharp pleasure-pain. He gripped her hips through the fabric of her skirt just the way she liked, his claws piercing the fabric, lifting and then lowering her down on his cock slowly, letting her feel every inch sliding into her core.

"Cheongul," she whined as the sweet tension built within her, making her muscles shake.

His response was a growl. She could feel a sense of urgency in him. Min-su opened her eyes, unaware she had closed them. If silver could be described as burning, it was epitomized in Cheongul's eyes. The overwhelming need to feel his fangs in her flesh came over Min-su.

She slowed the working of her hips again, pressed firmly against him. With gentle fingers, she stroked his lips, probing until he opened and revealed the glistening length of his fangs. She caressed one with a single finger, and he jerked within her. He grabbed her wrist, holding her gaze with his own. Min-su couldn't have looked away even if she wanted to. She was mesmerized by the way he nuzzled her wrist tenderly. He slowly swirled his tongue, and she watched it dance over her skin, the rolling of his hips matching the leisurely movement of his tongue. His other hand lay flat over her pelvis, and he shifted it to keep her rocking in slow motion.

Cheongul's eyes fluttered closed, and he slowly sank his fangs into her wrist. Min-su moaned at the sensation, white-hot, with just enough pain to sharpen the pleasure. Her breath stuttered, and she bucked her hips erratically, matching his movements, as a hot rush filled her. Min-su couldn't breathe for the sensations battering against her, all running in tandem with the languid draw of his mouth on her wrist. Cheongul launched her, sending her flying, even as he anchored her with his fangs in her wrist.

When she was younger, Min-su had planned to keep her virginity until she married. Being turned changed all that. Her body made demands she was unable to resist, no matter how hard she tried. She was not inexperienced, but the feel of Cheongul inside her, the feel of his fangs and the pull of his mouth on her wrist, it was the most amazing experience she'd ever had. Nothing could compare to it, nothing would ever measure up to it. In that moment she felt herself fall all the way. There was no turning back. She loved Cheongul. The realization was both amazing and catastrophic. There was no way he could feel the same.

CHEONGUL

CHEONGUL HAD always resisted the urge to feed from a Shifter, a respect for the departed sort of thing. He'd had sex with them but never taken blood. When he needed to feed, he chose humans or other Vampires, never a Shifter. Min-su tasted... amazing. He'd never gotten such a buzz from feeding before. It was as if his entire body were overflowing with energy. One last pull, and he licked the puncture wounds, two flicks of his tongue resulting in another moan from the amazing woman straddling his lap.

He turned to Min-su, saw the heat in her eyes, how they burned brilliant red. She was incredible. Cheongul curled his hand around the back of her neck and pulled her down for another kiss. Shivers raced through him as she nipped at his lips, just enough to sting, but not draw blood. When breathing became necessary, he let her up with a reluctant chuckle.

"What?" she murmured as she laid her head on his shoulder, playing with the hair at his nape.

"This was not the location I would have chosen for our first time together," he said. "I was hoping for a more... romantic setting, not an empty studio."

"So you're saying you were planning to seduce me, huh?" she asked, tugging a strand of hair. "Strategizing ways to get in my pants?"

"Well, I... that's not, damn," he muttered, letting his head fall back. Her giggle brought his head back up, and he bumped his shoulder, making her lift her head. She was smiling.

"I'm not complaining about the location at all," she purred before kissing him slowly. "Romance is all well and good, but let's be honest. Neither one of us was thinking about romance when this started. We weren't even thinking protection. We were thinking hot, dirty, monkey sex, and that's what we had, and it was incredible. Don't you dare go regretting it, or so help me, I'll smack the shit out of you."

"I don't regret the sex, just the setting. As for protection, Spiritual Beings can't transmit diseases. With Vampires and Shifters, our bodies attack and kill any human pathogens. I'm not sure about other species. Pregnancy would only be a concern if you were in heat, which, if you were, we would not be talking right now. We'd still be fucking," he said with a smile. "And please don't smack me. HanYin gets all worked up over the bruises you leave behind, and I can't always keep him from pinning me down to make sure I don't have any other injuries."

"You let HanYin hyung pin you down? Well, isn't that just a kinky little thought." She giggled again. She was so freaking adorable when she giggled.

"HanYin is…. he can be very persistent when he wants to be, and he gets very stubborn when it comes to making sure his family is okay," Cheongul said, growing serious as he considered the reasons why HanYin was how he was. "We…. None of us have bright, shiny pasts, but I'd be hard-pressed to say which of us had the worst of it. I would have to say it was a toss-up between Ki-tae and HanYin. They're my brothers, and if I could erase the pain they've experienced, I would do it in a heartbeat."

"That's how I feel about Jin-woo-ya and Jong-in-a," Min-su said, putting her head back on his shoulder. "Oppa…."

"Just Cheongul," he said quietly. "I would be pleased if you would drop the honorifics."

"Then you have to do the same," she said, and he could hear the pleasure in her voice.

"What were you going to say?"

"Where do we go from here?" She spoke so quietly he almost didn't hear her.

"We take it one day at a time," he said as he wrapped his arms around her. "I am… no good at relationships. I can, as I've been told on many occasions, be very difficult to deal with, especially when I'm in a foul mood. I… I'm not, I have…. The only way to put it is I have anger management issues, and it has resulted in horrible things. I have a tendency to get… physical if I lose control."

"One day at time, hm?" she said, shifting in his lap and making him groan. He gripped her hips to hold her still, and Cheongul just knew she was smirking. "I think I can manage that. I'm not always easy to get along with either. I didn't used to be that way. When I was little, my mom said I was such a laid-back child, happy and well-behaved. That all changed when we were attacked."

"It wasn't just you?"

"No, and I don't think I want to talk about this right now," she said, sitting up, her face full of sadness. "Maybe some other time."

"Would you have dinner with me tomorrow night?" he asked suddenly, not sure what he was thinking. He was more of a hookup sort of guy, and that had worked for him for centuries. Now, for her, he wanted to be a date kind of guy, and he wasn't sure exactly how to do that.

"I… sure, that would be great." She smiled, and it lit up his world. Cheongul knew he was in deep trouble. Min-su wasn't like the other women he'd had sex with. She wasn't like any woman he'd ever encountered. Yes, he was definitely in trouble.

After they finally parted and straightened themselves out, Min-su went to get her things and then return to the studio. He headed home, and now, Cheongul paced back and forth across his living room. He looked around, wondering if Min-su would like it, or if she would think it was too dark, too masculine, too modern. Cheongul sighed. He'd never worried about his apartment before. He loved it. The only place better than his was Soon-joon's, only because that was his home. He lived there just as much as he lived in his apartment.

Cheongul didn't need a lot of space, so he'd chosen a relatively small apartment. He just had a single bedroom, living room, kitchen, and the bathroom. When he'd first moved in, there was a second bedroom, but he converted that into a home recording studio. He did a lot of his work there and then sent the files to BLE when he was ready to polish them up or if he had some tweaks he wanted to make that he couldn't do at home. He felt it suited him, but he wondered what Min-su would think of it.

Then there was the fact he had no idea what she liked to eat. He was partial to pork, but that didn't mean Min-su liked it. Cheongul wanted to throw something. This was going to drive him insane. Hookups were easy and relatively uncomplicated. Not much thought went into it beyond "Damn, she's hot" and "You wanna?" Dating was a whole other ball game. He didn't know what constituted romantic, and he was loath to ask for advice, mainly because he knew his brothers would never let him live it down.

Yet if he wanted to make the date memorable for Min-su, he was going to have to step out of his comfort zone, which meant risking near-constant ribbing from Ki-tae and HanYin for about the next century, if not longer. Giving in to the inevitable, Cheongul pulled his phone out and dialed Ki-tae's number. If he wasn't currently involved in seducing Jin-woo, Ki-tae should pick up on the first or second ring.

THIS WAS not supposed to be happening. He was not supposed to be with someone else. He was supposed to realize where he belonged and be obedient. His actions were deplorable. There was no room for anyone else in his life, in his heart. There was only space for one, and that one was already chosen. He turned to the wall, examining the music venues again. An updated schedule was required. They had changed so many events that what he currently had was no longer accurate. Simply unbearable.

He yanked pins from the board and tossed them aside angrily, heedless of where they landed. Once all the errors were removed, he was much calmer. He could focus. He nibbled on his thumb as he walked back to the desk and tapped a few keys on the laptop. Then he took his seat and began typing. Clearly another message had to be sent, and this one needed to make a more significant impression, make him understand obedience was expected, demanded.

No, no, he would give him a chance to make reparations, one chance and one chance only. Then if that failed, he would deliver another message.

JIN-WOO

JIN-WOO AND Ki-tae were working companionably in the kitchen, Jin-woo only having to occasionally avoid wandering hands, when the door chime rang.

"I'll get it," Ki-tae said as he sucked juice off his thumb, winking when he caught Jin-woo staring.

"Evil bastard," Jin-woo muttered, but his tone conveyed how much he didn't mean it. He was just putting the rice into a bowl when Ki-tae came back into the kitchen. He looked very serious. "Ki-tae? Is everything all right?"

"HanYin is here," Ki-tae said. "He wants to speak to you, says he owes you an apology. What happened between you two? Why would he need to apologize?"

"He doesn't, really," Jin-woo said with a sigh. "He was just being the protective brother he is."

"What happened?" Ki-tae asked again.

"Nothing actually happened, Ki-tae," Jin-woo said. "It was shortly after we had gotten to the office. Shin-bai hyung brought me to Huijang-nim's office. You were out of it, and when I tried to check on you, HanYin hyung stopped me. He said something to me in what I can only assume was Mandarin, growled it, actually, and wouldn't let me near you. Soon-joon-nim explained why. There's no reason for him to apologize."

"Yes, there is," HanYin said quietly from the doorway. When Jin-woo looked over, he saw HanYin's hands filled with a package wrapped in red fabric. He walked over to Jin-woo and bowed low. "Please forgive my behavior this afternoon."

"HanYin hyung," Jin-woo said quietly. "There's really no need. I understand you were protecting your family."

"It was unacceptable for me to treat you in such a fashion," HanYin said.

"HanYin hyung...."

"Jin-woo," Ki-tae said from his spot on the other side of the counter. When Jin-woo looked at him, he shook his head.

Jin-woo sighed and took the offered package. It felt like a wooden box of some sort. With that done, he bowed to HanYin, smiling in thanks, and set the gift on the counter.

"I must get going. I will see you two tomorrow," HanYin said with another small bow, and then he quickly left. The door closed almost silently behind him.

"What was that all about?" Jin-woo said.

"Open it," Ki-tae said as he pulled a bottle from the wine rack and grabbed the corkscrew.

Jin-woo carefully untied what turned out to be silk cloth. Inside he found three round bamboo boxes. He lifted the first lid, and the delicious scent of steamed dumplings filled the air, making Jin-woo's mouth water. The second contained dwaeji bulgogi, spicy marinated pork, one of his favorite dishes. Jin-woo looked at Ki-tae, who gave him a small smile, and then turned to the last container. He gasped in surprise when he saw six manju, one of his favorite sweet pastries, arranged inside.

"Do you know what this means?" Ki-tae asked as he poured two glasses of wine.

"He asked either Min-su-ya or Jong-in-a about my favorite foods," Jin-woo said, feeling a little bit overwhelmed by the thoughtfulness. "I've never had anyone do that before. Min-su-ya could burn water, and Jong-in-a is too busy to cook for himself, let alone anyone else."

Ki-tae said, "When he is worried or happy or sad, or when someone is sick either physically or emotionally, HanYin cooks."

"Wait. You mean HanYin hyung cooked for me because...." Jin-woo couldn't even finish the sentence, his throat was so tight.

"He will talk at great length about general things, impersonal things, but when he wants to truly say something important to him, HanYin speaks with his cooking. He is saying you matter to him. Your happiness matters to him."

That did it. The tears slid down his face, and Jin-woo turned away from Ki-tae, embarrassed. Ki-tae wrapped his strong arms around him, and Jin-woo turned, burying his face into Ki-tae's chest. Really he felt like such an idiot, crying over something like this. Yet it had been so long since anyone had told him, even indirectly, that he mattered to them. Rationally he knew his friends cared, but little gestures like this, even it if was meant to be an apology, were a rare thing.

When Ki-tae chuckled, Jin-woo smacked him on the chest. It took a few more minutes before he could compose himself, and then Jin-woo stepped back. He grabbed two of the containers, pulling the dumplings out of Ki-tae's eager reach, earning a pout, and took them over to the table. While Ki-tae took the last box, he gathered up their rice bowls and the rice and placed them on the table. It was nice eating with someone. Usually he ate alone in his apartment. This was weird, but in a good way.

"I wonder if you realize exactly how much danger you were in this afternoon?" Ki-tae asked as they ate.

"What do you mean?"

"We're Vampires. We're faster, stronger. Our senses and reflexes are sharper than any human's," Ki-tae explained.

"Are you saying HanYin hyung would have hurt me?"

"Had he perceived you as a threat to me, he would have killed you," Ki-tae said softly.

"I don't understand. Are you trying to make me afraid of him? HanYin hyung is one of the sweetest people I know," Jin-woo said with a huff. "He's your brother. Why would you talk about him like this?"

"Precisely because he is my brother, and I love him," Ki-tae said. "HanYin *is* very sweet. He is caring and funny and mischievous. He's also one of the most dangerous Vampires I know. I'm not trying to make you afraid of him. I just want you to realize we're not like the people you've dealt with most of your life. We don't always think as humans do. Today HanYin was protecting his family, something extremely important to him. Had he considered you a threat, he would have killed you, and he would have hated himself for it. That day I sent you for HanYin, when Cheongul was… having a bad day? It was because Cheongul was having a hard time controlling his anger. He was close to losing that control, and when that happens, things bleed, things die. HanYin and I had the best chance of calming him down, or at least containing it to just us. It would have killed a little more of his spirit if he had hurt someone."

"And you?" Jin-woo asked, looking at Ki-tae. "What about you, Ki-tae?"

"I… get panic attacks," Ki-tae said softly. "Of a sort, at any rate. There are certain things, certain concepts that trigger me. I also… don't always wake up nicely."

"What does that mean?" Jin-woo cocked his head to one side, studying the serious expression on Ki-tae's face. It was clear this conversation was very important to him, but Jin-woo couldn't figure out if they were talking about what was really bothering Ki-tae.

"I'm not always awake when I start moving," Ki-tae said, and it seemed as if he struggled to find the right words. "It takes a few moments for my mind to register my surroundings. It's worse if I'm on my stomach and someone startles me awake. I don't deal well with being crowded or being touched or grabbed from behind. It gets a sort of fight-or-flight response, but for me, it's almost always fight."

"I always wondered why you guys had the same positioning whenever you were out in a crowd. You were always between Cheongul hyung and HanYin hyung, with Shin-bai hyung behind you and then two bodyguards on either side of the three of you. There was always at least a foot of space that seemed to be a sort of no-man's-land," Jin-woo said.

"We've gotten better with the crowds," Ki-tae said with a small smile. "Not many people are brave enough to try pushing past Shin-bai-ssi."

"You woke up fine this morning," Jin-woo pointed out as he took a bite of rice.

"I did indeed," Ki-tae said with a husky chuckle. "Another fact indicating you're a special person, Jin-woo."

"Me? I'm nothing special."

"You don't realize how special you are," Ki-tae said. Then he bit his lip, letting it slowly slide from between his teeth, and Jin-woo lost all thought of what he was doing. He shook his head and then glared at Ki-tae.

"Finish your dinner before it gets cold," he said with a huff.

"Only if I can have you for dessert," Ki-tae purred, licking his lips.

"Dammit, Ki-tae," Jin-woo whimpered softly. "You are evil!"

Jin-woo managed to make it through dinner without jumping Ki-tae. He was quite impressed with himself. As he put the last dish away and hung the towel up to dry, he felt Ki-tae press up against him, wrapping his strong arms around his waist and pulling him back against his chest. Jin-woo smiled. Ki-tae just nuzzled his neck, and it was so adorable. He wasn't looking for sex at that moment. Apparently Ki-tae just wanted to snuggle, and Jin-woo was all for that. Not that he minded sex—he loved sex—but snuggling was one of his favorite things, and he didn't get to do it often. Yet Jin-woo couldn't shake the feeling there was something on Ki-tae's mind.

"What are you thinking about?"

"Every Sunday we go to Abeoji's house for dinner," Ki-tae said quietly. "Would you be willing to come with me?"

"You're inviting me to family dinner?" Jin-woo was a little surprised. While he had gotten friendly, or relatively so, with Cheongul and HanYin, he hadn't spent much time associating with Soon-joon, crying on him notwithstanding.

"You don't have to if you don't want to," Ki-tae said, releasing his hold. Immediately Jin-woo grabbed his wrists and pulled Ki-tae's arms back around him.

"Don't pull away from me," Jin-woo said quietly. "I've never been invited to a family dinner before, and it was a bit surprising. I'd love to go."

"You would?"

Jin-woo could hear the smile in Ki-tae's voice and looked up at him, placing a kiss on his lips. "Yes, I would."

"Perfect," Ki-tae said before lifting Jin-woo off his feet and carrying him through the apartment to the bedroom. "Now I can focus on dessert."

"You are a sex fiend," Jin-woo laughed.

"Am I?" Ki-tae asked, pausing beside the bed. He set Jin-woo down, and that didn't sit well. "Does it bother you?"

"Yes, I'm going to complain about having lots of sex with a man I've been fantasizing about for years." Jin-woo snorted as he pulled Ki-tae's shirt out of his pants. "I love how much you want me. It makes me feel... special, desirable."

"I want you all the time. It's just...." Ki-tae stopped, and Jin-woo had the feeling there was a lot behind that deliberate act.

He looked up from his self-appointed task of unbuttoning Ki-tae's shirt to study him. There was something in his eyes, something fearful, almost panicked. Could this be what he was talking about earlier? Was there something about their current discussion that set Ki-tae on edge? Jin-woo wanted to ask, but he wasn't sure how to word the question. He gave a soft sigh as he brushed Ki-tae's shirt off his muscled shoulders. God, his arms were amazing, smooth, sleek muscles.

"Ki-tae," Jin-woo said as he placed a kiss on his sternum. "I get the impression there is something we need to talk about, but for whatever reason, the topic really sets you on edge. I know I overreacted earlier, and the truth is, I really don't like secrets, but I've realized trying to force the issue doesn't work either. We were both hurting today, and it was my fault for not giving you a chance to explain. This is clearly something that bothers you a lot, and I'm pretty sure it has something to do with what you told me earlier, so I'm going to do my very best to wait until you're ready to talk about it. I won't push you away, and I won't walk away again. I promise you that."

Ki-tae stopped the movement of his hands, holding them against his chest. He leaned down and touched their foreheads together. A shaky sigh puffed against Jin-woo's face. "Thank you."

That was it. No other words passed his lips, but what he had said was enough. Ki-tae wasn't ready, and Jin-woo was going to wait until he was. It was going to be hard, but Ki-tae was worth it. Surprisingly the whole atmosphere changed, and instead of another round of sex, they merely undressed and climbed into the bed.

It was a measure of how much things affected Ki-tae that he laid his head on Jin-woo's chest, wrapped his body around him, and after placing a gentle kiss on his skin, slipped into sleep. At that moment, Ki-tae was the one who needed to be held, needed to be comforted, and it made Jin-woo's heart ache. He gently stroked the silky strands of Ki-tae's hair, caressing the outer furl of his ear, and held him. Jin-woo was relatively short and often the one being held. It was... nice to be the one doing the holding, the one giving the comfort when it was needed, especially to someone as powerful and confident as Ki-tae. Soon Jin-woo drifted off to sleep, Ki-tae still firmly held in his arms.

CHEONGUL

HE'D PUT it off for as long as he could. Now it was no longer avoidable. He had to meet Min-su at the office soon, and he wasn't close to being ready to have her in his apartment. Cheongul sighed and hit the Call button. On the second ring, Ki-tae's voice came across the line.

"*Yeoboseyo?*"

"I need your help," Cheongul said without preamble.

"What? Why? What's wrong?" Ki-tae's voice sounded panicked and angry at the same time.

"No, no, nothing's wrong, per se." Cheongul sighed. "I... invited Min-su to dinner tonight... at my place, and I have no clue what I'm doing, Ki-tae. I don't do the dating thing, and I need your help."

"A date? You asked Min-su dongsaeng on a date?" He could hear the amusement in Ki-tae's voice, and he wasn't happy about it.

"Yeah, I did, and I want it.... I want it to be special, Ki-tae, because she's special." Cheongul hated to admit that, even to his brother, but if he didn't explain to Ki-tae why this was so important to him, it would take forever to get the help he needed. "Please, Ki-tae."

That seemed to get through to Ki-tae, that please. His tone immediately changed.

"I'll be right there," he said, and then he hung up.

Twenty minutes later there was a knock on his door. Cheongul opened it to find Ki-tae and HanYin standing there. Ki-tae wrapped his arm around Cheongul's shoulders and led him into the living room while HanYin headed straight for the kitchen. Cheongul couldn't help his smile. His brothers were awesome. Most of the time, Cheongul sat at the small island that separated his kitchen from the rest of the apartment. However, he did have a small space where he had placed a table large enough to seat four people when he had company, not something that happened very often.

"Where are your linens?" Ki-tae asked.

"Linens?"

"Tablecloths, napkins... those things," Ki-tae said with a chuckle.

"Oh, they're over here."

He walked to the cabinets to the left of the kitchen area. He pulled out a dark blue tablecloth and matching napkins in a lighter shade. Running his hand through his hair, Cheongul watched Ki-tae set the table, including wineglasses. HanYin was busy at work in the kitchen. The smells were enough to make Cheongul's mouth water. He came up behind him and snatched a piece of meat. HanYin slapped his hand with the spoon when he reached for another, and Cheongul pouted.

"We're trying to make a good impression here. If you eat it, then there won't be anything left for your dinner with Min-su dongsaeng," he admonished.

"I can't help it," Cheongul said, snatching another piece. "You're an amazing cook."

"When do you have to meet Min-su dongsaeng?" Ki-tae asked absently as he eyed the table, shifting things here and there. Cheongul stared at it. Where had the flowers come from? And he owned a vase? He looked at Ki-tae, who shrugged and then winked at him. Cheongul looked at his watch.

"I have to leave in about forty-five minutes."

"Go get ready," Ki-tae said. "We'll take care of everything here and be gone by the time you get back."

"You guys… thanks," Cheongul said.

"You're our brother," HanYin said. "Of course we're going to help you."

"Min-su dongsaeng is special to you," Ki-tae said. "That's all we really need to know. Go on and get ready."

Cheongul nodded and then went into his room. He sat at the foot of his bed and put his head in his hands. He took several deep breaths. It had been so long since anyone had gotten any sort of real emotional reaction out of him. Yes, there was the pure animalistic lust; that went without saying. Being a Vampire didn't change his body's urges. In fact, it tended to sharpen them. After turning, he'd developed an allure that drew people to him, made it easier to hunt and feed. He had always used it to his best advantage, but he had never gotten emotionally involved with any of them… until that one time. Cheongul shook his head. He really didn't want to think about that, not tonight.

Pushing to his feet, Cheongul walked over to his closet and slid the doors open. He pulled out a pair of black dress slacks, a deep red shirt, a thin tie, and a black blazer. He grabbed his black dress shoes and set everything on the bed.

On his way into the bathroom, he grabbed a towel from the shelf inside the door. Much like the rest of his apartment, Cheongul's bathroom wasn't huge. The most prominent feature was the oval bathtub on a raised pedestal of gray marble, a material which covered the floor as well.

Cheongul placed his towel on the vanity and opened the shower door. He turned on the water, holding his hand under the spray to measure the temperature. When there was just enough heat to sting, Cheongul got undressed and stepped under the spray.

He luxuriated in the heat, feeling his muscles relax and the tension leaving his body. As much as he wanted to lollygag in the shower, he had to get things moving. Cheongul chuckled. It was one of his little quirks, taking way too long in the shower or the bath. Of course, there had been times in his life where he had to go for weeks without being clean, so when he got the chance to bathe, he made the most of it. Cheongul preferred baths to showers, and he never scrimped on that portion of his bathroom. The one in his apartment was almost as luxurious as the one at Soon-joon's house.

A few minutes later, he stood in front of his mirror, turning his head this way and that. Something in the routine helped Cheongul focus and regain his calm. It was odd, really. The little things made a difference. Soon-joon had often told him that, but he hadn't realized how much of a difference they made to *him*.

He took the mousse from the shelf and put a dollop in his palm. He worked it between his fingers and then into his hair. When he was finished, he had pushed the right side back while the rest of the longish strands went to the left and fell over his forehead. He put small gold hoops in his ears. He donned his black watch and two understated rings on the ring and pinkie fingers of his right hand. A dash of cologne, and he was all set. Back in the bedroom, Cheongul pulled on his clothes, making sure everything was in perfect order, and then he walked out into his living room. Ki-tae gave him a wolf whistle, and HanYin pretended to swoon. Cheongul punched him in the arm.

"Go get your lady," Ki-tae said, pushing Cheongul toward the door. He grabbed his keys off the half-circle table just to the left of his entertainment center.

Pausing at the door, he turned to look at his brothers, smiling. "Gomabseumnida."

"Go," Ki-tae said with a chuckle while HanYin shooed him out the door.

On his way to the offices, Cheongul stopped and purchased a bouquet of flowers from a street vendor, delicately scented so as not to be too much for her sensitive nose. He pulled into the parking garage, and once the car was parked, he made his way into the building. Cheongul tried to ignore the stares as he walked through the halls. He had arranged to meet Min-su at her desk at six o'clock. She wasn't there, and for half a second, he thought she'd stood him up until he remembered Cheong-bo had her working in the editing room that day. One of the things he had learned about her was Min-su was very precise. He placed the flowers on her desk and leaned against it, prepared to wait as long as necessary.

MIN-SU

MIN-SU SIGHED. She raised her hands high above her head and stretched. Then she looked at her watch.

"Oh crap!" she yelled as she jumped up from her chair and rushed out of the studio after shutting everything down. She ran back to her desk and skidded to a stop as she rounded the corner, her breath catching.

Cheongul leaned against her desk, looking as if he'd just stepped from the pages of *GQ Korea*. God, he was so beautiful. What had she been thinking, accepting a date request from him?

Min-su shook herself mentally. She straightened her spine. She'd survived the attack that killed half her family. Life was too short and too precious to waste on fear. She would not let it rule her.

Min-su walked toward Cheongul. He looked so serious standing there, but when he spotted her, his face lit up, and he smiled. Min-su felt her heartbeat quicken. There was no faking that expression. He was happy to see her.

"Min-su." His voice was soft, but she could hear it and the pleasure in it.

"I'm sorry I'm late," she said as approached. "I got caught up in editing. Do you mind waiting a few minutes while I freshen up?"

"Of course I don't mind. Take your time," he said as he rose and took her hands in his. That simple touch made her shiver. She felt her cheeks heat and ducked her head.

Nodding once, Min-su grabbed her bag from her desk and headed for the locker rooms. There was no way she was just going to freshen up, and she'd mastered being ready in fifteen minutes including a shower. Honestly she didn't understand why or how it took people hours to get ready to go out. Perhaps she was just a weird girl, but she didn't, generally, waste time when she had somewhere to be, and this time was no exception. She took one last look at herself in the mirror, turning this way and that to make sure everything was in place. She tucked her dirty clothes in a plastic bag and then into her backpack. Once she was satisfied she looked as good as she could, Min-su headed back to Cheongul.

"I'm all set," she said with a bright smile. He walked over to her and offered his arm. Why did that gesture just go right to her heart?

"You look so beautiful," he said softly.

"Thank you," she said and felt her cheeks heat again. She blushed way too much around him. "You look amazing."

"I try."

Min-su laughed, and from the twinkle in Cheongul's eye, that was his intention. As they walked to his car, Min-su and Cheongul talked about the video and what she was currently working on. It was nice how he paid attention to what she had to say, not dismissing her, as had happened in the past. Not the most recent past—the people at BLE were very good about actively listening to opinions and suggestions. She hadn't met a single person who thought their way was the only way to do things or that their idea was the only good idea.

When they reached his car, he held the door for her, and that gave her pause. It wasn't that she was offended by the gesture, just surprised. She smiled at him and then climbed in.

The ride to his apartment was just as... casual as the walk to the car. When he opened the door for her, Min-su stared up at his building. It was one of those luxury high-rises, lots of chrome and glass on the outside. She preferred the more traditional buildings, but it wasn't horrible. Some modern buildings were truly atrocious, and she questioned the aesthetics of the architects. Once more he offered her his arm, and they went inside. When they reached his apartment, Cheongul gave her a hesitant smile as he opened the door. He gestured for her to precede him inside.

Min-su had been prepared for an ultramodern apartment with a large amount of chrome accents, much like the outside of the building, enough to blind a person when the sunlight hit it. What she got was a tastefully decorated home in neutral tones of dove gray, charcoal gray, and black. She had expected his apartment to be large, with almost too much space, but it was... decidedly cozy. Min-su smiled. Cheongul was a simple man, it seemed, with simple tastes.

"You look surprised," he said as he closed the door behind him.

"I am," she said honestly. "I thought an idol would have a huge, almost ostentatious penthouse apartment. I'm pleasantly surprised to be wrong. Your place is warm, inviting, and, dare I say, cozy."

"I don't need a lot of space. I'm one person," Cheongul said with a shrug. "I have as much room as I need and no more."

"I like it. The tones and colors suit you too," she said as she walked into the small living room.

The wall opposite the door had a line of windows reaching three-quarters of the way up the wall. The top of the curtains was hidden by a box valance. The trayed ceiling provided further lighting, with alcoves running along all four sides while three recessed lighting fixtures shone down on the entertainment center. Beneath the mounted TV was a mirror reflecting the plants, sculptures, and electronics. Min-su smiled when she saw the PlayStation4. It didn't surprise her that Cheongul was a gamer.

In the middle of the space, he had a square table that reminded Min-su of black marble countertops she had often seen in magazines. Two armchairs sat to the right of the coffee table while the matching couch faced the entertainment center. The outside of all three pieces was a charcoal gray. The rectangular ottoman was a shade lighter and matched the floor-length curtains over the windows. The wrought-iron chandelier with flame-shaped bulbs emitted a soft, romantic light. Min-su smiled. She really liked the room.

"I hope you're hungry," Cheongul said, drawing her attention. She turned to see a table set for two and with a small vase of blue flowers resting in the center. They were pretty and sweet, and Min-su felt herself fall a little more. She walked over to the table as Cheongul set two plates down and then lit the two blue tapers. "I have a confession to make."

Well, that didn't sound good.

"And what is your confession?" she asked warily.

"All this, the table, the food, it wasn't me," he said, looking nervous. "Ki-tae set the table, and HanYin made the food. I'm no good at either of those things. I… don't generally date, but I wanted this to be… special. So I called them for help."

"It's not easy to admit, is it?"

"What?"

"Needing help. I don't like to admit it either, and that you would tell me this, instead of claiming credit for it, that tells me how much of a good and honest person you are, Cheongul," she said. "That you would do this for me, it…. Thank you."

Then he was standing in front of her, cupping her cheek in his hand. He kissed her gently, and Min-su felt it to her toes. "You're most welcome, but it is I who should thank you for even coming here to begin with."

"No more of that," she said, putting two fingers over his lips. "Let's eat before dinner gets cold. We wouldn't want HanYin oppa's efforts to be wasted, would we?"

"No, definitely not."

KI-TAE

"ARE YOU sure you want to do this today?" Ki-tae asked as he pulled on his hoodie.

"I can't keep putting it off," Jin-woo said. "I can't stay here forever."

"Why not?" Ki-tae hadn't meant for the words to come out as sullen as they did, but he liked having Jin-woo in his apartment. He suddenly found himself wrapped in Jin-woo's arms.

"As much as I love being here with you, I don't think we're ready to move in together just yet," Jin-woo said, giving him a gentle kiss. "We've been shoved together by circumstance, and I want to make sure this is… real, if that makes any sense."

"More than you realize," Ki-tae said with a sigh. He placed his forehead against Jin-woo's. "I… really like having you here."

"I want the chance to make that dinner I promised you for our first date."

"You can do that here."

"Ki-tae."

"All right." Ki-tae pouted, earning another chuckle from Jin-woo. "You're still coming to dinner on Sunday, right?"

"Of course. I wouldn't miss it," Jin-woo promised, and that eased some of the tension within Ki-tae. He didn't like the idea of Jin-woo back in his apartment, not while they still hadn't caught the person who'd broken in. Jin-woo had called the landlord earlier and was assured the locks to his apartment had been changed, but that still didn't reassure Ki-tae. How had the person gotten the keys to begin with?

"Min-su-ya is meeting us there. She says to help, but I think it's more of a matter of playing bodyguard," Jin-woo said as he pulled up his pants. Ki-tae grumbled as that very fine ass was hidden from his view. Jin-woo rolled his eyes. "Ki-tae, focus."

"I was… until you put your pants on," Ki-tae said.

"On what we're supposed to be doing, not my ass."

"But I like your ass."

"I know." Jin-woo smirked as he sashayed, actually sashayed, out of the room. That boy loved playing with fire. If he didn't watch it, Jin-woo would find himself bent over the couch. Ki-tae grinned. That wasn't a bad idea.

He stalked out of the bedroom, only to find Jin-woo in the kitchen, putting bottles of water and snacks into an insulated basket. Ki-tae slid up behind him and wrapped his arms around Jin-woo's waist as he went straight for his throat. Jin-woo's moans were the sweetest music.

"I love the sounds you make for me," he purred as he worked his way from one side of Jin-woo's neck along his nape to the other side. "I love the way you tremble in my arms."

"Ki-tae," Jin-woo whimpered. "We have to meet Min-su-ya."

"You're being responsible again," Ki-tae grumbled as he slid his hand beneath Jin-woo's waistband and stroked him slowly.

"One of us has to be, or we'd never get out of bed!" Jin-woo moaned, bucking his hips into Ki-tae's grip.

"And this is a problem because?" Ki-tae murmured.

"Because... dammit, Ki-tae... I can't think when you do that!"

"That would be the point. Thinking is overrated."

When they finally arrived at Jin-woo's apartment, Min-su was standing outside the door, arms crossed over her chest, eyebrow up, tapping her foot. She looked pointedly at her watch. "I'd ask what took so long, but I can smell you from here."

"It's all Ki-tae's fault," Jin-woo said.

"And he doesn't look the least bit repentant." Min-su chuckled.

"I'm not," Ki-tae admitted with a grin.

"The landlord recognized me, so he gave me the new keys. He had to go help his niece," she said as she unlocked the door. "I didn't want to go in without you. Didn't think I'd have to wait for over an hour and a half, though."

"Again, Ki-tae's fault," Jin-woo said.

Ki-tae could see him bracing himself to go into the apartment. It was hell to have a haven violated. His family had been burned out of a few homes when they had ventured out of Asia. It wasn't pretty, but they had survived and were still together, and that was all that mattered. He took hold of Jin-woo's hand, giving him an encouraging smile when Jin-woo looked at him. Then they all went through the door and around the little corner.

"Okay, now this is beyond all sorts of fucked-up," Min-su declared.

Ki-tae had to agree with the assessment. All the broken furnishings and knickknacks had been replaced with what appeared to be the exact same items. All the stuffing had been removed in addition to the shredded pieces of Jin-woo's artwork and lyrics. What made it truly disturbing were the pictures of Ki-tae all over every available surface, every wall, every table, taped to the stairs and the windows. Each one with angry red slashes all over them.

"Either someone really hates Ki-tae or really hates good art, or both," Min-su said quietly. "I'm going with both."

"These are *my* drawings," Jin-woo said softly. "Every one of them, they're from my stolen sketchbooks. They tore apart my sketchbooks."

Ki-tae muttered something very nasty in Japanese. He pulled Jin-woo into his arms and away from the second assault on his sense of safety. He could feel the trembling in Jin-woo's body. If he ever caught this person, there would be no mercy.

As he tried to comfort Jin-woo, he watched Min-su move through the room, sniffing so delicately it was adorable, even amid the macabre setting. When she returned to them, Min-su shook her head. There was still something messing with the scent markers that should normally be there. Whoever this was, they were clever.

"When did the landlord say he changed the locks?" Ki-tae asked softly, stroking Jin-woo's hair.

"The day before yesterday," Jin-woo answered as he lifted his head, wiping at his eyes.

"So this had to have been done before that," Min-su said. "Have you talked to the police?"

"They said they're still investigating." Jin-woo sighed, and then he pulled himself up straight and stepped out of Ki-tae's embrace. Ki-tae didn't like it, but he didn't fuss either. Jin-woo was pulling himself together, and that was more important than what Ki-tae might feel now. "I doubt they've made any real effort, though."

"Good thing we don't work that way," Ki-tae said as he pulled out his phone.

Five minutes later, Shin-bai walked into the room.

"This is not good."

"No, it's not," Jin-woo said, and his tone made Ki-tae look at him. He smiled at what he saw. Jin-woo was pissed, and that was a good sign. A scared Jin-woo was not a good thing, in his book, but Jin-woo looking as if he wanted to kick someone's ass? Yeah, he could get behind that. It meant Jin-woo would not let this color how he behaved. He would not let this get to him, even though it was an invasion and a violation. "This is my space, dammit. Who in the hell gave this asshole the right to come in and fuck it up? I'd like to meet them, because I have a few choice words."

"That's my Jin-woo-ya." Min-su laughed. "You aren't as meek and mild as you seem!"

"Tell me about it," Ki-tae purred.

"Not now, Ki-tae," Jin-woo growled, and then he tilted his head. "Maybe later, though."

"And that is my cue to… I don't know, go to the bathroom or something," Min-su said while Ki-tae just waggled his eyebrows with a smirk.

"This is an escalation," Shin-bai said as he moved through the living room. "More than likely the culprit was expecting you to be home when they returned. When you were not, they probably went searching to see where you had gone. I would say they probably found out about your work at BLE from the college. It is entirely possible they followed you to Ki-tae dongsaeng's place, and that triggered this response."

"Do we still think this relates to the attacks on me?" Ki-tae asked.

"It is hard to say," Shin-bai said as he tapped out a text on his phone and then began taking pictures. "It is still a possibility, although there is a chance they are unrelated, I would not eliminate the likelihood of a connection."

"I am not going to be run out of my apartment again," Jin-woo said.

"Of course not," Ki-tae said as he turned Jin-woo to face him. "If you'll let me, I'd like to stay the night with you, at least for tonight."

Jin-woo said, "I don't want this person thinking they've gotten to me, though."

"Just one night." Ki-tae didn't want to leave Jin-woo alone. He would probably only agree to one night, but there were other ways to keep an eye on him without being in the same room. Ki-tae didn't need that much sleep, anyway.

"I'll think about it."

"The police should be here shortly," Shin-bai said. "I have sent the photos to my team. We are still trying to get the security footage from the management company. They are not being very cooperative. I do not wish to involve Soon-joon-nim, but I will if I have to."

"Just sic Hyun-jo hyung on them," Ki-tae said. "That's almost as bad but equally effective as Abeoji."

"Is it just me, or does Hyun-jo seonbae seem to stand up a little straighter when Soon-joon-nim's around?" Min-su said absently as she wandered to the windows and looked out. "I think there's a little crush happening there."

"I noticed a little tension there too," Jin-woo said. "How long has he been with the company?"

"I…. Come to think of it, Hyun-jo hyung has always been around," Ki-tae said.

"He has been with Soon-joon-nim longer than I have. I know this," Shin-bai said.

"He has a way of getting exactly what Abeoji needs and or wants in the shortest amount of time," Ki-tae said. "If the company isn't responding to our security team's efforts, Hyun-jo hyung would be the next step… unless you want to handle it, Shin-bai-ssi?"

"His approach would be more… agreeable than mine," Shin-bai said honestly.

"Then call him," Ki-tae said. "We need that footage. If they were giving us difficulty, they probably gave the police just as much, if not more trouble. See if the detective in charge was able to get a copy of the footage."

Shin-bai nodded in response just as there was a knock on the door. He went to answer it while Ki-tae and the others waited inside. When he came back, it was with the same two officers from the previous break-in. He wasn't happy about that, but there was little Ki-tae could do. The questioning went along the same lines as last time, setting not only Ki-tae's teeth on edge, but Min-su's as well. Jin-woo wasn't as subdued this time around, and the officers seemed to respond to the change in his attitude differently. They weren't quite as demanding in their questions. It was as if they suddenly realized this wasn't some overreaction. Yet the second man, Officer Kim, seemed to take offense at even being called to the scene.

"Could this be an ex-girlfriend?" Officer Kim asked. "Some women get incredibly emotional and obsessed."

"It hardly seems likely, as I'm gay," Jin-woo said. He crossed his arms over his chest, as if daring the officers to say something about his sexual orientation. He was getting feisty, and Ki-tae barely contained his response to Jin-woo's aggression. Min-su slapped him in the arm as she covered her nose with the back of her hand. Ki-tae simply shrugged. He couldn't stop the way his body responded to Jin-woo, and he wasn't about to try.

"Did you lead any girls on? Give them the impression you were interested when you weren't?" Officer Kim asked. Ki-tae tensed.

"That has to be one of the most offensives questions I have ever been asked," Jin-woo said, his tone cold. "Have women expressed an interest in dating me? Yes, and I have very politely turned them down. If they ask why, I give them the honest answer. To imply otherwise is rude and insulting."

"I apologize for my colleague," Officer Lee said, glaring at his partner. "That was, indeed, an inappropriate question."

"You should not have to apologize for someone else's rudeness," Min-su said.

"It's an honest question," Officer Kim said.

"No, it really isn't," Ki-tae said. "You're trying to blame Jin-woo. He has no control over someone else's behavior. No one deserves to have their home invaded and their sense of safety violated. You've implied that, because he's gay, he is the type of person to lead another on, and thus is deserving of what this person has done. That isn't an honest question. That's a bigoted one."

"We're done here," Jin-woo said. "You've taken all the pictures and gathered everything that you could. I'll not be disrespected in my own home from someone who is supposed to be serving the public and protecting them from people such as this, but instead chooses to insult them."

"Now wait a minute."

"Gentlemen." Shin-bai stepped in, a pleasant smile on his face that was anything but reassuring. "Jin-woo dongsaeng has expressed the desire for you to leave. Any further communication with him will be done through our offices."

"Since when does a multimillion-dollar entertainment company handle such things for a small-time college student intern?" Officer Kim said.

"Kim Jang-gyo," Shin-bai said, and Ki-tae knew the honorific was left off on purpose. Shin-bai was annoyed, and that was never a good thing. "We of BL Entertainment take care of *all* our employees. We are not just a company. We are a family, and we take care of our own. Jin-woo dongsaeng may be one of the newest members of our clan, but he is no less than even the president. She would be most displeased to hear of his treatment at the hands of the local authorities."

"Are you threatening us?" Officer Kim demanded.

"I am merely stating fact, janggyo. How you choose to take it is entirely dependent on you," Shin-bai said. "Shall I walk you out, gentlemen?"

"That won't be necessary," Officer Lee said as he grabbed his partner's arm. "We have to talk to the landlord before we leave. Thank you very much for your time. We will make every effort to catch this criminal."

"I appreciate your efforts, Lee Janggyo-nim," Jin-woo said.

Ki-tae barely waited for the click of the closed door. Heedless of anyone else, he pulled Jin-woo into his arms and kissed him senseless, backing him up against the counter. Jin-woo wrapped his arms around Ki-tae's neck and opened to his kiss.

"Okay, our cue to leave, Shin-bai oppa. We really don't want to be around for this," Min-su said. "See you two tomorrow... maybe."

Ki-tae waved them away, not releasing Jin-woo's mouth. He kept him pressed firmly against the counter. When he heard the door click closed, he filled his hands with that delectable ass and lifted until Jin-woo wrapped his legs around his waist. Slowly he rocked his hips, grinding their erections together through their clothes. Finally they both had to breathe, so he shifted his attention to Jin-woo's jawline, placing small nipping kisses along the edge. He nudged with his nose until Jin-woo tilted his head, giving him greater access. Then Ki-tae licked along the line of his neck. He sank his fangs into Jin-woo's artery slowly, letting him feel the length of them, the sharpness.

"Ki-tae," Jin-woo moaned, bucking his hips as hot wetness spread between them. Ki-tae growled against his flesh as he came. He continued to draw from Jin-woo for a few moments before pulling his fangs free and sealing the wounds. Then he let his legs buckle, and they sank to the floor. Ki-tae tucked his head in the curve of Jin-woo's neck, panting.

"You made a mess of me again." Ki-tae lifted his head when he heard the amusement in Jin-woo's voice. He found him smiling broadly, a twinkle of mischief in his eyes. "You realize I'm going to have to return the favor at some point."

Ki-tae smiled. "You already did, but feel free to do it again. I look forward to it."

"Do you have any idea how incredibly fucking hot it is when you bite slowly?" Jin-woo asked as Ki-tae stood up, still holding him in his arms.

He took his lips once more in a leisurely kiss as he carried Jin-woo up into his bedroom. Gently he laid him on the bed and drew back. Jin-woo's hands still rested on his shoulders. His lips were kiss swollen and his pupils were blown. He was so incredibly beautiful he made Ki-tae's heart ache. A part of him felt guilty. He should tell Jin-woo about the bond, about how strong it was for Ki-tae. He didn't want Jin-woo to doubt his feelings, but how could he want that when even *he* doubted them? The desire had been there from the beginning. It was what caused the initial issue, but now Ki-tae was scared. He didn't know how much was actually him and how much wasn't. Yet when he should leave Jin-woo alone, not touch him, make love to him, until everything was out in the open, Ki-tae couldn't bring himself to do that. He wasn't that strong.

"What's wrong, Ki-tae?" Jin-woo furrowed his brow with his concern.

"Nothing. I... I can't talk about it, yet," Ki-tae said, feeling like a coward.

"Okay," Jin-woo said. He tugged on Ki-tae's neck, pulling him down for another kiss. The next thing Ki-tae knew, he was on his back with Jin-woo straddling his hips. "I believe it's my turn to make a mess of you."

"Don't you mean an even bigger mess of me—or rather, us?"

"Point taken. Now, shut it."

Ki-tae smiled and tucked his hands behind his head. Jin-woo bit his lip, letting it slowly slip from between his teeth, and Ki-tae's cock jerked. He knew exactly what that did to Ki-tae, and he was taking advantage of it. Ki-tae was inclined to let him.

With nimble fingers, Jin-woo made quick work of removing his hoodie. Ki-tae lifted long enough to let it be pulled over his head and tossed to the floor. Then he resumed his position. He watched Jin-woo's eyes rove over his chest before he placed his hands on Ki-tae's stomach, making the muscles jerk. Jin-woo gave him that smile, and Ki-tae knew he was going to enjoy everything Jin-woo did to him.

Jin-woo traced the ridges of Ki-tae's abdomen lightly, running his fingers over each curve and concavity as he moved upward. He traced the lines of Ki-tae's pectoral muscles, his thumbs barely caressing the tips of his nipples. Ki-tae hissed at the little shocks of pleasure. Along the outside of his chest muscles to his biceps, Jin-woo continued up his forearms until he wrapped his fingers around Ki-tae's wrists. He brushed his thumbs back and forth across the tender, sensitive skin there. Little shivers of pleasure raced along his arms and down to his groin, making his skin tingle. Ki-tae let out a low growl.

"How long do you think you can hold still?" Jin-woo whispered as he shifted and pressed their hips flush together. "How long can you keep from grabbing me and fucking me senseless?"

Ki-tae held Jin-woo's gaze as he leaned down to lick the outer edge of his ear. Ki-tae shifted restlessly, his hands twitching.

"I'm going to find out," Jin-woo promised.

Ki-tae turned his head, giving Jin-woo better access, and he worked sharp little teeth down along the furl to Ki-tae's earlobe. He gave it a gentle tug before moving along the line of Ki-tae's throat. The feel of his breath against his skin was making Ki-tae hypersensitive. The brush of Jin-woo's shirt against his bare flesh, the shifting of Jin-woo's weight, a heavy press on his groin, made Ki-tae's cock ache. As much as he wanted to grab Jin-woo, Ki-tae resisted. He wanted Jin-woo to make a mess of him, wanted it badly.

He wasn't expecting the nip to his neck, and Ki-tae bucked with a cry as pleasure shot through him. It was almost as intense as when Jin-woo licked his fangs. He was instantly hard and leaking in his pants. Ki-tae panted for breath, trying to regain control, but Jin-woo wasn't having it. He kept up the sharp nips as he pressed their bodies together from shoulder to hip. He rolled his lean body along the entire length of Ki-tae's, and Ki-tae growled, turning his head, forcing Jin-woo's head up so he could catch his lips in a fierce kiss. After only a few minutes, Jin-woo pulled back, smiling.

"Uh-uh, it's my turn, remember?" he teased.

Ki-tae couldn't have looked away. He held Jin-woo's gaze as he brushed his lips along Ki-tae's chest, zigzagging down his sternum until he slid them to Ki-tae's right nipple. Delicate kitten licks followed, flicking his dexterous tongue at the tip and swirling around it before Jin-woo latched on and worried it with his teeth. Ki-tae cried out, arching his back. Jin-woo slipped his hands down to Ki-tae's forearms, but still Ki-tae didn't grab him. He was hanging on to his control by a thread, but he was still hanging on to it. His fangs extended when Jin-woo licked his way across his chest to his other nipple. A loud hiss followed as Jin-woo subjected the small nub to the same treatment, much to Ki-tae's delight. Jin-woo's whimper vibrated against his skin.

"You like that, don't you?" Ki-tae purred, his voice low and husky. "You like knowing how hard you make me."

He gave a few thrusts of his hips, felt the full-body shiver that shook Jin-woo.

"You're trying to get me to give up control," Jin-woo said after releasing Ki-tae's nipple. He looked up and grinned. "It's not going to work. I want this. I want to give you pleasure the way you're always giving me pleasure."

"Every sound you make, every little tremor that wracks your body, gives me pleasure, Jin-woo," Ki-tae whispered. "I love how responsive you are to me. I love the way your eyes dilate the minute I smirk at you or bite my lip. I love how the scent of your arousal fills the air when I walk into the room and how you cry out when I slide inside you."

Ki-tae gasped when Jin-woo gave his belly a sharp nip. "Shush."

"What? You don't want to hear how good you're making me feel? You don't want to know how hard my cock is right now? I have a wet spot on my jeans."

"I want more," Jin-woo said as he flicked open the snap to Ki-tae's jeans. He slowly drew down the zipper. Ki-tae chuckled at his delighted smile when Jin-woo realized there was only Ki-tae beneath the denim. He tapped Ki-tae's hip, and Ki-tae lifted. Jin-woo pulled his jeans down. He gave an adorable little pout when he had to move to get them the rest of the way off. Now Ki-tae was displayed before him like a buffet. "Beautiful."

Ki-tae watched as Jin-woo ran his eyes from top to bottom, lingering on his eyes, his abs, and his groin. Jin-woo smiled as he slowly wrapped his fingers around Ki-tae's cock. Ki-tae slammed his head back into the pillows, his fingers clenched as he fought with himself. The strokes were long and firm, tight enough to make Ki-tae feel it, but not to hurt. The more Jin-woo stroked, the slicker and smoother the glide of Ki-tae's cock in his hand got, and the more Ki-tae snarled and growled and groaned. He had never professed to be a quiet lover, and he wasn't about to start. He let Jin-woo know exactly how much pleasure he was getting out of that single touch, how much he wanted more of it, more of Jin-woo. Yet he kept his hands behind his head. His fingers were clenched tight in his hair, but he wasn't reaching for Jin-woo, so this was good, as far as Ki-tae was concerned.

"Close your eyes," Jin-woo commanded softly.

"Why? I want to watch you," Ki-tae said as he shifted restlessly, trails of precum glistening on not only his cockhead and abdomen, but Jin-woo's hand.

"I want you to just feel," Jin-woo said. "Close your eyes... for me, Ki-tae?"

On a sigh, Ki-tae closed his eyes. Everything sharpened, particularly the smell of Jin-woo's arousal. Ki-tae would bet his car the wet spot on his jeans was getting bigger too. He just wished Jin-woo would take the damn things off. He wanted to be skin to skin. Hell, he always wanted to be skin to skin with Jin-woo.

The rasp of those same jeans against his thighs sent goose bumps over his legs. The edges of Jin-woo's shirt teased low on his hips. Then it was gone, and Ki-tae fought to keep his eyes closed. Had it been anyone else, he would have said fuck it, but this was Jin-woo, and he wanted to make Jin-woo happy.

He heard the rustling of fabric and something thumping against the floor. It sounded like... shoes? Ki-tae smiled. Apparently Jin-woo had decided to remedy his decidedly overdressed state.

When he felt the brush of smooth warmth, Ki-tae moaned in bliss. That was what was missing, the feel of Jin-woo's silky skin against his. He loved how soft it felt, with firm muscle underneath, how he was so warm. Jin-woo shifted above him, and Ki-tae got the impression he was reaching for something by the head of the bed. He heard a drawer slide open and then closed. Something small made a soft thump against the mattress. Ki-tae smiled. If he wasn't mistaken, *that* lovely little sound was a bottle of lube. Then Jin-woo wrapped long fingers around his shaft, and Ki-tae gave up thinking. He thrust as much as he was able, trying to get more stimulation. The sudden feel of cool slick made him gasp and his hips jerk. Jin-woo's chuckle danced along his nerve endings.

"You purr like a kitten," Jin-woo said just before Ki-tae heard the telltale click of a cap. "I love knowing I made you make those sounds."

"I'm not inclined to be quiet, and neither are you," Ki-tae chuckled huskily. "That's one of my favorite things about being with you: I know exactly when I've hit the right spot. Your body bows and your eyes roll back in your head. You claw at my shoulders or back and cry out so beautifully. I love the sounds you make when I'm pleasuring you."

As much as words were just a tool of their lovemaking, they weren't needed once Jin-woo wrapped his slick fingers around Ki-tae's cock once more. Ki-tae could feel how slippery and ready to be inside Jin-woo he was. He bucked in short thrusts, reveling in Jin-woo's touch. Then he felt Jin-woo rise to his knees. The anticipation was killing him with the need to touch. The sensation of his cock at the hot entrance to Jin-woo's body, hovering there as if waiting for some sign to continue, made him hiss again, and he struggled to not top from the bottom, but the way Jin-woo was thrusting his tongue into his mouth aggressively and stroking his fangs was a shock, and Ki-tae simply reacted.

His hands shot to Jin-woo's hips, and he thrust up hard, pushing into his passage until their groins slapped together. Jin-woo arched his back on a loud cry, raking his nails along Ki-tae's forearms. Thick ropes of seed spattered across Ki-tae's bare chest. He opened his eyes and kept moving, lifting, and then pulling Jin-woo down onto his cock, watching the tremors shake his body and listening to the cries echoing through the room. He functioned on pure instinct, unerringly hitting Jin-woo's prostate, keeping him flying. Jin-woo clenched around him, pulling his orgasm from him within seconds of Jin-woo's explosion. He drew Jin-woo's hips down one more time and held him there as he filled his passage.

Jin-woo collapsed against his chest, and Ki-tae's strokes stuttered until they stopped. Neither one of them moved, still joined and not inclined to change the fact. Hot breath puffed across Ki-tae's chest. He stroked Jin-woo's back, little aftershocks making his muscles twitch. Ki-tae was officially a mess, and he couldn't be happier.

"We should get cleaned up," Jin-woo mumbled against his chest.

"Do you want to move? Because I know I don't." Ki-tae chuckled. "I don't think my legs are going to support me anytime soon."

"Mine either." Jin-woo giggled and then slapped a hand over his mouth. Ki-tae gently pulled it away.

"I like your giggles," he said softly.

"You don't think they're girly?"

"No, they're adorable, and I love them because it means you're happy… or at the very least thoroughly fucked and sated," Ki-tae teased. "You giggle just before you fall asleep after we make love."

"I do not!" Jin-woo said in shock, sitting up.

"Yes, you do. It's the sweetest, most adorable sound I've ever heard and don't you dare try to change it," Ki-tae said.

Jin-woo grumbled and then settled back on Ki-tae's chest. Ki-tae reached out and pulled the comforter off the other half of the bed to wrap them in. He supposed he should get up to turn off the lights, but he wasn't inclined to let Jin-woo go or get out of the bed, so he left it. One night with the light on wasn't a big deal.

JIN-WOO

JIN-WOO SLOWLY opened his eyes. He stared across the expanse of Ki-tae's chest, watching it rise and fall for a few moments. Then his eyes registered the clock on the nightstand. Eight o'clock in the morning.

He smiled and let his eyes close, only to snap them open again. Eight o'clock? Shit, they were late. He sat up and gently placed his hand on Ki-tae's shoulder. He might be special, but he didn't want to find out what might happen if he startled Ki-tae awake. Despite what Ki-tae thought, he was aware of how dangerous he and the others could be.

"Ki-tae?" he said softly as he shook Ki-tae's shoulder. "Ki-tae, it's time to wake up. We have to go into the office, and I'm pretty sure you have a full schedule today."

"Meh," Ki-tae mumbled before turning toward Jin-woo and curling around him.

"I don't want to be the one to tell Soon-joon-nim you missed a commitment, do you?" Jin-woo said with a huff. And he thought he was terrible in the mornings. Ki-tae was the epitome of "not a morning person."

"Why do they have to schedule these things so damn early in the morning?" Ki-tae grumbled as he sat up. Jin-woo smiled at him and then kissed his cheek.

"It's eight o'clock already," Jin-woo pointed out. "And you've made me late again."

"I'm not the one who was in charge last night," Ki-tae purred, nuzzling his neck as he pushed Jin-woo back onto the mattress, coming to rest on top of him. "That was all you."

"Are you complaining?"

"Never." Ki-tae nipped his neck, sending pleasure zinging to his cock, and then hopped off the bed. When Jin-woo pouted at him, Ki-tae chuckled.

Jin-woo smiled, watching Ki-tae disappear around the corner and into the bathroom. He climbed out of the bed and pulled on his sleep pants. They actually weren't that late. He was just used to having to leave by seven to make it to school in time for class, but they took Ki-tae's car yesterday, so it shouldn't take that long to get there. Jin-woo paused at the bathroom door and knocked.

"I'm going to make breakfast," he said.

"Coffee?" Ki-tae called over the sound of the shower.

"Of course." Jin-woo laughed. He already knew better than to forget the coffee. Ki-tae was a bit of a grump without it. Then again, Jin-woo wasn't one to talk. He was downright antisocial before his first infusion of caffeine.

Jin-woo pulled open his refrigerator and stared at the contents, which weren't much. He had some eggs and cheese... and that was about it. There was some milk as well. He didn't want to hazard what was in the various containers and how old it was. He really should have cleaned out his refrigerator before this. Jin-woo sighed. He'd wanted to make Ki-tae breakfast, but that wasn't going to happen this morning. He'd have to plan better for another time. Of course, there was always the possibility the fucking bastard had tampered with his food while he was tearing up Jin-woo's sketchbooks and cleaning his house. He'd have to throw everything out just in case and then go grocery shopping. He still had their dinner date to look forward to, and he was positive that would also turn into breakfast the next morning. Jin-woo grinned as he set about making the coffee. He usually grabbed a cup from the coffee shop on the corner, but today he had the time to make it himself and had a fresh canister of coffee and a still-sealed container of creamer.

Ten minutes later he heard Ki-tae pad down the stairs and turned, coffee mugs in hand. He nearly dropped them. Ki-tae stood at the base of his stairs, shirtless, barefoot, with his jeans not fully done up and his thumbs in the front belt loops, pulling the waistband down just enough to show off the delectable line of his Adonis belt. His hair was still wet from the shower and tousled, as if he'd just run his fingers through it. Jin-woo swallowed—hard.

"You do this on purpose," Jin-woo muttered as he tried to compose himself.

"I smelled coffee," Ki-tae said with a smirk. The bastard knew *exactly* what he was doing.

"And you couldn't wait until you were fully dressed before coming down to get some?" Jin-woo sighed as he handed Ki-tae his coffee mug. "Almost made me drop them. We're going to have to grab breakfast on the way. I don't really have anything here."

"That's all right," Ki-tae said as he sipped his coffee. "I don't really eat anything heavier than coffee unless I have dance practice or a show. Well, unless HanYin decides I'm not eating enough, then he shoves food in my hands as soon as I walk through the door."

"He's taking care of you." Jin-woo smiled.

"He's like a mother hen sometimes, but I can't really complain. His food is amazing. I think if he didn't love music so much, he would be a chef somewhere or own his own restaurant," Ki-tae said.

"What do you guys do as hobbies? I mean, how do you relax?" Jin-woo asked as he sat down on his couch. "HanYin hyung cooks, I draw, Min-su-ya runs, and Jong-in-a.... I don't think Jong-in-a knows how to relax, or he doesn't give himself time to do it. I wish he did. I wish he'd talk to me."

"It's hard," Ki-tae said softly. "Of the two, HanYin is the easiest to get to talk. All I have to do is catch him in midbaking spree, and I can usually get the whole story out of him. Cheongul is a different story. He's the oldest of us, and I think he has the same mentality as Jong-in dongsaeng. He doesn't want to burden us with his problems. He'll disappear for a few days at a time. The thing of it is, when he's not happy, we're not happy. We want to help, but sometimes we have to force him to let us. The only person worse than him is Abeoji. We can't get him to talk for love nor money. I think the only person he confides in is Hyun-jo-nim. They've been together for a long time. I never realized it until you asked about him last night."

"So what does Cheongul hyung do to relax?"

"That really depends. Cheongul doesn't like to hold still," Ki-tae said, taking another sip of coffee. "When he's working on a beat, he'll make a playlist of songs in the style he wants—rap, R&B, rock—and then he'll go down to the gym and work out. He swims... a lot. I think the only thing he does that requires very little movement is photography. That print just inside the living room at my place? That's one of his."

"The lotus?"

"Yeah. He took that while we were on tour in Japan," Ki-tae said. "We had half a day off and went wandering around Tokyo. We went to Shinobazu Pond. It was amazing, and Cheongul filled up two or three memory cards with pictures. He has a couple of different cameras he uses. Whenever he gets a new phone, he must have the one with the best camera. I think he still has boxes of photographs from film cameras. When they came out with digital cameras, he was immediately in love."

"It's good to have something you love, and if you have more than one hobby like that, even better," Jin-woo said before he emptied the last of his coffee and went to rinse his mug. "You still haven't told me what you do to relax."

"I make music," Ki-tae said. "It's all I do."

"You can't make music all the time, Ki-tae." Jin-woo smiled as he turned to face him.

"I've always heard music in my head," Ki-tae said quietly. "It helped me... escape when I desperately needed to. It kept me sane when everything around me was conspiring to rip my mind apart. I... have no other outlet."

Jin-woo felt the tightness in his throat. Those words, said so softly, tore at him. Ki-tae had given him yet another peek into a deeper part of himself, and Jin-woo felt humbled. He could see how affected Ki-tae was by his own words. His whole presence seemed contained, as if he were curling in on himself, a way to protect himself. Jin-woo didn't know what to say. Perhaps there weren't any words that *could* be said.

He walked over to Ki-tae and cupped his cheek. When Ki-tae looked at him, Jin-woo kissed him gently, sweetly, and then pulled back, smiling.

"Why are you smiling?"

"Because you just confided in me, even if you didn't realize it," Jin-woo said. "You're beginning to trust me, be comfortable with me knowing these things about you. It makes me feel… honored, that I'm special to you, and that makes me happy because you're already very special to me, Ki-tae."

Before Ki-tae could respond, Jin-woo put his fingers against his lips. He shook his head. He didn't want Ki-tae to say the words because he did. He wanted Ki-tae to say them when he was ready to say them, because then Jin-woo would know they were real. It would take time, and it would take him being very patient. Ki-tae had lived centuries with keeping secrets, and he needed to continue, but Jin-woo hoped they would get to the point where Ki-tae wouldn't keep anything from him, where Ki-tae would feel he could confide in him as he did with his brothers.

Ki-tae pulled his hand down. "I can't give you those kinds of words, Jin-woo, not now."

"I know," Jin-woo said. "I just wanted you to know how I feel."

"Can you be patient with me?" Ki-tae asked. "Some men don't want to wait. If they say the words, they expect to hear them back."

"I'm not some men." Jin-woo shrugged. "Now we have to finish getting dressed, or we really are going to be late."

"There you go, being responsible again." Ki-tae sighed, but he was smiling, and Jin-woo knew the mood had passed.

When they arrived at the office, Hyun-jo was waiting for them. He bowed to them, which still seemed odd to Jin-woo. Clearly Hyun-jo was of a higher station in the office, and older, so why did he continue to bow to Jin-woo? It didn't make sense to him, but he hadn't gotten up the nerve to ask about it.

Given the conversations they'd had about Soon-joon's PA, Jin-woo took a moment to study him. Hyun-jo had very fine, almost feminine features. His nose was long and straight, thin. His cheekbones were high and delicately curved, much like the bow shape of his lips. His eyes were almost perfectly almond-shaped, with long, dark lashes. Today he wore a light gray pinstriped suit and matching vest that emphasized the lean lines of his body, not being an overly muscular man. He had paired the suit with a black silk shirt and matching tie. A black silk handkerchief peeked out from his breast pocket. Hyun-jo was always sharply dressed.

"You keep staring at him like that, and I'm going to get jealous," Ki-tae whispered in his ear, jerking Jin-woo's attention to him. He blushed and turned to Hyun-jo, mumbling his apologies.

"There is no need, Jin-woo dongsaeng," Hyun-jo said, his voice low and sweet-sounding, almost lyrical.

"It was rude of me," Jin-woo persisted.

"If you insist," Hyun-jo said with a small smile.

"Usually you and Soon-joon-nim are ensconced in some meeting or other, Hyun-jo-nim," Ki-tae said with a smile, although Jin-woo noticed he moved closer. "What brings you here to meet us?"

"Shin-bai hubae has asked that I look into the matter of security footage from the incident at Jin-woo dongsaeng's apartment. I require some information from Jin-woo dongsaeng before I proceed." Hyun-jo turned to look at him. "Shin-bai hubae informed me the management company has not been forthcoming with the information needed to continue our investigation. Is your building a secure one?"

"Not like Ki-tae's building. The front door is open, but then there's an interior door people have to be buzzed through. There's a button where you can call the maintenance staff or the landlord if it's a delivery or something. After that, you have to have a key to the apartments," Jin-woo said.

"Key? The building does not have an electronic system?" Hyun-jo asked, raising an eyebrow.

"I asked about that," Jin-woo said. "The landlord said he liked keys."

"Is there a front desk?"

"No," Jin-woo said.

"There is a security guard, surely? Most apartment neighborhoods have them," Hyun-jo said.

"If there is, I've never seen him," Jin-woo said with a shrug. "Its an older building and I don't think the company is really interested in upgrading it. It's relatively close to the university, but not within walking distance. It's not the most secure building, I know, but it was the first one I liked that my aunt didn't outright refuse. She doesn't approve of the dormitories or officetels near the university itself."

"Has she been notified of this situation?" Hyun-jo asked.

"To say my aunt and I do not get along would be an incredible understatement," Jin-woo said. "I haven't told her about any of this."

"So once through the interior door, no one marks the coming and going of nontenants?" Hyun-jo asked.

"No, I guess not," Jin-woo said. "There's a camera in the main lobby, and I think there's one on each floor. I don't know if there are any in the stairwells."

"Other than yourself, who has keys to your apartment?"

"Min-su-ya and Jong-in-a each have a set. Then there's the landlord and the maintenance staff. Well, they have the master key to all the locks in the building. Only Min-su-ya and Jong-in-a have copies specifically to my place."

"What are you thinking, Hyun-jo-nim? These questions have a purpose," Ki-tae said.

"Yes, they do," Hyun-jo said. "The landlord and the maintenance staff have, as you said, a copy of all the keys, more than likely on one master key ring. Unless the individual in question knew exactly which keys belonged to Jin-woo dongsaeng's apartment, they would have to match them to the door, which would require them to be in the hallway for an extended time, and other residents might also take notice. Either the landlord or the maintenance staff would notice the absence of their keys…. Therefore it stands to reason they are not the source of the copies. This means whoever made copies did so from either Min-su dongsaeng's, Jong-in dongsaeng's, or Jin-woo dongsaeng's set. Because there is a smaller number of keys to go through, it would not take as much time, and the theft of the keys may not even be noticed."

"Who would go to all that trouble?" Jin-woo asked.

"Someone who is obsessed," Hyun-jo said quietly. "However, this is only a theory. I will know more once I am able to obtain the security footage."

"Why didn't Shin-bai hyung ask any of these questions?" Ki-tae said.

"Shin-bai hubae does not present theories until he is in full possession of the facts and the evidence. Old habits die hard." Hyun-jo gave another small smile. "You asked me the question. I answered it only because you are... you. Had the question been presented by someone else, my answer would have been quite different."

"Do you need anything else from me?" Jin-woo asked, watching the exchange between them. He decided Hyun-jo was just as scary as Soon-joon-nim. The look in his eyes spoke of a keen and cunning intelligence, and that was just plain frightening, especially when he gave that small, mysterious smile.

"No, Jin-woo dongsaeng. Thank you very much for your time." Hyun-jo bowed and then headed toward the elevators. When he turned around and saw Jin-woo watching him, Hyun-jo did something completely out of character. He winked and smiled, and it looked as if he flashed fang. Then the doors closed, and Jin-woo wasn't sure if he saw what he thought he saw.

"That man is scary," Jin-woo said, turning to Ki-tae.

"You have no idea," Ki-tae said. "Want to see him terrifying? Threaten Abeoji in his presence."

"No, thanks. I choose life," Jin-woo said, making Ki-tae throw his head back and laugh.

He placed a quick, hot kiss on Jin-woo's lips and then headed back downstairs to meet Shin-bai and the security detail escorting him to his appointments that day. Ever since the second attempt on his life, Ki-tae did not attend any off-site PR events without at least four bodyguards, and Shin-bai rarely excluded himself from those details.

Jin-woo watched him go... well, watched a part of him. Ki-tae had to have the finest ass ever made.

"Caught you staring!" Min-su said, pouncing on him. Jin-woo jumped and then smacked her arm.

"Dammit, woman," he snarled. "Don't do that!"

"Why not? It's so much fun to watch you react." She grinned.

"What has you in such a good mood this morning?" Jin-woo grumbled.

"I had a wonderful dinner with Cheongul last night, and this morning, Cheong-bo seonbae said we are making excellent progress on both videos. Since Jong-in-a finished the mixes the other day, Cho-ree seonbae sent them to Hyung-jun seonbae. We get to start really putting this together today."

"Have you gotten a chance to work on your song for part two?" he asked as they walked to their desks.

"Yes, I've got the bare bones of it right now. I'm working on lunches and breaks," she said. "What about you?"

"I had to start all over again. I had several options, but they got shredded, the bastards," Jin-woo grumbled. "I worked hard on those, and it was a pain in the ass because I'm so used to focusing on Ki-tae's vocal style that switching to Cheongul hyung's and HanYin hyung's is a bit difficult. I have a couple of ideas, but nothing that I would even call bare bones at this point."

"I'm sorry, Jin-woo-ya. I didn't mean to remind you of that," she said as she tucked her arm through his.

"It's not as if I wasn't thinking about it anyway." Jin-woo shrugged. "Hyun-jo seonbae is heading over to my building, now. Apparently everyone thinks he'll be able to get the company to comply, and I'm inclined to agree. There's something both charming and frightening about him, something cunning and… dangerous."

"There's something about his scent, I don't know. It kind of reminds me of Jong-in-a. Anyway, we don't have a lot of time left before the songs are due. What are you going to do?" she asked as they entered the meeting room.

"I'm going to work on it every chance I get. I don't have a choice. I have to have a fully produced song within two weeks. Even that's still generous, but I'm having such a hard time coming up with an idea. I'll think of something. Whether it's any good will remain to be seen."

Once Cheong-bo and Hyung-jun arrived, their morning meeting began. As much as he was looking forward to working on the video, Jin-woo was still concerned about the song. He hadn't come up with anything decent since his originals were trashed, and that bothered him. Everything sounded canned, and that wasn't what he wanted. He wanted something people would tap their foot to without even thinking about, something they could relate to, something to make them feel. He had yet to find the words to do that. Shaking his head, Jin-woo brought his attention back to the meeting. There was still a lot of work to do before the release date. There was a knock on the door as Cheong-bo paused. It opened, and Soon-joon-nim stepped into the room. He smiled at everyone and took the seat at the head of the table.

"How is everyone today?" he asked. "I'm sorry to interrupt your meeting, but I have an announcement to make."

"What is it, Soon-joon-nim?" Hyung-jun asked. "Does it have something to do with the videos?"

"In a way, yes," Soon-joon said. "Bam Kiseu is scheduled to begin working on their next album soon. They've been home about a month now, and the fans are itching for a live performance. In two weeks Hyun-jo hubae and I will be at Jeonjin University for the second part of the BLE scholarship program. I was originally going to have the boys as judges, but as much as I know they will be professional and unbiased, many people will not think so, considering their exposure to Jin-woo dongsaeng, Min-su dongsaeng, and Jong-in dongsaeng. There is a good chance someone will protest should one of your songs win the scholarship."

"Does that mean we can't put forth our songs?" Min-su asked.

"No. You are part of the class, and it would be wrong to penalize you because you were talented enough to win the first part of it," Soon-joon said. "I am planning for eventualities."

"It makes sense," Cheong-bo said. "Most people don't know Bam Kiseu the way we do, so they have no way of knowing how Ki-tae dongsaeng will tell you if something's crap straight to your face, no holds barred. He does it to HanYin dongsaeng and Cheongul dongsaeng all the time. He's usually right, and they realize that after they've calmed down."

"Won't they claim bias anyway?" Jin-woo said.

"If they do, it will be from the safety of their computer chairs," Soon-joon said. "And we have a contingency for that. It is one of the reasons I chose Hyun-jo hubae. His duties do not often expose him to the production staff. He mostly deals with the business end of things, managing my calendar, dealing with venues, marketing, public relations. However, his dual degree in business management and music theory and composition make him an excellent judge."

"And we're okay with that. I'll be honest, Soon-joon-nim, Hyun-jo seonbae is… intimidating, for all he's a soft-spoken man," Cheong-bo said.

"And that is what makes him so effective." Soon-joon smiled.

"How does this relate to the videos?" Hyung-jun asked.

"Before they go into the studio to begin work on their next album, HanYin dongsaeng thought it might be a nice offering to the fans to have a local performance, a sort of flashback concert where they perform mainly their older songs, the ones that made people fall in love with them. He suggested releasing the performance version the day before the concert and then debuting the regular at the concert itself. Cheongul dongsaeng suggested they could perform the winning song as well, a little bit of new with the old."

"That's a great idea," Min-su said. "A lot of fans like going to concerts to hear the new songs, but they get really hyped when they can hear some of their old favorites too. The songs that made us fans to begin with, we still listen to them, even when there's new stuff. It just all gets added to the mix."

"I'm glad you think so, Min-su dongsaeng. The boys have requested that you, Jin-woo dongsaeng, and Jong-in dongsaeng perform 'Crossing Time' with them."

"What?" The word was out before Jin-woo could stop it.

"Cheongul dongsaeng figured since you three were forced to learn the choreography alongside them and came up with the concept to begin with, it was only right for you to be onstage with them," Soon-joon said. "All three of them were very adamant about it."

"I… I am very honored by the offer," Jin-woo said quietly, feeling the tightness in his chest at the very idea of singing in front of an audience. "However, that is not possible for me. If you'll excuse me, please."

Jin-woo got up and walked out of the room. He walked as fast as he could to the men's room and locked himself in one of the stalls. While there always seemed to be reminders in the form of hospital bills, Jin-woo tried not to think about his parents. The memories were bittersweet and painful. They had loved each other very much, but his mother's family had not approved of his father, especially his aunt. She had refused to speak to his mother for years because of their marriage, and she was still a bitter old woman to this day.

Fortunately his grandparents had not cut his mother out of their lives completely, even warmed up to his father toward the end of their years, and that allowed them to live comfortably, if not in the way his mother was raised. Yet they were happy. Singing had been their thing. They met when his father was performing in the park near his mother's home. A humble street busker with a voice to make the angels cry, that was how his mother always described his father.

Jin-woo wiped at his cheek, brushing away the wetness. During the summer months, they would sit in the park as a family and sing to the passersby. What money they collected was then distributed among the other performers who were not as well-off as they were.

That day was still so clear in his mind. It was just like any other summer day, bright and beautiful. They had just finished listening to the other performers and putting money in their baskets. Together, nine-year-old Jin-woo and his mom skipped ahead, singing one of the many songs they loved. His father came behind them, playing his acoustic guitar, the case slung across his back. Jin-woo and his mother turned, teasing him about how slow he was, calling him "lazy turtle," plodding along and taking forever.

Jin-woo couldn't stop the memory, He tried to push it away, but it wouldn't leave. He covered his face with his hands, but he could still see his father's eyes widen, see him burst into a run, dropping his guitar, and the way it splintered upon the ground. He looked up, saw his mother turn her head to look behind them just before she placed her hand in the middle of his chest and shoved, sending him tumbling into the ditch. Screams, screeching brakes, the dull thud of bodies hitting the ground, tumbling over and over, the nauseating sound of tires bumping over something—someone—and the sound of shattered glass. He slammed his hands over his ears, not realizing the screaming was him until strong arms yanked him forward. He struggled, striking out until finally Soon-joon's voice registered, its tone low, soft, soothing. Jin-woo collapsed, the tears streaming down his face.

He was floating in a daze of swirling numbness. Jin-woo had no sense of his surroundings. Then the movement stopped. He could hear voices, but he couldn't make them out. It was too much effort to try. He let the darkness take him, take away the pain, the memories, the feeling of horrified helplessness. The images flashed through his mind, so fast they blurred together, his parents, Ki-tae, cars and trucks and blood, so much blood, his father's staring eyes, and then Jin-woo accepted the offer of sweet oblivion.

SOON-JOON

SOON-JOON SAT next to Jin-woo on the couch and placed a cool washcloth on his forehead. He could still see the anguish in the boy's face. Gently he brushed Jin-woo's bangs to the side. Right now he reminded Soon-joon of the many times he'd tended his boys when their pasts came back to haunt them. So many times they, and he, convinced themselves they'd conquered it, that they were no longer affected by it, only to be proven wrong. The past had a way of reminding people they weren't as healed as they thought they were. The horrors they'd seen, the torment they experienced, that never really went away, not for Vampires or humans.

"Does this happen often?" he asked, turning to look at Min-su as she brought a fresh basin of water over to him.

"No, but you hit a real sore spot today," she said. "Jin-woo-ya hasn't sung in public since the day his parents died."

"How did they die?"

"Some idiot who was more concerned about deadlines than safety. He fell asleep behind the wheel. Jin-woo-ya's mother had just enough time to push him out of the way before she and his father were hit straight on. He was nine years old," Min-su said. "Jin-woo-ya prefers to stay out of the spotlight for that reason. He can manage public speaking, though if he gets too stressed about it, he'll pass out. But asking him to sing? Yeah, not going to happen. You're taking care of him as if he were your own son, Soon-joon-nim."

"He brings that out in me." Soon-joon smiled gently. "He is the type of person who makes you want to take care of him, even though he is strong enough to take care of himself."

"He's a good man with a good heart," Min-su agreed. "But everyone needs to be taken care of now and then."

"Yes, they do."

"Maybe we could just be introduced before they sing 'Crossing Time'? That would still acknowledge our work without traumatizing Jin-woo-ya... or scaring people with how badly I dance," she said.

"You do not give yourself enough credit, young lady," Soon-joon said.

"Or people give me too much. He's going to be okay," she said firmly. "Jin-woo-ya won't let stuff get him down for long. I think... with everything that's happened, this was just this side of too much."

"We'll let him rest here," Soon-joon said. "As much as I do not wish to leave him alone. We both have work we must attend to."

"When is the concert scheduled for?" Min-su asked after she leaned down and placed a kiss on Jin-woo's forehead.

"In one month. We have coordinated it to coincide with the beginning of the Dano Festival. Their performance will be the day before, at the Eumak Nabi Theater," Soon-joon said as he led the way out the door and motioned for one of the secretaries to sit with Jin-woo until he woke. "Let me know as soon as he is awake."

"Yes, Sajangnim," the young lady said with a bow.

"Won't it be difficult to coordinate all this within such a short time?" Min-su said, and Soon-joon smiled.

"Normally yes, but Hyun-jo hubae and I have been working on this for the last few days. The contract with the hall was just finalized this morning. We will begin the publicity within the next twenty-four to forty-eight hours, starting with social media. The boys will have three weeks to select the rest of the songs, speak with Rha Goo-ji hubae regarding any choreography changes they might want to do, although I doubt they will change anything. They'll have meetings with their stylist, LeiChen hubae, and go over the wardrobe for the show itself. They usually have all that wrapped up in the first week. Then the final two weeks before the performance will be nonstop rehearsals."

"This last month I thought they were busy. Now I see it wasn't the half of it," Min-su said. "They really do work very hard."

"All of our performers work hard or they do not stay our performers for long. There have been a few that felt the need to leave, stating they could not handle the intense schedule. We released them from their contracts," Soon-joon said. "A performer who is not happy is one who does not give their all to the product. Their heart isn't in it. There have not been many who have left completely. Our managers usually find other avenues where the artists are more suited. Some are better at and prefer the creating rather than the performing, such as Cho-ree hubae and Hyung-jun hubae. Others are more suited to a different branch altogether, such as acting. Overall we found that being willing to listen to our artists and willing to make adjustments, to be flexible, has helped both them and the company. This is why our people are so loyal. We want them to succeed. When they succeed, the company succeeds, and that only happens when we work together."

"You say you make adjustments. Do you go through another contract negotiation?" Min-su asked.

"Essentially, yes. The manager sits down with the artist and goes over the problem areas. They discuss what aspects the artist enjoys, what they dislike, what they are having trouble with but would like to improve. They review the initial contract, making adjustments to it as needed. Then the manager and the artist draft a new contract proposal. That is then presented to the department board. This renegotiation is available after one year unless there are serious health concerns. When that is a factor, the time frame is adjusted on a case-by-case basis."

"BLE really does care."

"Yes, we do."

HANYIN

"HOW LONG have I been out?"

Jin-woo's voice pulled HanYin's attention from the notebook he was writing in. "About forty-five minutes since I came in. I came to talk to Abeoji and found you on the couch. How are you feeling?"

"Drained and embarrassed," Jin-woo said, rubbing a hand through his hair as he sat up.

"Don't be," HanYin said. "Abeoji is used to taking care of us when things get... overwhelming."

"It's still embarrassing. I'm a grown man, twenty-three years old. I shouldn't be screaming in the bathroom from a memory, even an unpleasant one," Jin-woo grumbled.

"And I'm a five-hundred-and-twenty-five-year-old Vampire who shouldn't feel the need to fight for my survival in an age where no one is actively seeking to take my head, but I do. I'm human that way." HanYin shrugged. "It's a bitch, and it makes my life hell sometimes. It makes getting close to people difficult, and it makes them scared of me, but it's something I have to live with every day, and I can either let it kill me or rise above it."

"How? How do you rise above it?" Jin-woo asked.

HanYin remained silent for a few moments, seriously considering the question. "I have an alarm clock wake me up every morning. If I forget to set it, which is rare, either Cheongul or Abeoji will be the one to wake me up, usually because Ki-tae is always the last to wake up. I meditate. I practice wushu to expend the excess energy... and I cook."

"I draw," Jin-woo said softly. "And although I claim it's just for exercise, I dance. I haven't had an episode like this in a long time."

"I won't ask what happened, because you're just recovering." HanYin turned to face him fully. "You're human, Jin-woo dongsaeng. You have issues, just like everyone else on this planet. Yet you've maintained a positive view, and that's impressive. I've lived centuries, and I still fall into a depressive state when I have a setback. I... I wasn't going to pursue Jong-in because of it."

"What changed your mind?"

"He kissed me."

"Jong-in-a kissed you?" Jin-woo's voice was filled with surprise, and HanYin felt his cheeks heat.

"I asked him to, and he did," HanYin said. "The day Ki-tae was hurt, I tried to drive him away, but he wouldn't leave. He told me it was a good thing I didn't make his decisions for him."

"Now that sounds like Jong-in-a." Jin-woo smiled. "I'm glad. He's been smiling more lately, and I'm all for that."

"Those dimples are a killer," HanYin muttered, catching his lip between his teeth.

"Do you guys practice that in front of the mirror or what?" Jin-woo huffed.

"What?"

"Biting your lip and then letting it slide out," Jin-woo said. "I mean, Ki-tae does it *all* the time, and I know you and Cheongul dongsaeng do it in the videos, especially when you look into the cameras during the live performances."

"We're Vampires. Biting is very erotic for us," HanYin said. "And as far as the concerts, well, we're selling a fantasy there. We look at that camera, and the audience on the other side feels as if we're looking at them, seeing only them. We pull them into the concert, make them feel as if they're there."

Jin-woo raised an eyebrow "Can you guys even see yourself in the mirror?"

"Just superstition, mirrors work for us just as they do for everyone else." HanYin said. "When we're with someone special, well, it's pure erotica for us, Ki-tae is an expert at working the lip bite, and then he has that smirk."

"Oh no, it's not all Ki-tae," Jin-woo said, pointing at him. "I've seen you and Cheongul dongsaeng do it too. Every time you see Jong-in-a, you do this slow lick of your lips, and Cheongul dongsaeng touches the tip of his tongue to his top lip before pulling it back in his mouth when he knows Min-su-ya is watching."

"No, it's not all Ki-tae." HanYin laughed. "But to answer your original question: no, we don't practice it in front of the mirror. At least I don't. I can't speak for Ki-tae and Cheongul. Vampires are very… oral creatures. Kissing, drinking, not just blood but beverages, eating, these are all very sensitive activities for us. Stroke our fangs, and you're going to get a very visceral response."

"That one I know already."

Jin-woo blushed, and HanYin couldn't help but laugh. "Did it to Ki-tae, didn't you?"

"I'm not going to answer that!" Jin-woo protested.

"You don't need to. Your reaction is answer enough," HanYin said.

"How come you're so easy to talk to about this?" Jin-woo asked suddenly.

"Well, first, I know you're not out to hurt us. Second, you care about Ki-tae, more than care, I think, and you need to understand what he is. Third, you're the most open-minded person I've met, and so talking to you about this doesn't make me feel as if you're measuring me for a straitjacket. I'm… comfortable with you."

"We talked about it a little bit the other day," Jin-woo said quietly. "At first I thought he was trying to make me scared of you. I couldn't figure out why he would do something like that."

"Ki-tae knows me very well. We have similar... histories," HanYin said quietly. "If he warned you about me, it's because he knows how much it would kill me if I hurt you. I was very close that day. Ki-tae has been with us since he was about twelve. We honestly don't know exactly how old he was when Abeoji found him. It is his story to tell if he chooses. Suffice it to say, we tend to be overprotective of him, me especially."

"Would you have really hurt me?"

"If I had even an inkling you meant Ki-tae harm?" Jin-woo nodded. "In a heartbeat. I won't let anyone hurt him ever again, and I will destroy anyone who even tries."

HanYin couldn't have been more serious at that moment. It wasn't his intention to scare Jin-woo, but he was honest to a fault. There were many aspects of his life where he had to keep secrets, but with Jin-woo, that wasn't necessary. He had a feeling Jin-woo was going to be around for a long time.

"Damn," Jin-woo whispered. "I... I can't promise we won't fight and hurt each other's feelings, but I would never intentionally hurt him."

"I know, dongsaeng. Deep down, I know," HanYin said. "But when I'm in that mindset, rational thought is extremely difficult. I become very focused on removing threats to my family and myself, in that order. I won't ever fail in that again. I won't remain frozen while others hurt them. I will do everything, anything, even give my life, for my family."

"Would you do the same for Jong-in-a?"

"Yes," HanYin answered honestly. "I... love him. Whether he feels the same remains to be seen, but I am... hopeful for the first time in a very long time."

"Have you told him how you feel?" Jin-woo asked.

"No. It is not the time. There is too much going on."

"Don't wait too long. He needs to hear it," Jin-woo said.

"Have you told Ki-tae you love him?" HanYin gave him a pointed look, and Jin-woo looked away, blushing.

"Not in so direct a manner. I told him he was very special to me. I don't think he's ready to hear the L-word. Honestly there's something he wants to tell me, but he's not ready yet. It just seems as if every time I think he's about to tell me what it is, something stops him. He looks... terrified. Only for a second, but I see it. I don't want him to push himself. I want him to not only want to tell me, but to be ready to talk about whatever it is," Jin-woo said.

"You're being very patient with him," Ha-Yin pointed out.

"I'm not usually, not with stuff like this, but Ki-tae... he's worth it," Jin-woo said.

"He is," HanYin said.

"You are too, hyung. I think Jong-in-a knows that but fears he's the one who's not. He's always working, whether it's a job or on projects for school. I'm afraid he's going to put himself in the hospital. He pushes himself so hard. I wish I knew why and that he'd let me help him."

"Perhaps you should sit him down and tell him of your fears," HanYin said. He wasn't going to reveal Jong-in's secret. That was Jong-in's choice. HanYin knew it was hard to place that kind of trust in people, hard to tell those you love there was something different about you, something not human.

"That's not a bad idea," Jin-woo said with a smile.

"I have them every now and then, good ideas." HanYin smirked. "Now it's time for both of us to get back to work. There's not much time before the concert."

"About that." Jin-woo took a deep breath and then let it out slowly. HanYin turned to face him, concerned. "I can't perform in front of an audience, hyung, not singing and dancing. I… it's not that I don't want to or that I'm not honored you guys want us up there with you. It's just not something I am mentally capable of doing."

"I understand, dongsaeng, and it's okay." HanYin smiled. Then he pulled a box from his pocket and offered it to Jin-woo. "Pocky?"

Jin-woo laughed and took a stick. HanYin smiled and took one himself. The mood was effectively lightened. He rose and pulled Jin-woo to his feet. He pushed him out the door, and off they went. There was work to be done. HanYin paused at the door, and Jin-woo looked at him in question.

"I would be honored if you would use my given name and ask if I may address you more familiarly," he said. It sounded so very formal. Jin-woo smiled.

"I would like that very much, HanYin-a."

"Then I shall do so, Jin-woo-ya." HanYin returned his smile before sticking another piece of Pocky in his mouth and walking out the door.

KI-TAE

KI-TAE CLIMBED into the van, leaned back, and sighed. It had been a long fucking day. Interviews, a commercial shoot, meet and greets, and then more interviews. He didn't really mind them, but by the time everything was done, all he wanted to do was sleep. He closed his eyes and snuggled down into the seat.

"Is everything all right, dongsaeng?" Shin-bai asked as he climbed in the other side of the van.

"Just tired," Ki-tae answered.

"I received a call from Hyun-jo seonbae. He has the security footage."

"Hyung, you've been with us a long time. What do you think of the relationship between Soon-joon-nim and Hyun-jo-nim?" Ki-tae asked suddenly, opening his eyes to look at Shin-bai.

"I think there is a mutual respect there and trust," Shin-bai said. "They have been together for a long time. Before I came on board, at any rate."

"Hm. I've never seen Soon-joon-nim date," Ki-tae said as he turned to look out the tinted windows. "I don't ever see him with... anyone save Hyun-jo-nim."

"Soon-joon-nim is a private person."

"True," Ki-tae murmured, his eyes drooping closed. "Still, it would be nice if he had someone to take care of him for a change."

"Hyun-jo seonbae takes care of him."

"Not in a business sense." Ki-tae yawned. "I meant someone to love him."

"I know."

Soon-joon

"YOU HAVEN'T fed."

Hyun-jo's voice brought Soon-joon out of his musings. He turned from his windows to look at him. "I've eaten."

"That isn't what I meant, and you know it, Soon-joon," Hyun-jo said, dropping all honorifics in his annoyance.

He stalked over to Soon-joon and turned his chair until they were facing each other. Hyun-jo's eyes roved over him, glowing lavender orbs that still made him shiver inside. Hyun-jo unbuttoned his suit coat and shrugged it off his shoulders. He laid it neatly on the desk before unbuttoning his cuff and rolling up his sleeve to his elbow. Silently he held his wrist out to Soon-joon.

"Hubae."

"No, no 'hubae.' In private I am Hyun-jo, and you *will* feed." Hyun-jo's eyes grew hard. "I will not have you starve yourself like this."

"Hyun-jo."

"Do I have to take drastic measures, Soon-joon?" Hyun-jo murmured as he straddled Soon-joon's lap. "Do I have to give you no choice in the matter?" His eyes flared, and his short-cropped hair grew to its actual length, stopping at his waist, bleeding from black to white. His ears sprouted from the top of his head, twitching to dislodge the long strands from the tips, and his tails, all seven of them, flicked back and forth in his irritation.

Soon-joon took hold of the proffered wrist. "Stubborn Fox," he muttered.

"Yes," Hyun-jo hissed, his head falling back, his eyes going half-lidded as Soon-joon wrapped an arm around his hips and sank his fangs into his wrist, drinking deep.

In all his centuries, never had anyone tasted as sweet as Hyun-jo. No one had satisfied his hunger as thoroughly as Hyun-jo. No one had sacrificed more for him. He could feel Hyun-jo digging his claws into his skin, piercing through his coat, vest, and shirt to draw blood. He could feel the fine trembling of Hyun-jo's body as he tried not to move. Oh, how he tortured his sweet Kitsune.

Soon-joon yanked his head away, then quickly licked the wounds, cleaning the pale flesh as he did so. When he looked up, he could read the hurt and resignation in Hyun-jo's eyes, and it stabbed through his heart. Without a word Hyun-jo straightened his clothes and donned his suit coat, his hair back to its short cut, ears gone, and his tails hidden. The last to change were his eyes. They glowed lavender for a few more moments. He bowed low and walked out of the room, passing ChenBao on his way. Soon-joon wished his hearing weren't so keen. Then he wouldn't have heard the stifled sob and the quickening of Hyun-jo's feet.

"When are you going to make an honest Fox of him?" ChenBao demanded, hands on her hips. "Really, Táozi-chan, this is too much. He loves you beyond all things, and yet you still push him away, refusing to accept the love he offers you. It is mind-numbingly stupid."

"How can I take advantage of his devotion when he has lost so much because of me?"

"He didn't lose anything he wasn't willing to!" ChenBao said, throwing her hands up.

"His clan, his family, his position, all these things—Hyun-jo should have nine tails by now," Soon-joon said. "He should be immortal."

"Táozi-chan, if that was what Hyun-jo-chan wanted, do you think anything would have kept him from achieving his goals?" she asked as she sat on the corner of his desk. "He is steadfast, loyal, totally devoted to you. Whatever you want or need, he provides. He receives little in return, and yet he remains. How many centuries must pass before you realize he will have no other and will never leave you?"

JONG-IN

JONG-IN TILTED his head back against the building, eyes closed, letting the song play through his head. It had been a long day. After he left BLE, he went to his part-time job. When his hours there were done, he went to the campus to work on several other school projects. He got home at about two in the morning but wasn't able to sleep, so he laid the beat track for his scholarship entry. Now he was trying to work the melody. He made another notation on the sides of the sheet music.

The door banged open, startling him, and Jong-in looked to see who had found his little hideaway. The man looked vaguely familiar, and Jong-in figured he must have seen him around the building. He was about to turn back to his work when the soft sob grabbed his attention. He tilted his head, curious. Had he stumbled on someone else's little haven? The man, at least he thought it was a man, wiped at his face.

"Are you okay?" Jong-in asked.

The man whipped around to face him, and Jong-in was struck by how beautiful he was. He didn't compare to HanYin, but he was damned close. Immediately the man looked away, hastily wiping away any evidence of his tears. Then he looked at Jong-in and gave a bow.

"*Gomen nasai*, I did not mean to disturb you. I did not know anyone was here." His voice was soft, lyrical, and Jong-in could hear the sadness in it.

"It's no trouble," Jong-in said. "I'm Bak Jong-in."

"Rhim Hyun-jo. It is a pleasure to formerly meet you, Bak Jong-in dongsaeng," Hyun-jo said. "I am Soon-joon-nim's personal assistant."

"You must be very busy, then. He always seems to be on the move," Jong-in said with a smile. Something caught his attention, a scent on the breeze. He tilted his head, distracted by the smell.

"He does keep me very active." He paused. "I had not thought to meet another of my kind outside of Japan," Hyun-jo said softly, drawing Jong-in's attention instantly. When he looked at him, Hyun-jo's eyes flashed lavender.

"You... you're... like me?"

"I am," Hyun-jo said, his smile gentle and welcoming. "You seem surprised. You did not sense me in the area?"

"I'm not sure I know what you're talking about." Jong-in blushed. "Honestly I have no clue what I'm doing in that regard. It just sort of... overtakes me. Sometimes."

"Let me ask you this since there is no one nearby. How many tails?"

"Two."

"Two for one so young? Impressive," Hyun-jo said.

"But what does that mean? And what am I?" Jong-in asked, hearing the desperation in his own voice.

"We are Kitsune, Fox-Spirits," Hyun-jo said.

"HanYin was right," Jong-in murmured.

"He is a very intuitive man," Hyun-jo said as he moved to stand next to Jong-in. "The number of tails indicates our power and wisdom, how close we are to Celestial status and true immorality. Also it is a measure of our age."

"May I ask?"

"Seven," Hyun-jo said with a smile. "You have been alone for a long time, haven't you?"

"Yes."

Hyun-jo reached into his pocket and withdrew a business card. He handed it to Jong-in, who took it with both hands. "This is both my business and personal phone numbers. While extremely rare, it is not unheard of for a young Kitsune to have more than one tail. However, the level of spiritual energy can be hard to control. Indeed, it can be overwhelming to the point of making it difficult to control your form when in a high emotional state. If you feel this way, call me, and I will help you."

"Why?" Jong-in looked from him to the card and back again. "Why would you help me?"

"You are young and alone, with no mentor to guide you, as is tradition," Hyun-jo said. "Perhaps I am old-fashioned, but I believe it is the duty of the elders to teach the young, to help them understand the way, and to keep them safe until they have mastered their current energies."

"Oh."

"And you matter to HanYin dongsaeng. He is special to me as well, and so you are special too. For now I must depart, but we will speak again, Jong-in dongsaeng." Hyun-jo gave him a small smile. He turned to go, but Jong-in stopped him.

"Wait." When he turned back around, Jong-in had to ask. "Why were you crying?"

"The only thing worth crying for," Hyun-jo said as he reached out and caressed Jong-in's cheek. "Love."

And then he walked away. Jong-in watched him go, elated and saddened by the exchange. He'd never expected his life to change so much by winning a scholarship. The opportunities being presented at BLE were amazing. Even more amazing to him was HanYin. It still terrified him, and a part of him still wanted to hide away from it, to deny how he felt about HanYin, how much he wanted him. That part of him kept expecting to be pushed away. It had taken so much effort to show HanYin what he was without knowing exactly what that was, to expose himself like that. He had fully expected to be rejected. That HanYin accepted it so easily, still wanted to be with him, was such a gift.

And now this, someone like him: a Fox-Spirit. He hadn't put much thought into HanYin's words. He'd been too busy to think beyond the moment. There was so much on his plate, and he was trying to balance it all. Jong-in felt if he added one more thing, it would all come crashing down around him.

He was drawn from his thoughts by the vibration of his phone. He glanced down to see his timer. He had to go back to work now. Cho-ree had made him take a break, although Jong-in tried to resist. It hadn't worked, but he at least made the effort. He pulled open the door just as a text message sounded, and he smiled. When HanYin had called him the first time, he'd saved the contact and made a customized tone for his messages. The chorus to "Heat" echoed in the stairwell, and Jong-in hurried to turn the sound down.

HanYin: *Where are you? I brought you lunch.*

I just finished my break, heading back to the studio. What did you bring?

HanYin: *Steamed dumplings. Hurry before Ki-tae smells them!*

Jong-in laughed and jogged quickly down the stairs. He wasn't sure if Ki-tae was in the building today, but he wasn't going to risk HanYin's dumplings.

On my way. Guard them!

HanYin: *LOL*

FIVE BILLION won; that should be sufficient. It wasn't about the money, anyway. That would be just a little bonus. He needed to learn his lesson. Clearly he wasn't paying attention. Now it would have to be taken to the next level. Blood would have to be spilled, and it would continue until he learned and obeyed and never turned away again.

KI-TAE

"SEUNG-GI HYUNG!" Ki-tae called as he walked into the lobby. He pulled Seung-gi into a hug before setting him back on his feet, holding his shoulders. "What are you doing here?"

"I came to see Soon-joon-nim," Seung-gi said, smiling. "I have the initial layouts for Eumak Nabi Theater for him. Are you just getting your lazy butt into work?"

"Actually I went straight to an interview and then came here," Ki-tae said. "Eumak Nabi, huh? I like that hall. It doesn't have the capacity of the Olympic Stadium, but it still has a decent feel to it. Acoustics are really good too."

"They're easier to work with." Seung-gi paused, and Ki-tae turned to see what caught his attention, smiling when he saw Jin-woo walking toward the elevators, his nose in his notebook. "Hey, isn't that…?"

Ki-tae nodded. "Yes, it is."

"What have I missed?" Seung-gi demanded, crossing his arms over his chest.

"A lot. Let's catch the elevator, and I'll formally introduce you." Ki-tae laughed, and then he jogged toward the elevator, calling out to Jin-woo. The smile he received made him almost giddy. He got into the elevator and motioned Seung-gi to hurry up. Seung-gi gave him the usual look. He only hurried when he had to, and this wasn't one of those times.

"Did you finish your interview already?" Jin-woo asked as Seung-gi finally made it to the elevator.

"It wasn't a long spot," Ki-tae said. "At this point I could probably do these in my sleep. They all seem to ask the same questions." He gestured to Seung-gi and said, "This is Byun Seung-gi hyung. He's our stage manager. His job is to coordinate with the venue to make sure our marks are set, they have the right lighting, and everything is micced properly. Seung-gi hyung, this is Cheong Jin-woo."

"I also have the daunting task of keeping the artists safe, healthy, and focused while on tour. Some make my job more challenging than others. It's nice to meet you," Seung-gi said with a smile.

"It's a pleasure to meet you too," Jin-woo said with a small bow.

"There, now you two have officially met." Ki-tae chuckled.

"Officially?" Jin-woo asked.

"Ki-tae dongsaeng often thinks he's cute when he's just being annoying." Seung-gi sighed. "I arranged for you to be transported home from the last concert and checked that you were okay the next day."

"Seung-gi hyung is like Shin-bai hyung in that he's been with us awhile," Ki-tae said. "And I am cute."

"And annoying," Jin-woo huffed.

"It's part of my charm." Ki-tae grinned before stealing a kiss.

"Idiot," Jin-woo muttered, but his smile ruined it. "Behave yourself today."

"I make no promises." Ki-tae laughed as Jin-woo stepped off the elevator. When he looked back, Ki-tae licked his lips, and instantly he narrowed his eyes. Ki-tae winked as the doors closed, but he caught Jin-woo's growl.

"You like him a lot," Seung-gi said.

"It's a bit complicated, but yes, I do like him," Ki-tae said. "This is my floor. Meetings upon meetings upon meetings today. Are you going to be around for a while?"

"I'll be in and out over the next several days. The concert isn't the only project I'm working on at the moment," Seung-gi said. "I went right from your last show to another artist. It's been pretty steady for me this last month."

"You love every minute of it," Ki-tae said.

"I do," Seung-gi said with a smile. "But I haven't gotten a chance to spend as much time with my niece as I'd like. She's working really hard at university, and I like to take her out, give her a break every now and again."

"Bring her to the concert, then. It's right before the spring festival, so it's the perfect time," Ki-tae said. "Everyone loves Dano."

"I'll see if I can pull her out of her room long enough," Seung-gi said. "She has so many projects to do she's barely taking time to eat or sleep. Her mom only sees her for one or two meals a day."

"Sounds like she's very dedicated."

"She is." Seung-gi smiled. "I'm so proud of her."

"You sound like a father." Ki-tae chuckled.

"My brother and I were very close. It's only right that I take care of his family. And my niece, she's the sweetest girl in the world," Seung-gi said.

"I'm sure she is." Ki-tae clapped him on the shoulder and then stepped off the elevator. "Have a good day."

"You too, Ki-tae hyung. Behave!"

"Don't I always?"

"No!" Seung-gi said with a laugh as the doors closed.

Ki-tae met up with Cheongul and HanYin in one of the many small conference rooms. He gave Cheongul's pointed look at his watch the attention it deserved, which was none. He wasn't more than five minutes late. HanYin tossed him a bottle of water as he nibbled on a stick of Pocky. Once he was situated, Ki-tae pulled his tablet out of his bag and opened their song files. Each of them had a list of all the songs they'd ever recorded and performed.

"Right, so we already know we're doing 'Crossing Time,'" Cheongul began. "I think we should save that one until the intermission, sort of build up to it."

"I'd like to do 'Call the Dragon' and 'Heat,'" HanYin said.

"Do we want to do 'Master'?" Ki-tae asked as he looked at Cheongul.

"It was one of our chart-toppers," he said. "I don't see why not. What about 'Phoenix Rising'?"

"I can dust that one off." Ki-tae chuckled. "How many songs do we want to perform?"

"They want it to go for about two hours," HanYin said, checking the email they'd received. "We've got five songs now. Each song, if we perform the whole thing, is about three to four minutes long. We're looking at close to thirty songs altogether. If we space them out and get the crowd worked up in between, we can maybe pare it down to twenty-five."

"That's not the usual format, HanYin," Kit-ae pointed out. "We'd be singing almost nonstop."

"We could do a few instrumentals, a couple of dance numbers," Cheongul said. "That would give our voices a bit of a break."

"We could do it all," HanYin said.

Ki-tae could see the excitement in his eyes at the idea of doing something different. "If we still do Ments and VCRs, we're looking at about three hours. That's a long time to sit."

"It would make it an atypical concert," HanYin pointed out. "We keep to the regular format every other time we perform. This would make it something extra special for our home fans, give them a little something extra along with all the stuff they expect."

All three of them turned as the door opened and Soon-joon walked in. "I see you three are hard at work. How is the song list coming?"

"We've only been here for about five minutes," Ki-tae said. "Pushy much?"

Soon-joon shot him a look, but Ki-tae just grinned at him, completely unrepentant. Soon-joon shook his head with a smile and turned to the others. "I'm glad you're all together. I wanted to let you know we've received the second notice from our... industrious videographer."

"So? What is he demanding?" Cheongul asked.

"Five billion won to be delivered by Ki-tae alone."

"Wow, someone is certainly bold," Ki-tae said.

"Definitely," Soon-joon said softly. "What concerns me is the demand that you deliver it. I believe the money is an afterthought. This isn't about getting rich. It's about getting Ki-tae."

"That is *not* going to happen," HanYin said quietly.

"No, it is most definitely not," Soon-joon agreed.

"I don't want you three putting yourselves in danger for me," Ki-tae said.

"You're our brother," Cheongul said. "Family protects each other."

"I know," Ki-tae sighed. Soon-joon laid a hand on his shoulder. He looked up and gave him a small smile. "I think that just effectively killed my good mood."

"I'm sorry."

"It's not your fault, Abeoji," Ki-tae said. "It's part of this life. Sometimes there's some people who get too fixated on us. We've dealt with it before, and we'll deal with it again. It's human nature."

"It is an unpleasant aspect of human nature."

"But we've all experienced it," Cheongul said.

"This is getting morose," HanYin said. "We're not going to let this person ruin things for us. We're going to plan our concert, so let's get back to the song list. We've got a lot to do and not a lot of time to do it in."

"He's right," Ki-tae said.

Soon-joon took a seat at the table. Cheongul showed him the songs they had already chosen. The four of them settled into an easy discussion of what the performance would be like. By the end of an hour, they had twenty-five to thirty songs set for the performance. They hugged Soon-joon before leaving the room and heading down to the wardrobe department to meet with their stylist. When they arrived, LeiChen was already there, reigning over his assistants with true flair. He had several racks of clothing arranged in a semicircle. To the right was a three-way mirror, and to the left were individual dressing rooms. Three armchairs sat across from the racks. Set between them were two small tables, each holding water bottles.

"My loves!" LeiChen called out when he turned and saw them walking through the door. He rushed over and hugged them, ignoring any sense of personal space, but LeiChen was their sweetheart, so they allowed it. He was eccentric, but he knew his business, and he never let them go onstage looking anything less than perfect. "Oh, we are working the casual look today, are we? I never have to worry about what you wear off-stage. It is always perfect."

"You say that all the time, LeiChen-ssi." HanYin laughed.

"That is because it is true," LeiChen said with a shrug. "Now, clothing, the fashion, we must make sure you look simply fabulous during your concert. Is there a theme?"

"This is sort of a flashback concert," Cheongul said as he leaned on one of the armchairs. "Soon-joon-nim began a scholarship program at Jeonjin University. During the first part, the students had to come up with a music video concept for one of the songs we hadn't made a video for. We're going to release the remix at the concert, so we decided it would be a good idea to perform a lot of our old songs. The only new thing will be the song that wins the second part of the scholarship."

"And you're doing it right before the spring festival? Brilliant," LeiChen said. He was practically vibrating with excitement. "Spring is color! I love dressing you three in color!"

He turned from them to the rack and began pulling clothes, barking orders at his assistants as he went. Ki-tae looked at HanYin and then Cheongul, who just shook his head and took a seat. He had no idea what LeiChen had in mind, but Ki-tae knew it would suit them. That was LeiChen's talent. He didn't just go with all the fashion trends. He followed those trends and then made them unique.

The assistants scrambled around, their arms full of clothing. One of them had brought three empty racks labeled with their names. Then the others were able to unload their burdens. Ki-tae chuckled. It was better to stay out of the way until LeiChen was done selecting clothing. He was a bit... concerned with how bright some of the fabrics were. Ki-tae was not big on bright tones. A few minutes later, the flurry of activity stopped, and LeiChen spun around to face them. He smiled.

"Ah, Ki-tae-ssi, why such the worried face, my love? Do stop. It will give you wrinkles before your time."

HanYin snorted his water.

"I don't think I have to worry about wrinkles just yet, LeiChen-ssi." Ki-tae chuckled.

"You have such lovely skin, the three of you. I am jealous." LeiChen sighed. "Now clothing. This is Dano. It must be fun, light, and energetic. You will be under such hot lights, so the fabric must allow your skin to breathe. We must avoid too much white. It glows under the lights. It must not be too tight, just tight enough to tease, I think."

LeiChen winked at them, which even got Cheongul to lighten up. His leg had already started to bounce with restless energy.

"It has to be easy to get in and out of," HanYin added.

"Ah, so right, HanYin-ssi, and since this is also about looking back, we shall add touches of tradition," LeiChen said. Then he turned and raised his hands. "Come, my little peacocks, let us adorn you with feathers of fashion."

"We have to get Jin-woo, Min-su dongsaeng, and Jong-in dongsaeng in here," Ki-tae said as they rose. "I would love to see him try that with Min-su dongsaeng."

"Nah, everyone loves LeiChen-ssi." HanYin chuckled.

"Dropping honorifics already, Ki-tae?" Cheongul teased.

"Oh, don't go there, brother mine," Ki-tae said, pointing a finger at him before shrugging out of his coat. "I notice there's a more... intimate air about you and Min-su dongsaeng as well."

Before either of them could say another word, LeiChen swept them into a whirlwind of clothing. They spent several hours trying on outfit after outfit, sometimes two or three times with different accessories or shirts. The banter continued. There was no way to be sad in LeiChen's presence. The man simply wouldn't allow it. By the end, they each had six different outfits and three backups, should there be a wardrobe malfunction. LeiChen hugged them each in turn, placing a kiss on their cheeks.

"Ah, my lovely peacocks, you will be fabulous," LeiChen said, drawing out the word.

"Thanks to you, LeiChen-ssi," HanYin said with a bright smile.

"Well, of course, my dear. That is what you pay me to do: make you magnificent!"

Cheongul shook his head again, but he was smiling. They said their goodbyes and left. There was still a lot to do, and then the real torture began.... Dance practice.

JIN-WOO

JIN-WOO LEANED his head back after hitting the space bar on the keyboard to pause the playback. He rubbed his face with a sigh. He'd been at this for several hours, and it was starting to show. This one section was giving him fits. Every time he thought he'd gotten the timing the way he wanted for the dancing and the beat, he would review it, and it would be off. It was driving him insane.

Of course, it would probably have helped if he'd gotten a decent night's sleep. Last night was the first time he'd slept without Ki-tae beside him, and he had tossed and turned most of the night. Jin-woo tried to convince himself it was the newness of everything, but he knew that wasn't it. He hadn't slept well because Ki-tae was not there.

And then there were the dreams. Jin-woo shuddered just thinking about them. He'd never had such vivid ones before. Yes, he dreamed in color most of the time, and that was cool, in his opinion, but he'd never had dreams like this before. No, they weren't dreams. They were nightmares. Surrounded by darkness, jerking around, trying to find the source of a myriad of noises, the sound of heavy breathing and the coppery sweet yet musky scent of blood. Grabbed from behind and pinned down, he was helpless. Then that flesh, the weird scent it held, sickly sweet. Jin-woo had tried to turn his face away, to resist, but then a tight painful grip grabbed his hair and yanked his head back so far he thought his neck was going to break. His mouth was forced open, and that flesh pushed against his lips. Thick, syrupy, copper-tasting blood oozed into his mouth, bitter and vile, filling his mouth until he had no choice but to swallow or choke.

Jin-woo shook his head. He didn't want to remember that horrible nightmare, had experienced quite enough of it the night before. Every time he closed his eyes, in fact. The worst part about it was, in the dream, he was very, very young. He couldn't have said how old, but definitely a child, and the idea someone could or would do that to a child made his stomach twist. Jin-woo sighed. He needed more coffee. Then maybe he could get this timing to work. He made sure everything was saved and then locked the computer. As he closed the studio door behind him, he saw Min-su and Jong-in heading his way. He smiled and waved, waiting until they reached him.

"What are you two up to?" he asked as he joined them.

"If I don't get something sweet, I might just murder someone," Min-su said.

"I have to head to campus to meet with Seonsaengnim. Cho-ree seonbae cleared it because I haven't been able to have my progress conference with him, and it's way overdue," Jong-in said with a sigh.

Jin-woo studied him, seeing the dark circles under his eyes and the pallor in his face. "You need sleep."

"I don't have time to sleep." Jong-in sighed.

"If you put yourself in the hospital, you won't have time for anything," Jin-woo grumbled.

"You know, I get it. I'm not an idiot, but I have bills that need to be paid and projects that need to get done. That means I have to squeeze every second of time I can out of every day. Sleep isn't a priority," Jong-in said, his voice tense and angry as they stopped just outside the commissary.

"It's going to be a priority when you pass out in the middle of doing something!" Jin-woo shot back, frustrated and worried and tired of trying to hide it. "You're going to push yourself into either a hospital bed or a grave!"

"What do you expect of me, Jin-woo-ya?" Jong-in said softly. "I don't have the resources you do. I have to work to stay in school. I barely made tuition last quarter. If I miss it, I'm out. I don't have a choice. I just don't."

"This isn't helping, either of you," Min-su said. They ignored her.

"You could let me help you, dammit," Jin-woo said.

"No, I'm not a charity case," Jong-in said tightly.

"Oh my God, so damned stubborn! So I'm just supposed to sit back and watch you work yourself to death? I'm supposed to be okay with the fact you look so pale and drawn right now I'm surprised you're still upright?" Jin-woo said. "Well, I'm sorry, Jong-in-a, but I can't watch you do this to yourself. I just can't."

Jin-woo turned around and walked back the way he came. He had no desire to be around other people. The best thing was to try to focus on work. He would figure out a way to help Jong-in, even if the bastard didn't want him to. He wasn't going to let one of his dearest and only friends work himself into an early grave.

He walked back into the studio but didn't turn anything on right away. He just sat staring at the dark screen. Finally Jin-woo got to work. He'd consider ways to help Jong-in when he went home that night. Right now he had a timing issue to work out.

Ten minutes later there was a knock on the door. Jin-woo sighed. He knew who was on the other side of that door, and he really didn't want to deal with Min-su getting on his case about Jong-in. The door opened without him saying a word. He kept his attention on the computer screen, shifting between the two monitors and trying to get the timing down. The distinct thunk of a paper coffee cup hitting the desk caught his attention anyway.

"What's this for?" he asked warily.

"You were going to get some coffee, right?" she asked, taking a sip of her own drink.

"Yeah, doesn't explain what this is."

"I got you a coffee since you left without it," she said as she took the other seat. She was quiet for a good five minutes before she spoke again. "Jong-in-a was pretty upset when he left."

"Don't."

"Jin-woo-ya."

"Min-su-ya. I really don't want to get into it with you too, not today," he said. "Right now I'm not inclined to be the laid-back Jin-woo most people expect."

"You really upset him."

"And you think I'm not upset?" he demanded. Then he pulled himself up straight, closed his eyes, and took a deep breath. "No, we are not going to discuss this now. You are not going to bulldoze me into it either."

"What's gotten into you today, Jin-woo-ya? Are you twisted?" she said.

"Maybe I am. What, am I not allowed to be upset or angry?"

"No, but you're not allowed to be an ass to me when you are, and you're certainly not allowed to light into Jong-in-a like that. He's having a hard time as it is. He doesn't need us hounding him too," she said.

"Says the woman who probably browbeat him into telling her what was going on. Well, that's fine. Be his friendly ear. In the meantime, I'm going to figure out a way to help him," Jin-woo said. "Now if you'll excuse me, I have work to do. Thank you for the coffee."

"I'm going to pretend you didn't just talk to me that way," she said as she rose. "I'm going to get back work, but rest assured, you and I will be sitting down to discuss this like rational people."

"No, we won't," Jin-woo said firmly. "I love you, Min-su-ya, but this is not something I'm going to waver on, not now, not ever."

"And you call Jong-in-a stubborn." She snorted.

"I never said I wasn't. How else am I supposed to deal with my aunt?" Jin-woo shrugged and took a sip of the coffee. It was exactly the way he liked it, which didn't surprise him.

He didn't look when the door closed behind Min-su. When Jin-woo finally stopped for the day, he couldn't even enjoy the fact he'd resolved his timing issue and was three-quarters of the way done with the video. He'd be able to finish it up tomorrow morning and present it to Hyung-jun for proofing and critique. He just wanted a hot shower, a cool drink, and Ki-tae, not necessarily in that order. And he still had to figure out what to bring to dinner that Sunday. Even though he knew everyone who was going to be there, he was nervous. It was a formal family meeting. What exactly did one bring to a Vampire family dinner?

HANYIN

IT TOOK another few days of driving Jong-in to work after he was done at BLE before Jong-in showed HanYin where he lived. He walked through the door and immediately liked it. It opened onto a short hallway with a closet to the left. Just where the closet ended opened to a small kitchen on the right, with a short island separating it from the living room. To the right of the archway was a set of narrow stairs leading up to a loft-style bedroom. HanYin had expected dark, muted colors. He was surprised by the bright aqua blue of the living room wall that faced the door. A single shelf lined the back wall and wrapped around to the right. It was filled with books and little knickknacks. In the center was a small table with storage beneath and a Persian rug in an aqua one shade darker than the wall. It was cozy and cheerful, and Jong-in had made the most of the space. It was… perfect.

"I love it," HanYin said, turning to look at Jong-in with a bright smile. "It suits you."

"I...."

"You thought because of who I am now, I would be disappointed in such a small place." HanYin took Jong-in into his arms and kissed him slowly, thoroughly. "I have lived out in the wilderness with nothing but a cave to shelter me from the weather and in alleys with no shelter at all. This is just as much heaven to me as my apartment is."

"I keep forgetting you've lived a lot longer and have a wide variety of experiences I know nothing about," Jong-in said softly. Although he smiled, there was an aura of sadness about him. "It's both intriguing and intimidating."

"You can ask me anything," HanYin said as he took the bags Jong-in had been carrying. "While I cook."

Jong-in chuckled. "You're determined to feed me every chance you get."

"Just as much as you are set on eating everything I make." HanYin pointed at him with a bunch of scallions. "Now show me where things are and then sit down and relax for a few moments."

They spent the next twenty minutes chatting about little things. Occasionally Jong-in would snatch a piece of food until HanYin caught his hand and nibbled on his fingers until he yanked them back with a breathless laugh. HanYin smirked at him and resumed cooking. He then placed the food on the small island and joined Jong-in on the other side, taking the stool next to him. He gave in to the urge to feed Jong-in by hand and was happy when he gave no protest.

Later HanYin snuggled up behind Jong-in on his futon, wrapping an arm around his waist. He nuzzled his neck softly, placing little kisses on his skin. He could tell Jong-in was not happy. He didn't think he was the cause of it, but HanYin wanted to make it go away. Jong-in sighed.

"I have to go to campus tonight," he said. "I have a project due in a couple of days, and it's not finished yet."

"That isn't what is making you sigh, though, is it?" HanYin said and kissed his shoulder.

"No," Jong-in said. "I…. Jin-woo-ya and I fought earlier today. I haven't spoken to him since. The messages I sent didn't get a response, and when I called, it went straight to voicemail."

"What did you fight about?" HanYin asked, making Jong-in roll over and tucking him against his side.

"How much I work," Jong-in answered. HanYin didn't think Jong-in realized he was worrying HanYin's shirt in his fingers, twisting and clenching and then unclenching them.

"You do work a lot," HanYin said. "Jin-woo-ya is worried about you. He wants to help, but he doesn't know what is going on, so he doesn't know what to do, and that's frustrating."

"How do you know that?"

"We talked the other day," HanYin said. "He mentioned how he was scared you'd work yourself to death. I cannot say that I don't share his worry. I do see how hard you push yourself, but I also know a little of why that is."

"I'm worried."

"About?"

"I don't know how he'll react."

"Considering he knows about me and Min-su dongsaeng and the others, I can't see him being any more than fine with it."

"The others?"

"Cheongul and Ki-tae," HanYin said with a smile. "We're the same."

"You're the same, but you haven't told me exactly what you are," Jong-in said.

"We're Vampires," HanYin said.

"Well, at least now I know why you all smelled so different than other humans. Honestly, I have no way of knowing what I'm smelling. I could have walked by hundreds of Shifters and Vampires and I wouldn't have any clue. How do you identify a species by smell?"

"Exposure mostly," HanYin said. "The more you encounter wolf Shifters, for example, you'll realize there's an… earthy scent to them, an essence that identifies their species. It's not like each species has the same smell, just there is a common denominator in their scents."

"That makes sense. You and Ki-tae hyung, and Cheongul hyung each smell different, but with the same… otherness. It's not something I can identify specifically, like an earthy smell or a woodsy smell, but there is that common link."

"Exactly."

"What do I smell like to you?"

HanYin buried his nose against Jong-in's neck and inhaled deeply. "Delicious."

"HanYin."

"All right." HanYin sighed. "You smell delicious and smoky, like a campfire."

"Min-su-ya told me about being a Shifter. I... I couldn't bring myself to tell her." Jong-in buried his face in HanYin's chest. "I'm such a coward."

"You're not a coward." HanYin made him look up and kissed him. "Jin-woo-ya and Min-su dongsaeng, they matter to you a great deal, and so does their opinion of you."

"It isn't only that. I don't... I don't want them to see me as a charity case, as someone who needs to depend on them financially. I've been making ends meet, barely, but I've been doing it on my own."

"Your independence is one of the things I admire about you," HanYin said. "Yet it doesn't make you any less to accept help when it is offered. It took me a very long time before I allowed myself to depend on Soon-joon-nim and Cheongul when they first found me. I didn't want to be viewed as weak."

"What happened?"

"They didn't give up on me, and eventually I started to trust them," HanYin said quietly, remembering that time so long ago. "For years they put up with my fight response in the morning. One day after lessons, Soon-joon-nim came into the room with his hands behind his back. He'd been gone for a long time. Cheongul was with him. The tutor had left for the day, and I was just going over my lessons. I had a hard time learning to write. I was worried, thinking they were going to tell me to leave. I remember that. I think I started to shake a little as they sat down with me at the table. Without a word, Soon-joon-nim set a wrapped package in front of me. The paper was a brilliant red, with gold dragons all over it and a big gold ribbon. I looked at him. I didn't speak much back then. He told me to open it."

"What was inside?"

"An alarm clock," HanYin whispered. "When he'd heard about them, Soon-joon-nim had gone all the way to America to purchase one for me. He didn't need to say anything to me. I knew why he'd done it."

"Why?"

"Every time I'd hurt them, I'd cry for hours and hours. They were my family, and I was causing them pain," HanYin said, his voice tight. "It may not seem like much, considering there were times I forgot to wind it or set it, but Abeoji gave me that very first one and Cheongul said, 'No more tears.'"

"He did it so you could be in control of when you woke up and not hurt them, which made you cry," Jong-in said.

"Yes," HanYin said. "Jin-woo-ya and Min-su dongsaeng are not going to give up on you either."

"He hasn't responded... at all," Jong-in pointed out.

"Jin-woo-ya is one of those people who is very laid-back, but push him past that point, and his anger is something to be reckoned with. He is upset and worried, and you two just argued earlier today. He might not be ready to talk about it yet."

"Min-su-ya said he shut her down when she tried to talk to him about it afterward," Jong-in said. "That's rarely happened."

"I think people forget Jin-woo-ya has a backbone," HanYin said with a soft chuckle. "They see that sweet face and think he is easily manipulated."

"If he's easily manipulated, I'm the Emperor of the Joseon Dynasty." Jong-in snorted. Then he looked at HanYin from beneath his lashes. "You think his face is sweet, huh?"

"And I think your face is beautiful and sexy, and those dimples are my weakness," HanYin said, rolling him onto his back. "You are who I desire, who I dream of, who makes me hard simply with the sound of your voice and your scent on the breeze."

"You know how to make a guy feel special," Jong-in panted as they slowly writhed together.

"You are special, Jong-in," HanYin said and claimed his mouth in a hot kiss. "Let me show you."

Jong-in ended up not going to campus that night. HanYin kept him too busy with hours of lovemaking in the bedroom, in the kitchen, in the living room. Any chance he got to have Jong-in inside him, HanYin took it.

CHEONGUL

CHEONGUL LEANED against the wall between the elevators in the lobby, waiting. He crossed his arms over his chest and bounced his leg in agitation as he watched the door. When Jin-woo and Jong-in came in, surprisingly at the same time as his brothers, Cheongul moved without thinking. He shot forward and grabbed the two men by their collars amid HanYin's and Ki-tae's protests. He snarled something that made his brothers step back and dragged the two men off. When he found an open conference room, he threw them inside and slammed the door behind him, locking it.

"I don't mean to be rude, but what the fuck, hyung?" Jin-woo demanded.

"Last night Min-su came storming over to my apartment, furious and in tears... *in tears* because you two were fighting. Neither one of you would talk to her, and she didn't know how to help you," Cheongul growled, his eyes flashing silver and his fangs visible when he spoke. His nails had elongated into sharp black claws. "You two will remain in this room until you've worked out whatever problem you have with each other, and then you will go reassure Min-su that you're not going to abandon each other."

"What?" Jong-in said. "What gave her that idea?"

"She said you two never fight, not like this, not talking to each other, and worse, not talking to her," Cheongul said, barely controlling his anger. "I'm going to leave so you two can talk and so I can calm down, if that's even possible now. When you come out, you better have worked this shit out. Whatever is going on isn't worth your friendship. Don't let it ruin that."

Without giving them a chance to say anything, Cheongul left the room. He found HanYin and Ki-tae on the other side, looking none too happy. When he caught the low growling, Cheongul sighed. "They're fine."

"What the fuck, Cheongul?" Ki-tae demanded.

"Let's not do this in the hall." He led the way into the next conference room over.

"Explain, now," HanYin said.

"Min-su came over last night," he said with a sigh as he sat down. Faced with the anger in his brothers' eyes and the hint of their fear scenting the air, the anger drained out of Cheongul. "She was in tears because she was so worried about them and their fight. I just had to do something. I didn't think."

"Clearly, because Jong-in may not be ready to tell Jin-woo-ya what's going on. He shouldn't be forced to do that," HanYin said. "And Jin-woo-ya, he's already worried enough as it is about Jong-in and about Ki-tae, so throwing him into this situation wasn't a plus for him either."

"I said I didn't think, HanYin," Cheongul repeated. "What did you expect me to do?"

"I get it," Ki-tae said. "You wanted to make her pain go away, and that's all that mattered."

"Yeah." The next thing he knew, Ki-tae slammed Cheongul up against the wall, his baby brother lifting him off the ground, claws curled in his shirt.

"You *ever* do that to Jin-woo again, and I will kick your ass," Ki-tae growled. "Are we clear?"

"Yes."

"Good." Ki-tae let him go, turned, and stormed out of the room, leaving HanYin and Cheongul alone. It was then Cheongul spotted the claw marks on Ki-tae's neck and jaw. He looked up, and the emotion in HanYin's eyes stabbed through his heart.

"Ki-tae had to hold me back from going through the door. I hurt him," HanYin whispered. "That's how much Jong-in means to me."

"HanYin."

"Don't ever put us in that position again." HanYin's eyes glistened. "I don't want to hurt either of you."

Then he left too, and Cheongul hung his head. He had managed to anger Ki-tae, cause HanYin to hurt him, and upset HanYin with both actions, and all because he couldn't control his anger at the tears Min-su had cried.

What the hell was wrong with him? He wasn't an irrational person. With his issues, he tried hard to think first. Yet when he'd seen the tears in her eyes, he'd wanted to maul whatever had caused her pain, a disproportionate reaction as she hadn't had a chance to tell him what was going on. He'd managed to project an outward calm last night, but inside, he'd been seething. Now, he just caused more people pain. Why had he gone off the handle like that? He shouldn't have grabbed them and dragged them off. He should have used his head, thought things through before he acted. With the way his luck was going, Min-su would be pissed when she found out about it too.

Pushing off the wall Ki-tae had slammed in him into, Cheongul made his way down to the gym and started beating himself up in the healthiest way possible. They had an hour before they needed to head to dance practice, so he needed to get rid of as much of this angry energy as possible before then. He was going to be exhausted when they were done for the day, but if it made him unable to do stupid shit, all the better. He couldn't hurt anyone if he was passed out in his bed, asleep.

JIN-WOO

"I'M SCARED," Jin-woo said softly as he sat down in the chair at the head of the table. "I don't want to lose you, and all I can see is you pushing yourself until your heart gives out."

Jong-in joined him at the table. "There's something I need to tell you."

"What is it?"

"I'm not...." Jong-in stopped and took a deep breath and then started again. "I'm not human."

"Okay," Jin-woo said with a shrug. "So what are you?"

"That's it? 'So what are you' is your only response?" Jong-in looked confused.

"I'm dating a Vampire, and one of my best friends is a Shifter. How is this supposed to surprise me?" Jin-woo snorted. "So what are you?"

"A Fox-Spirit," Jong-in said, and the expression in his eyes lightened.

"Wait... did you think I was going to be upset about this, just like you thought I was going to be upset about you being gay?" Jin-woo narrowed his eyes. "Seriously? I should smack you."

"Please don't. This was really hard for me to say, and being gay is not nearly as upsetting as being a Fox-Spirit. Look, I don't have a lot of control over this. I mean, I get too upset, and I pop ears and two tails, and my eyes go lavender. Sometimes it happens all at once, and other times it's piecemeal, like I'll get just the ears. There are times when I get so overwhelmed with shit, I change completely, and I don't remember anything afterward, which is terrifying. Until just a couple of days ago, I didn't even know what I was, just that I wasn't normal."

Jin-woo scooched his chair around the table to Jong-in and took his hands. "You are one of my dearest friends, Jong-in-a. Being a Fox-Spirit doesn't change that, doesn't change who you are and have always been to me. I see you, your face pale, dark circles under your eyes and determined to do it all on your own, and it kills me to not be able to help because I don't know what's wrong."

"I don't want to be a burden."

"You're not," Jin-woo said, trying to make him see. "We care. *I* care. Min-su-ya was right. You could never be a burden to us. Tell me."

He held his breath as Jong-in stared at him as if searching for something in his eyes. He must have seen it because, slowly, Jong-in began to talk. The words were halting at first, but then grew smoother the more Jin-woo simply listened. He didn't interrupt, he didn't try to figure out how to respond, he just listened and that appeared to be the key. When he finally stopped, Jin-woo didn't say anything. He pulled Jong-in into his arms and hugged him tight.

"Thank you," he said softly.

"What for? Burdening you with my problems?"

"For trusting me, Jong-in-a," he said as he leaned back. "With all of it. I know you want to make it on your own. I feel the same way, and if I could live without having to have any interaction with my aunt, I would do it in a heartbeat. She's a miserable, bitter, bigoted, hateful old bitch. Thankfully my grandparents knew she would have never treated me well or helped me in any way if they hadn't set up the trust as they did. I only have to get through two more years before she's out of my life, but it's a long time. What I want you to promise me is that you'll come to me if you need help. I know you have to work—I get that. I just want you to take care of yourself too. It doesn't seem like it most of the time, but sleep is important. You need to give your body and your brain a break to be able to function. I don't want you to end up in the hospital, or worse."

"I'll do my best. That's all I can promise."

"That's all I ask."

"I got really good sleep last night," Jong-in said with a small smile.

"I can see that." Jin-woo couldn't resist. "I see you came in with HanYin-a this morning. Is he the reason you got such a... restful night?"

"Shut it," Jong-in said, blushing furiously. "Yes, he is, dammit."

"I'm glad you took the chance, Jong-in-a. He makes you happy, makes you smile, and I love seeing that."

"We're good?"

"Yeah, we're good." Jin-woo nodded. "Now we need to get to work, or we're going to be in trouble."

"We should probably arrange to have lunch with Min-su-ya and talk to her," Jong-in said.

"I suppose we're expected to apologize too." Jin-woo sighed.

"Probably."

"She cried."

"Yeah."

"That sucks."

"Yeah."

"She's going to hit us—hard."

"Yeah." Jong-in nodded. "But we'll live, and everything will be back to normal, or relatively, at least."

They walked out of the conference room, arms over each other's shoulders. It was good to not be at odds with Jong-in. Jin-woo had been scared and frustrated and angry, and now he could admit it hurt how Jong-in didn't seem to trust him. It had made him question their friendship, and Jin-woo hadn't liked that. Jin-woo rubbed his eyes, exhausted.

"You don't look like you're getting much sleep either," Jong-in said as they walked. "Is Ki-tae hyung keeping you up all night?"

"I wish, but no," Jin-woo said. "I've been having really disturbing dreams lately."

"Do you want to talk about it?"

"Later, I think," Jin-woo said. "I'm almost finished with the performance video. Once I get this last bit of timing right, I'll give it to Hyung-jun seonbae to go over."

"Okay. I'll see you at lunch, then."

"Sure. See you then." Jin-woo waved and then went to the studio.

Just before he walked through the door, a coffee cup appeared in front of him. He turned to Ki-tae and smiled. Ki-tae didn't look reassured.

"Are you okay?" he asked.

"Yes," Jin-woo said after taking a sip. It was perfect. "Jong-in-a and I talked and got things straightened out."

"You're not mad at me?"

"For what?"

"For letting it happen to begin with?" Ki-tae said softly.

"No, I think we were all taken by surprise, and I have some choice words for Cheongul hyung when I see him again."

"He wasn't thinking clearly."

"I know he wasn't, but that still doesn't give him the right to drag us around like that," Jin-woo said. "It was embarrassing and a bit frightening."

"I'm sorry he scared you."

"You're not the one who should be apologizing," Jin-woo said, putting a hand on Ki-tae's arm. He gripped Ki-tae's chin and turned his head to get a better look at the marks. "What the hell are these?"

"Nothing."

"They're not nothing, Ki-tae." Jin-woo glared at him. "You didn't have them this morning, so obviously, something happened between then and now. Don't keep things like this from me... please."

"Let's just say HanYin didn't appreciate Cheongul dragging you two off either and it would have gotten uglier if I hadn't stopped him from breaking through the door," Ki-tae said. "It really is nothing. They'll be gone in an hour, maybe two."

"I don't like seeing you hurt." Jin-woo could hear the trembling in his voice and hated it.

"I know," Ki-tae said as he pulled Jin-woo into his arms. "I don't like you being hurt either. I'm sorry."

"Apology accepted. Now enough of this. You're still coming over tonight?"

"Try and stop me," Ki-tae said with his sexy smirk firmly in place. "I have to go to a torture session now."

"Dance practice isn't that bad, Ki-tae." Jin-woo laughed.

"Gojira seonbae is nice to you. She thinks you're adorable. Me she has it out for. Miss one practice and that woman holds a grudge forever," Ki-tae said with a roll of his eyes.

"Yet none of you really complain, do you? She's damn good at what she does, and she has made you three some of the best dancers out there. Why don't you cut her some slack?"

"If we did that, she'd wonder what was wrong," Ki-tae said with a wide-eyed innocent expression before stealing a kiss and then hurrying on his way. Well, as much as Ki-tae hurried anywhere, leaving Jin-woo to his work.

Several hours later, Jin-woo was nibbling on his thumb as Hyung-jun got settled in the studio chair. Had it been just Hyung-jun, Jin-woo might not have been so nervous, but Soon-joon and ChenBao were there too. He wasn't expecting that.

"Relax, dongsaeng," ChenBao said gently. "It's going to be wonderful."

"I hope so," he murmured just as Hyung-jun hit Play.

Four minutes stretched on for an eternity as they watched the screen. No one made any comments, and Jin-woo didn't know if that was good or bad. When the video ended, they turned to him almost as one. He looked from one to the other, his stomach knotting as they continued to remain silent. He wanted to ask so badly, but he forced himself to wait.

"That was… beautiful," ChenBao said with a bright smile. "I love how it started with those forest sounds. The slight echo made them seem otherworldly and immediately set the tone."

"You used the sweeping camera shots perfectly, not overdoing them," Soon-joon said. "And you gave each performer an equal amount of screen time, not favoring one over the other."

"I know you were having trouble with timing the other day, but you worked it out perfectly. There's just one more thing to do," Hyung-jun said.

"What's that?" Jin-woo asked, not sure he could say anything further.

"Put your name on it," Hyung-jun said with a huge smile. "We'll work the credits a little later."

"Truly you have a talent for this business, dongsaeng," ChenBao said as she rose from her chair.

"I know you have school projects to work on before the spring festival," Soon-joon said. "That's why I am giving you the rest of the day off to work on them."

"Gomabseumnida, Soon-joon-nim," Jin-woo said with a bow. "I do have projects due this week. I greatly appreciate your generosity."

"Just promise me one thing, dongsaeng."

"What is that?" Jin-woo said.

"Get some rest," he said.

"I will try," Jin-woo said with another bow. "Gomabseumnida."

They left him alone at that point, Hyung-jun putting a hand on his shoulder before he walked out the door. Jin-woo flopped back into his chair. They had liked it. He punched his fists in the air and kicked his feet in delight. Childish, he knew, but he couldn't contain his joy. He had struggled with the timing and worried it wasn't up to par.

Glancing at the clock, he saw it was lunchtime and hurried to shut things down. He was supposed to meet Min-su and Jong-in. They had some things to talk about. As it was, he was going to be a few minutes late. After turning of the lights and leaving the studio, Jin-woo ran to the elevators. He hurried to the commissary and searched for Min-su and Jong-in. He finally spotted them way in the back by the windows and called out. When Min-su looked up, her face got all pouty. He hated it when she pouted. Flopping into the seat between them, he looked at her.

"Stop pouting at me," he said.

"No."

"It doesn't do any good, you know," he said. "You're still adorable, and I'm still stubborn."

"Did you two make up at least? It seems so since you're both sitting with me rather than avoiding each other," she said.

"You can thank your boyfriend for that!" Jin-woo said. "He dragged us off this morning and locked us in a room together. It was one of the most embarrassing things I've ever experienced in my life, thank you very much."

"He did what?" she said softly, sitting up straight in her chair.

"Cheongul hyung locked us in a conference room together, saying we made you cry and that we needed to work it out," Jong-in said and nibbled on a steamed dumpling.

"I... I didn't ask him to do that. I wouldn't ask him to do that," Min-su said. "I would have done it myself eventually, but when I went over to his place, I just needed someone to listen."

"He listened, and then he acted. He cares about you," Jin-woo said. "Now are the three of us good, because this is stressing all of us out, and we can't have that."

"Yes." Min-su looked down at her food, and Jin-woo could see the pink tinging her cheeks.

"Hey, take it as a good sign," he said. "He was seriously angry at us for making you cry."

"As sweet as that is and his intentions were good, he shouldn't have done that to you. I don't need someone to ride in like some proverbial knight."

"Here's the way I see it. We're both stubborn and it may have taken several days before either one of us bent enough to talk to the other. In the meantime, you would have been upset. Cheongul hyung, from what I've seen, is a man of action. He could have talked until he was blue in the face, not that he would, he talks only slightly more than I do, but we wouldn't have listened. Yes, it was not the best course of action, but it was effective and he didn't hurt us, just startled us a bit. In a way, I'm relieved he put us in that room. I didn't like being at odds with Jin-woo-ya one bit, but I felt I needed to stand my ground. Let it go. It's done, and it just shows how much he cares," Jong-in said.

"It just sounds like an excuse," Min-su said.

"Maybe a little bit, but I can see where Jong-in-a is coming from," Jin-woo said. "Cheongul hyung cares about you. You were upset. He knew what the problem was and had a solution which he then implemented. It wasn't the best solution and HanYin ended up hurting Ki-tae because of it, but it was the most expedient and it had the desired results. If you feel that strongly about it, talk to him, but when you do, remember who you're talking with. His thinking isn't necessarily going to be the most modern, is it?"

"No, I guess it won't be. He may look twenty-five, but as we know, looks can be deceiving," Min-su said.

"Communication is great, but sometimes, action is what's needed," Jong-in said. "Now, Jin-woo-ya, what's going on with these nightmares you were talking about earlier?"

"Nightmares?" Min-su looked at him.

Jin-woo sighed. "They started just after I went back to my apartment. It's not the same dream over and over again. Although it might as well be, because the differences are small. It always starts in the dark. I can hear voices, moaning. Sometimes, most of the time, the moaning sounds like the good kind, but intermixed with that, it sounds as if someone is in pain. I get grabbed from behind. I'm forced down onto this disgusting-smelling pallet face-first, pinned there by weight on my back. I'm so small, and I can tell I'm a child, a very young child. Then this person shoves their arm under my mouth. If I turn away, he grabs my hair and yanks my head back hard. I'm so small, so young, I can't fight him. He forces my mouth open and pushes his arm against it. He... bleeds into my mouth until it's so full I have to swallow or I'll choke. Everything gets hazy and warped, as if I'm on drugs. Only one thing is clear, one person, and he is... terrifying. I can think of nothing but—"

"Sashin."

Jin-woo whipped his head around to see Ki-tae and HanYin behind him. He was out of his chair the minute he saw the terrified look on Ki-tae's face, but Ki-tae stepped away, and pain lanced through Jin-woo's heart. It was as if he couldn't speak. Ki-tae shook his head, whispering "no" over and over again. Then he was gone. Jin-woo tried to go after him, but HanYin stopped him.

"HanYin-a, that's twice now," Jin-woo said. "Let me go. He needs me."

"He needs to process it first," HanYin said. "You don't get it, and he should have talked to you before this, but it is so hard for him."

"What? What is so hard for him? How did he know that name?" Jin-woo demanded.

"Come, I think it's best if we go talk to ChenBao-nim, all of us," he said, looking at Min-su and Jong-in as well.

"Why would we need to go to her? I'm not going anywhere until I get an *answer*, HanYin-a."

"Your nightmares, Jin-woo-ya. They were his reality."

Jin-woo stood, shocked, staring at HanYin.

"Come, we must see ChenBao-nim, and I must find Abeoji to let him know."

Without another word, HanYin led them up to ChenBao's office. Jin-woo felt numb, as if he were wrapped in cotton. He couldn't reconcile his dreams and his beautiful Ki-tae. In truth, he couldn't wrap his mind around the idea that anyone would be so evil as to do that to a child, any child. Children should be cherished, protected, loved unconditionally. They were precious gifts. It was inconceivable to him, simply unimaginable.

"I want to say something to lighten the mood, but there really isn't any way to do that, is there?" Jong-in said.

"No, there's really not, *xīn'ái*," HanYin said.

When they reached ChenBao's office, HanYin knocked and then opened the door. He ushered them inside. ChenBao was sitting behind the desk, and she wasn't smiling. The look on her face sent a shiver up Jin-woo's spine.

"What has happened?" They didn't even need to say anything for her to know something was wrong.

"Jin-woo-ya has been dreaming of Ki-tae's past, *Lǎodà niáng*," HanYin said. "I only wish it were not the worst part of his life. I must find Abeoji and let him know. Ki-tae has taken off, and it is imperative we find him as quickly as possible. I will need to enlist Cheongul too, but I am sure he is down in the gym."

ChenBao's eyes went completely white, and Jin-woo froze. That was seriously creepy. Min-su's soft "cool" and Jong-in's awed "holy shit" said he was the only one to think so. There was something so *powerful* about her. Then they returned to normal. It was only a few seconds, but Jin-woo still felt as if she were staring into his soul.

"Cheongul dongsaeng has finished his workout and is dressing now," ChenBao said. "Soon-joon-nim is on a business call to a venue in Busan."

"And Ki-tae?" Jin-woo couldn't stop himself from asking.

"How long ago did he discover this?"

"Not five minutes ago," HanYin said. "We were meeting Jin-woo-ya, Jong-in, and Min-su dongsaeng for lunch. We came upon the conversation at the tail end of Jin-woo-ya's description of his dreams. It only took those few sentences for Ki-tae to know."

"Qīngróu," ChenBao said. Jin-woo tensed even more as a slender woman in a sharp, pale yellow business suit materialized next to her desk.

"*Shi, Qíngfù?*" she said in a soft whisper of a voice. Jin-woo barely heard her. He started to feel light-headed. This was all getting to be a little much. He wanted, no, he *needed* to find Ki-tae.

"Stay with us, Jin-woo dongsaeng," ChenBao said. "This is Qīngróu. She is a *Fēng Líng*, a wind spirit, and has been my assistant for many years. She will help us find Ki-tae. He is no longer in the building. He moves fast in five minutes."

"I'm going to speak plainly, and I apologize ahead of time for being incredibly rude, but I don't give a damn what or who she is. All I want is to find Ki-tae," Jin-woo said in a rush. "Once I'm sure he's okay, then you and everyone else can explain this shit to your heart's content, but he is my priority!"

ChenBao laughed. "You are perfect for him, so devoted after such a short time. It is good to see. And I will forgive your rudeness because you are truly distraught over Ki-tae. However, to help you both, I need to know some details. Qīngróu and her siblings can search this city faster than even I can. They can also venture farther in a minute than I can in a day. Therefore I will trust the search for Ki-tae to her while you and I discuss your dreams."

"You really think I'm going to sit down and chitchat while he's out there, panicking and terrified?"

"Jin-woo-ya," Min-su hissed, grabbing his arm, trying to tug him down to the couch where she'd taken a seat.

"I think you really have no choice." ChenBao smiled, but it was a little less pleasant than before. "Unless you wish to beard the Dragon in her den, to coin a phrase."

That caught his attention. "Dragon?"

"Dragon."

"I thought you were a Vampire," Jin-woo whispered.

"I am. My mother was a Vampire. My father is a Celestial Dragon." She smiled. "Of my siblings, I am the only one who is both."

"No wonder you scare the shit out of me," HanYin muttered.

"Sūnzi, we will talk more later, just you and me," ChenBao said softly, and then she turned back to Jin-woo. "So, Jin-woo dongsaeng, what shall it be?"

"Don't be stupid, Jin-woo-ya," Jong-in said. "I may be clueless about this world, but I'm pretty damn sure messing with a Dragon is suicidal."

"I will tackle your ass before you get two steps," Min-su warned. "You won't do Ki-tae oppa any good if you push this."

"I'm the only human in the room. What choice do I have?" Jin-woo muttered, feeling weak and helpless and useless to the man he loved with all his heart.

He sat down on the couch and put his head in his hands. He just couldn't take not knowing where Ki-tae was, what he was thinking, not being able to help him. What could Ki-tae possibly see in him when he was so weak compared to everyone around him? He was just human. There was nothing special about him. He couldn't even compete with his best friends. What the fuck was Ki-tae doing with him?

KI-TAE

KI-TAE PERCHED atop the Beopjusa Palsangjeon, the Hall of Eight Pictures, staring up at Songnisan. The cherry blossoms were almost in full bloom and the pine trees would soon follow in summer. The urge to disappear into the forests of the mountain was strong. It was quiet and peaceful there. He'd disappeared amid them before, just for a few days when he was many years younger. There was no stress among the trees and waterfalls. He wouldn't have to worry about hurting his family if they had to wake him up. He wouldn't hurt Jin-woo, taint him with the horror of his past. He wouldn't have to think about Sashin. There were plenty of animals for him to feed on. He could survive there in relative peace.

The wind caressed his face, bringing Ki-tae out of his thoughts. He heard soft murmuring as he looked around him. He couldn't be seen from the ground seventy-four feet below, perched as he was at the base of the crowning spire. People tended not to look up. At any rate, the clouds were threatening rain. Not many people would remain outside when it started.

"Ki-tae?" Soon-joon's voice was soft and soothing as always.

"Abeoji." He could hear the tears in his own voice. "He knows."

"He does not understand," Soon-joon said. "He fears for you enough to challenge ChenBao-nim."

"Fears for me, or fears me?"

"He thinks only of finding you," Soon-joon said. "Come, *segare*, let us go home."

"Do I have a home with you?"

"Always."

Ki-tae took Soon-joon's offered hand and allowed himself to be pulled to his feet. Soon-joon wrapped him in a hug, and the next thing he knew, they were at the house. He didn't let go of his father for a long time, and the tears flowed in silent waves. He wasn't ready for Jin-woo to know of his past. He wasn't ready to remember the darkness he'd known for most of his childhood. His earliest memories were of Sashin and that place. After his rescue, there was a period of time he couldn't recall at all. It was a permanent gap in his memories, a nebulous blankness separating his hell from his salvation.

"I'm not ready," he cried against his father's shoulder.

"I know," Soon-joon said. "ChenBao-nim and your brothers will be here soon. They are bringing Jin-woo dongsaeng, Jong-in dongsaeng, and Min-su dongsaeng with them. Would you like me to put you to sleep so you may actually rest?"

"Yes," Ki-tae whispered, feeling like a coward for taking that escape from his nightmares, but he was so exhausted, and if he closed them, Sashin's face immediately appeared behind his eyes, that cruel, sensuous mouth grinning in triumph. Soon-joon placed his hand on Ki-tae's forehead. Ki-tae barely registered the whispered chant before blackness claimed him.

Soon-joon

AFTER HE put Ki-tae to bed, Soon-joon changed out of his suit and into something comfortable. He had picked up some habits from his boys and donned a pair of worn jeans, a long-sleeved shirt that went past his wrists, and bare feet, carrying his shoes over to the shelves by the door. In truth they got the bare feet from him. As a boy he hated shoes, and that carried through his life. He wore them when he must, but if he had a choice, he would not don shoes or socks. He padded into the kitchen and began pulling ingredients from the pantry and the refrigerator. Ki-tae would be hungry when Soon-joon woke him, and he wouldn't do that until everyone was here.

Never had he had so much going on with his family and business at one time. He saw his sons struggling with their pasts and their fears all at once, and he didn't know how to help them. He struggled with his own mistakes, and desire warred with guilt. For a long time, he confided in no one, but with ChenBao's return from solitude, he found his desire to confide in her as he once had very strong. Even when she yelled at him about Hyun-jo, he could still feel her love for him.

Soon-joon was not prone to indecision, especially where his family was concerned, and to see his sons falling in love filled him with joy and trepidation. Cheongul had not opened his heart to another in centuries. Yet Min-su brought out something in him, something Soon-joon had feared lost. She was not a demur woman, docile and subservient, and perhaps that was exactly what Cheongul needed. Perhaps he needed a woman who would stand beside him, who would be his strength when he had none left, and who would always speak her mind to him whether or not he wanted to hear the words.

HanYin had spent the night with Jong-in. That in and of itself was an achievement. Never had he risked such a thing. He had taken a chance on Jong-in, and it seemed to be working out. His middle son was smiling more, his chatter bright and cheerful. Yes, there were some dark moments in the last several weeks, but the change in HanYin was obvious. He was in love with Jong-in, and he was reaching out for that love. It made Soon-joon proud to see HanYin actively pursuing his own happiness, rather than focusing all his efforts on making sure his family was happy. That part of him wouldn't change, but that he now felt he could have happiness for himself was a wonderful thing. Jong-in had brought that out in him, had made HanYin think more of his own wants and needs.

Of his three sons, Ki-tae was the one he worried about the most. Ki-tae's greatest fear had happened: he was bound once again. Yet this time was different. The person was different. Jin-woo was nothing like Sashin, may that bastard fall

to the depths of Mugen Jigoku, the eighth and deepest circle of Jigoku, never to
return. When Ki-tae had a nightmare or awoke in a state of aggression, Soon-joon
found himself wishing he'd made the bastard's death last longer. Sashin had not
suffered enough, not when compared to Ki-tae's continued misery.

Ki-tae didn't remember the time when he went through blood withdrawal,
but Soon-joon did. They all did. He almost died several times, struggling to return
to that place, to seek out the source of his addiction. He escaped into the mountains
at one point, wearing only the clothes on his back, searching for a way back to
Sashin. There were times when they had to restrain him, and he fought them.
Oh, how Ki-tae fought them. It had been a daily struggle to see him through the
physical and mental trials addiction and withdrawal placed on a person.

Yet Soon-joon had hope for him. As he watched the interactions between Ki-
tae and Jin-woo, he saw a change in his youngest son, a change for the better. The
way Jin-woo looked at Ki-tae, the love Soon-joon saw there, gave away how he
felt. He didn't know if Jin-woo had acknowledged it in himself, but if his reactions
earlier today were any indication, the answer to that question was yes.

Soon-joon suspected Ki-tae had planned on telling Jin-woo about the bond
on Sunday, when he would have his family around to support him if the worst
happened, but it had been taken out of his hands now. He would have to tell Jin-
woo tonight. He would still have his family around him, though.

Soon-joon paused in his preparation of miso soup and sukiyaki to grip the
counter. He snarled as his fangs descended and the need for blood made his belly
clench. He did not have time to go out, not now. His family needed him, and his
needs would have to wait.

"Did you think you could sneak out of the office and not feed?"

He looked up to see Hyun-jo walking toward him, clad in a traditional
kimono, his hair long but still black and pulled up away from his face in a simple
style, the rest hanging down behind him. He came down the two steps and around
the island. Soon-joon should stop being surprised Hyun-jo appeared when he
was in need. Yet every time he saw his sweet Kitsune, guilt dug its claws into
his chest.

Hyun-jo turned Soon-joon to face him, and he couldn't look away from
Hyun-jo's lavender eyes. Then he stepped close, so close Soon-joon could feel his
body heat, and he dropped his eyes to Hyun-jo's mouth, the corners curved ever
so slightly. Slowly Hyun-jo raised his arm, letting his sleeve slide down to bunch
at his elbow. Soon-joon turned his head, brushing his lips across that bared skin,
causing Hyun-jo to whimper softly. He sank his fangs into Hyun-jo's wrist and
drank until the need was sated. Hyun-jo cupped his face, and Soon-joon looked
into his eyes as he licked his lips. They were filled with determination and the
flames of his fox-fire.

"I am done waiting for you to get over your guilt. You will feed only from me, but that is the last time you will feed from my wrist," Hyun-jo said. "Consider yourself forewarned, *Wŏ de àirén*."

"Hyun-jo."

"And I am not leaving tonight, nor am I sleeping anywhere save next to you," Hyun-jo continued as if he hadn't said anything. Soon-joon huffed. "I am also done hiding what I am and my relationship to you from your sons."

"You are full of demands," Soon-joon said, pointing at him with a spoon.

"I am out of patience. A millennium of waiting for you to pull your head out of your ass is quite enough, thank you very much," Hyun-jo said as he set the table, moving around with easy familiarity.

"Hyun-jo."

"No, Soon-joon, I have waited far too long, and I will wait no more," he said as he placed the last plate on the table and turned to look at Soon-joon over the island.

Hyun-jo sighed and came to stand before him once more. When he cupped Soon-joon's face in almost delicate hands and pulled him down for a gentle kiss, Soon-joon could not resist. Without conscious thought, he wrapped one arm around Hyun-jo's waist and pulled him close. When they broke apart, they were both breathing heavily.

"I am yours, and you are mine. I have no regrets. I cannot return to my clan, this is true, but I don't want to, and that is what you fail to see. It is you who makes me happy, Soon-joon, you who brightens my day with a single smile, you who turns me into a quivering mass of want when I catch your scent. It is *you* who means everything to me, and I am not going to stand idle anymore. I am going to pursue you until you finally give in and realize you love me just as much as I love you."

"I already know that," Soon-joon said softly. "I just do not feel worthy of your love."

"If you were not, you would not have it, and you know it. Stop being so damned stubborn and accept this love between us, in all its benefits and beauty," Hyun-jo purred as he nuzzled Soon-joon's neck. "When we retire tonight, I'm not going to let you sleep for a *very* long time. We have many, *many* years to make up for."

"There are more important issues we must deal with than our intimacy," Soon-joon said after swallowing hard—twice.

"Why do you think I said 'after'?" Hyun-jo smirked at him. "Do you recall how I prefer to wear my kimonos?"

With those teasing words, he walked out of the kitchen, leaving Soon-joon with a mental image he was hard-pressed not to react to. With a shake of his head and a very determined mental push to clear the erotic images from his mind, Soon-joon turned back to the food. He wanted it ready when everyone arrived, and he needed to think about something other than Hyun-jo in his bed once more.

JIN-WOO

JIN-WOO SAT in the car next to Min-su, staring out the window. He couldn't stop thinking about Ki-tae. It didn't take Qīngróu long to find Ki-tae, and Soon-joon called shortly thereafter to say Ki-tae was home and asleep. Now they were on their way to Soon-joon's house, and Jin-woo was incredibly nervous, not to mention antsy. They assured him Ki-tae was physically fine, but that didn't stop him from worrying. He wouldn't be satisfied until he saw Ki-tae for himself.

The car slowed and then turned. Jin-woo straightened.

"We're here," HanYin said quietly. He hadn't smiled since lunchtime, hadn't spoken much either. Jong-in sat next to him, their fingers intertwined. It was good to see, but it made Jin-woo sad. Would he have that level of comfort with Ki-tae ever again? Did the nightmares ruin all that? He didn't know, and it was making him sick to his stomach.

Shin-bai opened the door in silence. No one had said much of anything, in fact. It was weird and disconcerting. HanYin exited first, then Jong-in. Finally Jin-woo climbed out, followed by Min-su.

"Welcome to our home," HanYin said and then waved an arm to usher them forward.

"I thought you lived at the apartment?" Jong-in asked. Jin-woo suspected it was to break the continued silence.

"I do, but this is my true home," HanYin said. "We have lived here for years before getting our own places. Sometimes we need to be by ourselves, and our apartments allow us to do that, but we still think of this as our home. You see, Soon-joon-nim is our father as much as he's our sire."

"I don't understand."

"He found all of us as young children. Well, HanYin and I were in our teens. We figure Ki-tae was about twelve, still a child, when Abeoji found him," Cheongul said absently as he came up behind them and set pace with Min-su. He had ridden in a different car. "We'll explain it all when we get inside. I really want to take these damn shoes off."

"Me too," HanYin grumbled. "And Abeoji's been cooking. I can smell the sukiyaki from here."

"Means there's miso soup too," Cheongul said with a small half smile.

"Your father is a very good cook," ChenBao said. "He learned from the imperial bakers and from his Japanese grandmother. They all adored him. He was such a precocious child, always sticking his nose into every little thing to find out what it was, how it worked, such curiosity."

"Trying to keep these relationships straight is making my head hurt." Jin-woo sighed. "I just want to see Ki-tae."

"You will, Jin-woo dongsaeng," Cheongul said.

"Given the situation, can we all agree such formal speech is no longer necessary?" Jin-woo said, rubbing at the ache in his temple. "At least when we're in private?"

Everyone nodded.

Cheongul started walking again. "Abeoji has had him sleeping since they returned from Busan. When we get inside, we'll wake him up."

"I don't understand why we had to wait so long before coming here," Jin-woo huffed.

"Ki-tae needed the rest," HanYin said.

"I know," Jin-woo said as they paused outside the door. "I can't settle until I see him for myself. Does that make any sense? I mean, I trust you all, so why would I doubt you in this?"

"Because you love him," ChenBao said with a shrug. "And until you see him with your own eyes, check him yourself, you will not feel at ease with the idea he is okay."

"But he's not okay, is he?" Jin-woo said as HanYin opened the door and they went inside. "Physically, maybe, but that's it. Whoever this Sashin person is, the very thought of him terrifies Ki-tae, and he's part of those dreams."

"Jin-woo, patience," ChenBao said, laying a gentle hand on his arm.

"I'm going to change and get comfortable. These shoes are beautiful, but after several hours, I can't wait to take them off," ChenBao said as she slipped them off and carried them with her.

Jin-woo sighed once more, put his shoes in the shelf with everyone else's and followed them into rest of the house. He couldn't even appreciate the simplistic beauty of the décor, how it seamlessly blended three cultures. Soon-joon met them in the living room, looking so casual Jin-woo almost didn't recognize him. While he smiled, it didn't reach his eyes, and he looked very tired. Jin-woo felt his tension ratchet up another notch.

"We need to change too," Cheongul said. He placed a kiss on Min-su's temple and then followed ChenBao down the hall. HanYin followed suit, though his kiss was to Jong-in's mouth, making him blush.

"Please, make yourselves comfortable," Soon-joon said. "It is going to be a long and probably stressful evening."

"Ki-tae doesn't like to wear shoes either," Jin-woo murmured when he looked down at Soon-joon's bare feet. "Or socks."

"Neither does HanYin."

"Or Cheongul." Min-su tried to smile. "That's your fault, isn't it?"

"Guilty as charged, I'm afraid." Soon-joon did smile. "Occasionally we might don some house slippers, depending on how cold it is, but for the most part, we walk around like this. Would you like something to drink?"

"I...."

"Jin-woo." Soon-joon stopped him. "Ki-tae is waking up naturally as we speak. I know you're anxious to see him, but we need to give him that time. This is going to be incredibly difficult for him."

"Everyone keeps saying that as if I don't know it already," Jin-woo said. "I saw his face. I saw how terrified he was, and it's killing me to not see him. Please, Soon-joon-nim, please let me see him."

He could see Soon-joon wavering and resisted the urge to push.

"Of the people in this house, Jin-woo dongsaeng is in the least danger of being hurt," Hyun-jo said as he walked into the living room from the garden. "Let him see Ki-tae dongsaeng. It can only help them both."

"Hyun-jo seonbae," Jin-woo whispered, staring at the man in confusion. Robes, long black hair, and a warm smile were not what he was used to seeing from him.

"It is a night for truths," Hyun-jo said before turning to Soon-joon. "Take him to Ki-tae dongsaeng, xīn'ái."

Soon-joon stared at Hyun-jo for a few more moments before he sighed and inclined his head toward the hall. Eagerly Jin-woo followed him, leaving his friends in Hyun-jo's capable hands. He had only one thought in his mind. The hallway was long and seemed to go on forever, even though that wasn't possible. Soon-joon turned right at the crossing hall and paused at a door on the left. He looked back at Jin-woo.

"I know you and Ki-tae have spent the night together. I can only assume he woke up easily with you."

"He did."

"However, he was not in the same mental state as he is now, so I ask you to move slowly and carefully when you wake him. If he reacts aggressively, do not move at all. Let him scent you first. Call his name softly and let him come to you."

"You act as if he's an animal," Jin-woo said stiffly.

"That is a very accurate comparison," Soon-joon said. "You see, he will be acting on pure animal instinct if he startles. He will be defensive and aggressive at the same time. He won't be fully awake when he starts to move. That's why you stand still. The first thing Ki-tae does is scent the room. Since he spent so much time in the dark, unable to see, his other senses were heightened by that experience, even as a human child. It is why they are so much stronger now that he is a Vampire. Once he scents you, he can process it and identify you. Since your scent is intimately known to him, it may only take a few seconds, which is a good thing, but you *must* give him that time."

"How did he function with his other lovers?"

"Easily. Neither he nor they ever spent the night," Soon-joon said. "And he has never brought any of them here. Now go."

Soon-joon opened the door, and Jin-woo stepped inside. He walked the tiny hallway past Ki-tae's closets on the left. He paused at the end and stared at the bed. When he saw the steady rise and fall of Ki-tae's chest, Jin-woo felt a weight lift from him. He took a few steps closer.

"Ki-tae?" he called. "Ki-tae, wake up."

Glancing over his shoulder, Jin-woo moved closer and sat on the edge of the bed. He reached out and brushed Ki-tae's bangs from his forehead. He found himself pinned to the bed, a snarling, growling, silver-eyed Ki-tae on top of him with his wrists pinned next to his head. Jin-woo froze immediately, silently cursing himself for his need to touch.

"Ki-tae, it's me, Jin-woo," he said softly, surprised his voice wasn't shaking. Dammit, why hadn't he listened?

Ki-tae buried his head in his neck, and Jin-woo braced himself for the bite that never came. Instead he heard a very loud inhale, and then Ki-tae completely relaxed on top of him. He wrapped the arms that had just pinned him to the bed around him tightly, and hot tears splashed against his neck. He put his arms around Ki-tae and held him close, stroking his hair soothingly.

"Shhh, it's okay, Ki-tae. I have you," he whispered, placing kisses on his hair. "I'm here, and I'm not leaving, ever."

KI-TAE

KI-TAE BREATHED in Jin-woo's scent, letting it soothe him. Jin-woo was here. He hadn't run away. He was in Ki-tae's arms, and he wasn't struggling to get free. Ki-tae sighed and let the tears fall. He couldn't make out the words now, but the tone was what mattered, the quality of it. He rolled onto his back, taking Jin-woo with him. When Jin-woo made a move to leave, Ki-tae opened his eyes to see his smile.

"You awake now?" Jin-woo said, his tone teasing.

"Yes." Ki-tae's voice was rough, as if it hadn't been used in a long time. "You're here."

"Where else would I be?"

"Running far away from me," Ki-tae whispered.

"Never," Jin-woo said, placing a kiss on his nose. "I'm sorry I startled you. I couldn't help it. I had to touch you, to make sure you weren't my imagination, and that you were truly okay."

"I'm sorry I pinned you to the bed," Ki-tae said.

"Well, I didn't mind that so much." Jin-woo blushed, ducking his head against Ki-tae's chest.

"We have things we need to talk about," Ki-tae breathed. "And I'm starving. Otherwise I wouldn't let you out of this bed."

"Ki-tae, if you're not ready...."

"No, you're having nightmares. That's my fault, and you deserve to know why," Ki-tae said as he shifted Jin-woo off him and sat up. "Are the others here?"

Jin-woo nodded. "Cheongul-a, HanYin-a, Soon-joon-nim, ChenBao-nim Min-su-ya, and Jong-in-a. And oddly Hyun-jo seonbae, who looks *completely* different from what I'm used to seeing. His hair is long, for one thing. Why in the world would he wear a wig? And he's dressed in a kimono."

"That's not a wig." Ki-tae managed to chuckle. "That's his actual hair. Unlike the rest of us, he refuses to cut it, so he casts a glamour to hide it when he is out in public."

"So he's a Vampire too? I really am surrounded," Jin-woo groaned. "Did you know ChenBao-nim is a freaking Dragon? Well, Vampiric Dragon, which really just seems wrong, but damn, that woman has power to spare!"

"I didn't know the Dragon part, but it makes sense, with the aura she gives off," Ki-tae said. "C'mon, I need to change out of these clothes."

Jin-woo scooted up to lean against the headboard of Ki-tae's bed, crossed his ankles, and put his hands behind his head, grinning wickedly. "Okay, go ahead."

"Oh, you're going to enjoy the show, are you?" Ki-tae said, feeling his mood lighten with Jin-woo's teasing.

"Hell yeah," Jin-woo said.

Ki-tae smiled as he turned and walked toward his closet. He pulled out a pair of jeans and a long-sleeved shirt and then tossed them to the storage trunk at the foot of his bed. He slowly drew his shirt over his head as he walked back toward Jin-woo. He pitched it in the general direction of his hamper before reaching for the button at his pants. Jin-woo's eyes were riveted to his hands, and he peeked out that devious little tongue to sweep it over his lips. It made Ki-tae feel hot and desirable. He hooked his thumbs in the waistband of his pants and his underwear, drawing them down at the same time. Ki-tae chuckled as Jin-woo adjusted himself with a soft whimper. His pupils were blown, and he kept biting his lip. When Jin-woo crawled down the bed and reached for him, Ki-tae stepped back.

"If you touch me right now, I will not let you out of my bed for the rest of the night and probably into tomorrow morning, possibly not until Monday," Ki-tae growled. "I want you badly."

"I can see that," Jin-woo said, eyeing his erection. "You're hard and leaking for me."

"Jin-woo."

"Do you really want to go out to talk with your family like this?" Jin-woo purred, advancing once more.

Ki-tae continued to back up until his back hit the wall. Jin-woo dropped to his knees and took him deep in one swallow. Ki-tae cried out as he buried his fingers in Jin-woo's hair. He gripped the shelf above his head, bucking his hips involuntarily as Jin-woo worked him expertly. All too soon Ki-tae spilled down his throat, shaking with the strength of his orgasm. When he opened his eyes again, Jin-woo sat back on his heels, licking his lips. Ki-tae groaned. Jin-woo was going to be the death of him.

"You are...."

"I am... what?" Jin-woo grinned.

"Amazing, wonderful, evil, sexy as hell, beautiful, pick one," Ki-tae chuckled breathlessly. "You realize everyone knows exactly what was going on, right?"

"Hadn't thought about that, honestly," Jin-woo said as he rose and leaned into Ki-tae once more. He could feel Jin-woo's erection pressing against him and walked him back toward the bed. When his knees connected with the storage chest, Ki-tae gave his shoulders a little tap and sent him sprawling across the bed. Then he pounced and returned the favor until Jin-woo almost passed out.

"And I'm the evil one." Jin-woo laughed.

"You are," Ki-tae agreed.

"I suppose we need to clean up a little bit." Jin-woo sighed. "They're waiting for us, probably."

"Yeah," Ki-tae said.

Twenty minutes and several hot kisses later, they walked into the living room together to find everyone staring at them. Soon-joon shook his head. Cheongul, HanYin, Min-su, and Jong-in had their noses covered with the backs of their hands. ChenBao simply smiled, and Hyun-jo, well, there was no other way to describe the look on his face as anything other than a self-satisfied smirk.

"Feeling better?" he asked. "More... relaxed, Ki-tae dongsaeng?"

"Definitely."

"Good. Come, dinner is ready," Hyun-jo said.

Ki-tae tilted his head as he watched Hyun-jo bring food to the low table in the formal dining room. It was odd but right to see Hyun-jo in their home as if he'd lived there all his life. Ki-tae glanced at Soon-joon to see his father shake his head. It was a discussion for another time. Ki-tae shrugged as he took his seat to Soon-joon's left, pulling Jin-woo down to sit next to him. Normally Cheongul sat to Soon-joon's right, if not at the other end of the table. Tonight Hyun-jo took that space, and ChenBao sat opposite Soon-joon. Once everyone settled, they began to eat in relative silence broken only by the occasional clink of plates, chopsticks, and serving spoons. Ki-tae smiled as Soon-joon and Jin-woo piled his bowl with food.

"You're going to make me fat," he said looking between his father and his lover.

"Eat," they said.

Cheongul laughed. "That is too funny."

Despite the reason that brought them together, the mood lightened, and conversation flowed more freely. They would have to get to the topic eventually, but they could eat in relative peace until that time came.

"It is good to see you among us once more, Hyun-jo-kun," ChenBao said before throwing a glance at Soon-joon. "It has been too long."

"It is good to be back."

Hyun-jo

WHEN DINNER was over, they moved to the living room. Hyun-jo and HanYin stayed behind to clean up but shooed Jong-in into the living room with the others. They worked in silence for several moments.

"You have something you wish to ask, dongsaeng?" Hyun-jo asked without looking up from the dish he was washing.

"Yes," HanYin admitted. He turned to face Hyun-jo after putting away the plate in his hands. "There seems to be something very different about you, and there is a change in Abeoji as well."

"There is," Hyun-jo agreed, giving HanYin the courtesy of his full attention. "I have made my intentions clear to your father, and he is not quite sure how to deal with it yet. There will be a full explanation once things with Ki-tae dongsaeng have been resolved."

"So how long have you loved him?"

Hyun-jo smiled. "Millennia."

"That long?" HanYin looked surprised. "I didn't realize either of you were that old."

"The only person in this house older than Soon-joon and me is ChenBao-chan," Hyun-jo said.

"You've loved him for so long, but you haven't lived here for as long as I can remember. Yet Lǎodà niáng's words imply you once lived with him."

"Soon-joon is a complicated man, and sometimes he thinks too much and allows himself very little in the way of happiness he feels he does not deserve. Your father is confident in most every aspect of his life, save where I am concerned. In this he doubts himself. I have been waiting for him to come to terms with it on his own. I am done waiting."

"This should be interesting," HanYin said.

"Yes," Hyun-jo said as they turned back to their task and finished it in short time.

HanYin went ahead, Hyun-jo following slowly behind. He looked at the people spread about the room and felt both happy and sad. What had brought them together this evening was a chilling part of Ki-tae's past. It bled through in aspects of his life even now. Cheongul still fought to control his anger, pulling away from forming true relationships to do so. At least until this tiny little slip of a woman with a feisty temper and a strong will turned his world upside down.

"Okay, I can't take it anymore," Jin-woo said suddenly from his spot tucked against Ki-tae's side. "Hyun-jo seonbae, Ki-tae tells me that's not a wig, but since we met, your hair has been short. What is with the traditional robes?"

"Ah, so you wish the truth of me?" he asked as he glanced at Soon-joon. "Then I will share it. I would be honored if we would speak more familiarly with each other."

They all nodded and he let his glamour completely fall, feeling the weight lift from him. In the last several years, it was rare for him to remove it, and to do so was... freeing, somehow. He swished his tails back and forth and twitched his ears as he shook out his hair.

"Oh wow," HanYin said. "You're a Húli jīng."

"My ears aren't white, but we have the same eye color," Jong-in said.

"You're not old enough," Hyun-jo said, ruffling his hair as he passed on his way to Soon-joon. "You need to reach five hundred years of age before your fur will change color."

"It was you," Ki-tae said quietly.

Hyun-jo simply nodded as he made Soon-joon move or permit him in his lap. Soon-joon chose to move, and he pouted at him slightly before taking a seat.

"You used to curl up with me when the nightmares were really bad," Ki-tae continued. "I thought I was dreaming about the white fox."

"I do not recall this," Soon-joon said.

"You did not know. Therefore, you cannot remember," Hyun-jo said, and he couldn't keep the sadness from his voice. "You had sent me from the house shortly after Cheongul-a came to live with you. I returned to watch over you both, and then HanYin-a, and finally Ki-tae-ya."

"Wait." Cheongul held up a hand. "Just exactly what is your relationship?"

"Shall I tell him, or do you wish to do so, xīn'ái?"

"You will not let this go, either of you?" Soon-joon asked. They shook their heads. He shot a glare at ChenBao when she chuckled.

"I warned you to make an honest Fox of him, repeatedly. Had you listened, you would not be in this position nor would you have been miserable for the last millennium," she said primly. "This is why children should listen to their mothers."

"Hyun-jo and I met during the Kamakura period of Japan," Soon-joon began. "I came across a secluded pond and heard singing. I paused and then followed the sound until I found the singer. He was lazing on a rock in the sun, singing to the butterflies and other animals around him."

"You always did interrupt my sun naps," Hyun-jo groused. Soon-joon had always woken him in the most pleasurable ways.

"You slept more than Ki-tae. You needed interrupted naps. To continue, he heard me and darted away into the woods. I only caught the flash of his tail, a beautiful shade of ebony." Soon-joon caught a lock of Hyun-jo's hair between his fingers, and it made him shiver, though he contained it as best he could. He doubted Soon-joon even realized he'd done it.

"I had been traveling awhile, moving between the shogunates, and I was tired, so I camped by that pond for several days. By the third day, I had piqued his curiosity, and he came to the edge of my camp. He was such a curious Fox, asking so many questions, and we began a conversation," Soon-joon said. "Eventually I won his trust, and we became friends and finally lovers."

"He built a small hut to live in." Hyun-jo picked up the story, almost lost to the memory. "He told me what he was, and I allowed him to feed from me. We were happy. And then my sister discovered us, and when Soon-joon refused her, she told the clan chief, our father, about us. She always was a jealous little thing, which is why she's probably still a mousy brown to this day."

"Hyun-jo-kun," ChenBao admonished, but it was halfhearted at best.

"Not long after she left, our cottage was discovered by bandits. In the attack, Soon-joon was fatally injured, and I was hard-pressed to keep them at bay. That was when my father and the other warriors arrived. They drove off the bandits," Hyun-jo said, his voice hitching. He could almost feel Soon-joon's blood on his hands as he tried to staunch the bleeding. He couldn't step away long enough to get the necessary herbs. "I begged my father to heal him, but the shaman stepped forth and said only by someone giving qi could he heal such a wound on a Vampire. My father made me choose. Either I leave Soon-joon to die and return to my clan and my studies, or I save his life and be exiled forever. There was no choice."

"Hyun-jo gave the qi needed to heal me, and in return lost two hundred years of his life. He was still a Kitsune, but without his magic for those two centuries," Soon-joon said. "He gave up his clan and his family for me. If he had gone with his father, he would be a Celestial Fox by now and truly immortal."

"A fact you have held as a shield for the last millennium." Hyun-jo snorted.

"Okay, that just made *my* brain hurt," Min-su said. "Suffice it to say, you met, fell in love, and have been together for a really long freaking time. Then Soon-joon-nim sent you away, but it still doesn't really explain what your relationship is now."

"When I gave my qi to save him, Soon-joon became my bonded mate as he was meant to be. Otherwise, the bond wouldn't have taken," Hyun-jo said with a smile, and then it turned feral. "And now I'm reclaiming my place in his life... whether he likes it or not."

"So all that time, and you've just been on the sidelines?" Min-su looked at Soon-joon and narrowed her eyes. Cheongul slapped his hand over her mouth before she could say anything else.

"Please remember that is my father you're about to rip into. Please also recall he is much older and stronger than HanYin, Ki-tae, and myself, as well as you. His patience is vast but finite."

Her response was muffled, but her eyes spoke volumes.

"Good for you, Hyun-jo-kun. Now that we have that straightened out, we need to turn this conversation onto a significantly less pleasant but no less important topic," ChenBao said softly. She looked at Ki-tae. "I know this is very difficult for you, Sūnzi. Please take your time."

JIN-WOO

WHEN KI-TAE turned to look at him, Jin-woo wanted to mimic Cheongul and put his hands over Ki-tae's mouth to prevent him from speaking. He knew this was going to hurt Ki-tae, and he wanted to prevent that pain. He didn't want to put Ki-tae through this.

"After we were turned, we learned how to survive as Vampires. We were taught how to feed and where to feed from," Ki-tae said slowly. "Abeoji always stressed feeding from the wrist or the thigh if we were... being intimate. If those options weren't available, we could take from the neck, but only the right side."

"Why?"

"To feed from the left side of the neck is to take blood straight from the heart," Ki-tae said. "We are not sure why this position changes the rules, but when we feed from the left side, there is a chance we could be bound to the person we fed from."

Jin-woo's eyes widened. "At the concert you... fed from my neck, the left side of my neck."

"Yes," Ki-tae said, his voice so soft Jin-woo almost didn't hear him, but he did hear the fear in it. "And when I did, I bound myself to you without realizing it."

"I don't understand. What does that mean?"

"For those first three weeks, I was pulled into your dreams. We call it dream walking. I kept wanting to search you out, to find you," Ki-tae said. "I became... agitated."

"He became a grouchy ass, tired and cranky," Cheongul said. "Well, more so than usual."

Ki-tae threw a pillow at him, but Jin-woo saw him smile, and Jin-woo decided he would thank Cheongul later. The comment had succeeded in pulling Ki-tae up a little bit. Then he remembered his dreams shortly after the concert and felt his cheeks heat.

"Wow, I didn't know he could turn that shade of red," Jong-in said.

"Shut it," Jin-woo growled, and then he turned back to Ki-tae. "So you shared all those... dreams with me? Why didn't you say anything?"

"I didn't know how to, and I.... Bonds are.... It wasn't an easy situation for me to deal with. Your...." Ki-tae took a deep breath, and Jin-woo reached for his hands. He smiled when Ki-tae looked at him. "I've fed from you, from your neck, several times. I think... I think it made my bond to you stronger, and now my memories are bleeding into your dreams."

"Tell him all of it, Ki-tae," HanYin said. "No secrets."

Jin-woo waited, his heart rate picked up. Ki-tae remained silent, his eyes wide. And then Cheongul was behind him, wrapping his arms around Ki-tae's shoulders, and HanYin was leaning against his legs on the floor. Ki-tae pulled one of his hands away and buried it in HanYin's hair. He seemed to relax a bit, and then he started talking again.

"When I was very small, I was sold to a man called Sashin," Ki-tae said quietly, his voice flat, distant. "He kept me in a dark room, chained to a bed in his brothel. It was not like those found in the larger villages. The... tastes there were outside of what was permitted in the pleasure houses closer to the cities. Each time he woke, Sashin would come to my gilded cage with its silk curtains and moldy mattress. He would... he would press me down into the mattress face-first... and force me to drink his blood."

"Oh my God," Jin-woo said, seeing the image as clear in his mind as when he dreamed it.

"I was bound to him. All I could think of was him. My sole purpose was Sashin. He could do anything he wanted to me, anything at all. There was... there was nothing of me inside." Ki-tae hiccupped. "The older I got... the more...."

"Ki-tae," Soon-joon said. When Jin-woo looked over at him, his eyes were gold. "That is enough. You do not need to say more."

"Abeoji," Ki-tae whispered.

"I stumbled across that brothel in my travels." Soon-joon's voice was cold, emotionless, and frightening. "Sashin was a Vampire and, seeing what he thought to be someone like himself, offered me what he called his rarest treat. He took me to a room deep within the building. As I stood in the entryway, he lit the lamps around the room, the central focus of which was a large canopied bed, often called an opium bed. What I saw on that bed both infuriated me and made me sick to my stomach. A small boy, naked and chained, with lifeless, blood-colored eyes, yet he still lived. I knew he was a blood addict, and I lunged for Sashin, but he ran. I followed until I caught him in the main room, and there I tore him apart until there was nothing left but gore. Then I went back for the child. Anyone who willfully opposed me died. Those who could not help themselves were incapacitated, and those that did nothing were left alone. I sent men I trusted to help Sashin's victims but carried Ki-tae out of there in my arms, wrapped in my coat, and he has been with me ever since."

"When Abeoji told me I was possibly bonded to you, I... I freaked out," Ki-tae said, leaning his head back against Cheongul, his eyes closed as if he couldn't bear to look at anyone while he spoke. Jin-woo's chest constricted. He held Ki-tae's hand tighter.

"Those panic attacks you told me about?"

"Yes. I... really lost my shit," Ki-tae said. "I didn't want to be bonded to you. No, not to you specifically. I didn't want to be bonded at all. I didn't want to lose myself again. I begged Abeoji to find a way to break it, to free me from it, but there were only two options he knew of."

"What were they?" Jin-woo said.

"I...."

"What were they, Ki-tae?"

"I could either turn you... or kill you."

"Well, shit."

KI-TAE

KI-TAE DIDN'T know how he was still breathing, the weight on his chest was so heavy. He didn't know how he was still able to put words together. Just thinking of Sashin could send him into a panic. Yet he was still functioning. Having Cheongul and HanYin so close helped, but so did Jin-woo's hand in his. He hadn't run screaming from the house. That was a good sign, wasn't it?

"Keep going, Ki-tae," Cheongul said softly. "You can do this."

"We're here." HanYin pressed closer to his leg.

"I begged Abeoji to find another way. It wasn't fair to punish you for my stupidity," Ki-tae said. "I didn't want to hurt you."

"I certainly appreciate that." Jin-woo's mouth quirked up on the side in a half smile.

"This is where I come in," ChenBao said. "Soon-joon wrote to me of the situation, but before I could advise him, I needed to see you and Ki-tae together."

"Why?"

"We do not turn people at random or kill them on a whim. When a Vampire bonds with someone, it is a voluntary and special commitment between the two. Often the Vampire's partner is a Spiritual Being, such as Min-su-ya and Jong-in-a. Our most sacred and rare bond is that of the Xuè Huǒbàn, the Blood Partner. The bonding begins when a human with no spiritual blood freely offers blood straight from his heart to the Vampire."

"Wait. What?"

"When you and Ki-tae were together at the concert, you tilted your head. You offered him your neck. You offered him blood straight from your heart. When he accepted, it started the bonding."

"I didn't mean to, Jin-woo," Ki-tae said, his voice edged with panic even he could hear. The look on Jin-woo's face was…. He didn't know how to describe it. So much had been shoved at him all at once. Ki-tae tightened his grip on Jin-woo's hand, struggling not to use his full strength in the face of his fear. He wanted to pull Jin-woo into his arms, but he couldn't, and that was probably a good thing. If he held him now, he would never let him go, and it had to be Jin-woo's choice.

"So to break the bond, Ki-tae would have to either kill me—not a fan of that one—or turn me—not sure about that one either," Jin-woo said. "I'm squeamish as it is. The last option, and it's only because of what I am, is Ki-tae and I can become… Blood Partners?"

"Yes," ChenBao said. "You would eventually cease to age, and you would live as long as Ki-tae-ya does, and vice versa. You would sustain him with your blood, and he would sustain you with his qi."

"That is... a lot to take in," Jin-woo whispered.

Ki-tae felt his heart drop.

"Don't even. I can see the resignation in your face, just like I heard it in your voice when you thought I regretted meeting you," Jin-woo said suddenly, pulling his hands free and cupping Ki-tae's face. "I am not rejecting the idea or you. It's just a big change to my life, and I'm not sure how to take it."

"You don't have to if you don't want to," Ki-tae said. Jin-woo kissed him hard.

"Silly Vampire, don't you know I love you already?" Jin-woo said with his sweet smile before he kissed Ki-tae senseless.

"And that's our cue to, well, yeah, so... night!" Cheongul said as he rose and pulled Min-su with him out of the room. HanYin and Jong-in soon followed. ChenBao giggled and disappeared, literally, leaving Soon-joon and Hyun-jo the last in the room with Ki-tae and Jin-woo. Hyun-jo stood and looked down at Soon-joon before grabbing his hand and dragging him down the hall. Ki-tae barely noticed.

KI-TAE ROSE from the couch. Then Jin-woo jumped and wrapped his legs around his waist. He palmed that incredible ass, kneading and squeezing as he carried Jin-woo, never releasing his mouth.

When they reached his room, Ki-tae set Jin-woo on his feet. Slowly he undressed him, kissing and licking every inch of bare skin he exposed. He nipped at his collarbone before moving down to capture one taut nipple in his mouth. Jin-woo cried out, digging his fingers into Ki-tae's hair and holding him against his chest. Ki-tae worried that tiny little nub with his teeth, scraping it with a fang before sucking hard. Jin-woo grabbed the back of his neck with his other hand as Ki-tae stroked the insides of his legs from behind, teasing along the line where thigh met buttock before venturing higher.

"Ki-tae... too many clothes," Jin-woo murmured, pulling at Ki-tae's shirt. It was removed in short order, as was the rest of Ki-tae's clothing.

Wrapping his arms around Jin-woo's thighs, Ki-tae lifted him once more and carried him into the bathroom. The dying light of evening poured through the sheers lining the windows, muted but still providing some light. As he reached for the door handle, Ki-tae let Jin-woo slide down his body, growling as their erections rubbed together. He attacked his mouth, thrusting his tongue deep as he maneuvered Jin-woo into the shower area.

Almost absently Ki-tae turned on the faucets and then guided Jin-woo beneath the water. Soft green light made the water droplets glitter as they fell over Jin-woo's body, and the sight made Ki-tae's gut clench. He smiled when Jin-woo tilted his head up and laughed as the water fell like a summer rain on his face.

Ki-tae reached over and flipped another switch. In seconds Jin-woo was standing in his own personal waterfall and looked absolutely stunning in the shifting LED lights. Looking had to be followed by touching, and Ki-tae followed Jin-woo into the rainfall, placing almost gentle kisses on his lips before moving to his jaw, following the line of it to the sensitive skin behind his ear. He nibbled his way down the length of his neck, feeling how each nip made Jin-woo shiver, hearing the little moans and whimpers that drove Ki-tae crazy. He worked his way down Jin-woo's body, following streams of water until he was on his knees.

Looking up, he watched Jin-woo close his eyes as he pushed his wet hair back off his face. He opened his eyes, and Ki-tae growled at the heat in them. Holding his gaze, Ki-tae leaned forward and gently touched the tip of his tongue to the line running between Jin-woo's abs, tasting the water on his skin flavored with Jin-woo's unique taste. Again and again he flicked his tongue against Jin-woo's skin, earning gasps and moans, all the sounds that told Ki-tae he was on the right path.

One of his favorite places on Jin-woo's body was his navel. When Ki-tae licked it just so, Jin-woo squirmed and moaned, the skin sensitive, and he loved to play there. Slowly he swirled his tongue around the edge, and Jin-woo's muscles quivered with pleasure. He dipped his tongue inside and made tiny circles in that delicious indentation. He nipped around it, catching small bits of skin between his teeth but never breaking through.

Ki-tae reached up and slid his nails lightly down Jin-woo's sides before gripping Jin-woo's hips as they bucked involuntarily. Jin-woo's body was, for the most part, hairless. Ki-tae loved the smoothness of it, and he loved how just at his belly button was the start of Jin-woo's treasure trail. It was light and silky, and Ki-tae adored following it down—treasure trail indeed.

Jin-woo was already leaking profusely, fighting to move his hips beneath Ki-tae's hands. Then he took Jin-woo's hard shaft deep, letting it slide easily into his throat, reveling in the loud cry that tore through the room. Ki-tae worked Jin-woo's cock, steadily bringing him closer and closer with the hard suction and long slides along the length of his erection. He savored the precum coating his tongue as he slowly pulled off, wrapping his fingers around Jin-woo's cock.

"You damn well better not stop there," Jin-woo hissed as Ki-tae flicked the tip of his tongue over the head of his cock. Ki-tae smiled up at him but didn't say a word.

As much as he wanted to be inside Jin-woo, Ki-tae didn't change his pace. He wanted this slow and sensuous and special. He never ceased moving his hands, even when he filled his mouth with Jin-woo's cock once more. He caressed his legs, teasing behind his knees and up to the curve of his buttocks, the water slicking the way, flowing down Jin-woo's body to splash against Ki-tae. Jin-woo's legs shook with the effort to hold him upright as Ki-tae delved between his cheeks to stroke his anus, pressing slightly.

"Yes, more," Jin-woo moaned, parting his legs as much as Ki-tae would allow.

Just Jin-woo's responsiveness and the sounds he made, the way he begged and demanded in turns, were enough to shove Ki-tae over the edge. When he pushed a second time, he could tell Jin-woo's body wasn't quite ready to accept him. He would have to change that... as soon as he fully tasted Jin-woo.

"Let me taste you, Jin-woo," Ki-tae purred along the length of his cock as he rolled his balls in his fingers. He stroked the sensitive skin behind them and pushed back to press against him. "The sounds, the whimpers and moans, they make me so hard I could cum just from listening to you."

"Ki-tae," Jin-woo whimpered, seeking purchase with his hands on Ki-tae's slick shoulders. Ki-tae took him in, slipping the tip of his tongue into the slit, tasting him. Then he pushed forward, pressing his tongue hard along the underside of Jin-woo's cock, and buried his nose in the silky hair at the base of his shaft as he allowed the head deep into his throat. He withdrew, inhaled, and then sank on him once more.

"Ki-tae, I can't. I'm...."

Ki-tae's only response was to continue the torturous slow suction. Just as he teased his finger against Jin-woo's passage, the trembling increased, his cock jerked in Ki-tae's mouth, once, twice, and then erupted. He held Jin-woo to him, just deep enough for his cum to coat the back of his tongue and throat. He swallowed every bit of it and then licked his lips to catch any he might have missed before the water could wash it away. Feeling Jin-woo's legs start to give out, Ki-tae caught him.

"Don't pass out on me now, Jin-woo," Ki-tae said as he slowly rose to his feet, letting his body brush against Jin-woo's, kneading with his hands, savoring the resulting aftershocks and the little cries of pleasure. "I'm not done with you yet."

"I...," Jin-woo panted. "You... didn't."

"I will once I'm inside you," Ki-tae said as he turned Jin-woo, aligning their bodies back to front.

He pressed him against the wall, nuzzling his hair, then placing gentle kisses along his shoulders and nape. Ki-tae worked his way over Jin-woo's back, brushing his lips against his skin, interspersed with slow, sensuous bites and gentle leisurely swirls of his tongue. He loved the way Jin-woo quivered with pleasure.

Ki-tae followed his spine on the return journey. Jin-woo turned his head, his eyes half-lidded, watching as Ki-tae gently scraped his fangs over the curve of his shoulder. His breath came in short pants; his lips were swollen from their kisses, his cheeks flushed. Water droplets hung from Jin-woo's lashes, slid down the fine curve of his cheek to cling to his chin before dropping into what little space remained between him and the wall. He pushed back with his hips, and Ki-tae groaned at the contact, that flawless ass cradling his aching cock so perfectly.

"Ki-tae," Jin-woo murmured when he leaned down to kiss him, Jin-woo turning and lifting his head at the same time, his hands tucked into his torso as he shifted restlessly. Ki-tae could see the desire in his eyes. He could smell the wet scent of it perfuming the steam-filled shower room. Tiny shivers shook Jin-woo's body, and Ki-tae was awed. He was so responsive to him, so vocal in his desire for Ki-tae, it was amazing.

Reaching for the lube he kept on the shelf with his shampoo and conditioner, Ki-tae slid his thigh between Jin-woo's legs. He loved the way Jin-woo moaned, and smiled when he saw Jin-woo catch his bottom lip between his teeth as Ki-tae slipped slick fingers between his cheeks, stroking his opening gently before pressing inside with one finger. God, he was hot and tight as always. Ki-tae bit his shoulder without breaking skin, keeping the movement of his finger slow and steady. When Jin-woo started to push back with short little whimpers, one finger became two, and then three.

"Ki-tae, please, I need you," Jin-woo moaned, thunking his forehead against the tile.

Without a word, Ki-tae replaced his fingers with his shaft and pushed deep in one slow thrust. A satisfied moan of pleasure echoed through the room. Jin-woo parted his legs wider, shifting his hands to brace against the wall. Ki-tae stroked up his hips, along his sides, claws teasing and leaving pale white trails. He caught a giggle when his fingers danced past Jin-woo's armpits and continued up until he laid his hands over Jin-woo's on the wall. They twined their fingers together as almost an afterthought as Ki-tae retreated, only to thrust forward again. The pace was maddening for him. He wanted faster, harder, but he wanted Jin-woo to explode from the pleasure; he wanted the screams and the cries and the curses as Jin-woo came apart in his arms.

Suddenly Jin-woo shoved away from the wall and stepped free of Ki-tae. Ki-tae stumbled backward, staring, a yawning pit of dread opening in his chest. Jin-woo leaned back, letting just his shoulders touch the tile, making his body arch enticingly, the water raining down on his torso and hips. He reached up to wrap his fingers around the bar where Ki-tae hung his washcloths. Then he smiled such a wicked smile it was like a kick to the gut. He inclined his head, signaling Ki-tae to come closer.

"I want to see you," he purred. "I want to watch your eyes bleed silver and your fangs slide down. I want to see how you bite your lips and then lick the blood from them. I want to see as well as feel how much you want me."

JIN-WOO

THERE WERE only about three steps separating them, but Ki-tae stalked across them, his head dropped low like the predator he was. Watching the way his muscles glided beneath his skin in a way that really should be illegal was almost enough to make Jin-woo cum again. His first desire was met when Ki-tae passed beneath the waterfall spray, his eyes bleeding from brown to silver in that one step. He smiled, and his fangs slowly slipping down was as erotic as the feel of his fingers earlier. God, Jin-woo loved his fangs! The only thing better than seeing them come out was feeling them piercing his skin. He started to let go of the bar, but Ki-tae shook his head.

"Hang on," he growled as he reached down and wrapped claw-tipped fingers around Jin-woo's thighs and hauled him upward.

Jin-woo gasped at the sheer strength and the feel of Ki-tae between his legs once more. He held that silver gaze and smiled, breathless. Then Ki-tae was pushing, thrusting inside him, and Jin-woo couldn't recall his own name. He shook his head, getting his hair out of his eyes. Ki-tae was watching him, watching his reactions, and it was the hottest fucking thing Jin-woo had ever experienced. He lunged up for a kiss, Ki-tae meeting him halfway.

As much as he wanted to comply with Ki-tae's demand he hang on, Jin-woo wanted, no, he *needed* to touch him. He wrapped his arms around Ki-tae's neck, the sudden shift moving them beneath the water. It splashed around them, teasing his skin, heightening it, making it more sensitive to every sensation, and Jin-woo reveled in it, reveled in Ki-tae, the feel of him thrusting hard into his ass, filling him, the taste of him, still salty from Jin-woo's orgasm earlier. Even the pinpricks of Ki-tae's claws only made him hotter, made him roll his hips to match Ki-tae's.

Jin-woo tore his mouth from Ki-tae's and turned his head to the right, knowing exactly what he was doing. The minute Ki-tae's sharp incisors pierced his flesh, Jin-woo exploded, spilling between them, his body clenching Ki-tae tight, and he screamed Ki-tae's name as he felt the rush of heat deep inside.

JIN-WOO'S EYES fluttered open to see the bare expanse of Ki-tae's chest and the windows beyond. It was still night. He smiled and snuggled closer. He felt as well as heard Ki-tae's soft chuckle.

"Proud of yourself, are you?" Ki-tae asked. "I wanted to make it last for you, to draw it out all night long."

"I can't wait that long," Jin-woo said with a smile. "The feel of you inside of me is too perfect."

"Pushy."

"Maybe a little."

"For a second I thought you were going to send me away," Ki-tae whispered.

"I needed to see you," Jin-woo said. "I needed to feel you at the same time, if that makes sense."

"When you smiled at me...," Ki-tae groaned. "The way you make me feel, the way you make my body come alive, just your scent gets me hard."

"Must be tough walking around the office." Jin-woo smirked.

"Ha, I've seen you do some not-so-discreet adjusting just from me licking my lips." Ki-tae laughed. "At least you have some warning."

"Yeah, that evil glint in your eye just before you make me decidedly uncomfortable, with no hope of relief for a long time!" Jin-woo said, straddling his waist.

"I get blindsided in the elevator, the hallway, Abeoji's office, the recording studio.... Anywhere you've been, I catch your scent, and I have to put on my sunglasses, clamp my lips closed, and make sure my shirt hides my hard-on," Ki-tae said, rolling Jin-woo beneath him. He couldn't complain. It was one of Jin-woo's favorite places to be. He wrapped his arms around Ki-tae's neck and pulled him down into a hug.

And then it hit him: he could have this man forever, literally forever. His best friends were Spiritual Beings too. The very idea was overwhelming. It was a big decision to make, and he would need to think about it. But Ki-tae, having Ki-tae forever, was such a temptation to him. His heart was screaming *yes*, but his head was saying *stop, think, make sure this is a good choice*. He really wanted to tell his head to go to hell.

MIN-SU

MIN-SU WATCHED Cheongul move around the room in nothing but a pair of boxer briefs. He was such a beautiful man. Tonight had been full of revelations, and amid it all, she had seen love and devotion. There was no doubt in her mind Jin-woo would choose to complete the bond with Ki-tae. He already loved the annoying bloodsucker to distraction, much as Min-su loved Cheongul. She drew her legs up and wrapped her arms around her knees.

"You seem thoughtful," Cheongul said, pausing to look at her. "Is there something wrong?"

"No, nothing is wrong," she said. "I'm just debating with myself."

"About?"

"Everything we heard tonight," she said with a sigh. "It makes me feel like a coward that I haven't told anyone what happened. I mean, honestly, it's nothing compared to what happened to Ki-tae. The attack occurred so fast it was done before we even realized what was going on. Ki-tae lived with that for years... as a child. And let me tell you, if Soon-joon-nim hadn't already done it, I would have hunted the bastard down and gutted him... slowly. As much as Ki-tae annoys the crap out of me on occasion and assaults my nose with his damned pheromones every time I freaking turn around, he's still mine now."

"Oh, he's yours, is he?" Cheongul chuckled as he sat down on the bed next to her. "What about me?"

"It's different," Min-su huffed. "Ki-tae is like another brother. Annoying, obnoxious, but no one gets to hurt him but me, and those are only love taps. You're mine, end of story."

"Define 'mine,'" Cheongul murmured as he leaned in and kissed her.

"Well, this is, of course, assuming you agree," she said. "I guess it's just best to come right out and ask. Are we dating? I mean, we have sex... a lot, but we never really talked about what we were to each other."

"I love you," Cheongul said quietly. Min-su stared at him in shock. He said it so simply, no grand, flowery speeches, no grandiose announcement, just a simple statement of fact... and it was perfect.

"I love you too," she said. Then she grabbed his hand and pulled him farther onto the bed. He shifted until he was leaning against the headboard and she was cradled against his chest.

For a few moments, Min-su said nothing. Taking a deep breath, she began. "Abeoji loved to hike and camp, and he loved it best when he was doing it with his family. Every summer he would take us to Taeanhaean National Park. It was the best part of summer. I never hated it like most of my friends would have. I loved being outside. I loved running through the woods with my family. Eomeoni would show me all the plants that were useful, and we'd make note of them in our herbal books. We'd collect them, drying them when we got home, and she'd use them to treat just about everything. She was really smart about plants and things."

She paused to take a breath and Cheongul tightened his arms around her. "You don't have to tell me if you are not ready."

Min-su shook her head and continued. "Min-seok and Abeoji would fish, always catching enough for dinner. That's how we worked. I mean, we brought stuff from home, but there was nothing like having fresh fish for dinner."

"Can't say I love fish," Cheongul said. "It's okay, but I prefer pork."

"The year I turned thirteen, we did our normal camping trip. We had just come back from hiking a trail, and Eomeoni was sorting the plants we'd picked along the way. Min-seok, my older brother, he was sixteen, was helping Abeoji clean the fish. Maybe that's what drew his attention. I don't know.

"We were all laughing and joking, and the next minute, Eomeoni was screaming and Abeoji was yelling, pushing her down onto the ground, covering her. I could see underneath Min-seok's arm as this huge dark thing tore at him, but he wouldn't move. He just wouldn't move, Eomeoni pinned beneath him, covered in his blood. She fainted, I think, because her screaming stopped. Abeoji wasn't moving, and Min-seok was shaking, but he wouldn't move either, and it came at him, knocking him over before turning to look at me, eyes red and glowing. It lunged for me, claws digging through my sweatshirt, ripping the hell out of my side. I threw my arms up, trying to push it off. Gods, its breath smelled horrible, like rotting meat and blood. It was so strong. I knew it was going to kill me. I was going to die there with my whole family."

Min-su could see it all. It played in front of her eyes like some personal horror movie. She hated horror movies. She was cold, but there was heat at her back. She snuggled into it, not realizing she started talking again.

"Min-seok hit it with a camp chair, beat it until it turned its attention to him. In the blink of an eye, he was beneath it, its muzzle buried in his stomach. He screamed, screamed at me to run, but I couldn't. I couldn't move. All I could hear was my brother's screams. All I could see was his face distorted with pain. I think there was a loud bang, but I can't be sure. Everything went black."

"Min-su," Cheongul whispered, and she felt his lips against her hair.

"I woke up in the hospital, Eomeoni in the chair next to my bed. She was using her arm as a pillow, and she had a death grip on my hand," Min-su said. "We were the only ones left. Abeoji and my brother were dead, died protecting us. But could that fucking thing be satisfied with that, with killing them? No, the fucking thing had to turn me too."

"Things changed between you and your mom?"

"Not really. I mean, I changed, but it took a while to figure out why," she said with a sigh. "I was more aggressive, more prone to fight. The first time I changed, I was at my grandma's house in Busan. She lives outside the city proper. I woke up in her shed, bare-ass naked with what looked to be rabbits sort of gutted next to me. *Halmeoni* found me in there, shaking and crying, covered in dirt and rabbit bits. She took me into the house, cleaned me up, and put me to bed. Then she talked Eomeoni into calling her friend, a priestess. That was a weird conversation, let me tell you."

"I can imagine." Cheongul chuckled. "I've always found priestess and spiritualists to be an odd bunch. I guess it comes from having that connection to the spirit world."

"Anyway, while *Mudangnim* was quite the eccentric, she knew what she was talking about, and she helped Eomeoni and me adjust to what was going on." The look on Cheongul's face puzzled her. "What?"

"Did Mudangnim give you anything? A charm or anything like that?" he asked.

"She gave me this jade earring," Min-su said showing the small jade hoop she never removed. "She said never to take it off."

"Would... do you mind removing it now?"

"Why?"

"With my exposure to Shifters, I should have been able to identify you as one at first meeting. While not all Shifters smell the same, the different species have certain scent markers that link them together. I think that earring is actually a charm to disguises your scent."

"Okay." Min-su didn't quite understand what he meant, but she removed the earring. His nostrils flared wide and his eyes went silver. "I'll take that as a yes, this hid my scent."

"Almost completely masked it, in fact," Cheongul agreed. "It definitely prevents other Spiritual Beings from identifying you as a Shifter."

"Why would she think I needed the protection? I mean she just said don't take it off."

"Did you express any interest in learning more about what you were? If not, then the charm would have prevented them from finding you by scent."

"No definitely not. I didn't want to have anything to do with the thing that made me this way." Min-su growled. "But Mudangnim, she didn't know any other Shifters, so I still had to learn most of this on my own. There's things I still don't understand, but there's one major rule for me. Getting mad is not a good thing."

"That is something I'm all too familiar with," Cheongul said softly. "Saying getting angry is bad for me is like saying a monsoon is a little wet."

"What happened?"

"Ah, it's my turn, now, huh?" Cheongul said dryly.

"Only if you want to."

"I fell in love with a woman, Mikiko," he said. "We were living in Japan at the time, just Abeoji and me. I spent months courting her, bringing her gifts, helping her with anything she needed, just being there. I worked her family's fields just to be near her."

"Sounds pretty serious."

Cheongul stared at the small black lacquered box on his dresser before turning back to look at Min-su. "She was so beautiful, elegant, demure, and soft-spoken."

Min-su winced inwardly. This woman was everything she wasn't.

"I was one hundred and seventy-five years old, and I thought I had found the one person I wanted to spend the rest of my life with." He sighed, and Min-su looked down as he caressed her hand gently. "I was a fool."

"Cheongul."

"I was so happy," Cheongul said, leaning his head back.

Min-su wanted to make him stop but didn't. He needed to talk about this just as much as she had needed to tell him her story.

"There was this young man I hung out with, Tashi. He was a Shifter, and we were best friends. I told him of my girl, and he shared that he, too, was in love. When we weren't courting or working, we were together. He was like a brother to me."

Min-su knew where this was going.

"I found them together by the pond at the edge of her family's land, a place I had thought special to us," he said quietly, his voice catching. "She sat there, tears rolling down her cheeks, saying nothing when I confronted them. Tashi told me they had been betrothed as children and were in love. He asked me to understand as if he'd known all along and said nothing, but what man lets his betrothed step out with another man? I couldn't understand that. I couldn't understand why she hadn't told me at the very beginning. I was furious, beyond furious. I punched Tashi, sending him flying into the tree I had found them under. When she slapped me and ran to him, I blanked out. The next thing I recall is standing in the middle of our home and Abeoji telling me it was time to leave."

"You killed them," she said. It wasn't a question, but a statement of fact. "That's why you left me that day because you thought I was with Jong-in and messing around with you."

"Yes and no," he said, pulling her closer into his chest. "You are so very different from Mikiko. I was young and foolish, and she was beautiful. I wanted to give her everything. I make no excuses for what I did. There are none. The guilt, however, that's another thing entirely. It eats at me still, haunting my dreams. The anger is a beast inside me, clawing its way out of me. It's been a part of me for as long as I can remember, even before I was turned, coloring everything. I can push it down, lock it away for a time, but eventually it breaks loose. On top of that, I have… no luck in relationships and stopped looking for one about three hundred years ago."

"What do you mean, no luck in relationships?" she asked.

"I'm terrible at reading feelings," he said after a few moments. "It's different when it's just lust. That I can smell and there's no way to fake that, so I know when someone wants me in their bed. Most of my encounters were hookups, but every couple of decades or so, I would meet someone I wanted to have more with. Either they were playing me for the fool or they ended up marrying someone else, mostly as part of a family arrangement. There weren't a lot of love matches in those days. That wears on you, having such a pisspoor track record in finding someone who both wants you and is free to be with you."

"I guess I can see that."

"I started focusing more on hookups and less on long-term partners, but I also started in with drinking. And then I found the pit fights. I almost want to say they helped, but it was more like a Band-Aid than a real solution."

"Pit fights? Against humans?" Min-su asked.

"No, one of my old compatriots brought me to this seedy little place in Shanghai, a dark, dank place that reeked of piss and rice wine, and blood. In the back, they had a big room with a dirt floor. It had four pillars in the center with thick ropes wrapped around them. Everyone inside was a Spiritual Being. Most were audience members, but a good portion were participants. My first match was that very night and not only did I take home a healthy chunk of money, but I found an outlet for the rage."

"How was that supposed to help?" Min-su asked. "I mean you're still getting violent."

"It was a controlled violence. I have to focus because my opponent is just as capable of kicking my ass as I am of kicking his, but killing each other is less likely. Most of the fighters are Shifters and you guys are notoriously tough. Not to mention there were guards to pull the fighters apart if things went too far. From that point on, it was nothing but hookups for me. I was alone, but I wasn't getting hurt or hurting people either. Well, not much. I stopped seeing Mikiko and Tashi every time I closed my eyes after about a century or two, but I still feel the pain. I killed them. There's no getting around that. I felt betrayed and in that instant, I let my rage loose, I wanted them to hurt as much as I was hurting, and I made that happen. I can't even say it was an accident."

"You're not the first person to lash out at the people who hurt you, and you won't be the last," she said quietly, placing a kiss on his bare chest. "You have to forgive yourself. It's hard. I know that from personal experience, but you can't let this keep you from being happy."

"I'm working on it," he said. "I've been working on it for centuries, even went so far as to spend time in a monastery."

"You and sitting still? How did that work out for you?" She smirked, trying to lighten his mood.

"Yeah, it didn't," Cheongul said, his smile faint but there. "They had some good ideas, and for HanYin and Ki-tae, they might have worked. But I cannot sit still for long periods of time. I won't say I didn't take anything away from their teachings. I learned better control over my body."

"What about the anger?"

"As the years passed, I got better at pushing it down and holding it inside. There have been times when I've lost it, different situations," Cheongul said quietly. "Shortly after HanYin joined us, the bastard that had slaughtered his family in front of him kidnapped him. We went to get him back and when I saw him in that fucking cage, yeah, I lost it. I don't recall much of what happened. The first thing I remember was carrying HanYin into his room and curling up in the bed with him, holding him while he shook and cried. When Abeoji brought Ki-tae home, I spent three days in the pits because of the things I wanted to do to Sashin, because of the rage his actions triggered in me. There were others, too many to say I had mastered my emotions."

"You know, you're entitled to feel, Cheongul," Min-su said quietly. "Everyone is and I doubt there's a person on this planet who has mastered their emotions, except *maybe* the Dalai Lama."

"Sometimes, it's just too much," he said.

"What about relationships? Have you completely given up on them?"

"Over the years, I've stayed away from docile and demure. In the beginning, it was because all I could see was Mikiko's face as she sat there and cried, instead of explaining why she hadn't been truthful with me. Then I began to value the women I was with because there were no pretenses. We were both in it for the sex and there were no expectations beyond that. I prefer feisty and petite, straightforward, mostly the straightforward part and until you, I haven't looked for a single relationship. I didn't want to risk being hurt again. Honesty is a hard quality to find in people nowadays."

"Well, it's a good thing you love me, then, isn't it?" She looked up at him and flashed him her cheeky smile. "I'm honest to a fault and I'll tell you when you're being a Neanderthal."

He kissed her nose. "A very good thing, indeed. *Gomaweoyo*."

"Why?"

"For trusting me with your story," he said softly as he kissed her lips.

"You're welcome," she said with a sigh and opened her mouth to his kiss.

Their lovemaking was slow and gentle and perfect. She could feel the love in every touch, in every caress of his fingers lightly over her skin. He took his time, made sure she was out of her mind with pleasure before letting her cum, following behind her. As she drifted off to sleep, she heard his voice, his breath tickling her ear. "I love you, Min-su."

"Love you too," she murmured before sleep claimed her completely.

JIN-WOO

WHERE HAD the last two weeks gone? Jin-woo ran across campus toward the conference room. He had about ten minutes to get his ass there and turn in his song. It was all Ki-tae's fault he was late… again. He wrenched open the door and only slowed his pace because of the people in his way. Were he a car, Jin-woo would have drifted through the door to the conference room, but he had five minutes to spare, and that was way better than being on time. He took a deep breath and then walked calmly over to where Teacher Kim, Soon-joon, and, surprisingly, Hyun-jo sat. He smiled and bowed and then presented his USB drive.

As he turned, he caught Min-su waving at him from her seat in one of the upper rows. Jong-in sat next to her. When he reached them, Jong-in moved over to let him squeeze between them.

"Made you late again, didn't he?" Min-su teased.

"Shut it," he grumbled good-naturedly. He could never be upset about Ki-tae desiring him. "Is it just me, or is this more nerve-racking than the video?"

"Maybe just a little bit," she said. "This isn't a collaboration. It's just us."

"It's harder for us to put ourselves out there as individuals," Jong-in admitted. "I almost didn't hand mine in."

"What?" Jin-woo stared at him.

Jong-in sighed. "Remember when we talked about HanYin?"

"Yeah."

"I wrote the lyrics that night. Everything came out in one long rush," Jong-in said. "The words, I mean. It was… what I was feeling at the time, and it's personal, but I knew it would be powerful because *it was personal*. Or at least that's what I'm hoping."

"Did we all write from our recent experiences?" Min-su asked. "I tried writing from the very beginning and got crap-all. But after things happened, the words came. After that the music was easier because I could hear it in my head."

"I wonder why the guys aren't here, though. They're the ones who will be singing the song," Jong-in said.

"Think about it," Jin-woo said. "The three of us have been around them for over two months now. If one of our songs is chosen, someone would cry foul. As it currently stands, the only one from BLE who we've spent any time with is Soon-joon-nim. This way it will be fairer."

"Makes sense," Min-su said.

"Still sucks," Jong-in added.

"Yeah." They sighed.

Jin-woo chuckled. "We sound like we just stepped out of some sappy romantic comedy."

"There should be little broken hearts and sad faces floating over our heads." Jong-in snickered.

"And silly sad background music." Min-su grinned.

"How about some manga chibis?" Jin-woo added.

"Oh no, no chibis!"

Twenty minutes later the three of them were tempted to bang their heads against the desks. It was that or walk through the room smacking one or two people for being completely oblivious of Bam Kiseu's vocal styles and music trends. So far they'd heard American country, Japanese Kyoto style, and some genres Jin-woo couldn't even identify and they were only a third of the way through the presentations. What part of pop did these people not get? Clearly they hadn't taken Teacher Kim's advice to do some research. It wasn't that the songs were bad. The technical skill was clearly there, but they just didn't match Bam Kiseu's style. Experimentation with genres was all well and good when that's what your client asked for, but that hadn't been the parameters of the project. Song after song played, and Soon-joon's expression grew darker and darker. Hyun-jo's face was impassive, but he kept shooting side glances at Soon-joon. Hopefully, the submissions would get better after the first break. Jin-woo glanced at the clock on his phone—five minutes left.

Jin-woo met Min-su and Jong-in on the stone wall running along the walkway of the building. They sat in silence for a few moments.

"Some of that was absolutely horrible," Min-su said. "Well, not so much horrible as not fitting the parameters of the assignment. The Kyoto was actually kind of cool. I liked how strong the drum beats were. It had potential."

"American country…." Jong-in shuddered.

"I figure they were trying to step out of the expected genre, trying something different. Some of it wasn't bad. I liked the Kyoto drums too. Let's hope the next group is better," Jin-woo said. "We have a lot of talented people in our class."

Ten minutes later, they were back in their seats, waiting for the presentations to begin. Jin-woo crossed his fingers. He knew his classmates could do this. He wasn't sure what the first six people were thinking, but he hoped the others did well. Then the next song began and Jin-woo smiled. Yeah, this one got it. Strong beat, energetic melody in major, tempo switching up before hitting with another drop, and they mixed a little blues in too. He leaned over to Min-su.

"I like this one," he said. "Tae-ri hubae did a great job."

"He did," she said with a smile. "I like the blues, gives it a different sound than what we're used to hearing."

Jin-woo cast a quick glance at Soon-joon as he straightened in his seat. His expression wasn't as dark as it had been before the break. That had to be a good sign. The next two songs were really good, very much pop, and had a palpable energy to them. They were positive, happy, good-times songs that he could picture listening to while driving to the beach. Most of Bam Kisue's music had a sultry overtone to it, but there had been a couple pieces at the beginning of their career that had the same type of feeling, so these songs were still in keeping with their style, just their earlier style.

By the time they reached the second break, Jin-woo was tapping his foot and bobbing along with just about every song. He couldn't help the smile that lit his face. He knew they could do it. And then the most discordant sound ever hit his ears. It was so sharp it was painful.

"Oh my God, who made this and can we make them never do it again?" he gasped as the notes crashed into each other, conflicting in tone and pitch. Hell, the song didn't even stay in the same key from beginning to end, and it wasn't as if it was a smooth transition. The damn thing skipped like a rock on a lake.

"Make it stop." Jong-in's voice was close enough for him to hear. Jin-woo turned to see him curled in his chair, his hands over his ears as if he were in pain. It wouldn't surprise Jin-woo if he was. This wasn't music; this was noise, chaotic noise. Then it hit him. Shifter hearing, Jong-in really was in pain. Jin-woo rubbed his back, not sure what else to do to help Jong-in.

"I don't get how she willingly made something like this," Min-su said. "Mei hubae's always been fairly good with her engineering, if a bit repetitive."

"Mei hubae made this crap?" Jin-woo was shocked. "Was she drunk at the time? Stoned? Both? Please tell me there's a logical reason for this."

"If there is, I have no idea what it is," Min-su said as she rubbed Jong-in's back as well.

Fortunately a minute later, the sound stopped and the silence was deafening. Jin-woo looked for Mei only to find her staring at him with an unreadable expression. It was as if she was there, but not, and it was decidedly creepy. Then she shook her head and smiled at him brightly, which was somehow more disturbing.

As the winners of part one, Jin-woo, Min-su, and Jong-in's entries were last. Jin-woo would have to say about 20 percent of the songs submitted were in no way geared toward Bam Kiseu's style. That gave them the advantage. They knew the music, loved it, in fact, even before their internship. However, the other 75 percent had been damn good. Well, except for Mei's. There was no way anyone in their right mind would have even dared to call that music, let alone good music, and even the other songs that weren't in Bam Kiseu's style were better than that audio chaos.

As if you saw right through me,
Saw deep into my heart.
Your words, meant only for me to hear.
You reach out your hand, draw me near.
Your eyes so deep and dark, your voice so sweet and low.
You caught me, now, don't let go.

As Min-su's submission played, he could picture her writing it, staring at Cheongul's face all over the wall behind her desk... and across from her bed. Jinwoo wondered if she'd taken him to her apartment yet but wasn't about to ask. She'd hit him. The song was poppy and energetic, a fun sound, but with some hard beat drops that conveyed the "take no shit" attitude Min-su had.

Caught me, in your eyes
You've caught me now
You hold me, do you know
Are you going to love me anyway?
Are you going to tell me to go?
Tell me what you want from me
Tell me what you need
I'll give my heart, give you every part of me
But I don't share and I don't play games
Take me as I am or walk away
Your eyes may have caught me
But I'm not the type you can play.

The lyrics flowed, conveying both the worry and the determination of the singer. He found himself bouncing to it and could totally see Gojira's choreography in his head.

Caught me, in your eyes
I'm afraid of your hold
Caught me, in your smile
I'm scared you'll let me go
Caught me, in my heart
Can you promise me
We can take this slow

Jin-woo liked it a lot. He elbowed her and smiled brightly.

"That is freaking awesome," he said, bumping her shoulder. "I love the way you added those hard drops. It screams 'Min-su-ya' to me."

She blushed. "Thanks. I can't wait to hear yours and Jong-in-a's. You guys are better than me at the musical portion."

"Don't sell yourself short. Soon-joon-nim looks a little bit happier now!" Jin-woo laughed.

"He was looking a bit... stormy," Min-su said. "I would be too. I thought some of our classmates would make more of an effort, but it looks like they didn't even bother, just did the songs according to what they liked. I'm glad the rest took this seriously. I think Tae-ri hubae's song was awesome. I'd produce it."

"That's not going to work in their favor in this industry," Jong-in said and then took a sip of his coffee. "Did you see Hyun-jo ya taking notes? I think they've made a list of people to watch for. I think Soon-joon-nim started tapping along. His fingers were moving."

A distance hope well beyond my reach.
When I close my eyes, I see you before me.
You take my hand, the faintest brush,
Your fingers against mine.
Yet that simple touch,
Sends pleasure through me in a rush.
I feel so alive, but you're only a dream.

Jong-in slouched down in his seat as the first notes of his composition played, pulling his hood up. Jin-woo's throat tightened as he listened to the words. The song was in minor, lending such a sad tone, an almost hopeless feeling to it, but there were parts of the melody that lifted it.

I can't speak the words.
They won't cross my lips.
A moment, a blink in time,
Where everything was perfect.
Imagining you were mine,
But that was just imaginary.
You'll forget me soon.
A crazy wistful dream,
To think I mean anything to you.

The notes were complex, the beats subtle until the drop for the chorus.

Untainted, unsullied, untouched,
Your smile is a fantasy.
Untainted,
Your love is a ghost.
Untainted,
You're a dream,
Best left untainted by reality.

It was beautiful, and Jin-woo could only picture one person singing it: HanYin. There could be no other singer. This song was written for and about HanYin.

I can't keep you,
No matter how hard I try.
I'm bound up in my dream,
Smoke and mirrors, a lie.
You were the one bright spot,
The one shining star.
But it's not meant to be,
I can't take it that far.

Jin-woo took his sleeve and wiped the tears from his eyes.

"Didn't mean to make you cry," Jong-in said when he sniffled.

"It's a sad song, but I detect a note of hope in it, and I'm glad that hope happened," Jin-woo said. "You two are good together."

"Yours is next," Jong-in said. "Wonder what you wrote about."

"It's nothing."

By the middle of his song, Jong-in and Min-su were gawking at him, their mouths hanging open. Jin-woo's face heated, and he slouched just like Jong-in had done. Min-su grabbed his arm and yanked him up as the chorus began. "You wrote a freaking duet?"

"It didn't start out that way," Jin-woo mumbled. "It just sort of happened."

"You sang both sides," Jong-in said. "You changed your octaves. What the hell is your range?"

"I don't know."

"Bullshit," Min-su said succinctly. "What is it?"

"I never really thought about it. I guess it's four at most, maybe. No big deal." They gaped at him and Jin-woo felt the urge to squirm. "What? My dad taught me."

Before they could respond, Jin-woo noticed the silence of the room. He looked around and saw everyone staring at him. He felt the panic kicking in, the anxiety and lightheadedness. He couldn't take this. He really wanted to get up and leave, but he knew if he stood up, he was going to fall flat on his face. That would just top his day. Spots danced before his eyes.

The next thing he knew, Min-su yanked his chair out with one hand, and Jong-in grabbed the back of his head and shoved it between his knees. It served the dual purpose of snapping him out of his panic and relieving the resulting nausea. He was spared from further scrutiny by the clearing of someone's throat. Teacher Kim stood in front of the seats, his hands folded in front of him. He didn't look too happy. Jin-woo straightened up and pushed his hair off his face, trying to ignore how he'd just embarrassed himself.

"Soon-joon-nim, Rhim Hyun-jo dongsaeng, and I will retire to one of the smaller conference rooms to deliberate on these submissions. Before we do so, however, I feel I must express my disappointment. I specifically advised researching the band you were writing for. I was clear in what factors needed to be taken into consideration when you were composing these songs. I heard several submissions that showed a blatant disregard for the men who would be performing the winning piece. It smacked of disrespect, and that is unacceptable," he said. "If I can take the time to do the research to adequately judge the music I am listening to, I expect no less from my students. We will be discussing each submission at our next series of conferences. Rest assured some of you will not be receiving full credits for them."

With those words hanging in the air, the three men left the room. Once the door closed behind them, everyone started murmuring. Several people shot glances his way, but Jin-woo couldn't be bothered to notice. He kept choking up, thinking about his mom and dad. He knew they would be so proud of him, and he had wished, more than once, they were here to see this.

"I've never heard you sing," Jong-in said.

"I don't sing in front of people anymore," Jin-woo said quietly. "I haven't in a long time."

"I've said this before, but I'll say it again. Your parents wouldn't want you to hide your gift," Min-su said.

"I'm not hiding it," Jin-woo said. "I just… I can't sing in front of other people. If you think my panic attacks are bad now? Put me in front of a live audience, and I will turn into a quivering pile of screaming, crying crazy. You saw what happened at the very idea of singing 'Crossing Time' with Bam Kiseu in a few weeks."

"You're going to *perform* with them?" The strident voice made Jin-woo jump. He snapped his head up to see Mei standing in front of him. Her entire body was tense, and the fury in her eyes was completely out of place.

"It's rude to eavesdrop," Min-su growled.

"Tell me that's not true, Jin-woo," Mei demanded, ignoring Min-su. "Tell me you're not going to belittle yourself by performing with… them."

"Firstly, I did not give permission for you to speak to me so familiarly," Jin-woo said. "Secondly, I don't have to tell you anything, and thirdly, it's really none of your business to begin with."

"What are you freaking out for, anyway?" Min-su said. "Bam Kiseu is our favorite band. To be onstage with them would be an honor and damned fun."

"Of course *you* would think so." Mei snorted before turning her attention back to Jin-woo. Seriously, what was her problem? She pressed closer, and he was glad there was a desk separating them. He didn't think she would have stopped before she was right in his lap—ew. "You won't perform with them, right, Jin-woo? You are so much better than that, so much nicer and sweeter."

"You need to step back," Jong-in said. "And he already told you he didn't give you leave to address him so informally."

"I'm not talking to either of you!" she snapped. "I'm talking to Jin-woo."

"And now you're done," Jin-woo said coldly. "I refuse to talk to someone who is rude and disrespectful to not only my friends, but to me as well. You should return to your seat. Try practicing consistent pitch and tone or something, maybe staying in the same key throughout a song. I don't know. Just do it somewhere away from me."

Mei looked as if he'd slapped her, and in a sense, he had. However, she had been told twice not to address him inappropriately and hadn't listened. If she hadn't been rude to Min-su and Jong-in, he might have been a little less cold, but Jin-woo didn't think so.

She'd gone flat in several spots, and the key changed from verse to chorus, sometimes midverse. The melody was discordant, and Jin-woo didn't think that was on purpose. No, either she hadn't paid attention in any of the classes on composition, just didn't care, or had no skill. As he'd heard some of her previous work, he knew it wasn't a lack of skill or attention. He wasn't sure what it was, beyond painful to listen to.

She narrowed her eyes and the muscles in her jaw tensed. Then she turned and walked away without another word. He sighed in relief and relaxed in his seat. "What is with her lately?"

"I don't know, but I don't think that girl is playing with a full deck," Jong-in said. "I...."

"What is it?" Jin-woo asked.

"The way she acts toward you, the way she's gotten more... obsessive, Jin-woo, is it possible she's your stalker?" Jong-in said.

"Could she have done all that damage? Smashed my coffee table? The couch? All that stuff and then cleared it all away? She's about my height, but skinnier," Jin-woo said. "I mean unless there's something... special about her, she just wouldn't have the physical strength, right?"

"I don't know. It's just she's gotten really weird."

"She is definitely stressed out, but you can talk to Soon-joon nim and see what he thinks," Min-su said. "Why would she participate in this scholarship if she didn't like Bam Kiseu? Did you hear how she referred to them? As if they were tainted or something. Girl is definitely not a pop fan."

"I wish they would hurry up." Jin-woo sighed. "I have so much other work to do."

"Work? You just want to see Ki-tae-ya." Min-su chuckled, and then she sobered a little bit. "Cheongul's been so tired lately. They're working really hard to be ready for this concert."

"HanYin said they were looking at twenty-five to thirty songs," Jong-in said. "That isn't really surprising. They're known for that, with just enough breaks spaced out through the concert to make sure they don't overdo it. Still, that's a lot."

"That's about two hours of performing with crowd popping," Min-su said. Jin-woo smiled. He loved that term "crowd popping." She used it when referring to the idols getting the crowd worked up between songs. "Plus they're going to perform whichever song is chosen here. They'll need to work that in along with any new choreography. Goo-ji unnie is working them hard on the older dance moves as it is."

Jin-woo nodded. "I caught a rehearsal the other day. Now I know why they call her Gojira."

"Ever wonder if she knows they call her that?" Jong-in asked.

"She does." Min-su chuckled. "The funny thing is she loves those movies."

"How do you know that?" Jin-woo asked.

"We've hung out a couple of times, talked on the phone. She's really pretty cool." Min-su shrugged. "She knows what they're capable of, and she refuses to let them do anything less than their best. Still, sometimes I wish she would take it easy on them."

The door opened and all sound stopped. The tension shot up as Teacher Kim, Soon-joon, and Hyun-jo returned. They stood in front of the room and said nothing for a few moments. It went on long enough for people to start squirming in their seats. Then Teacher Kim stepped forward.

"It was a bit problematic to narrow down our choices of songs," he began. "There were many we listened to a second and even a third time, but in the end, it came down to four. This is where our task became difficult. We had to choose between Tae-ri dongsaeng's 'Swept Away by You,' Min-su dongsaeng's 'Caught Me,' Jong-in dongsaeng's 'Untainted,' and Jin-woo dongsaeng's 'Invisible.' Each one fit perfectly with Bam Kiseu's genre. Each one addressed the vocal styles of the members, and each one was a high-quality finished product. This tells me they put forth a great deal of effort, knew their client, knew their engineering, and knew their music. Yet we can only pick one. Our choice, by unanimous vote, is 'Invisible' by Jin-woo dongsaeng."

Jin-woo froze in his seat, unable to move. And then Min-su was hugging him tightly.

"It's going to be all right," she whispered in his ear. "You've got this."

He hugged her back. When they parted, he nodded to her, smiling his thanks, and rose to his feet. Then he was walking down the aisle to stand with Teacher Kim, Soon-joon, and Hyun-jo. He bowed and shook their hands.

"It is a beautiful song, Jin-woo dongsaeng," Hyun-jo said softly.

"Gomabseumnida," Jin-woo said. He couldn't seem to get any other words out.

"Your performance was nothing short of amazing, Jin-woo dongsaeng," Teacher Kim said. "I was awestruck with the changes in your vocals. It blended seamlessly with the changes in the melody and rhythm."

"I am very impressed," Soon-joon said. "You really know their voices, and it showed. Thank you for the pleasure of hearing you sing. I feel this was rather difficult for you, and I thank you for continuing on, seeing it through to the end."

"They are my favorite band," Jin-woo said softly. "It is only because I've listened to them so much that I know their styles so well. I know my song will sound even better when they sing it."

Jin-woo appreciated how Soon-joon didn't bring up the idea of him performing the song at the concert. It showed how much of a decent man he was. He knew of Jin-woo's… issues with singing and didn't hold it against him. After a few more minutes of chitchat, Jin-woo returned to his seat. Most of his classmates congratulated him, but some were unhappy. Mei kept shooting him dark looks. Others muttered under their breath. Yet he couldn't bring himself to worry about that. Their issues were precisely that: their issues. He had more important things to deal with. When they were finally dismissed, Hyun-jo stopped them by the door. He waited until the other students had left before he spoke.

"Soon-joon-nim is working out next year's details with Seonsaengnim, so he asked me to convey his request."

"You're always so formal and polite," Min-su said with a smile. He simply bowed with a soft smile.

"What can we do for Soon-joon-nim?" Jong-in said.

"Well, in effect, this request is for you and Min-su-ya," Hyun-jo said. "He was very impressed with your songs, and he would like to have Bam Kiseu record them as well, if you will allow."

"Pinch me," Min-su said softly. Jin-woo reached out and pinched her, as per her request. She jumped a little and then glared at him while rubbing her arm.

"What? You told me to pinch you," he said with a shrug.

"Why did you have to do it so hard?"

"For all the times you smack me in the head."

"Learn to dodge."

"Are you two finished?" Jong-in said with a sigh.

"For now," they answered. Jin-woo giggled. He couldn't help it. He was feeling good. Hyun-jo smiled at their antics.

"Of course we're going to permit it," Min-su said, putting her arm through Jong-in's. "We wrote the songs for them to begin with. I just didn't think we'd be offered something like this."

"Had we been able to choose more than one winner, rest assured, you three and Tae-ri dongsaeng would have been standing up there together," Soon-joon said as he came over to them. "I could not let those songs go. We'll see if they want to work all three of them into the concert. I also need to speak with Tae-ri dongsaeng. I think he might do well with a pair of trainees I'm working with."

"Live? You want them to perform them live?" Jong-in said softly.

"We'll see what they say. I've always been a firm believer on receiving input from the artists themselves," Soon-joon said. "Now I know you three have other work to do. We'll see you tomorrow at the office."

"Soon-joon-nim?" Jin-woo said suddenly, remembering what Jong-in had said as he felt the prickles on the back of his neck.

"Yes."

"I need to talk to you about my other situation," Jin-woo said, shooting a quick glance to see if Mei was watching him. "Could I meet with you tomorrow morning?"

Soon-joon looked at Hyun-jo.

"Your first meeting is at ten o'clock," Hyun-jo said with a smile. "I will let Hyung-jun hubae know you will be meeting with Jin-woo dongsaeng at nine o'clock if that is agreeable with you both?"

"That is fine," Soon-joon said, and Jin-woo nodded.

"How do you remember it all?" Jong-in asked.

"Practice." Hyun-jo smiled.

They said their goodbyes, and then Soon-joon and Hyun-jo walked out of the room after pausing to speak with Tae-ri. Soon-joon handed Tae-ri his business card before they left. Jin-woo nudged Min-su and then gestured to the departing couple. She smiled when she saw Soon-joon's hand resting at the small of Hyun-jo's back. Jin-woo wondered if Soon-joon even realized he was doing it. He didn't think so.

"They make such a good couple," Min-su said softly. "He's waited so long."

"He'll get his way in the end," Jong-in said. "Now we've got to get to work."

"Not before caffeine," Jin-woo insisted. "I've had one small cup, and that is so not enough to get me through this day."

"Agreed."

Walking arm in arm, they made their way out of the building and headed for the nearest coffee shop, heedless of the eyes that followed them.

KI-TAE

"THIS IS definitely yours," Cheongul said as they listened to "Untainted." Jong-in's lyrics were poignant, his mix complex.

"It wouldn't be right for either of us to sing it," Ki-tae agreed.

"It's…. I don't know what to say," HanYin murmured. "It's almost too… intimate, too personal to perform before an audience."

"It fits with 'Yes or No,' doesn't it?" Ki-tae said.

"I… I hadn't thought of that," HanYin said.

"This is a flashback concert, but I don't see why we can't debut more than one new song," Cheongul said with a shrug. "It's just before the spring festival, a time of renewal and new beginnings. Makes sense to do a few new things, doesn't it?"

"It does." Ki-tae grinned. "Let's move on to the next one."

"Hyun-jo-nim said this was Min-su-ya's composition," HanYin said as he queued the song. He pressed Play, and they all leaned back in their seats to listen, eyes closed.

"Holy shit, my girl can drop a beat." Cheongul laughed as his chair rocked forward and nearly shot him out of it. "And she raps too!"

"A match made in the studio." HanYin snickered. Cheongul threw a stress ball at him, which HanYin deftly caught.

"One word: piano!" Cheongul said pointedly, smiling when HanYin blushed furiously.

"'Your girl,' huh?" Ki-tae chuckled. "Going to tell her that anytime soon?"

"Leave off," Cheongul said. "This is a bit… new for me, and you know it. Besides, I already told her."

"You did? And? What did she say?" HanYin demanded.

"She loves me too." Cheongul smiled.

"Then I'll stop busting on you about it for now," Ki-tae said. He turned his attention back to the music. "This has got a lot of energy. It's upbeat but still has the solid drops."

"Add it?" HanYin asked.

"Add it," they said.

"Now for Jin-woo-ya's. His was the winning selection. Hyun-jo-nim said we should brace ourselves," HanYin said. Then he hit the space bar, and they resumed their positions, but not for long.

"Holy shit," Cheongul murmured. "Is that…. I thought they had to do this by themselves, no collaborations."

"That's all Jin-woo," Ki-tae whispered, awed by the layered vocals. "That's all him. He's got a what... four, four and a half-octave range?"

"No, that's a solid five," HanYin said. "You can hear it at the end of the notes. He's hitting middle five."

Cheongul said, "Two points of view, each looking at the other but feeling invisible."

"Ironically that's the title: 'Invisible,'" HanYin said, glancing at the email.

"Listen to the tones. When he finishes a verse, he drops his pitch to match the music, a sort of natural fade," Ki-tae said, shifting in his seat.

"The harmonies, they are *tight*." Cheongul moved closer to the speakers. "The buildup, you almost don't even notice it amid the strings. It's like riding a roller coaster, and when you hit the top, there's that almost imperceptible stop before you drop."

"Amazing," Ki-tae said. "And it suits us. This is a duet, though."

"Yeah?" Cheongul said.

"Um, there's three of us, remember?" Ki-tae said sarcastically.

"So what, we've done solo songs before. I always take the lead in 'Master.' I don't see why this has to be any different," Cheongul said. "Jin-woo-ya can."

"No, he can't," HanYin said with a shake of his head. "Jin-woo-ya cannot perform this in front of an audience."

"What do you mean?" Ki-tae demanded, turning to face him. "Why wouldn't he be able to do this with me?"

HanYin said, "It's not my place to tell, so I'm not going to say any more than that. Just don't ask him to do this."

"How do you know that?" Ki-tae asked.

"It was while you were out of the building all day. I guess Abeoji brought up the idea of them singing with us at the festival, and Jin-woo-ya had an adverse reaction to it. I was sitting with him when he woke up," HanYin said.

"Okay," Ki-tae said. "I guess I need to talk to him about it."

"Don't push, Ki-tae. You know how we get, and Jin-woo-ya's just as proud as the rest of us," HanYin said.

"I know when not to push, HanYin," Ki-tae said. "I just... I don't understand why I don't know this about him."

"It's not easy to tell people about what hurts us. You know this," Cheongul said. "Ask him about it, but if he's not ready, you have to give him the time."

"It hurts," Ki-tae said.

"I know," Cheongul said. "I... I told Min-su about Mikiko and Tashi, and she told me what happened to her. It was hard on both of us. The pain is still close."

"We're getting maudlin, and it needs to stop," HanYin said. "You guys remember this one?"

Ki-tae hadn't noticed HanYin fiddling with the computer while he was talking to Cheongul. What played on the screen was one of their oldest music videos. It didn't look like much now. They didn't have Gojira when that video was done. Otherwise their dancing would have been tighter, more precise. Still, it was a feel-good video that was fun to make. Soon they were laughing at their own antics.

"Oh my God, look at my hair!" HanYin laughed at the bright orange locks he sported. "Who convinced me to do that?"

"I believe that was our first stylist, Anyi seonbae, who I still feel was in need of serious medication. She was way too… much," Cheongul said.

"And LeiChen-ssi isn't?" Ki-tae chuckled.

"LeiChen-ssi is at least amusing and sweet, and he just doesn't care what other people think. Not only that, but he has incredible fashion sense and knows what it's like to be under those stage lights, so he doesn't layer us in fabric," Cheongul said. "I swear Anyi seonbae was not all there."

"She had her quirks," HanYin said. "That color doesn't look good on me at all."

"Not in your hair, at any rate," Ki-tae said. "I personally think the purples and blues suit you better."

"That more reddish purple works for you," HanYin said. "Remind me never to do orange ever again."

"Don't do orange ever again," Ki-tae and Cheongul said in unison. HanYin winged the stress ball at Ki-tae. He snagged it immediately.

"So we have three new songs to perform and one remix," Ki-tae said. "Do you want to do 'Yes or No,' HanYin?"

"Let's put it in for now, and I'll make a final decision closer to the concert," HanYin said quietly. Ki-tae tilted his head and studied his brother.

"What is it?"

"I wrote that song when I was uncertain about Jong-in," he answered. "I'm still a little uncertain. I don't know if he's going to stay. He's been trying to be a normal guy, and I'm so far from normal it's laughable."

"Have you talked to him about it?" Ki-tae asked. "Maybe Jong-in-a is just as unsure as you are."

"It's hard to have the time. He works so much, but if I offer to help him, he's going to get upset, just like he did with Jin-woo-ya." HanYin smiled. "He's so proud and determined and strong-willed."

"You're a goner," Cheongul said with a small smile. "You love him."

"I do," HanYin said softly. "But the question is, does he love me?"

"Only one way to find out," Ki-tae said.

"I don't know if I'm strong enough to hear the answer."

Ki-tae pulled HanYin to him, chair and all, and hugged him tight. Two seconds later it was a three-way hug. "We found some pretty amazing people, ones we can be completely honest with about who and what we are. We're not letting them go."

"What if they walk away?" HanYin whispered into Ki-tae's neck.

"They won't," Cheongul said.

"I... I can't lose him." HanYin's tears wet Ki-tae's neck. "It will kill me."

SOON-JOON

SOON-JOON LOOKED at the envelope sitting on his desk, Hyun-jo standing next to him. He had a bad feeling about this and was loath to open it. Yet he knew he had to. They needed to know what level of threat they were facing.

"Shall I?" Hyun-jo asked, setting a hand on his shoulder. Soon-joon could feel the soothing energy flowing into him.

"No," Soon-joon said. He reached out for the envelope, taking Hyun-jo's hand. "Just… be here."

"If I haven't left in over a thousand years, what makes you think I'm going to leave now?" Hyun-jo muttered. "*Baka.*"

Soon-joon chuckled softly as he tore open the envelope. He dumped the contents onto his desk. Three pictures poured out, one in pieces. All of them were Ki-tae, and they were very candid shots. It was clear Ki-tae did not sense the person following him. Either that or he did not consider that person a threat. *I warned you* was scrawled in red across one of the whole pictures. A chill went through Soon-joon, and then he got angry. His claws shot from his fingertips, piercing through the photo paper. Someone dared threaten his son.

"Easy, xīn'ái," Hyun-jo murmured. "We will find this person, and they will no longer be a threat to our family."

"It cannot happen soon enough for me." He sighed.

"I know," Hyun-jo said. "We have a threat from two sides, and it is aggravating."

"How is that investigation going?" Soon-joon asked.

"The footage is not the best quality, and I believe the perpetrator knew of the cameras. Their movements were too deliberate for them not to know. They made sure their face was not seen in more than a one-quarter view, making it difficult to do any sort of composite." Hyun-jo moved behind him and massaged his shoulders as he spoke. "The clothing was very loose, but if I were to hazard a guess, I do not believe we are seeking a large male as the destruction of the furniture would imply. While knives are typically a male weapon of choice, it is not out of the realm of possibility that Jin-woo-ya's stalker is female."

"You do not guess, Hyun-jo," Soon-joon said drily.

"I do not have all the information yet, therefore I will not commit to anything beyond a possible theory," he said.

"Your theory may be more valid than you think," Soon-joon said.

"Oh?" Hyun-jo said. "Your meeting with Jin-woo the other day?"

Soon-joon nodded. "One of his classmates, Byun Mei dongsaeng, has him concerned. He said she has often displayed... overfamiliarity and a distinct lack of personal boundaries with him but has gotten worse over the last several weeks. I would like you to look into it please."

"Byun? Any possible relation to Seung-ri hubae?"

"Possibly. He started caring for his sister-in-law and niece after his brother was killed in that train accident several years ago. Honestly, I am hoping there is no connection. Seung-ri hubae adores his niece."

"I will look into it," Hyun-jo said, his lilting voice as soothing as it was arousing depending upon his Fox's mood. "Now relax, or I will have to use drastic measures... again."

Soon-joon chuckled. He wondered if Hyun-jo realized that was not a deterrent.

JIN-WOO

THE FESTIVAL of Dano approached faster than anyone truly wanted. In between their multitude of meetings, promotional events, and rehearsals, Ki-tae and HanYin were in the studio with Jin-woo and Jong-in preparing "Invisible" for its debut. Cheongul worked on Min-su's song. HanYin spent extra time not only at the offices, but his home studio, rehearsing "Untainted." Each wanted to make sure these songs were perfect, and the stress was getting to them.

Jin-woo stretched out on his bed, his body as exhausted as his mind. He had returned to his apartment infrequently in the past several weeks. With all the work they'd been doing, he hadn't had a chance to think about his break-in. He wasn't sure the police were making any real effort to solve the case, but he knew Shin-bai and Hyun-jo were working on it, and that made him feel better.

Tomorrow night he would be at Eumak Nabi Theater. The venue had sold out in mere hours after the announcement was made. The social medial sites were all abuzz with the news. On more than one occasion, he and Ki-tae were stopped by fans while they were out. Ki-tae would smile, sign autographs, and take pictures with them. A few had gotten too intense, and Shin-bai quickly stepped in. Since the last envelope, Shin-bai did not leave Ki-tae's side until he was safely in his apartment, at the house, or with Jin-woo in his apartment. Even then he was outside watching, keeping them safe. It was terrifying to think someone wanted to hurt Ki-tae. It made his little stalker seem almost insignificant. At least there wasn't a threat to Jin-woo's life.

Jin-woo sighed as he sat up. He needed a shower, and then he needed to get some rest. Tomorrow was going to be hectic from beginning to end. Yet there was an energy that seemed to fill all the people involved, a certain level of excitement as they prepared for the performance. They hadn't done a flashback concert before. Bam Kiseu occasionally pulled out an old song during a tour, but mostly they performed the new music. It was going to be interesting to see how the fans reacted. Jin-woo thought it was awesome, but he was a fanboy, and everything Bam Kiseu sang was incredible, as far as he was concerned.

Half an hour later, Jin-woo crawled back into bed. It was empty without Ki-tae beside him, but Ki-tae needed a full night's rest, and they both knew resting wasn't the first thing they did when they climbed into bed together. At least not usually. There were a few nights where they were just too exhausted to do more than cuddle and go to sleep. Jin-woo smiled. Ki-tae was such a snuggler. One wouldn't think so, looking at him, but Ki-tae liked to wrap himself around Jin-woo, his face pressed in the curve of Jin-woo's neck. He would give this soft little sigh right before he fell asleep.

After grabbing his phone off the nightstand, Jin-woo swiped the lock screen and put in his code. He couldn't go to sleep without wishing Ki-tae sweet dreams. Including a kissy face emoji, Jin-woo chuckled and then hit Send. He set his phone back down, only to snatch it up two seconds later when Ki-tae's text tone went off. He opened the message to find only an attachment. Confused, Jin-woo downloaded the file. Once it was done, he pressed Play and then groaned as his gut clenched. Ki-tae's mouth close-up, his bottom lip caught between his teeth. Slowly that full lip slid out, and then he swiped that teasing tongue across the top one.

"Sleep sweet, xīn'ái," Ki-tae purred.

"Damn him," Jin-woo said. "I really need to learn Mandarin. What the heck did he just call me?"

Surprisingly Jin-woo fell right to sleep, the pillow Ki-tae always used cuddled to his chest.

"MAKE. SOME. Noise!" Cheongul shouted. The crowd screamed, Bam Kiseu lights waving frantically in the darkened hall. He ran out onto the stage, Ki-tae and HanYin right behind him. "I can't hear you!"

"Scream!" Ki-tae yelled as he raised his arms high, and the crowd obeyed his command.

Then HanYin launched into their very first single, "Kiss Me." The crowd chanted his name as he moved back into position. They moved in sync, not missing a beat. Every movement was precise, from the hand gestures to the hip rolls.

Watching from backstage, Jin-woo couldn't stop himself from bouncing with the music. Though it had been a long time since he last listened to this song, Jin-woo still knew all the words. Had he been alone, he might have sung along, but he was too conscious of all the people around him.

The musicians were just as hyped-up as Ki-tae and the others, bouncing as they played, smiling and singing. They blended right into the energetic beat of "Like You Do." It started out fast with a trance beat, and mixed it up with just enough dubstep to keep it interesting. Cheongul's voice carried over the music clearly, his bass rich and deep.

That's it, baby, bring that body over to me.
Love the way you move, so sweet and sexy.
Face so cute, body so fine,
Bring it over here, baby, let me make you mine.
I'll make your world shake,
All night long, I'll give you all you can take.
I'll make the stars dance.
I'll give you all my love, given half a chance.

HanYin's clear tenor blended so well with the third and fourth line of the verse, and the smile was nothing short of wicked, but Ki-tae had that smirk, and he licked his lips just before he took the fifth and sixth line. Then that harmonization on the last two lines, it always killed Jin-woo when he heard it. He waved his hand in front of his face, but there was no cooling himself off. The second verse started the same as the first, the beat picking up speed until it dropped into the hard dubstep on the chorus, a perfect blending of Ki-tae's baritone with HanYin's tenor and alternating with Cheongul's bass on the first word.

Move—like you do.
Talk—like you do.
Dance—like you do.
Love—like you do.
No one has me crazy—like you do.

Ki-tae took the lead on the third verse, and the crowd went wild. Jin-woo couldn't blame them. His ability to slide from tenor to baritone to bass gave the song a sexy, seductive feel.

Jin-woo smiled. They were going to dance to that song at some point and let things go from there. The crowd joined in on the last run of the chorus. Every single voice in the hall was in perfect sync. It was impressive and a little bit disturbing how they sounded almost like one voice. Then the music faded. The crowd went wild as Cheongul, HanYin, and Ki-tae stood on the extension to the main stage that put them in the middle of the crowd. They were smiling and waving.

"Are you having fun?" HanYin asked with a bright smile. "Do you like the old tunes?"

"Ah, you know you do!" Ki-tae laughed as the crowd screamed.

"We dusted off these tracks just for spring," Cheongul said.

"That's right," HanYin said. "Dano starts tomorrow. Everyone excited?"

"Of course you are!" Ki-tae said. "We plan to celebrate, starting tonight!"

"You know who we are, but we're going to introduce ourselves anyway," Cheongul said as he stepped forward. "I'm Cheongul. I'm the leader of Bam Kiseu. How you doing, Seoul?"

"It's your boy, HanYin!" HanYin said as he bounced up and down. "We've missed you, Korea!"

"And here's the baby of the group!" Cheongul said, wrapping an arm around Ki-tae's shoulders from behind.

"I'm Ki-tae. Did you miss us?" Ki-tae said with a smile. The crowd screamed so loud Jin-woo could feel it. "It's only been three months since our last concert, but that was at the end of our world tour. Tonight, Korea, this is just for you! Spring is about to be sprung! Get up! Stand up and throw your hands in the air!"

"Ki-tae, HanYin, what say we turn up the 'Heat'?" Cheongul said just as the heavy beat started.

Ki-tae took the front position. He looked out over the crowd, his head tilted down slightly and the right corner of his mouth kicked up.

There's just something about you,
The way your hips sway,
The long lines of your legs,
A glance over your shoulder,
You lick your lips as you walk away.
If anyone was made for sin, it's you, baby.
The temptation is too much to resist.
I'm not trying too hard because you're it.

If it were possible, the screaming got louder. The choreography suited the sensuality of the words. Jin-woo figured they could thank Gojira and other factors for that. Ah, the joys of being a Vampire with enhanced reflexes and the oddly intoxicating aura of "otherness." He loved the way they so easily switched positions onstage, their movements tight. They were just starting, and the energy was already so high. This, the ability to keep the crowd hyped from beginning to end, was what made Bam Kiseu so popular.

HanYin's voice rose above the roar of the crowd, sensual and sweet.

How can someone look as sweet as you?
And be so wicked inside,
Such a deceiving little package,
With little devil horns to hide.
They think you can do no harm.
They've never spent a night with you, baby,
Burning in your arms.
But what a way to go, I must admit.
I'd spend forever, pressed against you,
And think nothing of it.

"God, his voice is so damn hot," Jong-in groaned, pressing his head against the wall.

"Just his voice?" Jin-woo teased, his eyes fixated on Ki-tae's ass as he rolled his hips to the music. How anyone could have thought this song was about the weather, Jin-woo didn't know. He grabbed Jong-in's arm and pulled him away from the wall. "Here it comes."

They grinned like idiots as they listened to the buildup, dancing along. The music moved faster and faster until it just stopped, and then that beat slammed into the audience. The beat was heavy on the kick drum, a throbbing, pulsing sound that drove the beat forward into the chorus.

You're a fire in my blood,
Burning beneath the skin.
You're a fire in my body,
Give me your… heat.

"Can they get any hotter?" Jin-woo asked with laugh. Being able to see the concert from backstage was cool, but a part of him wanted to be out in the crowd, wanted to see Ki-tae head-on while he sang. Now HanYin's comment about pulling people in through the cameras made more sense. When you were in the crowd, you could imagine they were looking right at you, even if they weren't. Backstage he only got a side view, and while it was still a fantastic view, as far as he was concerned, Jin-woo preferred to see Ki-tae's eyes.

He glanced over when Jong-in elbowed him in the side. Jong-in gestured toward the stage, and Jin-woo looked over just in time to catch Ki-tae's eyes as he began the third verse.

I love the way you moan for me,
The way you cry out in delight.
I love the way you claw at me,
As if you really want to fight.
You're a feisty little demon in an angel's guise,
And only I will ever know it's all lies.

Jin-woo gasped at the heat in that one short glance. At that moment he felt as if Ki-tae were singing just for him, even if he wasn't standing in front of him. His heart swelled. He really did love him.

"It's written all over your face, you know," Jong-in said as he put his arm around Jin-woo's shoulders. "How much you love him."

"I'm that obvious, huh?"

"To those who know you? Yeah, you are," Jong-in said. Suddenly he tensed beside Jin-woo, digging his fingers into his shoulder. "Crazy bitch alert."

"What?"

"Jin-woo!" Mei's voice carried over the music, acting like nails on a chalkboard to Jin-woo's ears. Seriously? What in the world was she doing here?

He turned with a sigh, and she immediately grabbed his arm. He shoved at her hands, but she was like a lamprey.

"Mei-ssi, what are you doing here?" Jin-woo said tightly, still trying to break her grip on his arm. "I thought you didn't like Bam Kiseu."

"I'm here with my uncle," she said, her smile bright. "I didn't know you'd be backstage."

"Your uncle?" Jin-woo said.

"Byun Seung-gi-nim is my uncle," she said. "He invited me so I could see what it's like. It's busy."

"Please let go of me," Jin-woo said, still trying to pull his arm free, but she wasn't letting go. It was as if she didn't hear him, but he knew better.

Just as he was about to say something, his arm was pulled free. He looked to see Ki-tae holding his wrist and dragging him toward the dressing room area. "I need your help," Ki-tae growled, and his eyes flashed silver. Oh, his Vampire was not happy.

"Thank God." Jin-woo chuckled in relief. He hadn't wanted to start something at the concert, but she had gone too far.

Looking back, he saw Mei staring at them, her eyes narrowed. He felt it like a stab to the chest, only she wasn't looking at him. She was glaring at Ki-tae.

The minute they were inside the dressing room, Ki-tae pressed Jin-woo up against the wall and claimed his mouth. The kiss was hot and savage and just what Jin-woo needed. He felt as if Ki-tae was restaking his claim on him.

When they pulled apart, they were both breathing heavily. Then Ki-tae stepped away and stripped off his costume. Jin-woo moved as Cheongul and HanYin came through the door. They ignored him as they, too, began to undress.

"Who was she?" Ki-tae asked as he pulled a brilliant blue vest on over his bare chest.

"A classmate," Jin-woo said and bit his lip. He wasn't sure he should tell Ki-tae Mei might be his stalker. If he did it would, at the very least, piss Ki-tae off and he needed to focus on the concert. Besides, there was no concrete proof it was her. "She's been acting weird every time I've seen her."

"She needs to keep her hands off you." Ki-tae dropped the leather pants and stepped out of them.

"Believe me, her hands are not the ones I want on me," Jin-woo said as he adjusted himself.

"Enough! I don't need the assault on my nose." Cheongul laughed. "Save it for after the concert. Then you can fuck each other all night long!"

"Because that's an image I wanted in my head," HanYin said as he pulled on a pair of red pants to go with the mesh shirt he was wearing. On more than one occasion, Jin-woo and Min-su had commented on the possibility of a tattoo below HanYin's waistline. Now he knew. A dragon weaved its way from his left hip along his lower back to curve around his right hip, dipping low.

"The lot of you are way too visual," Jin-woo grumbled. "Stop picturing us naked and get back onstage!"

"You're as pushy as Seung-gi hyung!" Ki-tae laughed, catching him up and giving him a hard kiss, slapping his ass in the process. Jin-woo yelped, jumping away and rubbing his cheek. He followed them out the door and back toward the stage. Their jog had them quickly outpacing him. Once he finally reached the entrance to the stage, he found Jong-in by himself.

"Please tell me she left," he said as he approached.

"Stomped off muttering something under her breath," Jong-in said. "The more I see of her, the more she's starting to creep me out."

"You're not the only one." Jin-woo gave a shudder. "Even if I were into women, I wouldn't want her."

Min-su pounced on Jong-in before he could respond, jumping onto his back and hanging there. "Oh my God, this is so amazing!"

Jin-woo laughed. "It's so different from being out in front."

"I was just in the sound booth. Cho-ree seonbae is running the board. He asked me to send you over, Jong-in-a," she said after hopping off his back.

"Me?"

"Yes, you. Go! You're going to be amazed by their setup." She laughed as she pushed him toward the side passage.

"You're just in time," Jin-woo said as another song started.

Min-su's eyes got wide as the first chords of "Can't Beat Me" flowed over the crowd and Cheongul practically growled the first verse. It didn't happen often, as Ki-tae was the main rapper of the group, but Cheongul had his own flow. Ki-tae and HanYin joined him on the chorus, but he took each verse just the way it was originally produced. The cool thing was the song really worked that way. It still had a pop beat but had just enough heavy guitar to give it an edgier feel. Then Cheongul screamed that bridge, and it was a punch to the ears. The smooth vocals of the chorus soothed the way for the final verse.

"I forgot he could rap," Min-su said with a chuckle.

"Ki-tae said he was ecstatic when he heard your rap," Jin-woo said, nudging her. "I believe he said Cheongul-a's exact words were 'My girl can drop a beat! And she raps too.'"

"Seriously? He liked it?" she asked.

"I think 'like' is not strong enough a word. 'Loved,' yes, 'loved' is much better," Jin-woo teased.

"Oh, hush, this is 'Master.'" Min-su scooted forward until she had a clear view of the stage. She bounced along just as he and Jong-in had with the earlier songs.

Faster than time, they say speed can kill,
Terrifying anger, this definitely will.
Enraged like a lion but far more deadly,
He's half man and half beast.
The master is ready,
And you will never be free.

"It took me a while to really figure out what this song was about," Min-su said, glancing back at Jin-woo.

"Well, it's definitely not the circus," Jin-woo said with a grin, trying to keep the mood light. He could see the serious expression on her face.

"It's about his temper," she said quietly. He almost didn't hear her. "It's about how his anger can burst out of control and hurt the people he cares about. The first two verses and the chorus are about how he feels controlled by it, by his inability to manage it. He feels as if he's in a cage, someone else pulling his strings. In the end, that last verse? It's about finally getting a handle on the rage, mastering it."

But what is this?
Have the tables been turned?

Did you find the strength within you?
You have broken your chains.
Now you stand before me, blood in your eyes.
Is it the end, my friend?
Half man and half beast,
You stare at me as if you want to feast.
Finally you realize… the master isn't me.

"I wonder what makes him feel that way," Jin-woo said. "Most of the time, Cheongul-ya seems so in control."

"He feels he has to be. He can't let himself get upset because he hasn't gotten control of his anger yet. He hasn't figured out how to keep it from hurting the people around him," she said.

"It sounds like someone else I know," Jin-woo said softly. "And now it makes more sense to me."

"I… we're not…."

"You are, Min-su-ya. In a way, you two are alike." Jin-woo hugged her from behind. "And the thing of it is this. You're a good couple because you know what it's like to have something inside you that you feel you can't control. And you're damned adorable together."

She laughed. "We are cute."

"When this is over, tell him," Jin-woo said. "Reach out to him and let him help you deal with what happened to you."

"How do you know I haven't?"

"Because I know you well enough to know you keep these things to yourself because you refuse to be pitied. Ki-tae says Cheongul-a has had the most exposure to individuals with the same concerns. He might be able to help you get a handle on this or find someone you can learn from."

"Look at you, being all responsible and sensible and sweet and shit," she grumbled. "Shut up and watch the concert."

Jin-woo laughed. He knew it might take her some time, but Min-su would talk to Cheongul about what happened. Min-su was perfect for him. She would stand up to him verbally and physically. She was a strong woman with a good heart. If anyone could help Cheongul, it was Min-su. They could be each other's strength. They needed each other.

"I already have," she said. Jin-woo whipped his head around to look at her. Then he smiled and hugged her tight.

"Good."

Song after song, set after set, Bam Kiseu kept the crowd hyped and the energy level high. Even when they weren't singing and just interacting with the audience, they never stopped moving, and they never let the energy lag. They were walking around the stage, reaching out to fans in the front rows, shaking hands, touching fingers as they could. Slowly each of them moved back together.

"Are you having a good time?" Cheongul said, and the crowd screamed, "*Yes!*"

"You love the old stuff?"

"*Yes!*"

"We love the old tracks too," Ki-tae said. "But we've got a surprise for you tonight!"

Behind them a curtain parted to reveal a large video screen, their logo spinning around on it. To the right and left of the stage, more monitors turned on.

"Two months ago BL Entertainment began a two-part scholarship program with Jeonjin University's Digital Media Faculty. Three songs were selected from our albums," HanYin said.

Cheongul continued, "Part one of the program had the students presenting music video concepts for one of those songs. The winning concept would be produced by BL Entertainment."

"Tonight we present to you the winning entry, along with a remix of an old track," Ki-tae said. "Here it is, Korea. 'Crossing Time.'"

"I want to throw up," Jin-woo murmured.

"None of that." Min-su whipped around and rubbed his back. "It's going to be fine."

"People can be assholes," Jin-woo pointed out. "We've seen it before."

"True, but you're going to be fine," she repeated. "Listen. The crowd is singing along with them. They wouldn't do that if they didn't like what was on the screen."

"True."

"Is it the video, or is it the idea you're going to be standing on that stage in about two minutes?"

"Yes," he answered.

"You're not going to be singing, Jin-woo-ya," she said. "All we're going to do is walk out there, smile, wave, and then walk back off-stage."

"I'm sorry you and Jong-in-a didn't get to sing it with them."

"We wouldn't do it without you," she said. "You contributed just as much, if not more than we did."

"Still."

"Jin-woo-ya, stop it, or I'm going to smack you."

"Okay."

Jong-in arrived just as Cheongul came to their side of the stage. He extended his hand to Min-su. She smiled and took it. Ki-tae just grabbed Jin-woo's hand without preamble. There was a moment's hesitation before HanYin offered his hand to Jong-in.

"Hey, Korea!" Cheongul said. "Did you like it?"

The screaming rose.

"Let us introduce the people who brought you that amazing video," Cheongul said. "This is Min-su-ya."

"Jin-woo-ya," Ki-tae said, holding up Jin-woo's hand. He tried to pull it down, shooting Ki-tae a look. He waved with his other hand, hoping his smile didn't look as strained as it felt.

"And Jong-in-a," HanYin said, throwing his arm around Jong-in's shoulders just as he would with Ki-tae or Cheongul.

"They brought this concept from beginning to end," Cheongul said. "We had a blast filming it, although I'll admit, not a big fan of wigs!"

Ki-tae laughed. "He kept having to blow strands out of his face!"

"HanYin was the most comfortable!" Cheongul said. HanYin just smiled and shrugged, that sweet expression on his face, and the crowd started chanting his name.

Jin-woo listened to the banter and smiled. This was typical Bam Kiseu. Finally they were released and returned backstage. Once he was out of the spotlight, his body relaxed. He'd probably have a headache tomorrow, but if it held off until then, he was good. Then the music played, and he froze once more. Ki-tae's voice rose in his smooth baritone.

You don't know me, but I see you.
You don't see me, but I'm always near,
Watching over you from the shadows,
Keeping you from harm.
In the night, I am sleepless.
In the daylight, I am hollow.
But still you draw me to you,
You give me hope for more.

It was his song. The one he'd written about Ki-tae. He couldn't bring himself to turn around. The rational part of him knew Ki-tae was going to hear the song. Hell, Ki-tae was going to perform the song, but the other part of him appeared to be in denial. They hadn't talked about his song at all. Now he was hearing HanYin's sweet tenor singing his point of view, and he was frozen.

I could stand in front of you,
But you would not see me.
One face among hundreds,
Nothing to set me apart,
Nothing to draw your eye.
But still I will protect you,
You're the owner of my heart.

A part of him had yearned for that, something to set him apart from the sea of faces Ki-tae saw at every concert. He wanted to be the one to catch his eye. He never thought such a thing was possible. Now he was living it, and it still felt like a dream. Being here, being with Ki-tae, it was all surreal. The bridge flowed effortlessly into the last verse and final chorus. They harmonized so beautifully. Jin-woo wiped his cheek, feeling wetness on his fingers. He wished he were strong enough to sing this song with Ki-tae. But it was HanYin singing his words, baring his heart to Ki-tae.

Do you see me, hunting through the night?
Do you hear me, offering my heart?
I am not what they think.
I am more than they believe.
I am the shadow that follows you,
The beast that guards you.
I am what they fear, do you see me?
I'm the one who holds you gently,
And sings you to sleep.
I am the light to lead your way,
If only you would see me.

Would he ever be able to sing in front of someone again?

KI-TAE

KI-TAE STRUGGLED to keep his voice even as he sang. These were Jin-woo's words, and he wanted to hear them in Jin-woo's voice live. He stared out over the crowd, seeing more than one fan wiping tears from their eyes. He tried to put as much emotion into it as he could. He wasn't quite sure how Jin-woo had figured out some of his feelings, but they were in that song. Perhaps it was the connection between them that allowed such an insight into Ki-tae's thoughts. Either way, it made this duet beautiful and touching. Jin-woo was his light.

When they finished, the hall was silent. For the first time, the crowd was not screaming or chanting. It was as if they had all lost their voices. It was intense and nerve-racking. Yet he couldn't think of anything to say to bring the crowd back up. It started out so slow he almost didn't catch it. The roaring of the crowd built up into a great wave of sound as they cheered riotously. They loved it!

Riding that wave, Cheongul moved forward. He joined them, and the first verse of "Caught Me" filled the hall.

Ki-tae and HanYin slipped to the back, coming in only on the chorus. From there they slid into "Sweet Angel" and then "Knew You Were Bad." The energy rose back up, and the crowd bounced in their seats, lights waving, hands in the air, singing along with the ones they knew. Ki-tae loved to see them get so energized. When they were in the United States, it was so different. The audiences there did not stand still. They got up out of their seats. Some were dancing in the aisles. They moved and screamed and chanted. But Korea, there was a different energy here. He felt it every time he stepped onstage.

When they left the stage for a set and costume change, Ki-tae searched for Jin-woo. He found him tucked in a corner, his arms wrapped around his torso, his head down. Ki-tae approached him slowly, not sure what he was going to do. Gently he tucked his finger under Jin-woo's chin and lifted his face until he could see his eyes. He smiled and then slowly leaned forward and placed his lips against Jin-woo's, feeling the soft sigh that escaped him.

"It was beautiful," he said quietly against his lips. "And I loved singing it for you."

"I... I wish I could have sung it with you, but...."

"Shhh, Jin-woo," he said, pulling back slightly. "Someday you will sing it with me."

"I don't know if I'll ever be able to sing in front of anyone again."

"Then I'll sing it to you." Ki-tae smiled. "I don't have your vocal range, but I'll do my best."

"Ki-tae dongsaeng," Seung-gi said softly. When Ki-tae looked at him, he seemed to be upset at having to pull Ki-tae away. "Set change is almost complete. You have to change."

Ki-tae nodded and turned back to Jin-woo. "Tonight I want you in my arms. I don't want to sleep without you again."

Jin-woo nodded.

Not even a minute later, Ki-tae was running out onstage once more, clad in red and gold as he launched into "Phoenix Rising." He had written the song after a particularly bad patch. He'd just started going to therapy sessions. While he had to hide certain details about his... experience, such as the actual time frame, he was able to start talking about it the tiniest bit. That didn't last long. He'd felt as if he was being reborn, just as the phoenix died and yet gave life back to itself.

He never stood still on the stage. He ran from one edge to the other. HanYin and he passed each other, pausing to grab each other's hand and bump shoulders. HanYin was clad in black and white, and he'd follow this song with "Call the Dragon." Cheongul would finish the set with "Tiger Pride." They never managed to write the fourth song for this set. The words hadn't come to them yet, but eventually they would.

There was a loud groan of protesting metal and then the screech of it tearing. The shove came out of nowhere, knocking Ki-tae across the stage. He landed hard on his left shoulder and slid another few feet until he almost went over the edge. He turned just in time to see HanYin get hit by the truss swinging down from above, a deadly pendulum slicing through the air, sending him spinning. The smell of blood flooded the air. Vampire blood.

JONG-IN

JONG-IN FLEW out of the backstage area across the stage, screaming, "HanYin!"

He slid the last few feet on his knees as he reached the unmoving body. Touching his back, Jong-in's hand came away bloody, and fear made his gut clench. He shook him.

"HanYin, wake up. Dammit, wake up," he cried, tears streaming down his face. "HanYin."

There was a groan, and Jong-in felt the muscles beneath his hands shift. He helped HanYin roll into a sitting position, his face white and his eyes silver. Jong-in cupped his face, heedless of the blood. He stared into HanYin's eyes and acted before he could think, taking HanYin's mouth is a passionate kiss. When he pulled back, HanYin's eyes were wide with shock. He reached up and caressed Jong-in's cheek.

"I… I thought—" Jong-in couldn't get the words out.

"Jong-in." HanYin's voice was a growl punctuated by another groan and screech of metal.

"Get him off the stage!" Cheongul shouted as he dodged debris. "It's coming down!"

He reached Ki-tae at the same time, dragging him from the stage. HanYin spun Jong-in around and covered his body with his own as the truss broke free, the last bolts unable to hold the full weight of the lights. They shattered against the stage, glass and filaments and metal shards shooting in all directions. Screams filled the air; chaos reigned. Security scrambled to get the musicians and fans to safety. He could hear Min-su's voice rising above all the others, screaming his name.

"We have to move." HanYin's voice was guttural, making Jong-in look at him. His fangs were fully extended. "Now."

"Then move, dumbass!" Jong-in snarled. "I'm fine. You're the one that's injured!"

"You're the only thing keeping me from losing my shit," HanYin said. "Don't let go of me."

"Never."

CHEONGUL

"MOVE, MOVE, move!" Seung-gi yelled, coordinating the evacuation of the technicians. "I want everyone out of this area until we know if the rest is going to come down! I want a list of every single person who was up in that rigging, and I want it fucking yesterday!"

"Status," Shin-bai barked as Kyung-soo, his second, appeared at his side.

"Security Team C is managing the evacuation of the fans farther away from the stage, but the crowd is panicked, hampering efforts to get them out safely. Team B is administering medical aid to those caught by the first break, and Team D is with those caught in the last fall. First responders are already on their way. Team A has evacuated all the musicians. They're accounted for and secured in the VIP room."

"Get me a status on HanYin dongsaeng and Jong-in dongsaeng. I want this place on lockdown now," Shin-bai said. "What's Cheongul dongsaeng's and Ki-tae dongsaeng's status?"

"Unknown. Cheongul dongsaeng pulled him from the stage on the other side."

"Unacceptable! You find them now!" Shin-bai growled.

"We're here, Shin-bai hyung," Cheongul said.

He struggled with Ki-tae, feeling the trembling in his brother's body. The low growling was not a good sign. He could still smell HanYin's blood in the air and knew there would be no getting through to Ki-tae until he no longer smelled it. A part of him desperately wanted to find HanYin and make sure he was all right. However, HanYin had been moving, so Cheongul had to make do with that for the moment. If he let go of Ki-tae, a lot more blood was going to be spilled on his hunt to find the source.

"Shit," Shin-bai said succinctly. He turned to Kyung-soo. "Get Team B to assist with the evac of the fans. Team D stays with the injured. Work with emergency services when they arrive. Find the head of security and get the footage for every fucking inch of this backstage area. If he gives you any shit, you tell him he'd much rather deal with you than me at this point."

Kyung-soo nodded before turning sharply on his heels to carry out Shin-bai's commands. Cheongul had to admire how efficiently they worked together, but he could do that later. Right now he had to focus on Ki-tae, who was starting to struggle harder.

"There you are!" Min-su's voice was like a balm to his ears, but he really didn't want her around Ki-tae now. She approached quickly, but he held up his hand. "What?"

"It's… not safe." He inclined his head toward Ki-tae, hoping she'd get the message. Min-su raised an eyebrow and then strode forward. Before Cheongul could react, she cocked back her fist and let fly straight into Ki-tae's jaw. His body sagged.

"Now it is. Don't you ever do something like that again! Racing across the stage with shit falling everywhere, scared me near to death, you ass!" she said, punching him in the arm. It was totally out of place, but Cheongul couldn't help his laugh. He leaned forward and kissed her hard before scooping Ki-tae into his arms. "Don't think that gets you out of trouble."

"Of course not," Cheongul said. "We have to get Ki-tae somewhere contained. He's still too close to the stage, and as strong as the scent is, I don't know how long he's going to be out."

"This way, Cheongul dongsaeng," Shin-bai said. "The dressing room is just down this hallway. The musicians are in the VIP room, so this area is clear of non-BLE people."

"Where the hell are Jong-in-a and HanYin-a?" Min-su demanded as they walked. "I saw HanYin-a shove Ki-tae-ya, and then it was all exploding lights and tearing metal. And where the hell is Jin-woo-ya?"

Cheongul froze, dread filling him. "What do you mean, 'Where's Jin-woo-ya'? I thought he was with you. That's where I saw him last."

"One of the techs came over and said something, and then Jin-woo-ya went off with him," Min-su said. Her eyes got wide. "Oh shit."

"Fuck," Cheongul said.

Shin-bai pulled the radio from his waist and starting barking orders. As they continued, four men came up behind them, forming a barrier around them. Shin-bai opened the door to the dressing room and cleared it before he let them inside.

"This building better be sealed up tight! No one leaves without clearance until we locate Jin-woo-ya. Am I clear? No excuses!"

SOON-JOON

SOON-JOON STORMED through BL Entertainment headquarters. It was only through sheer force of will that he maintained his current visage. Hyun-jo silently appeared beside him. "Status?"

"Social media has been flooding with stills, and the video has gone viral within a matter of minutes," Hyun-jo said. "The gossip sites are running with it."

"There's something you're not telling me," Soon-joon said.

"There's been an incident at the concert," Hyun-jo said. "At this time we do not know if it was deliberate, but knowing Seung-gi hubae as we do, I cannot see it as being anything else. Soon-joon, HanYin-a has been injured."

"My HanYin?"

"What?"

The sibilant hiss was something Soon-joon had not heard in many centuries, not since the last time his sire got enraged. He turned to see ChenBao pass through the window in her Dragon form, phasing through the glass. Then she was before them in her human form, barefoot, white eyed, and furious.

"And Ki-tae?" Soon-joon said carefully.

"It is not good," Hyun-jo said. "We need to get to them immediately. Cheongul-a can only do so much with Ki-tae-ya. He's strong, but Ki-tae-ya...."

"And we are still standing here why?" ChenBao demanded.

By the time they reached the hall, he and ChenBao had regained their composure. Police cars and ambulances filled the parking lot. Fans huddled in groups for solace and comfort. ChenBao ignored the police officer guarding the door. He let her pass, but the BLE security guard was not as lax. When he reached to stop her, she simply looked at him, and he moved away.

Once inside, Soon-joon passed her, quickening his pace as he scented HanYin's blood. He followed the trail and found his son sitting with Jong-in, who was pressing his shirt to HanYin's back and side. They had found a small side room. Soon-joon had no idea what it was used for, but it appeared to be perfect for avoiding the human medical personnel. It wouldn't do for them to try to assist HanYin when he was in such a state. The healing sleep would make them panic and he would be rushed to the nearest facility for treatment, and that would lead to a whole other mess of complications. Fortunately, those EMTs, police, and firefighters were distracted by the many other injured people in the main theater. Soon-joon moved closer. HanYin looked incredibly pale. There were tears in his eyes as he looked at Soon-joon.

"*Wǒ shìguòle*, Fùqīn," he said softly. "Dàn wǒ bù zhīdào rúguǒ wǒ chénggōngle."

"Shhh, *wǒ de érzi*," Soon-joon said as he knelt and gently pulled HanYin forward. He hissed at the damage.

"Jiānbǎng suì liè," HanYin said, his voice so tired. "Jǐ gè chuígǔ bèi pòjiě, gǔpén gǔzhé, chāoguò yībǎi gè lièkǒu."

"What is he saying?" Jong-in said.

"He is listing his injuries," Soon-joon said. "We can identify them because of how in tune we are with our qi."

"You have a piece of metal sticking out of your side that you won't let me take out," Jong-in said, his voice shaking. "Don't you dare leave that one out."

"Our medical team is waiting at the backstage entrance," Hyun-jo said. Soon-joon looked at him. "I called while we drove."

"Méiyǒu yīyuàn," HanYin said.

"I know, *Èrzi*, no hospitals."

"You're going to one!" Jong-in said.

"He can't," Soon-joon said. "Not a normal one."

"I didn't think," Jong-in said.

"It is all right, Jong-in-a," Hyun-jo said. "We often do not think when those we love are injured in such a way."

"He'll recover best at home, but he's going to need you to do it, Jong-in-a," ChenBao said softly, laying a gentle hand on his shoulder. It was a direct contrast to the fire in her eyes, but Soon-joon had never known his sire to unleash her fire on someone who did not deserve it, at least as far as she was concerned.

"Anything," Jong-in said without any hesitation.

"We'll take him out in an ambulance to avoid suspicion," Soon-joon said. He reached out and touched his fingers to HanYin's forehead. "Sleep, Wǒ de érzi."

HanYin's eyes slid closed, and he slumped. Soon-joon reached for the shirt, but Hyun-jo stopped him. Soon-joon snapped his head around, almost snarling. Hyun-jo just raised an eyebrow. "Jong-in-a and I will see to HanYin-a. You need to find Ki-tae-ya."

"You are right." Soon-joon sighed. He leaned down and kissed the top of HanYin's head. Then he looked at Jong-in. "Take good care of my son."

"Always," Jong-in responded. Soon-joon liked that answer. It was a very good one.

"Opposite side of the theater," ChenBao said. "Cheongul-a, Min-su-ya, and Shin-bai dongsaeng are with him."

Soon-joon didn't waste any more time on words. He strode in the direction she pointed, a wave of energy flowing before him, pushing people out of his way.

With everything that had been happening since shortly after the concert started, it was too much of a coincidence. No, this was a deliberate attack on his family, and it would not be tolerated. As they approached the other side of the theater, he could hear Shin-bai ordering his men about. Seung-gi was railing at someone. The minute he and ChenBao stepped through the door, all sound stopped. He walked right up to Shin-bai.

"Ki-tae dongsaeng and Cheongul dongsaeng are safe in the dressing room. Min-su-ssi is with them. Ki-tae dongsaeng is currently... sedated," Shin-bai said carefully. Then he looked down. "We have not located HanYin dongsaeng and Jong-in dongsaeng."

"They are secured," Soon-joon said. "Hyun-jo and Jong-in-a are getting HanYin to the ambulance as we speak. What happened?"

"As far as we can tell at this time, the truss supporting the front row of stage lights broke," Shin-bai said.

"Broke my ass!" Seung-gi said as he approached them after shooting a glare at the man he'd been yelling at. "I checked all the trusses myself. They were doubled-checked and triple-checked, as is our standard procedure. When I did my last run-through, they were bolted tight."

"What are you saying, Byun Seung-gi dongsaeng?" ChenBao crossed her arms over her chest.

"I'm saying this was deliberate, Huijang-nim," he said. "Someone tried to kill Ki-tae dongsaeng."

"How do you know Ki-tae dongsaeng was the target?" she asked.

"Because if HanYin dongsaeng hadn't pushed Ki-tae dongsaeng out of the way, the truss would have hit him straight in the chest as he turned for the next step in their choreography. The metal edge of the lights would have hit him in the throat."

"There is something else, Huijang-nim," Shin-bai said.

"And that is?"

"Jin-woo dongsaeng is missing. We suspect he's been taken." Shin-bai hung his head once more.

JIN-WOO

JIN-WOO SHOOK his head with a soft moan. He opened his eyes slowly and looked around the room. It was small, he could tell that much, probably a break room or a meeting room, possibly another dressing room. He reached up to rub the back of his head, only to find he couldn't. What the hell was going on? He struggled against the ropes binding him to the chair.

Jin-woo froze as fingers sifted through his hair. It sent chills down his spine.

Frantically he ran through the last things he remembered. He'd been with Min-su, watching the show. One of the techs had approached him, but not a BLE one; there was no logo on his shirt. Jin-woo cursed silently. He'd been fooled by such a simple thing as a fake phone call.

A monitor flicked on, drawing his eyes. That hand still stroked his hair. Jin-woo's heart froze as he saw the truss fall. The explosion of light blinded the camera for several seconds. When it cleared, Ki-tae was nowhere in sight.

"No," Jin-woo whispered. "No, Ki-tae!"

"Do not say his name!" that voice snarled, strident and high-pitched. Where had he heard it before? He wished he had Jong-in's ear right now. A thin hand grabbed his chin and pushed his head back. Then next thing he knew, his lap was filled with... Mei?

"What. The. Fuck?" he demanded.

"Do not say that name. Ever. Again," she hissed, and he saw the crazy in her eyes but also the cunning. Then her whole demeanor changed. She started pouting, and her eyes got all wide and sad. "I'm afraid I have to punish you now. You didn't obey, and that can't be allowed. But once your punishment is over, we'll be quite happy together. I have the perfect place for us."

"Not. Ever. Going. To. Happen," he said.

She tightened her grip. "Oh, you are a naughty boy, Jin-woo," she giggled. "But I'll fix that, and you'll never be bad again."

"If you've hurt Ki-tae, I swear to God, I will bury you," he promised.

"You will not speak of him! That disgusting, perverted demon, he tried to take you from me," she snarled, digging her nails into his neck. "He wouldn't listen. Twice I warned him away, and he was too stupid to take the hint. He kept sniffing around you as if he had the right to do so. He didn't respect a girl's territory. But it's okay now. He's gone, and it's just you... and me."

She leaned forward, and Jin-woo's stomach roiled and his temper surged. Fuck. This. He leaned back and then snapped his head forward, slamming his forehead into hers, sending her tumbling off his lap onto the floor.

"I would rather die a horrible lingering death than let you kiss me, or do anything else, for that matter. Reality check, bitch. I'm gay!" Jin-woo snapped. "I will never desire you in any way, shape, or form, even if you weren't batshit crazy!"

"Sit here and think on your words," she said coldly as she rose to her feet. "You will regret them."

She walked out the door, and Jin-woo heard the click of the lock. He pulled against the ropes, trying to get his hands free. The words he heard through the door chilled him.

"When there's no one left, you'll love me."

"Oh hell no," he snarled. "I will fucking kill that bitch first!"

KI-TAE

NEED. WANT. Need. Want.

The coppery sweet scent filled his lungs, driving all other thoughts from his head. His body shook. He needed. He wanted. Ki-tae burst into motion, launching himself off the sofa he'd been lying on. Scents swirled around him, so many scents, but not the one he wanted. Not the one he needed.

"Holy shit, he's fast."

The female voice.... No, she wasn't it. Where was it? Find it. Need it.

"Back away, Min-su. You're strong, but Ki-tae, he's not himself right now."

That voice, familiar, but not it. Not the source. There. That way.

"Really? I never would have guessed. What do we do now?"

"Hope Abeoji is on his way. I can't put him to sleep like he can, and Ki-tae and I are evenly matched as far as strength goes, but we have to keep him here."

Want. Need.

"Where's he going to go? It's still chaos out there," she pointed out. Ki-tae zeroed in on her. Red eyes, tiny, strong. He sniffed. Shifter, not it, not the source.

"He'll hunt HanYin down and drain him dry, given half the chance," Cheongul said.

"What?" Min-su's voice rose a full octave.

"Focus, Min-su. If he gets out of this room, more people will be hurt."

Want. Need. Need. Want.

Ki-tae lunged at Min-su, drawing Cheongul away from the door. He shot in the other direction and slammed against the wood. It groaned under the impact but didn't give. Ki-tae roared in frustration. Arms grabbed him from behind. The weight behind him pushed him forward, trying to pin him against the door. He brought his foot up and took the impact before pushing hard, sending him and his attacker flying backward. He rolled with the momentum, tearing out of the restraining grip.

"Nimble little bastard." Min-su growled, and then a full-grown wolf slammed into his chest. He grabbed at the ruff, digging his claws through the fur to the neck. Min-su yelped and jumped away, slicing his shoulder with her claws as she did so.

"Dammit, Ki-tae," Cheongul snarled.

Need. Want.

He launched himself at the door again, satisfaction filling him as it shattered. Ki-tae paused only long enough to get a good sniff. The delicious scent of blood filled his nose, near orgasmic in its sweetness.

"Ki-tae!" The voice was familiar. Warm. Safe.... Need. Want.

"Soon-joon, he does not hear you." That voice, power, threat, danger.

"He hears me but cannot hold the thoughts against the need."

The woman walking toward him smelled of no fear. Ki-tae crouched low, surveying the scene. Three filled the hallway, standing between him and his desires. He snarled, the sound rumbling up from deep within his chest. The female was small, the two men larger, but she radiated power. Ki-tae lunged for her. As he got close, she reached out, and he dropped, sliding between her braced legs, and passed all of them.

"Clever boy, but I don't need to touch you to stop you." The voice slithered through his brain, and his entire body stopped. He couldn't move. Ki-tae struggled. He tried to push forward, moving his foot just the barest of inches forward.

Want. Need.

Blackness claimed him, and he slumped, arms catching him before he could hit the floor. A single word slipped from his lips.

"Jin-woo."

JIN-WOO

JIN-WOO DIDN'T know how long he'd been in the room. Mei hadn't come back, and that scared him a little bit. If she was there, she couldn't be out hurting the people he loved. He was starting to lose hope anyone would find him. He hung his head again, thinking about Ki-tae, his beautiful Ki-tae. His bright smile filled Jin-woo's mind, and the tears slipped down his face. He didn't know if Ki-tae was all right or not, but something told him his Vampire was suffering. Was Ki-tae looking for him? Had Ki-tae been hit by the crashing lights? Was he okay? Was everyone else okay? Not knowing was killing him.

"Cheong Jin-woo dongsaeng? Cheong Jin-woo dongsaeng, can you hear me?" He didn't recognize that voice, but the one after it was beautifully familiar.

"You have keys for these doors, I presume," ChenBao said curtly.

"Here! I'm here! ChenBao-nim!" he yelled, his voice hoarse from the shouting he'd done after Mei left. The sound of running feet was music to his ears. The only thing better would be Ki-tae's voice. He heard the rattling of keys outside the door.

"If you cannot manage the simple task of unlocking a door, perhaps you should hand the keys to someone else," ChenBao said coolly, and Jin-woo could just picture her glaring at the poor person, her arms crossed over her chest, those eyes burning. He felt sorry for the guy.

Finally the door was thrown open, and people rushed into the room. Min-su was the first to reach him, shoving her way past everyone else. She cupped his face.

"Oh my God, Jin-woo-ya! Dammit, you scared the shit out of me too," she snapped, but there were tearstains on her cheeks.

"I didn't mean to. What happened to your neck?" he said softly. She touched their foreheads together. "Where's Ki-tae?"

"He's... he's not good, Jin-woo-ya. He needs you," she whispered.

There was the *snikt* of a blade, and Shin-bai was cutting the ropes free. Jin-woo immediately rubbed his wrists. The skin was red and raw, bloody in some spots from his struggles. Soon his legs and torso were free as well. Jin-woo stumbled as he tried to stand, Cheongul catching him easily, Min-su on his other side.

"Take me to Ki-tae," he said—demanded, really. "How badly is he injured?"

"Physically Ki-tae is fine," Cheongul said, his voice low. Jin-woo was reminded they were not necessarily free to talk. "He's having a hard time with what happened. HanYin was injured, but he's being tended to as we speak. How in the hell did you end up here?"

"You're not going to believe me," Jin-woo said.

"Try me, and let me tell you, whoever did this is going to wish they never messed with my family," Min-su said.

ChenBao chuckled. "A girl after my own heart. I like you."

Min-su smiled wickedly. Jin-woo didn't like the fact that they were both smiling the same smile, but he couldn't focus on that right now. He wanted out of that hall and into Ki-tae's arms. Someone had better make that happen—fast.

Shin-bai and his team surrounded them, leading them through the emergency medical teams and technicians. It felt as if Jin-woo couldn't walk another step. He sagged against Cheongul.

"I'm so tired," he whispered.

"I know, Jin-woo-ya," Cheongul murmured before scooping him up in his arms. "Rest. We'll get you to Ki-tae."

He must have slept, because the next time Jin-woo opened his eyes, Cheongul was lifting him out of the car. He thought about telling him he could walk, but it was too much effort. He laid his head against Cheongul's shoulder. Why was he so tired? It's not as if he had been able to do anything, tied to a freaking chair. It just didn't make sense. Jin-woo closed his eyes again, dozing.

When he came to again, Jin-woo was tucked in Ki-tae's bed, but Ki-tae wasn't with him. He sat up, rubbing his face with his hands. Ki-tae's scent filled his nose, and Jin-woo sighed. As good as it felt to be here, it wasn't good enough. Jin-woo threw back the covers and padded, barefoot, out of the room. He heard the murmur of voices and followed them until he reached the kitchen.

Soon-joon was at the stove making… something. He was very focused, and for the first time ever, Hyun-jo, sitting on one of the stools at the island, looked worried. This was not how things were supposed to be. Jin-woo looked around. He spotted ChenBao sitting outside by the Zen rock garden. Min-su was curled up on the couch with Cheongul, her head pillowed against his chest as he ran his fingers through her hair. No, this was not acceptable, and where were Jong-in and HanYin?

"Okay," Jin-woo said, putting his hands on his hips. "This is not how things are supposed to be. Jong-in-a and HanYin-a are missing, and where the hell is Ki-tae?"

"He's feeling better if he's getting twisted," Min-su said, her tone filled with relief. She wiped her cheeks, and Jin-woo knew she'd been crying again.

"Jong-in and HanYin are safe." Soon-joon's voice was… subdued. That was the only way to describe his tone, but his eyes kept flickering from brown to gold and back again. He was holding on by a thread, and it looked as if he wasn't even letting Hyun-jo near him. He just kept making plate after plate after plate of food. He put one in front of Hyun-jo and then set a second in front of an empty chair. Jin-woo felt his look stab through him as Soon-joon leveled that flashing gaze at him. "Sit down and eat."

"I'm not—"

"Jin-woo-ya," Cheongul interrupted.

When Jin-woo looked over, Cheongul just shook his head. Now was not the time to challenge Soon-joon. Without another word Jin-woo crossed the room, sat down, and began to eat. Soon-joon nodded. He shot one of those looks at Hyun-jo, who was merely staring at his food. When Hyun-jo looked up, Soon-joon nodded toward his plate as well and, surprisingly, Hyun-jo began to eat.

"You haven't said if Ki-tae is safe," Jin-woo said quietly.

"Ki-tae-ya is... contained, for the moment," Hyun-jo said softly. "You can't smell it, but HanYin-a's blood scent is heavy in the air. The amount of damage he sustained should take the better part of two days to heal. His body will start with the bones and internal damage first, so we've bandaged his open wounds as best we can. The problem lies in they are still open, and since he refuses to take blood, this makes it impossible for the scent to dissipate or for the healing to progress any faster."

"I still don't understand," Jin-woo said. "What does that have to do with Ki-tae?"

"Ki-tae is, for all intents and purposes, a recovering addict, Jin-woo-ya." Cheongul sighed, leaning his head back and closing his eyes. "Ki-tae used to struggle with even the most minor injuries, but as the years have passed, he has gotten much better at resisting and even ignoring them. What HanYin suffered today wasn't a small injury. With the scent of HanYin's blood saturating the hall and now here, it's too much too fast, and Ki-tae was in no condition to resist when all this fucking started."

"Cheongul," Min-su said, stroking his arm. He seemed to calm beneath her touch.

"I'm sorry. I just.... My brothers are suffering, and I can't fucking help them!" Cheongul snarled. "And in the process, you got hurt."

"I'm fine. It was just a little scratch," she reassured him, pushing her hair to one side and showing her neck. "See? All better."

"Still." He pulled her tight against his chest.

"Are you telling me Ki-tae would hurt HanYin-a?" Jin-woo whispered.

"Yes," Hyun-jo said. "His sole goal would be to get that blood, to consume it. He would hunt HanYin-a until he had drunk his fill. Addiction to Vampire blood is an all-consuming desire for the source. All the addict can think about is that person, the next sip, the next taste. They lose all sense of self."

"There is hope, however," ChenBao said as she closed the sliding door behind her. She walked over to the island and took a plate, then started nibbling the food almost delicately.

"Is there?" Soon-joon said. "I have never seen Ki-tae like this. He has never lost himself this completely in the desire for blood, not since the very first. He has always fought against it, always."

"Of course there is hope, my family," ChenBao said, and then she turned to look a Jin-woo. "You are our hope."

"What?"

"The last word Ki-tae-ya spoke before I put him to sleep was *your* name, Jin-woo-ya," she said. "There is potential in that."

"When can I see him?" Jin-woo felt the urgency building within him. He bounced his leg, and his fingers itched for a pencil or something, anything to occupy them. Soon-joon tapped his plate with a spoon.

"I will take you to him after you have eaten," Soon-joon said.

"Before we get on to that, there's one thing I want to know," Min-su said. "What in the hell happened? One minute everything was going great, the next, it's chaos. I mean, I know the lighting truss broke, but what the heck happened?"

"According to Seung-gi hubae, the truss did not simply break," ChenBao said. "It was sabotaged."

"Someone tried to kill my son," Soon-joon growled. "That is all I need to know."

"But who? Who would do something so... horrible?" Min-su asked.

"Mei," Jin-woo said quietly. "It was Mei."

SALVAGEABLE. THIS was salvageable. It might take another day or two, but she could work with this. Mei paced back and forth in her bedroom. The overturned lamp shone like a spotlight on her movements. She kicked the torn sketchbooks out of her way, sending paper flying like confetti. How could her sweet Jin-woo draw that.... She didn't even have a horrible enough word to describe Ki-tae. No, he was gone. She didn't have to worry about him anymore. All she had to do was get rid of Min-su and Jong-in, and then she would have Jin-woo all to herself. He would never leave her, never reject her, and he would be so good, so very, very good.

Mei turned toward her map and began removing pins, throwing them carelessly to the floor. She didn't need them anymore. There would be no more concerts for Bam Kiseu. They were ruined. No one would want to see such trash. Jin-woo would be happy with her now that *he* was gone. They'd move somewhere quiet, away from people. They would have many children, and he would draw only her, sing only for her and no one else.

But... Min-su and Jong-in had to go first. They could not be allowed to stand in her way, to take Jin-woo's attention from her.

Mei giggled and flung herself onto her bed, rolling until she could kiss the picture of Jin-woo that hung right next to her pillow. She looked up, her eyes jumping from picture to picture to picture. Jin-woo was the most beautiful person in the world. Oh, how she had loved taking his picture, following him, seeing all the things he liked. She accidently bumped the table at the foot of her bed, rattling all her tokens of Jin-woo. His pencil nubs, several pens, a can of his favorite drink, and a plate of his favorite cookies, all of them sat on the table in precise order, never shifted, never moving, the perfect shrine to her Jin-woo.

Suddenly Mei sat up. She hadn't been able to get Jin-woo out of the theater. She had to leave him there, and she knew they had stolen him from her. How to get him back? How long would they hide him? They couldn't conceal him forever. Eventually they would have to bring him out to deal with the social media storm she'd created. It was too bad her beloved Jin-woo would get caught up in that, but he *had* been naughty. Mei rubbed her forehead. Just like he'd been naughty in the storage room. That was not a nice thing to do to his beloved. She would have to devise an appropriate punishment for that, nothing too serious. He was her perfect man, after all, but something would need to be done.

Mei pulled on the sweatshirt he'd left behind in class one day, curling up in it. She sighed as she fell into an agitated sleep. "Naughty Jin-woo, you're only for me."

JONG-IN

JONG-IN OPENED his eyes slowly. He blinked a few times and then sighed. HanYin lay on the pillow next to him, his eyes still closed. His breathing was steady, though, so that was a good sign. He only wished HanYin weren't being stubborn about taking his blood. Hyun-jo had said he would heal faster if he drank, but the stupid man refused to take it from Jong-in. He hadn't given Jong-in a good reason why. As he noted the dark circles and the tight lines around HanYin's mouth, Jong-in resolved not to allow him to refuse much longer. Clearly going without was making it harder for him to heal, and Jong-in was so done with that.

He had fallen asleep shortly after HanYin slipped into his healing state. Hyun-jo had entreated him to come out of the room, but he refused. He wasn't going to leave HanYin to deal with this by himself. Besides, he was tougher than he looked. The next time HanYin woke, they were going to have a serious talk about this not-taking-blood-when-he-needed-it thing.

"You're frowning." HanYin's voice sounded so weak, but to hear it was the sweetest music.

"Of course I am. You're still being a dumbass." Jong-in snorted.

"Don't want to hurt you."

"Then don't," Jong-in said with a shrug. "If Jin-woo-ya is anything to go by, it doesn't have to hurt."

"I...."

"HanYin, what are you afraid of?" Jong-in demanded.

"I'm not afraid."

"Bullshit."

"You hang around Min-su-ya too much. Picking up her language," HanYin grumbled, wincing as he shifted on his stomach.

"I'll take that as a compliment and *not* tell her you said that, and that was a very poor distraction attempt." Jong-in scooted closer until their faces were barely inches apart. "You're in no condition to make love with me as you take my blood, but you're conscious, so you can feed and heal. Please, HanYin, it's killing me to see you like this."

"Stubborn Fox," HanYin muttered, but he shifted slowly until he could take Jong-in's proffered wrist. Jong-in shivered as HanYin brushed his mouth over the sensitive skin. His breath was hot, teasing, sending darts of pleasure racing straight to Jong-in's groin. And then he slowly sank those fangs into his flesh.

"Oh shit," Jong-in moaned as the darts became waves. He was hard in seconds and moving restlessly on the bed.

Still HanYin continued to feed, and it was the most erotic sight Jong-in had ever seen. He moved closer, pressing the length of his body along HanYin's uninjured side, careful not to jostle him too much. HanYin glanced at him with silver eyes before closing them once more, and Jong-in whimpered. He wished he were buried deep inside HanYin, bringing him as much pleasure as Jong-in was experiencing at this very moment.

Finally HanYin withdrew his fangs and delicately licked at the wounds. He looked at Jong-in, a small smile on his face before he slipped into the healing sleep once more. Carefully Jong-in maneuvered until HanYin's head was on his chest. He gently stroked his hair. He was never letting him go, ever.

SOON-JOON

SOON-JOON STOOD over the sink, washing the dishes, his mind carefully blank. If he thought about everything that had happened today, he would destroy his surroundings. The rage within him was nothing compared to the pain of seeing his sons hurting. He couldn't even begin to think about how to handle the mess those photos and video were causing. More importantly, how was he going to protect his sons and the people they loved from someone he knew nothing about? He had made a mistake in thinking Jin-woo's stalker and the threats to Ki-tae were unrelated. He should have known better and acted accordingly. He should have....

Gentle hands touched his, stopping his movements. He stared at them for a moment. Long, elegant fingers, fine-boned but strong, impeccably maintained. He looked into Hyun-jo's eyes.

"You've washed the same plate three times now," he said as he pulled Soon-joon's hands away from the sink. He put the plate in the drainer and then grabbed the dish towel, drying Soon-joon's hands. Hyun-jo pulled him from the kitchen and into the living room. Soon-joon allowed himself to be pushed into a chair and Hyun-jo to settle in his lap.

"I don't mean to push," Jin-woo said as he came into the living room. "No, that's not true. I do mean to push, but you said after I ate, you would take me to Ki-tae."

"I did." Soon-joon sighed.

He patted Hyun-jo's hip to get him to move, earning a pout. When he was able to rise, he gestured for Jin-woo to follow him down the hallway. He turned in the direction of Ki-tae's room. When he glanced back, he saw the confused look on Jin-woo's face.

"He wasn't in his room."

"No, he wasn't," Soon-joon said. He touched the top of the wooden panel across from Ki-tae's door, and it slid open silently. "He was underneath it."

"I don't know whether to be amazed or creeped out," Jin-woo said.

"It is a necessity," Soon-joon said with a sigh. He seemed to be doing that a lot. "Well, more precautionary than anything else. We haven't had to use it in quite some time."

"He's... he's okay?"

"Yes and no," Soon-joon said as he led the way down the steps. "He is not injured physically, but the blow to his self-esteem, to his mind, it will be devastating to him. He will not like knowing he hurt Min-su-ya and fought with Cheongul. He will not like knowing he was a danger to HanYin."

"So why tell him?"

"Because we try not to keep those kinds of secrets from each other," Soon-joon said. He punched a code into the panel next to the second door. "It would only add to his distress. He would feel as if we betrayed his trust, and I will not do that to him."

"I guess I can understand that," Jin-woo said. "It's so you don't add that pain on top of whatever it was to begin with."

"And there will be further stress to come. The attack at the concert was not the only strike against this family," Soon-joon said softly.

"I don't like the sound of that, but it's going to have to wait," Jin-woo said as the door slid open. "It's so bare."

"This is not a room to be comfortable in," Soon-joon said. "We keep the furniture sparse because when it is used, things are usually destroyed."

"I guess that makes sense too. I don't like the idea of him in here, though."

"Neither do I, Jin-woo-ya. Neither do I," Soon-joon said.

When he returned to the living room, it was to find only ChenBao and Hyun-jo remained. He returned to his seat, but Hyun-jo didn't join him.

"We're going to have to address this second attack at some point," ChenBao said.

"It cannot be tonight," Soon-joon said. "HanYin has not recovered, and you still have Ki-tae in stasis. Jin-woo-ya is with him now. It will not do much good if they cannot speak to one another."

"It is already done," ChenBao said, her eyes flashing white. "Still, this media attack is serious. This country is not quite ready to accept their idols may be attracted to the same gender, and Jin-woo-ya is caught up in it. His academic career is in jeopardy."

"As is Jong-in's," Hyun-jo added. "Although that was not so much an attack as a sign of relief."

Soon-joon looked at him, raising an eyebrow. Sometimes Hyun-jo liked to keep his little gems until the last possible moment.

"He kissed HanYin right onstage."

"Oh dear." ChenBao giggled. "Well, there's really no spinning that, and I really don't think we should try."

"No, it would be incredibly difficult and I don't think it would be right," Soon-joon said. "As for their academic careers, I would like to think Jeonjin University would not penalize them for this. It may not be a realistic thought, but it is a thought nonetheless. If the worst-case scenario happens in that corner, they will not have to worry. There is a place for both Jin-woo-ya and Jong-in-a, as well as Min-su, at BL Entertainment."

"Agreed."

"Enough for now," Hyun-jo said firmly, looking at them. "For tonight we focus on the healing of our family. Tomorrow we will face the threat to the company."

"Agreed," ChenBao said. She rose gracefully. Soon-joon smiled as she placed a kiss on his forehead, as she had done every day they were together since he was a small child. She did the same to Hyun-jo, ruffling his hair.

Then it was just him and Hyun-jo. Soon-joon studied him. Since his declaration, Hyun-jo had not returned to his own apartment to sleep. He had not taken one of the guest beds. And he had not allowed Soon-joon to feed from his wrist. In response, Soon-joon had simply not fed from him. He did not care for people telling him what he would or would not do.

"Shall we retire?" Hyun-jo asked as he rose from the couch.

Soon-joon continued to study him. He had lost his heart to Hyun-jo long ago. Hyun-jo had loved him, had stayed by his side for over a thousand years. Even after Soon-joon sent him away, Hyun-jo had not left him. He still did not feel worthy of the sacrifices Hyun-jo had made for him. To lose his clan, his family, and spend two hundred years powerless was too much to give. And yet Hyun-jo gave it without reservation. Was his guilt worth holding on to when it kept him from the man he loved? Perhaps it was time to let it go.

Soon-joon led the way to his room. He paused at the foot of the bed as Hyun-jo closed the door behind them. Keeping his gaze steady, Soon-joon slowly unbuttoned his shirt, then tugged it from his jeans. He slid it off his shoulders and let it fall to the floor. He never took his eyes off Hyun-jo, noted all the subtle shifts of his facial expression as Soon-joon removed everything. He caught the quickening of his breath, the shifting of his eyes from a beautiful brown to the gorgeous lavender, and the whitening and lengthening of his hair. Then he turned to face Hyun-jo, not hiding his erection. Still Soon-joon said nothing.

"*Saiai*," Hyun-jo whispered.

Soon-joon crossed the room in a blink and buried his fingers in the hair at the back of Hyun-jo's neck, yanking him forward to claim his mouth. He thrust his tongue deep, growling at the first true taste of his love after so many years.

In seconds he was as naked as Soon-joon. Soon-joon didn't let go as he maneuvered them onto the platform bed, kicking the blankets off in their haste. They writhed and twined together, touching every inch of skin they could reach. Soon-joon hissed as Hyun-jo dragged his claws down his back, bucking his hips forward. He grabbed Hyun-jo's hands and pinned them above his head with one of his own. He used his leg to spread Hyun-jo's thighs wider, giving him access to all the wonderfully sensitive areas between them. He reached for the lube in his nightstand and then set to the delicious task of preparing Hyun-jo. Soon-joon smiled at the little whimpers, moans, and yips that filled the room. He remembered those sounds, had loved them so long ago and still adored them now.

As much as he wanted to draw out the pleasure for Hyun-jo, Soon-joon needed to be inside him, needed to be one with him, to feel that connection solidify between them. He replaced his fingers with his hard shaft, pushing forward just the way he knew Hyun-jo liked, and the high-pitched cry confirmed his little Fox still loved to feel the slow stretch of his cock sliding inside him. "So tight, so hot, I love the way you feel around me."

"Soon-joon," Hyun-jo whimpered as he wrapped his legs around his waist.

He tugged at his hands, but Soon-joon would not let them go. He held them with both hands, staring into Hyun-jo's eyes as he slowly made love to him, each thrust a lingering invasion that only pushed the pleasure higher, increased the tension in every muscle. Yet he was the one brought to ruin when Hyun-jo turned his head to the right, offering his throat, offering blood straight from his heart, offering the chance of a deeper bond with him.

He placed his lips against his neck, brushing them back and forth as he spoke. "Are you sure, *watashi no kokoro*? It will be forever."

"Saiai, I have already given you over a millennium. How much longer are you going to doubt my love and devotion to you?" Hyun-jo said, his eyes glistening.

There was only one way to answer that question.

He gently pierced the skin, the rush of Hyun-jo's blood into his mouth heightening the pleasure of being buried deep within his body. He released Hyun-jo's hands and slid his arms beneath his back, lifting until he could sit back on his heels, driving his shaft deeper, and Hyun-jo cried out, clenching around him. Without conscious thought, Soon-joon moved his body to match the pull on Hyun-jo's neck. Hyun-jo dug his claws into his back and then clamped his sharp fangs onto his shoulder. He felt the magic surge across his skin, Hyun-jo's white-blue fox-fire searing his flesh, not with pain but with pleasure. Joy as he had never experienced before filled him. He would carry Hyun-jo's seal forever. Tears slid down his cheeks even as he pulled back and licked the wounds left by his fangs. He clasped Hyun-jo tightly to him, increasing the speed of his thrusting as he felt the trembling in Hyun-jo's body. His little Fox was close, and Soon-joon would have him reach his pleasure first.

He whispered into one delicate furry ear, "Cum for me."

Hyun-jo tossed his head back, his fangs glistening with Soon-joon's blood, so erotic, so intimate. He cried out, spilling between them, clamping around Soon-joon's cock. He followed Hyun-jo. He held on tightly, burying his face against Hyun-jo's neck as he came, filling that tight passage with his seed.

They collapsed against the bed, falling to the side as Soon-joon turned them. He remembered Hyun-jo didn't like lying on his tails. Yet he didn't release him either. They snuggled together, heedless of the mess, and Hyun-jo's little sigh sounded so content.

"*Aishiteimasu*, Hyun-jo," Soon-joon whispered. How long had it been since he last said those words? By the tears in Hyun-jo's eyes, it had been too long.

"*Shitteiru*." Hyun-jo smiled even as he wiped the tears away.

JIN-WOO

JIN-WOO STOOD by the door for several minutes after Soon-joon left. He wasn't sure how to begin. A part of him wanted to rush over to Ki-tae. He looked around the sparse room. There was a platform bed with a thick, solid base along the far wall. He slowly moved closer, and as he did so, Jin-woo noticed there were eyebolts sticking out of the end of the platform. Were they… what he thought they were? Secure points for chains? When he was close enough to touch the bed, Jin-woo saw he was, indeed, correct. There were two more at the head of the bed. Soon-joon hadn't been lying when he said this room wasn't for comfort, but rather containment, and it hurt Jin-woo's heart to think Ki-tae might have needed to be restrained so.

Sitting down on the end of the bed, Jin-woo studied Ki-tae's face. He could see the rapid movement of his eyes and knew Ki-tae was dreaming, but what was he dreaming of? He moved closer, climbing onto the bed and curling up next to Ki-tae, laying his head on Ki-tae's chest. Jin-woo listened to the steady beat of his heart, and it soothed him. Ki-tae wasn't dead, and that was all that mattered. Everything else they would deal with together. But he wanted Ki-tae to wake up. Jin-woo shifted until he straddled Ki-tae's hips. Leaning forward, he brushed Ki-tae's bangs off his forehead and then kissed him gently.

"Come back to me," he whispered against Ki-tae's lips before sitting back up.

Slowly Ki-tae's eyelids fluttered and then opened. They were silver, and Jin-woo held perfectly still. The next thing he knew, Ki-tae was hugging him tightly, and his shoulders shook. Wetness splashed against his neck where Ki-tae's face was buried, and Jin-woo's heart broke. Silent tears, silent sobs. There was no need to tell Ki-tae what happened. He already knew.

"Shhh," Jin-woo murmured, resting his head against Ki-tae's hair as he rubbed his back. "It's going to be okay. Everything will be fine."

"I hurt Min-su-ya," Ki-tae said. "I would… I would have…. HanYin."

"But you didn't," Jin-woo pointed out.

"I lost myself again," Ki-tae said. "There was nothing of me left but the need. It took over, that need, that insatiable need. If not for ChenBao-nim, I would have hurt anyone who got in my way. I would have… killed my brother."

"I can't begin to understand what it's like to live with such an addiction," Jin-woo said. "And I have no words to make your pain go away, although I wish with all my heart I did. I can only be here with you, hold you, and love you, and hope that's enough."

"I don't deserve you," Ki-tae whispered. "I don't deserve any of them. I'm a danger to them always."

"You *do* deserve us. You deserve to be loved." Jin-woo pulled Ki-tae's face away from his neck and made Ki-tae look him in the eye. "They are your family, and they love you. I love you."

"I am a monster," Ki-tae said. "You... you should...."

"If you tell me to leave, I'm going to smack you," Jin-woo growled. "I am never leaving you, Ki-tae."

"You're human, Jin-woo," Ki-tae said. "You will leave me eventually, whether you want to or not."

"We'll see about that," Jin-woo said softly. "Are you feeling up to getting out of this cage?"

"I haven't had to be in here for more than 180 years," Ki-tae said. "It is the only room in this house I hate because it means I've failed to win against my addiction again."

"You may be a Vampire, Ki-tae, but you're not perfect. There are going to be times when you succeed and times when you won't, but as long as you never stop trying, you can never truly fail."

"Such wisdom out of one so young," Ki-tae said, his chuckle lacking true warmth.

"Wisdom isn't exclusively the domain of the aged. It is a matter of experience and the things we've learned in the time we've been alive," Jin-woo said. "Now Soon-joon-nim locked the door behind me, and I don't know the code to get out. So how do we go about doing that? I'm not keen on the atmosphere in here."

"What...." Ki-tae paused and took a deep breath before trying again. "How badly... hurt was HanYin?"

"Well, as it was explained to me, he's been in that healing sleep you guys do, but because he refused to feed, the process is slow going. They tell me his scent is still in the air pretty heavily."

"Then I cannot leave just yet," Ki-tae said, putting his head back down on Jin-woo's shoulder.

"Would you like me to take your mind off things?" Jin-woo said, shifting slowly.

"I...." Ki-tae sighed. "Could we... could we just hold each other... for a little while?"

Jin-woo's heart clenched, and he hugged Ki-tae to him, kissing his hair. Then he pushed Ki-tae back down on the bed before shifting to lie on his back, and then he pulled Ki-tae to him, holding him as tightly as before. "Of course we can."

"It's not that I don't want you," Ki-tae insisted, trying to lift his head from Jin-woo's chest, but Jin-woo wasn't having it.

"I know that, Ki-tae," Jin-woo said softly. "But right now you don't need or want sex, and that's fine. Right now you need me to be the strong one, and so I'm going to be whatever you need me to be."

HANYIN

BY THE next morning, HanYin was completely healed, mainly because Jong-in guilt-tripped him into feeding whenever he woke. He had to smile at how persistent Jong-in was. It seemed once his man made up his mind about something, he charged full speed ahead, and damn anyone who got in his way. Still, looking at him now, sleeping in his bed, HanYin couldn't complain. He looked so sweet, so innocent, his dimples peeking out whenever his mouth shifted. They really were killer.

He reached out and brushed Jong-in's bangs. His little Fox was tired, and he would be hungry when he woke up. He had fed HanYin several times during the night. Now it was HanYin's turn. He slid out of the bed, careful not to wake Jong-in, and pulled on a pair of sleep pants. He closed the door quietly behind him and padded to the kitchen.

His mind still back in his bedroom, HanYin collided with a solid mass. Looking up, he caught the panicked look in Ki-tae's eyes just before his little brother tried to dart away. Always the faster of the two, HanYin reached out, grabbing Ki-tae's arm. He yanked hard, pulling Ki-tae to him, and hugged him tightly. Tears of relief streamed down his face as he held his baby brother. Ki-tae was stiff in his arms, but he could feel the fine trembling of his body.

"I'm so glad you're okay," HanYin whispered. "I thought…."

"How can you bear to touch me?" Ki-tae's voice was so soft HanYin almost didn't hear him. But he did hear him and only held him tighter. "If not for Cheongul, I would have…. I would have hurt you so bad, HanYin."

"You're my brother. I will always look out for you. I will always protect you. I will always be willing and ready to give my last breath to keep you safe," HanYin said, his voice strong, determined. "I love you. Nothing will change that—nothing."

Finally Ki-tae relaxed his entire body, and he wrapped his arms around HanYin's waist, squeezing tight. Though there was no sound, HanYin could feel his tears, feel the sobs shaking him. HanYin had never had an addiction, never knew the lengths the need would drive a person to, and he didn't have to know it. He saw what it did to Ki-tae anytime he lost control, anytime he had to fight that need. This time it was much worse because there was no struggle beforehand. HanYin may not have been conscious, but he knew how hurt he'd been, knew how strongly the coppery sweet scent of his blood had hung in the air, both in the theater and here in the house.

Finally they parted, and Ki-tae looked at him. HanYin smiled, and then, as he'd always done, reached out and brushed the tears from Ki-tae's cheeks with his thumbs. He put his arm around Ki-tae's shoulders, and they headed to the kitchen. Without a word, HanYin made Ki-tae sit in one of the island chairs and then began breakfast. He placed plate after plate in front of Ki-tae, smiling as he dug into the food. It was a common thing when Ki-tae first came to them to wait and wait and wait, a plate of food in front of him, but once he realized he didn't have to wait for express permission to eat, Ki-tae ate with all the enthusiasm of a small boy.

"If you weren't a musician, you could be a world-class chef," Ki-tae said after swallowing a bite of food.

"Maybe," HanYin said with a shrug. "But I prefer cooking for our family."

"I know. It's how you show you love us, by feeding us until we're all fat," Ki-tae said, and HanYin wanted to cheer at the teasing note in his voice.

"There isn't an ounce of fat on any of us, and you know it," HanYin said, tossing a biscuit at him. "We work it all off at dance practice."

"True," Ki-tae said before taking a huge bite of eggs. "How is Jong-in-a?"

"Still sleeping," HanYin said softly.

"He loves you, you know," Ki-tae said.

"I think you're right, but he hasn't said anything." HanYin sighed as he pulled bao buns from the steamer and plated them.

"He's not much of a talker," Ki-tae said. "Which is good because you talk a lot."

"I do not," HanYin said with a frown.

"Either way, I think he's the type whose actions speak louder," Ki-tae said, and then he paused, a bun halfway to his mouth. "Who the hell came up with that phrase, anyway? 'Actions speak louder than words'? It makes no sense."

"It means words are easily said, but it's harder to do something than it is to say you'll do it," HanYin said absently as he started some okonomiyaki. He knew how much Soon-joon loved it, and Hyun-jo had been known to steal a bite or two. "What about Jin-woo-ya? Still asleep?"

"Yeah." Ki-tae sighed. "It was... a rough night, I think. I feel as if I spent most of it restless."

"It was a hard time for all of us."

"How did you know?"

"What?"

"How did you know something was going to happen?" Ki-tae asked. "We were all so focused on the performance."

HanYin paused, thinking about the previous night for the first time since he'd woken up. There had been something, some niggling sense of dread.

"I honestly don't know. My gut kind of screamed 'look up,' and I did," HanYin said. "I saw someone up there, and the truss moved, and looking at it, I knew it would hit you."

"You saw someone?" Ki-tae whispered. "Someone sabotaged it?"

"Yes," Soon-joon said as he came into the kitchen area. He joined Ki-tae at the island and wrapped his arms around him tightly for a few moments, resting his cheek against Ki-tae's hair, eyes closed, as he had done earlier when he'd let Ki-tae out of the room. Then he took his own seat. HanYin placed a plate of okonomiyaki in front of him and a second one at the empty place next to him. Soon-joon raised an eyebrow.

"For Hyun-jo-nim." HanYin smiled. Soon-joon nodded before starting on his food.

"Is there more going on?" Ki-tae asked softly. "Something seems, I don't know, off."

"There is," Soon-joon said. "But we will wait until everyone is awake and fed before we discuss what is going on and our next course of action."

It didn't take long for the smell of food and, more importantly, coffee to draw the others from their slumber. HanYin moved the food from the island to the dining table, making sure everyone had everything they needed. He was trying not to think about the fact that Jong-in had yet to join them. Had he taken too much? Was he all right? Should he go check on him?

"You're thinking too much," Jong-in grumbled as he walked into the kitchen, his eyes half-closed, rubbing his head. HanYin bit his lip as he roved his eyes over Jong-in's state of dress... or undress. His sleep pants rode low on his hips, his chest and feet were bare, and his muscles rippled beneath his skin as he rubbed his head.

"Not in my kitchen," Soon-joon said without even looking up from his food, making HanYin jump guiltily.

Jong-in looked at him, and the little bastard smirked. He knew exactly what HanYin had been thinking. HanYin growled softly. He was going to make him pay for that later. For now HanYin settled for handing Jong-in the mug of coffee he'd made.

"You are a god," Jong-in murmured as he took his first sip. He moaned, and HanYin had to grit his teeth. Then Jong-in was kissing him, and he couldn't think of anything else.

"Dammit, I am not properly caffeinated yet. Either get a room or knock it off," Min-su grumbled from her spot next to Cheongul.

"You people really don't understand what it means to wake a Dragon before she's ready, do you?" ChenBao grumbled as she walked in and took her place at the table.

HanYin took a deep breath. Her power still intimidated him, but it was hard to maintain his fear of her when she sat at the table wearing adorable crimson pajamas with a big fluffy panda on them and a serious case of bedhead. He smothered a smile. Turning back to the counter, he picked up the small tea set and brought it over to the table. Without a word, he poured her a cup of tea, then set it before her just so. When HanYin turned to go to his seat, she grabbed his wrist. HanYin froze for a second and then turned to her.

"*Xièxiè*, wǒ de sūnzi," she said without looking up from the cup.

"*Bù kèqì…. Nǎi nai*," he answered. When HanYin looked up, his eyes zeroed in on Jong-in. The wink he received over the edge of Jong-in's coffee mug made him smile.

"Everyone eat up," ChenBao said as she took a bao bun. "We have much to discuss after the meal. These attacks on our family, both blood and corporate, will not go unanswered… or unpunished."

HanYin sat down, smiling when Jong-in joined him. Before he realized it, he had filled Jong-in's plate with a little of everything. The chuckling drew his attention, and HanYin looked up to find everyone staring at him. "What?"

"You're feeding him." Min-su giggled. "And he's letting you. It's too freaking cute."

"This is something I have been missing," ChenBao said softly as she looked around the table. "Perhaps isolating myself from the world for so long was not the best course of action."

"*Okasan*," Soon-joon said softly, putting his hand on hers.

"Why am I the last to know about food?" Jin-woo muttered. "Is there coffee left? Please tell me there's coffee."

"I have yours here, Jin-woo," Ki-tae said with a smile. He rose from his chair and guided the woefully undercaffeinated Jin-woo to the empty chair beside him.

With everyone at the table, they resumed eating. Talk of other things would wait until later. For now it was peaceful and nice just to be together as a family. They needed this bonding time. Things were going to get worse before they got better, as the saying went. It would be harder on Jong-in and Jin-woo than on HanYin or Ki-tae. As idols they were aware of the effects of what might be considered negative press and the influence of netizens. Yet they really didn't need their jobs. They had survived centuries in times much more physically challenging than this one.

However, Jong-in and Jin-woo? This could end their academic careers. It was not unheard of for classmates to bully gay and lesbian students to the point of dropping out or even taking their own lives. In fact, it probably happened more than people would like to think or acknowledge. Views were still conservative in Korea, and even if some progress was being made, it was a very slow process. In the meantime people lived in fear of their family and friends finding out, of being abandoned, bullied, or worse.

"You're thinking too hard again," Jong-in said softly. "Just enjoy this time, leave the other stuff for later."

"How do you know what I'm thinking about?" HanYin said.

"Well, you said it yourself: protecting your family is paramount to you. Someone has attacked them. You're not going to sit back and let that go," Jong-in said. "Plus you're growling."

HanYin chuckled. "I didn't realize it."

"I know." Jong-in smirked at him. "It's sexy as hell."

"Later," HanYin purred before kissing his cheek.

Unfortunately "later" was a long time coming.

JIN-WOO

JIN-WOO CURLED up on one of the ottomans by the windows, staring out over the yard. He didn't know what was going to happen now. Mei was still out there, and he knew she wasn't going to give up. Crazy never gave up, which meant she was a continued danger to Ki-tae. He suspected she was behind the leaked video and photos too. Considering she felt he needed to be punished for not being even remotely into her *and* for the added "offense" of loving Ki-tae, it made sense. How was he going to protect the family he never thought he'd have again?

Ki-tae wrapped his strong arms around him, and Jin-woo leaned into his embrace with a sigh. "This is all my fault."

"Nonsense." Ki-tae snorted. "You are not responsible for someone else's mental state."

"Perhaps not, but I'm the reason for all of this."

"Her obsession is the reason for all of this," Ki-tae said.

"It's still so surreal… and creepy," Jin-woo said as he looked up at Ki-tae. "There's a term for it, you know, much like 'sasaeng' for obsessed idol fans. She is what is called a '*yandere*.' Well, sort of because yandere is a term from manga and anime. Granted, it's referring to fictional characters, but since they basically do what Mei is doing, I think it fits. It scares me, the lengths she's gone to already. I can't help but worry about what she's going to do next. She's already tried to kill you three times, and before she left, she threatened Min-su-ya and Jong-in-a. She wants to take everyone I love from me."

"I won't let that happen," Ki-tae promised. "She has no idea what she's taken on with her attack."

"She is insane, Ki-tae. It isn't going to matter what you are. She wants you dead."

"I've lived almost three hundred years, Jin-woo, and I've encountered people who wanted to kill me before. Now that I've found you, there is no way in hell I'm going to let anyone take you from me or me from you."

"Do you think it's a good idea? This press conference ChenBao-nim and Soon-joon-nim want to hold?"

"I think so," Ki-tae said as he pulled Jin-woo into his lap and held him close. "It has always been company policy to face these types of things head-on."

"Bam Kiseu has never been under this kind of scrutiny before. While the fans love it when you guys do the Pocky thing, they've never indulged in rumors about your orientation," Jin-woo said. "I hoped—a lot—but it was never really in question before."

"Are you glad you were right?"

"Very much so." Jin-woo smiled. "Things here are better than other places in the world, but still not great. A lot of the fans may not stick around, hating the idea that you and I are together, or that HanYin and Jong-in are together."

"Then they're not the type of fans I want," Ki-tae said. "I love the people who listen to our music, who get it, and who are moved by it. I like knowing our music can help people through tough times, but I'm not living my life for them. I'm not letting other people dictate who I will and will not love."

"I was blessed that day."

"No, it is you who are truly a gift to me," Ki-tae said as he leaned down and then claimed Jin-woo's mouth in a slow, sensual kiss. Jin-woo whimpered softly, pushing his fingers into Ki-tae's hair. After a few moments, he pulled back, just a little, to breathe. "I love you, Jin-woo."

"I love you too, Ki-tae."

"Dammit, you two!" Min-su said with a sniffle, accepting the tissue Cheongul handed her. "Why do you have to be so damned adorable and sweet and romantic? Now I'm crying! Oh, I want to smack you both! I hate to cry!"

"You have your own, so go away," Jin-woo said, winking at Cheongul's raised eyebrow.

"Yes, but you two are like watching a drama while he is like being in an epic tale," Min-su said.

"I don't know if I'm being insulted or complimented," Cheongul muttered.

"Be complimented. There is nothing she enjoys more than epic tales." Jin-woo laughed.

The time came for everyone to go about their day. Hyun-jo had been on the phone since after breakfast, making the arrangements for the press conference, getting updates from the media teams. Qīngróu had flitted in and out, carrying reports and messages between the house and the office. Shin-bai remained with them yet still communicated with the security teams, keeping Hyun-jo informed as things came in. It amazed Jin-woo to see them like this. While he had seen them working before, there was always this air of casualness about them. They weren't as intimidating as they were right now. All pretenses were gone.

Jin-woo's phone rang, startling him from his thoughts. Without looking at it, he answered.

"Yeoboseyo?"

"Cheong Jin-woo dongsaeng?" He didn't recognize the voice, and a shiver of dread went up his spine.

"Yes."

"I am Lee Tae-hwa, secretary to the Jeonjin University Board," she said, her tone cool and just this side of polite. "They request that you come to the campus immediately."

"I'm sorry, but I can't do that right now," Jin-woo said, trying to keep the tremor from his voice. "I will be happy to arrange a meeting for a later time, but I cannot shirk my responsibilities to BL Entertainment."

"Dongsaeng, this meeting directly concerns your academic career. Which do you feel is more important?" she asked.

"My position at BL Entertainment also directly concerns my academic career," Jin-woo said, throwing her words back. "What kind of precedent would I be setting if I left my internship with little to no notice? I will confer with my on-site mentor and arrange for some time to attend the meeting, but it is not possible today. As I'm sure you're aware, a tragic event took place at the Bam Kiseu concert last night. If you would provide me with a phone number, I will contact you when I am available."

"I will speak with the board, dongsaeng," she said. "You may reach me at this number. I suggest you make these arrangements as soon as possible."

"I will take that under advisement," he said before disconnecting the phone call. He let out a sigh. That's when he felt it. Looking up, Jin-woo noticed everyone was staring at him. Well, everyone except Min-su and Jong-in. "What?"

Cheongul and HanYin walked up to stand next to Ki-tae. They threw their arms around his shoulders, still looking at Jin-woo. Then they turned to Ki-tae and said, "Keep him."

"It seems behind that sweet face is a backbone of steel." ChenBao smiled.

"You have *no* idea." Min-su snorted.

"We knew something like this was going to happen. However, I question the timing," Soon-joon said. "It should have taken at least a day or two before the university responded."

"More than likely the photos and videos were sent to the board directly at the same time as or shortly after the initial upload," Hyun-jo said. "This meeting was arranged within the last few hours."

"Regardless, I'm not going to let them shove me around like the schoolyard bully," Jin-woo said.

"Hyun-jo, you will accompany Jin-woo-ya and Jong-in-a to the university. Take our best men. Make sure nothing happens to them," Soon-joon said. "Shin-bai hubae will go with them as well. Ensure the best possible outcome."

"I will do my best," Hyun-jo said with a bow.

"The boys and I will head to the offices and confer with the media teams, see where things are at and what the majority opinion is," Soon-joon said. "We also need to keep in mind Mei is still a threat. We don't know who her next target will be."

"She'll go after Ki-tae," Jin-woo said quietly. "Once she knows he wasn't killed by the truss, she'll go after him again."

"What makes you say that?" ChenBao said.

"Min-su-ya and Jong-in-a were like an afterthought to her. It was as if she didn't see them until Ki-tae was out of the way. She didn't even want to hear his name, she hates him that much. Once it's made clear he survived, I think she'll lose what little sanity she has left. She sees him as an obstacle to me, the biggest obstacle, but not irremovable."

Cheongul snorted before putting Ki-tae in a headlock. "Clearly she has no idea how stubborn this little baka can be!"

"Leave off," Ki-tae grumbled, slipping out of the hold and smacking Cheongul in the head. "I'm not that bad."

"Yes, you are," HanYin said. "He once didn't speak to me for a solid month because I didn't make the steamed dumplings I'd promised. A whole month."

Before Ki-tae could respond, Jong-in came into the room. The devastation on his face had HanYin by his side before anyone could draw breath to ask what was wrong.

"Jong-in-a?" Jin-woo said softly. "What happened?"

"I...." He started to speak, but it was clearly difficult for him. The tears flowed down his cheeks. "My little sister... she called.... She wanted to warn me. I'm.... They're forbidden to talk to me or of me. I'm never allowed to see them again. She said Stepfather was furious. He... he saw footage of the concert."

HanYin pulled Jong-in into his arms. Jin-woo was across the room, hugging them both in seconds. "We're not going to let this go. They're your family."

"She said Eomeoni has been crying all morning, that he railed at her, saying it was her fault I was this way, that she should have known and drowned me at birth so I wouldn't be an embarrassment to him."

"Pardon my language, but.... No, don't pardon it," Min-su said. "That man is an asshole."

"This will not stand," Hyun-jo said, drawing all eyes to him. Energy flared in the room, whipping his long white hair back and forth almost as fast as his tails were moving. "He will not be allowed to take your family from you. I will *not* allow it."

"Easy, Saiai," Soon-joon said as he pulled Hyun-jo to him. "We will—"

"No," Hyun-jo said. "*I* will handle this with Jong-in-a."

"We can't do anything," Jong-in said.

"Do not underestimate me, *Sukoshi kitto*," Hyun-jo said. "We will take care of the university first, your family situation second. It will be all right."

Later, when they were climbing into the cars to leave, a bicycle courier pulled in and handed Soon-joon a package. Without looking at the contents, he handed it to Hyun-jo with a smile and a kiss. Then he got into the car with Ki-tae and the others. Hyun-jo joined them, a smirk on his face as he looked at the package before opening it and sliding several envelopes into his briefcase.

"I'm pretty sure if I asked what's in the envelopes, you'd tell me I'll find out soon enough," Jin-woo said, his arm around Jong-in's shoulders.

"You would be correct."

"I don't know who is more close-lipped, you or Jong-in-a." Jin-woo chuckled.

"I have had more practice, but it is a Kitsune trait. We do not reveal our tricks until the time is right."

"I am not looking forward to this," Jin-woo said. "I'm not even sure why they're holding this meeting. It's not as if I'm an authority figure or anything."

"It is the idea that the university would allow such a student to attend. While under Article Thirty-one of the Human Rights Committee Law, such discrimination isn't permitted, there is very little in the way of legal reinforcement of that article, or really any protections," Hyun-jo said. "There is a chance they may expel you both. However, it is more likely they will either ask you to quietly transfer or withdraw."

"They're going to have to kick me out," Jong-in said quietly. "I worked too hard for this."

"You and me both," Jin-woo said.

Hyun-jo said, "Progress comes from people taking a stand against such bigotry."

All too soon, it seemed, they arrived at Jeonjin University. Several men and two women met them at the front doors to the main building. The older woman, probably late forties, early fifties in age and dressed in a severe black pantsuit, stepped forward.

"Cheong Jin-woo dongsaeng, Bak Jong-in dongsaeng, I am Lee Tae-hwa. You will follow me, please," she said. As they all stepped forward, she stopped. "Only Cheong Jin-woo dongsaeng and Bak Jong-in dongsaeng may attend this meeting."

"Oh, I don't think so." Hyun-jo smiled pleasantly. "Huijang-nim has assigned me as advocate for both Cheong Jin-woo dongsaeng and Bak Jong-in dongsaeng. I am here to act in their best interests, as well as those of BL Entertainment."

"I do not see how this affects your company," she said.

"You are not required to see. Your role is to escort us to the meeting, as per your employer's instructions. If you insist on preventing not only myself but their security team as well, we will simply depart. Then your employer can explain your reasoning to Huijang-nim. I'm sure it will be an interesting conversation." Hyun-jo smiled.

Jin-woo had to turn away before he burst out laughing. Miss Lee's eyes got so wide he thought they were going to pop right out of her head. Apparently ChenBao had quite the reputation. How had he never heard of it? Jong-in elbowed him, and the small smile on his friend's face told him Jong-in was enjoying this as much as he was. Hyun-jo's tone was perfectly even and pleasant. Even his eyes didn't hint at the anger he'd displayed not a few hours ago.

Miss Lee turned on her heel and led the way into the building. Hyun-jo looked at them and winked before following her. Jin-woo and Jong-in looked at each other and let out their laugh but quietly.

Thirty minutes later, Jin-woo understood why Soon-joon sent Hyun-jo when he wanted something done quickly, efficiently, and to the best possible outcome. He was terrifying in his ability to control the direction of the meeting and the people in it. He and Jong-in barely had to say anything, which was a good thing because Jin-woo's nervousness was making his throat dry. As much as he wouldn't back down before this kind of treatment, he was still worried it wouldn't go their way.

"We simply cannot allow such a disruption to the education of our students," the chairman insisted.

"Yet you actively seek the disruption to the education of two of your students?" Hyun-jo said. "Does that not strike you as the least bit hypocritical? The issue in question has no bearing on anyone save the individuals involved. Should there be a disruption, it would not be a result of Jin-woo dongsaeng's or Jong-in dongsaeng's actions. They have been attending your university for the last three years, and there has never been an issue. Your... concern is disproportionate to the precedent set by both men."

"Still...."

Hyun-jo sighed. "I had hoped it would not come to this. However, it seems you will leave me with no choice."

Shin-bai stepped forward and took the envelopes. He handed one to each member of the board, and the last two he placed before Jin-woo and Jong-in.

"What is this?" the chairman demanded.

Hyun-jo simply smiled.

They tore into the envelopes. As they read, their eyes grew wider and wider. Some of them gaped, opening and closing their mouths like fish on land.

"Both men refuse to transfer or withdraw. Therefore you will be forced to expel them should you wish to engage in such discriminatory practices. Upon their expulsion, BL Entertainment and its subsidiaries, many of them sponsors of your university, will cease all funding and support of Jeonjin University. Any and all grants, endowments, scholarships, and future contributions will be terminated. All fund-raising activities will end. Our company will not have dealings with individuals and or entities which engage in actions that are discriminatory, in direct conflict with our company's mission statement. We will not support bigotry. We will not do business with an educational entity that displays disregard for their students. We will not associate with a university or business that actively seeks to persecute an individual for their sexual orientation, that places its reputation above its role of nurturing and educating the future of Korea. Furthermore, Huijang-nim is considering filing suit against Jeonjin University for discrimination based on sexual orientation. However, she is not an unreasonable woman. You have forty-eight hours to make your decision. Good day to you."

"Wait," the chairman said. "What about their envelopes?"

Jin-woo opened his. As he read it, he almost fell over.

"These are formal employment contracts with BL Entertainment. Jin-woo dongsaeng and Jong-in dongsaeng have displayed exemplary skill, natural talent, and a willingness to work hard. They have been model employees, much as they have been model students, with a curious nature and an easy personality. They have made many friends at BL Entertainment. They are part of our family now, and we do not abandon our family," Hyun-jo said. "Good day to you, gentlemen."

He walked out of the room. Jin-woo and Jong-in could only follow, completely flummoxed, and Shin-bai followed with a smile on his face.

"Welcome to the family," he said quietly.

Jin-woo couldn't even formulate the words to show his appreciation. Of all the possible outcomes, he had never considered this. He didn't know why, but he hadn't. It had been his dream to work for BLE, but he thought the fulfillment of that dream was further off. He wasn't sure how he should react. Honestly, as he climbed into the car, Jin-woo realized there was only one question he really needed to ask.

"When do these contracts become effective?"

"Optimally upon your graduation. However, given the current situation, if they choose to court ChenBao-nim's wrath, upon your expulsion," Hyun-jo said.

"Who drafted this?" Jong-in asked softly.

"ChenBao-nim."

"But," Jong-in said, "she hardly knows us. We haven't been with the company long enough."

"She's a Dragon." Jin-woo snorted. "I'm pretty sure she sees more than most people in less time."

"Again you would be correct," Hyun-jo said. "ChenBao-nim is thousands of years old. She has had many years to fine-tune her abilities."

"That document, though, it seems so harsh," Jong-in said.

"You will find ChenBao-nim can be merciless when she feels the situation calls for it," Hyun-jo said. "She will do whatever she feels necessary to protect her family, and she has no problem getting her fangs bloody in the process."

"Remind me never to make her angry," Jin-woo said.

"Same here," Jong-in said, and then he gave a small smile. "Yet it's hard to reconcile that image of her with the lady in the panda PJs from this morning."

"She does have her softer side." Hyun-jo smiled. "There are just certain things she will not tolerate. Now, Jong-in-a, we will go see your mother and sister."

"I don't see how that's going to do any good. He has forbidden them to speak with me."

"We will not know unless we try. Your sister called to warn you, and in that, there is hope. Sometimes people within a situation they feel is beyond their control need only be shown the way to take back control," Hyun-jo said. "Sometimes they need someone to help them take that step."

"Do you honestly think she will leave him after all this time?" Jong-in said. "For me? She hasn't left him yet. She didn't even stand up to him when he kicked me out of the house."

"She was a woman in love with a Kitsune," Hyun-jo said. "He was taken from her too quickly, with no chance to say goodbye. For many humans it may take years to recover from the loss. Some never recover. How long after your father's passing did he approach her?"

"I don't know," Jong-in said. "I remember Oesamchon ending the mourning period on the one hundredth day, and the feast they had. It seemed... wrong to me, as if Abeoji had not been properly grieved for. Eomeonim, she never really recovered. And he just sort of took over."

"Was he familiar with your family?"

"Yes, I guess so. I'd seen him around a few times," Jong-in said. "Usually when Oesamchon came to visit. They were friends from his university days. I know Abeoji didn't care for him much."

"Kitsune are very good at sensing the true nature of a person," Hyun-jo said.

"Is that why you fell in love with Soon-joon-nim?" Jong-in asked, his head cocked to the side in his curiosity.

Hyun-jo nodded. "I had encountered several outsiders before I met Soon-joon. I could tell they were not good men, and I made my exit as quickly as possible, losing them in the forest so as not to lead them to our village. Soon-joon was different. First, he didn't chase me. He let me come to him, showing patience. Second, our conversations were long and varied, showing his intelligence and compassion for many things. Thirdly, I could tell from his aura and his armor that he was a warrior, but not vicious or cruel. And fourth, well, you have seen the man himself."

"He is sexy as hell."

"That he is. The beauty of his face is matched by the beauty of his soul, and that is why I fell in love with Soon-joon," Hyun-jo said.

"Do you honestly think we'll be able to help Eomeoni and my sister get away from him? Do you think she even wants to leave?" Jong-in asked. He had never understood what his mother saw in his stepfather, never understood why she allowed him to treat her and her children the way he did, as if he owned them all. "I just don't understand how she could let him do those things."

"It is difficult to understand the mind of another, let alone for a child to understand the mind of an adult," Hyun-jo said. "Once we have resolved this issue, then you may talk to her, as an adult to his parent, but you must also listen to what she has to say without judging."

"I don't know if I'll be able to do that. I felt as if she betrayed me, not once, but twice." Jong-in looked out the window and tensed. "We're here."

HYUN-JO

JONG-IN RUBBED his hands against his thighs and Hyun-jo couldn't help his smile. For all his usual calm appearance, little gestures gave away Jong-in's true feelings. His leg bounced as the limousine stopped in front of a medium-sized gate.

"Jong-in-a," Hyun-jo said drawing his attention. "Everything will be fine."

"I haven't seen them in a year and a half." Jong-in said, continuing to stare out the window.

"Well, that ends right now," Jin-woo said as he wrapped an arm around Jong-in's shoulders.

Hyun-jo nodded as Jong-in took a deep breath. "Shall we?"

Without waiting for a response from either of them, he got out. After straightening his suit, Hyun-jo stepped aside to let Jong-in out. He turned his attention to the gate as it opened. The young girl who exited could only be Jong-in's sister. The two of them could have been twins. Her eyes went wide and flashed lavender for the briefest of moments as he spotted her brother. She shot a nervous glance through the gate before she rushed forward and pounced on Jong-in.

"Oppa!" she cried. "I'm so happy to see you, see that you're okay, but you shouldn't be here."

Jong-in held her, his eyes closed, tears on his cheeks. "Yeong dongsaeng, is he here?"

She nodded.

"Jong-in-a, put your sister in the limo," Hyun-jo said. "I will get your mother."

"No," Jong-in said as he released Yeong-hui. "I'm not going to wait in the limo."

"Very well."

"I'll sit with your sister," Jin-woo said. "You go get your mom."

"What's going on, oppa?" Yeong-hui asked. "Who are these people?"

"Friends, and I'll explain after we get Eomeoni."

"Okay, but I expect all the details," she said.

Hyun-jo waited while Jong-in hugged his sister again before nudging her toward the open limo door. She got in, and then Jon-woo followed before Shin-bai closed the door.

"Do you wish me to accompany you?" Shin-bai asked.

"I don't think that will be necessary," Hyun-jo said as Jong-in turned to face him. "Are you ready?"

Jong-in nodded. "As I'll ever be."

"Then lead the way."

Hyun-jo was proud of him. Once Jong-in had made up his mind, he didn't hesitate. He waked through the gate into a small, rather barren courtyard. Hyun-jo followed. He didn't like the feel of the place. It held an aura of oppression and fear and violence. He was hard-pressed to keep his fangs from emerging. Hate filled the air with heaviness. If Jong-in's mother and sister weren't being beaten, they were, at the very least, being emotionally abused. With the scent assaulting his nose, Hyun-jo was certain a spirit was involved.

"Jong-in-a, my son, what are you doing here?" the beautiful woman who turned to look at them said in a fearful voice. Petite, with thick black hair twisted up and pinned behind her head, she could only be Jong-ins mother. "You must go before he sees you."

"Not without you," Jong-in said. "Yeong dongsaeng is already in the car."

"He will not let me leave, and he will hurt you. You must go." She tried to push him toward the gate.

"Why do you stay with Kang-dae-ssi?" Jong-in said angrily.

"If I stay he will not hurt my babies," she said. "I must keep you safe."

"No, Eomeoni, I must keep *you* safe," Jong-in said.

"Jong-in—"

"Yeong-ja!" a deep chilling voice called from inside the house. Hyun-jo stepped closer to Jong-in and his mother. There was something off about that voice. It set his hackles rising. Jong-in pushed his mother behind him as a man came storming into the courtyard.

"You!" Kang-dae snarled. "What are you doing here? I forbade you to ever set foot in this house again!"

"I came for my family," Jong-in said. "I won't let you cage them anymore."

"She is mine!"

Hyun-jo moved, slipping past Jong-in to catch Kang-dae's wrist as he made to strike Jong-in. The minute he made contact, Hyun-jo's suspicions were confirmed. He could feel the spirit writhing inside Kang-dae.

"Jong-in-a, take your mother to the car," he said, never taking his eyes from Kang-dae. The man had yet to look at him. When he heard no movement, Hyun-jo gave a push of qi to nudge Jong-in. Even young as he was, he would feel it.

"Eomeoni, let's go."

"Are you sure?" she asked.

"You know what I'll do!" Kang-dae growled.

"Jong-in-a, go," Hyun-jo said. "Now."

Finally, he heard them leave and the gate close. "Now, Onryo, it's just you and me, and we're going to have a chat."

Kang-dae's eyes grew wide. "Gumiho."

"Yes," Hyun-jo hissed as he dropped his glamour.

"I will kill him! I will kill them all! She was mine! She *is* mine!" Kang-dae screamed until Hyun-jo wrapped his hand around his throat and dug his claws in.

"That's exactly what you *won't* do," Hyun-jo said. "She is Fox-touched and you should never have laid a hand on her or her kits."

"Kill me, kill him," Kang-dae said, only it was no longer his voice, but the voice of the spirit inside.

Slowly, Hyun-jo smiled. "You assume I care whether this body lives or dies. I assure you I do not."

"You don't scare me."

"You stink of fear." Hyun-jo snorted.

"I deserve to be married. She should never have left me."

"Your petty desires are of no interest to me." Hyun-jo gave Kang-dae a little shake. "I can sense this man's spirit has withered away under your control. You have until the new moon to set his business in order and then depart this realm. If you do not do this, I will hunt you down."

"You can't exorcise me if he let me in of his own freewill," Kang-dae said with another eerie high-pitched giggle.

"Oh, little spirit, you are very much mistaken," Hyun-jo said, letting his fire fill his eyes for the spirit to see. "And if I discover you had anything whatsoever to do with the Fox's death, you will beg to be released from this world, and I will savor your screams."

KI-TAE

KI-TAE, HANYIN, and Cheongul arrived at BL Entertainment headquarters to find a huge crowd waiting for them. On one side were those who supported them, signs declaring their loyalty and their love. On the other were those who felt betrayed, who were offended by their apparent lies, and who wanted them to stop immediately. The third group watched with ravening eyes, praying for some sort of conflict between the two groups, cameras and microphones at the ready.

"Why do they have to act like hungry vultures circling overhead?" Ki-tae muttered as he watched the reporters.

"For these types, it's their nature," Cheongul said. "No one gets out until Shin-bai hyung and his team are in position. Standard pattern from here to the door."

"We know the drill, Cheongul," HanYin said. "I just wish it wasn't even more necessary now."

"I know, HanYin." Cheongul sighed. "I wish the same."

"Min-su-ya is already inside?" Ki-tae asked.

"Yes. She went in with Halmeonim earlier this morning," Cheongul said. "Abeoji and Hyun-jo-nim are in the front car with Jin-woo-ya and Jong-in-a."

"I wish we could have ridden in the same car," Ki-tae complained. "I don't like having him so far away."

"Abeoji and Hyun-jo-nim will keep them safe," HanYin said, resting a hand on his shoulder.

"I know, but I still don't like it," Ki-tae said.

Before he could say more, there was a knock on the window, Shin-bai's signal that they were in position. The door opened, and Ki-tae stepped out into the sunlight. The black fabric of his suit immediately pulled in the heat, and he took comfort as that warmth started to chase away the chill he'd felt ever since Jin-woo got into the other car. He stepped forward several paces so his brothers could get out of the vehicle.

From the left, something came flying at his head. Before he could respond, Shin-bai snapped out his arm and caught the projectile. The crowd gasped. Shin-bai turned his eyes toward the crowd. He simply dropped the rock out of their path without a word. Then he moved them forward. Each of the six other team members were either Shifters or Vampires. They had the abilities needed to protect Bam Kiseu from any threat, and they had been trained to handle humans as well. They knew their job. They were the elite team and only ever assigned to Bam Kiseu.

Ki-tae looked over to where the other car stood. Everyone was already out, and he searched out Jin-woo. When he caught his eye, Ki-tae gave him a gentle smile. While he wanted to rush over to him, Ki-tae waited until they reached the door. At that point he couldn't resist. He reached out and took Jin-woo's hand, pulling him to his side. They walked into the building together.

The walk to the conference room was probably the longest walk over the shortest distance he'd ever taken. Jin-woo was correct the other night: Bam Kiseu had never been the target of such rumors before, and it was disconcerting, to say the least. It wasn't that he couldn't handle the situation. He'd been through much worse. It was the idea that people could consider such a private thing to be something they had a say in.

When they took their seats at the front table, the room was packed with not only reporters, but fans and protestors alike. It was surprisingly composed, unlike the atmosphere outside. Were these a different group of people? No, he recognized some of the faces from outside. Perhaps the feel of the building had changed them. Every BLE employee they ran into expressed their support and their displeasure at the rumormongers and haters. Now those who were there to persecute them were on enemy territory, and they were feeling the sting of that threat.

ChenBao nodded to Soon-joon. He rose and took to the podium.

"Good morning, ladies and gentlemen. I welcome you here today as we address recent events. As many of you know, I am Park Soon-joon, manager of Bam Kiseu. To my left is Lyang ChenBao-nim, owner and president of BL Entertainment, and my personal assistant, Rhim Hyun-jo hubae. To my right are the members of Bam Kiseu: Cheongul-a, HanYin-a, and Ki-tae-ya. Cheong Jin-woo dongsaeng, Bak Jong-in dongsaeng, and Yi Min-su dongsaeng, our interns from Jeonjin University."

"Why is Miss Yi present? It seems out of place for an intern not involved to be present."

"Questions and answers will be at the end of the conference," Soon-joon said with a smile. "I respectfully ask that you hold them until that time."

"You're avoiding the question." The reporter smirked. "What? Did she get knocked up by one of the band members?"

Min-su laughed, drawing attention to herself. She looked to Soon-joon, and he nodded. "I am here, sir, because Cheong Jin-woo-ya and Bak Jong-in-a are my best friends, as are all of the people at this table. I am here to show them my support, as any proper friend does. It is poor manners indeed to insinuate otherwise."

Ki-tae smiled. Min-su was in protective but professional mode. It reminded him of Hyun-jo. He wondered if all Shifters were like that.

"My apologies," the reporter said, looking a little less smug. Min-su simply nodded, neither accepting nor rejecting his apology.

"As I said, there will be a question-and-answer session afterward," Soon-joon said. "For now I will turn over the podium to Huijang-nim."

"Thank you, Soon-joon-nim," ChenBao said as she rose gracefully and he took his seat. "Good morning, ladies and gentlemen of the press and fans of our Bam

Kiseu. We appreciate you taking the time out of your day to be present. As many of you are aware, during the Bam Kiseu spring concert at Eumak Nabi Theater, a lighting truss crashed to the stage. It struck our dear HanYin, who, thankfully, did not suffer any major injuries. The resulting shrapnel from the breaking lights did, however, injure several fans. BL Entertainment has already been in contact with the hospital and will cover all medical expenses of the injured fans. All of those who had purchased tickets to the concert will be able to turn their receipts in for a free entry to Bam Kiseu's next show. We know you work hard, and you attend our shows to unwind. We are most sorry this time was interrupted in such a horrible fashion. We will open the floor to your questions now."

"Any idea what caused the truss to fall? Was it faulty?" one reporter asked.

"It saddens me to say this was a deliberate attack upon Bam Kiseu. The truss was sabotaged by person or persons unknown," ChenBao said. "We are working closely with both the venue and the authorities to identify the perpetrator and bring them to justice."

"Fan-cam footage shows HanYin dongsaeng shoving Ki-tae dongsaeng out of the way of the truss. Do you believe Ki-tae dongsaeng was the intended target?" another asked. It was a relief they were focusing on the attack, but Ki-tae knew it wouldn't be long before the more personal questions began.

"We believe that is a distinct possibility," she said.

"Could this be an attack by an antifan?"

"Also a distinct possibility," ChenBao said. "If we consider this was a deliberate attack on Ki-tae dongsaeng only, an antifan is someone who has an irrational hatred for a particular idol and will go to great lengths to harm that idol."

"Or is it possible this attack is a direct result of the video that went viral the same day? The video showing explicit relations between Ki-tae dongsaeng and a man?" the first reporter demanded.

"The level of planning and the timing indicates the two incidents could only be related if the culprit behind them both was the same individual. The video was released during the concert. That would not be enough time for an individual to see the video, get into the venue, learn the choreography well enough to know when Ki-tae dongsaeng would be at that section of the stage, and then remove the bolts to the truss," Hyun-jo answered at ChenBao's nod. "We are either dealing with one mentally unstable and cunning individual, or two individuals, possibly both deranged. Either is unacceptable."

Ki-tae watched the reporter. His eyes were calculating as he looked at everyone at the front table. He didn't like how the guy focused in on Jin-woo and smiled. "And you're sure it has nothing to do with the rumors that Ki-tae dongsaeng is gay? Isn't the other person in the video, in fact, sitting next to Ki-tae dongsaeng, Cheong Jin-woo dongsaeng? How will BL Entertainment address that issue?"

"There is no issue to address," ChenBao said.

"No issue? One of your star idols is gay."

"And? Does his sexual orientation affect his ability to sing? Does it make him incapable of dancing? Does it prevent him from writing the truly compelling lyrics or engineering the distinct sounds Bam Kiseu is known for? In truth it is a nonfactor to all of those things." ChenBao smiled. She glanced at Ki-tae and nodded. He straightened in his seat. Then he pulled his hand from beneath the table, firmly entwined with Jin-woo's.

"Yes, I am gay," Ki-tae said.

"And yes, I am the man in that video," Jin-woo added.

"Outrageous!" someone shouted. "Disgusting. You should be ashamed!"

"Why? Because I love someone who happens to be male? When is love wrong? And what business is it of anyone other than myself and Jin-woo?" Ki-tae asked. "I love my fans. I love knowing our songs help them, make them smile, get them up and dancing, and I love Jin-woo. I won't live my life the way someone else wants me to simply because they have issues with homosexuality. I will continue to write and produce music. I will continue to sing and to perform, and those fans that are truly fans will be in that crowd, cheering us on, making us smile with the joy on their faces as they dance and sing along with us."

"Jin-woo," the first reporter began.

"I did not give anyone save Ki-tae leave to address me so informally. Either use the proper form, or keep your questions to yourself," Jin-woo said. The reporter looked shocked, and Ki-tae smiled. His little angel had his fangs out.

"Jin-woo dongsaeng, aren't you concerned your relationship with Ki-tae dongsaeng will cause problems academically?"

"There is a chance it might. However, that remains to be seen," Jin-woo said.

"HanYin dongsaeng, you were filmed kissing another man onstage."

"Well, it's more of I kissed him." Jong-in smiled. HanYin blushed, and Ki-tae couldn't help his chuckle.

"Are you admitting to being gay as well?"

"I *admit* nothing," Jong-in said. "I simply am gay. It's not a confession, although too many people make it out to be some horrendous crime. We were born this way, but it is not the defining factor of our character. How we treat others, how we behave, how loudly our actions echo our words, these are the things that define our personality. I am a sound engineer. I love food, especially HanYin's steamed dumplings. I love my mother and my sister and my friends. And I am gay."

"HanYin dongsaeng?"

"You make being homosexual out to be some sort of deviation, some abomination that is a threat to your way of life, when, in fact, we couldn't give a damn about your life," he said quietly. "We are simply trying to live ours. We laugh, we cry, we live, we die, we mourn, and we celebrate, just like you. The only difference between you and me is the person I love is male. He is a remarkable man who has the most amazing voice and the most adorable dimples. He works hard, driving himself to succeed in everything he does. He cares for his friends and strives to make them smile when they're sad. He tends to be a man of few words, but his words are meaningful and precious in their rarity. As Ki-tae said, our true fans, the ones that really get our music, will wish us luck and celebrate with us that we have found these amazing people to love and to be loved by."

"Cheongul dongsaeng, you've remained silent through this entire conference. How do you feel about your bandmates being gay?"

"Wow, you're really trying to start something today," Cheongul said bluntly. "I couldn't give a damn who they love or sleep with. As long as that person never hurts them, he and I won't have issues. Looking at the two men they fell in love with, I don't see that ever happening. You see, Ki-tae and HanYin are my brothers, and I will defend them from all threats to my last breath. That's the kind of bond we have with each other."

"Are you gay as well?"

"No, I'm not." Cheongul smiled as he looked at Min-su. "But I am taken by this lovely lady at my side."

"Well, damn. There goes that fantasy," someone female grumbled loudly, causing a riot of giggles from the supporters.

"How is it that such a large company in the entertainment industry is taking such an open stance, contradictory to the popular opinion?"

"'Popular opinion' is precisely that: someone's opinion or a group's shared opinion," ChenBao said. "And that opinion is slowly changing. Here at BL Entertainment, that opinion has always been in favor of acceptance, tolerance, and understanding. Here we do not care what your sexual orientation is. What we care about, what we focus on, is the creative growth of our entertainers, production crews, and staff. Here we inspire loyalty in our employees because we give them the same. We earn their respect because we treat them with respect, we value their input, and we actively listen. This is what makes BL Entertainment a family, whereas all others are simply companies."

"So you won't be terminating their contracts?"

"Of course not." ChenBao laughed. "Not only are they extremely talented, loving individuals, but Bam Kiseu is the highest-grossing band in our family."

"Aren't you afraid there will be a drop in sales?"

"We know there will be, but we will continue to produce Bam Kiseu because there are people out there who love them, some who may even need them to get through the day, and we won't abandon those people any more than we will abandon these fine young men," Soon-joon answered.

"And you're on board with their... proclivities, Soon-joon-nim?" that first reporter asked, his face less smug and more frustrated. He wasn't getting the conflict he had been hoping to instigate.

"I am more than 'on board' with it," Soon-joon said as he looked at Hyun-jo before they too brought their clasped hands into view. Ki-tae smiled. Soon-joon's timing was impeccable as usual.

"My God, this is disgusting. This company in infested with abominations," a man railed from the back, his shirt spouting anti-LGBT slogans. "We'll put you out of business. You won't get a cent of our money. We'll see this den of perverts brought low."

"Sir, you are welcome to try," ChenBao said, standing her full height. "I have faced down better men than you in my day. I have defended my family and my friends from those who would see them destroyed, and I will do the same for the people of this company. We are BL Entertainment. We are a family, and we are strong. You face not just one of us, but all of us, and we will not back down. We will not surrender. We will not be coerced or manipulated into denying the very core values we hold dear. You, sir, can keep your hard-earned money and all that comes with it. We do not want it."

Ki-tae rose, bringing Jin-woo with him. Soon they were all standing strong with ChenBao, presenting a united front to those who would attack them. He hoped Mei was watching, because then she would know, in part, what she was facing. If she retained any sort of sanity, which he seriously doubted, she would quit now, but Ki-tae knew better. She wasn't going to stop until she either had Jin-woo, was in jail, or dead. And option one was no option, as far as he was concerned.

SEUNG-GI

IN OTHER news, two-thirds of the highly popular K-pop band Bam Kiseu came out today, identifying as gay at a press conference earlier this afternoon. Ki-tae hyung, the lead rapper and main sound engineer for the band, also introduced his lover from the notorious video leaked to the internet during Bam Kiseu's spring concert. Sources close to the two men say they are very much in love.

"Alive! He's alive!" Mei shrieked as she stared at the television screen. "How is that possible? I made sure it would hit him. I waited up there all through that horrendous noise to make sure I got him. How is he still alive?"

"Mei-ya?" Seung-gi stared at his niece, concern and fear lacing his voice as he took in her words.

"No. No! I won't allow it. I won't! I won't! I won't!"

"Mei-ya, honey, calm down," Seung-gi said gently as his sister-in-law backed away from her ranting daughter. He moved closer, trying to take her arm. "Everything is going to be all right. Just tell me what's wrong?"

"Didn't you see it? He's still alive. That... that *thing* is still alive!" she hissed, turning on him. "He can't have him. I won't allow it. He's mine, do you hear me? Mine!"

Before he could take another step, Mei bolted, and the front door slammed against the wall with how hard she yanked it open.

"Mei-lei-ya, call the police," he said quietly.

Then he went upstairs to his niece's room. Until now he'd never entered Mei's room without her permission, but he had a suspicion it was high time he did. When he opened the door, his stomach twisted. Photos of Jin-woo covered almost every available surface. The floor was blanketed with shredded papers, and a huge map hung on one wall. Pinned to it were the rigging plans for Eumak Nabi Theater.

"Oh, Mei-ya, what have you done?" he whispered, a tear sliding down his cheek. Then he pulled out his phone and dialed Soon-joon-nim's number.

JIN-WOO

JIN-WOO WALKED down the aisle of the campus auditorium, Kyung-soo next to him, alert and tense. Ki-tae insisted Shin-bai accompany him while Jin-woo insisted Shin-bai should be with Ki-tae. They compromised with Shin-bai staying with Ki-tae, and his second-in-command, Kyung-soo, going with Jin-woo. Jin-woo chuckled. If Ki-tae had his way, he would be surrounded by bodyguards anytime he was out of Ki-tae's sight. While a bit annoying, it was also very sweet.

"Seonsaengnim?" Jin-woo called as he reached the stage. "Are you here?"

"This is suspicious," Kyung-soo said as he rolled his shoulders. "We should leave."

"He may be backstage, and it's difficult to hear anyone out front," Jin-woo said. "Let's just check quickly. If he's not there, then we'll leave."

"Very well," Kyung-soo said. "I do not like it, though."

"I'm not too happy about it either."

Someone snaked a thin arm around his neck as they walked back toward the front of the auditorium after checking backstage, and Jin-woo immediately began to struggle. They tightened their arm, cutting off his air, but Kyung-soo had already turned. Then he felt cold metal placed against his temple.

"Make one move, and I will kill him," Mei said, her voice higher than usual and strained. "He's mine, and I will not let that monster take him from me."

"Ki-tae is not a monster. He would never hold a fucking gun to my head. He would never threaten the people I love. He would never harm other people the way you have. You're the monster, Mei, not him."

"Shut up," she hissed.

"Clearly she is not mentally stable. Perhaps antagonizing her while she has a 9mm semiautomatic pistol to your head is not a wise idea," Kyung-soo said in a perfunctory voice.

"We're going to leave, and you're going to let us," Mei said.

"I'm afraid that is not possible," Kyung-soo said. "It is my recommendation you put the weapon down and turn yourself in. This will not end well."

"Now who's antagonizing her?"

"I am stating fact."

"No, I have a better idea, a more fitting idea." Mei giggled. "Call him. Call that *thief*. Bring him here, and we'll end this once and for all. Bring them all here, and I will show them Jin-woo is mine and mine alone."

"Okay, I think that is a very bad idea," Jin-woo said.

"Very well," Kyung-soo said as he held up his cell phone, showing the active call screen. "They are already on their way. I must warn you, however. Ki-tae dongsaeng is very unhappy, and that is never a good thing."

"Don't say *that* name! *Never* say that name in my presence."

Jin-woo resisted the urge to chant Ki-tae's name, but just barely. The gun was still against his head, and as much as she wanted him, he figured she might pull the trigger on impulse. He felt slightly hysterical, not sure what to do, but not wanting Ki-tae anywhere near this crazy bitch. He had to try to keep Ki-tae away.

"Ki-tae, you damn well better not come here!" he yelled.

"Cheongul dongsaeng says he and Min-su dongsaeng are already gone." Kyung-soo shrugged before switching his attention to Mei. "I advised against this course of action."

"Don't forget Jong-in," Mei hissed. "He has to be here too."

"Now that is highly inadvisable," Kyung-soo said. "If harm comes to Jong-in dongsaeng, that will anger HanYin dongsaeng, and that is even worse than angering Ki-tae dongsaeng. You are a very suicidal woman, I think," Kyung-soo said.

"They won't do anything as long as I have my precious Jin-woo." She laughed. "I will eliminate them one by one by one, and then nothing will prevent us from being together."

"Don't you get it? I'm gay! I am not sexually attracted to women. I never have been, and I never will be!" Jin-woo said angrily. She tightened her arm around his neck and pressed her cheek against his, sliding the barrel of the gun along his neck in a disturbing caress. Revulsion raced through his entire body. "I wouldn't respond to you, not now, not ever."

"There are ways around that, my sweet Jin-woo, drugs I can use, and you won't be able to resist me."

"Over my dead body." Ki-tae's voice echoed through the auditorium.

"That's the plan." Mei giggled again, the sound grating against Jin-woo's ears. He frantically searched the auditorium for Ki-tae, zeroing in on him as he stepped from the shadows by the entrance doors. Joy and dread surged through him.

"No matter what you do, no matter what drugs you give him, you'll always know, won't you, Mei?" Ki-tae's voice was low, sibilant, and Jin-woo could see his silver eyes. He walked with his hands in his pockets, casually, as if he didn't have a care in the world, but Jin-woo could sense his anger, his agitation, and his urge to charge them.

"What are you talking about?" Mei said haughtily. "He's mine."

"No, he's not." Ki-tae chuckled. "He's mine in every sense of the word. I know him intimately in a way you never will, and even if you drug him into oblivion, even if you manage to get him to perform for you, you'll always know, in the back of your mind, that Jin-woo loves me, desires me, has given himself to me freely and with abandon. I have heard his moans. I have felt his caresses. I have watched him come apart in my arms, screaming my name in his pleasure. I have heard his joyous laughter, felt his kisses over every inch of my body, and you will never know the ecstasy of his love, of knowing his heart is yours... because it is already mine."

"Shut up! Shut up! Shut Up!" Mei screamed.

It really does happen in slow motion, Jin-woo thought. He watched her swing her arm away from him, felt a shove send him stumbling to the stage, the barrel pointing toward Ki-tae, and the flash as it fired. He hit the ground with a thud. Hysterical screaming filled the air. And then Ki-tae was at his side, pulling him into his arms, and the safety of it engulfed him. The screaming continued, and when he looked over, Jin-woo saw Min-su sitting on top of Mei, pinning her hands above her head.

"I swear to God, if you don't stop that screaming, I'm going to knock you unconscious, bitch!" she growled. Then she turned to look at Jin-woo. Her eyes were blazing red. "Are you okay?"

He nodded, leaning into Ki-tae's arms. "I am now."

Before anyone could say anything else, police flooded the theater. Behind them came Soon-joon, Cheongul, HanYin, and Jong-in. Then ChenBao entered, and Jin-woo could feel the tension and menace rocket upward. She was not a happy Dragon. Min-su hauled Mei to her feet and shoved her at the police officers.

"Kyung-soo hubae!" Shin-bai's voice was sharp with concern, and Jin-woo pulled his head from Ki-tae's chest. He spotted Shin-bai holding Kyung-soo at the end of the stage.

"I am sorry, Boojang-nim. I shouldn't have allowed her to put hands on him," he said, his voice strained and his hand clutching at his upper chest, over his heart.

"Nonsense," Shin-bai said. "You did your job well, contacting us immediately, and she is no longer a threat to Jin-woo dongsaeng and Ki-tae dongsaeng."

"I had to stand by, helpless to act."

"Shhh, Kyung-soo dongsaeng." ChenBao sat down next to him wrapped her arm around his shoulders, and kissed his temple. "You have always done your job well."

"He needs an ambulance," one of the officers said. "He's bleeding pretty badly."

"They are on their way." Jin-woo didn't see who spoke, but he didn't care. He hurried over to Kyung-soo.

"You did great," he said with a watery smile.

"I am sorry, Jin-woo dongsaeng."

"No, no apologies. She could have just dragged me off, but you kept her here. You wouldn't leave, and you tried to get her to give up. That's more than anyone could ask for."

"I am faster than she is," he said. "I could have disarmed her."

"But there's a chance she would have shot me, and you knew that, so you did the best thing."

Kyung-soo closed his eyes and sighed. For a second Jin-woo panicked, thinking he was watching such a brave man die, but then his chest rose again. He looked at ChenBao, and she winked at him. She had put Kyung-soo under.

"He will have to go to a hospital," she said. "But we have our doctors in every hospital in every city we travel to. It has nicked his heart, but he will be okay."

"How can you be sure?" Jin-woo asked, tears blurring his vision. She just looked at him with a raised eyebrow. "Right, forget I asked."

Jin-woo rose and turned toward Ki-tae with a smile. The shriek filled the auditorium, and he barely caught Min-su's "Thank you, God" before he was shoved out of the way again, and she launched herself off the stage. As he rolled over, he saw Min-su's fist slam into Mei's face as Mei rushed the stage, officers chasing her, a nausea-inducing crunch echoing through the air, and Mei collapsed to the ground.

"God, that felt good," Min-su said with a wicked smile. "I've been waiting to do that for months!"

Cheongul walked over to her and pulled her into his arms. "You're giving these nice officers nasty impressions of you."

She shrugged. "I'm just being honest. Even before she went batshit crazy, she was annoying."

It seemed to take forever before they could finally leave the auditorium. Jin-woo leaned heavily on Ki-tae, feeling so worn-out and tired. He just wanted to sleep, wrapped in Ki-tae's arms, and not think about the last week. Spring had not started off with the fun times they anticipated. After the press conference, things were truly weird. He and Ki-tae had a few run-ins with angry fans. Hence Ki-tae's insistence he have a bodyguard. After the third time in a single day, they stayed either in his apartment or Ki-tae's. The netizens were harsh and overreactive, but surprisingly, the support from other fans was just as prominent. One fan went so far as to apologize to him on Weibo, stating she was still going to "fantasize about his man, thank you very much." It made him laugh. He responded with a smiley face and a "Me too!" Ki-tae had blushed. It resulted in a very hot session on his couch.

"My place or yours?" Ki-tae asked softly as they climbed into the car.

"Soon-joon-nim's," he said. "As much as I love your apartment, I want to feel safe right now. In your arms at the house would be ideal."

"The house it is," Ki-tae said with a soft smile, pulling Jin-woo into his lap as the car moved. "I feel safest there too."

"Is it truly over, Ki-tae?" he asked, hating how his voice shook.

"Yes. It's over, my love."

"I love the sound of that," Jin-woo murmured, his eyes slipping closed without his permission. Then he was asleep.

JONG-IN

JONG-IN SAT on one of the rocks in the garden, the trickling stream a soothing sound in the evening light. He plucked at the strings of an acoustic guitar, picking out the melody to "Untainted." Softly he began to sing, remembering when those words had poured from his battered heart, as if that was all he was ever going to have. He was so scared back then. Back then. Had it truly been only a few months? It seemed so long ago. Now he was with the man he'd loved from the moment he heard him sing. His mother and sister were in a new home. It was surreal, seeing them again and not feeling a threat looming over him. His mother had cried, but when he tried to apologize for being gay, she smacked him, saying he was her son, and as long as he was loved in return, it did not matter if that person was male. Then they all cried.

During that conversation, Hyun-jo pulled things from his mother he'd never heard before, like she once dreamed of having her own restaurant. Within a few hours, Hyun-jo made that dream come true. Pogseu Paieo would open within a few months. His sister would transfer high schools, and his family would be close by. Every so often, Jong-in would pinch himself. Everything felt like a dream. Now all he had to do was figure out how to invite HanYin to meet his mother and sister. He wanted them to know the man who made him happy.

"Now who is thinking too hard?" HanYin's voice was a whisper on the breeze, and then he was there, lowering himself to sit next to Jong-in. "That song is both beautiful and heartbreaking."

"I'm sorry."

"Don't be. I love it." HanYin smiled. "May I?"

Jong-in handed over the guitar, confused at the request. His confusion didn't last long when HanYin began to sing. He sat, enraptured, hearing the words and knowing the feelings behind them. HanYin didn't look at him as he sang, even though Jong-in tried to catch his eye. Then the notes were fading, and the last chorus hung in the air between them.

Yes or no?
Will you tell me yes or no?
Will you hold my heart?
Will you let it go?
Do I take the chance?
I'm scared, but I want to know,
Yes... or no?

"Of course it's yes," Jong-in said softly. "There couldn't be anyone else but you, HanYin."

"It won't be easy," he said, still not looking at him. "Especially now that we've been outed. People will be stupid."

"People were stupid before, but I spent too long worrying about what other people would think, too long trying to be something I'm not, and I won't do it anymore. I love you, HanYin, and I want to spend the rest of my apparently very long life with you."

Jong-in took the guitar from his hands and gently set it aside. Then he climbed into HanYin's lap, cupping his face and forcing him to look at him. "You are it for me. Whatever happens, if we're together, I can take it."

"Zhēn?" HanYin shook his head and then tried again. "Truly?"

"Zhēn," Jong-in chuckled. "Although you're going to have to teach me Mandarin so I can understand what you're saying when you lose the ability to speak other languages."

HanYin blushed. Clearly he was thinking of the last time Jong-in made him unable to speak anything but Mandarin. Jong-in smiled and then kissed him slowly. When he drew back, they were both breathless. "Let's go inside."

"Shi," HanYin said. "That means yes."

Jong-in stood and offered his hand. HanYin took it, and, grabbing the guitar, they went inside. As they walked, he thought about asking but wasn't sure how to bring it up.

"What is on your mind, wǒ de xīn?" At Jong-in's raised eyebrow, HanYin ducked his head and then translated. "It means 'my heart.'"

"I never really thought about how beautiful Mandarin sounds. It's very... lyrical, almost melodic," Jong-in said.

"Some people say we sound like we're drunk when we speak because the words blend together," HanYin said. "But I agree, it's very musical. Nice try, by the way. What were you thinking about?"

"No hiding from you, huh?"

"No."

"I want take you to meet my mother and sister," he said in a rush. "Hyun-jo-nim has set them up with a new home, and he arranged for Eomeonim to have her dream restaurant, and I want her to meet the man who's made me so... so fucking happy it almost hurts."

"I would be honored to meet your mother," HanYin said softly. "I like to think if mine had lived... well, if mine had lived, we probably wouldn't be here."

"Will you tell me one day, when you're ready?"

"Someday. It is not a happy memory, and I do not like to revisit it."

"I can understand that, and I can be patient," Jong-in said as he led HanYin through the door of his room and then closed it behind them. "My mother's restaurant opens in a few months. She and my sister live above it, and, knowing her, she will be constantly working on it right up to opening day. Perhaps we could go over there someday before it opens."

"We usually have Sunday dinner here, but I do not think Abeoji will mind if we have one Sunday with your mother and sister," HanYin said as he pulled Jong-in into his arms. It was amazing how strong HanYin could be, the muscles shifting smoothly beneath his skin. And yet he yielded to him. It made Jong-in feel so very special. He kissed HanYin gently, bringing his arms around his waist to scrape along his lower back, sending shivers through HanYin's body. He loved how responsive HanYin was to his touch, loved making him whimper and writhe as they made love.

"I hope you ate well," he purred in HanYin's ear. "You're not going to be leaving this room for quite some time."

"Promise?" HanYin murmured as he nipped Jong-in's lip.

"Promise."

HANYIN

HANYIN STOOD in front of the full-length mirror. He tilted his head this way and that, studying his reflection. The dress slacks were okay, but he wasn't sure about the white button-up shirt. It wasn't comfortable, but he wanted to make a good impression. Sighing, he removed the shirt and hung it back up. Then he flipped through his shirts. What should he wear? Were the dress slacks too much? Should he wear something more formal? What type of restaurant was Pogseu Paieo? He went over to his bed and sat down, putting his head in his hands. The nervousness just wouldn't leave. Perhaps he should stay home. He reached for his phone just as there was a knock on his door.

"Come in," he called as he picked up his phone and unlocked it.

"If you are considering canceling, don't." ChenBao smiled at him from the doorway.

"Nǎi nai," he said softly, and she giggled.

"I love how you call me that," she said as she came farther into the room. Pausing before him, she ruffled his hair. "Your nervousness is palpable. I figured I would see if I could help."

"I want to make a good impression, but dressing up seems...."

"Fake?" she said. He nodded. "Then do not get all dressed up. That is not the true you. As an idol, there are times you must don a tuxedo or suit and tie, but this is not one of those times. This isn't a formal betrothal meeting, Sūnzi. Be yourself."

She walked over to his closet. In less time than it took him to inhale, she laid a pair of black jeans, a red summer-weight turtleneck, and a lightweight dark brown jacket on the bed. She then pulled out a pair of his black combat boots. "There. Comfortable, but not too casual and definitely presentable."

"I am scared," he said. "What if she doesn't like me?"

"That is every boyfriend's fear. What if the father or the mother doesn't like me? And it is understandable," ChenBao said as she sat down next to him. After the first time he made her tea, they had shared in that simple ritual every day they could. He had grown accustomed to her qi, to her scent, and to her presence. She was still intimidating at times, but she didn't terrify him anymore. He could feel her love for him. "I do not think that will be the case here. I think she will adore you, and you already have two things in common."

"Two?"

"You both love Jong-in-a," ChenBao said, holding up one finger and then a second. "And you both love to cook for your family."

"True." HanYin sighed. "It's been such a long time since I've done this, since I've allowed myself to love someone. Jong-in is... amazing."

"He is," ChenBao said. "You all are, and I am very proud to count you among my family, especially my grandsons."

HanYin looked at her. "Have you ever been in love, Nǎi nai?"

"Yes," she said quietly. "It is both joyous and bittersweet. You see, I have a tendency to fall in love with humans, and it is harder for me because, as a Dragon, I can only bond with someone who can handle my qi. I have yet to find that man. I have loved, but I have had to watch them age while I remain as I am. I do not regret my time with them or the joy we brought each other, but it breaks my heart every time I must let their spirit continue its journey."

"Your qi?" he asked, tilting his head.

"A Celestial Dragon has very powerful energy. It is like a raging fire within us. When we are... intimate, that energy is shared with our partner. If we are not careful, it will burn them from the inside out," she said softly. "It is a painful death and horrible to watch and know it is your fault. We must always be aware of our qi and keep it from consuming our partner."

"How would you know if someone could handle your qi or not?"

"My father once said it is known in an instant, from the first brush of fingers. He said when he met my mother and touched her hand, peace settled over him, and his fire was banked. That's how he knew she was the one." ChenBao smiled. "They were very happy together, and my siblings and I never doubted their love for each other or us."

"How many brothers and sisters do you have?"

"There are twelve of us: six men and six women," ChenBao said, standing. "Now enough about me. You must get ready for your date. Once you have won over his mother, you must bring them to the house for dinner sometime."

"Xièxiè, Nǎi nai," he said with a smile. She leaned down and kissed his forehead.

"Bù kèqì, Wǒ de sūnzi."

He had just stripped off his shirt when his phone rang. Anxiously he snatched it up as Jong-in's ringtone played. "Yeoboseyo?"

"Hello, HanYin." Jong-in's voice sounded... annoyed. "I have some news."

"She doesn't want to meet me," he said, a rock settling in his gut.

"What? No, no, it's not that." Jong-in sighed. "It's just not going to be you, me, and my family. Apparently Min-su-ya and Jin-woo-ya stopped by the other day looking for me, and she invited them too. And she said they could bring their boyfriends. So it's all of us."

"So it's still you, me, and your family." HanYin chuckled.

"Well, yeah, I guess it is," Jong-in said. "I just... I was hoping to keep it small."

"I'll be honest, I'm happy Cheongul and Ki-tae will be there. I'm nervous as hell as it is." HanYin gave a dry laugh. "I've… never been introduced to someone's mother before."

"You're going to do fine, and she's going to love you," Jong-in said. "I know I do."

"I love you too."

"So hurry up and finish getting ready. I bet they're already waiting for you," Jong-in teased.

"Are you kidding? Have you ever timed how long it takes Ki-tae to get ready? I have, and it's never been under an hour." HanYin snorted. "About the only one who is going to be ready before me is Cheongul, and that's only because he has no idea how to not do anything."

"Did that even make sense in your head?" Jong-in laughed.

"I meant he can't sit still. He always has to be doing something," HanYin huffed. "Oh, hang up and let me finish getting ready, *yi saekki*…. I love you."

"I love you too, HanYin."

After they finally hung up, HanYin was quick to dress, changing out of the dress slacks and then pulling on the turtleneck. He kept the accessories to a minimum, donning only a small dangle earring in his right ear and a simple stud in his left. He put an unassuming silver ring with red stones on his right hand and a silver bracelet on his left wrist. Pulling on the jacket, he examined his reflection. Yes, this definitely suited him better. He took a deep breath and then walked out of his room. When he reached the living room, he found Cheongul fiddling at the piano, and it made him smile.

"Waiting for Ki-tae, as usual," he said.

"Yup," Cheongul said absently, most of his attention focused on the music. HanYin joined him on the bench.

"What are you working on?"

"It's been stuck in my head for the last day or so," Cheongul murmured. "I almost have it, but this middle piece right here. It doesn't fit."

HanYin closed his eyes as Cheongul played it again. Then he put his hands on the keys. "Try this."

He played the song from the beginning, making his tweak to the middle section. "How's that?"

"That's it." Cheongul smiled, bumping his shoulder, and HanYin couldn't help but return it. Cheongul didn't smile like that often, with his whole face.

"Are you two done playing? We have somewhere to be," Ki-tae said as he walked into the room.

"We're waiting on you," Cheongul said.

"As usual," HanYin teased.

"Shut up and let's go," Ki-tae grumbled.

Soon they were on their way to Pogseu Paieo, and HanYin felt as if he were going to be sick. He stared out the window, watching the scenery pass, trying not to think about it. Would she like him? Would she hate him? Would he be okay, or would he make a fool of himself somehow?

"Stop," Ki-tae said softly. "She's going to love you."

"You don't know that."

"HanYin, of the three of us, you're the most personable," Cheongul said. "People love you on sight."

"Still."

"It will be fine," Ki-tae reassured him.

He should have listened to his brothers. Within five minutes of being introduced to Jong-in's mother, Yeong-ja, she was hugging him and dragging him into the kitchen. Jong-in tried to follow, but she shooed him away. The food smelled delicious, and he could see several bowls already prepared.

"My Jong-in, he's a good boy," she said as she handed him a spoon and gestured to one of the pots. "He tells me you cook well and that you make him eat. This is good. He will forget if someone does not remind him."

"I try to take care of him," HanYin said. "He doesn't always let me."

"He is a stubborn boy too." She smiled. "He has his father's pride."

"He makes me very happy," HanYin said softly as he stirred.

"You make him happy too," she said. "This is all a mother wants for her children, for them to be loved and happy. Thank you for giving him that."

"He is very easy to love." HanYin smiled. "And his dimples are killer. I see where he gets them from."

"Oh, now you flirt with this old lady, a handsome young man like you!" Yeong-ja laughed. "You are a good man, I can tell. My son is special as his father was special. So are you. It is good. He needs someone who will wear him out so he will rest."

HanYin stared at her in shock, and she just grinned at him, making him blush. She reminded him of ChenBao, and he wasn't sure that was a good thing.

"Come, we must feed them. They are too skinny," she said with a grin. "So are you. I best see you eating at least three helpings, such a skinny boy!"

The food was amazing. He could really taste the love in it, and the company was superb. Having his brothers and friends around made it easier for HanYin to relax. There was laughter and joy and teasing all around. It was such a wonderful experience he almost wished it didn't have to end.

Just as everyone was finishing the main meal, Jong-in's phone rang. When he looked the caller ID, he frowned.

"Who is it?" HanYin asked, but Jong-in just shook his head. He rose from his seat and would have walked away if HanYin hadn't caught his wrist. "Are you okay?"

"Yeah, I just need to take this call," he said, giving a smile that didn't reach his eyes. "I'll be right back. You guys finish eating. Then we can have dessert."

HanYin let him go, but he didn't like it. His gut was telling him this was a bad idea.

JONG-IN

JONG-IN WALKED out of the restaurant as he answered the phone. "What do you want?"

"I want my wife and my daughter back, you little shit," Kang-dae demanded.

"They were never yours," Jong-in said, his shoulders tensing up. There was something off about Kang-dae. His voice didn't sound right. It sounded like the whispers from the cemetery, but it was hard to tell over the phone.

"She was always mine!"

The blow came out of nowhere, striking Jong-in solidly in the cheek. He stumbled. Before he could regain his footing, he was knocked to the ground and then dragged into the alley. Kang-dae grabbed him by the front of his shirt.

"I should have gotten rid of you the minute he was dead," Kang-dae growled, smashing his fist into his face again and again. "He had no right. She was mine from the minute I saw her. And now, now you humiliate me with that disgusting display on live television! Kissing a man, fucking a man. You're an abomination. You're a waste, useless, nothing but garbage."

"Fuck you!" Jong-in said as he swung wildly, catching Kang-dae in the jaw and sending him flying against the wall. He rolled to his knees. The alley was cold and deathly still. As Jong-in stood up, things shimmered as if he were looking at a double-exposed photo. Shadows darted here and there, moving all around, but he couldn't get a fix on them. Something was not right He spun around, trying to locate Kang-dae, but the alley seemed empty. It was so disorienting, nothing stood still like it should. The two-by-four slammed into his shoulders and he crashed into the ground, his head connecting with the concrete. His vision blurred, and he couldn't orient himself. Then the blackness crept in, and Jong-in collapsed, barely registering his stepfather's words.

"I'm going to kill you, and then I'm going to get my wife and daughter."

JIN-WOO

"NOPE, NOT doing it. Let's go," Jin-woo said, standing up from the table. Everyone stared at him. "What? He's been gone too long for a simple phone call. Something isn't right, and I'm not going to sit here and wait to find out what it is."

He left the table and hurried toward the front of the restaurant. The sound of chairs scraping against the floor followed. He didn't wait for them but simply headed out the doors.

The sound of fists hitting flesh caught Jin-woo's attention, and he ran, but HanYin was faster. He rounded the corner of the restaurant into the alley just in time to see Jong-in on the ground, unmoving and bloodied, his stepfather, Kang-dae, raining blows on him. A loud roar battered the air, and HanYin's kick sent Kang-dae crashing into the wall at the end of the alley, HanYin following. The growling and snarling coming from him was terrifying. But Jin-woo couldn't think about that now. He started toward Jong-in, only to have Ki-tae stop him. He looked at Ki-tae in question and saw him jerk his chin toward the other end of the alley.

When Kang-dae finally gave up trying to stand, HanYin stopped. He stood over the huge man, his chest heaving, clenching and unclenching his hands, bloodied. Jin-woo watched him visibly grab hold of himself. He turned and walked back toward them, his eyes still blazing silver and his fangs barely hidden. Though people had flooded the alley, no one got close. HanYin knelt next to Jong-in. Gently he touched his face and then scooped Jong-in into his arms, holding him close to his chest as he walked out of the alley. He didn't say a word to anyone. He didn't need to. No one stopped him or got in his way.

"HanYin will take care of him," Ki-tae said, draping an arm around Jin-woo's shoulders. "He's in the safest hands right now."

"I know," Jin-woo said, wiping angrily at the tears. "I'm not crying because of that. I'm crying because I'm so fucking angry right now I could seriously hurt that man."

"He won't be getting up anytime soon, not without assistance. I can hear his breathing from here," Ki-tae said quietly. "If HanYin hadn't stopped himself, the bastard would be dead, but Jong-in came first."

"Bastard is too kind a word for him," Jin-woo growled, wrapping his arms around Ki-tae's waist.

"He is," Yeong-ja said quietly. "He always has been. I should never have allowed him into our home once Jong-su had passed. I should have sent him away. Instead I allowed him to hurt my son and imprison my daughter and myself in his home."

"Don't blame yourself, Yeong-ja-nim. Some people are just jerks," Min-su said as she put her arms around Jong-in's mother. "You were grieving, and he took advantage of that."

"I should have protected my children," she cried.

She buried her face in Min-su's shoulder. Min-su looked at Jin-woo and Ki-tae, inclining her head toward the restaurant. Then she took Yeong-ja inside. Yeong-hui, Jong-in's sister, walked over to her stepfather. She stared down at him, and Jin-woo wondered what was going through her head.

"I used to be terrified of him," she said softly. "Now he looks so pathetic."

"Bullies often are when they meet someone stronger than they are," Cheongul said.

"You are like my brother and myself, aren't you?" she asked, looking at Cheongul.

"Yourself?" Jin-woo said, and she gave him that "duh" look all teenagers seemed to master the minute they hit puberty.

"I can see it," she said. "Min-su unnie is more like us than Cheongul oppa and Ki-tae oppa, but you're not like us at all, Jin-woo oppa."

"No, I'm not," Jin-woo said, feeling that difference keenly now.

"We're... similar but not the same," Cheongul said carefully. "Look, the police are here. Why don't we continue this inside after they've taken out the trash?"

"Are there more like us? Like Jong-in oppa and me?" she asked, and for a moment, she was a frightened little girl.

"Yes. We'll introduce you to him. I think you and Hyun-jo-nim will get along just fine."

"Hyun-jo oppa? He came with Jong-in oppa that day, the day we moved," she said as she blushed. "He's very pretty."

"He is." Jin-woo chuckled.

"Hey!" Ki-tae said. "What am I?"

"Handsome, sexy, adorable? All mine?" Jin-woo said. "Pick one."

"All of the above." Ki-tae grinned and pulled him into a kiss just as the ambulance pulled up.

Kang-dae was hauled away to the hospital with a police escort. One of the officers gently insisted they needed to see Jong-in. That was an interesting encounter. It took Ki-tae and Cheongul to convince HanYin to let anyone into the room. Jong-in had regained consciousness, but he really didn't need to speak. The black eyes, swollen lip, and darkening bruises all over his torso said plenty. Yeong-ja brought in a first aid kit and set about tending her son while HanYin hovered. Jin-woo was pretty sure if she hadn't been Jong-in's mother, she wouldn't have gotten within a foot of him. Ki-tae kept their attention off HanYin, as his eyes were still flashing back and forth.

When they were finally left alone, HanYin crawled carefully into the bed with Jong-in, heedless of his mother being right there. He curled around him, and that was that, but the smile on Yeong-ja's face said she had no problem with it. Clearly HanYin loved her boy, and that's all that mattered to her. Then she reached for HanYin's hand, and everyone tensed. He growled softly.

"Shush," she admonished as she dabbed at his bloodied knuckles. "Thank you for saving my son."

HanYin's growls quieted, much to Jin-woo's surprise. He glanced at Ki-tae, who simply shrugged. Then he pulled Jin-woo out of the room. "That was... the weirdest experience I've ever had.... Well, except for stalker bitch."

"She exudes calmness and love," Ki-tae said. "HanYin senses that. I think there's a little bit of spiritual blood on her side of the family."

"It wouldn't surprise me. I just wish none of this had happened. We were having such a nice time."

"True, but now he's out of the picture for good, and Jong-in-a won't have to worry about his mother and sister," Cheongul said from his seat at the table as they came into the dining room.

"What an ass," Min-su grumbled.

"Very true," Jin-woo said. "I think we should head out, give them some time to rest. Jong-in-a isn't going anywhere anytime soon, and neither is HanYin-a."

"You're right," Cheongul said. "We'll come back another time and bring Abeoji and Hyun-jo-nim with us."

They said their goodbyes to Yeong-ja and Yeong-hui and then to each other. Min-su left with Cheongul, and Ki-tae and Jin-woo headed back to his apartment.

They kicked off their shoes in the front hall, and then Jin-woo padded to the living room, going down the two steps and stretching out on the couch. He sighed, thinking about all that had happened over the last few months. The only thing hanging over his head was Mei's trial. He didn't really want to go through that. Given she attacked Bam Kiseu, sabotaged a concert hall, injured about thirty innocent people, and shot someone with a, more than likely, illegal firearm, tried to run over Ki-tae twice, destroyed and then cleaned his apartment, it was going to be a media circus. Ki-tae came over and pulled him into his lap, snuggling close.

"You look exhausted and sad," he said.

"I'm just thinking," he said, resting his head on Ki-tae's shoulder. "It seems like everything is over except the trial, and I really am not looking forward to that. I don't think she'll go to prison, anyway. They only have to listen to her talk to know she's insane. They'll lock her up in some institution instead."

"Either way, she won't be able to come after you and me again," Ki-tae said. "I think I can live with that."

"I suppose." He snuggled against Ki-tae's chest, yawning.

"So sleepy." Ki-tae chuckled as he stood and carried Jin-woo into the bedroom. "And here I thought I would get lucky tonight."

"Hm." Jin-woo laughed softly. "Maybe later."

"I can wait for later," Ki-tae said. He stripped them both, climbed into the bed, and pulled Jin-woo's back to his chest. "Is it later?"

Jin-woo burst out laughing. He rolled into Ki-tae's embrace, giggling against his chest. "You're such a sex fiend."

"Only with you," Ki-tae murmured, nuzzling his neck.

"You're obsessed with my neck."

"It's one of my favorite places to bite," Ki-tae purred. "Your scent is strongest there and here."

He slid his finger along the sensitive skin between his legs where thigh met hip. Jin-woo gasped as shivers danced over his skin. He parted his thighs wider and pulled Ki-tae to him by the shoulders as he rolled onto his back. He smiled up at Ki-tae. "It's later."

"Good," Ki-tae said before taking his mouth in a slow, sweet kiss.

Jin-woo whimpered softly, hooked his legs over Ki-tae's hips, and bucked upward, rubbing their erections together and spreading slick precum between them. He wanted Ki-tae inside him, but strangely, was in no hurry to get him there. He wanted this slow buildup. He wanted to feel the tension tightening inside him. He caressed the long line of Ki-tae's back, kneading his flexing buttocks as Ki-tae answered his movements with thrusts of his own. Fingers danced, teased, prepared, and then were replaced by the hard length of Ki-tae's cock sliding slowly inside him. He loved the way he could feel himself stretching to accommodate Ki-tae's length and girth. He loved the connection that seemed to grow stronger each time they made love, and Jin-woo realized he wanted this forever. He pulled from Ki-tae's kisses and cupped his face, holding perfectly still, though he wanted to writhe beneath him.

"Ki-tae?"

"Yes."

"How do we complete the bond?"

Ki-tae froze above him, his eyes wide with shock at first and then softening and filling with love. Jin-woo smiled.

"You... you want to complete it? You want to spend forever... with me?"

"I do." Jin-woo felt the joy bubbling within him, and it came out in a happy laugh. "I want to spend forever with you, Jung Ki-tae."

Ki-tae pushed up on his forearm and snatched his phone off the nightstand. It took him several attempts to dial the number he wanted. "Halmeonim, how do Jin-woo and I complete the bond?"

Jin-woo heard ChenBao clearly and laughed. Apparently she was ecstatic at the news. He couldn't hear what she said after her squeal, and yes, she squealed, but Ki-tae was being very attentive. "Can we do it now, or do we have to wait? Okay, yes. I understand."

Jin-woo watched Ki-tae blush furiously. "Halmeonim! Can we do the ceremony part later? Awesome. Gomabseumnida, Halmeonim!"

He hung up the phone and put it back on the nightstand. Jin-woo looked at him expectantly. "We don't need to do anything super special. Usually there's a ceremony involved, a ritual, but Halmeonim says it's not really necessary, as it really just acts as a guide for the energy itself."

"So? What do we have to do?"

Jin-woo gasped when Ki-tae wrapped an arm around his waist and then shifted into a cross-legged sitting position, pushing himself deeper. "Damn, so good."

"Since you're human, you don't have the same control over your qi as Spiritual Beings do," Ki-tae said in a low growl, clearly not unaffected by the change in position. "You'll need to take some of my blood to open the pathways for our energies to merge together."

"Drink your blood?" Jin-woo said softly.

Ki-tae smiled. "Don't worry. Halmeonim gave me a suggestion on how to take your mind off that part, not that I really needed it."

Jin-woo watched the silver slowly bleed into Ki-tae's eyes, and a shiver of anticipation shook his body. Ki-tae's lip kicked up at the corner, showing his fangs lengthening. It was so slow Jin-woo almost didn't notice it. Then Ki-tae was kissing him senseless.

He responded, thrusting his tongue deep and licking at Ki-tae's fangs. The resulting growl made his belly clench. Ki-tae thrust hard, nailing his prostate, and Jin-woo cried into his mouth. He met each upward thrust with a push of his hips, rolling them. He gripped Ki-tae's shoulders, digging in his fingers, felt Ki-tae's hands on his ass, teasing the stretched skin where they joined with his fingers. In all the overwhelming sensations, Jin-woo barely notice the coppery taste flavoring Ki-tae's kisses. He just knew he wanted to go on kissing and making love with Ki-tae.

Higher and higher they flew. When he had to breathe, Jin-woo pulled back to see the smirk on Ki-tae's face and the blood smeared around his mouth. Jin-woo's eyes went wide, and he licked his lips, tasting copper. Before he could react, the most amazing sensation flooded his body. He cried out as every nerve ending seemed to fire at once. Clinging to Ki-tae, Jin-woo rode out the amplified sensation of their combined orgasm, gasping for breath as he felt as if he were being torn apart and put back together again. It was too much, simply too much, and Jin-woo let go of consciousness to float on the cloud of pleasure swamping him.

HYUN-JO LISTENED to the Qīngróu's whispers as she gave him her report. It matched what the spirits had told him regarding Jong-su's train accident. Much as he wished otherwise, it had not been an accident at all. Now, it was time to hunt. The question was did he hunt alone or with another?

"Hyun-jo?" Soon-joon stepped out into the rock garden and carefully leapt to the rock he was sitting on. "What is wrong?"

"It is nothing."

"Saiai." Soon-joon's voice held a warning.

"Very well." Hyun-jo sighed. "Kang-dae was possessed by an onryo. He claimed Yeong-ja dongsaeng was his, had been his. He killed a whole train full of people just to eliminate Jong-su dongsaeng, Jong-in-a's father. It takes a lot to kill us if we have not reached full Celestial status, but it is possible."

"I recall that catastrophe," Soon-joon said as he wrapped his arms around Hyun-jo. "They never figured out what caused it, did they?"

"There was no way they could unless they could communicate with the spirits of the departed, and as far as I know, only Kitsune and Fèng-huáng can do so."

"The spirit is still within Kang-dae?"

"Yes. For all intents and purposes, the real Kang-dae is dead. The spirit has resided within the body for so long that the original spirit has wasted away. We will never know why he fixated on Yeong-ja dongsaeng, but he has caused their family nothing but pain. He terrorized the driver into losing control of the train." Hyun-jo growled. "I gave him until the new moon to set Kang-dae's affairs in order and leave. I told him what would happen if I found out he had anything to do with Jong-su dongsaeng's death."

"Will you tell Jong-in-a?" Soon-joon asked as he nuzzled Hyun-jo's temple. It had always soothed him in the past, but this time, Hyun-jo could not let go of his anger.

"Yes, and then… we will hunt."

Soon-joon simply nodded.

CHENBAO

CHENBAO FLOATED gracefully in the air, twisting this way and that sinuously. She loved the feel of the wind on her scales, pulling at her mane, and the kisses the wind spirits placed on her face. She had already checked on HanYin and Jong-in, sending healing qi into the young Kitsune to speed his recovery. Cheongul and Min-su were snug in bed at his apartment, curled around each other almost like puppies. Hyun-jo and Soon-joon were finally bonded and marked, so there were no worries there. Her son would not be so stupid as to let his little Fox go again.

Even Ki-tae and Jin-woo were settled. Well, almost settled. There was one thing that hung over their heads, and ChenBao was not inclined to let it remain there. Perhaps she was an old-fashioned Dragon, but there were some insults and injuries she could not let go unanswered.

THE CELL was dark and cold and lonely, and all she could hear was him singing. Singing, singing, always singing, sweet and light, an angel's voice. Her Jin-woo, her sweet, naughty Jin-woo. Mei giggled. She wouldn't go to jail. They'd lock her in some nice, quiet institution, and she'd play their game until she fooled them all. Then she would be released, cured of her "insanity," and she would find him, find him and punish him, and then live happily ever after with him. They would leave Korea, leave Asia, go somewhere where they would never be found, and he would love her, oh, how he would love her.

"Mei."

She sat up and looked around. Someone called her name. She turned to the cell door, staring hard into the deep shadows of the hall and then the darkness beyond the windows. She stared as two glowing points of white light appeared. They grew brighter and larger, coming closer and closer. Mei smiled.

"How pretty," she giggled. "Such beautiful lights, like fireflies, sweet fireflies. I will catch them for my Jin-woo."

The lights continued to come closer, and then a face appeared, but not a human face, a bestial one. It continued, heading straight for her, and when she thought it would crash into the window some ten feet away from her cell door, it merely slipped through like smoke. A shiver of dread filled her as the beast kept coming, its long, sinuous body weaving back and forth, its red and gold scales flashing briefly in the darkness as they caught the light from her one lone bulb. Then the head came to her door, and what passed through the bars was not a beast but a woman. She was elegant and beautiful and majestic. Her hair wove around her in inky black waves like a mane blowing in the breeze. Her lips were bloodred and her eyes snow white. A lotus blossom marked her brow in red, just between her eyes.

"Pretty," Mei whispered. "Are you here to take me to Jin-woo?"

"No." Her voice was musical and ethereal, echoing in the small space.

"Are you here to set me free?"

"No."

"Why are you here?"

"In your next life, remember this." She leaned forward, so close. She smelled of cherry blossoms and peaches. "Never harm a Dragon's family."

Her lips were hot, so hot. Yet Mei couldn't pull away. Fire filled her, heat as she'd never felt before. She opened her eyes, unaware she had closed them. The lady was farther away, not kissing her, not touching her, yet she still burned. Finally the agony registered in her brain. She screamed and screamed and screamed as the fire consumed her from the inside out until there was nothing left but ash and smoke and embers.

CHEN-BAO STARED at the remains, emotionless. It had been a long time since she last took a life in such a manner. That too was a case of someone hurting one she loved. Such an affront could not be forgiven nor forgotten. Turning, she passed through the cell bars and then through the window, shifting as she did so and winding her way into the sky. The mystery of Mei's death would baffle the masses, but those who knew, those who had encountered Dragons before, would know she had broken the law of the Celestials:

Never harm the clan.

E.T. MALINOWSKI is the youngest of seven girls. It was her love of reading that eventually led her to attempt writing. From there, a passion was born. She began writing romance in her early teens and, at that time, never dreamed of sharing her work with anyone. With the help of several dear friends, not to mention her ex-husband, she found the courage to take that last step toward publication.

As the single mother of three rambunctious boys, finding time to write is a bit difficult. Yet E.T. manages to do it, even if it's on break or lunch at a regular day job. She has found her place in homoerotic romance. To her, love doesn't recognize gender boundaries and is always special.

An avid reader, E.T. finds inspiration in all her favorite genres, from mainstream romance by her favorite authors to Japanese manga and anime. To her, even the classic fairy tales hold that spark of motivation, and if there is one thing she has learned from her many years of writing solely for herself, it's this: never deny the Muse, she gets cranky and pulls out the bullwhip.

Email: etmalinowski@gmail.com